Time's Up, Mr Darcy

FREDRICA EDWARD

Copyright © 2015, 2016 Fredrica Edward

This book was originally published in serial form on fanfiction.net from

3rd Apr 2015 to 11th Mar 2016.

All rights reserved.

ISBN-10:0-9946322-1-5
ISBN-13:978-0-9946322-1-0

DEDICATION

*This book is dedicated to Caroline Herschel,
Original author of the NGC catalog,
recipient of the Royal Astronomical Society's gold medal,
not awarded to another woman for almost 170 years
and Mary Somerville,
co-elected with CH as the first women members of the RAS in 1835,
pioneers in the field of astronomy.*

And also to my followers on fanfiction,
particularly those who posted constructive reviews,
especially *alix33, YepItsMe, tremu and JeanB.*
Finally, thanks to Betty Campbell Madden
for proofing the final drafts.
Any mistakes that remain are my own.

CONTENTS

1 The end 1
2 The bet 3
3 The ultimatum 8
4 The chemisette 13
5 The post-mortem 19
6 Miss Elizabeth's solicitude 24
7 Understanding Miss Elizabeth 32
8 Badajoz 38
9 Introspection 44
10 A soirée 50
11 By the River Lea 57
12 Scylla and Charybdis 64
13 The ball 71
14 The day after 80
15 Preparations 86
16 More preparations 92
17 Mr Collins' surprise 98
18 Complications 105
19 Guests at the wedding 111
20 North 120
21 A reprieve 127
22 Pemberley 136
23 The morning after 148
24 The dressmaker 156
25 An experiment 165
26 Church 173
27 Greensleeves 180
28 Exploration and adventure 192
29 Not Tuesday 202
30 Uneasy relations 209

31 A fairy tale	217
32 The Lakes tour	225
33 Travel plans	236
34 Christmas	247
35 Boxing Day	257
36 Richard joins the fray	264
37 Beggar My Neighbour	275
38 A honeymoon	282
39 Here's poison	288
40 Hatchard's	292
41 Old friends	299
42 Regret	304
43 Something wicked	309
44 Schemes	316
45 Confidences	324
46 Mr Bletchley	331
47 Revelations	339
48 The bandbox	347
49 The inn	356
50 Karma	362
51 Aftermath	368
52 Rapproachment	377
53 To get back up again	381
54 Visitors	386
55 Love blossoms	390
56 Of Georgie and Rosings	392
57 The season	395
58 Of things past	401

1 The end

Leaving her lover sprawled in her bed, Diana rose, pulled on a sumptuous wrap and tidied her auburn hair. Walking back to the bed, she contemplated the example of male beauty lying there. He looked so young when he was asleep, exhausted from their recent exertions. His magnificent body was that of a Greek god, though his unlined face, with its strong jaw and slightly hooked nose, was more reminiscent of Mars than Apollo. His dark curls were tousled adorably. Despite the opportunities that modern clothes afforded men to enhance their physiques, he looked best without a stitch on.

Dragging the bed hangings closest to the door shut noisily, she tugged the bell-pull and sat down on the mattress near him. He still did not stir.

A knock was heard and a maid appeared. Her eyes downcast, she placed a tray containing a bottle and two glasses on a small table just inside the door and withdrew.

Diana walked to the table, filled the two flutes with champagne and returned to the bed.

"Fitzwilliam," she said, shaking his shoulder.

Darcy opened one eye.

"Have some champagne," Diana said, handing him a glass.

He raised himself on an elbow.

"What's the occasion?" he asked. "Your birthday is not 'til next week."

"A celebration," she whispered with a wistful smile, "of our last kiss."

Darcy froze. "Why our last kiss?"

"I'm getting married."

"What!" Darcy bolted up. "To whom?"

"The Duke of Redford."

"Bertie Thomas?" blurted Darcy. "He's as old as the hills!"

The duke was, in fact, a respectable fifty-five.

"You can't be serious!" Darcy continued. "You're terminating our relationship?"

"He's going to make an honest woman of me, Darcy. He's made a very good offer."

"You can't do this! Marry me instead!"

"You know we can't do that, Darcy. I'm seven years older than you—too old to bear a child. The Duke already has an heir and several spares from his first marriage. You need an heir for Pemberley."

"You can't do this," he repeated stubbornly. "I love you!"

"I'm doing this *because* I love you. You'll thank me in the future."

"Please, Diana, no! Plenty of women over thirty-five have children."

"Some do. But you forget that I was happily married for over five years to the marquis without issue."

"It might have been him!"

"He had a child out of wedlock during that time, Darcy."

"I'll get a Special Licence. We can get married right away!"

"No, Darcy, we can't. Be sensible. Drink your champagne."

"I won't."

"You're being a child."

"I'm not."

"I think you had better go," sighed Diana. She had known this was not going to be easy, but she had been determined to do it in person—sending a letter was so shabby.

"This is because I don't have a title, isn't it?" he said softly.

"Don't be ridiculous," she replied.

"You married a marquis, and now you've worked your way up to a duke. Plain old Mr Darcy is not good enough for you."

"Please stop," she said, stroking his hand.

He was not to be mollified. "You do realise Pemberley is one of the grandest estates in Derbyshire? In England!"

"This is not about titles or estates, Fitzwilliam. It's about being sensible. We had seven good years. Now it's time to move on."

Darcy stood chewing his lip, his mind in turmoil. *It would be humiliating to burst out crying.* "This is not finished," he managed to croak. "My uncle has summoned me, but I will be back tomorrow to talk sense to you."

He moved to kiss her and she submitted. It was a passionate kiss that drew on all their sensual experiences of the past seven years. He was determined to show Diana how wrong she was.

Pulling on his clothes, he allowed her to tie his cravat. Then he fled downstairs, demanding his hat and cane.

After Darcy left, Diana cried on her bed for half an hour. When her tears were exhausted, she got up and retrieved his letters from her bureau. They were tied together with a red ribbon.

Lying back down on the bed she reread these love notes, most of them written from his estate of Pemberley where he withdrew for the summer to supervise the harvest. The letters were not poetic, but heartfelt. As she read she smiled and played with a locket round her neck that contained a curl of his hair. Finally, getting up, she walked to the fire and consigned the letters to the flames. Opening the locket, the curl followed.

Then she rang for her maid to ready her for Lady Montagu's soirée

2 The bet

Darcy walked along the square and turned the corner into Mount Street, wondering how his world had been turned upside down. How could something that had become so central to his life evaporate in an instant?

It had all started in his first season. After Darcy had finished the two years of a gentleman's degree at Cambridge, his professors had encouraged him to come back for a third year to qualify for the full degree. They said he had a first-rate mind. But his father had died of an apoplexy during that last year at university. Darcy had posted north immediately, his studies abandoned.

So began his new life. Just shy of his twenty-first birthday he had become Master of Pemberley and guardian of a nine-year old sister he barely knew. His uncle—the Earl of Matlock and one of his trustees—had sent him down to London to look for a wife. His aunt had arranged everything: the dancing masters, the new clothes suitable for balls and soirées, the valet. It was a foreign world. They had told him he was comely enough, handsome even; that he would be *a catch*, but he'd hated it all from the moment he attended his first ball at Almack's.

To be more specific, he hated the women. They seemed to fall into two groups: the insipids and the cats. None of them could hold a decent conversation about anything important to him. The notion of being shackled to one of them for eternity was repugnant.

He consoled himself by discovering the diversions that were available to a gentleman: Angelo's fencing academy, the Royal Society, and of course, White's gentlemen's club. These had seemed a revelation, and he began to think that if he could just get his aunt to arrange a marriage for him and forget the ballrooms, it might be tolerable.

Then his new life as a gentleman of society had all started to fall apart. He had been oblivious to it when he'd first walked into White's that day. Men were always laughing and whispering there. It took him a while to register the fact that the susurrus started as he walked into a room. To check he wasn't imagining things, he had walked into and out of the same room twice from different directions.

His cousin had clued him in. Darcy had been sitting alone, sipping a drink while he stared into space. Usually he thought about the changes he was making to Pemberley when he sat by himself, which was often. He would get out his notebook and start jotting down ideas with the pencil he carried in his pocket—a good Derbyshire pencil. But that day no ideas came, and he was relieved when Captain Richard Fitzwilliam finally arrived.

"You're late," Darcy said as Richard sat down. "I've been feeling very exposed sitting here without you."

"Sorry—had a problem on the parade ground that I had to get sorted."

"Is it my imagination or are people talking about me?" asked Darcy.

"They're talking. Don't get upset. These things happen all the time. Most of the fellows here get bored. Someone's put something in the betting book about you. Actually there are a few bets now. Basically they concern your virginity: when and how you'll lose it."

Darcy blushed red, both from mortification and anger.

"Don't show them you're annoyed," advised Richard. "It will make it worse."

"Do they always make such odious bets?"

"They're always betting about something, but it's usually something innocuous, like whether someone will ride a donkey backwards down St James Street."

"How do they know?" he hissed. "Is it stamped on my head?"

Darcy had realised as soon as the words were out of his mouth—*Wickham*.

George Wickham was the bane of Darcy's life, the one fly in the heir of Pemberley's ointment. Well, if you didn't count those dashed females. George's late father had been steward of the Darcy family estate, Pemberley, during the lifetime of Darcy's father. Indeed, his father had held his steward in such affection that he had stood godfather to George, and treated him like a second son after Mr Wickham's untimely demise. Two years older than Darcy, George had unceasingly shown himself to be a fierce rival to Mr Darcy's own flesh and blood for his paternal affections, always getting the better of the younger boy in various contrived situations throughout their childhood.

A couple of days earlier, Darcy had seen his childhood nemesis strutting along Bond Street, bowing and tipping his hat to the ladies who were shopping. He'd smirked when he saw Darcy, and now Darcy knew why.

Dammit! Wickham isn't even a member of White's and he's managed to infiltrate it!

Darcy's uncle, Lord Geoffrey Fitzwilliam, had been furious when he'd discovered the bets, and had some terse words with some of his cronies who were participating. But the bets could not be removed, no matter their repugnant nature. It was a strict rule at White's.

Richard had suggested taking Darcy to an establishment he used in Pall Mall—just to get it over with; but Darcy had refused to have his life ordered by innuendo. He'd almost suggested to Richard that he should let it be known that he'd dallied with a country maid when he was fifteen, but he couldn't bring himself do it—disguise of any sort was his abhorrence. So Darcy stuck his nose in the air and avoided White's.

The situation had gone on for an intolerable month before that night at Lady Sefton's ball. All his favourite places had become anathema to him. Suddenly the men had turned into a bunch of cats like their female counterparts. He had retreated to the library of his townhouse and was reduced to going to balls and soirées—the sort of functions he abhorred—just for the sake of social intercourse.

The din and the crowding in Lady Sefton's ballroom that night had been overwhelming. He'd gone out onto the terrace to clear his head. Hearing the rustle of silk skirts behind him, he had braced himself for more simpering.

"A lovely night, isn't it?" said a sweet voice. "I'm always enchanted by a rainbow round the moon."

He turned sharply to see a beautiful woman.

"I don't believe we've been introduced," he said stiffly.

"Lady Diana Bellingham, Marchioness of Frensham."

She held out her hand.

Darcy bowed over it but did not take it. He relaxed slightly on hearing she was married, but wondered where her husband was.

"And you are?" she twinkled at him.

"Fitzwilliam Darcy of Pemberley."

"Of course, Mr Darcy. I *did* know that, but we must obey the forms."

"Frensham," he said, reminding himself to be polite. "That is in Somerset, is it not?"

"Indeed, my husband's estate is renowned for its thoroughbreds."

Darcy nodded in recognition.

"But excuse me for disturbing your reverie," she said, flourishing her fan. "I feel I am *de trop*."

He did not deny it.

"You must take tea with us in Berkeley Square sometime," she said.

With a curtsey she had withdrawn, and he'd been grateful to have his solitude restored. So grateful, that when he had walked out of Angelo's after braving that establishment two days later and found himself at a loose end, he had wandered over to Berkley Square to pay a morning call.

The butler who took his hat, cane and card was a singular fellow with a broken nose and a cauliflower ear. He was a big man whose shoulders seemed to brush the edges of doorways and so tall that Darcy had to look up to meet his eye—a rare experience for someone who generally had the advantage of his fellow men in height.

Darcy had been ushered into a sitting room where he found the marchioness reading, accompanied only by a little dog. She was so elegantly dressed in silks that, had she been wearing a wig, she might have been mistaken for Madame Pompadour.

The butler announced him and withdrew, closing the door. This move rather startled Darcy.

"I beg your pardon," said Darcy, looking around. "Where is your companion?"

"Right here," she laughed, indicating the little dog, which yapped in reply.

Darcy looked anxiously at the door. "Your husband cannot like me being alone with you."

"Do not worry, Mr Darcy. He will not call you out. Please, will you have a game of chess with me?"

"I cannot like it in a closed room. Will you permit me to open the door?"

"Be my guest," she replied.

So they had their game of chess, which he had won, but not easily, while they talked of all manner of topics from science to politics, and took tea. It was the first sensible conversation he'd had with a woman outside his family. Some other callers had come towards the end of the game, and he'd subsequently bid the marchioness adieu.

Darcy had wandered back to Grosvenor Square quite pleased with himself, feeling he'd cleared some sort of social hurdle.

He had called on the marchioness at the same time a week later, and once again, had been disconcerted when the butler closed the door. He'd gotten up to open it again, when he felt the lady's hand close on his.

"Leave it, Mr Darcy," she said. "I wish to talk to you."

"What of?"

"Do you know my husband, Mr Darcy?"

"I know *of* him."

"But you have never met him?"

"No."

"Then I gather you do not know that he met with an accident two years ago."

"He's dead?" he asked bluntly.

"No, Mr Darcy. He was thrown from a horse two years ago—a particularly nasty stallion I begged him not to ride. He landed on an iron stake. It went up through his mouth and pierced his brain." She indicated this with her hand. "He has never been the same since: his mind has reverted to that of a child's, and it has affected his body also. He lives at Stanyon now."

"I'm sorry," said Darcy. "I didn't know."

"I was hoping we might be able to come to some agreement, Mr Darcy."

"I don't understand."

"I believe that you are the victim of a cruel bet, several in fact, at White's."

"How do you know such things?"

"Word gets around, Mr Darcy. You should end this soon before it creeps into polite circles."

He nodded. It was the same advice Richard had given him weeks ago, but he was curious that her statement seemed to exclude herself from polite circles.

"I, on the other hand, am missing male companionship. Can you be discreet Mr Darcy?"

He swallowed, realising what she was offering, then nodded.

"Excellent," she said, taking him by the hand and leading him to a door. "Come with me."

Afterwards they had discussed how they would end the betting. The marchioness was a very strategic thinker. She got him to discover the exact nature of the bets and who had placed them. They worked out who would profit by them, and how to end it in a way that was sufficiently unambiguous. For this purpose they chose Lord Verney. He was a friend of his uncle's who had a sense of humour. Verney had laid a counter bet in Darcy's favour, claiming he would lose his virginity on St Valentine's Day—more as a means of ridiculing the whole farrago. The odds were enormous against him.

On that evening in February, which was branded forever in his memory, Darcy walked into the club and sought out Verney, whom he found playing piquet. Opening his handkerchief, he dropped the used sheath into his brandy.

"You win," he said, and walked off.

3 The ultimatum

By the time Darcy had finished these musings, he had arrived at his uncle's townhouse in Grosvenor Square. The butler showed him into the study where he found the earl puffing away on a cigar while he paced up and down. His cousin, Richard, the earl's second son, was also present, leaning uneasily against the mantelpiece.

The earl rounded on them when the butler closed the door.

"I've summoned you both here to remind you that you need to get married."

The cousins exchanged a glance.

"Darcy you're twenty-eight and an only son. I don't object to you dipping your wick in Berkeley Square," he said, stabbing his cigar at him; "but it's time you set up your nursery."

Darcy frowned at the earl's taproom language. How had his uncle known? He thought he had been discreet...

The earl turned abruptly to his son. "Richard, you're thirty. Enough said."

"Why do *I* need to get married?" protested Richard.

"Because you're the spare, you dimwit," snarled his father.

"You seem to have forgotten that my brother is already married," retorted Richard.

"He's been married for ten years and has produced four daughters. My granddaughters may marry to preserve our name but they can't inherit the title. So you *will* marry, and soon."

"Just because he has four daughters doesn't mean he can't have a son—the odds are even every time," complained Richard, displaying a fine understanding of stochastic processes.

"This is not a game of dice," returned the earl. "That is overly simplistic. I've seen this happen before. Some men are incapable of siring sons, and I'm getting nervous. Both of you have six months to find a wife. *If* in that time, you have *not* found a woman to bear your children, I will find one for you. One of you can marry Anne de Bourgh for a start—that will keep Rosings in the family. Now get out. My mistress is waiting for me."

As the earl's butler ushered them out the front door, Richard vented his spleen. "Bloody hell," he spewed, as he clanked down the stairs in his spurs; "it's like a game of musical chairs! Whoever hasn't found a wife in six months gets Anne!"

Darcy grunted his agreement. He was so incensed by his uncle's ultimatum that he felt an irrational urge to spite him by offering marriage to the first eligible female he encountered. As they were walking across Grosvenor Square, it occurred to him that this was not such a wild threat. Better if he walked down Bond Street where he might encounter the daughter of a Cit or, even better, a shopkeeper's daughter!

"What has precipitated all this?" Darcy asked savagely as they continued across the square to his own townhouse.

"Mother," replied Richard sadly.

"Why would she do such a thing?"

"She noticed I'm going bald."

"Nonsense," said Darcy. "You've still got a full head of hair."

"If you look closely you'll see there's a bald patch on my crown the size of a shilling."

Darcy discreetly affirmed it was true. "Good Lord!"

"Thank you! I feel *so* much better!" sneered Richard.

When they reached Darcy's townhouse, they were informed that his friend Charles Bingley was waiting in the parlour. Darcy was decidedly not in the mood for socialising, even with his affable friend, but he could hardly kick him out.

Charles stood as soon as Richard and Darcy entered the room. He saw with some misgiving that Darcy appeared to be in a black mood.

"Forgive me, Darcy," said Charles, "I have some exciting news and your butler said he expected you imminently."

"Not a problem, Charles," said Darcy, rearranging his features into the customary mask he wore outside his own domicile. "Come into the study. Richard and I were about to have a brandy."

Suitably ensconced in Darcy's den of industry, the cousins sipped their drinks while Bingley delivered his news.

"I think I've found a suitable estate. It's in Hertfordshire—so, close enough to allow me to manage my investments in London and permit Caroline to travel back and forward between the Hursts and myself. The house is grand enough to satisfy Caroline, and the rent seems reasonable."

"Excellent, Bingley!" said Darcy, who had been encouraging his friend to lease before he made a purchase. "It sounds just the thing!"

"But I'm still not sure," said Bingley. "I am in no position to judge the land or the improvements. I was hoping you might be able to spend a day going over the estate with me before I signed."

Darcy frowned. "I'm sorry, Bingley. I'm dealing with a bit of a crisis at the moment."

"That's all right, Darcy," replied Bingley affably. "I didn't wish to impose upon you. I guess I'll have to stand on my own two feet sometime…"

Now Darcy felt guilty. "Perhaps…" he said.

Bingley leant forward eagerly.

"Can you wait a week?" asked Darcy. "I'd really like to help, but there is something I need to attend to."

"Thank you! thank you! my friend," said Bingley gratefully, grabbing Darcy's hand. "Let me know when you're available and I will arrange it all."

They finished their brandy.

When Bingley got up to go, the colonel, who was committed to a regimental dinner, accompanied him and Darcy was left to his own musings.

Darcy spent a troubled night. He had retired at ten, as was his habit, only to spend an hour staring at the canopy of his bed. When sleep was elusive, he had removed to the library where he could not find a single book that inspired him to open its covers. He then spent another hour pacing up and down, practising arguments he might employ with Diana to change her mind. Finally, he built up the fire and resorted to the brandy.

On the following morning, his valet found him asleep in a wing chair, wearing his banyan. Cautiously moving around the room while he set it in order, Finn finally decided to rouse his unresponsive master by cracking a blind.

Darcy woke with a jerk. "Goodness, what time is it, Finn?"

"Ten, sir. I thought you would not wish to miss your fencing practise."

"Damn, the fencing practise! I must look my best!"

Finn knew better than to raise an eyebrow at this.

After Darcy had bathed, Finn shaved and attired him to a nicety. Dismissing his valet, Darcy retrieved the box he had purchased last week at Rundall and Bridge. Opening it, he stared upon the jewels he had specially commissioned for his love's thirty-fifth birthday. It was a necklace and earring set composed of emeralds and diamonds, which had cost him a small fortune. He had chosen the emeralds to complement Diana's beautiful auburn hair. Snapping the case shut, he proceeded down the stairs.

Darcy had sensed Diana's increasing restlessness over the last few months, but attributed it to her approaching birthday. She had obliquely referred to her increasing age several times, and he had assumed that the midpoint of her thirties was some sort of mid-life crisis for her. He could not understand it. She was as beautiful as ever—more so. The portrait in the hall of the marquis' townhouse, which had been executed upon her marriage, showed a younger and more rounded face; but the intervening fourteen years had only better defined her cheekbones. She was exquisite, and Darcy had sought to show his appreciation by commissioning jewels worthy of her beauty.

As he was helped into his coat in the vestibule, Darcy slipped the case into a commodious inner pocket after pulling out the notebook that normally resided there and laying it on the hall table. The jewels were a fitting tribute to their first seven years, and now, he hoped, the beginning of a new phase of their relationship.

Diana's husband had died over a year ago. Of course, there had been some nasty rumours that her stepson had smothered his father in his sleep, but Darcy did not credit them. It was a sad tale, and the gossips always indulged their fancy for the gothic in such cases. The marquis had only lived a half-life since his accident, and it was a mercy to both him and his heir that he had moved on. *Rest in peace.* Diana had worn full mourning in public for a year. No husband could have expected better observance.

Darcy walked briskly towards Berkeley Square, ruing his reaction of yesterday. He had responded like the unseasoned youth he had been seven years ago rather than a man of the world. He should have stayed in Berkley Square until he had persuaded Diana that she was making a mistake instead of going off to his uncle's. Darcy had ever been punctilious, never missing an appointment. Overly concerned with his duty, he had not given the crisis the attention it merited.

"Damn the duke!" he muttered under his breath as he rounded the corner into Berkeley Square. *I was in line first!*

If he had known he had a rival, Darcy reasoned, he would have moved faster. He had not wished to impose upon Diana too soon after she came out of mourning. Her birthday had seemed the ideal date to move things forward.

Darcy ran up the steps of the townhouse; but he knew as soon as Leith opened the door that Diane's butler wasn't going to let him in.

"The marchioness is indisposed today, Mr Darcy."

He choked back his indignation. "You know I must see her, Leith," said Darcy, calling on all his natural hauteur.

"I'm afraid I can't allow that, Mr Darcy. I'm sorry," said the bruiser with quiet dignity.

"Then let me in so I can leave her a note," Darcy demanded.

The butler did not hesitate to accede to his request—Darcy was generally a man of his word. But even if his emotions got the better of him, Leith knew he could bustle Darcy out the door in a trice, if need be. He was taller and heavier than the younger man and had considerable experience in the boxing ring to draw on. He knew Darcy didn't spend time at Jackson's boxing saloon—like gentlemen of old, Darcy favoured swords and pistols instead.

Darcy put down his cane and leant over the hall table to inscribe the note. He wanted to propose in person, not in a letter, so after a moment's thought he simply wrote:

With all my love.
Happy Birthday.
D

Then he sealed the note, withdrew the box from his coat, and placing the missive atop it, handed it solemnly to the butler before taking his leave.

Frustrated, Darcy walked back to Grosvenor Square, wondering when it would be deemed polite to call again. Arriving back at his townhouse, he locked the door to his study and buried himself in his business affairs.

He waited for three days for a reply. Finally, a footman brought a parcel to his desk around evening. It was wrapped in brown paper, tied in black ribbon with a sprig of rosemary tucked inside it. Darcy paled when he recognised the shape of the jewellery case. The ribbon was knotted tightly and, in his impatience to open it, he picked up the Venetian stiletto his father had used as a book knife. Snapping open the case, he saw a letter sitting on top of the parure and quickly broke the seal.

> Dear F
> Thank you for your kind thoughts on my birthday.
> I was married yesterday at St George's by Special Licence.
> Obviously I cannot keep your beautiful gift.
> Accept my best wishes for your future happiness
> with a woman who is worthy of your heart.
> D.

Darcy's first wild impulse was to plunge the dagger that lay to hand into his heart, but sanity prevailed, and he flicked the wicked object off his desk with the back of his hand. He jumped up and started pacing back and forth as the daylight faded.

Once the light had leeched out of the study, he moved stealthily into the dimly lit hall and let himself out of the front door, pulling it closed behind him. Under cover of darkness, he ran down the front steps and sprinted across the square.

Reaching the footpath on the other side, he slowed to a more acceptable pace as a link-boy came up to him. Darcy flicked him a coin, directing him to Berkley Square, and when they entered their destination, dismissed him with another coin.

He walked alone in semi-darkness along the street, his progress lit only by the light escaping from the other townhouses. The marquis' townhouse was shrouded in darkness. Halfway up the steps he perceived the knocker was off the door.

Darcy realised belatedly that he had lost her. This townhouse now belonged to the new marquis, and he would not find Diana there anymore. She was Bertie Thomas's property now and he must accept that.

A heavy weight settled in his stomach as he wandered off unthinkingly towards St James. Nearing White's, he would not go in, passing to the other side of the street to avoid the bow window. At some point he noticed the same link-boy was following him at a discreet distance, and he acknowledged the futility of it all.

It occurred to Darcy that he was quite lost—he was in a street that was unfamiliar to him in the darkness. He tossed the boy another coin.

One hand released the torch and flew out to snatch it deftly. A silence stretched between them before the boy ventured, "Grosvenor Square, sir?"

"Yes," Darcy replied hoarsely, in a voice quite unrecognisable as his own.

4 The chemisette

The estate Bingley proposed to lease in Hertfordshire was inspected, and found to be appropriate. The house and furniture were very fine, but the property and tenants somewhat neglected. Nonetheless, for the rent requested, the estate was a bargain. The lease was duly signed, and Bingley begged Darcy's further assistance once he took possession of the property at Michaelmas.

Thus, three weeks later, Darcy found himself as Finn left him, in full ball dress, standing in a dressing room at Netherfield going over the same things that had been revolving in his mind for weeks:

He should have bought her more presents, earlier... But he had not done that because of the clandestine nature of their relationship. *Then ephemeral things—like flowers, champagne and tea...* Ditto, but they would have been delivered by proxy, and he'd wanted to see the expression on her face when she received them. *He should have told her how much he loved her...* But he had—every time he met her, every time he wrote. *He should have expressed himself more eloquently—in poetry perhaps...* It seemed so false and foreign to him.

He looked in the standing mirror and was disgusted by what he saw there—a stripling dressed as a man of the world. He knew that underneath his valet's handiwork was a fellow not far removed from that 21 year-old virgin who'd been bullied at White's, despite the seven years that had elapsed; a contemptible fellow who still loathed going to balls, despised polite conversation, and was uncomfortable with every eligible female bar one. And she, the goddess, the one who had laid a veneer of sophistication on him, had cast him off....

Moving like an automaton, Darcy returned to his bedchamber, sat down in the chair beside the empty grate and stared at the walls.

When the colonel walked into his cousin's bedchamber at Netherfield some half an hour later, he found Darcy sitting in his satin knee breeches, staring into space. Richard felt an uncanny sense of déjà vu, as his thoughts were cast back to their visit to Almack's several weeks ago, four days after his father's ultimatum, the night he had realised his cousin was in serious trouble...

When he'd arrived at Darcy House at seven, he'd found Finn and Mrs Flowers in anxious consultation in the hallway. They had approached him, asking for his help—the master was behaving strangely. The first inkling that Mrs Flowers had of a problem was when the master hadn't come to take his lunch in the dining room. At three, she'd knocked on his door, reminding him of the time, and asking if he wished to have a tray sent in. He'd replied that he wasn't hungry. Finn had thought it best to leave the master alone, knowing the colonel was expected that night.

Richard had immediately repaired to the study and tried the door. It was locked.

"Darcy!" said the colonel as he rapped on the door while Mrs Flowers and Finn apprehensively stood by.

Mrs Flowers fingered her chatelaine nervously.

"It's past seven!" prompted the colonel. "We're due at the Hursts' at eight."

Silence.

"Come on, man! All work and no play makes Jack a dull boy!" he coaxed.

Footsteps were heard within. At the sound of a key rasping in the lock, Finn and Mrs Flowers effaced themselves.

The colonel noticed Darcy looked very dull-eyed and pale. He was wearing silk stockings and satin knee breeches but lacked a coat and cravat. His black curly hair was sticking in all directions.

"Well," Richard said, wondering what the hell had gone wrong; "at least you're partly dressed. I thought you must have forgotten we are going to Almack's."

Darcy didn't reply.

"We've got a good half-hour before we're due at the Hursts'. Care for a drink?"

Darcy stood back to let his cousin in.

Watching Darcy out of the corner of his eye, Richard poured two snifters of brandy.

Finn arrived, trailed by a footman carrying Darcy's dressing case.

By the time they reached the Hursts', the brandy and Richard's unceasingly affable conversation had warmed Darcy's mood somewhat. It was not, however, sufficient to tempt him to eat. Darcy spent the meal cutting the food on his plate and rearranging it, while Bingley talked excitedly of the Hertfordshire property, and Bingley's sister, Caroline, cooed at him assiduously.

Then Hurst had called for his enormous town carriage and the six of them, fitting comfortably into it, headed off to Almack's.

The colonel had spent the evening watching Darcy behave like an automaton. When they arrived back at the Darcy townhouse, he frogmarched his cousin into the library. Darcy sat down in his wing chair near the dying embers in the grate. Once the footman had built up the fire, Richard shut the door.

Standing cross-legged, with his back against Darcy's desk, Richard confronted his cousin. "Right. Now you are going to tell me what is wrong."

Time's Up, Mr Darcy

He poured them each a brandy; then sat down opposite his cousin in front of the fire. It took quite a bit of Darcy's brandy and discussion of shared childhood mischief before the colonel managed to breach his cousin's defences. In fact, they were both thoroughly tanked.

"Diana..." slurred Darcy finally. "She m...married Bertie Thomas."

Richard let out a low whistle. "Heard he got married. Didn't realise it was Diana."

He tried to think of something sympathetic to say that wouldn't indulge his cousin's maudlin mood, but his mind was a blank.

They both fell asleep without managing another word.

When Richard awoke several hours later, he was considerably less drunk. Darcy was snoring very loudly, a sure sign that he was still under the weather. The candles had gone out. Richard stabbed at the embers with the poker to reanimate the fire, then replaced the candles in the candelabrum on the mantel. Opening the study door, he heaved Darcy to his feet. Richard had gotten his cousin halfway up the stairs in his state of semi-stupor before he regained consciousness.

"Why do things have to change, Richard?" said Darcy, his voice cracking. "Everything seemed fine, and then suddenly your father decides I need to be married yesterday, and the love of my life marries a duke..."

He couldn't go on.

"Nothing lasts forever," Richard had sighed.

...But that was three weeks ago and dark moods shouldn't last forever either, thought the colonel. *Hell! No woman was worth that!*

"Come on, man," said the colonel, returning to the problem at hand. "Bingley has called for the carriage. Time to survey the lovely ladies of Hertfordshire."

Darcy knew as soon as he stepped into the assembly room at Meryton that he was overdressed. He, Bingley and Hurst were wearing satin knee breeches, the formal dress of his father's generation, as demanded by Almack's. His valet, Finn, had assured him that it would be better to be overdressed than underdressed. Darcy envied Richard the trousers of his military uniform. Around him was a sea of pantaloons and practical breeches. The only other fellow he could see wearing satin knee breeches was now approaching their party.

"Ah, Mr Bingley," said the man approaching Charles. "How good of you to grace our little assembly, and with so many distinguished guests."

"A pleasure, Sir William," replied Bingley. "May I introduce my friend, Mr Fitzwilliam Darcy of Pemberley; his cousin, the Honourable Colonel Richard Fitzwilliam of the Life Guards; and my brother-in-law, Mr Randolph Hurst, whom you have already met."

"Sir William Lucas, Master of Ceremonies," the gentleman replied, shaking their hands.

"Allow me, also," continued Bingley, "to introduce my two sisters, Mrs Louisa Hurst and Miss Caroline Bingley."

The ladies curtsied and Sir William made an elegant leg in return. It would not have looked out of place at St James, but seemed a trifle over the top at a country assembly. Mrs Hurst bit back a titter, while Caroline maintained a dignified but bland expression, only sliding her eyes sideways to meet her sister's.

"You have already met my family, Mr Bingley, but I would be remiss as Master of Ceremonies if I did not introduce the other family of note in the area," he said, favouring the rest of the party with a glance that indicated that they, too, were to be included in this high treat.

As Sir William led the way towards a matron with an elaborate headdress, Mr Hurst walked off casually in the direction of the card room, while the majority of Mr Bingley's party remained in situ. Only Colonel Fitzwilliam accompanied Bingley in Sir William's wake.

Darcy watched as five ladies gathered round the matron as Bingley approached, like ducklings racing back to their mother. One of them was very beautiful with guinea gold hair, dressed in gold silk. Three of them were hardly more than girls. *What were they doing out?* The other one with dark hair was dressed plainly in sprigged muslin and was wearing an over-the-dress chemisette. ...*to an evening function?*

He looked around the room with disfavour. The music was too loud and ungenteel, the clothes of the participants were not sufficiently fine, and the whole room had the stench of too many unwashed bodies. Darcy felt his mind begin to immerse itself in syrup as he tried to block out the tedium of being there.

His thoughts drifted back to his last visit to Almack's, where he'd mused how stupid a ball was for finding a wife, with all the ladies simpering behind their fans. Darcy had decided that society had become too decadent. Trying to imagine how the Master of Pemberley might have got a wife before the London season existed, he'd envisioned all the maidens in the village of Lambton lined up so he could choose the prettiest... but decided that was just as frivolous as a ball at Almack's.

Now, standing in the assembly room in Meryton, he reasoned that the Master of Pemberley would have used a more practical test of their ability to bear him an heir... *he would have the maidens run round the Village Green, carrying a brick maybe, to test their stamina...*

Richard returned, interrupting his reverie. "Come on, Darcy; stop mooning about Diana," he hissed.

"She is the love of my life. I will never love another."

"Oh, come, Cousin, surely you are being too particular. Besides, we're just dancing, not getting married... *yet*. There are two gentlemen here, and both of them have daughters. Miss Lucas is a bit plain but both of the elder Bennet sisters are very good-looking and well spoken. Bingley is dancing with the prettier one. She *does* have an angelic smile."

"She's insipid," replied Darcy.

Richard rolled his eyes. "The two younger ones are comely too, and you could mould them to your will; same for the younger Lucas, Miss Mariah. The middle Bennet looks a bit strait-laced."

"And which would you choose?" asked Darcy sarcastically, knowing his cousin would flirt with them all and commit to no one.

"Second sons can't be too particular, Darcy. I've a fancy for Miss Bingley."

Darcy raised his eyebrows in surprise. "She's a cat," he muttered.

They stood in silence for a moment; Richard determined not to budge until his cousin had conceded to dance.

Fragments of a conversation between two shrill ladies sitting behind them drifted to their ears.

Richard heard "ten thousand a year" and deduced them to be discussing Darcy, before snatching "penniless second son of an earl" applied to himself. He burst out laughing.

"Damn! They've got my number!" he whispered.

He looked at his cousin, whose mouth was a thin line.

"I hate it," said Darcy through gritted teeth. "I hate attending these balls and being weighed up and down."

"Don't be silly," chided Richard. "Weren't we just doing the same? It's natural—just taking your opponent's measure. You wouldn't go into battle without assessing the competition."

Darcy vouchsafed no reply.

"Don't look now," said Richard, "but the second Miss Bennet is just behind us with Miss Lucas. Why don't you ask her to dance? She has such speaking eyes!"

"I already saw her," Darcy replied testily, unwilling to have his life organised for him. "She's not handsome enough to tempt me, and she's dressed like a dowd to boot," he added in an overloud voice.

Richard, who was more of a connoisseur of what lay beneath the clothes, was watching Miss Elizabeth with appreciation. He saw her eyes flicker at this pronouncement and realised she had heard his cousin.

"Well, tough bikkies then," said Richard. "I shall be before you."

Without further ado, he left his cousin to solicit Miss Elizabeth's hand for the next dance. This turned out to be *Mr Beveridge's Maggot*. As the orchestra was loud, the colonel ventured no more than a polite compliment to Miss Elizabeth before the progression, but at the end of the set, he reclaimed his partner's hand and led her to the punchbowl.

"I believe you may have heard something indiscreet my cousin said earlier, Miss Elizabeth," said the colonel. "I beg you to forget it. He is in a sad temper at the moment and is not normally so churlish."

Elizabeth looked at him in surprise. "You're very solicitous on your cousin's behalf, Colonel. I cannot fault his taste…"

This statement made the colonel stare at her.

"Compared to the ladies of your party, I must look sadly underdressed."

"Your beauty outshines your raiment," the colonel returned gallantly. "I hardly noticed what you are wearing."

Elizabeth's mouth twisted into a smile. "You are an accomplished flirt, sir. If you must have the truth, I never wear my best dresses to these assemblies. They are mostly attended by tradesmen who have a habit of standing on my hem."

"How gauche of them," replied the colonel. "But I see your sister is wearing silk…"

"Indeed, sir, she is the eldest, and must sacrifice her best dress to the occasion. As the second in line, I choose to marshal my resources."

"I see you are a strategist, Miss Elizabeth, and your modesty does you credit, but I can't help thinking…"

"Yes?"

The colonel got a bold look in his eye. "…that I could appreciate you better without that chemisette."

Elizabeth blushed and smiled. "I must admit it was not part of my original attire this evening. One of my sisters dripped some wax on me as we were about to depart, and the chemisette seemed the best solution to avoid further delay."

"Indeed?" said the colonel. "I applaud your resourcefulness and fie on your sister."

They turned, and he was about to escort Miss Elizabeth back to Miss Lucas, who had remained standing in the same place they had left her, when they were confronted by the two younger Bennet sisters, whose names the colonel had forgotten, not having much interest in the infantry.

"Are you really a Life Guard?" asked the more buxom one, her eyes glittering.

"My uniform declares me as such," replied the colonel.

"But you're not wearing a funny hat," she pointed out.

"I tend *not* to wear it at balls," replied the colonel, struggling to keep a straight face; "just on the parade ground, and it's useful for battles."

"The next set is forming," the girl said. "Would you care to dance?"

The colonel, struck speechless, broke into a wide grin and turned to Elizabeth.

She curtseyed. "Thank you for the dance, Colonel. I believe you have already been introduced to my youngest sister, Lydia."

5 The post-mortem

Being held in the country, the assembly finished at midnight, so the good tradespeople of Meryton could rise betimes in the morning. On the last stroke of twelve from the town clock, the musicians lay down their instruments partway through a reel. Mr Bingley protested loudly, but to no avail. Jane smiled at his enthusiasm and expressed a wish to see him again at next month's assembly.

The Netherfield party piled into Hurst's carriage. Bingley and Darcy were out of sorts as they arranged themselves inside: one vocal about not having danced enough; and the other quietly thinking that his dances with the Bingley sisters had been more than enough.

As the ladies declared themselves fatigued from boredom rather than exertion, the colonel shifted uncomfortably in his seat, wishing that Hurst had chosen to sit beside his wife as he had done for their forward journey. Instead, Richard had been forced to shoehorn himself between Hurst, who was a big man—tallish and stout—and Darcy on the backward-facing seat. Darcy had slim hips, but his shoulders were as broad as the colonel's, so the three of them were wedged in together—shoulder-to-shoulder. Bingley, a tall, slight fellow with sloping shoulders, was sitting comfortably between his sisters on the forward-facing seat.

The reason for the altered seating arrangement was evident. It had not surpassed the colonel's notice that Hurst and his wife were pointedly ignoring each other. It seemed they were having a tiff.

No doubt, thought the colonel, *she'd objected to her husband's taking himself off to the card room without standing up with her for a single dance.* The colonel could not blame her.

Fortunately, Bingley could not be out of temper for long, and they had scarce travelled one hundred yards before he had regained his equanimity and declared, "Well! I have never met with more pleasant people or prettier girls in my life! Everybody was most kind and attentive! There was no formality, no stiffness! I soon felt acquainted with all the room!"

The colonel grunted his assent. Having danced with both Bingley sisters, four Bennets and two Lucases, he was sanguine—though it had been a near run thing with Miss Jane Bennet. He thought any future efforts to extract her from Bingley's company might require a crowbar.

But Bingley's sister was of another mind. "You should be careful how you choose your friends, Charles. The company was unrefined," sniffed Caroline; "decidedly provincial."

Hurst complained they were no crab patties at supper.

"For my part," said Louisa, "I saw little beauty and no fashion."

"You must have been asleep, Louisa," declared Bingley. "Miss Bennet is an angel!"

"What think you, Colonel?" asked Caroline, simpering behind her fan.

"I saw plenty of beauty, Miss Bingley," replied the colonel. "After all, I danced with *you!* And of fashion—I'm sure you and your sister were the most modishly dressed in the room."

Caroline batted her eyelashes. One point in her favour, but she could not be happy until she had cast the competition into disfavour.

"And what think you, Mr Darcy?" she asked, extracting him from his brown study.

"The music was too loud," Darcy replied; "and I agree, for the most part, the clothes of the participants were not sufficiently fine—only Sir William was wearing satin knee breeches."

Caroline was not satisfied with an aspersion on male fashion. She could see Darcy was out of sorts, and she sought a more specific putdown. "And what of Miss Bennet?"

"She is pretty, but she smiled too much," replied Darcy.

This was too much for Bingley. "On my word, Darcy, you are in a foul mood! What ails you?"

Darcy did not reply. Caroline could see she needed to do a little fishing.

"I heard you thought Miss Elizabeth Bennet quite dowdy, Mr Darcy!"

Darcy raised his eyebrows at that. "You were eavesdropping, Miss Bingley?"

Caroline flushed but concealed her face with her fan. "Of course not. Her mother scolded her so loudly for incurring your sartorial displeasure, I'm sure half the room heard her!"

"I'm afraid Miss Elizabeth heard your comment, Darcy," explained the colonel. "In her defence, Miss Bingley, she apprised me that she did not wear her finest because the local lads are a bit oafish and tear the ladies' dresses when they tread on them."

Caroline was not pleased with the colonel for coming to Miss Elizabeth's aid.

"Given that déclassé partners are all she can garner," she replied tartly, "she may be forgiven the sprig muslin, though it cannot do her any credit; but what *can* have induced her to wear that dowdy chemisette?"

"I believe she was forced to adopt it when one of her sisters dropped some wax on her dress," added the colonel mildly.

"By hiding it under a chemisette!" exclaimed Caroline. "She would have done better to change the whole ensemble!"

"Undoubtedly," replied the colonel, mentally acknowledging that Miss Bingley would not have hesitated to make her whole party wait for half an hour or more while she executed such a change.

The colonel's lukewarm agreement to her criticism had to satisfy Miss Bingley. Her brother began to regale the company with pleasant reminiscences of the dances and conversations he had enjoyed.

Richard was glad when they reached Netherfield. He bid his host good night and thanked him for his hospitality—he would be off at daybreak to rejoin his regiment.

"Please feel free to join us when you can be spared from your regiment, Colonel," begged Bingley. "I have no doubt your cousin would enjoy your presence while he is working here. We plan a shooting party next weekend."

"Thank you, Bingley," acknowledged the colonel. "It would be my pleasure if I am able."

The ladies of Longbourn arrived home much later, having a greater distance to travel from Meryton than the Netherfield party and only two horses harnessed to their carriage instead of four. By the time they reached Longbourn, they had agreed on several points: that Mr Bingley was the most affable of the Netherfield Party; the colonel—the most charming; and Mr Darcy—the most handsome and disagreeable. Mr Hurst and the Bingley sisters hardly rated a mention, though Jane claimed the sisters were very pleasing to talk to—a piece of information that failed to interest anyone else.

Upon arriving at the manor house, they disgorged into the night and promptly invaded their father's study. Mr Bennet was, of course, making astronomical observations, which occupied him on any clear night. The light of the candelabrum carried by Mrs Bennet made any further observations on the faint objects that were of current interest to him impossible. He sat down in a wing chair, resigned to the tedium of a recitation of the night's entertainment.

"Oh! my dear Mr Bennet," exclaimed Mrs Bennet as she entered the room, "we have had a most delightful evening, a most excellent ball! I wish you had been there. Jane was *so* admired; nothing could be like it. Everybody said how well she looked; and Mr Bingley thought her quite beautiful and danced with her twice! Only think of that, my dear; he actually danced with her twice! and she was the only creature in the room that he asked a second time. And Mr Bingley brought with him two other unmarried gentlemen—a Mr Darcy of Pemberley, worth ten thousand a year; and an earl's son who is a colonel in the Life Guards! Such a charming man! He danced with all our girls except for Mary, who sat against the wall all night and refused to put herself forward! He danced the first set with Lizzy, and the next with Lydia; but then he was waylaid by Charlotte Lucas, and after dancing with her, he was obliged to stand up with Mariah; but then Kitty partnered him in the Boulanger—"

"If he had had any compassion for me," cried her husband impatiently, "he would have sprained his ankle in the first dance!"

"Oh! my dear, nothing could be like it! Mr Bingley was so taken with Jane, he hardly left her side, and he looked quite miffed when the colonel asked her to dance. But poor Lizzy was insulted by Mr Darcy, who refused to stand up with her, saying she was dowdy and not handsome enough to tempt him!"

"To her face?" asked an astonished Mr Bennet, shocked that someone had outdone him in incivility.

"No, Papa," replied Lizzy. "I merely overhead him. You know what they say about eavesdroppers! I will make sure I stand well away from him in future!"

"But I can assure you," added Mrs Bennet, "that Lizzy does not lose much by not suiting his fancy, for he is a most disagreeable, horrid man, not at all worth pleasing. So high and so conceited that there was no enduring him! He walked here, and he walked there, fancying himself so very great! Not handsome enough to dance with! I wish you had been there, my dear, to have given him one of your set-downs. I quite detest the man!"

Having said her piece, Mrs Bennet was content to retreat to her chambers, closely followed by four of her daughters who were eager to get to bed. Lizzy stayed behind to look at the objects her father was viewing through the telescope, and during this companionable occupation no more was thought or said of Mr Darcy.

The next week was one of unspeakable boredom for the party at Netherfield. With the colonel gone, every attempt by Mr Bingley to steer the conversation to pleasant topics was thwarted: by the consistently spiteful comments of his sisters on their sojourn in the country; the indifference of Mr Hurst; and the absence of Mr Darcy, who locked himself in the study with the estate's ledgers.

While Darcy was gainfully employed in overseeing business on Bingley's behalf, he was also ruing his behaviour at the assembly. He had let his black mood get the better of him, and he knew he had behaved childishly. Worse still, he had mortified a young lady, a complete stranger, for no good reason. He felt apologetic towards the second eldest Miss Bennet, whatever her name was. Unfortunately, apologies were not Mr Darcy's strong point, so his silent empathy was likely to be the only outcome of these ruminations, much good that did her.

A welcome respite to the general ennui was provided by an invitation extended to the gentlemen of Netherfield from the officers of a militia regiment that had encamped in Meryton following the assembly. The gentlemen were invited to dine in the officers' mess that had been set up in one of the private rooms at the Red Lion. Unfortunately, Colonel Fitzwilliam, who was undoubtedly the chief person of interest to the officers, had not yet returned, but the invitation was gladly accepted nonetheless.

Having declared the neighbourhood beneath her touch, Miss Bingley now repined about the lack of social engagements available to the ladies.

This exasperated Charles, who had spent the past week encouraging his sisters to pay a morning call to the Bennets.

The problem, as Caroline saw it, was that she and Louisa had decided that Jane was the only Bennet sister worth knowing, based on the fact that she wore silk to the ball; agreed with all their pronouncements during their short conversation at the assembly; and had done nothing vulgar, like asking a gentleman if he wished to dance. She was, they declared, a *sweet* girl.

Unfortunately, they could hardly demand Jane's exclusive company if they visited the Bennets; but they *could* enjoy it if they invited Jane to Netherfield. Their only qualm in pursuing such a course was their concern that their brother had been overly particular in his attentions to her at the assembly. Such a connection would never do! As a friend, Jane Bennet was passable in the rural confines of Hertfordshire, but she could *not* be contemplated as a sister-in-law.

As soon as Charles reminded Caroline that a few morning calls might elicit some reciprocal invitations, Miss Bingley realised the perfect solution to their dilemma had presented itself—with Charles dining out, they could invite Jane without exposing their brother! Caroline sat down to write at once.

The letter was soon delivered at Longbourn by a footman who waited for an answer. Jane read the invitation with pleasure, but Mrs Bennet's reaction far exceeded her daughter's. She was so ecstatic one might have been forgiven for thinking that *she* was to be the guest at Netherfield. Her elation was somewhat dampened when Jane related that the gentlemen would not be present, but Mrs Bennet instructed her daughter to accept post-haste, and her mind began to whir.

As the daughter of a tradesman, Fanny Gardiner had managed to land a very big fish over twenty years ago when she married the local squire, Mr Bennet. Time had not dulled her ambition. Mrs Bennet was not to be thwarted in her aspirations for her daughters. If the gentlemen were absent from dinner, she needed to contrive some way of extending Jane's stay at Netherfield. A look at the gathering clouds outside proved inspirational.

When Jane went upstairs to dress, fully expecting to make the trip to Netherfield in the Bennet carriage, her mother advised her to put on something appropriate for riding as she needed the carriage to visit Mrs Stitchcombe. This lady just happened to live several miles distant on the London road—the opposite direction to Netherfield.

Jane was halfway to Netherfield on the Bennet cob when the heavens opened up. She was soaked through and chilled to the bone by the time she arrived at the Bingleys' door. The rain continued the whole evening without intermission, and the Bingley sisters were obliged to extend their hospitality to an overnight stay for Jane, just as her mother had hoped.

6 Miss Elizabeth's solicitude

The Master of Pemberley was sitting in a tree. He knew Finn would berate him once he saw the state of his buckskin breeches, but he would have to lump it. The atmosphere in the house was decidedly close in more ways than one—Darcy needed to breathe fresh air.

Yesterday's rain had given way to a muggy atmosphere that pervaded Netherfield. Although Darcy had once again locked the study, Miss Bingley had abused the mistress's chatelaine several times to intrude on his solitude—there had been a cup of tea and a biscuit, a book she had forgotten, and finally, an offer to mend his pen.

Escaping outside after the last incident, Darcy had found a marvellous oak near the ha-ha and disappeared into it. Within the fastness of its leafy breast, he straddled a mighty branch and, leaning back against the trunk, was finally able to relax.

He thus was in a very privileged position to see the arrival of Miss Elizabeth Bennet at Netherfield after the rain. Darcy perceived her as an anonymous female in the distance, following a cow-track that ran down to the stream. Picking up her skirts, she forded the stream in several bounds, jumping nimbly from rock to rock. Reaching the other side, she continued across the long grass with her skirts held aloft.

By this time Darcy had positively identified her as the second eldest Bennet sister—she of the dowdy chemisette. He could see she was wearing sturdy walking boots, and once or twice he fancied he could see the flesh of her calves above them.

She proceeded to walk straight towards him, and it occurred to Darcy that she might be using the oak he was sitting in as a landmark. When she arrived at the ha-ha she paused, and her head disappeared beyond the edge of the wall. Then her fingers appeared on the capstones and her head rose above it. She scrambled nimbly up, and during this process Darcy was shocked to see her knees. Reaching the top, she stood upright and he could see that she had tied knots in the hem of her dress and her petticoats to free her legs as she climbed. It looked like her legs were wholly exposed below the knee; but as he was sitting above her, he was in no position to appreciate the view. She proceeded to let down her skirts and, after straightening her clothes and tidying the curls that had escaped her bonnet, set off towards the house, oblivious of his presence.

He could see as she walked off that she was carrying something heavy in a simple drawstring reticule that she was wearing on her back. Her arms were swinging freely at her sides.

At some point as he watched her retreat, Darcy felt slightly dizzy and realised he was not breathing. It occurred to him what a spectacle he would have made should he have been found unconscious under the tree after falling out of it. A similar incident from his childhood flashed into his mind. He had been playing a boisterous game of pirates in a large tree at Pemberley with his cousin Richard and Wickham, when he slipped and fell. Apparently he had been borne into the house unconscious by the servants and awoke to find his mother and Mrs Reynolds fussing over him. In the event of such an accident at Netherfield, no doubt the solicitous Miss Bingley would do the fussing. He shuddered to think of it.

Some time after Miss Bennet had disappeared round the corner of the house, Darcy climbed down a little more carefully than he normally would have, had this memory not intruded. After flicking out his tails and straightening his coat, he proceeded back to the study, entering the house by the terrace and the French doors.

Bingley was in the study.

"Ah, there you are, Darcy! The door was locked and I couldn't think where you had got to! I thought perhaps it was The Rapture and I'd been left behind!"

Darcy smiled. "That is heresy, Bingley."

"Well, at least I got a smile from you. I haven't seen many of those lately."

"I needed some fresh air."

"Yes, well, you and Miss Elizabeth Bennet! She's just walked from Longbourn to tend her sick sister—all three miles. She's an intrepid lass!"

"Don't let your sister catch you using that word," remarked Darcy while thinking: *Elizabeth, yes, that was her name!*

"Lass? Yes, Caroline doesn't want anyone to suspect we are descended from grubby tradesmen in Yorkshire! But I digress… lunch is served, or would you prefer a tray?"

"No, I'll join you," said Darcy before accompanying his friend out of the study.

There was no sign of Miss Elizabeth Bennet in the dining room, but she was soon the topic of conversation.

"Well, Mr Darcy!" greeted Caroline, "You have just missed the most entertaining spectacle! Miss Eliza Bennet just arrived in our drawing room with her petticoat six inches deep in mud!"

"She seems to have disappeared," said Darcy blandly, sitting down to table and immediately surveying the viands on offer. Darcy had to admit Miss Bingley kept a good table.

"She's gone upstairs to tend her sister," said Bingley. "Caroline did you offer to send a tray up?"

"*Of course*, Charles. I had already requested one for Jane, so they will add a little extra to that."

"I shall never forget her appearance," continued Caroline, not to be deterred from her topic. "She really looked almost wild!"

"Yes!" tittered Louisa. "And the gown which had been let down over her petticoats to hide it not doing its office!"

Darcy selected some slices of apple, a portion of cheese, and a roll, which he began to butter.

"I could hardly keep my countenance," said Caroline. "How nonsensical to come at all! Why must she be scampering about the country because her sister has a cold? Her hair, so untidy, so blowsy!"

"She came to look after her sister, Caroline," said Charles. "Surely her exertions on her sister's behalf outweigh any untidiness in her appearance."

Darcy sipped his ale.

"To walk three miles, or four miles, or five miles, or whatever it is, above her ankles in dirt, and alone, quite alone! What could she mean by it? It seems to me to show an abominable sort of conceited independence, a most country-town indifference to decorum."

"It shows an affection for her sister that is very pleasing," said Bingley. "Hurst, will you pass the pepper?"

Darcy selected some pressed tongue, chutney and a little of the cucumber salad.

"I am inclined to think that you, Mr Darcy, would not wish to see *your* sister make such an exhibition," said Caroline.

"Certainly not," said Darcy. "She would not be allowed outside alone."

Caroline smiled to herself—one point to her.

"I have an excessive regard for Miss Jane Bennet," said Caroline. "She is really a *very sweet* girl, and I wish with all my heart she were well settled. But with such a father and mother, and *such* low connections, I am afraid there is no chance of it."

"I think I have heard you say that their uncle is an attorney in Meryton," added Louisa.

"Yes, and they have another," said Caroline, "who lives somewhere near *Cheapside*."

"How apposite!" added her sister, and they both laughed heartily.

"If they had uncles enough to fill all Cheapside," cried Bingley, "it would not make them one jot less agreeable."

"But it must very materially lessen their chance of marrying men of any consideration in the world," replied Caroline.

"Too true!" agreed Louisa, as her husband belched loudly.

Darcy selected a slice of the apple and onion tart.

"If you don't mind, I should get back to the ledgers. I didn't get much work done this morning," he said, looking particularly at Miss Bingley.

Caroline did not take the hint.

"Let me refill your mug of ale," she said, as she motioned to a footman; "and help you take it back to the study. It goes very well with the apple and onion tart."

When they arrived in the hall, they encountered Miss Elizabeth descending the stairs with a maid.

"…if you could fetch a glass for the barley water I've left on the night stand, Sally, that will give Jane some immediate relief. I'll brew the tisane in the kitchens. It will be more powerful, but it will take me over half an hour to prepare it, and at least that amount of time to have an effect."

"Yes, ma'am," said Sally, effacing herself.

Miss Bingley bristled at this interloper issuing orders to her servants.

"Is there anything I can do to make you more comfortable, Miss Eliza?" she asked sarcastically.

"Thank you, Miss Bingley," replied Elizabeth, either not noticing or ignoring the barb in Miss Bingley's words. "I was hoping to procure something to read to my sister. I would have brought a book myself, but I couldn't fit anything else in my reticule once I put in the barley water."

"I believe," said Mr Darcy, "there are some books in the study. I hardly know what they are, but I would appreciate if you selected a volume now, as I would prefer to work uninterrupted this afternoon."

Elizabeth really wanted to get the tisane brewed as quickly as possible, but she acceded to his demand. She hardly wished to incur his further displeasure lest she be accused of being a pollywoggle, or whatever came below *dowdy* in degree.

All three entered the study, and Mr Darcy indicated Netherfield's poor stock of literature on the bookshelves, which mostly held ornaments and ledgers.

Miss Bingley stood at the door and tapped her foot.

"You need not wait, Miss Bingley," said Darcy as he sat behind the large desk. "I will lock the door once Miss Elizabeth leaves."

"Surely it would be improper to leave Miss Elizabeth unescorted," Caroline replied.

"It is not improper if the door is left open," said Darcy imperturbably.

Caroline had little choice but to depart.

Elizabeth quickly chose a volume of Shakespeare and curtseying, turned to exit, stage right.

"Which did you choose, Miss Elizabeth?" Darcy asked.

"Shakespeare, sir."

"But which volume?"

"Volume three of Mr Steeven's edition."

"Ah! The Comedies. There are some who consider them among Shakespeare's lesser works."

"I am not among them, sir. Everyone needs to laugh."

"Indeed," he said solemnly and following her to the door, he closed and locked it.

It was only when he turned back to the desk that he noticed the handkerchief lying crumpled on the floor.

Picking it up, he saw it had a crocheted lace edge. One corner was cut out and filled in with lace, and in the opposite corner the initials EB were embroidered in white. There was a spot of blood near the centre. He realized Miss Elizabeth had been holding it in her hand when she reached up for the book.

Darcy knew he really should give the handkerchief back to Miss Elizabeth straight away—having walked to Netherfield, it was probably the only one she had with her, but he *did* want to get back to work…

He stuffed it into his pocket.

Returning to his journals and ledgers, Darcy worked, blessedly uninterrupted, 'til dinner. Perhaps Charles had finally put a word in Caroline's ear…

Having administered the tisane, Elizabeth was gratified to see her sister's temperature come down in the afternoon. Jane felt well enough to wish to converse with her sister; but Elizabeth forestalled her, knowing she should rest her swollen throat. Instead, she entertained her sister for an hour or so by reading the play until Jane drifted off to sleep, exhausted by her illness and the disturbed night she had spent at Netherfield.

Seeing her sister's wan face lying on the pillow, Lizzy thought their mother had rocks in her head if she thought Jane could recommend herself to Mr Bingley in her current state, but she reckoned without that gentleman. Not half an hour later, Elizabeth answered a soft knock on the bedchamber door to reveal Mr Bingley with a bunch of beautiful red roses.

Elizabeth quickly held her fingers to her lips to indicate Jane was asleep.

Mr Bingley pointed his finger inside to indicate that he wished to enter.

Elizabeth was not quite sure how to deal with this request. It seemed improper to admit a gentleman to a lady's bedchamber, but she supposed she was present to chaperone. Nor did she wish to wake Jane by disputing with him. Surely it would not be improper if she left the door open?

Mr Bingley tiptoed in and stood a respectful distance from the bed, smiling beatifically upon Jane with his head tipped to one side. When it was clear that he did not immediately intend to quit this position, Elizabeth grew uncomfortable watching him. Pulling the bell rope, she instructed the summoned maid to fetch a vase. When this arrived, she managed to prise the blooms from Mr Bingley's nerveless fingers and distracted herself by arranging the flowers in it. Having completed this operation, Mr Bingley showed no sign of quitting his post, and she was obliged to motion him to the door.

Once Elizabeth had accompanied him outside, Mr Bingley asked her if she thought Jane any better.

"I gave her a draught and her temperature has come down," said

Elizabeth, "but I expect it will rise again towards evening. It is too early to expect an improvement."

"Oh, well, if you need anything, please don't hesitate to ask," he requested, smiling at her as he took his leave.

Some hours later, Miss Bingley finally appeared to fulfil her obligations as hostess. She was accompanied by her sister, Louisa. Jane was awake—her temperature having risen again; and she was much worse than when Elizabeth had first encountered her in the morning.

When Miss Bingley assured Elizabeth that she would have a maid sit by Jane overnight and offered her the carriage to return to Longbourn, Jane testified such concern in parting with her sister that Miss Bingley was obliged to convert the offer of the chaise to an invitation to remain at Netherfield for the present.

Elizabeth most thankfully consented, and a servant was dispatched to Longbourn to acquaint the family with her stay and bring back a supply of clothes.

Caroline was mollified when her reluctantly tendered dinner invitation was rejected. Elizabeth assured them she could not possibly think of coming down to dinner with Jane in her current state. Caroline then extended an invitation to take tea with herself and Louisa once the ladies had withdrawn if Jane was more settled.

Thus sometime around nine, a maid appeared at the bedchamber door offering to sit by Miss Bennet if Miss Elizabeth wished to join the ladies for tea. As Jane had fallen asleep after her temperature was again lowered by re-administration of the tisane, Elizabeth consented.

Miss Bingley's attempt to limit Miss Elizabeth's time in the gentlemen's company was somewhat thwarted when they removed themselves from the dining room in record time. This was no coincidence—Bingley had heard Miss Elizabeth's voice and suggested their early departure. Mr Hurst was in favour of the project as he wished to pursue his normal after-dinner occupation of falling asleep on the settee, and Mr Darcy make no demur.

When the gentlemen entered, the ladies were sitting in three armchairs arranged on an Aubusson rug near the fire. A tea tray rested on a nearby card table. Mr Hurst headed straight for the settee while Darcy and Bingley joined the ladies, arranging themselves standing with their backs to the hearth as Miss Bingley poured them tea.

Mr Bingley began the conversation with inquiries on Miss Elizabeth's sister's health. Not much liking the topic, Caroline sought to change it.

"And what of your sister, Mr Darcy? Is Miss Darcy much grown since the spring?" asked Miss Bingley. "Will she be as tall as I am?"

"I think she will. She is now about Miss Elizabeth Bennet's height or rather taller."

This comparison displeased Miss Bingley. "How I long to see her again!

I never met with anybody who delighted me so much. Such a countenance, such manners! And so extremely accomplished for her age! Her performance on the pianoforte is exquisite."

"It is amazing to me," said Bingley, "how young ladies can have patience to be so very accomplished as they all are."

"All young ladies accomplished! My dear Charles, what do you mean?" asked his sister.

"Yes, all of them, I think. They all paint tables, cover screens, and net purses. I scarcely know anyone who cannot do all this, and I am sure I never heard a young lady spoken of for the first time without being informed that she was very accomplished."

"Your list of the common extent of accomplishments," said Darcy, "has too much truth. But of what use are such abilities in a wife? Georgiana has created all the tables and screens I should want at Pemberley. I have no need of a woman who can make more."

"You forgot the purses, Darcy," said Bingley.

"You may have the purses, Bingley," smiled Darcy.

"Of course, your list is quite silly, Charles, as Mr Darcy rightly points out," interjected Caroline. "A woman must have a thorough knowledge of music, singing, drawing, dancing, and the modern languages, to deserve the accolade of 'accomplished'; and besides all this, she must possess a certain something in her air and manner of walking, the tone of her voice, her address and expressions, or the distinction will be but half-deserved."

"While a woman's ability to sing or play may have some entertainment value, I cannot think these things important either," replied Mr Darcy.

"Whatever can you mean, Mr Darcy?" asked Caroline, horrified to hear her expensive education at an exclusive ladies' seminary so summarily dismissed.

"A woman must be fit and strong to bear children. She must be able to care for the children, and nurse them through childhood illnesses and accidents; and she must be well-read, knowledgable and ethical to educate them to become valued members of society."

"Surely these are the roles of nurses and governesses, Mr Darcy," scoffed Miss Bingley.

"No, Miss Bingley. Nurses are uneducated women who need supervision. As for governesses, a child's character is largely formed ere they ever come near a governess. A mother is the preceptress of this important stage in a child's life."

"Should you ever find such a woman, Darcy, no doubt your children will be pattern cards," said Bingley; "but what of your own heart?"

Darcy was tempted to reply that he had no heart. Certainly it felt like it had been ripped from his breast, though he would never really expose himself by saying so, especially in front of Caroline. But Bingley had poked him in a tender spot and he relapsed into silence. He might have felt somewhat appeased if he'd known that his friend had already received physical retribution—Miss Bingley had stamped on her brother's foot for using the déclassé "pattern card" metaphor.

Mr Darcy's unlikely rescuer was Miss Elizabeth. She thought there was much sense in what he said, no matter how coldblooded it sounded. "I'm sure if Mr Darcy ever found such a paragon, his heart would be well-looked after," she said softly.

This surprised Mr Darcy who had not looked for kindness from a lady to whom he had been most unkind.

"You must excuse me," said Elizabeth, getting up. "I should return to my sister."

She was about to depart when a thought occurred to her. "Oh, Miss Bingley, I seem to have lost my handkerchief. It has my initials on it, should the servants find it."

Mr Darcy reached into his pocket and for reasons he could never fully explain to himself, pulled out his own handkerchief.

"Please, Miss Elizabeth, take mine," he said, holding it out.

"Oh, thank you, Mr Darcy, but I couldn't. I'm sure that mine will turn up."

"But you can't be without a handkerchief. It would not do. Please take it until yours is restored to you. I have plenty."

Miss Bingley scowled.

After a moment's hesitation, Miss Elizabeth took the proffered handkerchief and curtseyed, responding, "Thank you."

7 Understanding Miss Elizabeth

Upon retiring to the guest wing, Mr Darcy heard Miss Elizabeth's voice as he passed her room and paused briefly to listen at the door. She was reading the volume of Shakespeare, using different voices for the characters. When she adopted a booming voice, he immediately recognized a speech by Petruchio from *The Taming of the Shrew*.

"Thus in plain terms: your father hath consented
That you shall be my wife; your dowry 'greed on;
And, will you, nill you, I will marry you."

Darcy would have tarried to hear more, but the sound of a maid ascending the stairs forced him to move on.

Entering his bedchamber, Darcy could hear Finn moving about in the dressing room. He almost walked straight in to his valet before thankfully remembering Miss Elizabeth's handkerchief was stashed in his pocket. Looking around for a hiding place, he stuffed it under his pillow.

Once Finn had retired, Darcy paced the room, attired in his nightshirt and banyan. He felt alert, not at all sleepy, and restless. After several laps of the bedchamber, he retrieved the hanky and threw himself into a Hepplewhite carver that stood near the window. Unfolding the handkerchief, Darcy questioned his motives in withholding it from its owner. It made no sense. Staring abstractedly at the small blood spot, he wondered how she had injured herself. *Perhaps climbing the ha-ha?*

It was then Darcy realised he could still hear Miss Elizabeth's voice. When he raised the sash of the window, he discovered that it remained reasonably warm outside. Her voice was noticeably louder. *Perhaps her window was also open?*

Testing his theory, he leant out of the casement. Sure enough, her voice was more discernible now, but no light shone from the adjacent window. *She must have the window open and the curtain closed.* It seemed an unusual arrangement for a sick room...

Darcy concentrated on her voice, trying to discern her place in the play from the snatches he caught. The voice characterizations were quite good. She seemed to be a natural mimic. He listened for what seemed like half an hour with his elbows resting on the casement, all the time repetitively drawing the handkerchief with his right hand through a loop he had made with the finger and thumb of his left. He was rudely interrupted from this trance-like state when Miss Elizabeth's voice suddenly became louder and a flash of light beamed outside indicated she had drawn the curtain aside.

"I think that's enough fresh air!" he heard her call from next door. "It's getting cold."

His reaction to this change of the status quo was violent. He stood up suddenly, crashing the back of his head against the upper casement. Seeing stars, he stepped back into the room, unsure whether his eavesdropping had been detected. The crash had seemed quite loud, but his ears *were* attached to his injured head. When Darcy rubbed the back of his skull, he could feel a lump forming there, but there was no blood. He listened, but no further sounds were forthcoming, and the light had disappeared. It seemed his blundering had not been detected.

Darcy untied the belt of his banyan and flung it onto the Hepplewhite chair. Climbing into bed, he reached out to snuff the wax candle. It had burnt down far more than the half-hour he had perceived to pass, making him aware that he must have lost track of time.

Laying his head on the pillow, he fell instantly asleep.

There was no sign of Miss Elizabeth or her sister at breakfast. Darcy blocked out the chatter of the Bingley sisters as he ate, despite the fact that his opinion was continually sought. He answered their queries with, "Really?", "Indeed!", or by repeating the last phrase he heard, which he seemed to be able to recall from the aether, as a question. When Miss Bingley finally put him on the spot by demanding a more specific answer, he replied, "I'm sorry, my mind must have been wandering."

When Darcy looked up from his breakfast to find Charles grinning mischievously at him, he excused himself to the study.

At eleven o'clock, he heard a carriage draw up. The identity of its occupant was not long in doubt when Mrs Bennet's loud exclamations reverberated in the hallway—presumably she had come to reclaim her offspring. Darcy could not be sorry for it. He found himself thinking about Miss Elizabeth Bennet more than was warranted, and he still hadn't returned her handkerchief.

Mrs Bennet removed herself to the upper reaches of the house for half an hour, but when he heard her descend, the conversation outside the study door took a different tack to the one he had imagined.

"I do not think it would be wise to move her," declared Mrs Bennet. "Indeed, she might have a dangerous relapse!"

Miss Elizabeth's voice answered in a tone too soft for the words to be distinguished.

"I must agree with your mother, Miss Elizabeth," Charles replied. "The apothecary has advised bed rest until the fever has completely subsided."

"I'm afraid we'll have to impose upon your kindness and solicitude a little longer, Miss Bingley," said Mrs Bennet.

"You may depend upon it, Madam," said Miss Bingley, with cold civility, "that Miss Bennet will receive every possible attention while she remains with us."

"But you must take some tea while you are with us, ma'am," offered Charles, seeing his sister was not about to do so.

"Why, thank you, sir," replied Mrs Bennet. "It is most appreciated."

The voices retreated into the breakfast parlour, and Darcy tried to refocus on the ledger before him. But before he could do so, he heard a key scraping in the lock of the study door and looked up to see Miss Bingley enter.

"Oh, Mr Darcy, you won't believe it! The entire horde has descended on us! I invite one Bennet and end up with six! Please save me! I demand sanctuary!"

"Shouldn't you be pouring tea, Miss Bingley?" he asked.

"I'm sure Louisa can handle the situation," Caroline replied.

Seeing he couldn't shame Miss Bingley into resuming her post, Darcy stood. "I believe *I* would like a cup of tea."

"Oh, Mr Darcy, I'll bring a tray. You cannot wish to endure the tedium of their company."

"I would not put you to the trouble, Miss Bingley," Darcy said, walking round the desk.

Miss Bingley moved to block him, but he was too quick for her. With three long strides he was at the door and had escaped into the hall.

Darcy entered the breakfast parlour from the hall at the same time as the housekeeper, Mrs Nicolls, bore the tea tray through the opposite door. He found Mrs Bennet with Miss Elizabeth and the three youngest Bennet daughters. Charles was the only representative of the Netherfield party. Some moments later, Caroline arrived, breathless from keeping up with Darcy's loose stride.

Mrs Bennet was surveying the furnishings. "You have a sweet room here, Mr Bingley, and a charming prospect over the gravel walk. I do not know a place in the country that is equal to Netherfield. You know Jane and Lizzy spent several years here growing up."

Mr Bingley expressed his surprise.

"Yes, dear Lady Yardley treated them like her own daughters. She only had sons, you know, and always wanted some daughters to dress prettily and brush their hair. Such a comfort to me! I spent a good part of my confinements for my three youngest in bed and was unable to look after them myself."

"Indeed," said Mr Bingley, motioning the ladies to the seats. "Do tell us more."

Darcy watched the three youngest sit down together on the settee—one sat bolt upright on one end, while the other two proceeded to whisper, giggle and poke each other. Mr Bingley performed the office of a footman, helping Mrs Bennet settle into a carver. Elizabeth hovered between the Netherfield and Longbourn parties, whether acting as a barrier or an intermediary Darcy was not sure.

"I did not know Jane had lived here at Netherfield," added Mr Bingley. "How old was she when she resided here?"

"Well, they lived here for five years, from the time Lizzy was born. So Jane would have arrived here at Netherfield when she was two, and she returned to Longbourn when she was seven."

"And you were ill all that time?" asked Mr Bingley solicitously.

"Having children did not agree with me, Mr Bingley. I was all right with my Jane, but Lizzy really did me in, and I got steadily worse with each confinement, until Mr Griffith thought dear Lydia might carry me off. He was the apothecary before Mr Jones, you know. Then Mr Bennet said, 'No more, Mrs Bennet! No more! You have suffered enough!'"

"Lady Yardley was kind enough to look after Jane and me as small children when mother was ill," translated Elizabeth.

"Lady Yardley was so taken with Jane!" continued Mrs Bennet. "I do not like to boast of my own child, but to be sure, Jane—one does not often see anybody better looking! She was like a little doll when Lady Yardley took her away. I cried for a whole day! She doted on Elizabeth too, but she was but a baby and hadn't a tooth in her head at the time. She spent most of the time when she first arrived at Netherfield in the care of the wet nurse I hired."

Mr Bingley grinned at Elizabeth, before checking if one of his sisters was pouring the tea. Louisa, who had materialised from somewhere, was performing this office, handing the cups to Caroline to distribute.

"But the Yardley sons were very kind to Lizzy," continued Mrs Bennet, "particularly the two youngest, Fred and Bob."

"It was Albert and Edward, Mama! Fred and Bob are your nephews!" corrected Lizzy.

"Of course, that's what I meant, dear!" Mrs Bennet said before returning her attention to Mr Bingley. "When Lizzy was old enough to sit up, they used to cart her around in a hand truck with their little dog, although I've forgotten the name of the breed. It had a funny, pushed-in nose."

"It was a pug, Mama!" replied Lizzy.

"Indeed, she was most kind!" said Mrs Bennet. "Lady Yardley, I mean, not the pug. A true lady! Always willing to graciously condescend to her neighbours! Not like some I could name, who are too haughty to even make themselves agreeable at a local dance!"

Elizabeth blushed when she realized her mother's comments were directed at Mr Darcy.

"But I'm sure Mr Bingley is not interested in the details, Mama. Suffice to say we spent several years living here with Lady Yardley, who was most kind to take us in."

Belying her words, Elizabeth knew Mr Bingley was tolerating this onslaught in his usual affable manner; she was more concerned about incurring the censure of the other members of the Netherfield party—Caroline had a mocking look in her eye as she dispensed the teacups; and Mr Darcy? Elizabeth could not tell if his expression was one of disdain or boredom, but neither was good.

"On the contrary, Miss Elizabeth," objected Mr Bingley. "This is most fascinating! You must tell me more of Jane!"

"Well!" said Mrs Bennet, gratified to have the subject taken up by the man it was directed at. "Nothing would do for Lady Yardley but to have Jane dressed in the most beautiful costumes! I remember she came to Longbourn to visit for my birthday—she must have been six at the time, dressed in the most beautiful taffeta gown, cornflower blue, just like her eyes. Her hair was curled to perfection. She looked just like my Pandora doll!"

Caroline rolled her eyes at Mr Darcy, while Elizabeth watched them in growing dismay.

"No, she must have been seven then," reminisced Mrs Bennet, "because Lizzy came also and wore a similar dress, only green, which looked very well on her until she spilt her milk all over it!"

Lizzy blushed as Caroline suppressed a titter.

"What a droll story, Mrs Bennet!" Miss Bingley commented with a fake air of bonhomie. "Do you have any more?"

"Oh, yes!" gushed Mrs Bennet. "Once I recovered from Lydia's birth, the girls returned home, much to the disappointment of Lady Yardley, but I felt I had trespassed upon her goodwill for too long! The day Mr Bennet came to take them back, Bob, their youngest, did not want Lizzy to leave!"

"Edward, Mother," corrected Lizzy with an inward groan. *Not this story!*

"Edward, yes. He was ten at the time. They ran off together through the fields, and when the servants finally found them, Lizzy had mud up to her knees!"

"Not much has changed then," said Caroline, *sotto voce*.

She was heard only by Elizabeth and Darcy, who both shot a quick look at Miss Bingley to hear her contribution before realising the spiteful nature of her comment, whereupon they quickly turned away, but in opposite directions, so neither noticed the negative reaction of the other.

"But I digress," continued Mrs Bennet, "Jane and Lizzy often visited Lady Yardley after they departed Netherfield, and her Ladyship never failed to comment on Jane's beauty. I do not like to boast of my own child, but to be sure, Jane—one does not often see anybody better looking. It is what everybody says. I do not trust my own partiality! When she was only fifteen, there was a man at my brother Gardiner's in town so much in love with her, that my sister-in-law was sure he would make her an offer before we came away. But, however, he did not. Perhaps he thought her too young.

However, he wrote some verses on her, and very pretty they were."

"And so ended his affection," said Elizabeth impatiently. "There has been many a one, I fancy, overcome in the same way. I wonder who first discovered the efficacy of poetry in driving away love!"

"I have been used to consider poetry as the food of love," said Darcy.

"Of a fine, stout, healthy love it may," replied Elizabeth with élan; "everything nourishes what is strong already. But if it be only a slight, thin sort of inclination, I am convinced that one good sonnet will starve it entirely away."

Darcy only smiled; and the general pause that ensued made Elizabeth tremble lest her mother should be exposing herself again. She longed to speak, but could think of nothing to say; and after a short silence Mrs Bennet began repeating her thanks to Mr Bingley for his kindness to Jane, with an apology for troubling him also with Lizzy. Mr Bingley was unaffectedly civil in his answer and forced his younger sister to be civil also and say what the occasion required. Caroline performed her part without much graciousness, but Mrs Bennet was satisfied, and soon afterwards she ordered her carriage.

Upon this signal, the youngest of her daughters put herself forward. The two younger girls had been whispering to each other during the entirety of their mother's speech, and the result of it was that Lydia should tax Mr Bingley with having promised on his first coming into the country to give a ball at Netherfield.

His answer to this sudden attack was delightful to their mother's ear:

"I am perfectly ready, I assure you, to keep my engagement; and when your sister is recovered, you shall, if you please, name the very day of the ball. But you would not wish to be dancing when she is ill."

Lydia bounced up and down, causing the settee to creak alarmingly. She hugged her sister and squealed, declaring herself satisfied. "Oh! yes—it would be much better to wait 'til Jane is well because the men always want to dance with her, and by that method we can be introduced!"

When Mrs Bennet and her youngest daughters departed, Elizabeth returned instantly to Jane, leaving her own and her relations' behaviour to the remarks of the two ladies and Mr Darcy; the latter of whom, however, could not be prevailed on to join in their censure of her, in spite of all Miss Bingley's witticisms.

8 Badajoz

Elizabeth did not come down for lunch, and when Darcy escaped out the library doors in the afternoon, he once more sought the refuge of the oak. He had not been ten minutes in the tree, watching the leaves flutter in the breeze when he heard footsteps on the grass, and glancing around, saw Miss Elizabeth approach. When Darcy saw her object was the ha-ha, he thought she might intend escaping Netherfield, but she merely walked to the edge and sat on the capstones, dangling her feet over the side.

After a minute's indecision as to whether he should announce his presence, Darcy gave in to his more sociable side and said in a loud, clear voice, "I thought you were going to jump."

And jump she did. Swivelling her upper body round, it took her a moment to locate him in the tree.

"Mr Darcy, whatever are you doing up there?"

"Surveying the countryside. It is part of a steward's duties. May I join you?"

Elizabeth wasn't too enthusiastic about this idea, but between being spied on from the tree and his immediate presence, it seemed the lesser of two evils.

"Of course," she replied.

Being on show, Darcy jumped down boldly and athletically, then settled himself beside her on the capstones.

"Is this a favourite place of yours?" he asked.

"I could ask you the same thing," she replied.

"I asked first," he countered.

"I am a lady," she grinned in reply.

Darcy raised his eyebrows at this gambit. He had such a natural look of hauteur that Elizabeth blushed and cast down her eyes, feeling she had been terribly forward.

"Of course, ladies first," he muttered. "I like to sit in this oak when I have a need for fresh air."

After delivering this speech, he got a mischievous look on his face and decided to exact his revenge for being forced to go first.

"In fact," he drawled, "I was sitting here yesterday when you arrived at Netherfield. You scaled the ha-ha quite proficiently."

Her eyes still downcast, Elizabeth started, looked up, and blushed again. "I beg your pardon, but it is a good quarter mile extra to go via the carriageway and I thought I would be unobserved—you cannot see this part of the ha-ha from the house."

"Really?" he asked, swivelling around to look at the house. "I hadn't noticed that." *Well! My oak is a better hiding place from Miss Bingley than I had heretofore appreciated...*

"The house is situated so there is a blind spot here," explained Elizabeth. "The windows on the east front look to one side of the oak, and those on the south front to the other. So I thought I could save myself some time and energy without embarrassment."

"But surely there is an opening in the ha-ha somewhere," he ventured. "Some steps?"

"Yes, they are along that way," she pointed. "The path from the door in the middle of the south front leads to them. There is a gate at the bottom, but the key was lost years ago. Sir Laurence and Lady Yardley only ever went out in the carriage, so they didn't see the point in replacing it. The boys chose this place near the oak as an alternate entry and chiselled some footholds in the wall to help themselves scramble up."

A silence stretched between them.

Darcy tried to get the conversation going again. "So you eloped with the youngest boy when you were ten?"

Darcy's friends would have immediately recognized this as a joke, but he had a way of delivering such lines with a straight face, and Elizabeth was still smarting from her mother's visit.

"It wasn't an elopement!" she replied hotly. "I was five! Edward was ten. He didn't want me to go back to Longbourn, so we ran off together and hid. The poor servants spent most of the day looking for us. Edward decided to take me back in the afternoon because I got wet and started to sneeze."

"No doubt that was due to all the mud, or was it milk?" he replied light-heartedly.

Elizabeth blushed again. "I hope you will forgive my mother. Her tongue tends to run on wheels, but she means well."

"I'm afraid I didn't see that," he replied. "She seemed to spend all her time denigrating you at your sister's expense."

"That wasn't her intention. She was merely relating some stories of our stay here at Netherfield. Jane spent most of her time indoors with Lady Yardley, whereas I spent most of my time with the two younger boys and hence got dirtier."

"So you are a tomboy."

"Not at all. I liked Pug, you see, and once I could crawl was forever trying to play with him. The boys used to take Pug with them when they went outdoors, and so they started to take me also. This inevitably involved falling into a few puddles."

Darcy sensed his attempt to set Miss Elizabeth at ease had backfired and sought to change the subject.

"I understand Sir Laurence Yardley left Netherfield after his lady died. How many sons does he have? I must admit I have never met them."

"He had three, but they are all dead. That was why he remarried and let

Netherfield."

"I'm sorry. If you were close to them, it must have been like losing your brothers."

"It was, for the two younger. The eldest, Henry, I didn't know very well. He was already at Eton when I arrived at Netherfield. He was a bit of a scapegrace. But Albert and Edward... It was such a tragedy. They both joined the army and were killed during the Siege of Badajoz. Edward volunteered for the Forlorn Hope, so he took a risk. Nobody imagined it would be as bad as it was. And for Albert to be killed too... Jane and I were visiting when their names were published in the gazette. It was terrible. Lady Yardley collapsed. Jane and I stayed for a week to nurse her and would have stayed longer, but Sir Laurence thought it best to take her off to town—that there were too many memories here at Netherfield."

Elizabeth picked a stem of clover and began to tear the leaves from it.

"But worse was to come," she continued. "A month later, Henry was killed in a curricle-racing accident. Apparently Lady Yardley never got over losing all three of her children so quickly. She died of the grippe six months later. It is over a year ago now."

Darcy realised belatedly that Lady Yardley, whose passing he had mentioned so casually, was almost like a mother to Miss Elizabeth. He could see she was having trouble maintaining her equanimity and sought once again to change the subject.

"Well, your sisters seemed very eager for a ball."

Elizabeth winced. "I am sorry for my sisters' behaviour. They are a little young."

"Indeed, what was your mother thinking to allow them out of the schoolroom?" he blurted.

"They are out because they were never in. We never had any governess."

"No governess! How was that possible? Five daughters brought up at home without a governess! Is it possible you were educated by your mother?" he asked incredulously.

Elizabeth could hardly help smiling as she assured him that had not been the case. Her mother couldn't read and figured with her fingers, but she dared not tell Mr Darcy *that*.

"Then, who taught you?" he asked, thinking of her splendid rendition of *The Taming of the Shrew*.

"Jane and I were taught by Lady Yardley and the boys' governess, Miss Thraxton. Both of us could read by the time we returned to Longbourn. After that, father encouraged us to read and occasionally engaged tutors for us over the summer, mostly for mathematics and music. We taught our sisters to read, but it was done informally. Getting the two younger ones to sit still and apply themselves was sometimes difficult." *Especially when our attempts to teach our own mother to read resulted in her throwing up her hands and declaring it beyond her.*

"Aye, no doubt; but that is what a governess will ensure. Education requires steady and regular instruction. It is amazing you know as much as you do."

Elizabeth knew her education was spotty and was embarrassed about it, particularly talking to a man who had been to university.

Silence ensued, and it was Darcy who again spoke first, but perhaps not wisely.

"Regardless of their educational status, I question the wisdom of the younger girls being out. What was your mother thinking, to have all five of you out at once?"

Elizabeth's own opinion coincided exactly with Mr Darcy's, but she thought it was none of his business and proceeded to tell him so by giving a flippant answer.

"Don't you think it very hard upon younger sisters that they not have their share of society and amusement because the elder may not have the means or inclination to marry early? The last-born has as good a right to the pleasures of youth as the first. And to be kept back on such a motive! I think it would not be very likely to promote sisterly affection."

Darcy stared at her open-mouthed before realising she was not in earnest.

"You are pulling my leg," he said. "I believe Miss Bennet only recently attained her majority."

Elizabeth smiled and then got to her feet. "Excuse me. You remind me that I must return to my sister."

As she walked back, Lizzy thought Mr Darcy had certainly managed to make her feel small. She was dowdy and uneducated, and he had caught her behaving indecorously, climbing the ha-ha. Licking her wounds, it did not occur to her that she had discovered the haughty, university-educated Mr Darcy sitting in a tree or that he had condescended to get down from it to sit beside her on the ha-ha.

For his part, Mr Darcy thought this new information explained a lot about the Bennets. The two elder daughters were a world apart from the mother and the three younger ones.

The remainder of the day passed much as the day before. In the afternoon, Mrs Hurst and Miss Bingley made a perfunctory visit to the invalid, who continued, though slowly, to mend; and in the evening, Elizabeth joined their party in the drawing room after Jane fell asleep. Mr Hurst and Mr Bingley were at piquet with Mrs Hurst observing their game. Mr Darcy was writing a letter to his sister while Miss Bingley hovered near him, watching his progress, repeatedly complimenting the style and method of his writing, and making suggestions for its content.

Elizabeth sat down near the fire, pulled a small notebook and pencil from her pocket, and began to compose an acrostic to amuse Jane.

Despite Miss Bingley's solicitude, Mr Darcy finished his letter, although it took him half an hour longer than he had anticipated. He then picked up a volume from a side-table and, taking the chair opposite Elizabeth, sat down next to the fire.

This did not please Miss Bingley at all, and she asked if Mr Darcy would like some music. He replied pleasantly in the affirmative. When a polite request that Elizabeth should lead the way failed to dislodge her from her prime position near Mr Darcy, Miss Bingley moved with some alacrity to the pianoforte herself, determined to show how an accomplished lady could please a man.

Playing some Italian songs, Miss Bingley was gratified to receive a nod and smile from Mr Darcy at the conclusion of each piece, but she could not fail to appreciate that his attention was mostly elsewhere.

Despite Mr Darcy's ostensible object of reading, Elizabeth could not help observing as she wrote, how frequently Mr Darcy's eyes were fixed on her. She wondered if he was now finding fault with her penmanship or perhaps the grubby marks on her fingers from the pencil. She would have wiped her fingers on her handkerchief, but the realisation that it was *his* handkerchief in her pocket prevented her from doing so. Her only recourse was to do her best to ignore him, telling herself that she liked him too little to care for his approbation.

In truth, Darcy was interested to see Miss Elizabeth carried a notebook and pencil, just as he did. He would have liked to ask her what she was doing, *perhaps keeping a diary?*—but seeing Miss Bingley's hackles were raised, he dared not.

Miss Bingley saw, or suspected, enough to be jealous; and her great anxiety for the recovery of her dear friend Jane received some assistance from her desire of getting rid of Elizabeth. Noticing her attempts to draw Mr Darcy's attention were in vain, Caroline picked up an assortment of embroidery threads her sister had been untangling and, under the guise of sorting these, sat down on a footstool near Mr Darcy's chair, thus neatly inserting herself between the gentleman in question and Miss Elizabeth.

Having such long legs, Darcy had no need of this piece of furniture, but he suddenly wished he could place his boots on it.

When the tea tray arrived in the room half an hour later, Elizabeth took a cup for herself, but declared her intention to return with it to her sister. After she quit the room, Miss Bingley tried to provoke Darcy into disliking her guest by talking of their supposed marriage, and planning his happiness in such an alliance. Caroline thought the visit by Miss Elizabeth's mother and sisters that morning was surely enough to disgust him.

Not entirely satisfied with the mild disapproval Darcy expressed for

Miss Elizabeth's relatives, Caroline then proceeded to relate some gossip she heard from Lady Lucas during a morning call made by that lady and her daughters after the ball.

"Dear Elizabeth has my fullest sympathy, such a sad want of connections and prospects! You would think that living on a tidy estate, she might have a reasonable dowry, but alas! It is only a thousand pounds."

"Yes, so sad!" said Louisa, taking the place vacated by Miss Elizabeth in front of the fire, "and the estate entailed upon a cousin."

This last piece of information piqued Darcy's interest. "An entail?" he repeated.

Darcy had met Mr Bennet when he had first called on Mr Bingley. The squire was sixty if he was a day. He had also noted the deeply etched lines from that gentlemen's nose to his mouth that often indicated a heavy drinker. He thought of his own father who had died of an apoplexy at fifty-one. Suddenly he understood why all five daughters were out.

Darcy continued to try to read his book for the next half-hour, but the combination of the Bingley sisters' chatter and his own distraction prevented progress. In fact, his mind was full of Miss Elizabeth.

If Darcy had attempted to explain it, he would have said she was like a puzzle he was trying to solve—his mind would not let go of it. Unwilling to subject himself to the sound of her voice reading as on the previous night, he retired instead to the study and worked there until the candles were guttering in their sockets.

9 Introspection

In consequence of an agreement between the sisters, Elizabeth wrote the next morning to their mother to beg that the carriage might be sent for them in the course of the day. But Mrs Bennet, who had calculated on her daughters remaining longer at Netherfield, sent them word that they could not possibly have the carriage before Tuesday.

Against staying longer, however, Elizabeth was positively resolved—she asked Jane whether it might be possible to ask if Mr Bingley's carriage was available, and at length it was settled that their original design of leaving Netherfield that morning should be mentioned, and the request made.

The communication excited professions of concern from the Bingley sisters, which were as profuse as they were false, but they soon advised that the carriage would be made available directly after lunch.

The master of the house heard with real sorrow that the sisters were to go so soon and repeatedly tried to persuade Miss Bennet that it would not be safe for her—that she was not enough recovered—but Jane was firm where she felt herself to be right.

To Mr Darcy, it was welcome intelligence—Miss Elizabeth had been at Netherfield long enough. He thought about her more than he liked. Furthermore, Miss Bingley had noted his attention focused on her several times and was uncivil to her and more teasing than usual to himself. He wisely resolved to be careful to pay no further mind to her for the rest of the day, sensible that his behaviour during the previous day might have seemed over-particular. Steady to his purpose, he scarcely spoke ten words to Elizabeth before her departure, and when she sat down beside him for lunch, he would not even look at her.

It began to rain after lunch, and when the carriage drew up near the front steps, the sisters were escorted to it under an oilskin held by several footmen. From the study, Darcy watched, undetected, as the Bennets climbed into the carriage. The raindrops, chasing each other down the windowpane, obscured the scene.

Darcy was gripped by a melancholy during the afternoon, which threw him back to the mental state that had plagued him in London following his rupture with Diana. He steadfastly continued his progress through the ledgers, having resolved to check and summarise the contents of the previous seven years, but his mind constantly betrayed him with thoughts of his lost love—things he had said that made her laugh, things she had said to make him laugh, the touch of her skin, the flutter of her lashes. No escape to the oak was possible due to the rain, and by the time Miss Bingley called him to dinner, he had briefly lain his head upon his arms on the desk, wondering whether the rest of his life could possibly hold any joy for him.

Miss Bingley's voice calling out to him as her key scraped the lock snapped him out of the depths of his despair. He could not let Caroline see him in such a state.

Darcy talked little over dinner. The discussion was of the projected ball, a topic to which he had neither interest nor inclination to contribute.

"By the bye, Charles, are you really serious in meditating a dance at Netherfield?" sniped Caroline. "I would advise you, before you determine on it, to consult the wishes of the present party; I am much mistaken if there are not some among us to whom a ball would be rather a punishment than a pleasure."

"If you mean Darcy," cried her brother, "he may go to bed, if he chooses, before it begins—but as for the ball, it is quite a settled thing; and as soon as Nicolls has made white soup enough, I shall send round my cards."

"It is all very well for you," she replied. "As hostess, the bulk of the work in organising such an event will fall on me."

"And just think what a triumph for you it will be when you show them all how it is done!" grinned Charles.

This happy thought somewhat mollified Miss Bingley, and she spent the best part of the meal discussing with her sister how they could copy or outshine every good idea that had been employed at the balls they had attended in London during the last season, from the decoration of the room to the punch that was to be served.

After dinner, Darcy consented to play loo with the rest of the Netherfield party, a move that so pleased Mr Hurst that he decided to forego snoring on the sofa.

At eleven, Darcy declared himself exhausted and went to bed.

Darcy woke with a start the next morning, ready for violence. He had walked into the master's bedchamber at Pemberley to find Diana in his bed with the duke. He yelled at them, demanding what they meant by it. But they laughed at him and continued their carousing, whereupon he'd snatched a sword that was mounted on the wall.

Breathless, he found himself sitting up in bed, clutching the sheet.

Finn walked in. "Did you call, sir?"

Looking about him, Darcy recovered quickly. "What time is it?"

"Seven, sir. I had expected you to sleep another hour."

"I went to bed early last night," Darcy said lamely, hoping he hadn't yelled anything intelligible in his sleep.

He got up and cast an eye out the window. "It looks fine enough to ride. I'll head out before breakfast."

"Would you care for a cup of coffee before you depart, sir?"

"Thank you. Tell them not to bother to send it up, I'll drink it at the kitchen door."

Finn retreated through the dressing room to advise the kitchen before setting out his master's riding gear.

Darcy was back working in the study after lunch when Nicolls announced his cousin.

"Well, any luck?" asked the colonel as he strode in.

"With what?" asked Darcy, bemused.

"You seem to have a damnably short memory, Darcy! Finding a wife, of course."

"Oh, no. I will need to go back to London for that. I've been busy going through the ledgers for Bingley. The estate hasn't been badly run, but I think I can suggest some improvements."

The colonel rolled his eyes.

"Well, no doubt Pemberley will be the best-run estate in the kingdom, but Father is right, it will mean nought if you don't have an heir."

"And what of you?" retaliated Darcy. "How is *your* search going?"

The colonel smiled. "Well I passed a damned pretty wench carrying a basket in St Albans on my way here. I would have swept her up on my horse, but as I was wearing my uniform there might have been some sticky questions at the Life Guards."

"Very funny," replied Darcy. "So you're on your way to the north?"

"Yes, another communiqué for the general in Newcastle. Just thought I'd drop in and see how you're going, maybe get a drink. There's a stiff wind blowing outside."

Darcy smiled and poured his cousin a snifter of brandy. "It's only eleven o'clock you know."

"Tell that to the wind," retorted the colonel.

"When do you expect to return to Netherfield?"

"I am at the whim of the general's communications, but they usually turn me around in two days."

"There is a soirée at Lucas Lodge on Friday if you have a mind for it. Bingley's received an open invitation."

"If the general co-operates, it would be my dearest delight," replied the colonel.

After Richard finished his brandy, Miss Bingley persuaded him to stay for breakfast.

At Longbourn, the morning meal was turning into a memorable event.

"I hope, my dear," said Mr Bennet to his wife, "that you have ordered a good dinner to-day, because I have reason to expect an addition to our family party."

"Who do you mean, my dear? I know of nobody that is coming, I am sure, unless Charlotte Lucas should happen to call in—and I hope my dinners are good enough for her! I do not believe she often sees such at home."

"The person of whom I speak is a gentleman and a stranger."

Mrs Bennet's eyes sparkled. "A gentleman and a stranger! It is Mr Bingley, I am sure! Well, I am sure I shall be extremely glad."

Mr Bennet rolled his eyes at Lizzy.

"About a month ago I received this letter; and about a fortnight ago I answered it, for I thought it a case of some delicacy and requiring early attention. It is from my cousin, Mr Collins, who, when I am dead, may turn you all out of this house as soon as he pleases."

Lizzy could not be easy with the cruel nature of her father's teasing, but she knew it partly arose from his own depression on the topic.

"Oh! my dear," cried his wife, "I cannot bear to hear that mentioned. Pray do not talk of that odious man! I do think it is the hardest thing in the world that your estate should be entailed away from your own children; and I am sure, if I had been you, I should have tried long ago to do something or other about it."

Mrs Bennet continued her oft-repeated soliloquy, railing bitterly against the cruelty of settling an estate away from a family of five daughters, in favour of a man whom nobody cared anything about.

"It certainly is a most iniquitous affair," said Mr Bennet, "and nothing can clear Mr Collins from the guilt of inheriting Longbourn. But if you will listen to his letter, you may perhaps be a little softened by his manner of expressing himself."

"No, that I am sure I shall not! And I think it is very impertinent of him to write to you at all, and very hypocritical. I hate such false friends. Why could he not keep on quarrelling with you, as his father did before him?"

"Why, indeed; he does seem to have had some filial scruples on that head, as you will hear."

"Dear Sir,—

The disagreement subsisting between yourself and my late honoured father always gave me much uneasiness, and since I have had the misfortune to lose him, I have frequently wished to heal the breach; but for some time I was kept back by my own doubts fearing lest it might seem disrespectful to his memory for me to be on good terms with anyone with whom it had always pleased him to be at variance..."

"There, Mrs Bennet."

"...My mind, however, is now made up on the subject, for having received ordination at Easter, I have been so fortunate as to be distinguished by the patronage of the Right Honourable Lady Catherine de Bourgh, widow of Sir

Lewis de Bourgh, whose bounty and beneficence has preferred me to the valuable rectory of this parish, where it shall be my earnest endeavour to demean myself with grateful respect towards her ladyship and be ever ready to perform those rites and ceremonies which are instituted by the Church of England. As a clergyman, moreover, I feel it my duty to promote and establish the blessing of peace in all families within the reach of my influence; and on these grounds I flatter myself that my present overtures are highly commendable and that the circumstance of my being next in the entail of Longbourn estate will be kindly overlooked on your side and not lead you to reject the offered olive-branch. I cannot be otherwise than concerned at being the means of injuring your amiable daughters and beg leave to apologise for it, as well as to assure you of my readiness to make them every possible amends—but of this hereafter. If you should have no objection to receive me into your house, I propose myself the satisfaction of waiting on you and your family and shall probably trespass on your hospitality for a se'ennight, which I can do without any inconvenience, as Lady Catherine is far from objecting to my occasional absence on a Sunday, provided that some other clergyman is engaged to do the duty of the day.—I remain, dear sir, with respectful compliments to your lady and daughters, your well-wisher and friend,*

WILLIAM COLLINS"

"At four o'clock, therefore, we may expect this peace-making gentleman," said Mr Bennet as he folded up the letter. "He seems to be a most conscientious and polite young man, upon my word, and I doubt not will prove a valuable acquaintance, especially if Lady Catherine should be so indulgent as to let him come to us again."

"Mr Bennet!" exclaimed his wife. "You have had that letter for over a month! What do you mean by giving me such short notice of his descent upon us!"

"I did not wish to worry you unnecessarily in advance, my dear."

Mrs Bennet snatched the letter from her husband's hands and, passing it to Jane, asked her to read it again. She found herself more pleased on the second reading of the letter, saying: "There is some sense in what he says about the girls, and if he is disposed to make them any amends, I shall not be the person to discourage him."

"Though it is difficult," said Jane, "to guess in what way he can mean to make us the atonement he thinks our due, the wish is certainly to his credit."

Elizabeth was chiefly struck by the pompous style and extraordinary long-windedness of Mr Collin's correspondence. "Could he be a sensible man, Father?"

Mr Bennet sipped his tea, observing that his Lizzy had gone straight to the crux of the matter as he saw it. "No, my dear, I think not. I have great hopes of finding him quite the reverse. There is a mixture of servility and self-importance in his letter, which promises well. I am impatient to see him."

"In point of composition," said Mary, "the letter does not seem defective. The idea of the olive-branch perhaps is not wholly new, yet I think it is well expressed."

Mr Bennet smirked at his middle daughter's attempt at erudition. Her efforts to match her elder sisters' observations were just as pompous as Mr Collin's letter. To Kitty and Lydia, neither the letter nor its writer was in any degree interesting. Fixated on scarlet uniforms, they could have no interest in a clergyman.

Mr Collins was punctual to his time and was received with great politeness by the whole family. Mr Bennet achieved this by saying little; but the ladies were ready enough to talk, and Mr Collins seemed neither in need of encouragement nor inclined to be silent himself. He was a heavy-looking young man of five-and-twenty, whose figure, inclined to fat around the middle, seemed that of an older man. His air was grave and stately, and his manners were very formal. He had not been long seated before he complimented Mrs Bennet on having so fine a family of daughters; said he had heard much of their beauty but that in this instance fame had fallen short of the truth, and added that he did not doubt her seeing them all in due time disposed of in marriage. This gallantry was not much to the taste of some of his hearers, but Mrs Bennet, who quarrelled with no compliments, answered most readily.

The girls were not the only objects of Mr Collins's admiration. The hall, the dining room, and all its furniture were examined and praised. His commendation of everything initially touched Mrs Bennet's heart, for she really had done much to improve the shabby and dirty furnishings she had found at Longbourn when she first arrived—Mr Bennet's uncle, from whom he had inherited the estate by entail, had really let things go to a deplorable degree. However, when Mr Collins turned his cup over at dinner to examine the hallmark, Mrs Bennet's delight was tempered when it occurred to her that his interest might be somewhat mercenary.

During dinner, Mr Bennet, observing that Mr Collins seemed very fortunate in his patroness, found his cousin eloquent in her praise. She was all condescension; had given him advice on his sermons; had asked him twice to dine at Rosings; and had sent for him only the Saturday before to make up her pool of quadrille in the evening. She had even condescended to advise him to marry as soon as he could.

Mr Bennet nodded sagely and raised an eyebrow at Lizzy, who blushingly exchanged a horrified glance with Jane.

10 A soirée

Mr Collins was not a sensible man, and the deficiency of nature had been but little assisted by education or society—the greatest part of his life having been spent under the guidance of an illiterate and miserly father by whom his character had been set. By the time he entered university, he was not able to rehabilitate his mind through the intellectual environment he found there, but scraped his way through by rote. A fortunate chance had recommended him to Lady Catherine de Bourgh when the living of Hunsford became vacant.

In seeking a reconciliation with the Longbourn family, he had a wife in view, as he meant to choose one of the daughters if he found them as handsome and amiable as they were represented by common report. This was his plan of amends—of atonement—for inheriting their father's estate, and he thought it an excellent one, full of eligibility and suitableness, and excessively generous and disinterested on his own part.

Of this he apprised Mrs Bennet more fully the next morning over tea when all the girls had gone out to spend time in the garden.

Miss Bennet's lovely face, he averred to her mother, had confirmed his views over dinner and established all his strictest notions of what was due to seniority, such that *she* was his settled choice.

Mrs Bennet, immediately perceiving that if she played her cards carefully, she might very well have *two* daughters comfortably settled, issued him a caution against fixing on Jane. As to her younger daughters, she could not take it upon herself to say—she could not positively answer—but she did not know of any prepossession; her eldest daughter, she must just mention—she felt it incumbent on her to hint, was likely to be very soon engaged.

Mr Collins had only to change from Jane to Elizabeth, who was next to Jane in birth and beauty. It was done in the shake of a lamb's tail.

The invitation to attend the Lucases' soirée was duly extended to Mr Collins, and he found himself as the Bennet ladies' sole male escort on the night, Mr Bennet having abstained from the august event. Climbing down from the rumble seat of the carriage on their arrival, Mr Collins solicitously handed the ladies out, retaining Miss Elizabeth's hand far longer than her sisters' and smiling fatuously at her.

Upon entering Lucas Lodge, they found several select members of the town of Meryton and two officers of the militia standing in the vestibule. Of the Netherfield party, there was no sign.

In fact, Colonel Fitzwilliam and Mr Darcy were standing in a doorway leading from the vestibule, behind a curtain that Lady Lucas had untied to stop guests circulating through that door. It abutted an area of the foyer she had set up as a cloakroom. Richard had immediately spotted its possibilities for spying on arriving guests and guided his cousin there.

"Ah, ha! The Bennets are here, accompanied by a strange little man," whispered Richard.

Darcy strove to appear uninterested. "Really, Richard, must we stand here?"

"There is somewhere else in this room you would rather be?" Richard asked rhetorically. "Ah, Miss Bennet is wearing blue silk, matching her lovely eyes. Too late! Bingley has already snabbled her. Where did he come from? Ah, but Miss Elizabeth is looking radiant tonight!"

Darcy peered through the gap in the curtains. Elizabeth was wearing a sunny yellow dress with an ivory net overdress.

"You see? Miraculous!" said Richard. "She changes her dress, and your ugly duckling turns into a swan!"

Darcy had long realized that he had been unjust to Miss Elizabeth at the assembly, but he was not happy that his cousin had reminded him of his ungracious behaviour.

Sir William rushed to attend the Longbourn party, and Jane duly introduced their cousin. Mr Collins beamed unctuously upon a knight of the realm and proceeded to flatter him on the elegance of his abode—a topic sure to win Sir William's heart. It was during this interlude that some giggling was heard at the top of stairs and, after a short commotion and a yell, Little Johnny Lucas tumbled down the steps, landed unceremoniously on the tiles, and burst out wailing.

Sir William was quite flustered by this incident. He shot a scowling look at several children at the top of the stairs, who promptly effaced themselves. But he was saved from further embarrassment by his eldest daughter, Charlotte, who had come into the vestibule from the parlour, hoping her good friend Elizabeth had arrived. She helped her littlest brother up, straightened his short coats, and sitting down upon a chair, drew him upon her lap, whereupon he calmed considerably. Miss Elizabeth crouched in front of him, dabbing his knee with her handkerchief.

"Ah, yes. It does not look so bad under the blood," she said. "Shall I kiss it better?"

The child hiccupped and nodded.

She leant forward and planted her lips on his knee. Darcy unconsciously pouted his lips in sympathy.

Little Johnny miraculously stopped crying.

"Is it better now?" she asked.

"Yes," said the boy, wiping the tears from his eyes as he jumped from his sister's lap. He ran off, back up the stairs, as if nothing had happened.

"Magic!" said Charlotte.

"He just wanted some sympathy," smiled Elizabeth.

Sir William, whose dignity had been injured by this disruption, chose to ignore it.

"Come, come inside..., ladies, Mr Collins... Let me get you some refreshment." He bowed and gestured for them to precede him into the parlour.

Returning his attention from this scene, Darcy found his cousin watching him in amusement.

Richard puckered his lips in an air kiss. "Would you like a kiss too?" he joked.

Finally realising he was pouting, Darcy rearranged his face into his customary mask. "How much did you have to drink before we stepped into the carriage tonight?" he demanded of his cousin.

"Just enough to grease the wheels, Darcy. Come, I believe, we may abandon our espionage. The pretty girls have arrived."

"Miss Elizabeth, Miss Lydia, how do you do?" asked the colonel as they approached the Longbourn party. He'd already forgotten the names of the other two sisters.

Elizabeth smiled her understanding. "Very well, sir. You remember my sisters, Catherine and Mary."

"Of course, I had the pleasure of dancing with Miss Catherine at the assembly. And Miss Mary, I hope to further our acquaintance," he said, bowing.

"I am going to play the piano," declared Mary, flourishing some sheet music she held in her hands.

"Let me settle you at the instrument," declared Charlotte, taking her off.

The rest of the Bennet party merged with the other guests. Bingley drew Jane to a small group that included Lady Lucas and the Bingley sisters. The two youngest Bennet sisters made a beeline towards some young militia officers, leaving the colonel to conclude that his shine as a Life Guard had worn off; and they now considered him, at thirty, to have one foot in the grave. Cheerfully offering his arm to Elizabeth, they approached the rest of the Netherfield party with Darcy trailing behind.

"Ah, Colonel! Mr Darcy!" Caroline hailed them before turning to Lady Lucas and confiding: "The colonel has just returned from visiting his mother, our dear friend the countess."

Richard was glad there was nobody about who would retail this comment to his mother. He was fairly sure Miss Bingley's acquaintance with her was of the slightest. The countess's standard response to encroaching mushrooms was the cut direct, which was what Miss Bingley would receive if his mother ever got wind of Caroline's presumption—not so good for his matrimonial plans.

"Well, Caroline!" interposed Bingley, noticing the slightly raised eyebrows of the colonel. "I've just been enquiring of Miss Bennet's health, and she says she is right as a trivet."

"What wonderful news!" Miss Bingley replied with a forced smile. Her wish to befriend Miss Bennet had paled considerably following her sister's recent visit.

Jane, taking this pronouncement at face value, smiled back genuinely. Having never had a nasty thought in her life, she had a great deal of trouble recognising sarcasm, even when it emanated from her own father.

Bingley returned Jane's smile eagerly. Knowing his sister better, he recognised the barb in her words, but blithely chose to ignore it, continuing with: "So I believe we can shortly send out our cards of invitation."

Caroline quickly changed the subject to fashion. Her sister, Louisa, listened to her discourse and added her mite while playing with her bracelets and rings. Mr Collins, who had joined the group, had a surprising number of observations on the topic, most of them hinging on the elegance of dress of his patroness and her daughter. Jane attempted to take some part in this conversation, while Miss Elizabeth and the other males listened in a desultory fashion.

As they conversed, Mary Bennet played a long concerto. Unfortunately, Mary had neither genius nor taste; and though vanity had given her application, it had given her likewise a pedantic air and conceited manner, which would have injured a higher degree of excellence than she had attained. The first two movements went well enough since most of the guests were able to talk over the top of the music. But she played the dramatic last movement so loudly that Caroline gave up trying to speak and fanned herself impatiently until a crashing crescendo marked its end.

"Thank goodness for that!" Caroline said behind her fan.

The guests were saved any further torture by the intervention of the two younger Bennet sisters, who requested Mary play a jig. Although at first unwilling to divert from the second concerto she intended to play, Mary relented when two or three young officers praised her performance and added their entreaties. The officers then joined eagerly with the younger Bennet sisters and Miss Mariah Lucas in dancing at one end of the room.

"Good gracious!" remarked Caroline in disdain. "So much for discussing politics or reading poetry. The soirée has turned into an impromptu hop!"

Mr Collins agreed the dancing was lowering the dignity of the occasion.

Bingley, more careless of his sister's opinion, asked Miss Bennet to partner him, and she gladly acquiesced.

The colonel, who didn't have an interest in either politics or poetry, had been about to ask Miss Bingley if she wished to dance prior to her pronouncement, but bit his lip instead and smiled to himself. He then happened to glance at Miss Elizabeth, who was having difficulty keeping a straight face, and realized she had correctly discerned his intentions. Answering her smile, he threw caution to the winds, promptly asked her if she wished to dance, and broke into a full grin when she acquiesced.

Mr Collins watched them depart with chagrin. Having agreed with Miss Bingley, he could only watch helplessly as the lady he was trying to court was taken off by another man, and a devilishly poised one at that.

Darcy eyed their departure with envy. While he didn't particularly wish to dance, he liked standing around carping about it even less. He was sure they were having more fun at the other end of the room—Miss Elizabeth was certainly applying herself to the jig with some energy.

After enduring an hour of the inconsequential chatter of Mr Collins and the Bingley sisters, Darcy finally saw an opportunity to escape when Sir William Lucas approached them. Excusing himself and heading off in the direction of the convenience, he escaped through one of the French doors onto the terrace. It was cold outside and the terrace was deserted. There was a full moon with a rainbow round it…

He was staring at this and beginning to sink into one of his dejected moods when he heard a patter of slippers approach and turned to find Miss Elizabeth beside him.

"Miss Elizabeth," he said, noticing her low cut gown; "it is cold and we should not be out here alone."

"It is all right, Mr Darcy, your cousin is standing guard at the door and I only intend to be a moment," she said, pulling her hand from her pocket. "I laundered your handkerchief. Thank you very much for the loan of it."

Darcy extended his hand to take it, but then changed his mind. "Did your handkerchief turn up?"

"Not yet."

Of course it didn't. It is still in my pocket with a spot of blood on it. "Please keep mine."

"I can't do that, Mr Darcy. It would be most improper. It has your initials on it."

"But I'm sure you're a clever needlewoman. FD can easily be turned into EB."

She smiled. "So it can. But I still can't take it."

"Miss Elizabeth."

"Yes?"

"I believe you heard something—ill-tempered and… untrue, that I said at the assembly. Please take it as an apology."

Elizabeth didn't want to keep the handkerchief. Besides being improper, she didn't wish to be beholden to Mr Darcy in any way; but if she refused his token now, she would be guilty of rejecting an olive branch.

"Very well, Mr Darcy. Your apology is accepted. It is a very nice handkerchief and will make shift as an excellent picnic blanket."

Darcy smiled limply at her attempt at light-heartedness. "Well, perhaps you could turn it into four ladies' handkerchiefs—then you would only have to alter the embroidery on one of them."

Elizabeth smiled in return, curtsied and took herself off.

The Netherfield party arrived home shortly after midnight.

Not feeling quite ready for slumber, the colonel convinced Darcy to have a drink with him before bed—he needed to be gone at dawn and wouldn't be able to converse with his cousin in the morning. They retreated to Darcy's suite.

"You know she really is a gem," said the colonel. "What a pity she has no dowry!"

"I gather you are talking of Miss Bennet. I'm afraid I will have to counsel Bingley there."

"Miss Bennet? No, I am talking of Miss Elizabeth! And if I were you, I would stick to advice about his estate and let him take care of his own heart. He's not short of a penny and he could do a lot worse than Miss Bennet. She's charming and a beauty to boot."

"So when did you develop a tendre for Miss Elizabeth?"

"Around the same time I discovered I couldn't stomach Miss Bingley. You're right, she's a bitch."

"I didn't say that. I said she's a cat," corrected Darcy.

"Cats, dogs! You use your euphemism and I'll use mine," retorted the colonel.

"So what do you find so attractive about Miss Elizabeth?"

"Everything! She's everything I could want in a woman—pretty, vivacious, caring... she has a sense of humor... What more could you want?"

"Beauty," replied Darcy.

"Granted her sister is prettier, but I wouldn't want to marry a beauty anyway. I'd get jealous as soon as some other fellow spoke to her. Like Sophia Astley—a diamond of the first water, but the court cards cluster around her like flies around carrion. No, a pretty girl, like Miss Elizabeth, would do me fine. Mind you, I'm surprised you put beauty down as your first criterion, Darce. Mighty shallow of you."

"It's not my first criterion," replied Darcy defensively. "I just thought it would be at the top of *your* list."

"Don't read too much into my silly raillery. So what's at the top of Fitzwilliam Darcy's list?"

Darcy thought of all the things he admired in Diana. She *was* a great beauty, but what else? "Intelligent..."

"So you want to marry a blue stocking..." mocked the colonel.

"No, just a lady smart enough to have an intelligent conversation with. Well read enough to know that Euripides has nothing to do with a torn dress."

"What?" asked the colonel.

"A particularly inane conversation I had with Miss Bingley at the breakfast table yesterday..." explained Darcy.

"Anything else?" asked the colonel.

"Someone who could be a friend to Georgiana..."

The colonel tossed off the last of his brandy.

"Well, I think Miss Elizabeth fills all your criteria as well as mine. Pity about her lack of dowry; can't really ask her to live in the barracks. Too bad the Dower House is falling down at Wyvern Hall. But enough maudlin thoughts, I'm to bed. Let me know when Bingley sets the date of his ball. Who knows? Maybe some unknown Hertfordshire heiress will come to it."

"You have my promise," assured Darcy.

The colonel took himself off, and Darcy, having given Finn the night off, prepared himself for bed alone.

As he drifted off to sleep, Darcy dreamt he was walking through the fields of Pemberley towards the house when he spied a lady in the formal garden surrounded by three boys in short coats who were gambolling round her. His stomach was gripped by the certainty that this dream was somehow prophetic. He realised that the woman was his wife, and the children—his sons. Overwhelmed with curiosity to know the identity of this woman, he hastened forward, but no matter how many steps he took, he didn't seem to get any closer to her, and her bonnet hid her features. Suddenly the littlest child fell and started to cry. She scooped him up, and giving him a kiss, disappeared into the house with the other boys following at her heels.

Darcy woke with the sense of a lost opportunity.

11 By the River Lea

Darcy had plenty of time to contemplate his cousin's words and his own situation over the coming days. The Bingley sisters were thankfully occupied with writing invitations for the ball and, against their protestations, their brother took them off to personally deliver the invitation to the Bennets on the third day after Richard's departure.

Although he had assured the colonel he would return to London to look for a wife, Darcy now admitted to himself how ridiculous that notion was. Had he not been looking for the past seven years? Even if not done overtly, was that not the reason he had clung so desperately to Diana, hoping against hope she would be freed of her bonds? Had relief not gripped him, evil though it was, when he heard of her husband's passing?

He doggedly continued with the ledgers but had to force himself to concentrate while random thoughts of maidens dancing, running round the village square with bricks, and playing with children intruded. His patience was further stretched when a letter arrived from his uncle's man of business advising him of developments in a joint investment, to which the earl had added, as a postscript, a reminder of his marital duties. *Damn his eyes!*

Amidst this mental tumult, Darcy pulled the last stack of journals from the bookshelf. A cascade of folded paper hit the floor. He thought at first that one of the journals had fallen apart, but upon placing these upon the desk, he perceived that it was correspondence.

Crouching down to retrieve it, his hand first alighted on a letter with a black edge. When he opened this to reveal the King's coat of arms stamped on the paper, he knew what it must contain. Sure enough, it was the official notification of the deaths of the two Yardley sons at Badajoz. He reached for the rest of the scattered correspondence. Opening each folded sheet, he quickly scanned the direction and signature. They were letters from the sons to the parents, all from Badajoz, which the army had besieged for some time in the days leading up to the final battle. He expected they had arrived as a single packet with the death notice.

Darcy immediately saw that the last letter he had picked up was sealed. Turning it over, he discovered it was directed only to 'Elizabeth', and that the paper matched that of the other correspondence that had emanated from Badajoz. He walked to the window and carefully examined the seal. The letter appeared never to have been opened. The simple direction indicated it had been enclosed in one of the other missives. Comparison of the handwriting indicated the author was Edward. *Was he the older or the younger brother?* Darcy could not remember.

The location of the letters in the study suggested Sir Laurence had opened them but never passed on to Lady Yardley the correspondence addressed to her. It seemed likely the missive to Elizabeth was enclosed in one of the letters from Edward to Lady Yardley. A comparison of the folds of the opened letters supported this conjecture—the fold lines of one of Lady Yardley's letters were less distinct, and Elizabeth's letter fit neatly within.

Presumably Sir Laurence had not passed the correspondence onto his wife because he did not wish to further distress her. Had he withheld the letter to Elizabeth for a similar reason? Or perhaps he disapproved of correspondence between his son and a female who was not a relation? *But some allowance must surely be made for their having lived under the same roof for so many years...* It seemed likely her possible distress was his first consideration.

Darcy was then faced with the problem of what to do with the missive. Should he deliver the unopened letter to Elizabeth, or perhaps give it to Bingley to do so? Maybe he should he just return the correspondence to the state in which he'd found it, concealed behind the journals on the shelf?

Without quite knowing why, his fingers broke the seal.

> *Dearest Elizabeth,*
>
> *I write to you on the eve of what the Duke hopes will be our final conquest of Badajoz. The fortress is a mighty one, but God willing, we will breach it, as we did at Cuidad Rodrigo. I was selected to lead the Forlorn Hope. It is a risk, but I am eager to gain a command, and promotions are not handed out to those who hang back.*
>
> *Albert is sulking and will not speak to me because I did not tell him I had volunteered. But I hope he will forgive me before we are called to order.*
>
> *The campaign is definitely an adventure beyond any of our hijinks at home, and I am learning Spanish so I can barter with the peasants.*
>
> *Sometimes I wish I could fly back over the water to see your smiling face. If all goes well, I hope to soon get some prize money. Who knows? Perhaps sufficient to allow us to get married. There is not a day I do not think of you, my dearest. I hope you think of me.*
>
> *All my love*
> *Edward*

Darcy's hand fell limply to his side. Why had he opened it? It was unpardonable, but now he knew her secret. She had a broken heart too, and her love was even more unobtainable than Diana—buried in foreign soil.

He stuffed the letter mindlessly into his pocket. Walking back to the bookcase, he gathered the rest of the correspondence and hid it behind the ledgers he'd recently placed upon the shelf. Sitting down at the desk, he reached for a journal.

Three days later, Darcy had finally finished his work for Bingley and went out riding early in the morning. He rode south through Prior's wood, then proceeded cross-country until he reached the River Lea. It was his intention to pick his way west along the river until he came to the lane that headed back towards Netherfield.

As soon as he was alone, thoughts of Diana came crowding in, but he pushed them aside and, breathing deeply, detached himself from his emotions to consider his problem like a puzzle he was trying to solve.

Clearly, his long-held wish of emulating his parents' marital felicity by making a love match was no longer a possibility. He had only himself to blame—his time had run out and no ideal match had fallen into his lap. The simplest solution was a marriage of convenience. This was not so unusual; many families brokered such marriages for their children—to extract themselves from dire financial straits or to fuel family ambitions. He remembered briefly considering this prospect before he found Diana. It seemed such a foreign concept now that he had known love, but given his failure to project himself into the marriage mart, it appeared to be the best a man with an encumbered heart could hope for...

Time, however, was of the essence. If he waited too long, his uncle would step in, and he would find himself married to his cousin, Anne de Bourgh, or some other woman of his uncle's choice. Personally, he didn't find Anne that objectionable. Although he was not attracted to her, she was intelligent in her own quiet way. But could she bear him a child? He doubted it, and if she did, she would probably die doing it. Yet Anne was infinitely preferable to some unknown female his uncle might conjure. The earl would chose him a wife based solely on status and fortune; he might end up with a spoilt harpy—the Ton's equivalent of Caroline Bingley. Imagine living under the cat's paw in his own home...

As he reached a decision to take the initiative, Darcy came to open ground and urged his horse into a canter over the fallow fields. His mount gave a snort of satisfaction and adopted an easy rhythm, jumping the hedges on the fly as they encountered them.

Yes, thought Darcy, returning to his musings, *if I want to have control over the selection process, I need to act sooner rather than later, and to do that I need to be practical.* Thinking wistfully of his list of attributes for his paragon: beauty, intelligence... he mentally tossed it out the window.

He proceeded to pare back his requirements to the bare essentials. He needed someone who would understand his situation—intelligence was watered down to empathy. He needed someone who was willing to have his children and not cuckold him, even after she had borne him an heir—a trustworthy lady. *But how did one determine that on short acquaintance?*

On the whole, he thought, it would be better if his wife was content to stay in Derbyshire to bear and bring up his children. Keeping her far from the metropolis would also provide some constraint on potential extra-marital activities. *So perhaps a Derbyshire girl would be the best solution...*

His thoughts slid to Miss Choke, a local lass who, having failed to make a match in her three London seasons, had retired in favour of her younger sister. She was well spoken. He believed her to have a tolerable understanding. She was, unfortunately, very plain, but Richard was right—such a requirement was rather shallow. However... her parents were not without power locally and might object to their daughter living such a reclusive life at Pemberley. It might be viewed as neglect by her husband, which, he had to be honest, it would be.

As Darcy reached the edge of the meadow, the horse stirred up a thin fog that was still clinging to the ground. It thickened as he approached the river, 'til he could only see a few feet in front of his mount.

Darcy might have passed by without even seeing her, had he not glimpsed the movement of her cloak in his peripheral vision.

"Miss Elizabeth!" he said, pulling his horse up.

She had risen from a crouching position, carrying her bonnet in one hand. Her chestnut hair was untied and Darcy could see that it fell all the way down her back.

"Mr Darcy!" she replied, rather startled.

He dismounted. When he turned back to her, Darcy saw she had pulled the hood of the green cape she was wearing onto her head.

He looked around. "You are alone?"

"As you see."

"Surely that is unwise. You could be in danger."

"From whom? I'm not on the road, and there is no one in these parts of concern."

"Surely you cannot know that for certain. The militia, for instance, have recently arrived in the area."

"Mr Darcy, I know this area like the back of my hand; it is foggy, and I am wearing a green cloak. Who do you think would be at the greater disadvantage in a game of hide-and-seek: myself or a man in a bright red uniform?"

She is right, thought Darcy. *Those bright red uniforms certainly looked impressive on a battleground but the soldiers were at a decided disadvantage in a skirmish.*

When he did not reply, she ventured: "Are you implying I should be wary of *you*, Mr Darcy?"

His mouth twisted into a small smile. Lowering his eyes from her direct gaze, Darcy shook his head. His eyes fastened on the bonnet she was holding in her hand. He could see now she was using it as a basket to gather flowers.

Lizzy saw his eyes drift to her bonnet and moved her hand behind her back.

"Ah," said Darcy, clued in by her evasiveness; "I thought at first you were picking flowers, but I see you are gathering simples."

"Indeed," she said defensively. "I gather them for the local apothecary."

"You need not worry, Miss Bennet. I won't accuse you of being a witch. I am well aware of the usefulness of simples."

"Good," she smiled. "I assure you I won't take them off to a secluded hut on chicken legs."

He laughed. "Not chicken legs, Miss Bennet. Surely an honest English witch never thought of such a thing. I believe you have been reading Russian fairy tales."

"Indeed, Mr Darcy. My father collects such stories, and he used to read them to us at bedtime."

"Really? It is rather an unusual hobby for a country squire."

"My father was a fellow at Oxford before he inherited Longbourn."

Ah, the entail, thought Darcy. "And his specialty was folk stories?"

"Specifically, symbolism in folk stories."

Darcy raised his eyebrows at that, and the expression seemed to freeze on his face as the cogs whirred suddenly in his brain, as if anticipating striking the hour. *It all fit.* She was a country girl, one of five sisters... the entail—no doubt her parents would be eager for the match... She was healthy, caring, unattached...

To his own ears, his voice seemed to come from outside his head. "Miss Elizabeth, have you ever heard of Euripides?"

Lizzy looked at him in puzzlement. "You mean the Greek playwright?"

"Yes, Miss Elizabeth, the playwright!" he said eagerly. "I'm glad luck has thrown us together this morning!"

She looked at him in surprise. He was behaving like a lunatic. "I cannot imagine why, Mr Darcy."

Suddenly he became more serious. "My father died some years ago, Miss Elizabeth. I have been master of Pemberley these seven years. It is time I thought of marrying."

Lizzy wondered why he would talk of such a subject to her.

"You walked three miles across heavy ground, Miss Elizabeth, to tend to your sister."

"Indeed, Mr Darcy. I'm glad that you appreciate that fact. I thought you were rather focused on the impropriety of my climbing the ha-ha."

"I need an heir, Miss Elizabeth. I believe you are a caring person. You like living in the countryside. I believe you will be happy to bring up my children at Pemberley."

She stopped and stared at him. Was he asking her to be his wife or his governess? Both seemed equally preposterous. If this was a marriage proposal it was even stranger than the one she had received from Mr Filch, the undertaker, over a year ago. She decided to clarify things.

"Mr Darcy, is this a proposal of marriage?"

"Indeed, Miss Elizabeth, will you marry me?"

Ah, the bizarre workings of modern courtship! thought Elizabeth. She could remember mocking poetry to him in a recent conversation, but she could not help thinking that some attempt at it wouldn't go astray now.

"But you do not love me," she stated objectively, while thinking this was putting it rather mildly.

"No, Miss Elizabeth, I do not love you, but as my wife and the mother of my children I will treat you with respect."

"Forgive me, Mr Darcy, but I must question your motives in asking a dowerless daughter of a country squire to be your wife. There are surely many far more eligible females in London."

"The dowry means little to me, Miss Elizabeth. My estate is a rich one and in good order. I have trouble disposing of my money. I don't need to go searching for more of it."

She raised her eyebrows at this. "Aside from the dowry, I have no connections. Why would you choose a woman with no connections, Mr Darcy?"

"I do not wish to enter parliament, Miss Elizabeth."

"But a woman with no connections, Mr Darcy, is a woman without protection. Is that your design?"

Darcy stared at her. "Are you implying I intend to abuse you? You have affronted me, madam."

"I beg your pardon, Mr Darcy. I am merely trying to understand your thinking, as it is likely crucial to my future happiness, or lack of it, at your side."

"I can see I am going to have to be more open," sighed Darcy. "Miss Elizabeth, I need to marry, but I'm afraid I gave my heart away years ago to… someone else. It is not mine to give. And given that you…" He stopped in confusion, realizing he had almost exposed his impropriety in reading her letter from Edward.

"Well, that still doesn't explain why you have fixed on me," she retorted, filling the dangerous gap in his words.

Seeing her unexpected hesitancy, Darcy quickly recruited his scattered thoughts, and continued with slight pique: "I thought I had explained my criteria quite succinctly, but perhaps I can express myself more clearly in negatives: I do not wish to marry a wife who will fritter my fortune away at cards; or who will expect me to escort her to balls every night; or who will take up with some other gentleman when I don't escort her. I do not wish to be bothered at the breakfast table by vacuous conversation, or receive large bills for finery, or be required to tool you round Hyde Park at the fashionable hour."

Some of these last pronouncements reminded Elizabeth a little of things her father said to her mother. A small devil inside her prompted her to reply: "But Mr Darcy, there must be some error in logic. If your fortune is so large that you have trouble disposing of it, surely large bills for finery cannot be a problem?"

"I believe you are being pert," bristled Darcy, annoyed that his condescension in singling out this squire's daughter was being met with such flippancy.

"Does it make me ineligible?" asked Elizabeth hopefully.

He sighed again. Who knew that making a marriage proposal would be so damned difficult, for him, of all men? "Can I please have your answer?"

She wanted to decline such an outrageous proposal, but a small voice in her head, which sounded remarkably like Charlotte's, caused her to prevaricate.

"Can I please think on it a little longer?"

"How long do you require?"

"Could I have two days please?"

"Very well. May I ask you another question?"

"Yes."

"Have you reached your majority?"

"No, Mr Darcy."

"Then, do I have your leave to put my case to your father?"

"Could it not wait until I have formed an opinion?"

"I'm afraid not. I need to leave for London in two days time and I would like to have things settled before I go."

"Whatever is the rush?" she asked, startled.

"Merely that I have urgent business in London and would like to draw up the settlements and procure the marriage licence before I return."

"Provided your suit is successful."

"If my suit is not successful, Miss Elizabeth, I will not return. There would be no point."

"Surely your friendship with Mr Bingley is sufficient reason?"

"I merely accompanied Mr Bingley to Hertfordshire to help initiate him in the way of running his estate. I have spent the past three weeks assessing the estate and the ledgers. I have written a business plan, and I hired a steward yesterday. My contribution is complete."

"And you do not wish to sojourn here longer in the spirit of friendly camaraderie?"

"I have stayed for the Netherfield Ball *in the spirit of friendly camaraderie*," retorted Darcy. "I intend to leave directly after it."

"Very well, Mr Darcy. As you are in an unholy rush, I give you my permission to seek my father's opinion. I will be interested to see what he makes of it."

Elizabeth was fairly sure her father would say no. As for herself, she was fairly sure her own answer would match it.

"Then there is only one more thing for me to say, Miss Elizabeth."

"And that is...?"

"May I request your hand for the first two dances at the ball?"

"I am afraid, Mr Darcy, they are already taken."

He raised his eyebrows, wondering who had pre-empted him, but he was too polite to ask. "Then do you have the next two free?"

"Indeed, sir."

"Then, good day, Miss Elizabeth. I will see you at the ball."

"Good day, sir."

12 Scylla and Charybdis

After Mr Darcy remounted and rode off, Elizabeth walked back unsteadily towards Longbourn. The ground felt weird and spongy beneath her shoes. Had she dreamt the whole thing? It all *seemed* rather like a nightmare...

Elizabeth had escaped Longbourn early in the morning to avoid Mr Collins, who was also an early riser, on the pretext of searching for herbs. Her excursion was not unusual—Lizzy and her friend Charlotte Lucas gathered and prepared simples for the local apothecary, Mr Jones, who supplied them with free and discounted tinctures and ointments in return. Elizabeth used these mostly to treat the tenants of Longbourn who suffered various injuries and ailments and who could not afford to treat themselves.

Being cooped in the house with Mr Collins over the past couple of days had been horrendous—his attentions had become way too particular. Every time Lizzy had turned around, her cousin had been there, simpering at her. Perhaps it was a figment of her wild imagination, but she had gotten the distinct impression Mr Collins was stalking her, and she had done everything in her power to ensure they were never alone. Elizabeth had hoped her obvious indifference would encourage her cousin to cast his eyes in other directions, hopefully towards Mary, who had been watching him wistfully since his arrival.

Lizzy's escape into the morning air had felt like deliverance, but then, with that nasty trick of nightmares, her pursuer had suddenly transformed into Mr Darcy, who had sprung up out of the mist to propose to her.

When she reached the house, she went straight to the stillroom and locked herself in. With economy borne of habit, she began to sort the simples into those that must be dried and those distilled and started the burner Mr Jones had loaned her. Once she had tied and hung the bunches for drying, she stripped the leaves from the stems of the remainder and dropped them into neat piles. Macerating the first pile, she steeped them in alcohol and placed the limbek over the burner.

When she leant against the bench, Elizabeth realized she was shaking. Feeling weak, she sat down heavily on a nearby chair and burst out crying.

Elizabeth saw nought of Mr Darcy for two days. In his absence, the hope that it was all a silly mistake began to grow. Perhaps he suffered from some sort of mental illness like King George? Perhaps he had forgotten all about their conversation...

She was upstairs in the sitting room with her mother and sisters when this hope was snuffed. Elizabeth had retreated there to escape Mr Collins, taking some mending as her excuse. Jane had sat down beside her with her embroidery, and they were soon joined by Kitty and Lydia, who had fled the parlour when Mr Collins threatened to read Fordyce's sermons for their edification. Finding the object of his attentions beyond his reach in the ladies' area of the house, Mr Collins declared significantly to Mrs Bennet that he intended to seek Mr Bennet in his study for an *important* discussion.

Mrs Bennet subsequently burst into the upstairs sitting room, flapping her hands and whispering in a loud voice that great things were afoot. Mary trailed disconsolately behind.

The ladies of Longbourn were on tenterhooks for over half an hour when they were distracted by the sound of a carriage. Kitty jumped up to investigate.

"It is Mr Bingley," she declared from the window.

"Oh, lovely!" said Mrs Bennet, grasping Jane's hand. "Have both of his sisters come?"

"Neither," replied Kitty. "It is only he and Mr Darcy."

"Oh, Mr D'arsey!" said Lydia, rolling her eyes.

"Hush!" said Mrs Bennet, getting up. She cared nothing for Mr Darcy's sensibilities, but she did not wish to offend his friend.

"Well, I expect his sisters are very busy with the final preparations for the ball," she excused. "Indeed, I dared not hope we would meet him before tonight, but you see, Jane? He cannot keep away!"

The ladies of the house poured down the staircase to great the guests. Lizzy, who trailed reluctantly behind, saw Mr Darcy was attired in an outfit worthy of a London club. He wore a black coat of superfine with a grey watered-silk waistcoat, ivory breeches and black hessians with silver tassels. His cravat was a darker grey and a diamond pin nestled in its folds. His black curls were pomaded to perfection, and he carried a black cane with a silver top. Lizzy had never seen him look so handsome, or so formidable. In comparison, Mr Bingley's less formal attire looked that of a country squire.

Mr Darcy carried a book in his hand and met Elizabeth's round eyes with a direct stare. Transferring his cane to Mr Hill's waiting hands, he bent to kiss Lizzy's hand in the old-fashioned manner. "Miss Elizabeth, how good to see you again," he murmured.

This attention did not go unnoticed by Mrs Bennet, but as there was nothing lover-like in Mr Darcy's manner and his opinion of her second daughter was well known, she merely ascribed his behaviour to the manners of the Ton and ushered the gentlemen into the parlour.

Darcy lingered inside the doorway to address Elizabeth privately.

"I brought this book for your father, Miss Elizabeth. Is he available?"

She had scarce time to answer before she heard the library door open and the voices of her father and Mr Collins drift down the hall.

"...All in good time, Mr Collins, all in good time. I imagine you young people are eager for the ball."

"Most definitely, Mr Bennet. I do hope you will accompany us."

"Indeed, I cannot turn down an invitation to Netherfield. It is long since I have been there."

When her father and Mr Collins arrived at the parlour to find the unexpected guests, Mr Bennet's eyes flicked round the room, finding Mr Bingley at his usual station next to his eldest daughter. His eyebrows lifted infinitesimally when he discovered that *rara avis*, Mr Darcy, in his parlour, and he was further surprised when that gentleman approached him.

"Mr Bennet," said Mr Darcy, bowing, "your daughter tells me you collect folklore, so I thought this edition might interest you." He passed Mr Bennet the handsomely bound book.

Mr Bennet's eyes bulged slightly when he read the spine. Opening the front cover, he examined the frontispiece and the list of contents. "Indeed, Mr Darcy. The Grimm brothers were kind enough to share a copy of one of these stories with me, but this is my first glimpse of the published edition."

"I recently purchased it at Hatchard's," Darcy supplied.

That was true enough. Darcy had sent a letter with his valet post-haste to Hatchard's shortly after returning to Netherfield from his morning ride two days ago. His requirements were simple: any rare or valuable volume of folktales or similar, at any cost, immediately; and Mr Hatchard had been gratified to supply him with the recently published German book.

"Thank you," said Mr Bennet. "I am most eager to see the culmination of their work. Could you spare the book for a few hours? I could return it at the ball."

"My pleasure, sir. Do you have many other volumes of folktales in your collection?"

"Well, none so handsomely bound as this. I have print editions of Perrault's tales and one of the Grimm brothers' earlier works—Danish Tales; but the rest are chiefly manuscripts circulated by scholars."

He eyed Mr Darcy with some interest. "Would you care to see them?" he asked tentatively.

"Indeed, sir, if that is possible," averred the younger man.

Mr Bennet was highly gratified. He escorted Mr Darcy off to his library, leaving Mr Collins to take tea with Mr Bingley and the ladies.

Over half an hour later, Mr Darcy returned alone, and without his book. He sat down in the parlour and accepted a cup of tea from Mrs Bennet. When he thought no one was looking, he smiled tentatively at Elizabeth.

The gentlemen left half an hour later. Mr Bingley was reluctant to go, and Mrs Bennet reluctant to let him go; but they both yielded when Darcy gently reminded his friend they must attend to preparations for the ball.

After lunch, Mr Collins went off to inspect Longbourn's beehives, which were kept by one of the tenant farmers—beekeeping being a rather unusual hobby of the clergyman's. Mostly relieved to have their cousin out from underfoot, the ladies of Longbourn relaxed. Kitty and Lydia escaped outside, and Mrs Bennet retired to the chaise longue for her post-prandial nap while her elder daughters ranged themselves round her, engaged in various needlework. Mr Bennet sat down in front of the fire to read a book, an unusual move for him since he generally retired to his study, but not altogether unheard of. Soon after their mother started snoring, Mr Bennet waited 'til Lizzy looked up, crooked his finger at her, and retreated to his library.

Upon entering her father's stronghold, Elizabeth was motioned to a seat.

"Lizzy," said Mr Bennet. "You are a popular lady. I am in receipt of two offers of marriage for you."

Lizzy sighed. "Yes, one from a complete fool and the other from a madman."

"Granted, Mr Darcy's offer was unexpected, and there is an aspect of being between Scylla and Charybdis, but they are both good offers. If you marry the fool, you will one day be Mistress of Longbourn. If you marry the madman, you will be mistress of a far greater estate in Derbyshire."

"Must I accept either of them, Papa?"

"I'm afraid so, Lizzy. You know eligible men are thin on the ground in Hertfordshire, thanks to Napoleon and the delights of the metropolis. I cannot afford to send you and Jane to London for a season. You may never get another eligible offer."

"But must I marry at all, Papa? Surely one of us must stay to look after you and Mama in your old age?"

"Frankly I hope I pop my clogs quickly, Lizzy. I have been careful to husband my resources and repay the mortgages my uncle took out on parts of the estate, but I'm afraid my efforts have amounted to too little, too late. That is why I have lately let your mother have more of her way with finery. Her strategy is all that we have left to us now."

"What do you mean, Papa?"

"Marriage, Lizzy. Perhaps it was a godsend that I was blessed with five daughters. My son would have inherited a poisoned chalice. I have finally paid off the mortgages, but each year the income from the estate buys a little less. The industrialisation of the land means that only the larger estates will have sufficient income to survive in the future, and Longbourn is not large enough. I do not envy Mr Collins, although he does have one advantage I do not."

"What is that?"

"As a clergyman, he will also have the income from the living attached to Longbourn, once Mr Hammond passes. Still, even with that, I fear it will be no sinecure."

Lizzy's heart constricted as she felt the walls closing in on her.

There was a knock. Mrs Hill entered with the tea tray and, setting it down, quickly departed.

"Pour some tea, my dear," instructed Mr Bennet, "and let me lay the situation before you."

Lizzy poured and handed her father a cup. He picked up his teaspoon and began to stir his tea idly, not looking at his daughter.

"I spoke to your mother briefly before lunch. She favours Mr Collins. You know she took a set against Mr Darcy after the Meryton Assembly. *That* she has been vocal about. She does not say so, but if you were to marry Mr Collins, then she could likely stay here as the dowager after I am gone."

"No, Papa! You are still healthy!"

"Nonetheless, I have twenty years on your mother, and women who survive childbirth tend to live longer than men."

Elizabeth started to protest, but her father pursed his lips to shush her.

"I, on the other hand, favour Mr Darcy. He is a very wealthy man, Lizzy. Your mother has no idea. She merely judges him by his manners and his lack of title. It's here in the baronetage, my dear," he said, putting down his teacup to hand her the tome. "Look for yourself. Pemberley is one of the richest estates in Derbyshire, and Mr Darcy's wealth extends far beyond that. I have spoken with him about my concerns for the future. He has very generously agreed to provide a five thousand pound dowry for each of your sisters as part of the marriage settlement. This will allow them all to marry well, and it will leave your mother's five thousand pound dowry untouched to support her in her old age."

Tears had begun to trickle down Lizzy's face during her father's speech as she saw the ground shift beneath her.

"The choice remains yours, Lizzy. I have merely tried to present you with the cold, hard facts. I will support whichever option you choose, but you must choose one."

Lizzy shook her head and looked at the floor. She was close to losing her composure and did not want her father to see her face.

"I hate to pressure you, my dear," continued Mr Bennet, "but Mr Collins has sought my permission to ask for your hand tomorrow morning. You will need to decide one way or another by then."

Lizzy left her father's library with a heavy heart. Unable to bear company, she fled to the bedchamber she shared with Jane and, lying down on the counterpane, sobbed for a good half-hour.

But Elizabeth was never one to give in to despair, and soon composing herself, she thought carefully of the choices before her. Her thoughts went first to Mr Darcy. She considered herself a good judge of character, but his nature eluded her. He could be arrogant, as he had shown at the Meryton assembly; possibly selfish, based on his behaviour in the Netherfield library, wanting everyone to organise their lives around him; but he also appeared to be an independent thinker, judging by his words in the drawing room on the accomplishments of ladies—a practical man. He was responsible, competent—his work for his friend, Mr Bingley, demonstrated that; but… there was no other word for it—erratic; first dismissing her disdainfully, then seeking her hand in marriage. Or perhaps his agendas were too obscure for her to discern…

She sighed. *The man has more layers than an onion.*

Lizzy rolled over and thought of their few conversations, replaying the words in her mind, looking for more insight into his character; trying to understand his motives. He had said that his heart belonged to someone else: *Perhaps his love had rejected him; …or had married someone else; …or had died.* Memories of Edward intruded, but Elizabeth pushed them aside, whispering a brief prayer for his soul.

Again she tried to understand why Mr Darcy had singled her out after so short an acquaintance. He had seen her climb the ha-ha; knew of her slightly tomboyish expeditions with the Yardley boys; had caught her outside with her hair unbound and without a bonnet. Clearly he thought her a hoyden. And why was he interested in what she knew of Greek playwrights? *Oh, it made no sense!*

Elizabeth tossed again. *What would it be like to be stuck in a loveless marriage?* Mr Darcy owned a grand estate—no doubt she would have her own chambers, could lead her own life to some extent. The parsonage at Hunsford, on the other hand, would be a much humbler abode. She might even be expected to share a bed with her cousin every night. She shuddered. There would be no escaping Mr Collins then.

She was shaken from her reverie when Lydia came noisily along the corridor and burst into the room wearing a pelisse over her shift.

"Come on, Lizzy! There's warm water in the washtub. Mama says you have to get in next. She wants us as fresh as daisies for the ball!" Lydia paused and peered at her sister. "Do you have a headache?" she asked.

Elizabeth soon became convinced she *did* have a headache as Lydia and Kitty raced excitedly round the house, finding ribbons and slippers, giggling and exclaiming about the most trivial occurrences.

Lizzy had dutifully stripped down to kneel in the turbid water of the washtub. This was an ablution the sisters normally performed once a month, after their menses. Lizzy's daily ablutions employed the jug and ewer in her bedchamber. She dried herself with a small huckaback towel and gratefully pulled on the chemise and pelisse that Sarah held out for her—although the copper had been lit to warm the water for the bath, the air of the scullery still held a decided chill. The ladies then abandoned the washroom in favour of Mr Bennet. He chose to stand in the tub while Mr Hill dashed the last of the hot water mixed from the copper tub over his master.

Lizzy then retreated to her bedchamber to find Jane already dressed and urging her to make ready also, so Sarah could do her hair; the curling tongs were heating on the hearth. Jane was wearing her gold silk dress, which had been enhanced for the occasion by Mrs Bennet's pearl necklace and earrings.

Lizzy had hoped to disgust her suitors by wearing the sprigged muslin again, but Jane had laid out a new green muslin dress that she had been painstakingly embroidering with silk thread.

"Oh, Jane. It's beautiful. When did you finish it?" asked Lizzy.

"Not an hour ago. You did not think I would fail to have it ready for the ball did you?"

"But you must have stitched yards this week! The last I saw you had only started the bottom hem!"

"Indeed, I have, but the incentive of the ball gave my fingers speed. I dare say you did not notice because you have been too busy eluding our cousin."

Lizzy did not want to think of her cousin and, whispering *thank you*, gave her sister a hug. She busied herself with arranging Jane's golden curls while Sarah applied the tongs to her own straight chestnut locks.

When Mrs Bennet arrived in the room an hour later, Jane was arranging a sheer ivory shawl embroidered with golden pineapples around her shoulders.

"Oh, Jane, you look beautiful," exclaimed Mrs Bennet. "Surely Mr Bingley will succumb tonight!"

She then turned to her second daughter and was remarkably surprised. "Well, Lizzy, you look very well, too. That dress looks almost as good as Jane's silk! And Sarah has wrought wonders with your hair. Mr Collins will be swept away!"

Jane gave her sister's hand a reassuring squeeze upon this pronouncement, following which they descended to the coach.

Mr Bennet handed the ladies of Longbourn inside before climbing onto the box seat beside John Coachman. He shook his head at the loud twitterings of Lydia and Kitty, which emanated from the coach—the noises almost sounded like an altercation between two angry birds. With the aid of a footman, Mr Collins ascended to the rumble seat, where he did his best to look dignified as they wended their way towards Netherfield.

13 The ball

The Bennet carriage arrived at Netherfield in good time. Several footmen clustered round to assist the gentlemen to descend and pull down the step to allow the ladies to alight. In her eagerness to be first from the carriage, Lydia missed the step, fell into the footman's arms, and promptly burst out giggling. As the footman was a very handsome one, Kitty strongly suspected her sister had 'done it a purpose'.

Rolling his eyes, Mr Bennet handed his wife out, and then the other sisters emerged in a more seemly fashion assisted by Mr Collins. Elizabeth, who had waited 'til last to ensure Jane's cape did not snag on the door, realised her mistake when Mr Collins refused to relinquish her hand once her feet were on the ground. He placed it on his arm and kept his other hand firmly over it so there could be no escape. His proximity made Lizzy aware that her cousin smelt like turned milk.

Only four of the Netherfield party were manning the receiving line—Mr Hurst was nowhere in sight. Caroline stood at the head with Mr Darcy beside her. Elizabeth was immediately struck by how handsome he was. It was the first time she had seen him in pantaloons, and the lack of a horizontal line at his knee emphasised his long legs and overall height. Louisa stood next to her brother, who was at the end of the line. Although Mr Bingley was also immaculately turned out in the understated style popularised by Mr Brummell, he somehow did not manage the overall magnificence of Mr Darcy.

When Elizabeth's attention shifted to the Bingley sisters, she noted that they were even more ridiculously overdressed than usual. Caroline was very bubbly as she greeted her guests, continually glancing at Mr Darcy when she made a joke, and once even clutching his arm. Mr Darcy's expression was harder to read. It was serene, possibly bored.

As the Bennets approached the receiving line, two horses bestrode by officers of the militia entered the drive. Before Elizabeth had even identified them as Captain Carter and Mr Denny, Lydia and Kitty had broken away from their family and run to the end of the west front of the house to greet the officers. From this position, Lydia proceeded to halloo at them while both sisters bounced up and down on the spot. Mr Bennet frowned.

"Well, we always know when the Longbourn party has arrived!" remarked Caroline, as she greeted the remainder of the family with a saccharine smile.

"Oh, Miss Bingley!" gushed Mrs Bennet, oblivious of the intended jibe; "what a pleasure it is to be here and to see Netherfield lit up again like a fairyland! I have fond memories of attending several balls here at

Netherfield before Mr Bennet came along and swept me off my feet!"

Mr Bennet gave an embarrassed cough. He could not remember much sweeping.

Mr Darcy gave Elizabeth a civil nod as she followed her parents and Jane. She was sure that his eye contact with herself had differed not a skerrick from other members of her family, and it made her again feel that she had somehow dreamt his proposal.

Once the militiamen dismounted, Kitty and Lydia accompanied them back to the receiving line. Elizabeth's hope that her family might proceed inside before further embarrassing themselves was cruelly dashed by Mr Collins.

"Mr Darcy, I have found out," said he, "only yesterday, that you are a near relation of my patroness. Who would have thought of my meeting with, perhaps, a nephew of Lady Catherine de Bourgh in this assembly! I am most thankful that the discovery was made in time for me to pay my respects to you, and I trust you will excuse my not having done it before. My total ignorance of the connection must plead my apology."

Mr Darcy gave a slight inclination of his head.

"It is in my power to assure you," continued Mr Collins, "that her ladyship was quite well yesterday se'nnight; and your betrothed, Miss de Bourgh, the flower of Kent, was in her usual bloom. May I felicitate you on your excellent discernment in the choice of a bride and hope that as rector of Hunsford, I may soon preside over your nuptials."

That drew more of a response from Mr Darcy. His mouth drew into a thin line and his eyes flicked to Elizabeth.

Elizabeth knew not how to interpret Mr Darcy's reaction, but she could see that her cousin was holding up the receiving line, so she gripped his arm and pulled him into the vestibule while Mr Collins chattered about how Mr Darcy was so condescending, 'just like his aunt'.

The receiving line was just breaking up when a horse came galloping up the front drive and Colonel Richard Fitzwilliam jumped down from the saddle.

"Richard!" exclaimed Darcy, who had tarried behind the rest of the Netherfield party on perceiving his cousin, "I had despaired of seeing you."

"Sorry, Darce. Got a late start."

"No problem at the Life Guards I hope?"

"Won't say there wasn't, but can't say much more. Storm in a teacup anyway. Here now. What news?"

"I do have something to relate to you," whispered Darcy, leaning close to cousin, "if you have a spare moment later."

The colonel raised his eyebrows, but before he could question his cousin further, Miss Bingley returned from the ballroom to claim Darcy's arm.

"Come, Mr Darcy," cajoled Caroline. "The band is eager to strike up the first dance."

"Sorry, Fitz," said Darcy. "I must go. My valet has your things laid out upstairs. I expect he's still there tidying up."

"Good-oh," said the colonel, taking the stairs at a trot.

The colonel walked into Darcy's dressing room to find Finn and a footman in the process of emptying the bath.

"Leave be, man. I smell of horse," said the colonel.

"Yes, sir, but it's less than lukewarm. Will you let me top it up?"

"No matter," said the colonel shedding his mud-spattered uniform left and right. "It's wet."

Within half an hour, the colonel, attired to a nicety in his dress uniform, entered the ballroom. As Darcy was about to progress to Miss Bingley, Richard deduced that the first set was almost finished. He quickly scanned down the line, admiring the ladies and eyeing the competition, matching the original partners as he went.

Darcy was looking his usual impeccable self. His long legs were encased in form-fitting pantaloons that displayed a shapely calf above his dancing slippers. A well-muscled thigh was occasionally revealed as he moved in the dance. He was the tallest gentleman present, even exceeding his rake-thin friend, Mr Bingley, in height.

No doubt, thought the colonel, *my cousin will have a few ladies sighing over him tonight, regardless of the fact that he will probably treat them all with disdain.*

Miss Bingley was, as always, overdressed in an elaborate multi-coloured silk, bedecked with jewellery; her hair arranged in an elaborate coiffure with a gaudy tiara set in it. He wondered what his mother, always a stickler for proper form, would have to say about *that*.

Well, thought the colonel, *I suppose I will dance with her anyway if she has a set free, but I won't be pushing any other fellow out of the way.*

Miss Bennet was next to Miss Bingley in the proper formation. She looked her usual radiant self in gold silk, her perfect golden curls glinting in the candlelight. He saw she had begun the set with Mr Bingley. *No surprise there*, he thought.

The colonel determined he would ask Miss Bennet if she had a set free, directly after the conclusion of this one. Given the number of gentlemen present, she might already be engaged for the remainder of the ball; but even if that were so, he would still be able to partner her in the progression if he positioned himself cannily.

His eyes then skipped over several unknown females in the line of dancers, and two of the younger Bennet sisters, to settle on Miss Elizabeth who was near the end. It took him a moment to realise she had started the set with her cousin, the clergyman, who either had two left feet or was demonically possessed.

The music ended with a flourish, and Darcy performed a graceful bow to Miss Bingley before escorting her to her next partner, Colonel Forster—the commanding officer of the militia regiment that was stationed in Meryton.

Richard swiftly intercepted Miss Bennet, whose hand was about to be claimed by Bingley for the second set.

"Miss Bennet!" he said, performing a graceful bow. "I come late to the ball. Do I hope in vain that you still have a set free?"

Jane blushed prettily. "Of course not, sir. I have the supper set free," she said, naming her first free set.

The colonel grinned from ear to ear, knowing he could likely also claim Miss Bennet's company for supper. He bowed and left the field to Bingley, whose face was set in something very close to a scowl.

Indeed, Charles was regretting promising his sisters that he would not engage Miss Bennet for a third dance. Instead, he had to be satisfied to lead her into the second set.

Glancing around after ridding himself of Miss Bingley, Darcy perceived his cousin had entered the ballroom. As Richard had not yet engaged a partner for the second set, he drew him off near a curtained alcove. What Darcy didn't realize was that Miss Elizabeth had disappeared behind the curtain to pin up her hem, which Mr Collins had inevitably trodden on and ripped.

The skirt of Elizabeth's dress was quite ruined, all Jane's beautiful embroidery gone to waste in the first set. Possibly the dress could be salvaged by cutting off the hem and adding a flounce. *At least*, Elizabeth reasoned, *I now have an excuse to miss the second set and further mortification by my cousin's clumsy dancing.*

As the music struck up to signal everyone to take their places for the next set, Darcy spoke in a low voice to his cousin: "I've taken your advice and offered for Miss Elizabeth."

"Well! Knock me over with a feather!" exclaimed Richard. "How unprecedented for you to actually listen to some sense! Good man! May I be the first to congratulate you?"

"She hasn't accepted yet."

"Eh?" ejaculated Richard, more than a little surprised.

"And considering the behaviour of the younger Bennet sisters tonight," continued Darcy, "I feel I have been rather rash."

Not being aware of the earlier incidents, the colonel glanced round the room to discover Lydia tickling one of the younger militia officers, Mr Chamberlayne, while several others guffawed at her antics.

"Oh, come now," said Richard. "They are merry lasses and in high gig. Some allowances must be made for their youth."

"They are wild to a fault," retorted Darcy.

Behind the curtain, Lizzy had frozen in the midst of her pinning. On

Darcy's pronouncement of his 'rash' behaviour, she had blushed red and then white with anger.

"Where is she?" asked the colonel, searching the room for Elizabeth in vain.

"Perhaps she has gone to get some punch. I think she was engaged to dance with her cousin for the first two sets, but he is sitting over there with Mrs Bennet."

"Have you spoken to her father?" asked the colonel.

"Yes," replied Darcy. "He views the match favourably, but would not undertake to speak on his daughter's behalf. He promised me an answer by tomorrow morning."

"You cannot really think she will say no?" declared Richard.

"Well, it is an unusual situation," conceded Darcy, "and most young girls these days have the most ridiculously romantic notions; but I believe she fits my requirements, and I hope she will see what side her bread is buttered on."

Lizzy would have dearly liked to push Mr Darcy through the curtain, and make him fall flat on his face; but sanity prevailed, and she kept quiet as a mouse.

Having finished her torment of Chamberlayne, Lydia ran up to the gentlemen, closely followed by her sister, Kitty. "I would like to dance," she declared to the colonel, "but Lizzy says I must not ask gentlemen to dance."

"Or tradesmen," added Kitty.

"That's not relevant, Kitty," Lydia declared.

Darcy looked at the colonel significantly.

The colonel grinned. "Then may I have the honour of this dance, Miss Lydia?"

"Why, thank you, Colonel!" Lydia coquetted.

With a slight shrug to Darcy, Richard escorted his partner to the end of the line. Abandoned by his cousin, Darcy went off in search of Miss Elizabeth. When he could not find her by the punchbowl, he returned to the ballroom. He eventually discovered her talking to her friend, Charlotte Lucas, in a dim corner of the ballroom. As the second set was just finishing, he bowed very correctly to request her hand.

At that moment, Lizzy thought she would rather walk backwards to Jericho than dance with Mr Darcy, but as she was engaged to dance with him, there was no escaping—a torn hem had its limits as an excuse.

The hand that was extended towards her was well formed with elegant long fingers in pristine white gloves. As Mr Darcy took her gloved hand, Elizabeth appreciated for the first time how very large his hands were when her own hand seemed to disappear in his grasp.

Darcy steered Miss Elizabeth away from her friend to a quiet spot as the new set was forming.

"Miss Elizabeth, I hope you did not credit your cousin's words in the receiving line. I wish to reassure you that I am not betrothed to my cousin Anne. The match is a conceit of my aunt's."

"Let me also reassure you, Mr Darcy, that if you wish to withdraw your offer, I will completely understand," replied Elizabeth.

Unaware that Elizabeth had heard his own rash words to his cousin Richard earlier, Darcy reassured her he did not and hoped for a favourable answer by the morrow.

They took their place in the formation as a cotillion was announced. Elizabeth spent the first half of the dance stewing over her various embarrassments related to Mr Darcy, but sheer enjoyment of the dance soon overtook her, and by the end of the set she had to concede that he was a far superior partner to Mr Collins. They were both rather startled when the next set was announced as a waltz.

When Darcy glanced over the sea of heads to check for Caroline's reaction, his eyes first met those of Charles. His friend was grinning mischievously. His partner, for a *third* set, was Jane Bennet.

Turning back to his own partner, Darcy asked, "Are you familiar with the steps of the waltz, Miss Elizabeth? We can sit out if you are not."

"I am, Mr Darcy. Though I must admit, I have only ever danced it with my friend, Charlotte Lucas."

Darcy took Elizabeth's right hand in the distinctive grasp and rested his own right hand lightly at the back of her waist. As she was wearing short stays, the warm imprint of his palm penetrated her thin dress and seemed to sear itself onto her skin.

Lizzy fumbled the first few steps but soon found her rhythm. She quickly understood why the waltz was considered so scandalous, finding herself so close to Mr Darcy that she dared not look directly at his face. Glancing upward, she was confronted with his smoothly shaven, but well-defined, chin. She concentrated instead on one of his waistcoat buttons. She could smell his cologne, mixed with an earthier scent that could only be his own fresh sweat. It was a heady mixture that she found herself breathing deeply, whether from the exertion of the dance or her own volition, she knew not.

The dance made her feel extremely self-conscious. At first she attributed her unease solely to Mr Darcy's proximity, but she began to realise that the combination of stepping backwards and having her movements largely determined by her partner were also disconcerting. She had not been discommoded by the steps when she practised them with Charlotte. With her friend, the waltz had seemed more like the dances she was used to—a pairing of equals. Now, she felt overwhelmed by Mr Darcy's physique, and it occurred to her that should she miss a step or try to resist him, she would be swept about willy-nilly.

"The waltz," observed Mr Darcy, who seemed completely unaware of her unease, "is a dance where it is possible to speak to one's partner. Have you read any good books lately, Miss Elizabeth?"

"Well, I might say that books are not an appropriate topic for a ballroom, Mr Darcy, but I must admit I have been puzzling over your mention of Euripides in our previous conversation. In the context, I must wonder if you were having a slight poke at me. Do you think the proposed union will be a tragedy?"

He was silent sufficiently long that Elizabeth glanced up to check his reaction and found him frowning at her.

"I assure you no sinister meaning was intended, Miss Elizabeth," he replied gravely. "In retrospect, I admit my words must have seemed strange. The truth is that I had a bizarre conversation with a lady once who, when I mentioned the Greek playwright in passing, thought I was speaking of a torn dress. I resolved then and there to use it as a criterion for the minimum standard of education I would consider in a future spouse."

Without really knowing why, Lizzy felt her ire rise once more. "You set the bar rather low, Mr Darcy."

"Unfortunately, Miss Elizabeth, experience has taught me I have set it rather high."

"You think so little then of the intelligence of women?"

"I suppose it is more their education that is at fault."

"But that is hardly fair, Mr Darcy, as a woman's education is largely dictated by society. Women are not even allowed to attend university."

"Ladies are taught to read and there is nothing stopping them from picking up a book," he replied.

"Nor is there anything encouraging them to do so either," Elizabeth retorted; "lest they be labelled as blue stockings."

"That is a weak excuse for laziness, Miss Elizabeth."

"Not at all, Mr Darcy. You would not expect a hobbled horse to win a race."

"We must agree to disagree, Miss Elizabeth, but now I am curious…"

"What of?"

"Can you read Greek?"

"Certainly not. I would be at pains to recognise most of the letters," she admitted.

"And what of Latin?" he asked.

"I can read a little. The alphabet is, after all, the same. But do not ask me to conjugate a verb."

"I must admit that I only conjugate Latin verbs these days when I am trying not to lose my temper," replied Darcy.

"And does that happen often?" asked Elizabeth tartly.

"Only when I am forced to talk to exceedingly stupid people."

"Like now?" breathed Elizabeth.

Darcy blushed when he realised he had indeed been conjugating Latin verbs in the receiving line.

Unfortunately, Elizabeth interpreted his blush as an admission of his belief in her own intellectual inferiority. Having a father who was a former Oxford fellow, she was well aware of it.

They finished their dance in stony silence. She was only too glad it had come to an end.

Mr Darcy bowed very correctly and formally; Elizabeth tried to return a curtsey with equal grace before walking off, quietly seething.

She had not gone far before she encountered Charlotte.

"Lizzy, you looked so good dancing with Mr Darcy! He is such a handsome man, and you danced the waltz admirably! With such spirit!"

"We were having an argument."

"On what?"

"The stupidity of women."

"Oh, Lizzy," smiled Charlotte, "you do like to jest! I am having such a wonderful time! Colonel Forster has engaged me for the next set and Mr Collins for the one after! And here I was thinking I would be sitting against the wall all night!"

"I am glad the ball is graced with a few gentleman of discernment," replied Lizzy generously. "Here comes the colonel now."

Lizzy could only marvel at her friend's willingness to be pleased. Colonel Forster was a very well worn fifty years, having spent many years being weathered by the sun and strong drink in a militia posted to India.

She was met by her sister, Jane, who led her off down the hallway to the room that had been designated as the ladies' cloak and retiring room.

"Oh, Lizzy, my period has started early," whispered Jane as she closed the door.

"Are you wearing anything?" asked Lizzy.

"Yes, I felt some pain before we left Longbourn and tied on a girdle, but it has soaked right through. I suppose the dancing has been vigorous. I fear I will have to ask Caroline for assistance. How embarrassing! Do you have anything in your reticule?"

Lizzy opened her reticule and immediately spied Mr Darcy's handkerchief that she had been carrying with her, chiefly so that Sarah or Hill would not find it amongst the laundry.

Jane grasped it thankfully, but in the process of refolding it for her needs, stopped and looked at her sister. "Lizzy, this is a man's handkerchief, and the initials... Lizzy could this be Mr Darcy's handkerchief?"

"It is, Jane. He loaned it to me when I lost mine at Netherfield."

"I cannot use this! You will have to give it back."

"No, Jane. He asked me to keep it as a replacement for one I lost."

Jane looked at her sister in consternation. "Lizzy, is there something you are not telling me?"

"Indeed, Jane. I need your advice, but it must wait until we get home."

Jane would have requested her sister unburden herself immediately, but she stopped when she heard Mr Bingley's voice raised in agitation.

"Leave be, Caroline! I'll dance with Jane Bennet if I want to!"

Both the Bennet sisters froze. The voices were coming from an adjacent room. Lizzy looked stricken and would have pulled her sister away, but Jane leaned towards the interconnecting door. Caroline's voice was just discernible.

"There were to be no waltzes, Charles, and that was your third set with her! You are raising her expectations!"

"By all means let them be raised! She is a goddess!"

"She is portionless and she has relatives in trade. You will not throw yourself away on her! What would Father say if he were alive?"

"Must you always throw that at me?"

"I must since you do not have a sufficient sense of duty to think of it yourself," replied Caroline.

"Take your hands off me, Sister. The hostess should be out in the ballroom."

"Very well, Charles, but think of your family before you have our father rolling in his grave!"

A door slammed and two sets of footsteps retreated down the hallway.

Lizzy squeezed her sister's hand. Having roamed the house at Netherfield while her sister was confined to bed, she was well aware of the Bingley sisters' true sentiments. She had hoped that Jane's gracious nature would win them over, but it was now clear that those hopes were in vain.

They heard the music strike up for the supper set. Jane finished arranging her skirts and twirled for her sister's inspection, as if nothing untoward had occurred. Then giving Elizabeth a tight smile, she hurried back out to the ballroom to meet Colonel Fitzwilliam.

Lizzy trailed behind her sister down the hallway and then stopped to lean against the wall. She was not engaged for the supper set and frankly had no wish to return to the ballroom. Her heart was heavy for her sister. While her own expectations for the Netherfield Ball had not been great, she knew Jane had stars in her eyes for Mr Bingley. Now those hopes had been dashed most cruelly.

She touched the wainscoting in the hallway, so familiar, and the background to so many happy memories for herself and Jane as children, but tonight the scene of their mortification. She sat down on a bench and, closing her eyes, leant her head back against the wall.

14 The day after

Inside the carriage, the return to Longbourn was subdued. Kitty and Lydia, exhausted from their exploits, fell asleep on either side of their softly snoring mother. Mary was her usual taciturn herself, only making occasional mundane remarks on the quality of the supper and her father's unwillingness to let her perform more than one song during that interval. Lizzy and Jane, who had much they wanted to say to each other, were forced to sit in silence until they gained the privacy of their room. Lizzy longed to know Jane's thoughts on her potentially ill-starred relationship with the tenant of Netherfield. Despite Mr Bingley's protests to his sister, he had not engaged Jane for a fourth dance. For her part, Jane was bursting to know what information Lizzy had been keeping from her.

To Lizzy's mind, the evening was capped by a brief conversation with her father when they descended from the coach: "Oh, Father!" she said, recalling his promise to return the fairy tales at the Netherfield Ball. "You forgot to return Mr Darcy's book!"

"He made a gift of it to me, my dear," Mr Bennet replied sanguinely as he walked into the house.

Elizabeth ground her teeth. *Am I to be traded for a book of fairy tales?*

While Hill and Sarah attended the sleepier ladies of the Bennet household, the two elder sisters helped each other undress.

"Now, Lizzy, what have you been keeping from me?" asked Jane.

"Something that I hardly wished to acknowledge to myself. I must marry and I do not want to!"

"Has Mr Collins made you an offer?"

"He has spoken to Papa and intends to speak to me tomorrow morning."

"Oh dear," said Jane, "and I suppose Mama will insist that you take him since it will secure our future at Longbourn."

"That is not all. Mr Darcy has also made an offer."

"Mr Darcy!" said Jane, in shock.

When Lizzy, who had plonked herself down on the bed looking thoroughly dejected, did not elaborate further, Jane sat down beside her and took her hands.

"Of course! I forgot about the handkerchief! So when Mr Darcy came with Charles yesterday, it was to talk to Father?"

"Yes."

"How clever of him to use the book of fairy tales as a ruse to see Papa," mused Jane. "I never guessed, but I suppose I was a little distracted by Mr Bingley."

"It was more than a ruse," snapped Lizzy. "It was douceur."

"Oh, Lizzy, surely such a gift would have little influence on Papa for such a momentous decision!"

"You don't know Papa. It was exactly what he wanted and an expensively-bound edition to boot."

Jane mentally rejected this ridiculous notion. "But, Lizzy, how did this happen? Did something occur at Netherfield?"

"If you are asking if he compromised me, he did not. Quite the contrary, he showed no interest in me at all. His offer is a practical one. He seeks a marriage of convenience."

"But why has he settled on you? There must be so many females setting their caps at him—Caroline…"

"There's the rub. I cannot fathom it either. As best I can understand, he wants some female he can seclude on his estate in Derbyshire to bear his children, no doubt so he can gad about in London. Do you think Caroline would be happy to oblige?"

"I cannot imagine so. But is that all he had to say?"

"I am not to make vacuous conversation at the breakfast table."

"Now you are being flippant," sighed Jane. "Was there nothing else he said that spoke to you personally?"

"He said that he thought I was a sensible female; that he could not love me; that his heart was given to someone else… but he would treat me with the respect due to his wife and the mother of his children."

"Oh!" cried Jane, feeling her heart contract. "He must have a mistress—someone he cannot marry… someone from the lower classes; or… someone who is already married!"

Jane grasped her sister's hand in sympathy. Because of her beauty, Jane had always intended to marry and expected to marry well, preferably in a love match. Lady Yardley had hoped she might marry her eldest son and become the next mistress of Netherfield. Her sister, Lizzy, on the other hand, had shied away from the notion of matrimony. Although Edward Yardley had tender feelings for Elizabeth, Lizzy had refused to acknowledge they were deep, believing he would forget about her when he went to the Peninsula. Indeed, with the sole exception of a letter from Lisbon, nothing had been heard from Edward after his departure.

Considering their different prospects, Lizzy and Jane had made a secret pact: that Jane, being the attractive one, would marry, while Lizzy would live with her as a type of governess. While Lizzy did not exactly dislike men, Jane knew her sister abhorred the thought of putting herself in one's power; and a man who claimed no love for her—*that would be even worse.*

"Come," Jane urged her sister, "under the covers, and we will talk of it some more."

Lizzy dutifully got between sheets but did not wish to discuss her situation any further that night. "What of you and Mr Bingley?" she asked.

"Well," sighed Jane, "at least I know what I am up against: either he will follow his heart, or not. His actions will speak his mind. Let us see what he does in the next few days."

The long clock on the landing struck three in the morning, and taking what rest they could, the sisters sought refuge in sleep.

When the cock crowed around dawn several hours later, the two sisters were still snuggled together in slumber. Two pretty faces surrounded by beautiful tresses lay on the pillows: the dark and the fair. Lizzy greatly undervalued her beauty, but not without reason. She always suffered by comparison to Jane. Jane was truly stunning, and her guinea gold hair and cornflower blue eyes appealed to widely held views on the feminine ideal. Everyone in the family acknowledged that Lizzy was the first among the sisters in wit and intelligence, but Jane was the acknowledged beauty.

The chiming of the hour soon after cockcrow roused the sisters from sleep. As the coming day crystallized in her mind, Lizzy had the irrational notion of pulling the covers over her head and refusing to come out. Once again she surveyed her options. Either way, she reasoned, she would be marrying without love. She was sure that Mr Collins had no concept of the emotion. Based on the volume of his interests as expressed since his arrival at Longbourn, she was fairly sure that if she and Lady Catherine fell into a river, he would attempt to save Lady Catherine first. She recalled Mr Collins' hand imprisoning hers as they walked towards the receiving line. She tried to imagine kissing him and, smelling stale milk, felt slightly ill.

She thought then of Mr Darcy—of his arrogant words at the assembly. Despite his avowal that he would respect her, she thought it likely he would spend their marriage belittling her, just as her father subtly belittled her mother. *Could I endure that?* She tried to imagine kissing him and shuddered, feeling... *What?*

"Lizzy?"

From beside her, Jane's voice broke through her reverie.

"Lizzy, are you awake?"

A door slammed down the hallway, and giggling, Lydia and Kitty rattled down the stairs to breakfast.

Lizzy sighed as she sat up. "If I wasn't awake, I certainly am now."

"Have you had any more thoughts on your decision?" Jane asked timidly.

"The choice, Jane, is not whether I will marry for love or practicality. It is which of the two suitors I will be the least miserable with."

"Mr Darcy is very handsome, Lizzy."

"He is arrogant."

"He is very rich."

"He is very haughty."

Sensing that Lizzy had decided against Mr Darcy, Jane tried to find something nice to say about his rival. "I suppose Mr Collins might be more manageable than Mr Darcy. Looks aren't everything."

"He is a dolt," replied Lizzy, flopping back onto the bed.

Jane groped for something else positive to say about Mr Collins and found her mind a blank. She was spared from making a response by the arrival of Kitty.

"Papa wishes to speak to you, Lizzy; but he says get dressed first."

Half an hour later, neatly attired in a day dress, Elizabeth arrived at the base of the stairs. Her mother appeared at the door of the parlour in her dressing gown and cap, to mouth "Mr Collins", before disappearing back inside. Lizzy knocked and let herself into her father's library.

"Well, Lizzy?" said Mr Bennet, setting his coffee cup aside. "Have you made your decision?"

"Oh, Papa," said Lizzy, wringing her hands, "I am leaning towards Mr Darcy, but I hardly know him from Adam."

"It is true, Lizzy, but many marriages are arranged on such short acquaintance."

"I do not even understand why he has fixed on me."

"Well, he did speak somewhat to that question in our short discussion. He is chiefly looking for a mother for his children. He knows you are a sturdy and healthy lady, was impressed with how you tended Jane at Netherfield, and also how you dealt with Little Johnny Lucas."

"Little Johnny Lucas?"

"Did he not take a tumble at the Lucases' soirée?"

"He did, but Mr Darcy was not about when he did so."

"Well, perhaps your nursing skills were the talk of the soirée, my dear."

"Papa, it makes no sense. If Mr Darcy is as rich as they say he is, he could have his pick of eligible females. I do not understand why he has not offered for a lady of the Ton."

"Oh, Lizzy, how do I say this to you?" said Mr Bennet, glancing helplessly at the shelf of forbidden books in his library.

Lizzy waited in trepidation.

"...Mr Darcy has been to university," stated Mr Bennet.

"Yes."

"...and *I* have been to university."

"Yes," agreed Lizzy in puzzlement.

Then in a rush he concluded, "...and there are some men who prefer the company of men, but they still need heirs."

A slow blush crept from Lizzy's bosom and suffused her face. Stealing a glance at her father, she saw he, too, was blushing.

Her courage rose. "Did he actually say that to you, or do you just surmise?"

"It is a very delicate topic, Lizzy, but I have no doubt from my conversation with Mr Darcy that he will treat you with respect. Really, my dear, I think the situation he is offering you will suit your independent nature admirably. He won't live in your pocket, and you will be mistress of a grand estate."

Lizzy was at a loss as to what to say.

"Now come, Lizzy," said Mr Bennet. "Mr Collins is waiting to speak to you, so you must make a decision now. Which will it be?"

Lizzy thought she could still feel her cousin's greasy palm print on her skin, despite the fact she had washed her hands multiple times since the ball. She knew there was only one acceptable option.

"Then let it be Mr Darcy, Papa."

Mr Bennet hugged his daughter. "God bless you, Lizzy."

Then, as an afterthought, he went to his shelf of forbidden books and took down Patronius' *Satyricon*. It was Mr Burnaby's translation, which he kept next to a copy of the Latin text.

"Sometimes, Lizzy, I think young ladies are a bit too sheltered. No doubt your mother will give you a talk, but perhaps you ought to read this before you go to Derbyshire. No showing it to your sisters though, mind."

Lizzy accepted it, but was none the wiser when she looked at the spine. Thanking her father, she retreated from the library. When she spied Mr Collins and her mother lying in wait at the entrance to the parlour, she discreetly placed the book behind a pot plant in the hall.

Her mother quickly pounced on her. After closing the parlour door on her daughter and her suitor, Mrs Bennet retreated upstairs to the sitting room with glee.

The interview with Mr Collins was every bit as awkward as Lizzy had dreaded. It was all she could do not to cringe when he made his flowery proposal. Despite declining his offer politely but firmly, her cousin continued his persuasions at some length, even pursuing Elizabeth out into the garden when she tried to take her leave of him. She was saved from further torment by the arrival of her friend, Charlotte, who distracted Lizzy's determined suitor by inviting him to lunch at Lucas Lodge.

Having disposed of Mr Collins, Lizzy snuck back into the house by the kitchens, hoping to avoid her mother. She retrieved the book in the hallway and, tiptoeing to her bedchamber, distracted herself by reading it.

An hour later Mr Darcy arrived on horseback, summoned by a note sent by Mr Bennet. After a brief consultation in Mr Bennet's library, the pair emerged. Mrs Bennet was all astonishment when Mr Bennet shut his daughter in the parlour with Mr Darcy.

What a day! thought Lizzy, as the doors once more closed upon her.

Mr Darcy was again dressed in his immaculate and understated way, but he had taken it down a notch from the outfits he had sported yesterday. He was wearing top-boots, biscuit-coloured breeches with a matching waistcoat, an impeccably cut navy coat, and a linen cravat. Lizzy, who had attired herself in contempt of her situation, now felt hopelessly underdressed.

"Miss Elizabeth…"

"Yes, Mr Darcy?"

"Please, call me Fitzwilliam. May I call you Elizabeth?"

"Yes," she hesitated over the word, "…*Fitz-william*." *What a mouthful! Why did it sound easier in his cousin's name? Perhaps the word 'colonel' limbered you up somehow...*

"Elizabeth, thank you for agreeing to be my wife. I will leave for London immediately to visit Doctors' Commons and my attorney this afternoon. I expect the license will be issued tomorrow, or the day following at the latest." Darcy was sure he would not get the same treatment as Byron, who had been forced to wait over two days.

"Your father has already spoken to your parson, Mr Hammond, who has agreed to marry us on Wednesday, or Thursday, if need be. Are there any commissions you wish me to execute on your behalf?"

Good Lord! thought Lizzy. She had never imagined her father could move so fast. *He must have summoned Mr Hammond as soon as we walked out of his library.*

"Commissions?" asked Lizzy in a daze. "Wednesday? Are we not going to read the banns?"

"As I related to you several days ago, Elizabeth, I have urgent business. It is long since I set foot in Derbyshire," he explained. More accurately, Darcy was very conscious that his Aunt Catherine's parson was visiting the Bennets. Wishing to tie the knot quickly in case his aunt sought to intervene, he was completely unaware that he had a rival in that man.

Lizzy was dumbfounded. "But how can I possibly be ready in that time? I don't even have a dress..."

"The dress you were wearing last night was quite pretty," he suggested.

"It is torn, but perhaps it can be mended," replied Lizzy, depressed by both the dress's state and Mr Darcy's lukewarm compliment.

"I'm sure it will suffice," he assured her.

She nodded mutely.

"Your father," prompted Darcy, "thought you might wish to invite your aunt and uncle to the wedding... I would be happy to carry a letter..."

"Of course," said Lizzy, feeling rather numb. She sat down at the escritoire, picked up a pen and, discarding the notion of beginning with her usual greetings and family anecdotes, wrote a perfunctory invitation to her aunt. She would leave the explanations to Mr Darcy. Sanding and sealing this, she turned to find Mr Darcy staring abstractedly out a window. He turned when she approached him.

"Thank you, Miss Elizabeth," he said, tucking the missive into his pocketbook where another from her father rested. The two letters sandwiched a loop of wool supplied by Jane, sized on one of Lizzy's rings. "I mean, Elizabeth," he amended.

With a deep bow, Darcy retreated to the door, and without a backward glance, exited to the hallway. She heard him consult briefly with her father in the hall; and then, without further ado, he was gone. Walking to the window, she saw him mount and trot out the front gates. Had Darcy turned, he would have seen his betrothed standing at the window watching him, but he did not.

15 Preparations

Feeling a little numb, Lizzy sank down onto a chair.

Soon after, Jane peeked into the parlour. Seeing her sister staring disconsolately out the window, she came quietly in and sat down next to Elizabeth. "I saw Mr Hammond visit Father. Have they already arranged to read the banns?"

Lizzy burst out crying. After hiccupping a little and blowing her nose, she managed to get herself under control. "There will be no banns. We are to marry as early as Wednesday. He has gone to get the Special Licence."

"Wednesday!" repeated Jane. "Oh! No wonder you are overset! So sudden! But what will you wear?"

"I shall wear this!" said Lizzy stubbornly, indicating her day dress; "since he doesn't even care!"

Jane grasped her sister's hand.

Lizzy swiftly composed herself when Mrs Bennet burst into the room, closely followed by her other daughters.

"Well, Lizzy," her mother remarked, "I can't think that you've made the right choice, but at least you are getting married, and your sisters will benefit from it!"

"Yes, I'm sure that Captain Carter will be interested to know that I have a *five thousand pound dowry!*" said Lydia, swishing her skirts from side to side.

"I'm sure he will, Lydia," agreed Mrs Bennet. "This should bring Mr Bingley up to scratch, Jane! And with five thousand pounds, perhaps Mr Collins will consider Mary. She is just the wife for a clergyman!"

She rubbed her hands together before continuing: "I would have encouraged your cousin in that direction earlier, if I did not know what is due to my *elder* daughters," she sniffed. "Little though they consider *my* feelings!"

Looking around, Mrs Bennet asked in a perplexed voice, "Did Mr Collins go for a walk?"

Lizzy mentally rolled her eyes. Mr Collins would hardly have been present when she spoke to Mr Darcy, but she supposed that the parlour was the last place her mother had seen her cousin.

"He went to the Lucases for lunch," replied Elizabeth.

"The Lucases! What business can Mr Collins have with the *Lucases*?"

"He had an invitation for lunch, Mother," said Elizabeth. "I expect he will be back this afternoon."

"Well, I thought he was here to visit with family, but he is off gallivanting round the countryside! He could have had the decency to let me know to set one less place for lunch!"

"I'm sorry, Mother. No doubt, he intended me to tell you, but I have been rather distracted this morning."

Mrs Bennet smiled at her daughter. "Well, no harm done. I shall tell Hill directly, but first let us start our plans for the wedding! How many guests shall we have? With four and twenty families of our closest acquaintance there will be over one hundred on the bride's side. They will hardly fit in the church! And then there are the officers; and your aunt and uncle from London... Did Mr Darcy indicate how many of his circle he expected to attend?"

"Mama," intervened Jane. "Did Papa speak of the date to you?"

"Well, I expect that will have to be settled with Mr Hammond along with the reading of the banns."

"Mama, I believe Mr Darcy wishes to marry by Special Licence," said Jane.

"Ooh!" said Mrs Bennet. "A Special License! They're very expensive! Ooh! Imagine that, Lizzy! Married by Special License! What a coup!"

"Mama," interjected Jane. "Mr Darcy wishes to avoid the waiting period associated with banns."

"What? Sooner than banns? But I cannot possibly arrange a suitable function in less than three weeks! What is the point of marrying a rich man if one cannot appreciate it?"

Jane sighed at her mother's unrefined remarks. *Perhaps Caroline is right, I am unworthy of Charles.* "Mother, Mr Darcy wishes to marry on Wednesday."

"Wednesday! How can I possibly arrange anything by Wednesday? It is impossible!" Mrs Bennet shrieked.

Lizzy was about to explain that Mr Darcy had urgent business in Derbyshire, when, thankfully, Mr Bennet walked in.

"Mrs Bennet!" he commanded to bring his wife to order, and then in a quieter voice, "What *is* all this hullabaloo?"

"How *could* you have agreed to allow our daughter to marry on such short notice, Mr Bennet?"

"Indeed," replied her husband urbanely. "It was quite inconsiderate of me. There will be no time for you to order the carriage and spend all afternoon in Meryton bragging to your sister and friends."

"What can possibly be organised in such a short time?" she repined.

"A tolerable wedding breakfast, I would hope," retorted Mr Bennet. "Would it appease you if I gave you carte blanche to do what you may? I expect some extra servants will be required as a minimum."

"Well..." said Mrs Bennet, astonished by this extraordinary concession on her husband's part. "I suppose that will go someway towards helping..."

"Excellent," replied Mr Bennet. "Mr Darcy is the kind of man to whom I should never dare refuse anything which he condescended to ask. Now let us have lunch. Where, pray tell, is Mr Collins?"

"He has gone to the Lucases for lunch," replied Elizabeth.

"How very fortuitous," murmured Mr Bennet. Then, addressing the ladies of Longbourn he said: "I have one request to all of you. Pray keep Mr Collins in the dark regarding Lizzy's betrothal for one day will you?"

Following this pronouncement, he added, with a sly smile: "We would not wish to offend his sensibilities."

When Darcy arrived back at Netherfield, Finn was supervising the loading of his travelling carriage for the trip back to London.

"Almost ready to go, Finn?" Darcy asked.

"Yes, sir," replied Finn. "That is… I believe Mr Bingley wishes to speak with you, sir."

Bingley did indeed wish to speak to Darcy, for Caroline had been busy in Mr Darcy's absence. Although she rued his departure to London—for it temporarily suspended her schemes to beguile him; it allowed her to move forward another of her plans—to separate her brother from his latest inappropriate inamorata. While Charles had paid heed to her strictures not to dance a fourth set with Jane Bennet, Caroline knew him for the romantic recidivist he was.

An opportunity to put distance between Charles and Jane Bennet, which came in the form of a letter from his man of business in the City, was timely. This missive had requested Mr Bingley's presence before the next quarter day, which was still a month away. Nonetheless, during Mr Darcy's absence, Caroline had rung a peal over Charles on his neglect of his financial affairs, persuading him to accompany Mr Darcy back to London.

Upon speaking to Bingley, Darcy was quite happy to accept his friend's company on the journey to London and invited him to stay at his townhouse in Grosvenor Square during his sojourn there. Thus Mr Bingley's luggage was added to the carriage and both valets entered it, while their masters mounted their horses. Riding ahead of the carriage allowed Darcy and Bingley to set their own pace and have private conversation.

"Charles, I must tell you that my main purpose in returning to London is to obtain a Special Licence."

"A Special License!" exclaimed Bingley.

"Indeed, I hope to wed Miss Elizabeth Bennet on Wednesday. Will your business in London allow you to attend?"

"Well, good Lord, Darcy! When was this romance going on?"

"It is rather precipitate, but I believe she will suit me admirably," Darcy replied, displaying more enthusiasm than he felt.

"Well, congratulations!" laughed Bingley. "Won't Caroline be fit to be tied!"

"I have been very careful not to raise her expectations," replied Darcy stiffly.

"I know, Darcy, but she's damnably determined. I hope she didn't bother you too much during your stay," apologised Charles.

"Not at all," Darcy replied politely, but disingenuously.

"I must say it's rather short notice," said Charles. "Do you intend to get married in Hertfordshire or London?"

"In Hertfordshire," replied Darcy. "We will marry from Longbourn and return to Pemberley directly afterwards."

"Do you expect many of your relatives to attend?" asked Charles.

"Only my cousin, if his military duties will allow, and possibly my uncle. I hope Richard will stand up with me as best man. May I also ask you to act as a groomsman?"

Bingley was chuffed. "Of course, Darcy. I would be most gratified. You and your cousin will, of course, stay at Netherfield prior to the wedding?"

"Thank you, Bingley. I greatly appreciate it."

"And of course, you and Miss Elizabeth are welcome to stay at Netherfield for as long as you like."

"I appreciate the offer, Bingley, and may yet impose upon your good will if the weather is inclement, but I must admit I am anxious to see Pemberley again."

"Yes, and take your bride there, too, by Jove! No pun intended!" snickered Bingley.

Darcy blushed at his friend's coarse joke. "Indeed," he agreed quietly.

Having shared the information he wished to impart, Darcy urged his horse into a canter before Bingley could indulge in any further wedding humour. The rest of the journey passed quickly in a state of unspoken companionship. While Darcy planned what he needed to accomplish over the next two days, Bingley fantasised about racing off to Doctors' Commons with his friend and standing up with him for a double wedding next to a radiant and ravishingly beautiful Jane Bennet.

After daydreaming about this happy event for a good hour, Charles found himself anticipating Caroline's reaction. If he married Jane Bennet, he reasoned, he would be Darcy's brother! Surely the gain of the connection compensated for any lack of dowry? But he knew Caroline was going to be annoyed to find that Darcy had got leg-shackled; *and* to a female she considered inferior to herself. Her chagrin would likely be large. *Dammit! Why did she have to complicate things?*

His mind then proceeded to matters of familial diplomacy.

During lunch, Mrs Bennet expiated at some length on the various difficulties that faced her, which included the wedding dress, the wedding breakfast, and a trousseau. "I am not a magician, Mr Bennet! A worthy trousseau cannot be conjured from thin air!"

"Regarding the trousseau, Mrs Bennet," said her husband, "I hope your brother may help us. Mr Darcy was kind enough to carry a letter to Gracechurch Street with a draft from my bank. I have requested dress fabrics from your brother's warehouse appropriate to the station of the future Mrs Darcy. Clearly, there will be no time to have them made up, but I'm sure a suitable dressmaker can be found in Derby. On the other matters, I have every faith in your abilities."

"Regarding the wedding dress, Mama," added Jane, "I thought I might be able to refurbish Lizzy's ball gown or, perhaps, cut down one of my silks."

"You are too good, Jane!" cried her mother, somewhat mollified. "Do you take care of that, and I will see what can be managed for the wedding breakfast!"

It turned out that Mr Bennet had underestimated both his wife's ability to contrive at short notice and to brag. She set off to Meryton in the Bennet carriage after lunch with her two youngest daughters. Kitty and Lydia spent a pleasant afternoon flirting with officers under the guise of dispensing informal invitations to the wedding, while Mrs Bennet ensconced herself with her sister, Mrs Philips, to plan the grandest wedding feast the district had seen for some years. The Gardiner sisters then proceeded on a grand tour of the Meryton shops to make their purchases, place their orders, and generally gloat.

Mary contributed her mite on their return by writing out formal invitations on the pretty card that had been purchased before spending the evening practising music for the ceremony. For his part, Mr Bennet attended to the most important aspect of the celebrations from a male point of view, by walking to the local alehouse to determine what they could supply.

Upon reaching London, Darcy and Bingley sat down to lunch while they waited for the carriage following in their wake. Once arrived, the vehicle was quickly unloaded, cleaned, and the horses exchanged in preparation for their trip to the City.

After a brief stop at Drummond's Bank in Charing Cross Rd, the friends parted ways: Bingley to his man of business, and Darcy to his attorney followed by Doctors' Commons, agreeing to meet back at the carriage in two hours. It was Darcy's intention to then present himself at Gracechurch Street. Although the hour was an unusual one, Darcy had Mr Bennet's letter of introduction, and he thought it better to make the visit as soon as possible. It would allow the Gardiners time to respond to Mr Bennet's request and arrange their trip to Hertfordshire, should they wish to attend the wedding. He also believed the late hour should work to his advantage in finding Mr Gardiner at home.

After executing their business, the friends met as planned and wended their way to Gracechurch Street. Darcy had intended to send Bingley back to the townhouse in his carriage after finding his destination, while taking a hackney back to Mayfair himself. Instead, his friend pledged his support in seeking out Miss Elizabeth's relatives, despite their location near Cheapside.

Their arrival at the Gardiner residence was not without embarrassment, when the footman who opened the door betrayed they had interrupted the family dinner.

Initially shown into the study, Mr Darcy was surprised to find himself in a comfortably furnished room that not only confirmed Mr Gardiner as a businessman, and one who was rather better-off than Darcy had supposed, but as an amateur naturalist.

Mr Gardiner entered soon after, wondering what had drawn such an august personage to his door. He was acquainted with Mr Darcy through his business dealings and his attendance of public lectures of the Royal Society. Although they occasionally breathed the same air at stockholders' meetings and public venues of the arts and sciences, Mr Gardiner had been fairly sure that Mr Darcy was completely unaware of his existence. He had hardly believed his eyes when his footman presented Mr Darcy's calling card. After shaking Darcy's hand genially and greeting his friend, Mr Gardiner sat down to read the proffered letter.

Upon finishing this missive, he looked up in surprise at the young gentleman in front of him, whom he knew to be several years his junior. While reading Mr Bennet's letter, which began by asking his brother-in-law to welcome the gentleman to the family, it had occurred to Mr Gardiner that the precipitate nature of the match might have been determined by less than gentlemanly conduct on Mr Darcy's part. While his brother had not explicitly denied this, Mr Bennet's warm commendation of Mr Darcy seemed to belie it, as did Mr Gardiner's own knowledge of Mr Darcy's reputation, which was pristine.

"Well, this is a surprise," he said, looking up following his second perusal of the letter. "You could not have found a more worthy woman in all of England than my niece, Mr Darcy, but I *am* surprised you found her. I have often wished to bring both my elder nieces to London for the season, but it has, to date, not been possible. Let me congratulate you on what I am sure will be a truly felicitous marriage."

Given Darcy's own low expectations for his future happiness, he shook hands somewhat guiltily—clearly Mr Gardiner thought highly of his niece. Mr Gardiner offered the men a celebratory drink, which Darcy initially declined, apologising for interrupting his dinner.

"For news such as this, Mr Darcy," Mr Gardiner assured him, "I would gladly set down my knife and fork any day. I expect you are used to dining much later, but please feel free to sit down with us. We are having a roast and there is plenty to spare."

"Thank you, Mr Gardiner, for your kind invitation, but my cook is expecting us back in Mayfair, so I must decline."

"Then can I extend an open invitation for lunch or dinner tomorrow? I expect you will be returning to Doctors' Commons?"

Lunch was duly agreed upon, following which the gentlemen consented to a celebratory glass of brandy before departing. During the ensuing conversation, Mr Bingley declared himself an admirer of Mr Gardiner's *other* niece, while Mr Darcy was surprised to discover that Mr Gardiner's brandy was quite tolerable. The brandy was, in fact, as good as any of Darcy's own, and he was forced to admit that while Mr Gardner's occupation was not ideal, his tastes could not be faulted.

Noting Mr Darcy's hesitant first sip from the glass, Mr Gardiner explained that he was lucky enough to get his hands on some very good brandy recently through a connection: "When one is in trade, one barters, you know."

After handing over Elizabeth's note for Mrs Gardiner, the younger gentlemen took their leave. Once the front door closed, Mr Gardiner shook himself and went to relate the momentous news to his wife.

16 More preparations

At Longbourn, Jane had found the remnant of the muslin they had used to make up Lizzy's ball gown. Cutting the ruined dress short above the tear, she proceeded to trim the embroidered portion to a neat band and tacked this to the new section she would add as a flounce. After Lizzy donned the dress and the flounce was pinned in place, the sisters agreed the result might be tolerable. Once her sister had removed the gown, Jane proceeded to tack the flounce in place, then set Mary to stitch the hem while she and Lizzy assessed the state of their combined wardrobes.

Lizzy's contribution to her trousseau was meagre. Like her father, she did not pay much heed to finery and was sincerely regretting that oversight. She spent her money on serviceable boots and capes for her rambles, items that had no place in a drawing room. Unfortunately the sisters were quite different sizes: Jane was Junoesque while Lizzy was shorter and sylph-like, so there was little Jane could offer beyond some generic items. These included chemisettes, fichus, and an expensive silk shawl from Spitalfields, which had been a recent Christmas gift from the Gardiners. After some argument, Lizzy accepted the items, but would only take the shawl on loan.

"Although who knows when I will be able to return it to you," she despaired.

"Whenever you can will be soon enough," replied Jane. "It's important that you present a good appearance on your arrival in Derbyshire. Once it becomes generally known that Mr Darcy has married, you will have many callers come to pay their respects," said Jane.

"Aye, no doubt we will be besieged by quidnuncs as soon as word gets round. Well, I have several day-gowns and must somehow contrive to make them look different each day until my other gowns are made up. Perhaps if I purchase some lace or beads I may furbish up some of the fabrics the Gardiners are bringing as shawls."

"Indeed, but it seems a shame to spend your honeymoon sewing shawls, unless… Oh Lizzy, I've just had a wonderful idea—Mama's old gowns! Remember how I said it was a shame they were just mouldering in the attics, and that we should use the beautiful fabrics for something else?"

"I remember," replied Lizzy. "Mama said not to touch them because they may come back into fashion."

"They will never come back into fashion!" scoffed Jane. "Let us go up and see if there is anything suitable to make a shawl or two."

The sisters wisely donned older day-gowns before making the attempt. After breaching the attics, they quickly located the correct trunks, bringing them down the stairs to the landing. With some help from Sarah and Hill, they dusted them off.

The first trunk revealed two lovely robes à la polonaise: one with a beautiful tartan silk overskirt; and another with a lovely rose motif. A second trunk contained two silk robes à l'anglaise in autumn colours.

"Oh, Lizzy, these colours will look especially good on you," mused Jane, as she turned them around.

"Don't get too carried away, Jane," said Lizzy. "There are only a limited number of shawls we can hope to hem in the time we have available to us."

A third trunk was nevertheless breached, but the sisters agreed that the fabrics of the dresses it contained were less suited to Lizzy's colouring.

When the distinctive sound of carriage wheels crunching on the gravel of the drive heralded Mrs Bennet's homecoming, the sisters sped downstairs to get permission to wield scissors.

Upon arriving back at the Darcy townhouse, Darcy and Bingley parted to their respective rooms to prepare for dinner. When Darcy finally donned his dinner jacket, he enquired if Finn had been able to fulfil his commission, to which his valet advised that he thought he had found something suitable.

Because of the precipitate arrangement of their marriage, Darcy had not given Elizabeth a betrothal gift. His initial impulse was to buy some trinket at Rundall and Bridge—a brooch perhaps; but ultimately he had shied away from this idea, conflicted with thoughts of Diana. He had spent so much time and money selecting the parure for his love that it seemed a betrayal of his sentiments to return to the jeweller searching for a gift for another woman.

He decided instead to choose something from the family jewels. It occurred to him that this was a trifle miserly because, as mistress of Pemberley, his wife would have use of these jewels regardless. Darcy assuaged these thoughts by deciding to cede the chosen piece to her personally. That way Elizabeth could leave it as she liked in her will. Removing this hoard from the safe in his study before his trip to the City, he had instructed his valet to sort through it and make some suggestions.

"Well, sir," explained his valet, "I was thinking about what you might wear to the wedding."

Darcy nodded at this apparent *non sequitur*, indicating his valet should go on.

"I understand that Miss Elizabeth will be wearing the green muslin she wore at the Netherfield Ball."

"That was my suggestion, yes," replied Darcy.

"Well, there is a very fine pair of earrings and a ring that would suit it admirably," said Finn, holding out the case.

Darcy's heart almost stopped when he saw the jewels in question. They were green tourmaline earrings and a matching ring presented by Darcy's father to his mother on their tenth wedding anniversary. His parents had loved each other deeply, and when his mother had passed, he remembered his father tenderly placing the matching necklace on her as she lay in state—how the pendant had glittered in the light from the branched candelabra that had been placed round her bier. The necklace had gone with his mother to the family vault.

In the circumstances, it seemed a mockery to give what remained of a set of jewels that represented the strength of his parents' devotion to his own betrothed. But before he could negate his valet's suggestion, Darcy bit his tongue, realizing that as Mrs Darcy, Elizabeth would be entitled to wear the jewels in question anyway. He supposed he could put them away and never bring them to her notice, but this seemed churlish. Had he not pledged to respect her as his wife?

"Very well, Finn. They will do nicely," he affirmed, "and thank you for your consideration."

"The presentation box is a little mottled, sir, and there seems to be space for a pendant I could not find. Should I procure a new box?"

"If you would, Finn, it would be greatly appreciated," replied Darcy. "But keep the old box—it has sentimental value to me. Perhaps some of my own jewellery could be kept in it?"

"Certainly, sir," said Finn, giving his master's coat a final brush.

When Darcy entered the dining room, he found Richard awaiting him; warming his coattails by the fire.

"Excellent," said Darcy. "You got my message about dinner. Were you able to get leave for the wedding?"

"I was, but my father is unable to attend," replied Richard. "I went by Matlock House on my way here. Father said he would try to drop by to talk to you before midnight."

"I gather he has gone out," observed Darcy.

"Went to White's for dinner. I expect he'll visit his mistress afterwards and swing by here on the way back."

"So I take it you spoke of my wedding? I sent a note to his townhouse this morning advising him of it," said Darcy.

"Indeed, and I did my possible to reconcile him to it," replied Richard. "I hope I have done you a favour."

"How could you have not?" asked Darcy.

"I stretched the truth a little. I advise you not to let on it is a marriage of convenience."

"How can it be anything else? Coming so soon after…" Darcy could not finish.

"This is my father we are talking of," chided Richard. "He changes his mistress as often as his coat."

"He knows I am not like that," replied Darcy.

"And yet," observed Richard, "he still thinks like himself. If he believes it is a marriage of convenience, he'll want to know why you didn't opt for a bride with a larger dowry."

"You forget that his principal directive was to sire heirs," said Darcy. "I chose a wife on that basis. Surely that should be enough for him."

"You're still not thinking like my father," admonished Richard. "I told him you fell in love with her; that she and her sister are the local beauties. That is true enough. That the elder sister is truly ravishing, but that you preferred the colouring of the younger."

"Richard, was this *truly* necessary?" winced Darcy.

"I know my father, Darcy. He was ready to cavil, but once I started talking of beauties, he softened his attitude. I did what I thought was necessary to get his approval."

"I don't need his approval," retorted Darcy.

"Nor do you want his disapproval," countered Richard.

The cousins faced each other in silence.

"Very well," said Darcy, admitting the point. "Forgive me, Richard. Thank you for your efforts on my behalf."

Soon after the cousins had reached this understanding, Bingley walked in, and the gentlemen sat down to an excellent dinner. Withdrawing to Darcy's study afterwards, Richard proposed they celebrate Darcy's bachelor night.

"If all goes well, we will be at Netherfield tomorrow evening, and will have to keep it tame for your sisters, Bingley," reasoned the colonel.

"Well, goodness, Colonel Fitzwilliam," laughed Bingley. "What are you proposing? That we go out rabble rousing and box the watch?"

"Oh, yes!" scoffed Richard, "and get Darcy appropriately banged up for his wedding day. What a good idea! No, I was thinking more of telling embarrassing childhood stories while we wait for my father to turn up."

"Surely, Darcy doesn't have any," scoffed Bingley.

"Oh, ho!" said the colonel, knocking back the last of his bumper of brandy.

"Richard," growled Darcy menacingly.

"Let's see... There was the time we were chased by Mr Fletcher's bull and had to jump the irrigation ditch. You landed on that pitchfork, and it went right through your foot. Wickham and I carried you to old Vickers, the sawbones, and he said he'd have to take off your foot. Lord, you should have seen your face!"

"Yes, hilarious!" remarked Darcy. "What a card he was! No doubt scaring ten-year-old boys provided endless entertainment for him."

"And that time we were playing pirates," continued Richard, "when you fell out of the tree and knocked yourself silly. I thought you were dead then. Or there was the time we went skinny dipping at Matlock as youths. Remember? Lady Adversane took our clothes. Said if we wanted them back, we had to go ask for them, and Wickham did! Took his sweet time too. Anyway, better him than me. She was as old as the hills even then, despite her appearance. I'm sure she eats small children for breakfast..."

This continued for some time while Darcy wondered how he might shut his cousin up.

"Who is this Wickham?" asked Bingley drowsily.

"He was the steward's son," replied the colonel. "He was orphaned at an early age, or something like that. His mother may be still alive, but she ran off with some fellow. Mr Wickham died a few years later, and George was left to the care of Uncle Darcy, who stood as godfather."

Bingley looked to Darcy in question and received resigned affirmation.

"As a playmate, George wasn't a bad bloke when he was little," continued the colonel, "but he didn't improve with age. Got into the petticoat line. Your father ended up sending him away, did he not, Darcy?"

"Yes," affirmed Darcy. "He thought Eton would straighten him out. Little did he realise, George only got worse. I had to share rooms with him for a year at university. He was into every kind of debauchery. I never knew who I would find in our rooms, male or female. Once I arrived back from class to find him with the dean's wife, who was twice his age."

"Really?" asked the colonel, ignoring the shocking behaviour of the dean's wife, and latching onto the one new piece of information Darcy had imparted. "I didn't know he was that way inclined."

"Tutors," replied Darcy.

"Oh, ho," said the colonel. "I suppose that fits with the Wickham I know. Always the easy road with him."

Silence fell and Darcy looked at the clock. "It is way past midnight, Richard. I think your father may have forgotten us."

"Probably having too much fun," sighed Richard. "Perhaps we'll see him in the morning."

The gentlemen got up to retire. Bingley, being the slightest of the three, proved unsteady on his feet, but with some help from the others, he managed to reach his bed without tumbling headlong down the stairs.

The gentlemen had not long been at breakfast the next morning when the Earl of Matlock was announced.

"Well, Darcy," said the earl, swaggering in, "getting leg-shackled at last, eh?"

"Yes, Uncle."

"Well, good, good. What's the rush though? Afraid I night not like her if I see her?"

"I was more concerned that Aunt Catherine might try to intervene if I had the banns read," replied Darcy.

"No, no, my boy," assured the earl; "*I* am the head of this family, so you need not fear her sanction. It's a pity that Anne is so sickly. From a strategic point of view, it would have been a good match."

"I'm sorry you are unable to attend, Uncle," observed Darcy, attempting to change the subject.

"So am I, my boy, but we need the numbers in parliament; very important vote coming up. Must be there. It is too much to hope the vote will be taken today. I expect Lords Blenheim and Fothergill will want to say their mite, so we can kiss the rest of the day goodbye on that alone. What are your plans following the ceremony?"

"I'm away to Pemberley, sir," replied Darcy.

"Keen to show your wife the delights of Derbyshire, eh?" leered the earl, giving his nephew a good shake about the shoulders.

"Quite," replied his nephew primly.

"Well," said the earl, surveying the table. "Mind if I join you for breakfast? Always set a good spread, don't you, Darcy? Your father was the same."

"Thank you, sir," replied Darcy, glad to escape further teasing. "May I introduce my friend, Charles Bingley."

"Bingley, eh?" said the earl, settling himself in a chair and indicating to a footman to prepare him a plate. "So you're the one who purchased this property in Hertfordshire."

"Yes, my lord; or rather, I'm leasing it with an option to purchase," replied Bingley. "Darcy thought it would it be wisest."

"No doubt," replied the earl. "Ever the canny one, eh, Darcy? The apple doesn't fall far from the tree."

Darcy vouchsafed no reply.

"Well," said the earl, beginning to ply his knife and fork. "I hear these Hertfordshire sisters are something else!"

"Oh, yes!" gushed Bingley. "The eldest Miss Bennet is the most beautiful angel I have ever encountered."

The earl, who had been slightly sceptical of his son's glowing review of the sisters, was glad to have Richard's opinion confirmed by an independent observer; but he was also slightly amused that Richard appeared to have a rival in this wealthy tradesman's son. The earl raised his eyebrow infinitesimally in the direction of his son. The colonel returned a tight smile.

"Indeed," said the earl. "Five of 'em, ain't there? And you are betrothed to the second eldest, Darcy?"

"Yes, sir."

"And how did this wonderful romance proceed?" asked the earl, stuffing some ham into his mouth.

Darcy proceeded to replay the spiel he had rehearsed for Mr Bennet, assisted this time by his cousin and Bingley as chorus, affirming Miss Elizabeth's solicitous nature and healthy sprightliness.

"Well, I look forward to meeting her," said the earl. "Don't keep her holed up in Derbyshire forever."

"She's a country girl, sir. I expect she'll be happier at Pemberley," replied Darcy.

Well, thought the earl, *looks like my nephew plans to keep his wife pregnant in Derbyshire!*

Then, finishing the last of his eggs and ham, he gave a shrewd look at Darcy. "No doubt your Aunt Carissa will summon you to Matlock. I look forward to the report." Rising abruptly, he bid the young men good day and disappeared into the vestibule.

17 Mr Collins' surprise

Not long after the earl departed, Darcy heard the knocker sound again and assumed the earl had returned to impart further thoughts. However, they were all surprised when the butler instead announced the Bingley sisters and Mr Hurst.

"Caroline!" said Bingley, starting up from his chair in some alarm. "What has happened?"

"What on earth do you mean, Charles?" returned Caroline, simpering in the direction of Mr Darcy. "What could be more natural than to pay a visit to my dearest brother and his friend?"

"But why have you quit Netherfield?" demanded Charles. "Is there some problem?"

"Dear Charles, we became convinced after you left that your business in London could not be concluded speedily; and rather than pine away in Hertfordshire awaiting your return, we thought we could be of far more use to you here in London where we might help entertain you in the evenings. Thus we packed our trunks and here we are!"

During this speech Bingley's expression had steadily changed from consternation to tight-lipped indignation.

"Well, I hope you haven't unpacked them," he declared; "because you'll have to turn right back round. If all goes well, I expect to be heading back to Netherfield this evening."

"That's quite impossible, Charles," replied Caroline. "The house will be empty. They were placing the holland covers as we left; and Nicolls will have already turned off the servants!"

Charles did not reply to this sally, but had gone quite red in the face.

"Forgive me, Charles," said Darcy, rising from the table. "There are a couple of matters I must attend to before I leave for the City."

With a quick bow to their guests, Darcy retreated to the adjacent drawing room before exiting to the hall. In this manoeuvre he was closely shadowed by Colonel Fitzwilliam. Entering the study, Darcy closed the door behind them as a loud argument broke through the walls.

Assuming his place behind his desk, Darcy consulted his watch. Everything was, of course, already in order for his trip to the City, but he decided to make use of the half-hour available to him by opening the morning's mail. The colonel flung himself into a wing chair by the hearth; and grabbing a poker, proceeded to arrange the fire to his satisfaction. As Darcy systematically flicked the majority of the correspondence, which were invitations to balls and soirées, into a neat 'discard' pile, the low thrum of a dispute reverberated through the wainscotting, until a sudden high-pitched shriek of *"What?!"* pierced the woodwork.

"I believe," murmured the colonel, "that Miss Bingley may have just been apprised of your impending nuptials."

Shortly after, Charles poked a harassed face into the library. "Forgive me, Darcy. There appears to have been a slight miscommunication. I'm going to have to go off to make things right. What time did you intend to depart for Hertfordshire?"

"If the licence is ready, I hope to depart at half-past four," replied Darcy.

"Very well," said Bingley. "I will not fail, but you will have to give my apologies to the Gardiners."

"Certainly, Bingley," replied Darcy, "but if you are unable to make it back to Hertfordshire, I quite understand. Richard and I can always stay in Meryton at the Red Lion."

"Under no circumstances, Darcy. All will be well," replied Charles.

At Longbourn, Mr Collins' sensibilities were safe until breakfast. After partaking of lunch at the Lucases' on the previous day, he sent a note via a footman in the late afternoon advising Mr Bennet that he would be staying at Lucas Lodge for dinner.

This missive strangely pleased Mr Bennet, although it outraged his wife.

"What can he mean by it!" she expostulated. "How can Mary possibly fix his interest if he is forever at the Lucases'?"

But with the exception of Mrs Bennet, and possibly Mary, the rest of the Bennets bore Mr Collins' absence remarkably well.

Mrs Bennet had parted reluctantly with her beautiful dresses; but with her future looking more secure, she reconciled herself to the fact that not even a seamstress most gifted with gussets could alter them to fit their owner. Instead, she found some strange comfort in the fact that all of her daughters thought the styles quite silly.

By the time Mr Collins returned to Longbourn in the Lucas carriage a half-hour before midnight, most of the Bennets had retired. A sleepy Hill opened the front door to the clergyman who entered with all the stealth and satisfaction of a clandestine lover. Upstairs, the only candles still burning were in the bedchamber of the two eldest Bennet sisters.

"Well, that is one of the shawls finished," sighed Lizzy as she tied off the thread. "How goes the embroidery?"

"I've almost finished the left side," replied Jane. "You see? With the extra motif, you cannot notice the tear. Once the right side is done, I believe it will look as good as new."

When Mr Collins came down to breakfast on the morning following his unsuccessful proposal to his cousin Elizabeth, he was big with news. But he was not early enough to catch the two eldest Bennet sisters, who had already eaten and retired to the upstairs sitting room to continue their sewing. This was somewhat disappointing, but he contented himself with the rest of the Bennet family as his audience.

"You must felicitate me, ma'am," he said to Mrs Bennet with a vindictive smile; "for I am currently the happiest gentleman in Hertfordshire. Yesterday, Miss Charlotte Lucas agreed to be my wife."

"What?" shrieked Mrs Bennet, incredulous, "on the same day you proposed to Lizzy?"

Mrs Bennet might have gone off into a tirade if not for the timely intervention of her husband.

"I'm glad your sensibilities were not too wounded by my second eldest, Mr Collins," said Mr Bennet. "I felicitate you on your betrothal and your stoicism in the face of adversity."

This sanguine speech somewhat took the wind out of the clergyman's sails.

"La," said Lydia, administering the *coup de gras*. "You hardly had a chance against Mr Darcy. Even if he is high in the instep, he's very rich, and quite good-looking despite his age. The only thing you have going for you is Longbourn, and you don't even have that yet!"

Mr Bennet rolled his eyes. *Well, the cat has been let out of the bag, and with such decorum!*

Mr Collins was indignant. "You must be mistaken, Miss Lydia. Mr Darcy is betrothed to Miss Anne de Bourgh."

"He can't be," retorted Lydia. "Because he is marrying Lizzy tomorrow. Why do you think we are doing all this infernal sewing? You can't marry two ladies: that would be buggery!"

Mr Collins turned a deep shade of red while Mr Bennet's eyes rolled heavenwards, as if seeking divine help.

"I think the word you intended was *bigamy*, my dear," corrected Mr Bennet. "And might I suggest you spend less time in the company of the soldiers of the militia?"

"Is this correct, sir?" Mr Collins sputtered at Mr Bennet.

"Of course not," replied Mr Bennet, with his tongue in his cheek. "It isn't bigamy until you are actually married. As a clergyman, you would be aware that the civil courts may recognise a betrothal but it has no status in the eyes of the church."

"That is not what I meant, sir," objected Mr Collins coldly. "Is it true you are planning a wedding between your daughter and Mr Darcy?"

"Indeed, Mr Collins," replied Mr Bennet. "I cordially invite you to the ceremony, which is being arranged for the morrow."

"Then I counsel you strongly against it, sir," said Mr Collins, bristling. "Mr Darcy is destined for Miss de Bourgh."

"Mr Collins, that may be your patroness's wish, but Mr Darcy is a free agent. He wishes to marry my daughter, and I have given my consent to the union."

"You leave me no choice but to object at the ceremony, sir," replied Mr Collins stiffly.

"Do not make a cake of yourself, Cousin," replied Mr Bennet. "Your objections can hold no water, and you will certainly make a very powerful enemy in Mr Darcy. He will not appreciate having his nuptials interrupted."

This advice gave Mr Collins pause. "Then you leave me no choice but to write to Lady Catherine," he announced pompously.

"By all means, Cousin. Please invite her to the ceremony, the more the merrier," said Mr Bennet.

Mr Collins promptly retired to his room to write his letter and then hurried off to the receiving office to catch the morning mail. What he didn't realise was that Mr Bennet had been there before him, and greased the clerk in the fist to hold his cousin's letter over 'til the afternoon mail.

Satisfied that he had ensured Lady Catherine's timely intervention, Mr Collins took himself off to Meryton on foot, ostensibly to visit his betrothed, but more precisely to distance himself from the scene of the crime. A man with nicer morals might have removed himself to the Red Lion for the duration of his stay, but the lessons of his miserly father deemed such an action too extreme for the clergyman.

Shortly afterwards, Mrs Bennet headed off to Meryton in the carriage with her two youngest daughters. It was lucky that the right of way across the fields taken by Mr Collins separated him from the road, else Mrs Bennet might have ordered the coachman to give him a scare, acquainting him with the ditch on one side of the road or the hedge on the other. She was still quite out of charity with him. Fortunately out-of-sight was out-of-mind for Mrs Bennet and instead she chatted with her daughters of her plans for the afternoon. Her mission was to collect her sister, as well as supplies for the wedding, and to check if the agency had been successful in procuring more servants. Kitty and Lydia had been tasked with filling the remaining hole in Lizzy's wardrobe—that of shoes and stockings. The selection in Meryton was not great, but the ladies' commission was simple: they were entrusted with obtaining silk slippers and stockings in colours that would complement Lizzy's wardrobe. In this, the older sisters inherently trusted them—as silly as Lydia and Kitty were, they had a decided eye for fashion.

Arriving in Meryton, Mrs Bennet dropped off the girls at the haberdashery; and then, after picking up Mrs Philips, set off with her sister in the carriage to fulfil her own tasks.

The whole party arrived home to Longbourn shortly before noon, with two kitchen maids on the rumble seat and a footman on the box. Mrs Bennet had been pleasantly surprised that the agency had found help so quickly. She might have been less gratified if she knew the servants had been turned off from Netherfield the previous day.

The maids were sent to the kitchen to assist Hill while the footman busied himself with unloading the supplies from the carriage. Another footman, three more kitchen maids, and a chambermaid turned up in the afternoon. The latter was set to polishing the silver.

Darcy arrived promptly at Doctors' Commons at noon and was rewarded with the requested Special Licence. His next stop was his attorney where drafts of the marriage settlements were obtained. A footman, brought with him from Darcy House especially for the purpose, was promptly dispatched with a copy of the settlements and a note bearing the news of his success in obtaining the Special Licence to Hertfordshire. The footman tucked the note into his waistcoat where the jewellery case containing the earrings and ring already resided, and set off for the nearest posting house.

Darcy and the colonel then wended their way to Gracechurch Street, where Mr Gardiner himself greeted them at the door upon Darcy's knock.

"Mr Darcy," said Mr Gardiner, stepping back to allow both gentlemen to enter. "How good to see you! Forgive me for answering the door myself, but I have sent both footmen off on errands in anticipation of our departure to Hertfordshire."

Darcy bowed in reply. "Mr Gardiner, may I introduce my cousin, the Honourable Colonel Richard Fitzwilliam, who will be my best man at the wedding. Mr Bingley was unable to accompany me today due to urgent business."

"Colonel Fitzwilliam," bowed Mr Gardiner. "Edward Gardiner, at your service. How do you do?"

The colonel bowed in return, and Mr Gardiner led the gentlemen into the parlour where a well-dressed lady awaited them, surrounded by four small, but elegantly attired children. The youngsters looked a little uncomfortable in their formal clothes.

"May I introduce my wife, Madeleine Gardiner," gestured Mr Gardiner.

The lady smiled and curtsied; and at her signal, the four children did the same. The smallest one achieved this with such grace for his size that Darcy found himself smiling in return.

"My dear, may I introduce Mr Darcy, who has brought his cousin, the Honourable Colonel Richard Fitzwilliam."

The cousins bowed very correctly, and Mr Gardiner waved them to be seated. This gave Mr Darcy a chance to take in his surroundings. He found himself in a very elegant parlour decorated in the French manner with an Aubusson carpet, several gilt fauteuils and a settee. It was far grander than he had expected, but escaped being pompous by the accoutrements of its inhabitants, which included a sewing basket and a box of toys.

"Colonel Fitzwilliam," said Mrs Gardiner as she took her seat, "are you related to the Earl of Matlock?"

"I am his second son, ma'am," replied the colonel. "Are you acquainted with my father?"

"No, sir," replied Mrs Gardiner, "but I was born in Derbyshire and lived there as a girl, so I know of the family."

"In Derbyshire?" echoed the colonel. "Well, what a coincidence, Darcy! And here I thought we would be dining with foreigners!"

Darcy smiled weakly at the colonel's jest. "From where in Derbyshire do you hail, Mrs Gardiner?" he enquired politely.

"From Lambton, sir," she replied.

"Why," cried Darcy, forgetting his dignity, "that is not five miles from Pemberley! I used to ride there when I was a boy to buy barley sugar. My housekeeper always told me my teeth would fall out!"

"Indeed, I remember seeing you there once or twice," recalled Mrs Gardiner.

"You did?" he asked, somewhat surprised.

Looking at the children, Darcy realised Mrs Gardiner must be a similar age to himself. He had imagined Miss Elizabeth's aunt and uncle to be much older people.

"Well, perhaps you didn't notice the villagers, Mr Darcy," remarked Mrs Gardiner, "but you cannot expect that the villagers did not notice you."

"I remember some boys there," replied Darcy. "One of them was very big. I believe my groom told me he was the smith's son."

"Ah, yes, that would have been Joe Green," observed Mrs Gardiner. "He has largely taken over the business from his father now."

"Nobody ever spoke to me," remarked Darcy.

"Well, everyone knew you were Mr Darcy's son, so I expect at most there would have been some tugging of forelocks."

"Indeed, no, Mrs Gardiner, such actions were reserved for my father, but I have not set foot in Lambton since I left for Cambridge."

"You will find it largely unchanged, Mr Darcy," Mrs Gardiner replied.

Darcy might have pursued this interesting topic, but the parlour door opened, and a maid dropped a curtsey in the direction of the lady of the house.

"Well, gentlemen," said Mrs Gardiner, standing, "our lunch is ready."

The lunch turned out to be as grand as a dinner: with a baked sole, a rabbit pie and a fricassee of veal; and for dessert, an apple cobbler with fresh cream and tea.

It was three o'clock by the time Darcy and the colonel took their leave. The conversation had been surprisingly easy, ranging through the more recent lectures at the Royal Society to plays at the theatre. Darcy even thought he might have got on quite well in the absence of Richard, but he appreciated his cousin's easy repartee nonetheless. Mrs Gardiner made pertinent contributions throughout, and once the eldest Gardiner boy made an intelligent remark on a scientific topic, which made the colonel raise his eyebrow.

Upon the gentlemen taking their leave, Mr Gardiner wished them a safe journey, and assured them he would see them at Longbourn on the morrow.

"Well," said the colonel, once they were ensconced in the Darcy carriage and wending their way to Mayfair. "I challenge Miss Bingley to hold a conversation as intelligent as that. It would seem she has severely underestimated the company to be had at Cheapside."

"Indeed," said Darcy, but he did not elaborate any further.

Mr Gardiner's footmen arrived back in Gracechurch Street soon after Mr Darcy's departure. They had been sent to the warehouse with instructions to the staff for the two-day duration of Mr Gardiner's absence in Hertfordshire; and to retrieve the trunk of silks requested by Mr Bennet. These had been selected yesterday by Mrs Gardiner from the bolts, to be cut and packed by the following morning. As their wedding present to the Darcys, the Gardiners had doubled the value of the silks requested by Mr Bennet.

The footmen added the trunk to the luggage already residing on the carriage being prepared for Hertfordshire. Meanwhile upstairs, Mrs Gardiner sent the children to use the chamber pot before they departed.

"Well," said Mr Gardiner as Nurse closed the door behind herself after herding the last protesting child out—he was sure that he didn't need to pee-pee; "one day Mr Darcy walks through the door, and the next day we are dining with him and a peer's son. Lizzy has certainly done well!"

"It has all been so sudden," replied Mrs Gardiner. "Lizzy said nothing in her letter. She's been as close as an oyster. I hope nothing is wrong."

"Now, my dear," protested Mr Gardiner, "there was nothing in Thomas' letter to indicate a problem, and you see how perfectly amiable and gentlemanly Mr Darcy is. He could not have been nicer."

"The colonel was very affable, my dear, and Mr Darcy's manners could not be faulted, but after conversing with him for two hours, I still feel I hardly know him."

"Oh, women!" chided Mr Gardiner, with a smile. "You always make things more complicated then they really are!"

"Edward," replied his wife evenly, "you are a master of the quick decision; hence your success in business, but I think Mr Darcy is a complex man. I hope he will be right for our Lizzy."

Mr Gardiner was tempted to retort that he was sure Mr Darcy was a right one, but he respected his wife's intelligence more than that. Instead, he squeezed her hand.

"Come, I believe the carriage is ready," he said. "Say a prayer that everything will be all right, and let us be off."

Herding the excited children ahead of them, Mr and Mrs Gardiner descended the steps to the carriage.

18 Complications

When the Darcy carriage arrived back in Grosvenor Square, the cousins mounted the steps of the townhouse in order to refresh themselves for their longer journey to Hertfordshire. Footmen and stable hands swarmed around the carriage, bent on their own preparations. Finn and Crimplesham began supervising the loading of the trunks of all three gentlemen. Upon Darcy's enquiry, Mr Bingley's valet divulged that Bingley had not yet arrived back from his mission to placate Caroline and reverse her earlier directions to vacate Netherfield.

By the time the cousins re-emerged from the townhouse half an hour later to assess their situation, the pair already in the traces had been baited, and two fresh leaders, which had been harnessed in front of them, were stamping the ground, eager to be off. Darcy, who had consulted his watch several times in the past fifteen minutes, had begun to despair that they might have to depart without Bingley, when his friend entered the square on horseback from Grosvenor Street.

"Sorry, Darcy. I'm good to go," said Bingley, as he approached them.

Satisfied that all was in order, the valets entered the carriage and two stable boys mounted the offside horses, ready to bring the team on to Netherfield at an easy pace after the first change. The coachman gave the order and the grooms stood away from their heads, both of them swinging up behind the coach as it passed them by.

"Can I offer you a drink before we set off, Bingley?" asked Darcy, earnestly hoping his friend would decline.

"Thank you, Darcy, I am fine 'til the posting house," replied Bingley. "It's probably better if we get there earlier rather than later. I've sent a note on ahead to Nicolls, though heavens knows what we'll find when we get there. We may have to dine at the Red Lion. I deeply apologise for the mix-up."

The colonel eyed Bingley askance as he pushed his chapeau-bras onto his head. He thought Bingley needed to read his little sister the riot act.

"Think nothing of it, Bingley," said Darcy, as he and his cousin mounted the horses that had been led up to them. "I'm grateful you are able to accommodate us at all."

As Darcy settled into the saddle, his mare, Juno, danced playfully underneath him, obviously also eager to be off. "So are your sisters returning to Netherfield, Bingley?" he asked as they headed out of the square.

"They've sent their apologies, Darcy," said Bingley. "I'm afraid they can't make the wedding. Caroline has taken one of her nasty turns. Her heart troubles her occasionally—just like mother; God rest her soul. I've consulted several Harley Street physicians, but they can't seem to pinpoint the problem, and merely recommend laudanum and bed rest. She must have exerted herself too much yesterday, directing the packing and then the journey... Louisa, of course, would not think of leaving Caroline's side."

"Of course not, Bingley," replied Darcy. "I hope your sister recovers soon."

The colonel merely rolled his eyes at Darcy's polite disingenuousness, but Bingley returned his sincere thanks.

Shortly after they crossed Oxford Street, the colonel urged his horse into a canter and his companions followed suit. They passed their valets in the Darcy carriage on Hampstead Heath.

No more conversation was to be had until the first posting stop when Bingley went off to relieve himself. The cousins dismounted to stretch their legs and accepted the ales offered by a boy who ran out.

Darcy flicked him a gold coin in return. "Another for my friend who just went round the back."

"Yes, sir," nodded the boy, scuttling off to comply.

"Heart problems, my foot!" muttered the colonel, as he wiped some manure from his boot. "More like shit on the liver."

Darcy grimaced at his cousin's use of this cant term, which he often employed to describe some of the starts of his irascible major-general, but he was sympathetic to the sentiment.

"Yes, I'm glad you abandoned that pursuit—a man would be a hostage in his own home with Caroline as a wife," returned Darcy.

"Here, here," said the colonel as he upended his tankard to drink the dregs.

Bingley returned shortly after and manfully downed his tankard in one go, causing the colonel to mentally elevate him one notch above the prissy jellyfish he thought him to be.

Rather than swap to posting nags, the gentlemen decided to remount their own horses, which were showing no signs of tiring, but dropped the pace back slightly to give them a rest. Just over an hour later, the gates of Netherfield were in sight, and Bingley dismounted to parley with Mrs Nicolls who had appeared at the front door.

"It's all right!" Bingley yelled cheerfully to Darcy, as he skipped back down the steps. "Mrs Nicolls has managed to arrange dinner, though there is only a skeleton staff at the moment. I dare say we will manage with our valets."

"Excellent," replied Darcy as the cousins dismounted.

The Darcy coach arrived an hour later. Due to the lack of footmen, Mrs Nicolls was forced to enlist the services of both valets and the grooms to unload the coach, before she hurried back to the kitchen to supervise the completion of dinner.

Once Finn had deposited Darcy's trunk in his dressing room, he sought out his master, who had retired to his bedchamber to refresh himself and rest before dinner. He found him scribbling in his notebook as usual. Easing the well-fitted coat of superfine off Darcy's shoulders, Finn was already thinking of the following day.

"Sir, would it be possible to ascertain whether Miss Elizabeth will be wearing the green dress or some other gown to the ceremony?"

"You are thinking of what I should wear?" asked Darcy.

"Indeed, sir," replied Finn. "I brought a selection of waistcoats and cravats in the hope of preparing an outfit that would complement her gown. It would look best at the altar."

Darcy smiled. "We will have our backs to the congregation, Finn. Only the parson will be able to appreciate your efforts."

"There will be the wedding breakfast also," prompted Finn. "Please, sir."

"Finn, you make me feel trapped already," Darcy sighed. Then seeing his valet's woebegone expression, he relented, "*Very well*, I'll send a note to Longbourn, though who shall carry it, I know not."

In the end, one of Darcy's grooms volunteered, setting off on Bingley's horse. As Mr Bingley did not ride much above ten stone, the groom judged it to be the least tired of the horses available.

The gentleman ate a tolerable dinner before Bingley produced the brandy.

"Well, looks like my prognostication of having to keep ourselves in order tonight was a little premature," said the colonel with a grin.

"Speak for yourself, Richard," said Darcy. "I'm not arriving drunk for my wedding, and I have a long journey to Derbyshire tomorrow. Just one for me and then I'm for bed."

By the time Darcy had downed his tot, Richard and Bingley clearly hadn't finished their toasts, and Darcy left them as the colonel tossed off his third bumper. He hoped his groomsmen would be able to stand on the following morning.

As Darcy ascended the stairs, he could only be glad that Charles had managed to foil the machinations of his sisters. Spending his last night as a bachelor at the Red Lion would have been thoroughly depressing. *One bullet dodged,* he thought to himself. He only hoped that Mr Bennet had been as successful in handling his cousin—the last thing Darcy wanted was for his Aunt Catherine to arrive at his wedding.

Earlier in the day, Longbourn had been a hive of activity—with all the ladies engaged in sewing and cooking for the wedding, and Hill running in circles organising all the extra servants. By the time Mr Darcy's footman arrived from London with the settlements, afternoon tea was being served, and Jane had just finished the embroidery on Lizzy's wedding gown.

Taking his tea to his study, Mr Bennet perused Mr Darcy's missive before penning a note to Mr Hammond, confirming the ceremony for nine o'clock the next morning. He then settled into his wing chair to peruse the settlements. These were more than generous: besides the five thousand pound dowries offered by Mr Darcy, of which Mr Bennet had informed his family; there were the other terms that Mr Bennet had negotiated but kept to himself.

There they were in black and white: an income of five hundred pounds per year per child underwritten by the Pemberley estate to be made available to Elizabeth should she choose to live separately after the birth of the second son; or failing the birth of two sons, after the tenth wedding anniversary; a property in Yorkshire to be ceded to her at said time; and the ability to take any daughters of the marriage with her to live separately, to be raised at the expense of Mr Darcy.

Mr Bennet was sanguine that should his Lizzy be miserable with her husband, she could at least retreat to a comfortable retirement. The settlements were in triplicate as he had requested. He quickly signed Mr Darcy's copy before setting aside the copies for himself and Mr Gardiner, who he would ask to oversee the arrangement in the event of his own early demise.

Finally he picked up the jewel case and the associated note. Opening the case, he saw the box contained another note, this one addressed to Lizzy, sitting atop a demi-parure of tourmalines. Snapping the case shut, he summoned Hill, handed her his empty teacup, and requested the presence of his wife.

"See here, Lizzy," cried Mrs Bennet as she entered the upstairs sitting room shortly after, trailed by her two younger daughters. "A message has just arrived from Mr Darcy. He has obtained the Special Licence, so your father has arranged the ceremony for nine, tomorrow morning. But look what he has also sent!"

The jewel box was duly presented, and Mrs Bennet urged her daughter to open it. As the Bennet ladies crowded round to see the jewels, Lizzy opened the box to find the note from her fiancé. Handing the open box to Jane, Lizzy unfolded the missive.

Dear Elizabeth,
Please accept this late betrothal gift.
If you are wearing your green dress tomorrow,
I hope the jewels will complement it.
Fitzwilliam Darcy.

"Oh, Lizzy!" cried Mrs Bennet, eyeing the jewels. "They are very fine!"
"Are they emeralds?" cried Kitty.

"Of course not," replied Lydia. "It is jade, but there is no necklace."

"No girls, I believe they are tourmalines," stated Mrs Bennet authoritatively. "It is a shame there is no matching necklace, but you can wear my pearls, Lizzy."

"No, Mama. What will Jane wear?"

"It doesn't matter, Lizzy," said Jane. "All eyes will be on you."

Still Lizzy protested, and in the end Mrs Bennet fetched her jewel box and discovered a pendant of smokey-yellow topaz she had completely forgotten about. This jewel in no way matched the quality of the stones of the earrings and ring that Mr Darcy had given Elizabeth, but everyone agreed that it matched the embroidery on Lizzy's gown and balanced the ensemble. Thus it was agreed that Jane would wear the pearls.

"You had better finish off the invitations now, Mary," decreed Mrs Bennet, "and send them off with two footmen."

Mrs Bennet then asked her younger daughters to leave the room because she had something important she wished to discuss with Lizzy. Kitty and Lydia giggled conspiratorially and made a great show of effacing themselves. Lizzy, not unnaturally, dreaded she was about to get The Talk, but her mother's confidence turned out to be of a different nature.

"Lizzy, I don't know what to do. Mr Darcy has asked both Mr Bingley and Colonel Fitzwilliam to be groomsmen, and I am at a loss as to who should be your second bridesmaid. Mary wants to play the piano, and if I ask Kitty, Lydia is sure to feel left out."

The sisters immediately appreciated their mother's dilemma.

"Perhaps Charlotte?" suggested Lizzy.

"Charlotte Lucas!?" squawked Mrs Bennet. "After she stole Mr Collins! Over my dead body!"

Jane sought to intervene. "Mama, you can hardly blame Charlotte for accepting Mr Collins' proposal. She, too, must make her way in the world. Now that we all have dowries as good as your own, I'm sure we can all find very eligible matches. Charlotte *is* Lizzy's best friend..."

"Oh, very well," said Mrs Bennet begrudgingly. "I suppose the blue silk she wore to Netherfield will look well enough with your gold and green gowns."

Then she got a mischievous look in her eye. "It will be interesting to see what Mr Collins will do about his betrothed's participation in the ceremony."

"Mama," scolded Lizzy in jest. "I think you have been living with Papa too long!"

Mrs Bennet gave a surprisingly girlish giggle. "Yes, I believe some of him must have rubbed off on me!"

Lizzy and Jane tried not to think too hard about this declaration.

A note was quickly sent off to Lucas Lodge begging Charlotte to be one of the wedding party, and a gratified acceptance duly returned, all with Mr Collins none the wiser.

The Gardiners arrived at Longbourn around seven in the evening; and dinner, which had been held off for them, was quickly served. The children, who had all fallen asleep in the coach, were quickly roused from their torpor; but some difficulty was experienced in packing them off to bed later after their revivifying nap.

When the children had finally achieved sleepy-bobos, Mrs Bennet appealed to Mrs Gardiner to support her in explaining her marital duties to Elizabeth. Depending on whether she believed her mother or her aunt, Lizzy understood these to be either uncomfortable and undignified, or a special bond of intimacy with her husband that would bring her much joy.

As Lizzy lay down to sleep beside her exhausted sister, the words of her mother and aunt revolved in her head. These were inexorably mixed with her father's contribution to her knowledge of the world, revealed through such parts of *The Satyricon* glimpsed in the half-hour spared to her since learning of her impending marriage. This had been sufficient to grasp the gist of the book, and as she had sewed during the past day, she had re-parsed every interaction she had witnessed between Mr Darcy and Mr Bingley in the light of this new paradigm.

These musings left her none the wiser—perhaps, she thought, because her memory of them was too imperfect. As she fell asleep, she mentally resolved to watch these two gentlemen very carefully on the morrow.

19 Guests at the wedding

The day of the wedding dawned.

At Netherfield, one might have been forgiven for thinking that Mr Bingley was the gentleman getting married. On Bingley's instructions, his valet had attired him long ago. Bingley then proceeded to wear a path between the colonel's dressing room, where Crimplesham was helping Darcy's cousin into his dress uniform, and that of the groom at the other end of the hall, supplying regular updates to both parties. Crimplesham could only wince as he watched his master scuff his boots.

If the colonel and Bingley thought they were last to bed after their brandy fest, they were wrong: that honour went to Finn, who spent his evening preparing his master's raiment and that of the colonel for the wedding. His painstaking efforts and attention to detail were now becoming apparent. Thankfully Miss Elizabeth was to be attired in the Netherfield Ball gown, as Finn had hoped, granting the valet's wish to produce an exemplary matching outfit. Darcy's hair was pomaded to perfection and his black hessians shone. Above ivory breeches, a pale green watered silk waistcoat lay next to a darker green cravat, fastened by a pin with a single large diamond nestled in its folds. Darcy held out his immaculately manicured hands as Finn fastened the cufflinks.

"I don't recall seeing these before, Finn," remarked Darcy.

"No, sir, they are tourmalines to match those being worn by Miss Elizabeth. I selected them after you approved the jewels for her."

"They come from Rundall and Bridge?"

"Yes, sir. I saw them when I obtained the wedding ring."

Darcy had forgotten about the ring sized with the piece of string obtained from Jane Bennet. He had passed that errand onto Finn, ostensibly so he could dine with the Gardiners.

"Thank you, Finn. They look very well," said Darcy, turning his wrists over to admire the cufflinks as Finn eased the tailcoat of dove grey onto his master's shoulders.

Finn gave the coat a final brush as Darcy surveyed himself in the mirror. Satisfied with his valet's efforts, Darcy gave him a brief smile before turning to go.

"One more thing, sir," said Finn, opening another jewel box and holding it out to his master.

Darcy perceived the box contained a large solitaire diamond set in a ring. It had belonged to his father.

"Just for today, sir? To replace the signet?" begged Finn.

Darcy hesitated, twisting the signet on his left hand, which he used for sealing his letters. He had seen the diamond ring so often on his father's hand, it seemed sacrilege to put it on himself, but he supposed it was somehow appropriate to wear something of his father's at such an important event.

"Very well," he said.

Darcy met Richard in the hall. His cousin looked resplendent in his full dress uniform, with his helmet under his arm and his dress sword hanging by his side.

Richard gave Darcy one look over and fluttered his eyelashes: "Lovely!" he pronounced.

"He does look something else, does he not?" grinned Bingley. "You will have all the ladies sighing over you today, Darcy!"

"They are only sighing over my wallet, Bingley," said Darcy, unwilling to take the compliment.

Bingley rolled his eyes at the colonel and then added belatedly, "You also look resplendent, Colonel."

The colonel had no illusions about his own appearance. He was not a handsome man like his cousin, but he knew he looked to his best advantage in the full magnificence of his dress uniform.

"You have the ring?" asked Darcy.

"Yes, Finn gave me two of them," said the colonel, patting his breast pocket.

"Two?" queried Darcy.

"Finn says one of them is for your pretty finger. No doubt, he wants to show off that rock you're wearing to the congregation."

"Oh," said Darcy. "Well, it is a trifle unusual, but I suppose that betrothed couples wear gimmel rings. You will have to square it with the parson when we get to the church."

The gentlemen donned their coats in the vestibule and climbed into the carriage. Darcy spent the journey to Longbourn meditating on what his father might have thought of his arranged marriage. Having shared a deep love with his mother, Darcy could not think his father would have approved.

Outside the church, Jane and Charlotte stepped carefully down onto the pattens that Sarah had placed at the carriage step, watched by as many of the villagers as could spare themselves from their occupations for such a grand event. This seemed to be mostly everyone. The church was an easy walk from Longbourn's manor house, but not one to be attempted in silk slippers, hence the use of the Bennet carriage. Lizzy handed her bouquet out to her sister and then followed her bridesmaids down. Slipping her feet into the pattens, she joined the others as they minced their way to the church door.

Mr Collins was standing just outside the narthex, wringing his hands.

"Cousin Elizabeth, please reconsider your rash actions. Mr Darcy is betrothed to Miss Anne de Bourgh! You risk the wrath of one of the most distinguished families in Kent. You must proceed no further!"

Several village boys, who had caught his last words, booed; and one, who was standing behind Mr Collins tossing a small pebble from hand to hand, successfully lobbed it at the back of the clergyman's knee. Mr Collins jumped and swung round to confront his assailant, who had already disappeared round the corner of the church.

Turning back to the group, the clergyman stretched himself up to his full height and appealed instead to his betrothed. "Miss Lucas, you cannot aid and abet such a miscarriage of justice. I demand that you do not participate."

"Mr Collins," replied Charlotte in her kindest voice; "you cannot expect me to desert my friend in her hour of need. Does not *Proverbs 17:17* counsel us to be a friend at all times?"

If Mr Collins knew his scriptures better, he might have had an appropriate retort for his fiancée, but he did not. Outgunned, he subsided, but still refused to enter the church.

"Charlotte, that's amazing," whispered Lizzy as they entered the narthex. "Did you think of that just now?"

"I'm afraid not," murmured Charlotte. "I went to the rector of Meryton last night and we found it in his concordance."

Jane stifled a giggle. "That's forward planning, Charlotte," she whispered as they stepped out of their pattens.

Mr Bennet, who had been awaiting his daughter in the narthex, entered the church to ensure all was ready, before returning to take Elizabeth's arm.

Bach's *Air on a G string* washed over them as they stepped into the nave. The church, surprisingly, was full. Important residents of Longbourn and Meryton, along with representatives of many of Mrs Bennet's four and twenty families, primarily occupied the bride's side; while officers of the militia sat together as a bright red splash on the groom's side, with a backfill of tradesmen and their wives from both Longbourn and Meryton.

The congregation stood to honour the bride's passing, and Lizzy smiled left and right in turn as she progressed down the aisle. Halfway down the nave she almost stumbled when she perceived her fiancé standing at the altar staring at her. He was immaculately dressed and looking decidedly handsome in an outfit that, she realised, blended well with her own; but he was disconcertingly grave as he stood there. His eyes seem to bore right through her.

Happily, a movement to the right caused her to look at Colonel Fitzwilliam, standing beside Mr Darcy, resplendent in his dress uniform; and then to Mr Bingley, also becomingly attired in his best. The colonel grinned at her disarmingly, and Mr Bingley also gave her an encouraging smile of such sweetness that she regained her poise immediately. Her father felt only a slight wobble; but he placed his free hand over Lizzy's smaller one that clasped his arm and gave it an encouraging squeeze. She beamed gratefully back at him.

After they arrived at the altar, the rector announced the couple's intention of marrying and asked the congregation if there were any objections, despite the Archbishop's approval on the Special Licence. As Mr Collins had stayed outside, no voice was heard; and Mr Hammond requested the couple to kneel. Lizzy handed her bouquet to Jane and lowered herself to join Darcy on the embroidered cushion at the altar rail. Even kneeling, the groom towered head and shoulders above his intended bride.

As Darcy turned to look at Elizabeth, he was momentarily struck by a resemblance to his mother. He mentally shook himself, convinced that his mother's earrings and the way Elizabeth had arranged her hair had elicited a chance comparison.

The responses were performed without error on either part, and the colonel surrendered the rings without pretending he had lost them, as he had done recently at the wedding of a fellow officer. Darcy pushed the smaller ring onto his bride's delicate hand. Without question, Elizabeth, in turn, pushed the larger matching ring next to the diamond solitaire on Darcy's left hand. The parson led the wedding party into the vestry, where the couple signed the register, witnessed by the colonel and Mr Bennet.

As they returned to the nave, the rector declared them man and wife, and the congregation rose to congratulate the couple as they walked down the aisle. The colonel quickly offered Jane his arm and surged ahead of the newlyweds, leaving Charlotte and Bingley to attend them. With a nod, Colonel Forster followed them to the narthex where Jane retrieved her pattens and picked up a basket of small calico bags filled with barley. These she began to distribute among the waiting villagers as the colonels ranged themselves on either side of the church door.

Mr Collins, who was still outside, was now hopping from foot to foot. Colonel Fitzwilliam placed his helmet carefully on his head before turning towards him and drawing his sword rather dramatically, causing Mr Collins to give an odd squeak and retreat in the direction of the village tavern. The two colonels chuckled to each other at the success of this sally while several villagers cheered, and even Jane had to bite her lip to suppress a giggle.

Crossing their swords, the colonels formed an arch for the newly wedded couple to step through. As Darcy was not a military man, this was not strictly necessary, but Colonel Fitzwilliam had agreed it would make a nice effect when Colonel Forster had suggested it to him.

Upon emerging from the church, Darcy donned a shiny black beaver before stooping to step through the arch with Elizabeth. They were immediately inundated with barley. Darcy's raiment allowed him to shake this off easily, but Elizabeth was not so lucky—some of the grains lodged in her hair; while others slipped down her dress and into her décolletage before a few insinuated themselves beneath her stays.

She giggled as the cold grains made her shiver—one could only laugh at such a predicament. Her husband looked at her quizzically, amazed at her light-heartedness, and supposed she must be nervous. She was, of course, a little—but she felt she could hardly explain her grainy dilemma to a man she hardly knew, even if he was now her husband.

Congratulations and well wishes were duly made by those gathered outside, continually supplemented by the congregation streaming from the church. When the time came, Elizabeth aimed her bouquet at Charlotte, not wanting to give Kitty and Lydia any encouragement in their flirtations with the officers. The villagers cheered when Miss Lucas caught the flowers, not realising that she was already engaged. But alas, Mr Collins was not there to appreciate his status as the gallant suitor in waiting.

The ladies of the bridal party were then assisted into the carriage, along with Mrs Bennet, who giggled girlishly to be among them for the short trip back to the manor house.

The more genteel elements of the congregation followed the carriage back to Longbourn for the wedding breakfast while the rest of the crowd repaired to the alehouse, where Mr Bennet had paid for a keg to be distributed as largesse—a fact that had quickly become common knowledge amongst all the villagers.

The wedding breakfast that Mrs Bennet had contrived with her sister on short notice was generally agreed to be delicious. Unfortunately, Mr Hurst missed out on the best crab patties Mr Bingley had ever tasted. The champagne punch, assembled with the help of several bottles transported from London by the Gardiners, was also pronounced top-notch, especially after Colonel Fitzwilliam surreptitiously emptied a bottle of rum into it.

Elizabeth, swept up by the celebratory atmosphere, had hardly time for reflection until at noon Darcy approached her, suggesting they should soon be off in order to make good time on the road north.

At this point, the colonel stepped forward to make a speech in which he praised the groom's reliability and the bride's beauty before wishing them many happy years together and demanding Darcy seal the arrangement with a kiss before the toast.

Darcy, suspecting the colonel was well oiled, glared at him before planting a chaste kiss on his wife's cheek as Elizabeth blushed furiously.

Bingley followed with a toast praising Darcy as 'the best of fellows', who had married a lady from the prettiest family of sisters to be found in Hertfordshire. His gallantry earned him a blushing smile from Jane and some excited giggles from Lydia and Kitty.

Finally, the father of the bride was called upon to say his mite. Lizzy was surprised to see her father wipe a tear from his eye as he declared her to be the quickest and wittiest of his daughters, before saying: "Mr Darcy has told me somewhat of his library, so I am reasonably confident that you will have much to entertain you in Derbyshire, Lizzy..."

Several members of the audience broke into lewd chortles, which Mr Bennet acknowledged with a tight smile and a nod of his head.

"At least," he said, raising his hands for silence; "it will give me an excuse to visit soon, I hope."

Lizzy valiantly did not burst out crying, though she hugged her father to hide the contortions of her face. Having composed herself, Lizzy remembered to divest herself of her mother's topaz pendant in the vestibule as she donned a bonnet and her best Sunday pelisse. Then she let her father lead her out to the Darcy coach. Upon stepping out onto the gravel drive, Elizabeth saw that her trunks had already been loaded onto the coach. With a kiss for her mother and all her sisters, and an especial hug for Jane, she allowed her husband to hand her into the carriage.

Lizzy waved goodbye to her family as the grooms stood away from the horses' heads and swung up behind. Then the coach threaded through the gates and headed off through the village, closely pursued by a gaggle of village boys, who gamely kept pace until the outskirts of town.

As the crowd began to return to the feast, Bingley regretfully called for his horse, before turning to Jane.

"Miss Bennet, forgive me, but I must also say farewell."

"You are going so soon, Mr Bingley?" asked Jane in dismay.

Bingley blushed and shuffled his feet. "I regret I must return to London, Miss Bennet. You may be aware that my sisters have already done so."

"Indeed," replied Jane, "we heard from some of the servants we hired to help with the wedding. I hope nothing is wrong?"

"Unfortunately," replied Bingley, "Caroline has taken quite ill, and I promised Louisa that I would return to London directly after the ceremony. I fear that I have stretched the definition somewhat by delaying until the Darcys departed, but as a groomsman, I felt I could hardly leave before the toasts..."

"Certainly not," reassured Jane. "You have done just as you aught. I hope it is nothing serious?"

"Well, it is a recurring problem," said Bingley quite truthfully; "but she generally recovers after a few days' rest. I hope to return to Netherfield as soon as I may and will keep you informed of events via Caroline or Louisa."

"Then God's speed for your journey, Mr Bingley, and my prayers for your sister's quick recovery," said Jane.

Mr Bingley took the liberty of kissing her hand. Then mounting his horse, he walked it slowly along the drive. He stopped to look back and wave at the front gates before urging his mount to a trot and disappearing through them.

Jane sighed. Finding herself quite alone, she turned towards the house, only to be met by Colonel Fitzwilliam stepping down from the portico.

"Miss Bennet, I have come to find you. Some of the officers have cleared a space in the parlour so that we can have some dancing. Are you free?"

"Certainly, Colonel," replied Jane, taking his proffered arm.

The officers thus spent a merry, though slightly raucous, half-hour in this delightful pastime until a grand carriage drew through the front gates. Perceiving it through the window, Colonel Fitzwilliam went out to greet his father.

"Father, you made it after all!" exclaimed Richard as the earl emerged from his coach. "But I regret you have missed Darcy."

"What, off to Derbyshire already? He's eager!" guffawed the earl, quite unperturbed at missing his nephew. "I thought he would spend his wedding night in Hertfordshire before taking himself off."

"Well, you know Darcy's not one for parties," replied his son. "But come in, there is still plenty of food and drink."

"Indeed," replied earl; "just what I was hoping for."

Lord Geoffrey Fitzwilliam, the tenth Earl of Matlock, was immediately presented to Mr and Mrs Bennet, causing Mr Bennet to raise his eyebrows slightly, and Mrs Bennet to almost swoon with delight. The colonel could not have been more gratified with his parent's reception.

After adjusting the feather in her turban in the nearest mirror, Mrs Bennet hastened to introduce the earl to her daughters. Jane, who had stepped into the kitchens to ensure more food was on its way when the colonel had excused himself to greet the carriage, was the last of the remaining Bennet sisters to be introduced.

"And this," explained Mrs Bennet grandly to the earl, "is my eldest daughter, Jane. As she is also the most beautiful, I thought for sure she would be the first married, but there is no accounting for tastes!"

Jane blushed faintly at her mother's gaucheness.

The earl's eyes glittered, and his lips descended on Jane's fair hand, not long ago touched by the parting kiss of Mr Bingley. The earl was tall, and although his face was well worn, Jane could see he must have been a handsome man in his prime. He had a cleft chin, and his mid-blue eyes, which had a darker blue ring 'round them, stared at her appraisingly in a self-assured manner.

Jane's blush deepened. She bowed her head and curtsied.

"Miss Bennet," purred the earl; "what a shame I missed meeting your sister. You must forgive my tardiness—parliament is sitting."

"Yes, my lord. I'm sure there are many demands on your time."

"Indeed, 'though some of them are more pleasant than others," replied the earl purposefully.

"Would you like some punch, my lord?" asked Jane; "And perhaps a crab patty?"

Lord Matlock accepted these politely and tossed off the punch disdainfully before raising his eyebrows as the alcohol burned its way back up his nostrils. He glanced at his son, who grinned back mischievously.

"Another glass, my lord?" asked Jane, who had filled her own glass with ratafia.

The earl accepted the refill and treated it with more respect. "So my son tells me he has been enjoying his stay in Hertfordshire," he commented. "He tells me much of the beauty to be found."

"Oh, yes," replied Jane, oblivious of the earl's flirting. "The countryside is very fine and there are many lovely walks hereabouts."

"Indeed," said the earl drily, "It's a pity I can't stay longer to enjoy the views, but the gardens outside looked very pretty. Would you care to take a turn?"

Jane cast her eye about anxiously and spotted Charlotte.

"Indeed, my lord. I was about to step outside to take the air with my good friend, Miss Lucas, when you arrived. May I introduce you?"

This duly occurred, and Charlotte was drafted to make a foursome on a tour of the gardens. It was from the vantage point of the rose garden that the colonel spied a second carriage arrive through the front gates, also familiar but unwelcome. He excused himself with a glance at his father and hastened to the front of the house with a quick stride, but only arrived in time to follow his aunt into the parlour.

Lady Catherine confronted the gathering in the parlour with Mr Collins at her elbow. "Where is my nephew?" she demanded. "I must see him immediately!"

"If you are looking for Darcy, Aunt," said Colonel Fitzwilliam coolly, coming up behind her; "he is off to Derbyshire with his bride."

"What?" she exclaimed, spinning round and almost knocking Mr Collins' wide-brimmed clergyman's hat flying. "*You*, here! So you have aided and abetted this scheme! You will be sorry for it, Nephew!"

The colonel mentally rolled his eyes at this dramatic pronouncement but deigned not to reply.

"And you!" she rounded on Mr Collins. "How could you have let this farrago proceed?"

"Your Ladyship, I did all that was humanly possible," wheedled Mr Collins.

Lady Catherine turned back to her nephew. "This cannot be. You will ride after your cousin and bring him back immediately! He is betrothed to Anne. If he has a Special Licence then it is *Anne* he will marry, not Miss Nobody from Nowhere!"

"You are rather after the fact, Aunt," explained the colonel. "Darcy is already married."

"These things can be altered. Go now!" barked her ladyship. "The marriage has not yet been consummated."

Mr Bennet was watching this all in astonishment, when the earl walked into the parlour.

"*Siss*-ter!" drawled Lord Matlock.

Lady Catherine swung round as if stung. "What are *you* doing here?"

"Minding my p's and q's for one thing," said the earl drolly. "There is a very prettyish wilderness outside. Would you care to take a turn in it?"

Lady Catherine opened her mouth to object, but before she could do so, the earl had taken hold of her elbow and directed her towards the door.

"The fresh air would really do you good, Catherine."

Mr Bennet's eyes were now filled with amusement. He lifted his glass to his lips to hide a smile and glanced at his wife. Mrs Bennet's mouth was open in shock. He found the silence quite comforting.

The earl and his sister were still not out of the Bennets' earshot when Lady Catherine let loose with: "How *could* you have let Darcy marry this upstart?"

"Darcy is his own man," replied her younger brother in a lower tone as he pulled her further away. "I can only be glad he has married. I was a little worried that he had fallen in love with his mistress. I asked him to do his duty and set up his nursery, and he has. Enough said."

Having put a sufficient distance between his sister and the house, the earl let go of her elbow and stood back to survey her down his nose.

"He was betrothed to Anne!" she railed.

"Do cut line, sister," said the earl. "Clearly his preferences didn't lean that way. Where *is* Anne?"

"She's in the carriage."

"Well, what is she doing there? Bring her in so I may say hello to my niece."

Lady Catherine stamped her foot in frustration.

"I have no intention of staying here to celebrate such a mésalliance! I am going back to Kent, Brother."

"Very well," said the earl dismissively. "I will not argue with you, since I can see you're going to be a killjoy. Let me come out to the coach to see you off."

Viewing the tête-à-tête from a window, Richard saw his father had bested the dragon. He watched as the earl and Lady Catherine walked round the side of the house towards the drive, emerging from the house to join them as they reached the portico.

But upon arriving at the coach, the earl found Anne lying unconscious in her companion's arms. Mrs Jenkinson was ineffectually plying her with smelling salts.

"How now," said the earl climbing into the carriage. "What has happened to her?"

"It is nothing," said Lady Catherine before Mrs Jenkinson could open her mouth. "She does not travel well."

The earl began slapping his niece's hands to little effect. He looked at his sister, quite horrified. "You can't take her off when she is like this!" he exclaimed. "We must get a physician to her immediately!"

"She will be right presently. You fuss too much, Brother," retorted Lady Catherine.

The earl shooed Miss Jenkinson off the bench seat, and taking her place, drew his inanimate niece onto his lap and then into his arms. She remained unresponsive.

"Richard! Take her inside!" he said, passing Anne's limp form to his son, who stood near the carriage door.

20 North

"Oh dear!" exclaimed Mrs Bennet, as the colonel appeared in the parlour carrying the prostrate form of his cousin. "No wonder, my lady is so overset!"

Richard paid no heed to this piece of politeness or silliness, he knew not which; but mutely appealed for a horizontal surface on which to deposit his cousin. Jane quickly cleared a place on a settee and asked Hill to find the apothecary, Mr Jones, who was amongst the guests.

The earl was aghast once his niece was laid down. In the better light of the parlour, he could see that Anne looked dreadful. She was as thin as a rake; her skin was the colour of chalk, and her lips blue. Dressed in an elaborate pale blue silk court dress, she looked as if she might be laid on a bier. Jane had stepped forward to straighten Anne's skirts when Richard set her down; and she too became so concerned at Anne's appearance that she took her hand and felt for a pulse.

Mr Jones, who had been in the drawing room with some other revellers, arrived promptly. Taking Anne's hand from Jane, he felt her pulse before whispering to her: "Miss Bennet, did Lizzy leave any digitalis?"

"There were some medicines," replied Jane. "They are in the stillroom with a note for you."

Charlotte, who was hovering nearby, stepped forward. "I'll get them."

"I'll come with you," said Jane.

"Wait," said Mr Jones, and then murmured softly to Miss Bennet.

"Hill," said Jane, pulling a chatelaine from her pocket. "Will you open the stillroom for Charlotte? Colonel Fitzwilliam, Mr Jones has requested to transfer the lady to a bedchamber. Will you follow me?"

Gently scooping his cousin up again, the colonel followed Jane up the staircase. As the habitable guest rooms of Longbourn were filled with Gardiners, Jane led him to the only bedchamber she felt she could immediately offer, which was, of course, the one she had, until last night, shared with Lizzy.

As he stepped across the threshold, the colonel's nostrils were filled with the most delicious scents of honey, musk and lavender. "This is your room?" he asked, eyeing the double bed.

"I shared it with Lizzy," replied Jane, quickly gathering their dressing things that had been left on the counterpane. "Please lay her on the covers."

Hill, Charlotte, and Mr Jones arrived soon after with the medicine.

"If you could hold up by her shoulders, Colonel, and let her head tip back," instructed Mr Jones.

Miss de Bourgh's mouth fell open, and Mr Jones began to drop a tincture onto her tongue with an eyedropper.

"Lay her flat again," said Mr Jones. "Ladies, I need you to loosen her dress and stays so that I can access her upper body unimpeded. The colonel and I will step outside. Please cover her with a shawl and recall me."

The apothecary's instructions were followed to the letter.

"Miss Bennet," Mr Jones asked as he returned to the room; "do you have some writing paper?"

This was quickly procured, but before Jane could offer Mr Jones a pen, he had rolled the sheet into a tube. Twisting the shawl into a circle to preserve the lady's modesty, he inserted the tube into the centre of the shawl and laid his ear to it. Silence reigned as they watched the apothecary hopefully. Jane had to remind herself to breathe.

Finally, Mr Jones stood and addressed the colonel: "It is as I suspected—she has a heart murmur. Is she currently being treated?"

"Well, she has a physician, but as to the details, I hardly know," replied the colonel.

"Does she carry any medicines with her?" asked Mr Jones.

"My aunt is downstairs," replied the colonel. "Perhaps I should fetch her."

When Richard reached the bottom of the stairs, he found his father leaning against the wall with his arms crossed.

"The apothecary would like to ask Aunt some questions," said Richard.

His father snorted in reply. "You'll need to bring him out to her carriage."

On arriving there, they found Lady Catherine sitting stiffly inside with Mrs Jenkinson and Mr Collins. Rather than have an unseemly altercation with his sister in the open, the earl climbed inside, showed Mr Collins the door with his thumb, and upon that gentleman's alighting, indicated the apothecary should take his place. Richard stood at the open door.

Upon Mr Jones' enquiries, Lady Catherine explained indignantly that Anne was seen regularly by the best physician to be had in Kent. But when Mrs Jenkinson handed over the reticule containing Anne's medicines, these were found to be laudanum, sal volatile and Hungary water. Dismayed by these pointless prescriptions, Mr Jones thanked Lady Catherine and climbed from the coach. He retreated within the vestibule of the house and waited for the earl, who joined him shortly after, followed by the colonel.

"Well?" asked the earl, not mincing matters.

"These are useless restoratives, my lord," said the apothecary, still clutching the reticule. "There are more powerful modern medicines that will benefit her more."

"And will they cure her?" asked the earl.

"No, my lord, but they may keep her alive, whereas these," he said, shaking the bag, "most assuredly will not."

"How do I obtain these medicines you speak of?" asked the earl.

"I have already given her a dilute tincture of digitalis. Hopefully by the time we return to the room, it will have had some effect. But she will need to be seen by a London physician to confirm the diagnosis. I can name several in Harley Street who are familiar with the latest advances. One of them should be summoned immediately."

"So she is not fit to travel?" asked the earl.

"Certainly not," replied the apothecary.

Upon returning to Anne's bedside, they found her still unconscious, but her lips were now a purple shade rather than blue, and her skin less alarmingly white.

"I think she is recovering a little," said Jane, who had taken a chair beside the patient and was feeling her pulse.

The apothecary retrieved his paper roll and listened again to her heart.

He pursed his lips before looking up: "I should fetch a more powerful distillate from my home."

"Do you live in the village?" asked the earl.

"No, my lord," replied Mr Jones. "In Meryton, a mile off."

"Wait," said the earl. "I should summon the physician immediately. Do tell me the names before you go."

"It's all right," said Charlotte, who stood up from a nearby settee whence she had retired. "*I'll* fetch the medicine. I can use my father's carriage."

"Thank you, Miss Lucas," replied the apothecary, pulling some keys from his pocket. "You know where I keep it."

"Take my carriage," offered the earl; and then, turning to his son, "Richard, will you see to it?"

Colonel Fitzwilliam nodded and ran down the stairs ahead of Charlotte. By the time she had donned her bonnet and pelisse, the earl's carriage was drawing up in front of the house, and one of the newly hired footmen had raced out to open the door.

Spying his betrothed escaping in a foreign vehicle, Mr Collins emerged precipitately from Lady Catherine's carriage.

"Miss Lucas!" he yelled, in evident alarm, "where are you going?"

Charlotte waved her hand impatiently at him. "I'll be back," she said as the carriage door closed and the horses set off at a brisk pace.

As the coach sped out of Longbourn towards Meryton, Charlotte found herself sitting in the lap of luxury, on plush squabs sumptuously upholstered in red velvet. At twenty-eight, and with several grown-up brothers, Charlotte could only reflect that the interior of the earl's coach closely resembled what she imagined an expensive brothel might look like.

Meanwhile, on the road to Derbyshire, Darcy and Elizabeth sat in silence as their carriage wended its way north. At Longbourn, Elizabeth had moved over to the left side of the forward-facing seat when she had been handed into the carriage, expecting Darcy to sit beside her on the right; but he had taken the backward-facing seat on the roadside, so they were sitting as far from each other as the carriage would allow. He then proceeded to stare out the window in an abstracted fashion. They had not gone a mile before Elizabeth could stand the silence no longer.

"I beg your pardon, sir. I fear I must be sitting in your seat."

"No, no," he replied, waving his hand dismissively. "As the lady, you are entitled to that spot. Granted I sit there when the carriage is otherwise empty, but the seat does not have my name on it."

"But surely you cannot like travelling backwards?"

"Men get used to it," he said, turning to face the opposite window once more.

Elizabeth gave up and focused on the passing scenery herself.

They headed directly for Dunstable in Bedfordshire before passing through Hockcliffe. This was the extent of Lizzy's prior travels to the north, twelve miles from her home. The Darcy carriage was exceptionally well sprung, much better than the Bennet carriage; but still her heavy earrings began to bother her, and she slipped them from her ears and into her reticule.

Darcy's team was a strong one and well acquainted with the journey north; so the travellers pushed on to Brickhill in Buckinghamshire for the first change.

Unbeknownst to them, sometime before the newlyweds reached the next posting stop at Stoney Stratford, Lady Catherine had arrived at Longbourn. Call it serendipity, but she had been in her nephew's thoughts since he'd opened his eyes that morning. Darcy knew his aunt was too used to getting her way, and the possibility that she might seek to disrupt his nuptials had made him wish they had arranged the ceremony for eight instead of nine. He had breathed a deep sigh of relief when they'd signed the registry, but could not be completely at ease until they'd left Longbourn entirely behind. As the miles between himself and Kent increased, he began to relax. He could only be glad that his aunt had not embarrassed him at his wedding.

Lizzy's thoughts were more mixed. Mentally, she relived packing her trunk; sure she had forgotten something, or worse, inadvertently taken something of Jane's. She also reflected on the wedding ceremony, mostly with fond remembrance at the goodwill that had been directed towards her; but also with amusement at some of the silly things that had happened— she had been obliged to slip up to her room briefly to remove the last of the barley grains from beneath her stays. Mr Collins' behaviour had also been farcical, and she could only be glad that she had not been forced into marriage with such a ridiculous man. *What if Mr Darcy had not come along?* It did not bear thinking about. This thought directed her attention to her husband, and she glanced quickly at his profile as he gazed determinedly outside the carriage.

Her observations of the interactions between her groom and Mr Bingley had been fruitless. Towards Mr Darcy, Mr Bingley exhibited a playful subservience, much like a dog with his master; in return, Darcy seemed to view his friend with a detached fondness. Mr Bingley had spent most of his time talking and gazing at Jane, only occasionally glancing at Mr Darcy, as if seeking approval. She could find nothing lover-like in their interactions.

Now, as the sun became lower in the sky, Elizabeth began to get nervous, wondering what the night with Darcy would bring.

As the carriage passed the last milestone for Stoney Stratford, Darcy finally broke the silence. "Shall we stop to refresh ourselves?"

"That would be welcome, sir," replied Elizabeth. She knew she had drunk a little too much of the champagne punch.

Darcy tapped on the roof with his cane to signal the driver before enquiring of Elizabeth, "Would you like some coffee or tea?"

"Something warm would be nice," she replied.

The posting house was soon gained, and the landlord bustled into the yard once he saw the occupants of the carriage intended to descend. As the proprietor of the best posting house in Stoney Stratford, Mr Stubbs had immediately recognised the handsome equipage and liveried servants as those of Mr Darcy—carriages of that quality generally had insignias or escutcheons on the doors; Mr Darcy's carriage was recognisable by its lack of decoration.

Mr Stubbs watched as Mr Darcy handed the lady out of the carriage, immediately perceiving she was not Mr Darcy's sister, who had dark hair like her brother. He waited patiently to present himself.

"Good afternoon, Mr Darcy. May I help you?"

"A private room, if you have one free, or the coffee room else," replied Darcy.

"Certainly, sir; a private room it shall be."

Mr Stubbs stepped ahead to show the lady the way to a small, but comfortable, private dining parlour. By the time they arrived, Darcy had already removed his gloves and the landlord's eyes quickly spotted the diamond solitaire Darcy was wearing, and beside it, the wedding ring.

"What can I get for you today, Mr Darcy?" he asked.

"Some ale for myself, and some tea, or perhaps coffee, for the lady," he replied, turning to Elizabeth in enquiry.

"Tea, please," said Elizabeth.

The landlord hurried out to comply.

"There is a washroom over there," said Darcy, indicating a narrow door set into the wall, as he ranged himself in front of the fire.

When Elizabeth returned to the parlour, Darcy took his turn to use the convenience. Not long after he closed the door, the proprietor reappeared with the drinks, and Elizabeth sat down at the little table and began to remove her gloves. Mr Stubbs put down Darcy's ale and then made a great show of transferring the tea things from the tray to the table in front of Elizabeth: placing the cup and saucer, arranging the teaspoon just so, putting down the teapot and swivelling the handle around towards her, followed by the sugar and the milk.

Elizabeth watched all this in some bemusement. What she didn't realise was that all the while the landlord was surreptitiously watching her face. Once he was finished, she thanked him with a small smile, and this encouraged him to venture:

"Do I have the pleasure of serving *Mrs* Darcy?"

Elizabeth thought this a little impertinent since she hadn't been introduced, but she was amused rather than annoyed.

"Yes, you do, sir." she replied.

"Ah! Just so!" he bowed. "John Stubbs, proprietor of the Rose and Thistle, at your service."

Elizabeth nodded in return and he bustled out again. She busied herself with pouring the tea and had just added the milk when Darcy returned.

Sitting down, he took a draught from his mug of ale before transferring his gaze to Elizabeth's hands. As he watched her raise her cup to her lips, he noted that the bases of her fingernails were blue.

"You are cold," he stated.

"It is getting chilly. This tea is certainly welcome," she replied, taking a sip.

"Forgive me. I had not felt it. There are blankets in the seats. I will get them out when we return to the carriage."

Elizabeth had only time to mechanically say "Thank you", before there was a discreet knock at the door, and the landlord re-entered on Darcy's summons.

"Forgive me, Mr Darcy, but my wife has just baked this apple pie and wondered if you would like a slice, on the house, like."

Darcy looked at Elizabeth, who gave an enthusiastic nod in return. The pie certainly smelt delicious.

After the landlord placed the pie on the table, his wife entered with a tray holding plates, cutlery and a jug of cream. She proceeded to cut two generous portions, managing to serve these while looking intensely at Elizabeth all the while. Curiosity satisfied, the pair effaced themselves, happy in the knowledge that Mr Darcy's tip always encompassed anything accepted 'on the house'.

The pie still smelt of the oven, although it had obviously sat long enough to cool a little and maintain its integrity when cut.

Elizabeth ate around half of her slice before putting down her fork and declaring, "This is indeed delicious, but I think this slice is large enough to feed two people."

"Really?" asked Darcy, looking at his own empty plate.

Elizabeth laughed. "Or perhaps only two women. Would you like mine, Mr Darcy?"

He gladly took the plate and polished it off. "Thank you, Mrs Darcy."

She blushed and bit her lip.

Darcy looked at her and frowned. "Is there something wrong?"

"Please don't call me 'Mrs Darcy'," she murmured, looking at her saucer.

"But you called me 'Mr Darcy'," he replied.

She rolled her eyes. "But that is your name!"

"Ah!" he said. "I think I see the difference; but if you wish me to call you 'Elizabeth', you will need to call me 'Fitzwilliam'."

Elizabeth blushed again. She had not meant to bite his nose off. "Very well, Fitzwilliam. I'm sorry. I guess I'm a little sensitive about it. My father calls my mother 'Mrs Bennet' when he wishes to belittle her."

"And does he call her by her Christian name else?"

"No, never. She is usually 'my dear' when she is blameless, but even that seems to be a euphemism of sorts."

"For what?" he enquired.

"'Stupid'," Elizabeth said, casting her eyes down.

"Oh," replied her husband. "Well, I will refrain from using 'Mrs Darcy' outside of introductions and will try to remember not to use 'my dear' lest it be misinterpreted."

Unhappy with the infelicitous turn the conversation had taken, Darcy consulted his pocket watch. "It is getting late. Perhaps we should go?"

They returned to the carriage, where Darcy remembered to retrieve the carriage blankets before setting out, spreading them solicitously over his wife. For one breathless moment, Elizabeth thought she might even be tucked up, but her husband withdrew to his corner of the coach and rapped on the roof with his cane. The blankets turned out to be fur-lined. Elizabeth felt decidedly pampered as she snuggled into her corner of the carriage.

Inside the Rose and Thistle, Mr and Mrs Stubbs watched from the window of the parlour as the Darcys drove off towards Northampton.

"Well, she's a pretty lass and polite too," said Mrs Stubbs.

"Yes," agreed Mr Stubbs, sliding the guinea that had been left on the table into his pocket. "And he's in a good mood. I think he almost smiled."

As they were alone, he gave his wife a squeeze. "Mayhap, they'll need a bigger carriage soon."

His wife, who was pregnant but not yet obviously showing, replied only with a giggle.

21 A reprieve

At Longbourn, the earl folded and sealed the missive for the doctor just as Richard returned to the bedchamber. Jane noticed the colonel had fitted his spurs to his boots.

"Ah!" said the earl, spying his son, "summon one of my grooms will you?"

"They've both gone with the carriage," Richard replied.

"What? For such a short journey? I need one of them to go to London. Well, I suppose I can purloin one of Catherine's."

"I'll go," offered Richard.

"It's not necessary," stated the earl curtly. "I'll send a servant."

"I *want* to go," replied Richard. "It's for Anne."

"I don't see why you should be racing all over the countryside delivering messages like a servant."

"Father," said Richard drolly, "that is what I do in the army."

"Well," said the earl, much struck. "I suppose so."

"Is that the letter for the physician?" asked Richard, returning to the point.

"Yes, I've described Anne's condition and requested that he wait on me here at his earliest convenience. And this," said the earl unfolding an unsealed page, "is a list of three physicians Mr Jones recommends. Go to them in this order and bring the first who is available."

"Very well," said Richard. "Can I borrow your hat?"

"Where's *your* hat?" the earl sputtered indignantly.

"I left it at Netherfield. I wore my helmet to the ceremony."

"Well, I don't know if I should give it to you," said the earl, handing over his tricorn regardless. "It could be amusing to see you charging down Harley Street in full battle regalia."

"Hilarious," said Richard, as he headed off down the stairs.

Richard's horse was at the ready. With a skip he was in the saddle; and no sooner were his feet in the stirrups, than he was out the gate, sending grit from the drive flying.

The earl came down the stairs more slowly behind him and approached his sister's carriage. He found the clergyman, once more, back inside, sitting next to Anne's companion and nodding solicitously while Lady Catherine let loose a diatribe on the licentiousness of men and their mistresses.

This, thought the earl, *is no doubt a chapter in the larger book of my nephew's iniquities. A more blameless youth,* he reflected, *would be hard to find. It is a pity my eldest son does not take a leaf or two from Darcy's book.*

The earl opened the door, indicated for Mr Collins to alight with a dismissive flick of his wrist, and climbed in beside Anne's companion. His sister did not pause, and her words continued to wash over him.

"Silence!" barked the earl.

Beside him, Mrs Jenkinson quaked, and sincerely wished that she, too, had been ordered from the carriage.

"How long has Anne been like this?" demanded the earl.

"It is nothing but a fainting fit," sniffed Lady Catherine; "and no more than can be expected after the shameful way that Darcy has treated her."

"Rubbish," said the earl. "Who is her physician?"

"Dr Robbies is the best physician in Kent and was the personal physician to the Duchess of Wessex!"

"The Duchess of Wessex is dead," replied the earl dryly, not able to resist such an easy point.

As a matter of fact, the duchess, who must have been at least eighty at her decease, had had a pretty good innings. Whether this was due to her physician was another question.

Lady Catherine's eyes glittered at her brother's tactics, but he had temporarily succeeded in stemming her malicious diatribe.

"I have summoned a physician from London," he stated.

"That was completely unnecessary," Lady Catherine countered. "I demand you return Anne to the carriage this instant."

"I have been advised that if I do so, it may kill her," replied the earl. "What do you mean by dragging her all over the countryside in such a condition?"

"What else am I to do if Darcy acts in such a clandestine fashion?" retorted Lady Catherine.

"Enough! There was never any binding arrangement between Anne and Darcy. It is possible she is no fit bride for any man. She certainly won't be if she is dead."

Lady Catherine bridled in indignation, but the earl continued relentlessly. "She is in no condition to travel. She will stay here while I get the opinion of a Harley Street physician."

He looked distastefully at Mrs Jenkinson. "Is this woman yours or Anne's?"

"Anne's, of course," snapped Lady Catherine.

"Very well," said the earl, mentally noting that Mrs Jenkinson had not moved from the coach when Anne had been carried inside, insensate; "then she will attend her mistress here. With regard to yourself, I understand there is decent accommodation in the nearby town of Meryton. I suggest you remove there to await developments."

"I am not staying in a dirty inn in a market village!" shrieked Lady Catherine.

"As you wish," said the earl balefully. "Then I suggest you remove yourself to my London townhouse. I will apprise you of events when I may."

"And how am I to travel without female companionship?" snapped

Lady Catherine.

The earl eyed Mr Collins with a nasty smile. "Perhaps your clergyman will lend you countenance."

An hour after Lady Catherine departed, Charlotte returned with the digitalis, which was promptly administered by Mr Jones. Sometime later, the apothecary was gratified when Miss de Bourgh finally opened her eyes.

Anne was confused but comforted by the familiar presence of Mrs Jenkinson and was able to recognise the earl when he was summoned to her bedside from the festivities below, though she spoke little and did not ask for her mother.

Meanwhile the majority of the wedding guests continued to celebrate. Those who had seen Anne being carried about by the best man merely thought the lady had fainted in the crowded room. Upstairs, Jane and Charlotte took turns watching over the patient after she regained consciousness, while Mrs Jenkinson stationed herself on the chaise longue and produced some knitting from her reticule.

Mr Jones returned occasionally to check on Anne's progress. Despite the small improvement in her condition, he dared not give her any more of the distillate retrieved by Charlotte. It was powerful stuff, and not being familiar with such a case, he knew not how to judge when it would be safe to administer more. He anxiously awaited the physician's arrival.

Almost two hours after their departure from Stoney Stratford, the Darcy coach crossed the River Nenn and entered Northampton. Instead of proceeding to the posting inn, the carriage stopped at the receiving office. One of the grooms stepped inside and returned with a note that he delivered to his master.

Darcy scanned this quickly before nodding to the groom and remarking: "Onto Kingsthorpe then."

As the coach proceeded, Darcy explained to Elizabeth. "Finn has managed to secure accommodations for us at Kingsthorpe. It is a pretty village not far from Northampton."

She nodded her understanding.

He bit his lip before continuing. "I have taken two chambers, so I will not impose upon you tonight. We will be much more comfortable at Pemberley."

Elizabeth blushed and nodded again.

"I hope you will join me for dinner?" continued Darcy. "If you are not too tired?"

Lizzy wondered why she should be tired—all she had done was walk up an aisle, eat too much, and sit in a coach half the day. "Thank you, sir. Although after the wedding breakfast and the apple pie, I am not sure I can manage much more."

When the coach pulled up, Finn appeared to supervise the unloading of the trunks. He had travelled ahead in a hired post-chaise with the bare minimum of Darcy's possessions.

Elizabeth was shown to her room by a chambermaid, who undertook to wait on her before and after dinner. She was rather unnerved by the special attention.

"Do you not have other duties?" asked Elizabeth. "With the exception of my stays, I'm sure I can manage myself."

"Oh no, ma'am. Mr Finn said I was to wait on you special. I'll be paid to do so. Sometimes I wait on Mr Darcy's sister when she passes through, even though she has a companion. Mr Darcy is never scaly."

The maid could see that Mrs Darcy wasn't at all starched up and they talked of all manner of things—the weather, the inn, and the barges on the River Nenn, while Elizabeth washed and put on a fresh day gown. Her wedding gown was sadly crumpled from the journey.

As the maid finished putting up Elizabeth's hair, she ventured, "We were so glad to hear that Mr Darcy had married. So handsome and so rich! It seemed a waste he wasn't hitched. He's such a nice man. I hope you'll be very happy."

Elizabeth smiled and took this in the good part it was intended. It did not quite tally with the Mr Darcy she knew, but she supposed that civility and generosity went a long way with servants. Wrapping one of her new shawls round her shoulders, she descended the stairs for dinner.

The White Horse was a rather large inn of some antiquity—the maid had proudly related that Charles the Second had lodged there. Elizabeth had supposed she would be eating with her husband in the large public dining room, but she was instead directed to a private parlour. Darcy was standing in front of the fire, wearing an elaborately embroidered silk dressing gown over his shirt and breeches. Gone were the hessians, replaced by slippers and stockings that revealed the shape of his calves. Having never seen him so informally dressed, Elizabeth felt some embarrassment.

"I took the liberty of ordering you a bowl of chicken soup," he said as she entered the room. "It was the lightest fare they had on offer."

"Thank you," Elizabeth replied as she moved to join him by the fire. The hall had been quite cold.

They stood in an awkward silence with their backs to the hearth until a servant entered following a knock to begin arranging their dinner on the table. Darcy had ordered a hearty meal for himself—roast beef with vegetables. A tankard of ale was placed beside it, and a basket of fresh-baked rolls midway between his plate and Elizabeth's bowl of soup.

Having unloaded the tray, the serving maid looked up to enquire: "Would the lady like some tea?"

"No, thank you," replied Elizabeth, "but I'll take a little wine if you have it."

The maid curtsied and effaced herself.

Elizabeth moved to take her place at the table and was surprised when Darcy moved behind her to push in the chair. Not used to the offices of a footman at table, she sat down carefully but with reasonable grace.

Not long after they began their meal, the serving maid returned with the wine and a pat of butter. "Will there be anything else, sir?" the girl asked.

"No, thank you, " Darcy replied. "We won't take cheese or dessert."

"Very well, sir," she smiled; knowing Mr Darcy had married that morning. "The port is on the sideboard, as you know. Good evening."

After they finished eating, Darcy got up to broach the port. In response, Elizabeth got up to withdraw.

"Would you like some?" he asked.

Although Elizabeth had tasted port from her father's glass, she had never been offered a glass of her own.

"Perhaps, just a little?" she ventured.

He handed her a glass and gestured for her to sit down in front of the fire.

Elizabeth had half-expected they would talk of the wedding, but Darcy drew a book from his pocket.

"I found this book in my room, and it seemed somehow appropriate. I must confess I heard you reading *The Taming of the Shrew* to your sister at Netherfield. You dramatised the parts very well. I thought perhaps we could take turns reading this tonight."

He duly produced a volume of Shakespeare's sonnets. "Perhaps the first seventeen?" he asked.

Lizzy laughed and gestured for him to go first. She never imagined she would spend her wedding night reading Shakespeare's *Procreation Sonnets*.

Thus Darcy opened the book and read:

"From fairest creatures we desire increase,
That thereby beauty's rose might never die,
But as the riper should by time decease,
His tender heir might bear his memory:
But thou contracted to thine own bright eyes,
Feed'st thy light's flame with self-substantial fuel,
Making a famine where abundance lies,
Thy self thy foe, to thy sweet self too cruel:
Thou that art now the world's fresh ornament,
And only herald to the gaudy spring,
Within thine own bud buriest thy content,
And, tender churl, mak'st waste in niggarding:
Pity the world, or else this glutton be,
To eat the world's due, by the grave and thee."

By the time they had read the seventeen sonnets in turns, Lizzy had finished sipping her port. Getting up from the fire, Darcy offered his wife his arm. He really would have preferred to continue drinking port by the fire, staring at the flames: but it was his wedding night; he was staying in a public inn, and he knew he didn't have the luxury of neglecting his wife—eyes were everywhere; people would talk. So he escorted Elizabeth back down the corridor to her room, where he whispered goodnight to her, and planted a chaste kiss on her forehead.

This kiss rather startled Lizzy. She had frozen like a cornered rabbit when she'd belatedly realised his intentions as he bent towards her at her door. Although Darcy only touched her cheek briefly, his lips were hot, and she walked into her room feeling rather like she had been branded.

After dismissing the chambermaid, Lizzy retrieved *The Satyricon* from the bottom of her trunk and climbed into bed. She read for half an hour 'til her eyes began to droop, whereupon she snuffed the candle and lay back on the pillow. But sleep would not come.

Again, she twisted the puzzle of her husband round in her head. *The Procreation Sonnets… What a strange choice…* She knew it was a marriage of convenience, but it almost seemed as if he was egging himself on… Then he had kissed her voluntarily for the first time. The kiss at the wedding breakfast, she reasoned, didn't count because it was done under duress. But this second kiss had been surprisingly passionless. It certainly lent weight to her father's suspicions.

Oh, well, she sighed. *I am married now and will have to make the best of it.* At least Darcy had been polite—no sign yet of any disrespect. She supposed she would have to be content with that. And with that thought Elizabeth finally drifted off to sleep.

Some time earlier, back at Longbourn, the Bennets, Gardiners and Philips were sitting down to dinner with a few remaining guests who were apprised of Anne's condition—the earl, the Lucases and Mr Jones. Enjoying the triumph of her wedding breakfast, Mrs Bennet had been in a high flutter all afternoon; and it was only as they took their seats that she realised Mr Collins was missing. Before she could comment on it to her sister, the sound of an unfamiliar carriage drew them to the window of the parlour.

Colonel Fitzwilliam had returned and in the company of a singular gentleman. As Richard handed his horse to the groom who had come up from the stables, they watched in surprise as a man they could only suppose to be the Harley Street physician climbed down from a curricle and four. He was tall and was wearing a natty beaver and three-caped greatcoat, making him look even more impressive.

When he shed his greatcoat in the hall, they discovered the raiment he bore underneath was expensive but sober, and precise to a pin. He bowed

Time's Up, Mr Darcy

to the earl, whom he immediately perceived to be his client.

Richard performed the introductions. "Dr Hector Douglas, my father—Lord Geoffrey Fitzwilliam, tenth Earl of Matlock."

The earl recognised the first name on the apothecary's list. "Dr Douglas, I appreciate your efforts in coming here. I am very worried about my niece. She collapsed this morning after a long journey. She is a sickly girl and her mother believed it to be a fainting fit only. As an apothecary was present, he attended her, and it is on his advice that I have summoned you."

Mr Jones was duly introduced, and after a brief consultation with him, Dr Douglas wasted no time in seeking out the patient with Mr Jones in attendance. The earl and Richard followed them upstairs.

Dr Douglas had brought a box of his own instruments. After asking Anne some questions, which she answered in a whisper, he produced a wooden tube through which he listened to her heart. When he enquired about her current physician and care, the reticule with Anne's medicines was produced. He then suggested the gentlemen remove themselves from the sickroom to discuss the situation. Jane showed them into her father's library, which he had nobly offered for the occasion.

Dr Douglas addressed the earl. "Mr Jones is quite correct," he said, nodding to the apothecary; "your niece has a heart murmur, and it will need to be managed with digitalis."

"So you can cure her?" asked the earl.

Dr Douglas shook his head. "I'm afraid not. She has a small hole in her heart. The condition is serious and not curable. We can only hope to extend her life using the medicine. She will need to be managed very carefully—no more jaunting about the countryside."

"How long has she got to live?" asked the earl, horrified. Despite the apothecary's earlier advice, he had not expected such a grim diagnosis.

"Who knows?" replied Dr Douglas. "She could have died today. She could live another twenty years. It all depends on luck and good management."

The earl met his son's eyes, before turning back to the doctor. "How has this happened?"

"It is congenital," replied Dr Douglas. "She has had it from birth, but it would have been less obvious when she was small; she might not have fainted, but she may have been a restful child. It will worsen with age."

"And what of her prior treatment, these other medicines she had with her?" asked the earl.

"I believe her current physician must be aware of her situation. Those medicines are appropriate remedies, but they do nothing to improve the situation. The digitalis is more powerful. It cannot cure, but it can ameliorate the condition. It was discovered relatively recently. If her current physician is older, he may not be aware of it or may not ascribe to it."

The earl paced up and down. "So," he said, swinging around. "You may think this indelicate, but can she ever marry? Have children?"

"I would not recommend attempting children. Pregnancy would likely kill her. As to marriage, if she had an understanding husband, one who would be sensible of her limitations… I cannot see why not."

"Very well, doctor," said the earl. "I would like to secure your services for her treatment. I believe Mrs Bennet has undertaken to keep some dinner aside for us. I presume you have not eaten."

"Thank you, it is much appreciated," Dr Douglas replied.

Before leaving the library, the physician sat down to write a prescription that he handed to Mr Jones after a brief discussion.

Over dinner, accommodations were discussed. It was too dark for the doctor to return to London in his curricle. Indeed, as his last scheduled house call before he left London was after dark, Dr Douglas would not have attempted the journey to Hertfordshire before morning without Richard's escort. After securing the physician's services in Harley Street, Richard had called on the master of Netherfield at Hurst's townhouse in Mayfair to apprise him of the situation. Bingley had placed Netherfield at Richard's disposal, assuring him that he and the earl were welcome to stay indefinitely and had written a letter for him to carry to Mrs Nicolls. Richard thus offered Dr Douglas accommodation at the estate.

However, Mrs Bennet had other ideas. She had been eyeing the handsome and obviously well-to-do physician appreciatively since he walked in the door—he would do very nicely for one of her younger daughters. *How convenient that useless Mr Collins has taken himself off!* Thus it was decided. Dr Douglas was offered and gratefully accepted accommodation nearer his patient.

Meanwhile, Sir William, seeing the party breaking up, finally called for his carriage and the Lucases returned to Meryton.

Such insinuating people, thought Mrs Bennet, as she watched the Lucases leave. She had been obliged to offer them dinner after a hint from Jane. Mrs Bennet had not thought this necessary, regardless of any heroics performed by Charlotte on mercy missions. She thought the Lucases had eaten quite enough of her food at the wedding breakfast and could not wait to be rid of them, especially that grasping Charlotte. She supposed she would have to endure attending *her* wedding soon! *The next mistress of Longbourn! How humiliating! No doubt, Charlotte too, would soon be examining the hallmarks on the china!*

Thus, after an eventful day, the Fitzwilliams departed Longbourn. As the earl's carriage swayed towards Netherfield, Richard decided to test the waters regarding Miss Bennet.

"Well?" he asked his father. "What do you think of her?"

"She clearly is in no condition to marry either of you," replied the earl.

Richard sighed, realising his father was talking of Anne. "No, I don't know what Aunt could have been thinking."

"I know what she's thinking," growled the earl. "She needs an heir, but so do I, and I'll be damned if I'll sacrifice you to her ill-starred plans."

"What can be done?" asked Richard.

"I need to think. An heir to the Rosings estate must be found by some other means; perhaps I can get Anne to adopt one of my granddaughters. The trouble will be getting Catherine to agree."

The sound of the horses' hooves filled the silence before Richard decided to broach the subject of Miss Bennet again, praising her solicitude toward Anne and her beauty.

"You're right," agreed the earl. "She is a diamond of the first water. What is her dowry?"

"Five thousand pounds," replied Richard, glad that he could claim that much due to Darcy's beneficence.

The earl grunted. "Not much."

"Father, we've been through this before," complained the colonel. "How can I offer for a lady of the Ton, when I have no expectations. *Dear Miss Lack-Nothing, please come and live in the barracks with me on half-pay?*"

"They haven't downgraded you to half-pay yet," growled the earl, "and I'll keep the pressure on so they don't."

"You know what I mean."

"I do, and I agree that something should be done, if…"

"If?"

"If she bears an heir for the earldom."

"Now we are back at point non-plus," sighed Richard.

"I see your dilemma, but there is nothing I can do for you at the moment. Most of the property is tied to the earldom and will go to your brother. My hands are tied. You're right. At the moment, you have nothing to offer even a country squire's daughter."

"You make me feel so much better," said his second son.

"If you can get her to marry you, I will give you my blessing. That will have to do for the moment."

"Thank you, I'll take it from here," said the colonel.

That night, Richard dreamt of entering Jane Bennet's bedchamber carrying a prostrate female, but it was not his cousin he placed tenderly on the counterpane.

22 Pemberley

Darcy had arranged to start early from Kingsthorpe so as to reach Pemberley before dark. Thus shortly before eight, Elizabeth climbed into the carriage as the horses stamped in the frosty morning air. Stepping into the carriage after his wife, Darcy arranged the fur-lined blankets over her before settling once more onto the backward-facing seat. He himself was not cold, wearing a thick scarf tucked into his greatcoat, top-boots and dogskin gloves.

"They've put a hot brick in the box at your feet," he said. "Let me know if you'd like it changed at a posting stop."

She smiled and nodded, feeling the warmth radiating through her thin kid slippers. Then the eager horses took off with a jerk, and she was obliged to grab at the strap.

Setting off over the Union Canal towards Brixworth, they passed through Loughborough before crossing into Derbyshire where the land became hillier. Elizabeth found the changed landscape very beautiful.

They had lunch at the posting inn at Derby before continuing through Belper and Matlock. The country continued to become more rugged and Elizabeth felt a strange affinity for it.

"Richard's father's estate is over there," said Darcy just outside of Matlock, indicating the grim grey stone building of Wyvern Hall set into a hillside.

The carriage continued on through a pretty village called Lambton before taking a crossroad. Elizabeth knew they must be getting close to Pemberley, and her spirits were in high flutter. As the carriage turned into a well-tended drive at a lodge and made its way through an ancient wood, she realised they must have arrived. She glanced at her husband for confirmation, but he was still staring abstractedly out his window of the carriage.

Elizabeth turned her eyes to the scene outside her window. As they drove along, she saw many large trees whose size proclaimed their antiquity, including an oak so large she wondered if it predated the Conquest. *If Mr Darcy's name does not proclaim his noble Norman lineage,* thought Elizabeth, *surely these woods do.*

They gradually ascended for half-a-mile before her husband rapped on the roof and turned to her.

"I thought you might like to see the view from this point," Darcy explained as the carriage drew to a halt. "When I was young," he continued as she divested herself of the rugs; "I only left Pemberley occasionally to go to Matlock or, sometimes, London. Whenever we returned, my father would always stop here. He told me when I was seven that this would all be mine someday. I think he stopped here from then on to remind me of that."

After one of the grooms opened the carriage door and let the step down. Darcy climbed out, offering Elizabeth his hand to alight. Once she found her footing, he released her and walked several paces forward.

Following him, she found herself at the top of a considerable eminence where the wood ceased. The eye was instantly caught by Pemberley House, situated on the opposite side of a valley. The land beyond this point seemed to descend quite steeply, with the road winding back and forth into the valley. The house itself was a large, handsome stone building, standing well on rising ground and backed by a ridge of high woody hills.

Elizabeth was astonished at what she saw before her. When she had set out from Hertfordshire, she had been expecting Pemberley to be something like Netherfield, which was a far grander house than Longbourn. From the time they had passed the lodge, the ancient woods had sent her mind along a different path toward the gothic, and she began to wonder if she might be headed for a Tudor, half-timbered manor house. But she had not been expecting this—what stood before her was a large sandstone building in the modern Palladian style. It would not have looked out of place in London, in some prominent position on the Thames. It could be a palace, and here it was, sitting in a valley in Derbyshire. She felt decidedly foolish. She knew Mr Darcy's income was around twice that of Mr Bingley's, but this was extraordinary—Mr Darcy had a residence fit for a prince.

In front of the house was a lake, which reflected the colours of the stone. This body of water was so pleasantly disposed with respect to the house that it seemed it must have been altered to suit the building's proportions or the house built to suit it. Despite its symmetry, it looked quite natural. Its banks were neither formal nor falsely adorned. She had never seen a place for which nature had done more or where natural beauty had been so little counteracted by an awkward taste.

Elizabeth was struck dumb, feeling slightly weak at the knees. She turned her head to look at her husband, who was staring into the distance. She knew it behoved her to say something, but as she watched him, she saw a flood of emotions cross his normally impassive countenance. Then his face seemed to crumple, and he turned his head slightly away from her.

She knew not the source of her husband's distress, but in consideration, she turned her own gaze back to the building and, composing her voice said, "It is very beautiful, sir."

When he turned back towards her, she could see that he had mastered himself. Grasping for something else to say, she followed with: "It cannot be very old."

"No," replied Darcy in a slightly strained voice. "My father built it from the ground. There is an older house behind it, where my parents lived before it was finished, but it cannot be seen from this viewpoint. The older residence was meant to become the Dower House, but of course my father outlived my mother."

"She was younger than your father then?" Elizabeth asked.

"Yes, by more than ten years," he replied softly.

"And where are the outbuildings?" asked Elizabeth, trying to turn the subject.

"The stables are hidden behind that copse of trees over there," he said, pointing.

"And what are those?" she asked, pointing to some animals in the distance.

"Fallow deer," he replied. "There are several hundred in the park. The gamekeeper will slaughter one the next time we have guests."

"And is that often, sir?" she enquired.

"Not often; we entertained more frequently in my mother's day. But my aunt may visit when Georgiana returns. My sister is currently staying at Matlock." He paused for a moment before asking, "Shall we return to the carriage?"

As dusk fell, their coach descended the hill, crossed the bridge, and drove towards the door. While examining the nearer aspect of the house, Elizabeth observed that servants were trooping from the portico and disposing themselves in two lines stretching towards the door: males on one side and females on the other.

Darcy jumped out before the step was let down and then waited to hand Elizabeth out. "We will not bother with introductions," he confided. "There are too many. The important people are at the end of the line. The others you will meet in the coming days."

He offered her his elbow and they walked in a stately fashion towards the house. At the end of the line was a thin old woman, dressed in a prim apron and neat as a pin. Behind her stood a young maid.

As they reached these two, the older woman curtsied. "Good afternoon, Mr Darcy. Welcome home to Pemberley."

"Good afternoon, Mrs Reynolds. May I present my wife, Mrs Elizabeth Darcy, née Bennet, formerly of Longbourn in Hertfordshire. Elizabeth, this is Mrs Reynolds, who has been housekeeper at Pemberley these thirty years."

Elizabeth smiled at Mrs Reynolds and nodded, and the lady curtsied again, "Mrs Darcy."

The abigail was introduced as Elizabeth's new maid, Jenny.

"Jenny's grandmother was one of my mother's maids," said Darcy. "Her mother is currently handmaid to my aunt, the Countess of Matlock."

Again, Elizabeth smiled, and Jenny returned a curtsey: "Mrs Darcy."

Darcy proceeded into the house with Elizabeth on his right arm and

Mrs Reynolds to his left. Elizabeth could hear her maid pattering behind.

The vestibule was part of a wide, carpeted hall, hung with large paintings—very fine, realistic landscapes. The atmosphere was one of restrained luxury. The hallway, lit in the near part with a pair of glass lanterns, stretched off to the left into darkness; while to the right, it lead to a well-lit foyer.

"Dinner is ready to proceed at half-past seven, Mr Darcy. Would you like anything beforehand?" asked Mrs Reynolds.

"No, thank you," replied Darcy, before remembering he was speaking for two. "Although Mrs Darcy might appreciate something warm."

Awed by her surroundings, Elizabeth finally found her voice. "A cup of tea would be delightful, Mrs Reynolds."

"Certainly, ma'am," the housekeeper replied. "Jenny will accompany you to your room." Mrs Reynolds picked up a candlestick and walked off to the left into the dim hall.

After Darcy had taken off his hat and shucked his greatcoat with the help of a footman, he turned to the right, offering his arm once more to Elizabeth to escort her through the house. Tall, handsome windows were disposed along the right side of the hall, but as the darkness had already descended, these merely reflected the candlelight.

Traversing the hall, they arrived in a circular foyer. A wide spiral staircase twisted around its walls, illuminated by a large chandelier. The staircase was carpeted, with brass rods securing a rug to the steps, which, Elizabeth realised, must have been woven especially to fit the curve of the stairs.

Arriving at the top of the steps, Darcy stopped and picked up a candlestick from a console table. "The guest wing is down there," he said, indicating the right hallway with a gesture. "The family wing is this way."

Elizabeth could see the stair ascending to the next level was narrower and assumed it led to the servants' quarters.

"The first door on the left leads to my bedchamber," Darcy explained. "The door opposite is my sister's suite. The subsequent major doors on the left are our shared sitting room and your bedchamber. There are smaller service doors concealed in the wainscoting that access the dressing rooms. Jenny will show you your room. I look forward to seeing you at dinner at half-past seven."

He left her then, and Jenny, who had acquired her own candlestick from somewhere, led her on down the hall. Stepping into her chamber behind her maid, Elizabeth could see a large canopied bed looming there. The hearth was already burning, and Jenny moved quickly, lighting several more candles that stood at the ready. One of these she disposed in the dressing room before lifting the top of a pretty piece of furniture, which Elizabeth had assumed to be a small chest of drawers, to reveal it was a commode.

Elizabeth quickly divested herself of her bonnet, which her maid took before assisting her with her pelisse.

"Let me know when you are ready, ma'am. I'll fetch the hot water."

Once Elizabeth had used the chamber pot, she closed the commode and poked her head round the corner where her maid had disappeared. This revealed the rest of her dressing room, which was cavernous. In the middle of it stood her trunks, which the footmen must have somehow spirited up the stairs before she had even got there. Jenny was giving them a wipe over prior to opening them.

"The larger trunk contains my clothes, Jenny. The smaller one is full of stuffs for the making of new dresses."

"Oh, that sounds exciting, ma'am," replied Jenny. "Perhaps we can open it tomorrow in the better light."

Elizabeth approached the bowl and ewer on the washstand and tested the water. Jenny had already mixed in the hot water, but more stood at the ready in a brass pail at the side.

"Shall I undo you at the back, ma'am?" asked Jenny.

"Thank you," said Elizabeth.

"Would you like a fresh chemise and stays?" asked the girl.

"Definitely a fresh chemise, but I only have the one pair of stays."

"Very well," replied Jenny. "There is still an hour 'til dinner; perhaps you could put on the new chemise and a wrap while I prepare your clothes. Did you have a preference for a particular dress?" she asked, as she opened the trunk.

Elizabeth's favourite sprig muslin lay on the top—the notoriously 'dowdy' one of the Meryton assembly. A small devil prompted her to choose this gown. She wondered if Darcy would notice.

When Jenny took the garments away to be prepared, Lizzy removed *The Satyricon* from the bottom of her trunk and sat down to read in front of the hearth. She had barely settled in the chair when she heard a knock, and Mrs Reynolds appeared in answer to her summons.

"Here we are, Mrs Darcy," said Mrs Reynolds, placing the tray down on a nearby table. "I took the liberty of adding some shortbread in case you are hungry from your journey."

"Thank you, Mrs Reynolds. It is much appreciated," replied Elizabeth. "I must admit I am accustomed to dine at six at Longbourn, so I am a little peckish."

"Indeed, we dined earlier at Pemberley in old Mr Darcy's day, but the young master goes frequently to London and has adopted town hours. We certainly burn a few more candles these days."

Mrs Reynolds' confidence and her open manner almost prompted Elizabeth to give the glib reply that she supposed that he could afford them, but she bit her tongue and smiled instead.

After adjusting the hearth, Mrs Reynolds curtsied and left, and Elizabeth once more returned to her book.

Elizabeth was several minutes late for dinner. The journey must have fatigued her more than she wished to admit, for when Jenny returned with her clothes, she found the mistress asleep over her book in a chair near the hearth. There was a mad scramble to get Elizabeth into her clothes so that Jenny would have enough time to dress her hair. But Darcy suspected nothing of this when she walked into the dining room looking neat as a pin.

The dining table was a huge affair that could seat twelve people. Two places were set at one end of it. Its size caused Elizabeth to smile to herself, contemplating a mental picture of them sitting at opposite ends, a metaphor for their relationship.

"You find something amusing, Elizabeth?" said Darcy, as two footmen seated them.

"Pardon me for being provincial, Mr Darcy," said Elizabeth, as napkins were disposed upon their laps. "This is rather a large table."

"Hmm," said Darcy; "this is in fact the *small* version of this large table. It has several more leaves which Mrs Reynolds keeps somewhere."

The housekeeper soon arrived, followed by a footman bearing a tray, and a leek soup was served for the first course. This was very tasty. Elizabeth cleaned her plate, and felt herself quite sated on top of the shortbread. But the second course was roast partridge with poached pears and cress, which she felt obliged to at least sample. Elizabeth could not do justice to the dish, but her husband did, and asked Mrs Reynolds to pass his compliments to the chef. Finally, a chantilly cream was placed on the table with a plate of cheese. Elizabeth watched in amazement as Darcy polished off a portion of the dessert while she contented herself with a little of the cheese and a biscuit with her wine.

Throughout the repast, Elizabeth kept up a stream of inconsequential conversation, to which her husband occasionally added a curt remark. Once the servants withdrew she gave this up, afraid she had strayed into the realms of vacuous conversation. As the end of dinner approached, she was beginning to get decidedly nervous.

They sat in silence for a while as Darcy finished his wine, then he stood and helped her from her chair before accompanying her back to the door of her bedchamber.

"Prepare yourself and then come to me," he said, before leaving her at her door.

Entering her room on slightly shaky feet, Elizabeth found Jenny in her dressing room, arranging her gowns on hangers.

Darcy had fortified himself with a brandy and was pacing up and down. He had tried to cast his mind back to his early experiences with Diana, but for the life of him, he could think of nothing that would help him through this ordeal. He could only remember Diana kissing him; the thrill he had felt when she placed her hand above his heart on his naked chest; the way her gown had gaped when she had pushed him backwards onto the bed.

His passive acceptance of her caresses failed to instruct him on how he should initiate lovemaking now. Of course, later in their relationship he had been more assertive in bed, but he'd been completely at ease with Diana then, which was certainly *not* the way he felt now he had to confront a different woman—his wife.

There was a tiny knock at the sitting room door.

"Enter," he said in his deep resonant voice; then took a deep breath in anticipation.

He felt a wave of heat pass over his face as Elizabeth stepped into the room and could not understand if it was embarrassment or anger. There she stood in a loose cambric nightgown with her hair in a plait. The gown, which reached past her knees, somehow dwarfed her. She looked like she had escaped from the schoolroom. *My God, she looks no older than Georgiana. How am I to do this?*

For her part, Elizabeth was struggling to come to terms with Darcy's déshabillé. He also was wearing a loose cambric gown that resembled an oversized shirt. She had never seen his neck exposed before. It rose in a thick column from his broad shoulders. When he swallowed, she watched in fascination as the huge Adam's apple bobbed in his throat. *My goodness, it really is the size of an apple!* she realized.

Darcy saw her face flush as he stared at her, before she lifted her chin defiantly. *Lord! This is so awkward!* he thought, as he grasped for something to say.

"Do you not have something more becoming than that gown?" he blurted superciliously.

Lizzy blushed and stuck her nose further in the air. "I'm sorry, sir, but our wedding was very precipitate."

He frowned. "Do not young ladies sew pretty nightwear for their marriage?"

"Indeed, I've been helping Jane with her trousseau!" retorted Elizabeth.

"In anticipation for her marriage to Charles?" asked Darcy knowingly.

Elizabeth blushed again, realising she had, perhaps, divulged too much. "Jane is the eldest," she retorted lamely, wondering why she should have to defend herself on such a topic. "It was likely she would marry first."

A silence stretched between them.

Feeling confident he had somehow gained the upper hand, Darcy stepped towards Elizabeth and grasped her slim upper arms through her nightshirt. As he stooped to kiss her, the difference in their heights was glaringly apparent, even more so than when he had waltzed with her at the Netherfield Ball. His right hand moved automatically to tilt her chin up, but it was not enough, and he found himself bending at his knees to bridge the gap. Diana *had* been very tall...

Darcy heard Elizabeth gasp as his lips touched the side of her mouth. For some reason, this reaction gave him courage, and he pressed his mouth closer to the centre of hers in his next attempt. He felt her lips part and her breath tickle his chin, but before he knew what was happening, she lurched in his arms. Tightening his grip, he steadied her and pulled back to look at her face. Her eyelashes fluttered open, and she stared back at him wide-eyed.

"Oh!" she gasped. "I felt a little dizzy. Perhaps you tilted my head too far back."

"I'm sorry," he apologized in return, ashamed that he'd manhandled her so clumsily. Then feeling he'd somehow lost the ascendency through his mea culpa, he added: "Perhaps we should get in bed before you fall over."

"Perhaps you will fall first, sir," she retorted, "since you are stooping so much!" She was too polite to add that she'd smelt the brandy.

Darcy stared at her face, trying to read her expression. He wasn't sure if she was joking or being antagonistic, perhaps both? She was a blank page to him.

Placing his hand in the small of Elizabeth's back, he pushed her gently in the direction of the bed. When they arrived at their destination, Darcy discovered that the top of the mattress was higher than her hips. While he was wondering whether he should be so bold as to lift her onto the counterpane, she hoisted herself up with a little jump and scrambled backwards, crab-like, towards the pillows, until her back was resting against the headboard.

Darcy stared at his wife's lean and shapely calves. He supposed they were honed by all the walking she did.

Seeing his eyes did not meet her face, Lizzy twitched the sheet and pushed her feet beneath the blankets, pulling the covers defensively up round her waist.

Wondering how on earth he should approach her, Darcy prevaricated by snuffing out the candle on the bedside commode table before walking round the foot of the bed to snuff out its mate on the opposite side. Then, in the more comforting dimness of the light from the hearth, he pulled the covers back and swung himself into bed beside her.

Lizzy bit down on the gasp that almost escaped her mouth when Darcy's knees and hairy shins were presented to her, but thankfully these disappeared under the covers before she could think too much about them. Now there was just that bare neck again, disturbing her sensibilities.

Darcy rolled onto his side and lowered himself to his elbow. Taking his wife's arm, he gently tugged her down beside him. Her eyes were twin pools of darkness, glinting in the light from the hearth. Sliding his hand down over her hip, he found the hem of her gown and threaded his hand beneath it, running it upwards over her smooth outer thigh. He bent his head down to engage her lips once more, but before he could do so, she squeaked into his ear when he grasped one cheek of her bottom.

Elizabeth was struggling to come to terms with having a large hand groping her backside, but when Darcy shifted his fingertips to her inner thighs, his invasion of her privacy started to feel rather heavenly. He was touching her down there, stroking her, and she felt him gently push his fingers into her flesh. Then he shifted his position so that he was looming over her, the musky scent pouring from his gaping shirt filling her nostrils. He leaned down to kiss her again as he moved against her. His breathing was laboured, and as his lips enveloped hers, the spiritous fumes of the brandy were thrust into her mouth along with his hot breath. She felt a dull pain and gasped. Then her world seemed to tip sideways.

The next thing she knew he was inside her. It hurt. Starting slowly, he nudged against her until she felt him fill her up. The pain subsided as he continued to kiss and fondle her. He began to thrust rhythmically into her, and she found herself arching her back and moaning in response.

His movements became more frantic. Then, with a cry, Darcy shuddered and fell on top of her. When her elbows were pushed into the mattress Elizabeth realised she was holding him by the shoulders. His body was slick with sweat—his nightshirt clinging damply to him. Lizzy became conscious of his weight and pushed at him to get off her. As he rolled to the side with a groan, she felt warmth flood over her bottom. Reaching down, afraid she might be bleeding, she brought her hand up, saw the fluid was clear and sticky, and realised it was from him.

She got to her elbows, wondering if she should return to her own bed.

"Stay horizontal," came the muffled command from the pillows.

"I beg your pardon?" she asked.

He lifted his head slightly from the pillow, his eyes still closed.

"You need to stay horizontal to aid conception," he said groggily.

"Oh," she replied, while thinking: *Surely I don't have to sleep in this sticky damp patch?*

"Could I move, just a little bit?" she asked, turning her head towards him.

Darcy replied with a quiet but distinct snore.

When it was clear he wasn't going to respond, Lizzy slid sideways and rolled onto her side, facing away from him. *So that was it, the wedding night.* Well, it hadn't been so bad—though she could see why her mother had described it as undignified and uncomfortable. But as to bringing her much joy, surely her aunt was guilty of hyperbole. She reasoned it to be about halfway between their prognostications: there were elements of truth in both.

Elizabeth felt a tear slide down her cheek, but couldn't really understand why. Perhaps she briefly mourned her maidenhood? She lay in the darkness for some time, listening to the crackling of the fire in the hearth before the sound of her husband's regular breathing finally put her to sleep.

Darcy's slumber was quite disturbed. He first woke, feeling overheated, an hour or so after falling asleep, judging by the flames still flickering in the hearth. He was not used to wearing a nightgown to bed in his own house, preferring to sleep naked—and the covers of his bed had been adjusted accordingly. When he kicked off the blankets, he discovered his nightgown was not his only problem—another thermal impediment was his wife, who seemed to have clamped herself to his back like a barnacle. Gently prising her fingers from his shoulders, he threw most of the blankets over her, hoping this would discourage her from seeking out the warmth of his body. All this was performed in a state of half-stupor before he fell back asleep again.

He woke again some time later. The room was still dark, but the dying embers suggested it was closer to morning. Darcy was fully awake now and knew he would not be able to fall asleep again. He turned to view his wife, who was huddled under the pile of blankets with her legs drawn towards her chest. Clearly she was still cold. He rearranged the blankets to cover her more fully, and without waking, she unfurled a little. He felt rather guilty for denying her the heat of his body—such a small thing. Would it have killed him to let her cuddle him?

Turning away from her again, Darcy felt distinctly disgusted with himself. It had not been much of a wedding night. His performance had left much to be desired: he had come so quickly and then gone out like a light. She had overwhelmed him. *How?* His first thought was to blame the lack of a sheath. It was the first time he had made love without one—Diana had been quite insistent about that. Certainly the sensation of flesh upon flesh had been incandescent. It was if he'd been drawing squares on paper for the last seven years that had suddenly turned into cubes. He never wanted to wear a sheath again. But as soon as he came to this conclusion, he knew immediately that it had been more than that. Elizabeth had been so tight. She had been a maiden—he supposed that accounted for it.

He sighed. *Hopefully, it will be different next time. No going off like a squib, then collapsing, seeing stars.* Lord, he never imagined he would be so mortified when reflecting on his wedding night. *Did she realise? Perhaps not.* He could only hope her theoretical knowledge was no better than her experience.

Darcy pushed these thoughts to the back of his mind and rolled over to face his wife once more. She looked so young and innocent. He wanted to reach out and touch her face, *so smooth and perfect*. But he didn't. He felt like a lecher. He knew he had to get out of there.

Getting up circumspectly, he quietly pulled the bed curtains round his slumbering wife before ringing for his valet. Finn materialised in his dressing room shortly after with a pail of hot water and helped him don his riding clothes.

As his valet finished adjusting his cravat, Darcy finished timetabling his day in his head: "Tell Jenny that I will breakfast with Mrs Darcy, if it pleases her, at nine," he said before striding out.

Darcy took a cup of coffee at the kitchen door, a practice he'd developed in his youth. When he strode out the side door into the courtyard, Healy was waiting with his favourite stallion, Ajax. The groom was one of the new staff, who had come from the village.

"Morning, Healy," Darcy said, as he threw his leg over the horse.

"Sir!" said Healy, as he tugged his forelock.

Darcy walked the horse over the cobbles of the courtyard and through the arch. As soon as he hit the gravel of the drive, he rose into a trot and Ajax, familiar with the routine, responded.

Reaching the grass, Darcy set off on a bruising ride over his demesne, jumping hedges and scattering deer. The fresh Derbyshire air calmed him like oil on water, but his unquiet thoughts still roiled underneath.

He realised now he had made a mistake starting the affair with Diana seven years ago. He had been determined not to let his life be ordered by innuendo, but when the opportunity arose, he had just caved. He had sinned, and look what had come from it—only heartbreak.

Now, he was doing the right thing. He had married. Did his soul feel cleansed? *No! It is worse, infinitely worse!* He felt like such a lowlife. Elizabeth had seemed so poised and mature in Hertfordshire: tending to her sister, deflecting Miss Bingley's nasty comments with grace, comforting the Lucas boy. With her hair up and covered from neck to toe, she passed as an adult. But she was a child. He'd deflowered a child.

After finishing the circuit of the park, Darcy returned via the folly that was separated from the house by the formal gardens. He sought out his favourite place—a small lake behind the folly that could not be seen from the house, not more than a pond really. He used it as a swimming hole in summer. The mist hung above the water as he walked out onto the pier. Kneeling down at the end, enveloped by the mist, a huge sob wracked him, and he fell to quietly crying. This continued for some minutes as he dwelt on his iniquities; then he calmed himself, and drawing a huge breath of the cold damp air, he sat down cross-legged and thought.

Elizabeth was young, but only seven years younger than himself, the same number that he was younger than Diana. Was there not some strange symmetry in that? Had his father not been ten years older than his mother? It was done, and he had done it for good reasons. He would have to make the best of it now.

He pulled himself up taller, making his spine erect, straightening his arms as they rested on his knees. Putting his feelings in a box, he thought of Pemberley: what needed to be done next, the improvements he would make, and lost himself in plans for the future.

Across the lake, hidden in the shade, Finn watched his master. He had come here especially to do so. It was his guilty pleasure to watch Darcy swim here in the summer, *such a perfect body*. But today, Finn had come to view his mind.

Finn knew that Darcy had had a long-term mistress in London. Who she was, he did not know; but he knew it had ended badly, after he bought her that expensive parure. Of course, Finn knew there were letters but, as a gentleman, he never opened them, even though, as Darcy's valet, he had every opportunity to do so. It had cut Finn to the quick to see his master in such flat despair; to see him cast down by a worthless female who had dallied with him and then tossed him aside. Finn had worried for Darcy's sanity for a while there, afraid he might do something silly.

When Finn saw Darcy take an interest in Miss Elizabeth at Netherfield, he had breathed a sigh of relief. The way Darcy had carried her handkerchief around and kept hiding it was so sweet. She seemed a sensible lady. Finn approved and had done what he could to make things run smoothly.

Now he was perturbed to see his master upset again. Had the wedding night not gone well? But as he watched, he saw Darcy straighten himself and adopt a pose that reminded Finn somewhat of Eastern mystics—he was thinking. Of what he contemplated, Finn knew not, but Darcy's face became serene, and time blurred as he gazed upon his master's beauty.

Then Darcy rose and composedly walked back down the pier, grabbing the reins of his horse, which was grazing by the pond. As his master led his mount through the folly and proceeded back to the house via the formal gardens, Finn skirted round it, and walked briskly back behind the southern wall of the garden on which fruit trees were espaliered, satisfied for the moment that a crisis had been averted.

23 The morning after

When Elizabeth woke she found herself alone. Sitting up, she got the distinct feeling she had overslept. Someone—her husband, she presumed—had drawn the curtains round the bed. She supposed that accounted for it. She opened the curtains closest to her and slid off the mattress, straightening the hem of her nightgown. A fire had been built in the hearth, taking the chill off the air, but the floor was still cold when her feet touched it.

A quick peep around the curtains at the end of the bed ascertained the room was empty. Elizabeth was about to head for their sitting room, when Darcy's dressing-room door opened. But instead of her husband, Finn walked into the room. She dived back round the curtains at the end of the bed.

Finn turned swiftly about, and she heard: "I beg your pardon, ma'am," as the dressing-room door closed again.

Skittering across the rug of Darcy's bedchamber, Elizabeth opened the door to their shared sitting room. The fire was unlit there, and it was cold, so she skipped quickly across the cold floor to her own bedchamber.

Opening the door, she thankfully found her room much warmer, and immediately perceived her maid, Jenny, arranging flowers in a vase.

Upon seeing her mistress, Jenny greeted her, curtsied, and pulled a bell rope, all before Elizabeth had time to blink.

"Oh dear," said Elizabeth, by way of apology. "I fear it must be quite late."

"It is not quite half-nine, Mrs Darcy," replied her maid, consulting an ormolu clock on a dresser.

"Goodness!" replied Elizabeth. "I suspected as much! The curtains were drawn round the bed. I suppose I have missed breakfast."

"Not at all, ma'am. Mr Darcy breakfasted at nine, but we can ask for a tray to be sent up anytime."

Elizabeth blushed, realising the staff had probably ascribed her tardiness to her wedding night.

"I thought you might like to start with a bath, ma'am," suggested Jenny.

Elizabeth immediately realised this was a good idea. "Yes, please."

"Very well, ma'am," Jenny said, leading the way to the dressing room.

Her maid pulled the curtain across to give Elizabeth some privacy using the commode while she mixed some water in a basin for her mistress's ablutions. Finding the temperature to her satisfaction, she placed a large huckaback towel on the washstand.

Elizabeth emerged from behind the curtain in time to see Jenny put a brass pail in the wardrobe and slide a small door shut. She immediately realised the aperture was not a cupboard, but a pass-through. On the other side of the wall, she could hear footsteps.

"If you'd like to wash and slip into this dressing gown, ma'am," said Jenny; "I'll see to things next door. Just ring the bell when you're ready," she said, pointing to a small hand bell on the dresser before walking out through a door that Elizabeth had not noticed the night before.

Elizabeth did not recognise the pale pink dressing gown. Made of the finest silk, it was undoubtedly the most expensive garment she had ever had on her body. This, she thought as she slipped it on, was rather ironic considering its function—her dresses were not anywhere near so fine. The silk felt wonderful next to her skin.

When Elizabeth rang the bell, Jenny opened the door to reveal that it led into a short hallway with daylight streaming in from beyond. After traversing the hall past a curtain that had been pushed aside, Elizabeth found herself in a narrow room dominated by an enormous copper bathtub from which steam was rising.

"Goodness!" she exclaimed.

"It's marvellous, isn't it?" beamed Jenny. "Old Mr Darcy had all the modern conveniences installed when he built the house. There's a closed stove in the kitchen, too!"

"Yes, marvellous!" said Elizabeth, wondering how one went about getting in. "We certainly didn't have one of these at Longbourn."

"No, nor do they at Wyvern Hall, ma'am—that's the earl's residence near Matlock. It's a lot more work for the servants over there. I was so glad when I got the position here," said Jenny, testing the water once more. "Not that I mind working hard," she amended, "but it's possible to do so many more useful things with the modern conveniences."

"Of course," said Elizabeth, slipping off her gown.

The air in the room was quite warm—both from the steam and a fire that crackled in a hearth in one corner. She stepped gingerly over the side. The water felt quite heavenly as she immersed herself in it.

"Would you like me to shampoo your hair, ma'am?" asked Jenny.

"Shampoo?" echoed Elizabeth.

"It's this new thing from London for washing the hair," said Jenny. "Mr Darcy's man says it's much nicer than egg whites and vinegar. Would you like to try it?"

"Why not?" said Elizabeth, feeling adventurous.

"Then, do you paddle there while I get it, ma'am," said Jenny cheerfully, as she disappeared out a side door.

What followed was an adventure for both mistress and maid. Jenny, not accustomed to shampoo, used a little too much, and more water had to be called for before she was satisfied she had rinsed it out properly. The maid ended up nearly as wet as her mistress.

By the time a freshly scrubbed and wrapped Elizabeth emerged into her chamber, having had the bathing experience of a lifetime, she was thinking there were decided advantages to being married to Mr Darcy.

Jenny had arranged a stool next to the fire to allow her mistress to dry her hair. Meanwhile a tray had been sent up from the kitchens with breakfast.

"Begging your pardon, ma'am," said the chambermaid as she set it down. "Mrs Reynolds hoped tea and a muffin would suffice, since lunch is at one."

"Yes, of course," Elizabeth replied, picking up the muffin to nibble on, while Jenny lifted her wet tresses with a comb to help dry her hair.

"Where did this wrap come from, Jenny?" asked Elizabeth conversationally.

"It's one of Miss Georgiana's, ma'am," replied Jenny. "Mrs Reynolds thought you could make use of some of her things 'til more of your own gowns are made up."

This embarrassed Elizabeth a little, but she was determined not to show it. "Goodness! Surely my new sister won't appreciate my raiding her wardrobe while she's away!"

"No, ma'am," laughed Jenny. "I didn't explain properly. These are things that Miss Georgie has grown out of. They are generally sent to her cousins at Chaseley—that's the viscount's residence south of Matlock—but it seems a shame to waste them on girls who are not yet out. Some of them are terribly fine, beautiful gowns."

"I gather Georgiana is taller than I," remarked Elizabeth.

"About the same height, ma'am, but she is stouter, or," Jenny amended, "p'rhaps I should say, you are slimmer."

"And is she full grown?" asked Elizabeth.

"Well, her brother is very tall, so maybe she's got a way to go yet," said Jenny. "She's just turned sixteen, ma'am."

"And I gather she is out?" interpolated Elizabeth, considering Miss Georgiana's wardrobe.

"Well, no, ma'am," replied Jenny. "Mr Darcy thinks she is ready to come out, but Miss Georgie doesn't want to."

"Is she shy then?" asked Elizabeth.

"Very shy, ma'am," said Jenny. "Tho' I know not why. She is quite pretty. Not so beautiful as you, but still very comely. No doubt the gentlemen will be falling over themselves to make her acquaintance."

Elizabeth was about to retort that she was not beautiful, but she bit her tongue. She hoped to invite Jane to visit, possibly in the New Year, and she'd let her maid realise her mistake then. Instead, she contented herself with examining her bedchamber in the better light of day. It was a very large room painted a duck egg blue with soft furnishings in pinks and peaches. Not colours she would have chosen—she thought the blue a little cold; but she had to judge the overall effect quite pleasing. The canopied bed was a very fine one with thin barley-twist posts.

Once Elizabeth's hair was dry, they returned to the dressing room to select a gown. Miss Georgie's cast-offs had been hung to one side for her perusal. She could now see why Mr Darcy had declared her favourite sprig muslin dowdy. Although he had not said anything last night, perhaps he'd had a quiet word to Mrs Reynolds. Elizabeth eventually selected a charming ivory silk, mainly on the basis that it was cut in such a way that allowed Jenny to sew her into it. The other gowns would need to be altered before she could wear them.

Shortly before one o'clock Elizabeth found her way back to the dining room, wearing the ivory silk gown. Her hair was expertly coiffed in a new style bound with a green ribbon, and she wore a matching spencer and silk slippers.

Darcy was standing near the mantel with his back to the fire, staring at the carpet five feet in front of him.

"Good afternoon, sir," said Elizabeth as she came into the room. "I'm sorry I missed you at breakfast. I slept in."

"Good afternoon, Elizabeth," he replied, still looking at the carpet; "It is no matter." He dared not ask if she had slept poorly, since he knew there was every likelihood that she had, and that *he* was responsible.

When Darcy finally turned his attention from the very interesting rug he had been surveying to his wife, he stared at her for a moment. "You look very good," he blurted.

Elizabeth thought she detected a note of surprise. She watched as Darcy blushed slightly.

"Have you toured the house yet?" he asked, regaining his composure, and coolly changing the subject.

"Not yet," she smiled. "So far, I have had a bath."

"That must have been *some* bath," he replied, raising his eyebrows.

"It was," she assured him. "There was not a square inch of floor dry by the time we finished."

Darcy smiled to himself, but before Elizabeth could enquire as to the source of his amusement, Mrs Reynolds appeared, followed by a footman carrying a tray, and they took their places at table.

Lunch was a simple meal consisting of cold meats, fruit and cheese, served with bread and chutneys. The fine china on which it was served somehow belied its simplicity.

"I hope," ventured Elizabeth, as she buttered some bread, "that your morning was more fruitful."

"I went riding early on," said Darcy, "but I've spent most of the morning with my steward."

"Has it been long since you were last at Pemberley?" asked Elizabeth.

"Several months," he replied. "I correspond with my steward, but there are always some things that are best dealt with in person or not worth writing about. I will need to spend more time with him today, but I hope to show you the library later in the afternoon if you are free. Your father will not forgive me if I don't, and you must put a description of it in your first letter."

"Certainly," she replied, relieved he didn't intend to only meet her at mealtimes or in bed. "I look forward to seeing it."

After lunch, Mrs Reynolds was scheduled to take Elizabeth on the promised tour of the house. Once her husband excused himself to his study, Elizabeth walked to the windows of the dining room to await the housekeeper, admiring the view while a footman cleared away the lunch things. The room afforded a beautiful prospect of the hill, crowned with wood, which they had descended yesterday. It looked even steeper at a distance. She wondered what it would be like to descend the road in an open carriage, possibly vertiginous. Elizabeth felt a sense of calmness descend upon her as she admired the view. Every disposition of the ground was good, and she looked on the whole scene, the river, the trees scattered on its banks and the winding of the valley, as far as she could trace it, with delight.

Shortly after, the housekeeper arrived and apologised for keeping her waiting.

"I have spent my time well, Mrs Reynolds, admiring the beautiful view."

"Aye," the housekeeper replied, "I do not think there is a single window in this house that affords a bad view. Old Mr Darcy planned it most carefully. But before we start, Mrs Darcy, let me give you the mistress's keys," she said as she pulled a beautiful chatelaine from her pocket and presented it to Elizabeth.

"It is just as the former Mrs Darcy left it, ma'am. The keys mostly open the mistress's private rooms. I hardly know which is which. But this one," she said, pointing to a rather plain key, "opens the stillroom. That I *do* know, since I have a copy myself. Many of the rooms opened by the other keys have not been used since she died. Those were old Mr Darcy's wishes, and the young master has not varied them; so you may find some of the rooms in a parlous state. Just give me your directions, and they will be ordered as you wish."

From the dining room, they passed into other rooms where different views of the same prospect greeted them. The rooms were lofty and handsome, and their furniture suitable to the fortune of its owner; but Elizabeth saw, with admiration of Darcy's taste, that it was neither gaudy nor uselessly fine, with less of splendour, and more real elegance, than the furniture of Netherfield.

"I thought," said Mrs Reynolds, "that I would confine myself to the working part of the house today, ma'am, and introduce you to some of the servants."

After touring the withdrawing room and a breakfast parlour, which, Mrs Reynolds assured her, caught the morning sun beautifully, they descended to the kitchens where Elizabeth met the chef and a large number of maids and footmen who were just finishing their lunch in the servants' hall.

They viewed the scullery, the pantry and the stillroom before proceeding outdoors to the kitchen garden, which contained mostly herbs.

"There is a succession house and a larger vegetable garden beyond the stables, which I will gladly show you another day, if you are interested, ma'am."

"Certainly," replied Elizabeth. "I hope to go walking everyday and am keen to find my way around the estate."

"Well, I thought you might like a brief tour of the estate tomorrow morning before you visit Lambton, but I know that Jenny is eager to broach your trunk of silks this afternoon, so I'll return you to your chamber, if I may."

"Very well," acquiesced Elizabeth, casting a wistful glance outdoors.

They returned along the hall to the main staircase. On reaching the spacious lobby above, Mrs Reynolds hesitated and turned toward the guest wing.

"Perhaps I'll show you one more room, if I may, Mrs Darcy, before I hand you over to Jenny."

She led Elizabeth into a very pretty sitting-room, lately fitted up with greater elegance and lightness than the apartments below and informed her that it was but just done to give pleasure to Miss Darcy, who had taken a liking to the room when last at Pemberley.

"This is the first room that has been redecorated since the house was built," said Mrs Reynolds. "I thought young Mr Darcy might have redecorated his own rooms or the study once he became master, but he is always so busy working. But as you see, he is never too busy to look after his sister. He thought it would give her more confidence to have her own space to order just as she liked, and he purchased the piano as her Christmas present."

"He is certainly a good brother," said Elizabeth, as she admired the new instrument.

Mrs Reynolds anticipated Miss Darcy's delight when she should enter the room. "And this is always the way with him," she added. "Whatever can give his sister any pleasure is sure to be done in a moment. There is nothing he would not do for her."

"Indeed?" asked Elizabeth, trying to imagine where this more loving and solicitous man might be hiding in her husband. She stroked the delicate fretwork of a music stand.

"Do you play, Mrs Darcy?" asked the housekeeper.

"Very poorly, I'm afraid," replied Elizabeth. "My sister, Mary, is the best pianist among my sisters, but I don't consider any of us to be truly accomplished on the instrument, whereas I hear that Miss Darcy is."

"Oh! yes—so accomplished!—She plays and sings all day long, but like her brother, she is a little shy. I hope you can manage to draw her out a little. Her new companion has made some progress, but I can't help thinking that someone closer to her own age, and as bright and sprightly as you are, might not succeed more easily. It has been so hard on both of them, losing their parents so early."

Elizabeth made a non-committal answer, fully believing that she would find Miss Darcy to be an unpleasant combination of her husband and Miss Bingley, who seemed to be her chief admirers.

Mrs Reynolds soon escorted her back to her chamber, and Elizabeth spent a pleasant afternoon with Jenny, going through the silks and several issues of *Costume Parisien*, planning her new wardrobe in preparation for the trip to Lambton on the morrow.

At half-past four, a wizened footman arrived at her door to escort her to the library.

"I'm Stevens, ma'am," he said, bowing. "We met this morning."

After Jenny had quickly adjusted her costume, Elizabeth followed Stevens into the hall. She was glad she had added a shawl to her ensemble as she descended the stairs and traversed the atrium following him. A cold wind had sprung up in the afternoon, rattling the windows, and although they had remained snug in her chamber, she could feel the temperature had dropped several degrees in the rest of the house.

Stevens opened a door and bowed. "Mrs Darcy, sir," he announced before retreating.

Her husband stood from behind a large desk and bowed. The room Elizabeth had entered was a spacious one, lined with bookshelves. It had a handsome floor of chequered marble over which a huge Turkish carpet had been spread.

"Good afternoon, Elizabeth," said Darcy, as he walked to the hearth and tugged the bell pull. "Mrs Reynolds has undertaken to bring us some tea in the library."

"It is very beautiful, sir, " said Elizabeth, walking further in and fixing her gaze on a pair of candlesticks on the mantel in the form of sphinxes.

"Ah! Forgive me!" said Darcy, realising her mistake. "This is my study. The library is next door."

Offering his arm, he escorted her through a set of double doors. Lizzy had to suppress a gasp—the room they entered was twice as large as the study, and the bookshelves, which had been surmounted by a series of paintings in that room, went all the way to the high ceiling here.

"I can see why my father was interested in your library," she managed.

"Indeed," said Darcy, "and you may use it as your own. There is a stair over there that leads to our shared sitting room."

Lizzy looked more closely at the narrow stair he indicated, which was set against the wall. It was symmetrically disposed about the hearth with a movable set of library steps executed in the same style, and she had originally assumed that was its function. But she could see now that it was fixed in place, with a second flight of stairs let into a dark aperture in the wall.

"Will I not be disturbing your work?" Elizabeth asked.

"Not at all. I do all my work in the study and only come in here for leisure."

Looking around, Elizabeth stepped towards an interesting device executed in wood and brass.

"That is an orrery," Darcy remarked.

"Indeed," Elizabeth replied; "a very fine one. My father has a small one in his study. Did you notice it when you visited him?"

"Yes, we spoke of it," said Darcy. "This one was a present from my mother to my father."

"Your mother?" echoed Elizabeth. She could not remember her mother giving her father a present at all, but she supposed Mama had better uses for her pin money.

There was a knock, and Mrs Reynolds entered, followed by a footman carrying a tea tray. The tea things were disposed on a low table, except for a kettle, which Mrs Reynolds placed on a small hob set into the hearth. She indicated to the footman to arrange the fire.

"Shall I pour, Mr Darcy?" the housekeeper asked.

"Thank you, Mrs Reynolds, I believe we can take care of ourselves."

The housekeeper curtsied and effaced herself, followed shortly by the footman.

Elizabeth was already aware that Darcy took his tea with a little milk but no sugar. Taking her place at the teapot, she reflected wryly as she poured that this was one of the few things she actually knew of her husband.

"Would you like some seed cake, sir?" she asked.

"Thank you," he replied as he took his cup.

Elizabeth cut two slices of the cake before serving herself tea, and then settled into the second wing chair by the fire. They sipped their tea in silence for a while: he observing the flames while she surreptitiously observed him. Finally, Darcy drew his teacup to his lips and took a deep breath behind it.

"I hope you are not too uncomfortable after last night?" he asked.

"Uncomfortable?" she echoed, not quite understanding his meaning.

"I understand there is often some physical discomfort, the first time..." he trailed off.

"Oh! No!" Elizabeth replied, blushing as she took his meaning. "It hurt a little at the time, but I feel fine now."

"I'm sorry. I couldn't ask at lunch because of the footman."

"Of course," she replied, toying with her seed cake.

There was silence again before he ventured. "I won't bother you tonight. I've decided to visit you once a week, and I'll come to *your* chamber."

Elizabeth digested this. She supposed this would allow him to escape to the privacy of his own room afterwards, since she must *remain horizontal*. "Very well," she replied, taking a bite of seed cake. She watched him chase a few crumbs round his own plate, and divining he wished to say something more, waited expectantly.

"Would Tuesdays be all right?" he asked.

24 The dressmaker

After finishing drinking their tea, Darcy gave Elizabeth a quick tour of the library, pointing out its architectural features, some of its older books, and the sections containing Shakespeare and more modern works. These contemporary tomes consisted chiefly of volumes of poetry. Modern books concerned with the business of the estate and his investments were kept in his study. When asked, Darcy admitted there might be some novels in the house, but that these were not worthy of the library.

"So you do not read novels, sir?" Elizabeth asked.

"Not if I can help it," he replied curtly.

"Goodness, whoever have I married?" she joked.

"You might have discovered that I do not generally read novels before it was too late, if you had been willing to discuss books in a ballroom," he parried.

"Ah, but I believe I heard the qualifier *generally*," Elizabeth retorted.

On closer interrogation, Darcy admitted he *might* have some satires by Swift and Voltaire, which *likely* inhabited his bedchamber. These had been given him by *his sister*, but he could remember nothing of their plots or even if they were worth reading.

With this valedictory speech, Darcy took himself off to his study before he might be forced into any further embarrassing confessions. Once her husband departed, Elizabeth poured herself another cup of tea, topping up the dark lukewarm brew that came from the teapot with hot water from the kettle on the hob.

She then returned to the chessboard she had noticed on her tour of the library. In the game in progress, Darcy had informed her, he was beating Richard Fitzwilliam, but his cousin refused to concede defeat. Richard, Darcy had declared, had not made a move in months, insisting he was still thinking. Elizabeth supposed that the colonel must regularly visit his mother at Matlock and frequent Pemberley when he did so.

Surveying the chessboard, Elizabeth could see that white was in a very bad position, but the situation was not hopeless, and she thought the colonel quite justified in not conceding. Indeed, she thought it would be out of character to any soldier who had fought under Wellington.

She recalled a similar game where she had almost bested her father when he had not been paying full attention—reading a book while making his moves. Like Darcy, Elizabeth had believed she had reached a similarly unassailable position before her father, realising his danger, had put his book down, employed his full faculties, and defeated her. When she had reflected on that game, Elizabeth realised it had always been in her power to win, but she had made some silly mistakes in response to some bold moves by her father.

Studying the pieces on the board, she wondered if it might be possible to turn this game around. Her husband seemed quite sure he could not lose, and Elizabeth thought it might be possible to take advantage of his arrogance. Drifting towards the bookshelves, she began to turn a couple of ideas over in her mind.

Meanwhile, to establish her borrowing rights to the library, Elizabeth retrieved a volume of Shakespeare, his comedies again—she dearly loved to laugh. Then, pulling the bell rope to let the servants know they could clear away the tea things, she ascended the library stairs to the sitting room, and thence proceeded to her chamber. She found Jenny sitting in front of the fire, altering one of Miss Georgie's dresses.

"Could you try this one on again, ma'am?" asked Jenny on seeing her mistress reappear. "I think it should be ready to wear to Lambton tomorrow, barring no further mistakes on my part. I've already had to unpick one seam."

Elizabeth dutifully complied and admired the dress in the pier glass as Jenny surveyed her handiwork and rearranged pins. The ensemble consisted of a salmon silk underdress with a pink spencer adorned with a muslin skirt worn over it. Both pieces were beautifully decorated with gold thread.

Jenny chatted while she worked. "I've divided Miss Georgie's dresses into those which I can alter myself, ma'am, and those which will need to be altered by a professional—I'll package those up so we can take them to Lambton tomorrow."

"Thank you, Jenny. You are very skilled with needlework," remarked Elizabeth, as she shed the altered garment.

"My pleasure, ma'am," replied Jenny. "It is wonderful to work on such beautiful pieces."

They sat down together in front of the fire to while away the time before dinner. Jenny resumed her sewing, and Elizabeth decided to read the Shakespeare aloud, as she had so often done while Jane plied a needle. Elizabeth had little taste for needlework and had mostly contented herself with doing the family's darning. In that work she was quite skilled.

Dinner was again delicious, but her husband was in a bad mood and did not talk much. Apparently he'd had to step in to resolve a long running dispute between two tenants during the afternoon—a duty that was not to his taste. Elizabeth was glad when she could politely escape to her own chambers, leaving Darcy contemplating the brandy decanter.

Once Jenny helped her mistress into her nightgown, she took herself off to the servants' hall to have supper, taking her sewing with her.

Finding herself alone, Elizabeth reflected sadly that she and Jane would have been brushing out each other's hair at Longbourn at this time of the evening, and she wondered briefly if Mary might be brushing Jane's hair right now. Then, directing her maudlin mood to something constructive, Elizabeth picked up the lap desk and settled herself in front of the fire to write a letter to her sister.

An hour later, she felt she had summarised the events so far with as much humour and discretion as she could muster, and she curled up in bed with *The Satyricon*. As she read, Elizabeth could not help thinking that her husband's timetable for conjugal relations lent some credence to her father's theory, despite the fact that she had as yet seen no evidence of a male lover.

Awaking early, Elizabeth rang for her maid and had soon donned one of her old day gowns and her walking boots. Pulling her cloak round her shoulders, she headed for the kitchens, hoping to cadge a piece of toast and a saucer of tea before heading out. She arrived to find she had been pre-empted by her husband, who was standing just outside the kitchen door sipping a cup of coffee.

"Good morning, Elizabeth," said Darcy upon seeing her. "I take it you are catching the morning air."

"Yes, sir, I thought I might walk out past the stables to view the kitchen garden. Do you have any suggestions as to where I might walk from there?"

"Well, I could accompany you and show you round," he suggested.

Elizabeth had not failed to notice the riding crop under his arm. "I would not wish to disrupt your plans, sir. I gather you are going for a ride."

"I am, but I do so every morning and can miss one day," conceded Darcy.

"They have probably already saddled your horse, sir," remarked Elizabeth. "Let not their efforts be in vain."

He did not argue, instead suggesting she might like to return to the house via the formal garden and ensuring there was a footman to accompany her, before departing for his ride. But in this, Jenny had been ahead of him. Elizabeth was finishing her tea when Stevens materialised in the hall, dressed for the outdoors. It had not occurred to her that she would not be alone on her walk, and Elizabeth could not help but think that having a servant trailing her somehow inhibited her freedom. But she did not protest, knowing her parents a little lax in failing to supervise her morning walks in Hertfordshire.

Stevens kept a discreet distance. Were it not for the occasional crunch of his boots on the gravel, Elizabeth could imagine herself to be alone.

The winter kitchen garden turned out to be no great thing. It was the succession house that piqued Elizabeth's interest, but she found it to be locked. It occurred to her that there might be a key on her chatelaine, but she had left it behind. Circumnavigating the periphery of the sward along a gravel track, Elizabeth noted various branches of the path, which she could explore on future walks. She found the formal garden more interesting. There was a folly at the far end which separated the garden from a tranquil pond, and she was delighted by the fruit trees espaliered along a brick wall to catch the warmth and sun.

Elizabeth arrived back at the house in time to change her dress before breakfast, her walk slightly abbreviated because she had not dressed warmly enough. Derbyshire was definitely colder than Hertfordshire and getting more so every day. True to her word, Jenny had the pink ensemble ready and once more tied up her mistress's hair becomingly to expose her slender neck.

She preceded her husband to the breakfast parlour. When Darcy walked in at nine exactly, having freshly arrived back from his ride, his face was flushed, and Elizabeth could only surmise that he had ridden hard and fast on whatever circuit he had pursued.

After greeting her husband pleasantly for the first breakfast they had shared together at Pemberley, Elizabeth requested a plate of ham and eggs, which was placed in front of her along with a pot of tea. She was surprised when a bowl of porridge was placed in front of her husband.

"Would you like some tea, sir?" she enquired, as he proceeded to drizzle honey onto his porridge.

"Thank you, I'll wait for the ham and eggs," he replied, following the honey with milk.

"I see," she remarked. "So the porridge is only the first course."

He looked at her under his brows. "You disapprove of porridge?"

"Oh, no, no!" she said airily before admitting, "Well, I suppose it was not exactly what I expected you to eat for breakfast."

"My father didn't approve of my eating what he called servants' food, but when I was younger, my stomach couldn't quite wait until nine, so I used to sneak some porridge in the kitchens before breakfast. I grew rather fond of it. Have you tried it?" he asked.

She admitted she had not, adding that it did not look very appetising.

"Well, it's the sort of hot breakfast that does well when sent up on a tray," advised Darcy. "Unlike toast, which always arrives cold. So you may wish to try it next time you sleep in."

Unconvinced, she made a mental note to never sleep in again when her husband was ordering breakfast.

By the time his porridge was finished, Darcy seemed to have taken the edge off his hunger, and Elizabeth noticed him sneaking looks at her whenever he thought she wasn't looking. Finally, when she caught him at it, she raised her eyebrows at him.

"That is a nice dress," he remarked casually, studying the tea he was pouring for himself.

She wondered if he recognised it as his sister's. "It is, is it not?" responded Elizabeth.

"Pink suits your complexion," he remarked by way of explanation. "You should wear it more often."

"I prefer green," remarked Elizabeth. "'Though I suppose that wearing it constantly is rather boring of me."

Then realising her answer was hardly conciliating, she thanked him for the compliment and said she rather thought there were some pink silks in her trunk, before adding, "I am going to Lambton this morning to visit the dressmaker."

"To Lambton?" he replied. "I did not realise there *is* a dressmaker there. I thought a passable modiste might be found in Sheffield or Derby."

"My aunt assures me the dressmaker is quite good, and I hoped my great aunt might accompany me."

"Your great aunt?" he asked in puzzlement. "I did not realise you had relatives in Derbyshire."

"Technically, she is my great aunt by marriage, the aunt of my uncle's wife. You visited my uncle near Cheapside, did you not? The Gardiners? My aunt is formerly of Lambton and her aunt still lives there. I sent a message yesterday and had hoped to hear from her before I set out."

Darcy rang a bell on the table and Mrs Reynolds came bustling in.

"Did any message come for Mrs Darcy?" he asked.

"Why yes, sir," the housekeeper replied. "I put it right there on the table."

The note was eventually found under the teapot trivet.

"Oh! Who was the silly widgeon who did that!" exclaimed Mrs Reynolds as the missive was abstracted, none the worse for wear, but cosily warm.

"No matter," Lizzy reassured the apologetic Mrs Reynolds before remarking the colour of the paper was difficult to distinguish from the tablecloth.

Mrs Reynolds retreated; relieved she had not disgusted the new mistress with her incompetence.

"Ah!" Elizabeth said, as she scanned the note. "My aunt is most gratified to accompany me and invites me to morning tea beforehand."

"What is your great aunt's name?" asked Darcy.

"Amelia Polkinghorn," replied Elizabeth.

"The vicar's daughter?" said Darcy.

"Why, yes. Do you know her?"

"Well, no," admitted Darcy, "but I know *of* her; the living of Lambton is disbursed by the estate. Her name is on the Christmas list. We send a gift to Miss Polkinghorn every year to honour her father's service to the family. He died five years ago, 'though the curate gave his sermons for some time before he passed away. I believe he had a stroke."

Lizzy found it a little strange that her husband gave gifts to people he had never met. She could only assume he had never attended church in Lambton or, if he had, had never met the vicar's family.

Shortly after ten, Elizabeth set off for Lambton in the Darcy coach, feeling ridiculously over-accompanied. Jenny sat on the backward-facing seat, guarding two large packages and looking very pleased with the expedition, which was her first in the Darcy carriage. A groom and Stevens stood up behind.

Elizabeth reminisced on similar expeditions to the haberdasher in Hertfordshire, which had involved walking the mile or so to Meryton. At the time, the company of her youngest sisters had always been slightly irksome, their hijinks and hoydenish behaviour during any encounter with an eligible young man regularly embarrassing the party; but as they drove along in silence, Elizabeth found herself missing the sound of their vacuous conversation, which had always reminded her of excited birds.

Finally they arrived at the gate of her aunt's cottage, and Stevens let down the step. Elizabeth was unsure of her reception, having never met her great aunt before. She had sent her Aunt Madeline's letter of introduction with her missive yesterday.

By the time Stevens had opened the gate, a lady had stepped out the front door to greet her. By her age and her dress, Elizabeth could only assume this was her aunt. She looked a pleasant lady, definitely past middle age but younger than Elizabeth had imagined her. Her figure was that of a young lady and her dress, while modest, was fashionable and well made.

"Aunt Amelia?" Elizabeth ventured as she got closer.

"Mrs Darcy, welcome to Lambton!" greeted her aunt, "Come in, come in."

Elizabeth entered the hallway, where Jenny helped her out of her bonnet and pelisse. Her aunt then ushered her into an elegant parlour where they sat down to tea with her aunt's companion, another spinster, who was introduced as Miss Dorsey. Elizabeth could see why this lady had never married—she had a face as long as a horse's. During tea, she also discovered Miss Dorsey had an unfortunate laugh. In fact, if a horse *could* laugh, then Elizabeth imagined it would laugh much like Miss Dorsey did. In short, she had a disturbingly accurate name, worthy of Sheridan.

During the course of tea, which was accompanied by sweet cakes which her aunt, surprisingly, called madeleines, Elizabeth discovered that the house was owned by Miss Dorsey, who was the sister of Lambton's former physician, now sadly departed. Aunt Amelia had, of course, formerly lived with her father at the vicarage and had continued to do so until the new vicar had arrived. Then, given the choice between departing to live with one of her two married sisters elsewhere and remaining in Lambton, her aunt had gladly accepted the offer to move in with her friend. Their joint incomes allowed them to live very comfortably with a single servant.

"Did you name these cakes after Aunt Gardiner?" asked Elizabeth, accepting another of the shell-shaped treats.

"No, my dear," laughed her aunt; "my brother-in-law fell in love with these little cakes in France and brought the tin moulds back from his grand tour. He loved them so much, he named his first daughter, Madeleine."

"How bizarre," replied Elizabeth, never having heard this story of her aunt's christening before.

"Yes, I suppose it is a little strange," agreed her aunt, "but it is a popular name on the Continent."

After tea, Elizabeth's aunt accompanied her to the carriage for the ridiculously short trip to the dressmaker. Elizabeth was very tempted to walk the short distance to the shops, but they were obliged to return to the carriage for their packages anyway.

These were shortly opened by the dressmaker's assistant to reveal that one contained Miss Georgie's dresses to be altered, while the other contained some of the silks they had selected for the new dresses, along with the issues of *Costume Parisien* they had consulted. Jenny had carefully marked the selected designs with strands of embroidery floss that matched the colour of the silk to be used.

The dressmaker, Madame Lafrange, did an admirable job of appearing completely unfazed by the unexpected patronage of Mrs Darcy. When the package of silks was opened, they were seen to be very fine, and Madame was in a fever of trepidation that she would be quite unequal to the task of clothing the mistress of Pemberley—her patrons were generally more of Miss Polkinghorn's station in life. The garment the lady was wearing was much finer than anything she had previously made.

However, when the second package was opened to reveal the gowns that needed to be altered, Madame immediately perceived they were the work of an expensive modiste. She realised that she could study the designs of these dresses to produce garments of similar quality herself, and she quickly set to work planning their alteration as Mrs Darcy tried each of them on. In between these fittings, she discussed the design of the new gowns with Mrs Darcy's maid, and with Miss Polkinghorn, who was full of good ideas.

By the time the ladies left the shop over an hour later, Madame Lafrange had discovered that Miss Polkinghorn was a relation of Mrs Darcy; that Mrs Darcy was the daughter of a country squire from Hertfordshire; that she had spent little time in London and expected to spend most of her time in Derbyshire. All of these facts gave Madame confidence that she was equal to the task of making Mrs Darcy's gowns; and that if she did her job well, might reasonably expect to continue to enjoy Mrs Darcy's patronage.

The fact of the matter was that Madame Lafrange was really Miss Julie Dubois, who had been apprenticed as a lowly seamstress in a Parisian fashion house before the revolution. This had been rather a depressing career. After working there for a year, it was clear she would spend the rest of her life barely making ends meet in her occupation and could look forward to the indigent retirement enjoyed by her grandmother. Julie had thus decided that her best hope for advancement lay in engaging the interest of one of the many tradesmen in the district who were delighted by her charms. At sixteen, she had been an exceedingly pretty girl. Her problem was that she wasn't really interested in these tradesmen or men in general.

Around the same time she had been noticed by the son of a French nobleman on the verge of quitting the unrest in Paris for England. To be more precise, she had almost been trampled by his horse. In one of those life-defining moments, he had decided she might make pleasant company on his journey, and Julie had not resisted. Six months after arriving in London, he had established himself in society and, having tired of her company, paid her the handsome sum of two hundred pounds to go away.

Deciding on a life outside the very dirty metropolis of London, Julie had caught the first stage leaving to the North. Liking the country in Derbyshire, she had alighted in Derby, from whence she proceeded by enquiry to the village of Lambton—a pleasant town that, crucially, lacked a seamstress. Revising her age to twenty-one and styling herself as the widow of a much older French émigré, she had opened her shop under the assumed name of Madame Lafrange.

Her life in England had been pleasant and comfortable, and Julie did not regret her hasty decision to climb onto that nobleman's horse twenty years ago, although she did occasionally suffer pangs of guilt when wondering what had become of her grandmother. Julie could only hope she had caught the attention of some amiable man, for her grandmother had been still passably good looking, despite her failing eyesight.

Now, surveying the bounty of the art of stitchery before her, she carefully laid the first of Miss Georgie's dresses on the cutting table, produced a large sheet of paper, and proceeded to make some patterns.

During the extensive waiting periods when Mrs Darcy and her maid visited first her aunt and then the seamstress, Harry, the coachman, passed the time whittling toy soldiers for his son, while Stevens employed himself by getting to know the new groom, Healy, who had joined the estate from the village.

After discovering the details of Healy's lineage, Stevens decided to ease the new fellow into the job by describing his master's many virtues and few peccadilloes, the latter of which chiefly consisted of being very precise and particular about everything. He then proceeded to give Healy all manner of sage advice on how to get along at Pemberley, which principally involved navigating the shoals of the personalities of the other servants. This enumeration eventually arrived at the person of Darcy's valet, Finn.

"You steer clear of him, young shaver. He's bent," said Stevens, using the vernacular.

"What's that s'posed to mean?" asked Healy.

"He's a bloke who likes blokes," explained Stevens.

"Oh," replied Healy, considering this novel prospect. Well, maybe not so novel. It wasn't like he hadn't fooled around with the other boys in the village when they were swimming and the like; but that was more in the way of relieving the tension 'til you got a girl. It hadn't occurred to him that there might be men who actually *preferred* to fool around with other men.

"So is he dangerous?" he asked Stevens.

"Finn? Nay! He won't force himself on ya, if that's what yer mean. I'm just putting you on your guard, cause you're a handsome young fella, and you don't want to be drawn into any ungodly practices, unawares like."

Healy preened himself slightly on this compliment before reflecting that any practices that didn't involve his own hand would be welcome. There was a short silence before another thought occurred to him and Healy ventured: "So have you, eh… been with him then?"

Stevens gave him a stern look. "Nay! But he used to have a thing wif one of the footmen here, but the other fella went off to work for the earl. Anyways, you steer clear of Mr Finn. Goodness knows what he gets up to in Lunnon. That be a den of vice."

The conversation was cut short when Mrs Darcy emerged from the shop with Miss Polkinghorn and decided to stroll past the other shops in the village. Jenny trotted faithfully behind, but it was Stevens' job to provide an escort, so he was obliged to get down from the back of the coach and follow his mistress at a discreet distance.

Their perambulation down the village street caused much interest amidst the inhabitants of Lambton. Elizabeth first noticed the gawkers across the street, who considered themselves sufficiently far away to be invisible. She then became aware of the faces, which kept appearing and disappearing in her more immediate vicinity—at windows, and around corners. Finally, Elizabeth discovered she had attracted a gaggle of village children who seemed to be engaged in a game of *sly fox*—every time she turned to view them they froze, but once her back was turned they crept along behind her to maintain their distance. In short, the advent of Mrs Darcy to Lambton had caused a stir.

"Are people always so curious about strangers hereabouts?" she asked her aunt when they had returned to her gate on foot.

"Of course not, Elizabeth," said her aunt, who had moved to first name terms at her niece's insistence, "but they are very curious to see the new Mrs Darcy. The Darcys are like royalty around here, and they hardly ever appear in the village."

"But my husband doesn't even have a title," remarked Elizabeth, somewhat surprised—the Bennets experienced nothing like this in Hertfordshire. *Or did they?* Certainly all the gawkers had turned up for her wedding. Perhaps she'd just become inured to it and only found it strange among strangers.

"Nonetheless," replied her aunt, "he is the local feudal lord, as the Darcys have been for centuries. His marriage was bound to be of interest to the villagers."

Mentally acknowledging this is to be true, Elizabeth thanked her aunt for her company, returned to the carriage, and wended her way home.

25 An experiment

On returning to Pemberley from Lambton, Elizabeth was gratified to discover a letter from her sister had been delivered, but upon hearing that the master had delayed lunch pending her return from the village, she hurried up to her room to wash.

Darcy was once more waiting for her in front of the hearth in the dining room. Elizabeth apologised for keeping him from his meal, and they soon sat down to dine.

Having only recently consumed morning tea, Elizabeth's hunger was soon sated, and she enquired if Darcy would mind if she read Jane's letter while he continued to eat his lunch. Withdrawing it from the sleeve of her spencer, she was soon immersed in her sister's missive and making various exclamations as she read.

"Do you intend to share your news?" asked Darcy drily, "or are you saving it for Christmas?"

She laughed and apologised, adding, "You know that is just the sort of thing my father would say."

She returned to her letter before summarising, "Well, Jane starts off with the usual greetings which I will not bore you with, including some belated felicitations on our marriage from one of Aunt Gardiner's sisters who lives in Somerset. But here is something more of interest to you: apparently your aunt and uncle arrived at the wedding after we departed."

Darcy stiffened. "Which aunt?"

"Ah, well, I am not so sure," replied Elizabeth. "The uncle is named as the Earl of Matlock. Is that Richard's father?"

"Yes," affirmed Darcy. "I thought he was busy in parliament, but maybe he was able to make it belatedly."

"It would appear so," replied Elizabeth. "Jane says she did not get to meet the aunt—her daughter became ill after she arrived and she had to go off. But what's this? Perhaps I have read it wrong; but no, that is definitely what she has written. How strange!"

"What?" asked Darcy somewhat impatiently, beginning to think that he could now detect a resemblance between Elizabeth and her voluble mother.

"Well, it appears the daughter stayed at Longbourn after the mother departed because she was quite ill and unable to continue her journey," replied Elizabeth. "Perhaps they were late to the wedding because of her illness. Though what could be so urgent for the mother to go off leaving her daughter behind I can only guess."

"What is her name?" asked Darcy, wondering if his first suspicions were wrong. It seemed unlikely that Aunt Catherine would allow Anne out from under her thumb for a moment. Perhaps it was in fact his Aunt Carissa, the countess, who had decided to attend with her daughter-in-law; though this pairing seemed slightly improbable, and as far as he knew, his aunt was still at Matlock with Georgie. He supposed she *might* have got wind of the event through Richard.

"Miss Anne de Bourgh," replied Elizabeth.

Darcy took a deep breath. "Go on," he urged, dreading that his aunt had made a scene.

"Well, your cousin is still at Longbourn. Apparently, she was seen by a London physician in the evening, who advised she should not be moved for at least a sennight; and Jane is taking turns nursing her with Charlotte. Dear Charlotte! One can always rely on her in a fix, though why she should…"

"Why she should…?" prompted Darcy.

"Well, the least said about that the better," said Elizabeth. "I'm afraid I was only going to say something nasty about my cousin, Mr Collins."

Darcy had not the least interest in Elizabeth's obsequious cousin. "And what of my aunt?" he prompted.

"Well, it is not clear," said Elizabeth, rereading the end of the letter. "Maybe I wrong her. Perhaps she went off to fetch the physician. Apparently, the earl and Richard are staying at Netherfield, so she may also be staying there. The Gardiners and Mr Collins would, of course, have still been at Longbourn. I'm afraid Jane has written the letter very ill, but I suppose if she was nursing someone she might have been somewhat distracted. Likely she wanted to get a letter off to me quickly. I sent a letter off to her this morning, so hopefully she will send another soon."

Then turning the letter over Elizabeth remarked, "But look, I believe that your uncle, the earl, has franked this," and she handed the letter to her husband so he could examine the outside.

Retiring to her room after lunch, Elizabeth realised she would attend church on the morrow, and it occurred to her that, like her trip to the village, she would be on show to the locals. Thus when Jenny arrived in her chamber to resume her stitchery, Elizabeth asked whether it might be better if she changed from the salmon dress into something more comfortable, so that it might be furbished up to wear to the service.

Jenny answered with a broad smile. "I've got two more gowns almost ready, ma'am: one for church and the other for dinner tonight."

Elizabeth duly tried on the gown proposed for dinner. It was a beautiful pale green muslin worked with silver thread. The asymmetric hemline, chased with silver, had a slight train. More silver adorned the tiny cap sleeves, and a ribbon of silver circled the under-bust. Such it looked on the hanger, but when Elizabeth tried it on, it took on a new aspect.

"I think the bust is a little tight, Jenny," she remarked, gazing at her prominent décolletage.

"Well, no, I think it is fine, ma'am," reassured Jenny, "as you will see if you raise and lower your arms. The neckline is perhaps, a little lower than what you are used to, but I'm sure your husband will not object to it."

Elizabeth glanced suspiciously at Jenny before turning her attention back to the mirror.

She felt almost naked. "I can't," she sighed. "Besides, I will freeze."

"But, there is this beautiful little spencer to go with it," added Jenny, producing a garment in which she was still stitching darts.

Elizabeth looked at the mirror again as Jenny draped the spencer over her shoulders. Despite covering the nakedness of her arms, her bust still bulged alarmingly. She shook her head.

"I don't understand how Mr Darcy could allow his sister to get around in such a thing," marvelled Elizabeth.

"Well..." replied Jenny, biting her lip; "I did say Miss Georgie was still growing. I saw her wear it once. It looked a bit different on her."

"I'm afraid I don't dare, Jenny," said Elizabeth, turning round to allow her maid to undo the tiny buttons at the back.

In the mirror, she saw her maid looked quite crestfallen and felt a little guilty.

"No matter, ma'am," replied Jenny, pretending nonchalance. "Do you slip on this wrap, and I'll furbish up the pink gown you are wearing now."

Elizabeth would have preferred to put on an old day gown and go walking outside, but the afternoon weather had, once more, turned rather nasty. She dutifully slipped on the wrap and sat down near the hearth with the lap desk. Sharpening her pen, she proceeded to relate the Lambton trip to her sister, while Jenny took herself off to perform her duties.

When Jenny arrived back with a footman bearing afternoon tea, she woke her mistress, who had fallen asleep in front of the fire after finishing her letter. Elizabeth felt slightly guilty for being so indolent. She had slept well the night before and could only presume she'd fallen asleep from boredom rather than need. What would she have done to witness a good spat between Lydia and Kitty for entertainment? ... a really trivial one about a lost ribbon or shoe rose!

Elizabeth dutifully took a macaroon with her tea, so as to not offend the chef, but hardly felt able to eat it after the madeleines she had consumed in the morning.

During the long afternoon, she read again from Shakespeare while Jenny continued her stitchery. Elizabeth still felt a little guilty about rejecting the green gown after all Jenny's hard work. During the course of her reading, an idea occurred to her. Her uncle Gardiner was an aficionado of natural philosophy. Whenever she met him, which had been at least twice a year— at Christmas and Easter, he regaled her with tales of amazing scientific experiments, both present and past: tales of Sir Robert Hooke pumping the air from a chamber and killing the poor canary within; and Sir Humphrey Davy's demonstrations with phlogiston. She wondered then if she might wear the green gown as a type of experiment, to test her husband's sensibilities. If Darcy really *was* disinterested in women, then he wouldn't notice what she was wearing, would he?

Still she wavered. Was she *game* to wear it?

When she got up to dress for dinner, Elizabeth's courage rose. She decided to wear the green gown after all. Telling Jenny, she had the felicity of seeing her maid flush pink with pleasure.

Jenny had not, however, finished stitching the green spencer, which she had temporarily abandoned in favour of the gown she was preparing for church on the morrow. While Jenny bit her lip wondering if she could possibly pin the spencer together, Elizabeth remembered the new shawls she had brought with her from Hertfordshire. Pulling these from a drawer, they were gratified to discover that one of the plain ones Elizabeth had stitched in Hertfordshire, which shone green from the warp and blue from the weft, suited the gown admirably.

Once it was draped round her shoulders, Jenny thought it very pleasing, indeed, declaring it would be nothing short of perfect if a silver fringe was added for future wear. She slipped some silver bangles onto Elizabeth's arms to complete the ensemble. Staring in the mirror, Elizabeth could only see her disconcertingly exposed bust; but she took a deep breath and, gathering the shawl close round her shoulders, proceeded downstairs.

When she walked into the dining room, Darcy once more had his back to the hearth and his eyes fixed on the carpet. *Perhaps*, she thought, *he is thinking when he adopts this pose and when he stares antisocially out of windows*. In Hertfordshire, she had always thought him too stiff-rumped to participate in the conversation.

Elizabeth let the shawl slide a little down her arms after Stevens took himself off; then greeted her husband pleasantly, asking him how his work had fared in the afternoon. She saw Darcy glance towards her to answer her question, but the words seemed to freeze on his lips. He was staring at her with his mouth slightly open—"catching flies", Charlotte would have said.

Feeling a little embarrassed for him, Elizabeth pretended to adjust the silver bangles on her arms. *At least*, she thought, *that answers one question—my husband is not indifferent to the charms of women*. When she looked up again, Darcy had regained his composure, though the tips of his ears were pink. They were both saved from the awkward situation when Mrs Reynolds entered with a footman bearing the first course.

During the subsequent meal, they carried on a rather stilted conversation, the bulk of which was conducted by Elizabeth. Starved for a decent topic, she discussed *Much Ado about Nothing*, the play she was currently reading to Jenny. For his part, her husband gave rather distracted answers, and Elizabeth was tempted to make a May game of him by saying increasingly outrageous things to draw his notice. However, it occurred to her that this was just the sort of disrespectful thing that her father did to her mother when she didn't understand a point he was trying to make. Determined not to go down that path, Elizabeth struggled to innocuously continue what was, essentially, a monologue.

The change of service between courses gave Elizabeth some respite. The movement of china on the table and the presence of the servants somehow lessened the necessity for speech. As the dessert was placed on the table, Elizabeth finally became aware that her husband was studiously avoiding her person, and she wondered if her conclusion on his initial reaction to her gown had been too hasty. Perhaps he was not *indifferent* to women but found them *distasteful.*

It was true that Darcy was having some difficulty in deciding where to direct his looks. He had never been one to ogle ladies and despised men who did so. He believed that one should always be careful not to expose one's baser nature in public. But now he found his eyes relentlessly drawn to his wife's anatomy and was forced to study remote corners of the room, such as the cornices, to keep himself in check.

If he looked at Elizabeth's face, his eyes drifted downwards. As soon as he glanced at the potatoes, his eyes slid across the damask tablecloth to her creamy breasts, especially to that dainty pink mole that surmounted the mound of her left orb just above the low neckline. Of course, it was impossible to eat while staring at the cornices. Darcy pushed his food to the left side of his plate with his knife, trying to get his wife's décolletage out of his field of view.

By the time dessert was served, he was sure Elizabeth had noticed his distraction. He then began to mentally kick himself for being such a looby. She was his wife after all, was she not? They were alone after all, were they not? Still, after reaching that mental waypoint, he found that continuing the journey, by appreciating his wife without staring at her, very difficult.

When dessert was removed and the brandy decanter put on the table, Elizabeth excused herself and got up.

Her imminent departure finally galvanised Darcy. "Please, Elizabeth, don't go. I am afraid I have neglected you sadly today. Would you sit with me while I have a little brandy?"

He offered her a measure also, but she declined it; instead picking up her wine glass, which she had failed to empty. When Darcy suggested they should sit by the fire, a footman duly moved two carvers close to the hearth before effacing himself.

Acknowledging her experiment to be a dismal failure, Elizabeth pulled the shawl up round her neck as she sat down, pretending she was cold. She was rewarded when she saw her husband visibly relax.

"I'm sorry," apologised Darcy as he settled himself in his chair. "You asked me about my business today, but I was rather... distracted. I'm considering becoming a partner in Bingley's textile mills. We spoke of it at Netherfield. His man of business sent the details today, and I have been going over them."

"I had heard Mr Bingley made his money in trade. I did not realise he was still involved in it."

"He is not involved directly. His father started several successful mills in Yorkshire, but he educated his son as a gentleman. Nonetheless, Bingley is still part owner of these mills. Aside from the money he inherited from his father, a large part of his income derives from them."

"Well, this is all very educational," remarked Elizabeth. "Why does he wish for you to become involved, aside from *friendly camaraderie?*"

"They wish to upgrade the steam engines in the mills to the new high pressure variety," replied Darcy. "They use less fuel, but there is a significant cost in acquiring them."

"So in return for assisting in the purchase of the new engines, you would become a part owner?" asked Elizabeth.

"Yes," Darcy said, pleased with her ready understanding. So few women understood business. Despite their heritage, Charles' sisters were remarkably ignorant.

"And how do you feel about going into trade, sir?" she asked coquettishly.

He laughed. "I am already *in* trade, Elizabeth. My father became a partner in many of the reworked lead mines in Derbyshire. Those ventures were so successful that he built this house with the profits."

"Really?" said Elizabeth in surprise. "I don't understand. I thought the lead was found on the surface and that it belonged to the King."

Again she had surprised him with her superior understanding. "How do you know these things?" he asked.

"You forget my Aunt Gardiner comes from Derbyshire, sir."

"What you say is true," replied Darcy, "or at least it was in the past. All the easily accessible lead was mined years ago, down to the water table. Then some clever schemes were devised for clearing the water from some of the mines by draining it off elsewhere, but this depended on the local geography and was not always possible. With the steam engine, it became possible to pump the water out."

"Of course, all these schemes cost money," he continued, "and were not feasible under the old arrangements where the King issued licences to extract the Crown's lead to individuals. That is why mining withered in Derbyshire, and England was becoming increasingly dependent on lead mined elsewhere. When new deals were struck with the government, companies could procure mining licences, allowing mining to flourish once more with the new techniques."

During his exposition, Darcy had pulled a pencil from his coat-pocket and Lizzy watched in fascination as he proceeded to twirl it adeptly between his fingers, much as jugglers did with large sticks at fairs.

"Every year, the portion of my income that comes from the mines is larger. Pemberley is becoming increasingly dependent on it. But there is only a finite amount of lead that can profitably be obtained, and it would not be wise of me to become too dependent on it. Since the income to be derived from crops and livestock seems likely to diminish further in the future, I need to find new investments."

To Lizzy, the latter part of her husband's speech sounded disturbingly like the talk her father had used to convince her of the wisdom of marrying Darcy. It seemed these new machines, introduced into mines and mills, were somehow fundamentally changing things, changing society in unprecedented ways. Never having seen a steam engine, or a mine, or a mill, it was difficult for her to imagine; and she could only envision something like a huge black kettle crouching in a dark room under a factory—society's bête-noire.

However, Lizzy immediately appreciated a crucial difference between these two speeches despite their similar content: her father had conceded defeat in the face of the changes; while her husband seemed determined to ride this black beast.

Elizabeth nodded her understanding. "And do you think you will join Bingley in his venture?"

"I will sleep on it, but it is my current intention to write back to his man of business to request a tour of the mills. I prefer to see things before I pledge my money."

"These mills are in Yorkshire? asked Lizzy.

"Yes, in the North Riding. They originally made cloth from the wool and linen produced there, but they manufacture many different fabrics now: which incorporate cotton from the Americas and silk from the Indies."

"So you will be going to Yorkshire soon?" she asked.

"It is yet to be arranged, but I promise not to leave you until Georgiana returns from Matlock."

"Very well, thank you for your consideration," Elizabeth replied, unsure if she was happy or sad to be bereft of her husband's presence so soon after their marriage. Their interactions were decidedly awkward, but she was a social person, and the thought of being alone in such a large house, with only the servants for company, was rather depressing.

They chatted on for a good hour about his investments, and their conversation again impressed upon Darcy his wife's superior understanding. Although she knew nothing of mills and mines, she listened attentively and asked intelligent questions. She did not criticise him for prosing on about a technical or déclassé topic as a cat like Caroline Bingley did when her brother spoke about the mills, or titter about how *smart* he was to *understand* such things, like that insipid Louisa Hurst, or Caroline, *when addressing him*. For unlike the Turkish treatment she meted out to her brother, whenever Darcy spoke on similar topics, Miss Bingley sheathed her claws and pretended she wasn't a cat. Darcy was percipient enough to realise that Caroline would have reverted to type soon after marrying him.

For Darcy, his conversation with Elizabeth was a brief period of amity, which he had no wish to end; but fearing to wear out his wife's interest, he accompanied Elizabeth to her bedchamber door before ten.

Reaching the second floor, Darcy suddenly wished he had not timetabled his intimate time with her. He felt a sudden urge to pull Elizabeth into his bedchamber or enter hers; but he did neither of these things and simply kissed her on her forehead when they reached her door. His lips lingered momentarily, hovering above her skin, as Darcy inhaled the now familiar scent of her before tearing himself away, and retreating to his room.

Elizabeth noticed his hesitant manner, which initially reminded her of their first uneventful night together in Kingsthorpe. *Perhaps there was a difference... Is it my imagination, or did his lips dwell longer on my forehead?*

Lizzy found her maid waiting eagerly in her room, ostensibly for a final fitting of her church dress, but it soon became apparent she hoped for news of Darcy's reaction to the green dress Elizabeth had worn to dinner.

"Did Mr Darcy like the dress, ma'am?" Jenny asked casually as she helped her mistress out of the gown.

"Well, he didn't specifically say anything," Elizabeth temporised, before noticing the disappointed look on Jenny's face.

"But I think he was much struck," Lizzy added, before spoiling her circumspection by bursting into a giggle—the look on his face when he had first noticed what she was wearing *had* been rather funny.

Jenny joined in with a little giggle of her own.

26 Church

As Elizabeth dressed for church in the morning, she was again impressed by the quality of Miss Georgiana's gowns. The dress she had donned was a sprig muslin, but one that put her favourite day-gown completely in the shade. The muslin was very fine, and the sprigs were embroidered in gold thread rather than just printed on the fabric. The hem was trimmed in gold lace and an asymmetric split down the front of the gown was edged in a silk brocade. The modest round neckline was finished in the same brocade and incorporated a multi-stranded pearl necklace—whether these were genuine or the new false pearls made from shell, she knew not; but the effect was most pleasing. The under-dress was a heavy silk damask embellished with a wide band of the maroon brocade round the hem.

Jenny had dressed her hair in a matching snood embellished with more pearls, which had been crocheted by one of the chambermaids. The effect, Elizabeth decided, was very pleasing, and decidedly Tudor.

Finally, when Jenny passed her psalter, Elizabeth discovered it had gained a matching silk damask slipcover.

"Thank you, so much, Jenny," breathed Elizabeth, hardly recognising the lady who stared back at her from the mirror.

Descending in state down the spiral staircase with her maid in tow, Elizabeth discovered her husband pacing in the vestibule.

"Am I late?" she asked, as she consulted the tall clock that resided there.

When she turned back to Darcy, she found him staring at her once more, although this time, at least, his mouth was not open. He was looking very handsome, dressed almost entirely in black, which made him look thinner and somehow younger. His impeccably shaved chin was framed by a high white collar that emphasised its squareness.

"No, no," he replied, replacing his watch in his pocket.

The awkward silence was broken when Mrs Reynolds entered the vestibule in her Sunday best. "Mrs Darcy!" she curtsied. "May I say, how nice you look?"

"Thank you," replied Elizabeth, flashing an appreciative smile at Jenny.

Darcy's valet helped him don his greatcoat, while Jenny clasped a warm black wool cloak round her mistress and pulled the attached calash over her coiffure. Even in this formless garb, Elizabeth presented a pretty picture, with her heart-shaped face and cherry-red lips framed in black.

Wordlessly, Darcy offered his arm, and they set off down the back steps and across the formal garden, followed closely by Finn, Jenny and Mrs Reynolds.

Passing behind the south wall of the formal garden, they walked towards the Dower House, offering Elizabeth her first glimpse of this structure. It was, of course, a much smaller house than the current manor house, of mixed heritage. The newest portion, which contained a magnificent front door set in a gothic arch, was double-storied and, together with an adjoining wing, embraced a small garden. The older wing contained only a single rank of much smaller windows.

Elizabeth had little chance to scrutinise the house any further before the chapel came into sight. A small group of people, who were likely tenants, were milling about the entrance. Upon the approach of the master, all heads were turned in their direction. Consulting his watch once more, Darcy slowed his pace. Elizabeth glanced at him curiously, but his face was directed forward, and a look of serene hauteur had overspread his features.

As they arrived at the chapel, the men at the entrance tugged their forelocks, while the women, who had been surveying Elizabeth curiously, suppressed their smiles, cast their eyes down, and curtsied. These gestures of obeisance were recognised by Darcy with a curt nod, and they proceeded to the narthex, where Finn and Jenny removed their coats, and Darcy relinquished his top hat.

Offering his arm to his wife, Darcy turned to the aisle to discover that the chapel was filled to overflowing. This he ascribed to the chill weather. Although his tenants were not permitted to do gainful work on Sundays, many of the men used the Sabbath to perform maintenance, sending their wives to church to tend their souls for them. Younger children were also often left in the care of their fathers so the womenfolk could pray in peace. In contrast, today's attendance seemed to be very much a family affair.

When he walked down the aisle with his wife, Darcy felt all eyes turned towards him. As there was nothing unusual in his being the centre of attention, Darcy might have remained deluded as to the real cause of such full church attendance, had not a high-pitched and overloud voice proclaimed in the hush:

"Is she a *princess*, mummy?"

The offending youngster was quellingly hushed, much to Elizabeth's amusement; but she preserved her countenance, and they proceeded down the aisle without further interruption.

When they neared the altar, Elizabeth was quite interested to perceive that the family pew was of the old variety—completely enclosed to shield the family from the *hoi polloi*. She remembered that her father had said the church at Longbourn had once had such a structure. Papa said it had been in such poor repair—his uncle being such a skinflint; that when the door had fallen off during a service, his uncle had the whole structure demolished rather than fix it. Mr Bennet had repined his uncle's false economy—declaring he would have welcomed the opportunity to fall asleep during some of Mr Hammond's more long-winded sermons. As a child, Elizabeth wished she had been there when the door had fallen off for the sake of the spectacle and to see the reaction of the rector.

Once Elizabeth and Darcy had settled in the pew, the aged clergyman ascended the high pulpit. He preached a sermon on the benefits of marriage before offering Mr and Mrs Darcy his sincere congratulations. Some scattered applause and a hurrah broke out before a stern look from the parson restored order. He then called for the hymn, which was *Love Divine*.

Elizabeth quickly discovered her husband sang in a rich baritone, and she accompanied him softly so she might listen to it. Behind her, she could also hear that Finn had a beautiful tenor voice.

Afterwards they followed the parson down the aisle into the bright morning sunlight. Darcy introduced Elizabeth to Father Ben, who welcomed her personally to Derbyshire. It transpired that the clergyman knew Mr Hammond, the rector of Longbourn, having studied with him at Oxford, and asked her to direct his greetings to her former parish priest.

When the tenants streamed out of the church behind them, a cluster of boys congregated to one side. Their purpose became apparent after Darcy bid the parson farewell. When Finn emptied a small purse full of shillings into his master's hand, Darcy tossed them into the scrum. The boys dived about to catch the largesse, to the general entertainment of the crowd.

Offering Elizabeth his arm, Darcy escorted her to the house for breakfast.

"You look very fine today, Elizabeth," Darcy remarked as they took their seats at table. "Dare, I say, *just like a princess?*"

Elizabeth smiled. "That was very funny, was it not? I'm sure it tops the time a very young Lydia asked loudly why the rector was wearing a dress."

Darcy smiled in return, sanguine that Lydia was far away.

After breakfast, he surprised Elizabeth by offering to stroll with her in the formal garden. They donned their coats once more and began traversing the paths as Darcy explained the design of the garden, which had been one of his mother's chief occupations.

"And how else did your mother spend her time?" asked Elizabeth, curious to learn more.

"Mostly over there," said Darcy, pointing to the far end of the family wing. "You see the glassed turret at the end? It was her observatory. She was interested in astronomy. Her younger brother is the Astronomer Royal."

"Your uncle is the Astronomer Royal?" asked Elizabeth incredulously. "Did you tell my father that?"

"I must admit it was not uppermost in my mind on the few occasions I spoke with him," replied Darcy.

They spent such a pleasant hour in conversation that Elizabeth was loath to say it was rather cold, until she suddenly shuddered. With dismay, Darcy noticed her lips were blue and finally realised she was shivering under her cloak. He apologised for keeping her outside.

Once they returned to the house, it became apparent to Elizabeth that her husband took the Sabbath most seriously and did not intend to disappear into his study, as had been his daily custom so far.

They spent a pleasant day in the library, even taking their midday meal together there and reading companionably for some time—he occupied with a book on ancient Egypt; and she, with a novel that had been sent by her aunt, of three sisters living with their mother in straightened circumstances.

In the afternoon Elizabeth decided to finish hemming one of the shawls, and Darcy offered to read some Scottish poetry to her. As the light failed before dinner, they played several games of backgammon, enough to establish they were evenly matched in strategy, leaving only the dice to determine the game. On the whole, it proved the most satisfying day Elizabeth had yet spent at Pemberley.

On Monday morning, Jenny raised the spectre of the coming Tuesday. She had just finished attiring her mistress for the day when she produced a peach silk gown, presumably another of Miss Georgie's cast-offs.

"Ma'am, I was wondering if this might serve as a night dress? It would go well with your wrap."

It had not occurred to Elizabeth to change her cambric nightgown, even after her husband's criticism of it. In all her life, she had never worn anything else to bed.

"It looks rather fine for a nightgown," she remarked, examining the garment. It was sleeveless and was clearly only part of an ensemble. "Where is the rest of it?"

"It was worn with a chemisette and a net overdress," replied Jenny, "but Miss Georgie's niece chucked up on the overdress and ruined it, and Miss Georgie still wears the chemisette."

Elizabeth considered the gown. It was a summer gown and looked very flimsy. "What do the other married women wear over at Matlock?" she asked her maid.

"Well, the countess just wears comfy cambric like you do, ma'am," replied Jenny, "but the viscountess, who sometimes visits, wears silk gowns. I waited on her once when her maid was sick. And some of the other ladies who visit—friends of the earl—they have terribly fine things. I've waited on a few of them, too. They have the most amazing nightgowns, expensive diaphanous things."

Jenny giggled, before continuing: "Some of them are a bit scandalous, but they *are* very beautiful."

Friends of the earl? Elizabeth wondered. She supposed they must be the wives of other peers. "Very well," she replied. "I'll try it on for size tonight, Jenny."

After breakfast, Darcy once again disappeared into his study. Elizabeth spent the day reading and writing; the weather was too miserable to venture outside. She did not see her husband again until dinner, when he apologised for spending the day with his steward.

Lizzy tried on the peach gown before bed. It was rather loose but she decided it looked well enough and would be uncomfortable to sleep in if it were any tighter.

"I'll wear it on Tuesday, Jenny, but I'll stick with my cambric tonight."

"Tuesday, ma'am?"

"Yes, Jenny, Tuesday."

"Oh!" said her maid, finally twigging.

The weather outside continued to be execrable, and Tuesday marched by in a similar fashion to Monday. Lizzy was heartily glad her aunt had loaned her the novel. It was too cold to venture outside.

On Tuesday evening after dinner, Jenny helped her out of her dinner gown and into the slip, for the gown was little more. Then she brushed out Elizabeth's hair, suggesting they leave it loose rather than confining it in the usual plait. Lizzy's hair was thick and glossy, and Jenny did not think it would become too tangled.

Feeling hopelessly underdressed, Elizabeth pulled on her wrap and climbed into bed to finish the book her aunt had sent, which had been far more entertaining than *The Satyricon*. Yet, as she turned the last page, she felt quite dissatisfied with the ending. She had hoped Elinor would marry the colonel, but he ended up with the flighty sister—whom Elizabeth could not approve of—while she thought the undiscerning and indecisive Edward somehow deserved his Lucy, who, like Elizabeth's own mother, could not read.

However, Elizabeth did not have time to dwell on it for long before there was a knock at the sitting room door. Hastily disposing of her wrap, Lizzy bid her husband come in and waited in some trepidation.

When Darcy rapped lightly on the door to his wife's bedchamber, it was with the confidence of a man who knew himself to be an experienced lover, a man who had broken the ice with his bride, a man for whom the unprecedented events of last week's disappointing wedding night were a one-off occurrence which he had attributed to his nervous lack of familiarity with his new wife. His confidence lasted two steps into the room. Gone was the girl in the cambric gown. On the bed was a siren in a peach silk gown that barely covered her generous breasts. Dark tresses spilled over her shoulders.

Darcy stopped dead in his tracks and blushed with all the embarrassment of a man caught staring salaciously at his wife. Then regaining command of himself, he took a deep breath and moved forward to blow out the single candle on the vacant side of the bed, indicating that his wife should do likewise to the candelabrum on her side.

Removing his banyan, he slipped into bed beside her. After reaching for her shoulder, Darcy slid nearer and feathered some light kisses on her lips. When Elizabeth sighed into his mouth, he pulled her closer, and his hand slipped down her arm, bringing the strap of her gown with it. The sight of her naked shoulder inflamed him.

Now acquainted with what occurred in the marriage bed, Elizabeth held no fears and did her best to appease her husband. She didn't squeak when he grabbed the cheek of her bottom and was so bold as to slide her hand under the back of his nightgown and mimic his action. She discovered he had a lightly furred behind that felt *very* firm. She supposed it must be all that riding. Her action provoked an exclamation from him, halfway between a groan and a sigh that tickled her ear.

After petting and stroking her a little between kisses, Darcy nuzzled her cheek as he introduced himself into her, before raising himself up on his palms to bear down on her with his weight. There was no pain, only an increasing sense of accommodation as he pushed repeatedly against her, until Lizzy felt they could be no closer.

Accepting this oneness, Elizabeth's hips began to undulate in sympathy with Darcy's movements; and from his backside, she ran her fingertips up his spine. This proved too much for Darcy. Groaning again, his thrusts became more urgent, and he bore down on her relentlessly, peaking in a short frenzy, before collapsing on top of her in the now familiar paroxysm.

With a cry of frustration, he brought his fist down on the pillow an inch from Elizabeth's nose. She could only be glad she had not decided to move in that direction. Lying pinned by his weight, Lizzy wondered at the source of his displeasure.

When he withdrew, Darcy gave a dissatisfied sigh and rolled away from her. Lizzy sidled from the wet patch and cast an anxious glance at his back. Had she committed some solecism?

"Fitzwilliam?"

"Yes, Elizabeth," he answered without turning.

"Did I do something wrong?" she asked.

He sighed and then rolled over to face her. *How did one tell one's wife not to squirm so enticingly?* "No, dear, of course not," he replied, without elaborating.

A silence stretched between them.

"It did not hurt," she offered him consolingly.

This comment, which was meant to set him at ease, only caused him mortification.

"One might hope for something more than lack of pain," Darcy said bitterly, before rolling away from her once more.

She heard his soft snore soon after and realised he had fallen asleep. Listening to the sound of his breathing, Elizabeth soon followed him into slumber.

Darcy woke an hour or so later to discover that his wife, once more, had clamped herself to his back. He could only wonder at her willingness to be so intimate with him, despite her state of relative innocence. He peeled her fingers from his shoulder next to the mattress and slid the arm that had encircled his waist down his back, before rolling over to face her.

It had been his intention to slip out of bed and return to his chamber, but the sight of his wife in the dim firelight stopped him. Her beautiful dark hair was splayed on the pillow. Long lashes rested on her cheek. His eyes drifted to her lush décolletage, and he noticed the strap of her gown, which he had pulled down, still encircling her naked shoulder. He felt himself stir.

Reaching out, Darcy carefully pulled the strap back onto her shoulder, shutting down the animal instincts that had been roused. He knew he should go, lest he be roused again. Then, without quite knowing why, he lay back down beside his wife. Giving her a nudge, Darcy encouraged her to roll away from him, which she did most compliantly in her sleep. Then, snuggling up to her back, he rested his chin on her shoulder, bringing his hand round her waist to cup her uppermost breast.

Sighing, Darcy fell back asleep.

27 Greensleeves

Darcy woke again an hour before dawn. Knowing he would not be able to return to sleep, he rose and pulled on his banyan. Then checking his wife was covered by the blankets, he stirred the fire and added a log to the embers before returning to his own bedchamber via the frigid sitting room.

After building up his own fire in the hearth, he performed his ablutions with the cold water in the dressing room, then pulled on the riding clothes Finn had laid out for him the night before in anticipation of a disturbed night. There was no point, Darcy had reasoned with his valet, in them both losing sleep.

He pulled out his notebook to pass the last half-hour pre-dawn in front of the fire before ringing for his horse, picking up his crop, and heading down the stairs.

Healy had almost arrived at the courtyard steps leading his horse when Darcy skipped down them. Ajax snorted in satisfaction upon perceiving his master, eager to be off on a gallop.

As Darcy headed off across the near paddock, the rain came mizzling down; but in his greatcoat and with an old tricorn of his father's on his head, he hardly noticed. Ajax was similarly heedless, glad to be temporarily out of the confines of his warm stable. For now he could kick up his hocks—oats and a rubdown awaited him at the end of his spree.

Elizabeth was piqued to awake alone once more. She had vague memories of being warm most of the night but had woken up near dawn from the chill. Fitzwilliam was gone.

On the whole, she thought Jane a far superior bed buddy: she didn't abandon her during the coldest part of the night, punch pillows, or soil the sheets; and she stayed long enough to say good morning.

As the fire in the hearth was burning well, Elizabeth assumed the chambermaid had already done her rounds. Pulling the blankets closer around her, she rolled over and went back to sleep.

There was no sign of Elizabeth at breakfast, and rather disappointed, Darcy sat down to his porridge alone. His thoughts were not sanguine. While he had managed to inseminate his wife a second time, the act had hardly been a stellar example of connubial felicity. Worse still, he had failed to behave like a gentleman afterwards, responding grumpily when Elizabeth had tried to set him at his ease. Clearly she had no idea that the act could be pleasurable, and just as clearly, this was *his* fault. In focusing on his own lack of staying power, he had failed to attend to her needs.

Diane had taught him plenty of tricks, but these were not related to conception; and as such, he had decided prior to his wedding to leave them in his slightly sordid past. In retrospect, he could not help feeling he should have employed some of them last night—if for no other reason than to save his pride.

Leaving the table, Darcy walked slowly along the hall towards his study, praying that he might encounter his wife coming down for breakfast; but he crossed the great desert of the vestibule and arrived at the study door without even glimpsing a servant.

His hand lingered on the handle while he waited, hoping to hear her voice in the stairwell, when a legitimate excuse to seek her company occurred to him—he had yet to give her his mother's jewels. Retrieving them from the safe near his desk, Darcy went in search of his wife.

Jenny had once more prepared the bath for her mistress. Lizzy cautiously stepped over the side of the tub and tested the water with her toe. Despite the steam, the temperature of the water was tolerable, although far warmer than the lukewarm swill she was used to bathing in once a month at Longbourn. Climbing in and sitting down in the water with a splash, she began to wash herself with the soap while her maid prepared to shampoo her hair.

After retrieving the toiletries and arranging the towels, Jenny looked at the service door in frustration. "I'm sorry, ma'am," she apologized. "I don't know what's happened to the footmen with the rinse water. I'll be back in a moment."

Stepping into the narrow corridor, Jenny closed the door softly behind her.

Elizabeth splashed her feet a little, marvelling again at how big the tub was. *Why, I believe I could lie down with my legs outstretched with room to spare!* Slipping down, she tested her theory.

Lizzy had never been swimming or bathed in water more than a few inches deep, so the sensations of immersing herself in the warm water and the buoyancy of it were new to her. *Such luxury!* She imagined she was Elaine of Astolat, floating down the Thames, rejected by her neglectful lover. This made her smile slightly at her own silliness. Although she was still annoyed about being abandoned before daybreak, Elizabeth was hardly pining over Darcy, who was certainly no charming Sir Lancelot. She was also sure the Thames was not so deliciously warm.

Laying her head back cautiously, Elizabeth closed her eyes as she immersed her ears, listening as the thickness of the water enveloped her, until she found she could rest her head on the bottom of the tub without submerging her nose. Reaching one hand up, Lizzy ran her fingers through the hair floating freely around her crown; then released the rest of her mane by lifting her shoulders.

Well, this is certainly a far superior way to wash one's hair! she thought. *No bending over basins while someone pours tepid water over your head!* She gave a small sigh of satisfaction and began to softly hum *Greensleeves*.

Darcy walked through the sitting room and knocked lightly on Elizabeth's bedchamber door. Receiving no answer, he entered and found it empty; but hearing the voices of his wife and her maid, continued through to the threshold of the dressing room and called softly into it. When there was no reply, he walked through the open door and, finding no one about there either, cautiously poked his head into the bathing room. Steam was rising from the tub, but of his wife and her maid there was no evidence. *Perhaps they left through the service door? How strange.*

Intrigued, Darcy entered the empty room to investigate the mystery of his wife's disappearance. Towels were laid out, unused. The floor was not wet. Reaching the tub, the conundrum was solved: lying full-length in the bottom was his wife, or a water nymph—he was not sure which. Her head was almost completely submerged, the water lapping at her cheekbones. Her long hair streamed out around her head like seaweed, and there was a small smile playing on her lips. As he watched, spellbound, she started humming softly to herself.

His eyes raked down over two nipples like carmine rosebuds, just poking above the water from her rounded and flattened breasts, to the impossibly narrow waist accentuated by the low navel, filled with water like some small grotto. He dwelt on the thatch of black hair, darker than her chestnut locks, before proceeding to the rounded and well-formed muscles of her thighs and calves, and thence to the tiny ankles and dainty feet. He felt himself harden instantly.

Elizabeth, suddenly prescient that she was not alone, opened her eyes, and seeing her husband staring at her, sat up abruptly with a splash.

The voyeur quickly retreated.

"I beg your pardon," Darcy said hastily over his shoulder as he disappeared into her bedchamber.

Lizzy collapsed against the side of the copper tub, hiding her nakedness from she knew not whom. Her husband was perfectly entitled to look at her, and he'd gone off anyway. There was no need for silly palpitations, but she had trouble stilling her heart for all that. She subsided once more into the tub, silently scolding herself for turning into her mother, but it was impossible to recapture her earlier calm.

"I'm sorry, ma'am," said Jenny, re-entering the room. "They're just coming with the extra pails now. I'm not sure what the trouble was."

"That's all right, Jenny," replied Elizabeth. "If you could just wash my hair, I think I'm almost ready to get out."

Once Elizabeth dressed, she returned to her bedchamber to eat her breakfast while her maid dried and styled her hair. When there was a knock at the door, Jenny opened it to find Finn standing there with a large decorative box.

"Miss Hitchin," announced Finn in a very formal tone; "the master thought you would like the Darcy jewels. He asked me to convey his apologies for not presenting them earlier."

"Thank you, Mr Finn," replied Jenny in kind, solemnly accepting the box.

After she closed the door, Jenny carefully placed the box near Elizabeth's breakfast tray before doing a little dance of glee. "Oh, ma'am, can we open it?" she chirped.

"Of course, Jenny," said Elizabeth, smiling at her maid's antics. "Let's see what treasures the Darcy coffers hold."

As a note had arrived the previous day from Madame Lafrange advising that some of Elizabeth's dresses were ready for their final fitting, Jenny dressed her mistress for the outing to Lambton. Lizzy was attired in a very pretty peach gown with a matching carriage cloak. Having sent a letter requesting her Aunt Amelia's company once more, to which her aunt had duly replied with another invitation to tea, Lizzy had set the finished novel next to her reticule, so she would not forget to return it.

The weather had cooperated nicely with the warmest day since their arrival in Derbyshire; but as it was approaching Christmas, this was obviously an anomaly. As she sat in the carriage watching Pemberley retreat into the distance, Lizzy rued her luck in having wasted the best day for a ramble since her arrival. It was clear she was going to have to find some way to exercise indoors. Suddenly remembering her unused chatelaine, she mentally apostrophised herself as a ninny-hammer for not appreciating the entertainment possibilities of finding the doors to match the keys. Recalling her Sunday walk with her husband, she instantly resolved to find the astronomy tower at the next opportunity.

In Lambton, Lizzy's aunt and her companion had once more set out a delightful morning tea that they all consumed while discussing the novel. Miss Dorsey jokingly bemoaned the lack of Colonel Brandon-like gentleman in the vicinity, and they spent a pleasant half-hour discussing the book's plot before Lizzy and her Aunt Amelia headed out to the dressmaker.

A small incident occurred upon leaving when Elizabeth caught her gown on the garden gate, resulting in a tiny tear, which she attributed to her own lack of attention. Her aunt apologised profusely for the state of the latch, but Elizabeth was eventually able to mollify her by pointing out that her carriage cloak effectively covered the flaw and by reassuring her that

Jenny was a first-rate needlewoman.

They proceeded to the dressmaker's on foot, where Elizabeth tried on half-a-dozen gowns—several of them altered gowns of Miss Darcy's, but also two gowns made up from the Gardiners' silks. One of the new gowns had been strikingly fashioned by Madame Lafrange in an unusual design. Elizabeth thought the dressmaker very clever when she explained her adoption of the bold design to complement the linear motif on the brocade she called a sari.

Seeing Mrs Darcy was impressed with her work, Madame Lafrange encouraged her to wear the new gown home, offering to mend the small tear in the gown Elizabeth had been wearing, gratis. When Elizabeth demurred, pointing out that her carriage cloak hardly matched the new garment, her Aunt Amelia offered a cloak of her own which she thought would suit it admirably; and before Elizabeth could protest, Jenny had been dispatched to her aunt's house with instructions for Miss Dorsey to retrieve it.

Madame had a slightly nefarious purpose in suggesting this small service to her prestigious customer for free—she intended to borrow yet another design from Miss Darcy's London modiste.

All was soon settled, and Elizabeth dutifully donned her aunt's opera cloak before returning to the carriage. Upon parting from her aunt, Lizzy extended an invitation to Pemberley, but Aunt Amelia was steadfast in denying the visit during Elizabeth's first fortnight in residence, insisting Mr Darcy would not thank her for imposing her maiden aunt upon his household during his honeymoon. Instead, Aunt Amelia promised to visit as soon as she may, and a tentative arrangement was made to send the Darcy coach for the projected trip—her aunt and her companion not keeping a carriage, but instead hiring the Tilbury kept at the Rose and Crown whenever they ventured further than the village, which was not often.

Arriving home to find her husband had gone out with Pemberley's steward, Elizabeth returned alone to her bedchamber where she ate a late lunch from a tray in front of the hearth.

Rather than having any urgent business on the estate, the truth was that Darcy had not felt sufficiently composed to have lunch with his wife after their embarrassing bathing encounter. When, during their morning meeting, his steward had noted that a bridge needed repair in the near future, Darcy suggested they ride out immediately to inspect it.

Elizabeth's own plans to explore the nether regions of the house with her chatelaine were delayed when Mrs Reynolds met her on her return from Lambton, offering to show her the picture gallery after she had eaten.

The gallery was a long thin room on the far side of the saloon that looked out upon the formal garden. The interior wall was painted a striking colour that Elizabeth fancied her uncle had once described as ox-blood. Several generations of Darcys lined the walls, but she was most interested in seeing how her husband had been preserved for posterity.

His portrait was very fine, obviously executed by a leading artist. He cut a handsome figure, his square chin and aristocratic nose captured perfectly; the pale colour of his breeches drawing attention to his shapely legs. His countenance was proud, but she thought it looked more open than the man himself, almost guileless.

"It is a very fine portrait, is it not, Mrs Darcy?" asked the housekeeper.

"Indeed," Elizabeth replied diplomatically. "Was it done recently?"

"Oh, no, ma'am. Quite some time ago, when Fitzwilliam was at Cambridge and old Mr Darcy was still alive. He was as pleased as punch with it—to see his son grown up so handsome. He died suddenly not a year after it was hung here. Such a shame, but he never was the same after Mrs Darcy died. She was the air he breathed."

"They were very close then?" asked Elizabeth.

"Yes, terribly. It was a real love match. She was the ninth Earl of Matlock's daughter and quite a bluestocking. She wasn't interested in getting married at first—didn't want a man telling her what she could and couldn't do. When her father died, she wanted to go keep house for her brother who is the Astronomer Royal. But Mr Darcy courted her so prettily she came round in the end."

"And how old was Fitzwilliam when his mother died?"

"Oh, he was twelve, and Miss Georgie just a baby."

"Did she die in childbed then?" asked Elizabeth.

"No, she caught a chill. She used to be up all night sometimes with her telescope. I tried to get her to wrap up better; it was so cold up there. She never seemed to notice when she was absorbed in her work."

After a respectful pause, Elizabeth diplomatically changed the topic. "And are there no portraits of Miss Georgie?"

"In this room, there is only this miniature which was done when she was a little girl," replied Mrs Reynolds. "She'll have a proper portrait done when she comes out."

Elizabeth walked over to view the miniature the housekeeper pointed out. It was one in a group of three, which looked to be the work of a local artist. One of the other miniatures was probably her husband as a youth, but the resemblance was not strong.

"And who is this other young man?" she asked. "Could it be Colonel Fitzwilliam?"

"Bless you, ma'am. Do you know the colonel? He would laugh to hear you say that. Or maybe not... That is a portrait of Mr Wickham, Mr Darcy's godson. He has the face of an angel, but... well... The colonel is not a handsome man, but his heart is in the right place."

Elizabeth was sure that the housekeeper had been on the verge of saying something else, but had changed her mind. Slightly regretful that Mrs Reynolds had not trusted her enough to talk unguardedly, she was too polite to pursue the matter further.

By the time Darcy finally returned to the house at sunset, he felt in no better command of himself than when he had set out on his unnecessary errand in the morning. He was saved from lamely excusing himself from dinner with a headache by the unexpected arrival of Colonel Fitzwilliam.

Darcy had dismounted at the stables and was walking back to the house when the sound of a horse galloping down the drive made him stop and turn to identify the reckless rider.

"What are *you* doing here?" blurted Darcy when his cousin came within hailing distance.

"Well, that is a nice greeting!" scoffed Colonel Fitzwilliam, pulling his horse up.

"Don't get me wrong; I'm very glad to see you," said Darcy, "but you shouldn't ride hell-for-leather like that down the drive—you'll break your neck."

"Tell that to the horse," retorted Richard, dismounting. "I let him set his own pace. He's been here before and was obviously eager to visit again."

Affirming the colonel's exculpation, the horse attempted to jerk its bridle out of the colonel's grasp when Healy approached from the stables.

"Hello, Belper!" greeted Healy, who received a nudge to direct him back to the stables in reply.

"Belper? That can't possibly be the horse's name," said Darcy, who always thought long and hard about naming his steed.

"Oh, that is a little joke of ours," said the colonel, surrendering the bridle to Healy with a conspiratorial smile. "He is 'Belper' when I'm going North, and 'Sheffield' when I'm going south. That is the name of every horse I mount from those posting houses, but I must admit I'm rather fond of this particular 'Belper'. He is quite a character."

"And what is his real name?" asked Darcy, turning back towards the house with his cousin.

"I don't know," quipped the colonel. "He won't tell me."

Darcy sighed in exasperation.

They crunched along the gravel in silence until Darcy reached the front steps and turned to direct a question at his cousin: "I thought you were taking some time off, before heading back to London."

"That was the plan," said the colonel; "but things changed a little. Let me put my feet up, and I'll tell you about it."

In front of the fire, fortified with a glass of brandy, Richard explained their cousin Anne's illness and subsequent enforced stay at Longbourn.

"So the Harley Street physician was able to make a definite diagnosis?" asked Darcy.

"Yes, apparently she has a condition that affects the working of her heart. That is why she is prone to these fainting fits and general lethargy."

"And is there a cure?"

"No, but he was able to prescribe a treatment more efficacious then any of the medicines she is currently taking. Your wife had a silent hand in that."

"*My wife?*" asked Darcy in confusion.

"Yes, it just so happened that the medicine that revived Anne after her initial fit was sitting in the stillroom at Longbourn. Your wife made it from the leaves of a local plant."

Darcy remembered that Elizabeth had been harvesting simples when he had proposed to her near the river. Perhaps the herbs she had in her hand at that very time had saved his cousin. This seemed ironic or fateful somehow—his bride unwittingly saving his 'jilted' cousin.

"The physician had the distillate tested," the colonel continued, "and it was apparently more pure than his own supply. He wanted to start purchasing it from the local apothecary, but both of the women who helped produce it are getting hitched, or *got* in the case of your wife."

"So why have you left Hertfordshire prematurely?" asked Darcy, dragging himself from his philosophical musings and retreating once more behind his wall of apparent indifference. "Did you find the local populace deadly boring?"

"No," said the colonel, rolling his eyes. "It just got rather crowded at Longbourn."

"How many constitutes a crowd? Don't tell me—your father is still there and you argued with him?"

"No, no, we were getting along quite amicably—*for once*—but yes, he stayed at Netherfield to ensure that Anne got proper care."

"Well, that is good of him. I must admit I'm a little surprised," conceded Darcy.

"Yes, well, I suspect Father's sudden solicitude for Anne is partly driven by a need to ensure the succession to the Rosings estate. But I honestly don't think he was aware how poorly Anne was. He was truly shocked at the condition in which she arrived at your wedding, *and* at Aunt's callous disregard for her wellbeing. I was carrying her round the house, Darcy. She was out like a light and weighs no more than a chicken."

"So is Aunt Catherine also staying at Netherfield?" asked Darcy.

"No, Aunt is currently occupying Father's London townhouse. She refuses to return to Hertfordshire, but sends daily messages to Longbourn demanding the release of her daughter—as if the Bennets had kidnapped her! These communications are delivered by her parson, who spends most of his day in the parlour at Longbourn, but who stays at Lucas Lodge."

"I see. So I suppose both you and your father have been visiting Longbourn daily as well."

"Yes, Mrs Bennet has graciously provided lunch for us every day, or *ungraciously* in the case of Mr Collins. The three of us might have been considered a sufficient imposition on Mrs Bennet's resources, but two days after you left, Bingley and his sisters returned."

"*Reeeaaally?*" drawled Darcy. "I thought Caroline was *indisposed.*"

"She made a *miraculous* recovery," returned his cousin in kind, "and insisted on supporting her brother at Netherfield while the earl is staying."

Darcy harrumphed. "And how did she discover that piece of information?"

"I was obliged to drop in to ask Bingley if my father might stay at Netherfield when I went to fetch the Harley Street physician. Bingley *did* leave the house at my disposal, but it seemed the polite thing to do."

"You have been busy," remarked Darcy.

"Not as busy as I might have been," clucked the colonel.

"And what do you mean by that remark?" enquired his cousin.

"Darcy, I've taken a liking to Jane Bennet, and I mean to court her if I may."

"So you are the latest victim of the beauty," observed Darcy. "And what does Bingley have to say of this?"

"Nothing. He has resumed his place at her side, when he may, for Jane spends many hours with Anne in her bedchamber and only comes down when she is relieved by Miss Lucas, or one of the other silly Bennet sisters. That is why I have come away. I can hardly court her when Bingley is sitting in her pocket."

"Indeed, and Charles may object to you courting her at all when he is so intent on it himself."

"I have no fear of it. He is such a harum-scarum fellow. He will soon be distracted or dragged off by his sister, who thinks the Bennets are beneath her, though the shoe is definitely on the other foot with respect to the elder Bennets. My only fear is that Jane will be taken-in by his overtures. She has such a tender heart."

"She is insipid," said Darcy dismissively.

"No, you wrong her. If you could see how she has taken care of Anne, you would acknowledge her superior qualities. I confess I was originally drawn to her by her beauty, but she has now captivated me with her soft and caring ways. I could find no better woman if I searched the world."

"High praise, indeed," said Darcy, surprised to see his normally happy-go-lucky cousin so lovesick. "So will you stay with us for dinner?"

"If you don't consider it an imposition on your honeymoon; otherwise I will ride back to Matlock before heading north in the morning. My main mission in coming here was to deliver two letters from Jane to her sister."

"No doubt she will be very glad of them," replied Darcy. "I must admit you have relieved my mind. When Elizabeth told me of Jane's first letter, I was sure that my aunt had made a scene which Elizabeth's sister would not relate to spare her feelings."

"No, my father spared us a full-blown tantrum by dragging Aunt outside, and I believe the discovery of Anne's condition somewhat shamed her into holding her tongue—at least, she was required to use it to defend her own actions in dragging her ill daughter all the way from Kent."

"What a relief he intervened!" sighed Darcy. "I was afraid she would claim there was a pre-existing arrangement, and insist the marriage be annulled or some such side-show."

"Well, I'm afraid she did get a few words out to that effect in the parlour before Father stopped her. She wanted to send me off in pursuit of you."

Darcy blushed in mortification.

"I apologise for not being able to stop her mouth," lamented the colonel, "but short of tackling her, I'm still not sure what I could have done. Despite being thirty, I still feel rather cowed by the old biddy from being yelled at when I was in short coats."

"Now you are just trying to make me laugh," said Darcy.

"Possibly," said the colonel, "but I tell you she struck more terror in me when I was a boy than French troops ever did."

Upon preparing for dinner, Elizabeth had decided to wear the new sari dress and a matching gold shawl. But when a message was sent up advising that the colonel had arrived and would be staying 'til morning, Jenny worried that a more conventional dress might be more appropriate.

"I'm sure the colonel isn't fussy, Jenny," reassured Elizabeth. "You must have met him before, when you were working at Matlock."

"It's not the colonel's opinion I'm worried about, ma'am. Mr Darcy will expect you to be extra-fine for guests."

Elizabeth was about to say she was not about to change her dress to suit her husband's notions of pomp and circumstance, when a more diplomatic solution occurred to her. "Perhaps if we added some jewellery, Jenny? Do you think that would help?"

"Oh yes, ma'am," her maid replied enthusiastically.

Upon searching the jewel box to find something suitable, Elizabeth immediately picked out some gold filigree bracelets she had admired in the morning, while Jenny's eye alighted on some lapis earrings that matched the blue of the sari admirably.

Tricked out in her gauds, Elizabeth descended to the dining room, wending her way via the roundabout route of the library.

"Well, you didn't tell me you had married an Indian princess, Darcy!" declared the colonel gallantly as she walked into the room.

"She has been declared a princess, but I was under the impression she was *English* not Indian," replied Darcy.

"What's this?" asked the colonel, bemused.

"Oh, something amusing one of the tenant's children said when we were in church," laughed Elizabeth.

"You have not given the tale its due, my dear," replied Darcy, almost causing Elizabeth to start at his use of this term of endearment.

"We were walking down the aisle of the church, with all curious eyes on us—you could have heard a penny drop—when Jem Miller's youngest daughter blurts out: *Is she a princess, mummy?*" mimicked Darcy in a very creditable falsetto.

Elizabeth stared at her husband. She was not aware that he was a comedian. The colonel guffawed appropriately.

They sat down to a very creditable meal during which Richard regaled the Darcys with an amusing account of the goings-on at the wedding breakfast after their departure, suitably sanitised of any mention of Aunt Catherine. He made much of the dancing and the short walk he had enjoyed with Jane, paying her many pretty compliments.

"But this cannot be all that happened, Colonel," protested Elizabeth. "Jane told me your cousin arrived ill at Longbourn. I regret we departed too early to meet her."

"Aye," conceded the colonel, "and she also expressed a regret at not meeting you. She was still at Longbourn ere I left, and in her bed, but there was some talk of taking her out to the sitting room if the doctor considered her sufficiently recovered."

The conversation continued so convivially, that for the first time since her arrival, Elizabeth began to feel she might be at home. Once the dessert had been removed, it was with regret that she got up to withdraw, asking the men to join her in the library when they were done.

This they both gladly assented to—the cosiness of that room being more appealing to them than the formal withdrawing room next door. But before Elizabeth left, the colonel remembered the letters he had been charged to deliver and sheepishly handed them over, apologising for not doing so upon first encountering her.

Elizabeth accepted them gladly, saying she now had some proper entertainment in her solitude, before laughingly departing.

Darcy poured out the brandy and the cousins spoke of their relative business, as was their custom: Darcy of fences and tenants, and the colonel of the other officers' peccadilloes, which was his chief occupation during peacetime.

It struck Richard during the course of this conversation that Darcy was more reserved in his wife's presence, despite his initial attempt at joviality when she had entered the dining room. But given their short relationship, he supposed this was not unnatural.

When they entered the library half an hour later, Elizabeth got up from her letters and rang for tea. She'd had time, of course, to read Jane's missives several times over, and was now busy inferring what was *not* on the pages from what was.

Returning to her seat, she glanced at the chessboard and exclaimed, "Why, Colonel, you have finally made your move! Fitzwilliam told me he had given up all hope of any action on your part."

"But I am a man of action, Cousin Elizabeth!" fenced Richard, before adding, "I hope I do not presume too much in calling you so?"

"Not at all, *Cousin Richard,* if I do not do so!" she replied.

Meanwhile, Darcy, who had stolidly ignored this raillery, moved to the chessboard to study the pieces.

"I do not know what you hope to gain by moving your bishop, Richard," he said. "This game had run its course months ago."

Behind her husband's back, Elizabeth winked at the colonel.

Richard, who knew he had not touched the chessboard, but who was always quick to perceive any other type of game, replied, "Well, I *did* tell you I was thinking, Darcy."

By the time tea arrived, Darcy had made his next move, and he sat down with Richard to a game of piquet, while Elizabeth picked up a play of Sheridan's and proceeded to regale them with a spirited reading. Her performance had Richard in stitches, and Darcy griping that his cousin was not playing proper attention to his cards.

Thus a very pleasant evening was passed.

28 Exploration and adventure

When Darcy came down for his morning ride on Thursday, he detoured via the chessboard and was surprised to find that Richard had already made another move; or to be more accurate, another *useless* move. Wondering if his cousin had spent a sleepless night coming up with this latest piece of ingenuity, he contemplated the board briefly before moving his own piece and heading out to his horse.

Before retiring on the previous night, Elizabeth had enquired of the colonel when he expected to be off in the morning and whether he intended to return to Longbourn. After assuring her that he would stay for breakfast, Richard replied that he hoped to visit Longbourn for as long as his cousin Anne remained there; and if she had any correspondence ready for her sister, he would be glad to take it with him.

Thus Elizabeth rose early and, after Jenny had attired her for breakfast, she sat down to finish her letter to Jane. She mentally reviewed all that had occurred since her pen had last touched the paper, choosing anecdotes or facts that might amuse or interest her sister, glossing over the slightly chilly relationship with her husband, and then letting the ink flow.

But her mind took a different path from her pen, recalling her husband's use of the term "my dear" yesterday when his cousin had arrived. Elizabeth had been a little shocked to hear these words issue from his lips after their conversation at Kingsthorpe, initially jumping to the conclusion that he had employed the term ironically as a cruel jest. But she almost immediately perceived her mistake in ascribing her father's behaviour to her husband. She recalled observing that guileless expression in his portrait. It seemed more likely that Darcy had completely forgotten his promise not to call her thus, and that he merely wished to pretend a better state of marital felicity to his cousin than actually existed.

She then began to dwell on how different her husband was in the presence of his cousin: gone were the stiffness and distance that had characterised his interactions with the Bennet sisters, and, yes, she had to include the Bingley ladies as well. Instead, his whole aspect seemed to relax, exhibiting a camaraderie and gentle sense of humour. But before she could ascribe his less pleasant aspect to misogyny, she remembered her observations of him with Mr Bingley and realised *that* relationship also lacked ease. She shook her head. *What a conundrum her husband was!* Just when she had congratulated herself that she had managed to understand human nature before attaining her majority, along came a character who defied categorisation. No doubt to puncture her hubris! What a fitting punishment the Fates had arranged for her—to be tied to him for eternity...

Concluding her letter with salutations to the rest of her family before folding and sealing it, Elizabeth descended to breakfast via the library.

The previous night, after they had all retired, she had snuck down to the library in her nightgown via the sitting room stairs to view Darcy's response to her first move. Satisfied he was not yet wise to her purpose, she had then moved her bishop again.

Viewing the board in the morning light, she saw he had already responded and moved one of her pawns.

Entering the breakfast room at quarter to eight, Elizabeth found Richard Fitzwilliam at leisure, reading the morning paper from Derby over a cup of tea.

"Good morning, Colonel," she said brightly.

"Now, now, Cousin Elizabeth, what have I done wrong? I thought we had decided on *Cousin Richard*," he said, folding up the paper and putting it aside.

"I beg your pardon, *Cousin Richard*. I quite forgot myself," she replied with a smile.

"So, before Darcy comes in," he said, lowering his voice conspiratorially; "do you entertain any hopes of actually *winning* that chess game?"

"Well," she returned in kind, "it *is* a bit of a long shot, but if Fitzwilliam continues to believe himself unassailable, I *may* be able to do it. Let us say the game would not be unparalleled."

"So you fancy yourself an aficionado of chess?" asked the colonel, leaning back in his chair.

"I have played several thousand games with my father, who was a master of the game at Oxford. He has declared me 'not contemptible'."

"Indeed? Then this could be interesting," smiled Richard, before taking a sip of his tea.

When Darcy entered the room at eight, he found Elizabeth talking affectionately of Jane while his cousin attended, rapt.

The three broke their fast over the next half-hour with all the amiability of friends of some years' standing, and it was with regret that the colonel called for his horse.

Richard was gratified when Elizabeth produced her letter and thanked him for taking the trouble to deliver it. It suited him well to cultivate this role of courier, for it would give him a legitimate excuse to visit Longbourn after his cousin Anne departed. Elizabeth's gratitude was icing on the cake.

As Richard pocketed the missive, Darcy protested that he thought himself rich enough to pay to receive the post, but his cousin dismissed this blithely with "Waste not, want not."

"So you do not intend to return here on your way south?" Darcy asked his cousin as they took their leave of Elizabeth and walked to the vestibule.

"I would not wish to impose further during your honeymoon," said his cousin, watching Darcy covertly as he pretended to pay all his attention to fitting his spurs to his boots.

Darcy had turned his face away, but his cousin could see his lips working as he rehearsed some speech in his mind. A footman helped the colonel don his roquelaure and handed him his chapeau-bras.

"It is not an imposition," Darcy finally replied. "It is only for a night, and I am sure Elizabeth enjoyed your company last night just as much as I always do."

"Excellent," said the colonel, heading down the steps. "You know I always love to visit, and Pemberley is so much more comfortable than that pile of stones at Matlock."

And with this dismissal of his childhood home, Richard Fitzwilliam mounted his horse and headed for Newcastle.

After watching his cousin until he disappeared round the bend in the drive, Darcy reluctantly took himself off.

Elizabeth spent the rest of the morning poring over yet more fashion magazines with Jenny, prompted by their satisfaction with the additional gowns that had been delivered by Madame Lafrange subsequent to Wednesday's final fitting. They had decided to entrust her with more of the silks.

She took lunch with her husband, who began, once more, to lapse into awkward silences between sentences. Elizabeth was having a little trouble filling in the rest of the conversation. Her mind was still full of fashion from her morning's employment, though she dared not discourse on that topic. Knowing her father's distaste of frills and furbelows, fashion—she was sure—was firmly in the category of vacuous conversation. She already missed Darcy's cousin. *At least,* she thought, *the colonel's visit reduced the awkwardness of encountering my husband after the bathing incident.*

Darcy, however, was having more trouble coming to terms with their unplanned rendezvous. Every time he looked at his wife, his mind seemed to strip off her clothes. As he ate his lunch, he imagined her slim form sitting there naked next to him at the dining table. He tried to focus on her face, and particularly the words coming from her mouth, but that became dangerous too, because all he really wanted to do was kiss those lips.

They parted after the meal without regret: he, glad to be rid of his wife's disturbing company, to his study; she, to her bedchamber, to prepare for her afternoon project.

Jenny helped her out of the new gown she had worn down to breakfast, and this was put aside to wear to dinner. Elizabeth donned one of her older day gowns and a cloak. Then, retrieving the chatelaine from her bedside table, she set out to explore the house.

From the viewpoint of the formal garden, Elizabeth had noted the former Mrs Darcy's observatory abutted the family wing. During her recent return trip from Lambton, she had been able to see from the carriage that the structure was not visible from the front of the house—no turret marred its classic square lines. This caused her to wonder if the observatory was an original part of the newer house, or whether its silo-like structure had been added as an afterthought. Leaving her bedchamber, Elizabeth mentally debated whether she should seek entrance to the observatory from inside the house or external to it.

As the afternoon weather had turned miserable again, she resolved to look inside first, and headed off down the hall, away from the central stairs. She was surprised to find the first door she encountered was locked. *Who locks a door in a hall?* she wondered, slightly annoyed to be thwarted fifty steps into her adventure.

However, upon pulling out the chatelaine, she was gratified to discover that the second key she tried gained her entry. Beyond the door, the hall opened up on one side, and she found herself in a large pleasant sitting room, much more cosy than any of the rooms she had visited downstairs. It felt strangely abandoned, though the air was not stuffy.

Walking further into the room, she surveyed it. The hearth was completely clear of ashes as if it was not used, although there were partly burnt candles on the mantel. The furniture had a light film of dust, suggesting it was cleaned regularly but not often.

A half-finished tapestry stood in a frame next to the hearth with a thread hanging from it, but no needle or workbox was apparent. On an easel next to the window sat a botanical painting in watercolours, but no paints or brushes were evident.

Elizabeth's attention was then drawn to several portraits on the walls, which included a number of kit-kats of children. These were less fine than the portraits she had viewed in the gallery downstairs. It was only when she noticed the beautifully drawn eyes in a portrait of an older boy that she recognised her husband. Stepping back, she realised she was looking at the last in a time series of paintings that became progressively more sophisticated; and she guessed these to be the work of an amateur artist who had improved with practice. There were a number of knickknacks about the room, but none of them looked contemporary. Some of these were toys suitable for older children.

Everything suggested that this was the Darcy family sitting room. Its general cosiness made Elizabeth feel slightly homesick for Longbourn. She wondered that her husband had not shown her the room, for its aspect onto the lake was extremely pleasant. *Perhaps he doesn't favour this place himself?*

She did a circuit of the room, idly looking left and right, before returning to two chairs before the hearth. One of these was leather and looked significantly more worn than the other. A book sat on a side-table near the chair. Wondering if it might have belonged to Mr or Mrs Darcy, Elizabeth picked it up. But upon turning to the flyleaf, she saw it was inscribed with "Fitzwilliam Darcy" and, recalling that Miss Georgiana had been named for her father, realized it was her husband's book.

Replacing the volume and stepping back from the hearth, Elizabeth realised there were two doors symmetrically disposed about it. Castigating herself for becoming distracted from her original goal, she set out to open them. Thinking that the one on the left was least likely to lead to the tower, she tried it first. It was not locked, and led to a nursery that could also be accessed by a set of servants' stairs. Although the furniture remained—a cot and a rocking chair; it was otherwise bereft of any signs of habitation.

Retreating to the sitting room, Elizabeth opened the door to the right of the hearth, but was disappointed to discover that it was only another bedchamber, painted blue. It seemed the observatory must be accessed from elsewhere. Looking around, she perceived this was a boy's room, but unlike the nursery next door, it still looked habitable. There was a counterpane on the bed, and books on a side-table. It seemed likely it had once been Fitzwilliam's.

Elizabeth had turned to leave when she realised that the room felt terribly cold and saw that a window had been left ajar. Walking over, she was about to close the latch, when it occurred to her to poke her head out the window to check the disposition of the observatory from that viewpoint. She discovered she was very close—so close that it appeared to be immediately adjacent to the room she was standing in.

Returning to the sitting room, Elizabeth was about to retreat to the hall to review her options from outside the house, when she spied a tapestry against the adjacent wall. It occurred to her that it might be an arras. Stepping up to it, she pushed it aside to reveal another locked door. Excited, she tried the keys on the chatelaine and was soon through to the next room.

Elizabeth smiled in delight at what she found before her. A large telescope stood in the centre of the room on a dais. It was not long and thin like her father's refractor, but looked more like the barrel of a cannon, mounted within a frame. Moving closer and examining the dais, Lizzy perceived it was suspended above the floor and held in position by a wooden peg. Removing this, she saw the dais could be rotated freely and secured in a new position with the peg.

Above her, the room was illuminated by daylight streaming in through panes of glass in the turret. These were quite dirty, but Elizabeth could see that each was hinged, allowing it to be opened so that every part of the sky save the zenith and the horizon was accessible. Turning back towards the door, she perceived a desk scattered with papers, the whole overlaid with a thick layer of dust. On approaching this, Elizabeth could see that some of the papers were letters, while others were lists and diagrams.

Drifting back towards the telescope, Elizabeth circumnavigated it, contemplating its strange design. Upon observing that the only thing that resembled an eyepiece was partway along the barrel, she deduced that the barrel must contain a mirror to direct the light to the side. Halfway round the instrument, Elizabeth noticed a set of stairs that descended into the tower, and curious, she followed them down.

The next level seemed to contain bookshelves, but it was very dim, lit only by narrow windows that were little more than arrow-slits, and none too clean either. Elizabeth walked around the periphery of the tower, stumbling on something—perhaps a crate—which slid under a table, until she met another flight of stairs. There seemed little point in exploring this level further without a light.

Descending again, she found herself on the ground floor. Light seeped in under a door and through more of the little windows, though it was darker still than the previous level. Approaching the door, Elizabeth saw it was barred, and she lifted this to poke her head outside. The door was concealed on either side by camellia bushes, but it was clear that it admitted to the formal garden. Turning back into the tower, she could now see with the benefit of the light streaming in from outside that the lower level was used for the storage of garden tools. The Dower House was quite close and it occurred to Elizabeth that the tower might actually predate the new house. Closing the door once more, she waited until her eyes had adjusted to the dimness before carefully proceeding upstairs.

Arriving back at the desk, Elizabeth began to pick up the books that were scattered upon it and blowing the dust off them, examined the spines. One of them proved to be a volume on telescope design, and thinking it might prove informative, she did her best to remove the bulk of the dust before carting it off to her bedchamber.

After washing and changing into another old day-gown—for she had become quite grubby during her adventure—Elizabeth spent the afternoon perusing the book. By the time Jenny came to dress her for dinner, Elizabeth had decided that the telescope was some sort of Newtonian reflector, and judging by its size, it must have been at the forefront of enquiry in its time.

At dinner, her husband was once again uncommunicative, but Elizabeth was better prepared for his reticence than she had been at lunch, relating all that Jane had conveyed in her letters. She managed to engage his partial participation in the conversation by asking for Richard's recollection of the events surrounding his cousin Anne's illness.

This second-hand tale Darcy was willing to supply, suitably expurgated of his aunt's callous behaviour, although he was unable to properly account for her continued absence from Longbourn. He therefore invented a fictitious accident that had befallen Lady Catherine in London, whence she had travelled to procure a doctor for her daughter. Fortunately Elizabeth didn't press him on the topic, and Darcy thought he had managed to imbue this farrago with enough uncertainty to be able to recant it in future if necessary. Whether he had departed from the truth to save Elizabeth's sensibilities or his own, he was not sure.

When his wife got up to withdraw, Darcy was greatly relieved. His afternoon had been spent very unproductively, trying to focus on his ledgers as a naked Elizabeth floated across the pages. He'd had a few drinks before dinner, to calm himself before encountering her.

Before Elizabeth was two steps from the table, Darcy had poured himself another bumper of brandy; and as the door clicked shut behind her, he sat down in front of the fire, determined to immerse himself in an alcoholic haze.

Elizabeth retreated to her bedchamber, intending to test her suppositions on the telescope's design. Donning her day gown and her cloak once more, she picked up the book and headed off down the hall.

She spent over an hour comparing the telescope with several etchings in the book that she had marked with strips of paper and re-reading the accompanying text. Then, approaching the telescope once more, Elizabeth removed the cover of the eyepiece and bent to look through it, so engrossed in what she was doing that she failed to notice the approaching footsteps.

"What are you doing here?" barked a voice behind her.

Elizabeth jumped, and turning, discovered her husband on the threshold in what appeared to be a towering rage. She had never seen him angry before.

"I was looking at the telescope," she replied mildly.

"That is my mother's telescope. You have no right to be here!" Darcy yelled.

Elizabeth opened her mouth to protest. She had been given the key on the chatelaine by Mrs Reynolds and told she could reorganise things as she liked. She wondered briefly if this had been done without her husband's approval. *Still, why the inordinate anger?*

Looking at his glittering eyes, Elizabeth fancied there was something more than just anger in her husband's countenance. Then she remembered the large amount of brandy he'd poured himself as she withdrew from the dining room. She had little experience of drunken men, *angry* drunken men; but there had been a few incidents outside the Red Lion after the assemblies before Sir William—or Mr Lucas, as he had been then—had appointed the beadle.

"I beg your pardon," she said, backing away from him cautiously as if he were a dog, foaming at the mouth.

When she came up against an obstacle, Elizabeth glanced back to discover it was the handrail of the internal stairs. Making a snap decision, she turned and fled down the steps.

At first she thought there was no pursuit. She had just decided to calmly walk round the outside of the house, re-enter it elsewhere, and seek out somewhere to stay hidden until her husband regained his senses, when she heard his boots start to thunder down the stairs after her.

Now, truly frightened, Elizabeth started to run. She unbarred the door at the bottom of the stairs and burst out of the tower. Picking up her skirts, she ran full tilt across the formal garden. As her kid slippers scrabbled to find purchase on the gravel, she wished she was wearing her boots.

"Elizabeth!" Darcy bellowed behind her.

She ran faster. Slipping round the wall on the far side of the garden, she came upon two figures in the dark, and was just in time to see Finn plant a lingering kiss upon Healy's lips.

She darted back in the other direction. *Lord! I wasn't expecting that! The head groom and Darcy's valet? Where to now?* Changing direction, she headed off towards the folly.

It was difficult to ascertain if Darcy was following her above the sound of her own laboured breathing. She sped through the folly and into the shadows, veering off to one side when she remembered there was a pond there.

Lord, it is as black as the ace of spades here! Elizabeth stopped and peered around as her eyes adjusted to the surrounding dimness. She could hardly see her hand in front of her face. She recalled that most men could not see so well as women in the dark. Then she thought of Finn and Healy. *Well, they didn't seem to be having too much difficulty getting around in the dark...*

She briefly thought she might have eluded her husband when she heard the sound of his boots crunching on the gravel, walking now. *Damn! He must have seen me enter the folly to have confidently lowered his pace thus.* She stepped back further into the gloom and focused on controlling her breathing.

"Elizabeth! Please come out!"

She did not move.

Darcy walked closer, peering around, trying to catch a glimpse of her.

"I'm sorry. Please come out."

Still no movement on her part; the run had warmed her up, but it was a cold night, and under her clothes, Elizabeth began to shiver. *He must be cold too,* she thought, *though he has the advantage of his boots and tailcoat. Still, it might be possible to wait him out.*

"Elizabeth, I'm sorry," he called. "It was unreasonable of me. You have every right to be in that room. Please excuse my behaviour and come back to the house—it is cold."

Elizabeth silently wondered if he could be trusted.

For his part, Darcy, who had been quite bosky prior to his outburst, had sobered quickly, helped by the exercise and the cold air, and was now only half-sprung. He had seen his wife run through the folly, and the horrible thought now occurred to him that she might have slipped silently into the cold water of the pond in the darkness.

"Elizabeth?" he called plaintively.

There was no mistaking the child-like distress in his voice. "I am here," she said, stepping out of the shadows.

"Thank God!" he said, rushing forward and smothering her with an embrace.

She shivered in his arms, partly from the cold, but also in reaction to the denouement of their standoff.

"You are cold!" he exclaimed.

"A little—the cloaks I brought from Hertfordshire are not quite sufficient for the rigours of Derbyshire. Let us walk back to the house."

Darcy released her partially, leaving his arm draped across the back of her shoulders and hugging her to his side. She could feel the warmth pouring from him like a balm. They began to walk slowly through the formal garden.

"Please forgive me—I'm afraid I can't think about that room very clearly as I associate it entirely with my mother," he whispered. "I wasn't allowed in the room as a child. Sometimes, when my father wasn't there, I would sneak out of bed when my nurse had gone to peek through the arras, watching Mother peer through the telescope, then make drawings and annotations in her journal."

Elizabeth looked up at Darcy's profile. His face was sadly pensive.

"The arras was removed when it was hot in the summer," he continued. "I would stand at the door and stare in at her sometimes, when I was supposed to be reading or playing with my toys. I was forbidden to step over the threshold. Sometimes, she let me stay there, but more often she was disturbed by my presence, and my father or the servants would be requested to take me away."

Elizabeth waited for him to continue, but when he did not, she ventured: "It is a very unique room. It is a shame to see it sitting empty and dusty. The same is true of the sitting room."

"You wish to refurbish it?" he asked, somewhat alarmed, but ready to concede anything if she would forgive his transgression.

"Not refurbish it," she explained; "but use it."

"I do use the sitting room a little. Mainly I go there to remember my parents, but I suppose it is maudlin to restrict it to such use."

"The observatory has the feel of a neglected museum," Elizabeth observed. "There are papers on the desk which should be filed for posterity. Would it not be better to make some use of the telescope?"

"I suppose so," Darcy agreed; "but I haven't the faintest idea how."

They had now reached the centre of the formal garden, which formed a small square, the corners graced by four statues representing the seasons. A mosaic of the sun and moon occupied the place where the paths crossed in the centre. As they stepped onto this, Darcy turned and hugged her briefly once more.

"Please, again, accept my sincere apologies. The rooms were locked, so I can only presume that Mrs Reynolds has given you my mother's chatelaine?"

"Yes, she did. But if she was wrong in doing so, then I will return it."

"No, the fault here is mine. Now that I think of it, I have a vague memory that she asked me for permission, but I was so absorbed in whatever I was doing that I had forgotten it until now."

He stared at her in the darkness and then bent to place a light kiss on the top of her head.

While Elizabeth was grateful for her husband's apology, she could not help thinking that Healy had got a better kiss.

"That will not do, sir!" she said slyly.

"I beg your pardon?"

"Surely a setting like this," she said, gesturing around, "deserves a more heartfelt kiss?"

Darcy was astonished. His wife was asking to be kissed? He bent down to engage her lips. Despite their chill, which seemed as cold as stone, they yielded delightfully to his touch; and pressing his lips closer, he proceeded to kiss her most voluptuously, until, overcome with a sensation like vertigo, he drew back and staggered slightly.

Elizabeth, who had enjoyed the kiss without giving in to it, bowed her head and smiled to herself: *Another brandy-infused kiss, but definitely an improvement on the first.*

She put her arm round her husband's hip and thus conjoined, they proceeded back to the house.

"You didn't see anyone else out here?" she asked as they reached the back steps.

"No," he replied. "I certainly hope none of the servants perceived our silly meanderings."

29 Not Tuesday

After stepping from the sandstone of the folly, Darcy's feet sank into the carpet of cool moss that surrounded the pool. He briefly wondered where he had left his top-boots, before remembering that Finn had taken them to the cobbler. Shedding his clothes, he walked along the pier and dived into the cool water, then paddled lazily about. He was enjoying the feeling of the sun on his skin, until it passed behind a cloud, and the warmth quickly leeched from the day.

He flinched when something cold and slimy touched his back, then slid to his shoulder. Shuddering, he twisted around violently to shake it off, before splashing to the pier like a madman and clambering out of the water in haste. When he turned and looked back at the reeds, he saw Elizabeth floating there naked; her long, dark hair streaming around her. Her lips were not crimson, but blue; and with a shudder, he knew she was dead.

Darcy woke with a jerk, banging his skull against the headboard. Sitting bolt upright in the pre-dawn light, he tried to still his palpitating heart. *It was just a dream*, he reassured himself before covering his face with his hands, trying to erase the images from his mind.

He got up quickly, splashed himself liberally with cold water in some strange sort of penance, then pulled on his clothes, rang for his horse, and grabbed his riding crop.

Once Darcy was cantering along on Ajax across green fields, he began to feel calmer and was able to put his dream in perspective. He realised the nightmare was more than a distortion of the erotic thoughts he had been experiencing towards his wife—it was a warning.

He shivered silently, thanking God that his stupidity last night had not resulted in his wife's death by drowning a week into their marriage. Scaring her into taking flight could have resulted in tragedy. Her death would have been more than a callous act on his part to a blameless individual—he would have brought indelible shame to the Darcy name. Although there had been plenty of deaths in childbed, no other Darcy had lost a wife in such an ignominious way.

Fitzwilliam was too honest to lay such an event at the door of bad luck or his cursed fate. By the time he had surrendered the reins to Healy on returning to the house, Darcy had silently vowed he would never drink to excess again.

Elizabeth woke late with a heavy head and sneezed. She felt as if her limbs were made of lead. *Ah*, she thought sluggishly, *scampering about in the Derbyshire night air has caught up with me.* She had half-expected to get a cold from her adventures, but so quickly! *And it feels like a bad one too.* She wished she had Jane and barley water.

A solicitous Jenny, who emerged from the dressing room, suggested Elizabeth stay in bed and asked if she might get Cook to brew a posset. Elizabeth didn't know what this was, but it sounded like coddling, so she agreed and drifted back to sleep.

The posset turned out to be a surprising mixture of milk, ale and rum. Clearly it was an acquired taste, but Elizabeth had to admit her throat felt slightly less sore after drinking it.

When his wife didn't arrive at breakfast, Darcy became worried and enquired of Mrs Reynolds whether Elizabeth had requested a tray. Despite their apparent resolution of last night's contretemps, he was concerned Elizabeth might be viewing his behaviour resentfully.

The housekeeper replied in the negative, but assured the master she would check on Mrs Darcy and bring word to the study. She had seen the lovebirds coming in from the cold last night and thought them a little foolish to be trysting outside in such cold weather.

When Mrs Reynolds reported that Elizabeth was laid low with a cold, Darcy was overcome with guilt. Seeing the master so concerned, the housekeeper assured him she would take up some flowers from the succession house, causing Darcy to start up and insist on accompanying her while she picked them. But when they arrived at Elizabeth's bedchamber, Jenny would not admit them, insisting the mistress was too ill for visitors. Darcy found no support from Mrs Reynolds, who told him it would be senseless for him to catch cold also. The bouquet was surrendered to Jenny, and Darcy reluctantly returned to the study.

When Jenny placed the blooms in a vase on the bedside table, Elizabeth was overcome with the irony of receiving flowers she couldn't even smell, but smiled at the gesture.

Darcy spent his enforced solitude in turmoil. While he had been reassured that Elizabeth's absence was dictated by illness rather than resentment, he felt guilty about his role in precipitating that illness. He wished to be with his wife, to re-establish goodwill between them, but her maid continued to hold him off.

This state of anxiety oscillated with feelings even more disturbing to him—Darcy could no longer deny that he was attracted to his wife in a carnal way. The knowledge gave him no pleasure. Since seeing her in the bath, he had been unable to think a pure thought; and that kiss in the garden had drawn him in like a vortex. Just thinking about it gave him vertigo.

Of course, the inevitable comparisons with his mistress obtruded. Elizabeth wasn't voluptuous like Diana—she was lithe, with generous breasts, not large—just a handful. *That was enough.* And those tiny crimson nipples, the same colour as her lips, like rosebuds—quite different to Diana's large brown aureoles. And the feel of her flesh... Diana had been soft, like a pillow, whereas Elizabeth was firm but pliant and *erggghh!*

He knew these comparisons were totally inappropriate and ungentlemanly, and they compounded his guilt. Worst of all, he had never felt such an overwhelming urge to rut. It eclipsed any stirrings he had experienced in his entire relationship with Diana. He felt hardly civilised.

Darcy's respect for Elizabeth had been steadily growing. She was adapting to her role with the calm dignity that he had detected in their earlier interactions. Neither insipid nor spiteful, Elizabeth was shaping up to be the worthy companion and potential mother he had hoped for when planning his marriage of convenience. Darcy did not want to think of her solely as a vessel for his seed, but it seemed he could think of nothing else. The last few days had been pure torture. One thing he did know: next Tuesday seemed an eon away.

Two days after their brangle, when Colonel Fitzwilliam briefly visited Pemberley on his way back from Edinburgh to London, Elizabeth had still not emerged from her bedchamber. Over brandy, Darcy poured his heart out to his cousin but did not get the support he craved.

"I think I'm going mad. I can't stop thinking of her," he moaned.

"How tragic," replied the colonel. "You've fallen in love with your wife."

"Not that way!" protested Darcy, as a footman entered the room with a tray of savoury biscuits. "I mean in a lustful way," he whispered out of the corner of his mouth as he watched the servant retreat.

"That's seems perfectly natural to me," replied the colonel. "Lust is the precursor of love."

"I cannot agree," Darcy retorted. "The Greeks identified them as two different emotions, eros and agape. I seem to associate eros with Elizabeth, and agape with Diana, and the two should be the other way round!"

"I do not think that love for a woman can be divided into distinct entities like atoms," replied the colonel. "It is a continuum of a range of emotions. How did you feel when you first started with Diana?"

"The two cannot be compared!" said Darcy hotly.

"Well, no doubt you will find yourself making those comparisons regardless," replied the colonel mildly. "But be fair to Elizabeth. You were with Diana a long time. Try to cast your mind back to the beginning. What were your feelings then?"

Elizabeth woke on Sunday morning feeling slightly better. Having spent three days in bed, she felt she really should make the effort to go to church. After performing her ablutions, she accepted a cup of chocolate from Jenny and sat dutifully in front of the mirror as her maid brushed out her hair.

"Oh, Jenny," she whispered, "I look like death warmed up."

"You do look a little pale, ma'am, and your lips cracked; but a little makeup should help. I've prepared another of Miss Georgie's church gowns. I'm sure we can make you look presentable."

The dress was another heavy brocade in pale green, chased with gold and silver. It was similar in style to the gown she had worn the previous Sunday, and her maid had found two elaborate silver hair-combs to complement it. Jenny did a creditable job with the makeup, but Elizabeth still found the painted face that stared back at her from the mirror unnatural. Her neck, too, seemed to have become scrawnier during her illness.

Sitting in church, she could only conclude that her husband was also not pleased with her altered appearance. Periodically throughout the service she felt him staring at her intensely, but on the few occasions when their eyes met, he frowned and averted his eyes.

Returning to the house, Elizabeth felt exhausted. When Mrs Reynolds and Jenny fussed over her, insisting she go straight back to bed, she submitted without argument. Breakfast was sent up on a tray, but she could not touch it; the chocolate she had drunk before church still sat heavily in her stomach. Elizabeth fell asleep, and when she woke again in the afternoon, she finally did feel a little hungry and was happy to nibble on a ploughman's lunch.

By Monday, Elizabeth was feeling much better and got up as usual. She greeted her husband cheerily at breakfast, but after he had made enquiries on the state of her health, he fell silent and then left the table abruptly. Elizabeth ate her ham and eggs slowly, re-parsing everything they had said, wondering if she had inadvertently offended him somehow.

After breakfast, she took herself off to the picture gallery, walking up and down briskly to get some exercise while staring at the pictures on one side, and the formal garden on the other. How she wished the weather would improve so she could walk outside!

She read until lunch, which Mrs Reynolds brought up on a tray, explaining her husband had gone out to deal with some new tenants. In the afternoon, Elizabeth sat down with Jenny in front of the fire, and they happily set stitches together for two hours until there was a knock at the door. Jenny answered it to find the master standing in the hall, still carrying his riding crop.

"Yes, sir?" Jenny asked when the master ventured nothing.

A silence stretched between them before Darcy managed, "Leave us."

Jenny wasn't sure what to do with such a peremptory command. Still blocking the door with her body, she turned to her mistress for guidance. When Elizabeth nodded silently to her maid, Jenny retreated to the dressing room rather than push past the master, who was still at the hall door.

Elizabeth stared at Darcy, who stood immobile in the doorway, wondering at the cause of this extraordinary visit. His expression looked rather grim. She recalled their recent altercation, took in the riding crop in his hand; and then putting her needlework carefully aside, she stood up.

Soon after she did so, Elizabeth heard the door to the service corridor click shut as Jenny left.

Her husband also must have been waiting for this, for he stepped forward, flinging the door shut behind him. Elizabeth started involuntarily as the door slammed. Darcy strode rapidly towards her, and with a groan of "Forgive me," he dropped the crop and buried his hands in her hair before proceeding to devour her lips.

Elizabeth's heart lurched as he laid hands on her, and it did not still immediately once she perceived his intentions were amatory, not violent. He grasped her body insistently, but without undue force.

"Forgive me," he repeated as he came up for air and waltzed her backwards towards the bed.

Before she knew what was happening, Darcy had lifted her by the armpits onto the mattress and was rucking her skirt up about her waist. She realised with some misgiving that he intended to take her with some urgency; and when he began unbuttoning his breeches, she lay down on the mattress, arching her back to push her skirt above her bottom and out of harm's way.

Darcy was relieved at his wife's easy acquiescence, as he hardly felt capable of explaining himself. When he undid the flap of his breeches, she lifted her skirt higher and as he parted her legs, he was able to view for the first time the source of all his desires.

Pushing into her urgently, Darcy almost came a cropper, but sucking his breath in quickly, he managed to restrain himself on the brink of release. His lashes fluttered briefly before he opened heavy lids as he leaned into her. Deeper and further he penetrated with each push until he had almost buried himself to the hilt and then, unable to hold on any longer, he gave in to ecstasy and collapsed on top of her.

Lying beneath her husband, Elizabeth could only think ruefully of the counterpane. She wished she'd had the presence of mind to flick it back before he had begun, but she had been so preoccupied with saving her skirt. "Oh, dear," she muttered under her breath.

"Yes, love?" she heard the tender reply.

Elizabeth started. She had erroneously assumed that Darcy had succumbed to his usual state of post-coital unconsciousness. "I was just wishing we had pulled back the counterpane, that's all," she replied honestly.

"Oh, well... I see," replied Darcy. And then, "Perhaps if you wound your legs around my waist?"

Wondering how this would help, Elizabeth dutifully complied and was then astonished when her husband took her by the shoulders and lifted her bodily from the bed. When she was laid back down again, he withdrew, and she saw that he had managed to flick the counterpane out from beneath her body before depositing her gently on the sheets.

Darcy had turned away from her after decoupling, and when he turned back she saw he had adjusted his breeches. He seemed to hesitate there, staring at her, and she realised with some embarrassment that with the exception of her stockings, she was naked from the waist down. As her husband was now fully clothed, she felt very exposed and reached for the sheet to cover herself.

Suddenly, Darcy seemed to come to a decision, and in a flurry he stripped himself of his waistcoat, cravat and shirt. Elizabeth stared at his broad chest and the rounded muscles in the tops of his arms.

My goodness, she thought, *he looks just like a Greek statue.*

Her husband then proceeded to behave in a very unstatue-like way when he grabbed a chair and commenced doing a little jig. This looked exceedingly funny and Elizabeth had to bite her lip to stifle a giggle. She could see he was trying to get his well-fitted boots off using the runners of the chair, and was completely amazed when he managed to do so. *That cannot be good for the chair,* she thought vaguely, as he placed it back down.

Then his breeches and smalls were off, and Elizabeth stared in astonishment at her naked husband. She couldn't help noticing that he differed from a Greek statue on a couple of key points. Firstly, there was that hair, which she had previously glimpsed on his shins—it continued all the way up his legs, and ran in a line from his navel to his crotch. And, of course, *that* was the other difference. The few Greek statues she had seen which were not obliterated or covered with a vine leaf, were considerably smaller. She looked shyly away.

Darcy, on the other hand, wasn't the least embarrassed about his unclothed state. He stared at his wife, wondering how he might similarly divest her of her garments. In this, he had little experience. The first time he had made love to Diana, she had merely lifted her skirts. Later, she had greeted him in negligées, so the business of removing a woman's underwear was largely unknown to him. Returning to the bed, Darcy threw himself on top of his wife.

If Elizabeth had previously been pleasantly aware of her husband's musky scent, now she was awash in it, she felt a thrill run through her body.

Feeling her quiver beneath him, Darcy plunged his tongue into her mouth. Elizabeth gasped at the unexpected assault and parted her lips to allow him better access. She felt overcome by a type of delirium. She had not imagined a kiss could be like this!

Darcy stroked and squeezed Lizzy 'til she wondered if he had seven hands. During this half-frenzy, he'd worked her gown up under her armpits, but not content with this, he wrestled it off somehow while she twisted her arms to assist him, as if doing some exotic dance. The gown was tossed unceremoniously aside. Darcy would have liked to similarly remove her half-stays and chemise, but his patience didn't stretch that far. He plunged into her again. She was slick from their first encounter; and when, heart thumping, he discovered he could enjoy himself without going off half-cocked; he plied her vigorously. With an almighty groan he spent himself once more and collapsed.

This time her husband really *did* go out like a light, but fortunately for Elizabeth he'd moved to the side, so his weight was largely on the mattress. Nonetheless, he retained a proprietary grip on her shoulders such that she was pinned to the bed. She vaguely wished she could reach her glass of water on the bedside table. Feeling a little like a mouse trapped by a playful but somnolent cat, she resigned herself to her current position, and after focussing on her husband's breathing, managed to lull herself to sleep.

She woke around an hour later when Darcy moved beside her. Opening her eyes, she found his face poised over the top of her, framed by his wildly dishevelled curls.

He kissed the tip of her nose. "Again?" he breathed.

Elizabeth stared at her husband in amazement. *What has come over him? It isn't even Tuesday!*

Unable to find her tongue, she merely nodded.

"How do you undo these things?" Darcy asked, pawing at her stays.

"They are laced at the back," she said, rolling over. "Just loosen it, and I will pull it over my head."

This was soon achieved and the chemise followed soon after.

"So beautiful," Darcy gasped, finally able to touch the vision that had been haunting him. Bending down, he began to suckle her nipples.

This felt rather heavenly to Elizabeth, and she ran her fingers through his dark locks, pulling his head closer.

Darcy began kissing his wife with determination, eager to acquaint himself with every inch of her body; but soon the need to join with her overwhelmed him once more, and he submitted to his desire.

Now they were deliciously skin-to-skin, with the hard muscles of her husband's body rasping against her stiffened nipples as he urged himself further into her. Giving in to the sensations, Elizabeth arched her back to press her breasts against Darcy and heard him groan in response. During one lucid moment, she became dimly aware that she had locked her ankles round her husband's waist before her mind became a haze of primal pleasure. Then, she felt something contract inside, and shimmer within, as waves of ecstasy washed through her.

Darcy felt his wife shudder beneath him and let himself go, yelling *Yes!* at the top his lungs. It may have rattled the windows, but Elizabeth was completely oblivious, floating in a sleepy paradise an inch above the sheets.

In the hall, a footman stopped mid-step at Darcy's yell, then smiled to himself and continued walking, while downstairs in the library, two chambermaids who were polishing the woodwork looked at each other in puzzlement.

When they decoupled, Darcy clasped his wife to him, rolling onto his back. He continued to pet and stroke her as he whispered ridiculous things that tickled her ear, like *So lovely! incandescent!* and *'peaches'*.

30 Uneasy relations

After leaving Pemberley, Colonel Fitzwilliam made a belated visit to his mother at Wyvern Hall. Richard noticed a look of relief flash across the butler's face when he greeted him at the front door.

Grieves bowed and ushered him in. "It's good to see you, Master Richard."

"Thank you, Grieves." replied the colonel, surrendering his hat and cloak.

"I've just taken some tea to Miss Darcy and a guest in the saloon. Perhaps you would like to join her?"

"I will, Grieves, but I cannot stay long. Is my mother about?"

"She is indisposed, sir, but I'm sure she'd like to see you. I'll enquire of her maid."

"Thank you, Grieves. And who is Miss Georgie's guest?"

"Young Mr Anstey, sir. I admit I was in two minds as to whether to admit him, but the Ansteys are old friends, and I do not think there is any harm in young Henry."

The colonel frowned. Georgiana was not yet out, and he could not approve of her receiving solo male guests, even under the auspices of her companion, Mrs Annesley. The Ansteys were a respectable family, and Henry probably thought the countess would be present when he made his call; but as one of Georgiana's guardians, along with Darcy of course, it was the colonel's duty to warn him off nonetheless.

In fact, Henry had not been in the saloon five minutes when the colonel arrived. Mr Anstey had recently returned home from his studies at Oxford after the Michaelmas term and, upon learning that Miss Georgiana Darcy was a guest a Wyvern Hall, had made haste to the earl's seat.

"Miss Georgiana," Henry had said upon first strolling into the room. "What a pleasant surprise! I rode over to pay my respects to the countess."

"Oh, Mr Anstey!" said Georgie, much discomposed and casting a look of appeal at her companion. "I'm terribly sorry, but my aunt is unwell and cannot see you!"

Henry took a step forward before stopping again. "I do apologise for intruding. I seem to be making a nuisance of myself."

"Not at all, Mr Anstey," replied Georgiana, remembering her manners. "Would you care for a cup of tea?"

Mrs Annesley nodded approvingly.

"Thank you so much, Miss Darcy," replied Henry affably, ensconcing himself in a chair.

When the tea arrived, Georgiana poured him a cup and offered him a tiny cake.

"*Soooo...* Miss Darcy," started Henry. "I believe you have been to the seaside?"

"Yes, Mr Anstey. Mrs Annesley and I visited Ramsgate in the summer."

"Did you go sea bathing?" he politely enquired.

"Oh, heavens, no!" replied Georgiana, quite shocked. "But we did go for several strolls along the promenade. It was most invigorating!"

During this speech Mrs Annesley had retired slightly from the table with her cup and saucer. She sat down in a chair to the side and slightly behind Mr Anstey.

"Yes," affirmed Mr Anstey. "The sea air is so… *healthy*."

Seeing she was to have no help from her companion, Georgiana ventured, "I mainly spent my time painting, even though my efforts are quite excrab…"

She noticed Mrs Annesley discreetly shaking her head. "Excellent!" she amended.

Mr Anstey broke into a wide grin.

"I mean, *not excellent*…" modified Georgiana, blushing, "but *working towards* excellent!"

To her profound relief, Grieves re-entered the room, announcing Colonel Fitzwilliam.

"Cousin Richard!" cried Georgiana in relief. "Would you like a cup of tea?"

Richard felt more like brandy, but he accepted graciously. "Thank you, poppet."

He shook Henry's hand with a curt greeting, before turning back to his cousin.

"How are you, Georgie? How was Ramsgate?" he asked, acknowledging Mrs Annesley with a nod.

"Fine, Cousin. My painting is still atrocious," replied Georgiana, lapsing once more into truthfulness, "but I got plenty of salt air."

Mrs Annesley gave an infinitesimal sigh.

"Would you like a cup of tea, Cousin Richard?" enquired Georgiana.

"Thank you," said Richard, disposing himself into a chair.

After dispensing the tea, Georgiana glanced at Mrs Annesley, who was raising her eyebrows at her suggestively. Georgiana frowned. Mrs Annesley flicked her eyes in the direction of the piano.

"I should play!" blurted Georgiana. Then, recalling herself somewhat, "I've just learned a piece by Herr Mozart! Would you like to hear it?"

Both gentlemen voiced their assent.

Gathering her silk skirts, Georgiana sallied forth to the instrument.

The gentlemen watched politely through this piece, which lasted roughly a quarter of an hour, before applauding her first rate performance. The colonel, aware that he needed to be on his way, suggested Mr Anstey accompany him to the study for a glass of brandy before he departed.

Georgiana heaved a sigh of relief once the door had closed and began to play by ear a more modern ditty she had heard at Ramsgate.

After disposing of Mr Anstey and suggesting he not return without a female companion, the colonel wended his way to his mother's apartments, following her maid who had advised him he would be received. The countess occupied the east wing of Wyvern Hall, whereas the earl, when in residence, occupied the west.

Richard found his mother lying abed, wearing an elaborate lace cap with long lappets that descended past her ears. He thought this ridiculous confection made his mother look like a poodle; but conscious she had likely pulled it on to cover her untidy hair for his visit, he made no comment on it. From beneath this monstrosity, his mother's wan face gazed at him, the remnants of her beauty still apparent in her good bone structure, despite the depredations that cosmetics had wrought upon her skin and sagging muscles. She did not look happy.

"Mother, are you unwell?" asked Richard, sitting down on the edge of the bed.

"No, Richard, just cast down. What is your father doing in Hertfordshire?"

Richard frowned. "Nothing untoward, I assure you. I came to apprise you of events."

"Then he does not have a house full of Cyprians at this Everfield place?"

"No, mother. Who has told you such a faradiddle?"

"Lady Scott was here yesterday, and she said it is the talk of the town! If it is not bad enough for him to be flaunting his mistress at the theatre!"

"It is nothing of the sort," replied Richard. "Father attended Darcy's wedding in Hertfordshire and has stayed behind because of Cousin Anne. Netherfield is leased by a friend of Darcy's, a respectable gentleman. I have been staying there also and can assure you nothing untoward has occurred. I do hope Lady Scott did not broach this topic in front of Georgiana?"

"I would not have put it past her, but fortunately Georgiana was out riding. And what of my niece, Anne?"

"She collapsed at Darcy's wedding and has been abed since."

"And why has Darcy not informed me of this?" asked the countess.

"It occurred after he left. Father has been supervising her convalescence, but I expect he will write to you eventually. Anne's health is much worse than we were led to believe, and Father has some notion of setting up one of Robert's daughters to succeed her to the estate."

"Well, that is sad for Anne," replied the countess; "but good news for us. Who knows how we are to contrive to respectably provide for the half of our granddaughters…"

A short silence followed this much-repeated lament that substituted for complaints on her first son's many deficiencies.

Richard got up. "I'm sorry, Mother. I have a communiqué and must go. Promise me you will get out of bed."

Kissing his mother's forehead, Richard prepared to take his leave.

"When will I see you again?" she asked plaintively.

"Soon, I hope," her son replied. "I intend to regularly volunteer to carry these despatches and will venture to visit you as frequently as my bum can stand the saddle."

The countess frowned at her son's vulgar expression but squeezed his hand fondly.

She sighed when he closed the door and called for her tire-woman.

Darcy woke up feeling like he had walked across a desert. He reached for his wife's water glass and emptied it in one gulp. Getting up, he began pulling on his clothes, but experienced some difficulty locating his smalls and stockings. When his cravat proved particularly elusive, he resolved to get a fresh one from his bedchamber.

Prior to leaving his wife, Darcy built up the fire before returning to the bed to survey her. She lay like sleeping beauty, with one naked shoulder exposed. Knowing how Elizabeth felt the cold, he reached for the covers. It had been his intention to pull them up round her neck, but by the time his hand had grasped the sheet, a small devil had taken possession of it, and he lifted the covers gently to view his wife's naked body. Darcy discovered that in his haste to remove her clothes he had overlooked her stockings, and these were the only garments she was now wearing. For some reason he found her state of partial nudity incredibly erotic, but he smothered these thoughts immediately. *Four times in one day—it would be barbaric!*

Resisting an urge to retie the bow that had come loose on one of her garters, Darcy took a deep breath, settled the covers over her again, and left.

Elizabeth woke feeling disoriented in her dim bedchamber. With increasing awareness, she realised it was dusk, not sunrise, and she had spent the afternoon in bed with her husband. This recollection caused a twinge in her loins.

Turning over, Elizabeth discovered with some disappointment, though not much surprise, that Darcy was gone. Finding his musky scent still lingered, she leant over to sniff the pillow and, drawing it to her, inhaled deeply. She felt incredibly energised, as if returning from a brisk walk. Reaching for her water glass, she found it empty and had to refill it from the jug beside it. She could remember being thirsty, but could not recall draining it. *How strange.*

Cuddling the pillow, she settled down again under the warm covers to review her eventful afternoon. She smiled. *So my aunt wasn't exaggerating about the joy of conjugal relations after all...* It astonished Lizzy that she had almost reached her majority unaware of this great mystery of life. Now she understood why young women were so carefully watched and closely guarded. If they had any idea of the pleasure to be had from congress with a man, they would no doubt all be eloping with the first pleasing young man to cross their path.

Elizabeth spent several pleasant minutes reminiscing on how her husband's warm large hands had roamed her body—squeezing, caressing, teasing, until she felt herself grow liquid with her thoughts. She stretched, feeling as satisfied as a cat with the raw feeling of just being alive.

When there was a knock on the door, her mind immediately flew to Darcy. She certainly would not say no if he chose to impose himself again—*even if it wasn't Tuesday*. But to her great disappointment it was Jenny, come to dress her for dinner. Sighing, Elizabeth sat up.

After retreating to his study, Darcy had ended his post-coital afternoon pacing in front of the hearth. It had been impossible to work. Rather than appeasing the devil throbbing in his loins, his unplanned visit to his wife seemed to have transferred the imp to his brain, where it was playing havoc with his head. To Darcy's disordered mind, what had occurred had come perilously close to a rape. But worse than that admission was the knowledge that he wanted to do it again. Rather than damping his feverish desires, congress with his wife seemed to have amplified them.

He had forced himself to sit down at his desk and pick up his pen, but the page that loomed before him became her pale, pliant flesh, and when he gave up and thrust the pen back into the inkstand, that also evoked erotic memories.

Ceasing his pacing, he looked at his watch—*still two hours to dinner*. Knowing that riding normally calmed him and allowed him to order his thoughts, Darcy called for his horse.

Upon entering the bedchamber, Jenny was relieved to find her mistress unharmed, and after sending for hot water for her ablutions, she retrieved her mistress's wrap from the dressing room so she could cover herself.

Returning, Jenny tripped upon an object on the floor and, picking it up, discovered it to be the master's riding crop. At that moment, she made the mistake of meeting her mistress's eyes. They were full of merriment and before either could dwell on the impropriety of it, they both burst out laughing: Jenny in a high-pitched giggle and Elizabeth in a more full-throated laugh. Jenny's outburst had arisen more as an outlet for the relief she had felt at finding her mistress unharmed; while Elizabeth was driven more by a general sense of well-being, but prompted by unholy amusement at the slightly outraged look that had passed over her maid's face on finding this evidence of male occupation in her mistress's sanctum.

"Oh dear!" breathed Elizabeth, clutching her belly as she finally managed to get herself under control.

"I suppose I should give it to Mr Finn," observed Jenny as she laid the crop aside.

"I think that would be best," agreed Elizabeth solemnly.

They then proceeded to dress for dinner without exchanging another word on the topic, although a sense of solidarity prevailed. As Elizabeth sponged herself behind the curtain, her maid set out the dress and accessories she had selected for dinner, while she proceeded to revise her opinion of the master. Jenny had thought Mr Darcy all that was prim and proper, but now it seemed he had a touch of the earl in him.

After dressing her mistress in a beautiful dusky pink gown adorned with black-figured lace, Jenny arranged Elizabeth's hair in front of the pier glass by the light of two candelabra. Then, satisfied with her efforts, she selected some jewellery and extinguished the bulk of the candles.

Elizabeth thanked her kindly and, drawing a black cashmere shawl about her, proceeded downstairs.

Jenny, meanwhile, began her search of the bedchamber for the clothing her mistress had been wearing in the afternoon, before calling for a chambermaid to help her change the sheets.

When Elizabeth walked into the dining room she saw, with some amusement, that Darcy was once again staring at the carpet. But before she could make some joking comment on his abstraction, she was overcome with the realisation that her husband was an extremely handsome man.

Of course, she had counted Fitzwilliam Darcy as a grand physical specimen among men from the time he had made his first appearance at the Meryton Assembly, but his obvious disinclination to make himself pleasing had somehow diminished his physical beauty in her eyes. She supposed a flower was just as pretty if one couldn't pick it and could only deem herself a practical person for her dismissal of him at the assembly.

Now, it seemed she looked at him with different eyes. Besides his tall, strapping physique, he had a refined masculine face—combining the strong chin and patrician nose, hooked near the bridge, so often associated with a commanding personality.

Unfortunately, her recollection of their first meeting had reminded Elizabeth of the very reason why she had dismissed Mr Darcy from her list of attractive men—he had insulted her at the assembly. Thus, while her first inclination upon entering the dining room had been to engage in light-hearted flirtation with her husband after their newfound intimacy, she checked herself; and upon doing so, noticed he wasn't looking happy at all.

In fact, Darcy wasn't staring at the carpet in his usual distracted fashion, thinking of estate or investment matters, but was steeling himself to look up and meet his wife's eyes. He couldn't believe that he'd imposed upon her in such an imperious fashion and could only cite temporary lunacy associated with the ache in his loins.

His evening canter had not restored his equanimity as he had hoped. He'd startled the groom with his unexpected request for his horse at such an unusual time of day, and once he mounted, his sense of wrong-footedness had been compounded by the realisation that he had lost his riding crop. When had he last had it in his hand? Ajax had also objected to the change in timetable, behaving with irritable defiance whenever Darcy tugged on the reins.

By the time Darcy had arrived back at the house, his mind was in a whirl. Stepping across the threshold, he realized that he smelt of horse and sex. Consulting his watch, he saw there was still an hour 'til dinner and decided to have a bath before dressing. Not wishing to further disrupt his household, Darcy assured Finn that cold water would suffice, but his valet only raised his eyebrows and remarked that he was sure there was some hot water in the kitchens.

As Finn poured the water over his head in preparation for the shampoo, Darcy closed his eyes and breathed deeply, trying to calm himself, aware that he would soon have to face his wife. But it was no good. His general feelings of shame were interrupted with flashes of erotic memories of his afternoon with Elizabeth. Leaning back against the tub, he groaned.

When Finn's hands finished massaging the shampoo into his scalp and descended to work on his tense shoulders, he made no protest, submitting to the comfort of having the knots worked out of his tight muscles.

As Darcy dressed, he noticed the riding crop sitting on a chair in the dressing room. "Did I leave it there?" he asked his valet, sure the crop had not been there when he'd searched for it earlier.

"Miss Jenny returned it, sir. I believe you may have dropped it in the mistress's chambers."

Darcy blushed profusely, wondering what his valet was thinking. He certainly hoped Finn did not believe he was one of those men who hit their wives for pleasure. Without saying another word to his valet, he went downstairs.

Dinner was an awkward affair. When Elizabeth noted her husband seemed to have returned to the stiff, haughty manner she had first encountered in Hertfordshire, she was bewildered, but determined not to show it.

Once more, she managed to maintain a one-sided conversation. Choosing a topic she thought sufficiently erudite to escape condemnation as vacuous, Elizabeth spoke of one of her father's theories on fairy tales, specifically the significance of the number three. While she dwelt on the characteristics of first, second and third sons, Darcy made desultory comments, and could only wonder if she was poking sly fun at him.

For a moment during her discourse, Elizabeth thought she perceived a slightly hurt look on her husband's face, and she almost reached out to stroke his hand, to ask what troubled him; but the look vanished before she was even sure it was there. The haughty look returned, and afraid of one of his cold rebuffs, she kept her hands to herself.

They bid each other a polite goodnight.

When Elizabeth arrived at the breakfast table on Tuesday morning, she found a note in her husband's hand propped against her teacup.

Wondering what its contents might be, she opened it.

Dearest Elizabeth,

Forgive me for my precipitate departure, but I have brought forward my trip to inspect the Yorkshire mills. It had been my original intention to wait until Georgiana returned tomorrow, but as Christmas is nearing, I thought it would be better to go sooner rather than later.

I regret I am unable to introduce you to my sister, but Mrs Reynolds has assured me she will perform this office. I do hope you will become fast friends.

I will endeavour to return for Christmas.

My love and respect
Fitzwilliam Darcy.

31 A fairy tale

Saddlesore, Colonel Richard Fitzwilliam arrived in Meryton after sunset, just in time to see his father's mistress depart in the direction of London in the earl's carriage. She recognised the second son of her lover as she stepped into the coach and gave him a cheery wave, which he returned reluctantly.

Richard caught up with his father, who was riding one of Bingley's horses, halfway back to Netherfield. "Father, you have just made a liar of me," he whinged.

"How so?" replied his father.

"I just reassured mother this morning that you were not dallying with any females at Netherfield."

"So you are not a liar," replied his father coolly. "I was dallying with a female in *Meryton*."

Richard sighed. "Using the Red Lion and your travelling carriage were hardly discreet."

"Surely you don't expect me to be a celibate?" sneered the earl.

"No, but couldn't you visit that high flyer in London?"

"I've been visiting Anne everyday," replied the earl, taking the moral high ground.

Richard thought it far more likely that he had been flirting with Jane Bennet.

"Are you not interested in your cousin's progress?" enquired his father.

"Yes, of course," replied his son with resignation. "What is her progress?"

"The doctor says she is well enough to be moved, though not a great distance. He thought perhaps she could manage London if she lay down during the journey. Alternately, the Bingleys have offered further recuperation at Netherfield. I'm inclined to accept their offer."

"Surely you are wishing to get back to London?" asked his son.

"While your Aunt Catherine is staying in my townhouse? I think not."

"Could you not stay at your mistress's townhouse?"

"*Now* who is being indiscreet? Besides I can only take her in small doses. She has a boring habit of nattering on about the latest fallal she desires."

They rode on in silence, but after passing through the gates of Netherfield, the earl thought it safe to broach a topic that could be conveniently terminated upon their arrival.

"How, by the way, did your mother get news of what I *was* or *was not* doing at Netherfield?" asked the earl, strongly suspecting his son had put his foot in his mouth once again.

"Lady Scott," replied Richard truthfully.

"That woman should have been strangled at birth," drawled Lord Matlock.

Richard accompanied his father and Charles Bingley to Longbourn in preparation for Anne's removal in the morning. He found his cousin downstairs for the first time since her collapse at the wedding. She looked happier and healthier than he had seen her for years. Clearly Dr Douglas's care was doing her good.

Despite the earlier hour, Charlotte Lucas was already present and tending to her patient, while Mr Collins praised his betrothed as a ministering angel. Mrs Jenkinson sat like a ghost against the wall. Jane Bennet remained in the background as she was so good at doing, although it was she who had done the bulk of the nursing during Anne's stay. She dispensed her Mona Lisa smile alternately on the earl and Charles Bingley as they vied to say pretty things to her. Richard ground his teeth.

After the doctor arrived from London in his curricle and four, Anne was finally settled in the earl's carriage to everyone's satisfaction, with Charlotte Lucas and Mrs Jenkinson in attendance. They set off towards Netherfield, with Mr Collins on the box, and the earl and Mr Bingley riding behind.

With a flurry of his whip, Dr Douglas departed for Netherfield in his curricle soon after, overtaking the cavalcade just outside the village. He intended to arrive betimes to ensure that everything was in order for Miss de Bourgh's reception.

"Do you have time for tea, Colonel?" asked Jane as they watched the dust settle from the portico of Longbourn.

"I'm afraid not, Miss Bennet, but I have a letter from your sister," he said, withdrawing it from his jacket; "and would gladly return for your reply in a week."

"Surely, now that your cousin has departed," said Jane, "Longbourn is out of your way?"

"What is ten more miles on the road to the north? I could never wish to cease to be of service to you and your sister, Miss Bennet. And who knows," he smiled, "Longbourn may be less crowded the next time I visit."

Jane returned his smile prettily, with more warmth than the polite smiles she had been bestowing all morning. *He is such a nice man,* she thought.

"Very well, sir. I will have a letter ready pending your return," said Jane; "and perhaps you will have time for a cup of tea, then?"

"You have my word," he replied.

Bowing, Richard mounted his horse and rode off.

Georgiana and her companion arrived at Pemberley sometime before noon to be greeted at the carriage by Mrs Reynolds. Georgie stamped her foot when the housekeeper explained her brother had gone on business to Yorkshire.

"Oh, it is too bad of him!" she declared. "He promised he would come to Ramsgate too, and he never turned up."

"Well, Miss Georgie," said Mrs Reynolds. "I know you love your brother and are disappointed, but be good now because I have your new sister to introduce to you."

"Oh!" said Georgiana casting her eyes about and perceiving Elizabeth hanging back in the vestibule.

She blushed prettily before approaching Elizabeth. "I beg your pardon. I thought you would have accompanied my brother to Yorkshire."

Elizabeth put on a brave face. "No, no! He has gone on secret men's business."

"Well!" declared Georgie with an air. "We are better off without him!"

When Elizabeth offered her arm, Georgie accepted it without hesitation, and they took themselves off to the saloon for tea. Following in their wake, Mrs Annesley could only be glad that her charge's temper tantrum had broken the ice. Normally Georgiana's shyness governed any new interaction.

Over tea, the sisters found themselves well pleased with each other. Elizabeth was surprised to find a rather gauche girl with pretty manners when she had been expecting, based on her knowledge of her wardrobe, a well-educated and pampered miss in the style of the Bingley sisters. Lizzy greatly admired Georgie's curly raven locks that had been tamed into ringlets. For her part, Georgiana had found the sister she had always wanted.

"I was so surprised when Fitzwilliam wrote that he was getting married. I had no idea!" exclaimed Georgie. "I wanted to come to the wedding, but he said you would be halfway to Derbyshire before I could even set out. He is as close as an oyster. I never even knew he was courting you!"

Elizabeth blushed, wondering what she could truthfully say in reply. "We met at an assembly in Hertfordshire and found we had a shared love of fairy tales."

"Fairy tales!?" repeated Georgiana in astonishment.

"Yes, my father was an Oxford don who studied fairy tales before he inherited the estate. Your brother gave him a large book of them."

"How strange! I never knew Fitzwilliam even liked fairy tales. I have trouble getting him to read novels! I love fairy tales and never get to hear them! Tell me a fairy tale!"

"Miss Georgiana," Mrs Annesley intervened. "There will be plenty of time for fairy tales later. Which part of Hertfordshire do you come from Mrs Darcy?"

"From Longbourn, ma'am, a small village near Meryton."

"I'm afraid I don't know it," replied Mrs Annesley; "being only familiar with the posting stops of Barnet and St Albans."

"It is on a post road, ma'am. So you have probably gone through it, between St Albans and Dunstable."

"Indeed, I do remember a small village with a church on the right and a villa with high walls on the left."

"That is our very estate, ma'am," cried Elizabeth. "How amazing that you should remember it!"

Thus, during tea, the conversation turned to more normal channels—of Elizabeth's family and her life in Hertfordshire.

Georgiana was not so easily deterred, however, and after retiring to rest after her journey, she renewed her request for fairy tales at lunch. Elizabeth promised to tell her a bedtime story.

After lunch, Mrs Reynolds showed Georgiana her new sitting room. Georgie was so delighted with it that she almost forgave her brother for not being there to present it himself. Mrs Annesley, who had been involved in the planning of the room, and thus had a better notion of the significant amount of time and money Mr Darcy had invested in it, pointed out its manifold charms, and Elizabeth added appropriate comments of appreciation.

The three ladies spent a pleasant afternoon in the sitting room. Georgiana, without any prompting, went straight to her piano, for it was her joy to play in solitude or for her intimates. Mrs Annesley quietly noted that despite their short acquaintance, Georgiana already accounted Elizabeth one of these. She was not surprised, for Mrs Darcy—who could surely not yet have attained her majority—had great charm of manner, and a pleasant face.

Elizabeth had started the afternoon by sorting silk threads—for her maid had found a beautiful pattern she wished to embroider as a border on one of the shawls brought from Longbourn and had requested Elizabeth to choose the colour scheme.

Once she had done this, Elizabeth made a cat's cradle and delighted Georgiana with her creations between each musical piece.

As the afternoon progressed, and Elizabeth joked and said many witty things, Mrs Annesley added esprit to Elizabeth's list of qualities. She could see how Mr Darcy would be drawn to such a warm and lively character, being a little dour himself.

The ladies of Pemberley were interrupted in the afternoon when a lady and two gentlemen called. Elizabeth was a little surprised by the hour of the call, but she put it down to country manners when it became apparent they were well known to Miss Georgie. The lady and the older gentleman were introduced as the Floreys, who had a small estate near Matlock, while the younger gentleman was Mr Henry Anstey, who was studying at Oxford.

Mr Anstey was very particular in his attentions to Miss Georgiana, which seemed to greatly fluster the girl. Elizabeth and Mrs Annesley both exerted themselves to smooth over awkward comments made by Georgie in her distress, while the Floreys watched the show in silent amusement.

By the time the unexpected visitors left an hour later, Elizabeth was heartily glad to be rid of them. She found covering for Georgie almost as tiring as doing so for her mother. Nor did she appreciate the Floreys' unwillingness to temper the social awkwardness.

After dinner, Elizabeth came to Georgiana's room, as promised, to deliver the fairy tale, and Mrs Annesley gratefully retired. Georgiana was sitting expectantly in the centre of the bed with a shawl round her shoulders.

Elizabeth looked doubtfully at the hard chair Mrs Annesley had vacated. "Move over then," she said to Georgie. "It's cold."

Georgie squeaked in excitement and made room in the bed, whereupon Elizabeth climbed between the sheets and started her tale.

"*Once upon a time there were three brother bears who all lived in a cottage in the forest. The eldest brother was a big hulking bear who made the whole house shake when he laughed. The middle brother was a serious bear who read aloud to his brothers in front of the fire each night. The youngest brother was a cuddly bear who liked to eat honey.*

One morning after the eldest brother had made their usual breakfast of porridge, the youngest bear remembered there was no more honey, as he had eaten it all the previous night and smudged his pillow with his dirty paws. When he declared he couldn't possibly enjoy his porridge without honey, the three bears decided to go find some before they sat down to eat."

"Oh, my brother likes to eat porridge!" declared Georgiana. "*And* he likes honey on it too!"

"Very well, shall we imagine him as the youngest bear?" asked Elizabeth.

"Oh no! He is very fastidious and would never smudge his pillow. I would think him more the serious bear."

"All right, the middle bear's name was Fitz."

"The oldest bear can be Richard," interpolated Georgiana. "He laughs loudly."

"Very well, and what shall we name the youngest bear?"

Georgiana got a mischievous look in her eye, before blurting, "Henry Anstey!"

This caused Elizabeth to chuckle. If she was worried that Georgiana had developed a tendre for Henry based on her gauche behaviour in his presence, her sister had just dispelled this suspicion.

"Very well,

Richard, Fitz, and Henry set off to raid their local hive. Meanwhile, a young lady who was walking through the forest came upon the bears' cottage."

"I thought it was an old lady?" interrupted Georgiana.

"I thought you had never heard any fairy tales?" retorted Lizzy.

"Well, not many," admitted Georgiana sheepishly.

"Well, that is a different story, anyway," explained Lizzy. "This was a young lady with raven locks, named Georgiana; but as she was travelling incognito, let us call her Sootylocks."

Georgiana blushed prettily and asked, "Why was she travelling incognito?"

"She was trying to escape the attentions of an unwanted suitor," said Lizzy slyly.

"Oh," replied Georgiana. "What happened next?"

"Well, the bears were very trusting bears who never locked their door, and Sootylocks walked straight in."

"Didn't she knock?" asked Georgiana, quite shocked.

"Yes, she knocked, but there was no answer."

"I still don't think she should have gone in then," replied Georgiana.

"Probably not, but people don't always behave sensibly in stories or in real life. You would do well to remember that," said Lizzy archly.

Georgiana gave a small smile and bit her lip.

"Well," continued Lizzy:

"It had been Sooty's intention just to sit down in front of the fire and rest awhile because she was very cold and tired, having walked a long way in shoes that were pinching her feet. But once she sat down at the hearth she smelt and saw the porridge and was overcome with hunger. She saw there was rather a lot of porridge, enough to feed an army, so she decided she would take a little to eat and leave one of the coins she had in her pocket.

When she went to the cupboard for a bowl, she found them stacked inside each other on a shelf. The outer bowl was huge; big enough to be a mixing bowl. Even the smallest bowl was much larger than the bowls Sooty used at home, but she thought it the most serviceable. But when she tried to retrieve it from the cupboard, she discovered the shelves were too close together to extract it—she would have to take all the bowls out at once and set them on the table. Alas! When she pulled them out, she found them much heavier than she expected, and the largest bowl fell on the floor and was shattered to pieces."

"Oh, no!" cried Georgiana, her hand flying to her mouth.

"Yes!" affirmed Lizzy:

"Looking around, Sooty saw a broom and set about cleaning up the mess. Unfortunately, this was a very recalcitrant broom owned by the fastidious bear, Fitz, and only he knew how to operate it. The broom had a loose handle, so it was necessary to push the broom and never pull it. But Sooty didn't know that, and as soon as she tried to sweep the shards towards herself, the broom fell to pieces."

"Oh, no!" cried Georgie, both hands now covering her mouth.

"...she cried," said Lizzy, ready for this interjection; *"I have broken the broom!*

So leaning the handle against the wall, Sooty crouched down and swept the shattered pieces into a corner with the head of the broom. Satisfied she had done her best to restore order, she found a small wooden spoon, which the youngest bear used as a teaspoon, and taking some porridge from the pot on the hob, she sat down and began to eat it.

She had only just set the bowl aside and was licking the spoon when she heard a noise outside; the knob of the door turned, and a huge bear entered, ducking his head so he did not strike the lintel. His brothers soon followed him."

"Oh, nooh!" cried Georgiana.

"Sooty was so shocked, she jumped up, dropping the spoon into the fire. She stood there, frozen, with all three bears staring at her, until the little one, Henry, saw his spoon catch alight and raced to snatch it from the flames.

"You burnt my spoon!" he accused.

Then the large bear, Richard, saw the small bowl near the fire and the middle-sized bowl on the table, and he correctly deduced that the shards in the corner were in fact his bowl.

"You broke my bowl!" he accused.

Then the middle bear, Fitz, seeing the state of his broom, chimed in with, "You broke my broom!" even though he knew very well he could fix it.

"I'm so sorry!" cried Sootylocks, horrified. Then pulling the pocket containing her money from her dress, she dumped it unceremoniously on the floor, burst out crying, and ran for the door.

But before she could run outside, the older bear relented, saying "Stop! Stop! Come back inside. You look like you have come a long way! I'm sorry if I frightened you!"

And he encouraged her back inside."

"He was a good bear, really," said Georgiana.

"Quite," replied Elizabeth.

"Then Richard said he would make her a cup of tea and asked how she came to be there.

Sooty first wanted to explain that the devastation she had wrought on their home was accidental, and she went on to describe the series of accidents that had befallen her upon deciding to eat a little porridge, which she had fully intended to pay for.

When she was given the tea, the cup was so huge that Sooty wondered that it had not occurred to her to use **that** as a bowl, thus avoiding the bulk of her folly. She accepted the tea gracefully, and as the bears ate their porridge—the eldest one straight from the pot—she explained her predicament.

Her father had received an offer for her hand from a local lord. He was very eligible, but she could not like him, and so she had run away."

"Why didn't she like him?" asked Georgiana. "Was he ugly?"

"Oh, no! Quite good looking! But... he didn't smile very much, and... he was haughty."

"Oh! Was he nasty to the servants?" asked Georgiana.

"Well, no," replied Elizabeth. "But he was *very* condescending."

"He didn't smile and he was condescending?" cried Georgiana.

"Sootylocks seems a bit severe!"

"Whose side are you on?" asked Elizabeth, arching her brows and causing Georgiana to giggle apologetically.

"Very well," conceded Elizabeth, "there was a bit more to it. Sootylocks overheard the lord insulting her at the ball."

"All right, now I don't like him," frowned Georgiana. "What did he say?"

"He said... that she shouldn't wear blue because it did not suit her complexion."

"That wasn't very gallant of him," commented Georgie. "He deserved to come unstuck."

"My thoughts exactly," said Elizabeth, before continuing:

The bears were very sympathetic to Sootylocks' plight.

"One shouldn't be forced to marry against one's will," said the oldest bear.

"No, one shouldn't!" interjected Georgiana vehemently.

"But remember," said Elizabeth coolly, "they were bachelor bears, so they might have been biased."

"So what happened?" asked Georgie.

The bears offered to escort Sootylocks home because they were concerned for her safety, and the oldest bear promised to speak to her father. Sooty didn't think this would do much good, but she agreed that she couldn't continue roaming the countryside. She did offer to act as housekeeper to the bachelor bears, but the older bear wasn't keen on replacing all the crockery, so he suggested that perhaps that arrangement might be viewed as slightly improper, given they were bachelor bears.

After the bears escorted her home, Richard Bear spoke to her father, suggesting he should not give his daughter's hand in matrimony 'til she met someone she really liked. The father argued that the suitor was a worthy man and that his daughter, being young and foolish like all girls, would soon grow to like her husband; but when he heard about the insult he relented. He conceded that if the suitor really loved his daughter, as he claimed, then he would have thought her beautiful in whatever she was wearing.

So the suitor was rejected, and the daughter and her father spent many happy years together before she finally met someone she liked and got married.

The End."

"That was a very good story," said Georgiana, "but I think the youngest bear would have argued in favour of matrimony."

Elizabeth laughed, and tucking Georgiana in, she blew out the candle and said goodnight.

Early the next morning, Elizabeth was woken early when Georgie climbed into her bed.

"What's the matter?" Elizabeth asked groggily. "Were you cold?"

"No," replied Georgiana, "I had a nightmare."

"What was it about?" asked Elizabeth.

"Bears," said Georgie.

32 The Lakes tour

Following the return of Georgiana to Pemberley, the house settled into a new routine. Like her brother, Georgiana liked to ride in the morning, although she set out after breakfast rather than before. She had several warm riding habits in velvet, of which Elizabeth particularly admired a black one. Georgie wasn't conventionally pretty, but wearing this, and with a small beaver perched on her glossy black locks, she resembled her brother, and managed to look rather dashing.

Georgiana had at first been rather taken aback to discover that Elizabeth did not ride. "But you must learn, Elizabeth!" she pleaded. "Then we can ride together!"

Elizabeth was not enthusiastic. She begged off on the excuse that she had nothing to wear, which was true, as none of her gowns were cut full enough to allow her to mount with decorum or warm enough, besides. Disappointed, Georgie had resumed her rides with Healy in tow.

While Georgiana might not have found the riding companion she had hoped for in Lizzy, in the week leading up to Christmas, Lizzy and Georgiana spent many happy hours together in Georgiana's sitting room.

Georgiana, under the guidance of Mrs Annesley, was tatting a bookmark as a present for her brother. Elizabeth was impressed with their efforts—for Georgie made so many mistakes that had to be corrected by Mrs Annesley that it was indeed a dual effort. Lizzy thought it so pretty that she decided to make a bookmark for herself under Mrs Annesley's guidance.

As Mrs Annesley reversed the damage of an ill-set or erroneous knot in Georgiana's bookmark, Georgie entertained them both with musical accompaniment. On the piano Georgie excelled, putting Elizabeth, and even her sister Mary, so much in the shade that Elizabeth vowed never to touch a keyboard again. It was quite clear that the level Georgie had obtained was achievable only through years of practice. Elizabeth simultaneously acknowledged she had no wish to spend an enormous amount of time in front of a keyboard or to make everyone cringe with her comparatively poor efforts in the meantime.

While Elizabeth's hands were occupied in tatting, her mind wandered in many directions. For one thing, she wondered on the reason for her husband's sudden departure from Pemberley. True, Darcy had raised his intentions of going to Yorkshire earlier, but she struggled to understand his unheralded disappearance. Possibly some deadline had arisen which he had failed to communicate; or, perhaps, she thought, his unwillingness to speak of his imminent departure beforehand arose from fear of being challenged in his intent. She had given no indication that she was likely to object when he had explained his plans, but Elizabeth realised that such secretiveness often arose from childhood habits rather than premeditation.

Other less pleasant explanations for his precipitate departure arose. She wondered if Darcy had a lover in Yorkshire, and if his passionate anticipation of his scheduled weekly visit with her had presaged a need to be reunited with his flame.

The gender of this spectre had alternated in Elizabeth's mind between male and female. While her father's wisdom conjured Darcy planting a passionate kiss on some obscure male in a scene that smacked of her nocturnal encounter with Finn and Healy, Lizzy's own imaginings placed him in the frilly boudoir of an enticing mistress. This female form of the wraith looked like her sister Jane but acted like a tigress. Elizabeth did not like the combination of these two characteristics and tried in vain to imbue the mistress with a different form. She could only suppose her imagination had invoked the greatest beauty she had encountered as the embodiment of her rival in a pathetic attempt to assuage her own feelings of inadequacy.

Elizabeth attempted to resign herself to this unknown third person in her marriage, trying to view her cup as half-full instead of half-empty. When a nascent wish for a nice hot bath intruded, she reminded herself she was residing at Pemberley in far greater luxury than she had ever enjoyed at Longbourn. Unfortunately she found little solace in sentiments more worthy of her mother. A more cheering thought was that the prospect of a lonely existence in the huge house had receded, at least temporarily, with the arrival of Georgiana. Certainly her sister was one thing to be glad for— Georgie was a good girl, and they were fair on their way to becoming boon companions. Imagine if she had been cooped up with the likes of a sister like Caroline Bingley! Still, Georgie was no Jane or Charlotte, for that matter, and Elizabeth could hardly take her into her confidence.

As she tied another knot in her tatting, thoughts of her husband continued to nag at Elizabeth. Had Darcy not been honest with her from the start? He had said his heart belonged to another when he proposed their marriage of convenience. She had gone into the marriage with open eyes, if somewhat reluctantly. Still, it hurt to be valued only as a broodmare.

In desperation, Elizabeth sought refuge against these thoughts by imagining herself married to her cousin, Mr Collins. This provided some temporary relief, particularly when she imagined him groping her bottom. Unfortunately it proved not enough to stem her ingratitude, and the dismal thought that she had been denied the felicity of finding someone who loved her, cherished her, still lurked.

Elizabeth reminded herself that it was very unlikely that she would ever have found such a man. In all her years, she had met only one person who expressed something approaching true regard for her, which she might have been able to reciprocate. That man, of course, had been Edward Yardley— a thought that led to yet more melancholy reflections. She began to think that passive occupations such as tatting did not suit her and that she really ought to be doing something more active to take her mind off her situation. But the weather remained frigid, and only short walks outside were possible on the odd day and pacing of the gallery on most.

Two days before Christmas, a large box arrived by courier for Elizabeth and Georgiana. When it was discovered it was sent by her brother, Georgiana became enraged.

"No doubt these are presents!" she spat.

"Miss Georgiana, there are few brothers in this world who are so considerate with gifts for their sisters as your own," said Mrs Annesley, trying to turn her charge's mind to a proper sense of gratitude.

"As sure as check, he will not be home for Christmas!" said Georgiana.

Mrs Annesley sighed. *Where did Miss Georgie learn such cant expressions?* She suspected Colonel Fitzwilliam was to blame.

"He did only say that he would *try* to be home for Christmas," said Elizabeth, recalling his note. "Perhaps he has been delayed. Cheer up. We could always open this box now. In fact, I think we should, because it might contain something perishable."

"The only thing I want is a new horse," pouted Georgie; "and I'm fairly sure there is not one inside."

Elizabeth laughed. "What is wrong with your current horse?"

"He is a slug and refuses to take the smallest jump. Brother promised me a cover-hack for my sixteenth birthday, and he didn't deliver!"

"Now, you know, Miss Georgie, that the last time you asked him, your brother said he hadn't found quite the right animal," remonstrated Mrs Annesley.

Georgie merely snorted in reply.

The first package to be retrieved from the box, which was directed to Elizabeth, turned out to be a beautiful woollen cloak lined with rabbit fur.

"Oh! This is just the thing!" she cried. "Now I shall be able to walk outside!"

A smaller package for Georgie turned out to be a sable muff.

"Another muff!" huffed Georgie.

"But the fur is so beautiful!" said Elizabeth, stroking it; "and look! It is lined with fur as well!"

Georgie grudgingly acknowledged it was an exemplary muff.

The last package was also directed to Elizabeth. It turned out to be another cloak, but a very fine one of mink trimmed with ermine. "For church" declared a note in Darcy's writing that fluttered out of it.

"Oh, it is very beautiful!" said Elizabeth, holding the fur to her cheek.

"Now I am jealous," said Georgie. "My best is not half so fine."

"Would you like it?" asked Elizabeth, looking at the two she had received and thinking how much she had benefited from Georgie's wardrobe.

"Oh, no!" said Georgie, abashed, but still eyeing the ermine covetously. "I was only joking. I have plenty."

In Hertfordshire, Jane had finally been able to reoccupy her own bedchamber after Lizzy's wedding, following Anne's removal to Netherfield. As she lay down to sleep, the familiarity of it calmed her, but her sense of relief was tinged with some sadness when she realised that it was her first night alone there following her sister's departure.

Of Miss de Bourgh she thought little. While her deepest sympathies had gone out to someone so young and so ill, Jane had not developed a close bond with Miss de Bourgh while nursing her—Anne was inoffensive to the point of insipidity. Remembering the appearance of Anne's dragon of a mother at Lizzy's wedding, Jane briefly wondered if Anne's timidity was due to her upbringing or was inherent, and what manner of man Anne's deceased father had been to choose such an overbearing wife. Finally, she decided Anne's illness had likely been crucial in deciding her temperament.

Suddenly it dawned on Jane that analysing people's characters was Lizzy's hobby, which she seemed to have taken up in her sister's absence, even imagining herself talking to Lizzy as she thought. Relieved of the burden of nursing Anne, Jane realised she missed Lizzy every day.

Of Mr Bingley there had been no sign since Miss de Bourgh's departure. Jane had begun to worry that *he* might be ill when she encountered him in the main street of Meryton towards the end of the week. He blushed profusely and begged pardon for his failure to visit Longbourn—his sisters had been caught up with the nursing of Miss de Bourgh and had been quite unable to spare the time to accompany him on a call. He hoped to visit the following week.

Jane replied politely to his assurances, but she could only be glad that she had guarded her heart against his gallantry after overhearing the Bingleys discussing her lack of suitability at the Netherfield Ball. It seemed that out-of-sight was out-of-mind with Mr Bingley. She even began to wonder whether his easy-going charm and fickleness were symptoms of a licentious nature.

Poor Mr Bingley would have been aghast had he known the direction of her thoughts. He was genuinely attracted to Jane and his intentions were quite pure, but it was true that she was one of a series of women he had been attracted to who had not found favour in his sisters' eyes. They had been at pains to keep him away from Longbourn, using their guest as an excuse. Instead, they employed every stratagem to throw their brother together with Miss de Bourgh, whose fortune and relationship to Mr Darcy made her a most eligible partie.

Jane's uncharacteristically dark thoughts on Mr Bingley had, in fact, arisen from her observations of the earl. At first, she had detected no difference in the earl's pretty compliments and attentions to those bestowed upon her by many other men. It was his son who had made her suspect that there was more to some of the earl's utterances than she at first appreciated.

Colonel Richard Fitzwilliam, she realised, had an interesting face. Upon their initial acquaintance, it had seemed open and bland. It was a comfortable rather than a handsome face, a face of stolid reliability that set one at ease. It was only after Jane became better acquainted with the colonel, when she began to understand his nuances of expression, that she suspected that some of the earl's pronouncements were not entirely proper. She started to carefully note each comment that elicited a slight frown or pained expression from the colonel.

Having no Lizzy to discuss these with, Jane turned to Charlotte. Following Miss de Bourgh's departure, Charlotte had resumed spending her mornings at Longbourn as had been her habit before Lizzy married. Although Lizzy, Longbourn's biggest attraction, was gone, the genteel female companionship to be had there still attracted Miss Lucas for her daily visit, much to Mrs Bennet's chagrin. With the departure of the last of the wedding guests, the mistress of Longbourn had hoped to finally rid her house of the presence of its next mistress—at least, temporarily.

Jane's sympathies were with her mother. She had always been slightly disapproving of Lizzy's friendship with Charlotte. Sir William and Lady Lucas had a tendency to puff themselves off in front of the Bennets, who were the most significant representatives of the landed gentry in their vicinity. Sir William, who had been a well-to-do merchant in Meryton before aspiring to the mayoralty, had renounced trade upon receiving a knighthood for his efforts in that office. He had built a grand house upon some land purchased outside the town, but there was no income attached to this property—his living was derived solely from investment in the funds. Thus while he was something more than *Mr* Bennet in having a title, he was also something less than *Squire* Bennet.

Charlotte, herself, did not put on airs; but her manners were not so nice as Jane would have liked. Nonetheless, at seven years older than Jane and with the advantage of several grown brothers, Jane suspected Charlotte was more worldly-wise than herself; and she had resolved to seek her counsel on the earl's manners. She was very glad that she did.

"I am so sorry to trouble you with these dark thoughts, Charlotte," she had begun. "I hardly know what is happening to me, I feel so depressed since Lizzy left."

"That is natural," replied Charlotte, unruffled. "You were very close and will no doubt miss each other greatly. Your other sisters are... different."

Charlotte had then gone on to explain potential double meanings in the earl's utterances that would have had Jane blushing if she had understood them at the time.

Then, disturbingly, Charlotte had concluded with, "Do not worry at having dark thoughts, Jane. Everyone has them. They are your natural defence against danger. It used to amuse me the way you and Lizzy divided up the good and bad between you: you, with your blonde hair, taking the part of the angels; and she, with her dark hair, being the devil's advocate."

"What are you talking about, Charlotte?" asked Jane bewildered. "What is a devil's advocate?"

Charlotte laughed. "Do not worry. Loving her as I do, I am not accusing your sister of being evil. It is a catholic thing to do with the canonisation of saints."

And she had gone off, leaving Jane thinking that perhaps Charlotte was smarter than she had previously realised.

Jane's sensibilities were spared further testing by the removal of Miss de Bourgh to Netherfield. The earl came no more and Jane breathed a sigh of relief.

The colonel returned as promised to pick up Jane's letter for Elizabeth on his way north and to take tea. She found him a very pleasant companion, and more easy in her company than she had noticed before. He began to make jokes.

Charlotte had been present for the morning's visit, and they had both walked out to the portico to see the colonel off.

"Well, he has taken quite a shine to you," said Charlotte as Richard disappeared through the gates.

"He is a very sweet man," said Jane; "but his solicitude is chiefly for Lizzy. His mother lives in the north not far from the Darcys. He says it is no trouble to take letters back and forth, for his work takes him in that direction anyway."

Charlotte smiled knowingly. "He seemed more cheerful this time. No doubt because he had you all to himself."

"What can you mean, Charlotte?" asked Jane.

"Merely that he used to spend a good deal of his time watching you while Mr Bingley and the earl vied for your attention. His manner reminded me of a small boy waiting for some bigger boys to forget a toy, so that he might have his turn."

"I believe you are mistaken, Charlotte," replied Jane stiffly.

"I know I am not. I had every chance to observe him while your attention was naturally focused elsewhere. I think you will see the colonel make his attentions more obvious now his rivals have disappeared."

Believing Charlotte to be drawing a rather long bow, Jane changed the subject by enquiring of her wedding preparations.

"Mother has everything in hand," replied Charlotte. "All I have to do is fit into the wedding gown—for she has made it rather tight—and say '*I do*'."

"I wish you every felicity, Charlotte," said Jane, trying to make up for some of her mother's incivility. "It must be comforting to know that your future is assured."

"Indeed," said Charlotte with a mysterious smile, "although I believe your cousin was within aims-ace of crying off when he heard he had lost out on a five thousand pound dowry by not offering for Mary."

"How came he by that knowledge, Charlotte?" asked Jane, shocked.

"Surely you jest, Jane," replied Charlotte. "It is the talk of the town."

"How odious," murmured Jane. "Is it possible that Kitty or Lydia has been indiscreet?

"I'm afraid so," replied Charlotte.

"And is it common knowledge that Mr Darcy is supplying our dowries?" asked Jane.

"It is rumoured, of course, but I managed to confound Mrs Winkworth by saying that it was always your mother's intention to supply a dowry to you all equal to her own."

Jane bit back a smile. "I suppose that is the truth, even if it is misleading."

Charlotte chuckled. "But I must be off to Netherfield. I promised to sit with Anne this afternoon to relieve Mrs Jenkinson."

"You are too good, Charlotte. What will happen when you marry next week? Will Mr Collins return to Kent as he originally planned?"

"It is undecided. Mr Collins has assured Lady Catherine that he would not think of leaving Miss de Bourgh's side if her ladyship desires him to stay. His curate is delivering the sermons he writes every week. We may yet be spending the first weeks of our marriage at Lucas Lodge."

And with this parting statement, Charlotte finished tying the strings of her bonnet, gave a cheery wave, and was off.

On the morning following the arrival of the furs at Pemberley, it rained. Thus it was not 'til after lunch that Georgie managed to set out on her daily ride, and Elizabeth decided to test her new coat by taking a walk. As the less expensive cloak had a hood, Lizzy pulled this onto her head as she left the house.

Elizabeth set out towards the succession house, with a poke about that as her first object. Unlike her prior expedition shortly after her arrival at Pemberley, this time she had the forethought to bring her chatelaine to open the locked door. She found a sole gardener tending the plants in the cold weather.

In winter, Old Matthew preferred to spend his time in the succession house rather than his cold hut, as his rheumatism bothered him less there.

Although he was perturbed to be discovered lounging about by the new mistress, he graciously offered to show her around and was quite in charity with her when she offered to take back a small basket of provisions the cook had ordered for dinner.

Elizabeth did not get far with the basket on her arm before Stevens divested her of it. Beginning to see the advantage of having a footman dog her steps, Elizabeth thanked him and set off on the rest of her walk, taking a circuitous route towards the formal garden.

She was making for the entrance in the north wall of the garden when she encountered Georgiana returning from her ride. Her horse was a very handsome one with a kind look in its eye. Remembering Georgiana's wish to replace her 'slug', Elizabeth wondered how she could bear to part with such an admirable animal.

"Where are you going, Elizabeth?" asked Georgie, eyeing the basket on Stevens' arm.

"Only to the formal garden. Do you care to come?"

"Certainly," replied Georgiana, dismounting and handing her reins to Healy.

Stevens took this as his cue to depart.

Elizabeth slightly regretted her offer when she saw Georgie gather her voluminous skirts over one arm. Georgie's riding habit was cut to make her appear decorous when mounted, but it looked quite cumbersome to walk in. Elizabeth could not imagine that Georgie could comfortably go far and decided to curtail her walk for her sister's sake.

After passing through the gate, they headed for the centre of the garden from whence Elizabeth intended to take the path back to the house. When they reached the central square surrounded by the statues of the four seasons, Georgie exclaimed. "I loved this square when I was a child. I used to pretend that the mosaic in the middle was magic, and it would grant your wish if you stepped on it while thinking of what you wanted."

Elizabeth smiled, thinking of the last time she had stood on the mosaic, when she had kissed Fitzwilliam after their mad scramble around the garden. "And did it ever work?" she asked.

"Yes," replied Georgie in all earnestness. "Fitzwilliam gave me a Diablo after I saw Henry Anstey playing with one."

Elizabeth laughed at the modesty of the girl's wishes, before reflecting that such trinkets were likely to be the only things that Georgie had ever lacked. "Perhaps it was a coincidence," she suggested.

"You have to believe in it," responded Georgie testily, having encountered the same degree of scepticism from her cousin Richard. Knowing her sister's interest in fairy tales, she expected better of Elizabeth.

Georgie then looked around. "Which statue do you like best?"

Elizabeth examined the four sculptures. "Well, they are all beautiful, except Winter of course, because he is portrayed as an old man; but I think I prefer Spring. She reminds me of my sister, Jane."

"Your sister must be very beautiful," remarked Georgie.

"She is," affirmed Lizzy.

"I like Autumn, because he reminds me of George."

Elizabeth examined the statue of the beautiful youth holding the cup. "Who is George?"

"He is the handsomest and nicest man I know," said Georgie. "He used to live here at Pemberley, but he has gone to study law. I have not seen him for years. His father was the best steward Pemberley ever had."

"He sounds quite the paragon," said Elizabeth.

"Yes, and I miss him terribly, but his studies have not allowed him to visit."

"Well, perhaps we should head back to the house," suggested Elizabeth, not displaying any further interest in George.

"Oh, no!" whined Georgie. "We have hardly begun."

"Surely walking in your riding dress must be tiring?" observed Elizabeth.

"Well, it is a little clumsy," conceded Georgiana. "But I am fine."

"I had hoped to explore the Dower House," said Elizabeth.

"Sadly it is locked. I have always wanted to go in there myself," added Georgie. "It was my parents' house before the new house was built."

"I have keys," said Lizzy, producing the chatelaine. "Do you think one of them will fit?"

"Oooohhh!" said Georgie. "That looks like my mother's chatelaine!"

"It is," replied Lizzy, archly. "You forget that I married your brother!"

"Oh, yes," mused Georgie as they walked towards the Dower House. "You must forgive me. It all happened so quickly and I have yet to see the two of you together!"

Reaching the entrance, Elizabeth tried several keys before finding one that fitted the lock.

"Oh, I feel like Sootylocks!" cried Georgiana as they pushed open the front door. "I do hope the bears don't come home while we are here!"

"Grrrr!" said a voice behind them.

Despite the encumbrances of her skirts, Georgiana jumped several inches into the air. Elizabeth swung round to confront their attacker, who turned out to be Richard.

"The look on your face, Cousin Elizabeth!" he laughed. "I believe my knees are knocking together!"

"Very likely," she mocked. "How did you sneak up so quietly?"

"I walked on the grass. It is an old army trick," he joked.

Elizabeth was about to abandon her exploration of the house when Georgie protested that Richard could well wait half an hour for a cup of tea.

Despite having ridden directly from Longbourn, Richard did not protest. He'd helped himself to brandy on his way through the main house in search of them, and expressed himself ready to explore the Dower House. "I have not been in here since I was in short coats," he added.

The Dower House turned out to be about the same size as Longbourn, although in considerably better repair despite the antiquity of parts of it. Although the rooms were a little dusty, it was quite clean—the furniture all under holland covers and the rugs rolled up.

"I believe Mrs Reynolds comes over here once a year to give it a spring clean," said Richard.

"I didn't know that," said Georgie.

"It is quite charming," said Elizabeth. "I could easily live here myself."

They abandoned their exploration of the house as the afternoon light failed, whereupon the three of them walked back to the main house for tea, chatting amiably.

"Where is Darcy?" asked Richard.

"He went off to Yorkshire shortly after you left for the south," responded Elizabeth.

"He didn't even wait 'til I had returned from Matlock!" complained Georgie.

A slight frown creased Richard's brow as he recalled the troubled state of Darcy's mind during their last conversation. He had thought his cousin's dilemma ridiculous, but perhaps he should have paid more attention—Darcy was a very intelligent chap, but prone to the occasional queer start. "Does he intend to return for Christmas?" he asked.

"He was non-committal on that point," replied Elizabeth. "I suppose it depends on his business in Yorkshire."

"He sent us some presents yesterday, so I am betting he is going to pike!" said Georgie.

"But he didn't specifically *say* they were Christmas presents," pointed out Elizabeth.

"Well, I must deliver the communiqué in my jacket, but I will be back on Christmas Eve and will stay several days," promised Richard.

With this, the ladies had to be content. The three of them passed two pleasant hours together in Georgie's sitting room with Mrs Annesley before dining together.

When the colonel rode off in the morning, the ladies were sad to see him go, very much missing male company.

Elizabeth waited to retire before reading her letter from Jane, so that she could do so in privacy. She was rather surprised to discover that Darcy's cousin had been removed to Netherfield, which was no closer to her home in Kent than Longbourn. She strongly suspected Caroline of trying to promote a match between her brother and Miss de Bourgh. Her suspicions were strengthened when Jane related she had seen little of Mr Bingley lately.

Despite her dislike of both Bingley sisters, and of Caroline, in particular, a part of Elizabeth had hoped that Jane's five thousand pound dowry would make the match more palatable to the Bingley sisters, for Jane's sake. But it appeared they valued themselves higher.

Sighing, Lizzy snuffed the candle and lay down to sleep.

Elizabeth was roused before dawn on Christmas Eve when Georgie once again climbed into her bed.

"Not another nightmare?" said Elizabeth sleepily.

"Yes," affirmed Georgie snuggling up to her sister and clinging to her back.

"Was it the bears again?" asked Elizabeth, thinking she would never tell Georgie another fairy tale.

No reply was forthcoming. Elizabeth was about to pose the question again when she realised Georgie was shaking. Turning over, she was astonished to find the girl crying. "Why, Georgie, ...what is the matter?"

"I had that dream again, about Fitzwilliam not coming back."

Elizabeth had not previously been aware of *that* dream, but it hardly seemed the time to question Georgie more closely.

"He'll come back eventually, Georgie," Elizabeth soothed. "He has to run the estate. He's only gone to Yorkshire."

"He can't come back," sobbed Georgie, "because he's dead. The highwaymen kill him."

Despite herself, a shudder of dread ran through Elizabeth. She hoped Georgie didn't notice. "Shhh," she said, hugging her sister and stroking her hair. "It's just a dream."

33 Travel plans

Darcy's business in Yorkshire prospered. Bingley's partners welcomed him with open arms, accepting without a blink his explanation for his early arrival. His tours of the mills were an entirely new experience for him. Darcy marvelled at the ingenuity of their enterprise, but he was also surprised at the hellish conditions the mill workers laboured in. The noise from the machines was atrocious, and the air on the manufactory floor seemed almost unbreathable—such was the lint and dust floating in it.

He gratefully accepted the hospitality of the mill-owners and was astonished at the level of luxury in their houses. One evening he dined off gold plate, a practice that had been abandoned in most homes of the Ton— his Aunt Catherine was one of the few holdouts among his acquaintances who had not adopted china. In another household, he used his first water closet.

By the mill-owners, Darcy was treated with a pleasing deference due to his money and station in life. Their manners were sometimes gruff and direct, but he felt an affinity for these captains of industry which he had never felt for many members of his own social circle, like that fritterer Hurst, whom Bingley called brother-in-law.

Darcy's mental decision to commit his money to the steam engines was made relatively quickly, but he continued his tour, partly to satisfy the wishes of Bingley's partners who welcomed the opportunity to describe their ingenious plans to such an avid listener, but also to defer making a decision on returning to Pemberley.

Elizabeth occupied his mind often. His erotic thoughts continued, but were thankfully confined to his dreams. Her absence had taken the edge off his lust. During the spare moments of his waking hours, Darcy mainly replayed their various conversations, dating from their first interactions at Netherfield. He even began to subtly alter the dialogue, allowing himself to say clever things that he had thought of afterwards but hadn't been quick-witted enough to say at the time. But any waking thoughts of his wife were always tinged with the guilt he felt about having imposed upon her in such a barbarous way.

As Darcy's tour of the manufactories came to an end, the question that was foremost in his mind was whether he could trust himself to return to Pemberley for Christmas. His home seemed to call to him, but a more rational part of his mind reasoned it would be better to stay away until his blood cooled.

When Darcy was spending two days in York finalising the paperwork committing him to Bingley's enterprise, the solution to his dilemma came to him. As his contribution to the project seriously depleted his ready cash, it would be necessary to correspond with his man of business to rearrange his finances. It occurred to Darcy that a trip to London would enable him to do so personally and give him a valid excuse to continue to avoid Pemberley. Thus, when his valet started to pack Darcy's trunk in preparation for his removal from York, he let him know of his travel plans.

"I've decided to go to London, Finn. Tell the driver we'll take the post road through Sheffield and Chesterfield. That way the horses can be sent back to Pemberley. We'll continue post from there."

"To London, sir?" repeated Finn in some surprise. He had hoped to spend his day off for Christmas in Healy's room over the stables.

"Yes, to London," said Darcy defensively, irritated at having his orders questioned.

"I beg your pardon, sir," replied Finn, resuming his packing. "It was not my intention to demur."

As light snow was falling when they departed York, Darcy rode in the carriage, with Finn occupying the backward-facing seat. As they passed through Sheffield, Darcy watched the turnoff to Baslow pass by with some regret. A glance at his valet showed he was asleep. Reconciling himself to his decision, Darcy settled back into his seat for the next stage to Chesterfield.

Colonel Fitzwilliam was delayed by unforeseen complications in Newcastle, but he arrived back at Pemberley just before sunset on Christmas Eve. The ladies had despaired of having any male company at all for Christmas by the time he galloped up the drive. The colonel was cold and dispirited by the inefficiency he had encountered in Newcastle. He couldn't believe the moulders he'd had to deal with were not already on half-pay now that Napoleon had been defeated. Why did the general prefer to surround himself with lickspittles who wouldn't lift a finger unless they could see some direct benefit to themselves? He wished he could visit Wellington upon them—that would set the cat among the pigeons!

Shaking the snow from his roquelaure and stamping his boots, Richard entered the vestibule where a footman helped divest him of his chapeau-bras and his outerwear. As he was donning a pair of slippers he kept at Pemberley for just such occasions, he heard Georgie running down the stairs. Richard made a show of staggering as she catapulted herself at him, although he was never in any danger of being knocked off balance.

"Richard, we thought you weren't coming!" declared Georgie.

"Now, Georgie, I said I would be back by Christmas Eve and I fully intended to be so, by hook or by crook! There were a few delays in Newcastle. That is all."

"Come upstairs," said Georgie, pulling her cousin by the hand. "We have a nice warm fire in my sitting room!"

Elizabeth, who had followed Georgie into the vestibule in a more seemly fashion, now intervened: "Perhaps your cousin would like some brandy to help him warm up, Georgie."

"Indeed I would, Cousin Elizabeth," affirmed Richard with gratitude. "I will join you upstairs shortly, Georgie."

Georgie dutifully let her cousin go, thus enabling him to relieve himself and down a bumper of brandy before walking into Georgie's sitting room.

Padding across the atrium in his slippers after Georgie and Elizabeth had departed, Richard headed for Darcy's study, hoping his cousin had arrived back from Yorkshire. He hadn't liked to question Georgie about her brother's whereabouts, knowing it would be a sore topic if Darcy was still absent.

Richard knocked on the door to Darcy's study and, when no summons was heard, let himself inside. The room was in darkness and no fire was lit in the hearth. Retrieving a candle from the hall, Richard helped himself to the brandy and the chamber pot before proceeding upstairs.

When he arrived in the sitting room to find Georgie once more seated at the piano with Cousin Elizabeth and Mrs Annesley in attendance, Richard resigned himself to ask the inevitable question at the end of her piece:

"Did Darcy not make it back from Yorkshire?"

Georgie erupted. "No, I told you he would not! His horses arrived back this afternoon from Sheffield. He is posting to London!"

"He sent a message saying he needed to rearrange his finances in London," added Elizabeth. "He decided to invest in Bingley's steam engines, which has depleted his cash reserves."

Richard nodded in understanding. Despite his disapproval of Darcy's failure to return to Pemberley, he was relieved that his cousin had at least notified his wife of his movements, which was something. Sometimes Darcy seemed to exist in his own little world.

"It is too bad of him not to come back!" continued Georgie with asperity. "I spent ages making a Christmas present for him! And Mrs Reynolds ordered venison to be readied for his return!"

"No matter!" said the colonel with an airiness he could not feel, "I shall eat his venison for him."

The snow had continued to fall lightly as Darcy made his way south from York early on Christmas Eve, but soon began to form small drifts. He could only hope that the weather stayed cold, so that it did not melt and make the roads slippery.

His team were good until Sheffield where they were unhitched and left in the care of a groom and one of the under-grooms, ready to make their way back to Pemberley in the afternoon. Darcy had penned a note for

Time's Up, Mr Darcy

Elizabeth at breakfast, explaining his decision to go to London and, as his carriage prepared to depart, he handed this to the groom bound for Pemberley. The post-boys mounted the offside horses and, with a crack of the whip, they were off, making good time on their journey south.

But the team were not five miles from Chesterfield when the carriage gave a jolt and a lurch before righting itself. When the coachman pulled up and jumped down, exchanging words with the post-boys, Darcy leant his head out the window.

"Is there a problem, Harry?"

"I'm sorry, sir," replied the coachman. "I hit an object hidden by the snow on the road. It must have fallen from a cart in front of us, for I was keeping to the wheel ruts of the other vehicles. Neither of the post-boys saw it either."

Darcy waved his hand dismissively at any perceived negligence on his coachman's part.

One of the under-grooms, who had jumped down from the back to search for the obstacle, now ran up to report. "It was a sack of meal, sir. Shall I pick it up? We may catch up with the cart it fell from."

"No, Tom," said Darcy, "just drag it to the side of the road. They may live nearby and turn back to look for it. Mark it with a branch or some such, to help them find it."

Then, turning back to the coachman who was inspecting the front nearside wheel, Darcy asked if there was any damage.

"Not that I can see, sir; but I was going pretty fast when I hit it. I'll slow down if I may, just 'til I'm sure it's all right."

Darcy sighed inwardly. "Very well."

But when the coachman got down to inspect the wheel at Chesterfield he did not have good news. "I can see a crack opening up in one spoke, sir. I dare not go much further on that wheel 'til the wheelwright has inspected it."

Darcy resigned himself to an early lunch while the coach was taken off to the wheelwright. "Very well, Harry. Let me know when you have an estimate of the delay."

Darcy was partway through a very tolerable repast at the inn when his coachman returned with bad news.

"There is not a spare coach wheel to be had in all Chesterfield, sir. Apparently the master wheelwright died suddenly a fortnight ago. They expect to get some spares from Sheffield this afternoon, but the apprentices say they won't be able to fit the new wheel until Boxing Day."

Darcy was damned if he was going to spend Christmas in an inn in Chesterfield. He pulled a small purse from his pocket, which he kept for just such emergencies. "Do what you can to get us on our way, Harry. Surely there is a coach that no-one is using that can spare a wheel 'til Boxing Day?"

"Yes, sir," said Harry, accepting the purse with a smile. He didn't fancy hanging round Chesterfield for Christmas either.

While this solution eventually enabled them to be ready to proceed, it was still several hours before the wheel was procured and fitted. By the time Harry announced that the coach was good to go, it was three o'clock. Knowing that he couldn't travel on Christmas Day and was not far enough south to make London by evening, Darcy finally resigned himself to the inevitable.

"We'd better make for Pemberley, Harry. I'll have to delay my trip to London 'til after Christmas."

"Yes, sir," replied his coachman with a straight face.

But after Darcy entered the coach there were grins all round—it seemed their broken wheel was a cloud with a silver lining. The bag of meal had been sent by providence—they would be spending Christmas at Pemberley after all.

When the inhabitants of Pemberley were about to sit down to dinner on Christmas Eve, a carriage was heard drawing up outside. The colonel abandoned his post at the head of the table to follow Mrs Reynolds into the vestibule to investigate. When he stuck his head back into the dining room to announce that Darcy had returned after all, the ladies promptly left the table.

As Darcy stepped into the vestibule, Georgie threw herself at her brother even more enthusiastically than she had greeted her cousin.

"Now, Georgie, what is the matter with you?" said Darcy, straightening his cravat. "Please behave with decorum!"

"Oh, Fitz, it is good to see you! I thought you had abandoned me again!" declared Georgie.

Darcy frowned, disliking being called out for his negligence.

Elizabeth, who had hung back, smiled to herself—Georgie could not be faulted on her devotion to her brother, even if she did behave a little like Lydia. Lizzy was genuinely glad Darcy had returned; in fact her heart gave the oddest little leap upon seeing him. Her husband seemed to have become a little handsomer since she last saw him, which she could not satisfactorily explain—*perhaps his hair was a little longer?* Sensing an enthusiastic welcome from herself would not be appreciated, she merely smiled at him.

Darcy flicked a glance at his wife, but quickly lowered his eyes once they met hers.

"So you changed your mind about London?" asked the colonel with a smile, as a footman helped Darcy from his greatcoat.

"We had a slight mishap with the carriage just outside Chesterfield," replied Darcy. "A spoke on one of the wheels cracked, and there was not a new wheel to be had in town. By the time a replacement was found, we could not have made London by midnight, so I changed my plans."

"Well, I'm glad they are short of wheels in Chesterfield!" replied Richard. "It's good to see you! We were about to sit down to dinner, and Mrs Reynolds has cooked venison!"

They all repaired to the dining room, with Darcy assuming his place at the head of the table. Elizabeth sat at his right, and Georgie at his left with Mrs Annesley at her charge's side. A new place had been set for the colonel next to Elizabeth, which suited him very well, as he merely got to sit on her right instead of her left; and could still claim her as a very pleasant dinner companion.

They partook of a feast very worthy of the master's homecoming—the venison having been hung for just the right amount of time. Darcy relayed details of his trip, explaining his tours of the factories, and, upon further prompting by his relatives, he spoke somewhat of his less business-like activities, including the water closet he had encountered. They were all rather bemused by this invention, which seemed hardly necessary if one could afford chambermaids, but deemed it an interesting curiosity.

When the ladies got up to withdraw, Darcy declared himself ready to follow them, to which the colonel gracefully conceded, knowing he could have some brandy before bed anyway. They all agreed to repair upstairs, as Darcy was eager to hear his sister play her Christmas present in her new sitting room.

Upon entering the sitting room, Darcy was gratified by Georgie's appreciation of her gift. She flew round the room pointing out aspects of the decor that had particularly pleased her, as well as explaining how they had slightly rearranged the furniture to dispose the settees and the piano in a more inclusive configuration. Georgie then sat down at the instrument and regaled them with the latest piece she had mastered. Darcy had to admit that the tone and volume of the piano was vastly superior to the other instruments they possessed, just as the salesman had promised in London and that the vast expense of purchasing the instrument and having it brought most of the way to Derbyshire by water was worth it.

During the course of Georgie's recital, Darcy's attention inevitably strayed to his wife. He had been considerably embarrassed upon first encountering Elizabeth in the vestibule and could not meet her eyes. He'd got a glimpse of a pink dress, but he was careful to ensure he did not look at her again, and thereby start his mind in an undesirable direction. Once they sat down at table, Darcy had gradually been set at ease by his relatives' unfeigned interest in his travels; so by the end of the meal he believed he had mastered any wayward thoughts of his wife.

After repairing to the sitting room, Darcy was momentarily disturbed by the thought of sitting next to Elizabeth on the settee and chided himself for the licentious thoughts that had erupted upon association of his wife with a horizontal surface. Thankfully, with Mrs Annesley present, it was only natural that they should dispose themselves as Quakers, with the men on one settee and the women on the other, facing them. Unfortunately, Elizabeth, who had sat opposite him, was now in full view, and his eyes slid over that slender neck he had kissed so recently, prompting him to swivel round and focus on Georgie's hands on the keyboard.

Upon his sister's completion of the piece, Darcy praised her heartily, and Georgie flew to give him a big hug.

"It is truly a beautiful piano, Fitzwilliam, and I am so glad you came back to Pemberley to hear it!" she gushed. "Now I must give you your Christmas present!"

Although Darcy protested that tomorrow would be fine, Georgie presented her brother with the bookmark she had tatted, upon which he smiled graciously and thanked her kindly.

Georgie's gift put Elizabeth in a rather unenviable position. She had not expected to see her husband for Christmas, being fairly sure the non-committal note he had left on his departure for Yorkshire had been the easy let-down before failing to return. The note from Sheffield had merely confirmed her expectations, although his intention of removing to London had been a surprise. Now she found herself in the embarrassing situation of not having prepared or purchased a gift for him. On the whole, she had felt rather relieved to be freed of the burden of thinking on it. Elizabeth hardly knew her husband and could not imagine that he lacked anything that could be purchased with her pin money.

It was at that point that Lizzy spied the discarded cat's cradle on a side-table. Picking it up, she declared her intention of entertaining them with some tricks. Requesting Georgie's assistance, she started the repeating two-handed sequence, with Georgie providing the second pair of hands.

The colonel clapped when they managed to return the cat's cradle to its original configuration, declaring he was sure they were tying it into a devilish knot. Darcy merely looked rather bemused at what his wife considered entertainment. He supposed he should be glad that such things amused her, living as she did in the wilds of Derbyshire.

After her demonstration with Georgie, Lizzy asked Fitzwilliam to help her with the next sequence as a prelude to giving him his present. Darcy protested, having never played cat's cradle before, but reluctantly agreed when urged by Georgie and Richard. He would have stood up to take Georgie's place next to Lizzy, but she requested him to stay seated.

Threading the cat's cradle onto her hands to produce a bridge, she asked Fitzwilliam to place both his hands through the hole in the centre. Once he had reluctantly complied, Lizzy released the string from all but her thumbs, pulling the cat's cradle tight, and capturing his wrists before jerking them downwards sharply. As quick as a flash, she lent in and kissed him briefly on the cheek.

Richard and Georgie burst out laughing at her trick. Darcy, on the other hand, blushed beet red, not from embarrassment, but from the heroic effort required to control his nether regions in response to this provocation.

He then became truly embarrassed when he happened to glance at Richard, who had a wicked look in his eye. Realising his cousin was getting more entertainment from his bound state than was seemly in front of three ladies, Darcy wrenched his hands out of the cat's cradle before Lizzy could perform the next step to magically unbind him.

She was pulled slightly off balance, but being reasonably athletic, recovered quickly. Elizabeth was slightly astonished at her husband's angry reaction. Clearly her playful trick had gone awry. She could not understand how the same man who had spent such a passionate interlude with her so recently could be embarrassed by an innocent kiss, such as one might give to a child, and could only think he objected to being kissed in front of his younger sister.

The awkward moment was broken by Georgie. "So where is his present?" she prompted.

"It was the kiss, you silly!" said Richard.

"Ooooh!" replied Georgie. "That was a good trick, Lizzy! Will you show me how to do it?"

"As long as you promise not to use it on Henry Anstey!" Elizabeth laughed.

Darcy and Richard both frowned at this allusion. Now it was Georgie's turn to blush. To hide her embarrassment, she poked out her tongue.

Mrs Annesley sighed and suggested that it was close to Miss Georgiana's bedtime. Darcy threw a grateful glance at Georgie's companion and invited the colonel to retire downstairs to have their brandy belatedly.

Taking a branch of candles, they made their way to the library where Darcy tended the fire while Richard poured two bumpers.

"Cousin Elizabeth is certainly a sprite," said Richard as he handed Darcy his glass. "I could have laughed out loud at your reaction. What have you and your wife been doing behind closed doors?" he asked, raising his eyebrows suggestively.

"You did laugh out loud, and none of your business!" retorted Darcy.

"I was laughing at her trick," said Richard, "not at your silly reaction. Count your blessings! I wish I could get her sister to do that to me!"

Darcy welcomed the opportunity to change the subject. "So, do you still have any plans in that direction?"

"You must think me as fickle as Charles Bingley; although I have to agree with him on one thing, Jane Bennet is an angel, and now that he has turned his attention elsewhere, I intend to do what I may to fix my interest with her."

"Oh? And to where has Charles turned his attention?"

"Why, to Cousin Anne, of course. She has been moved to Netherfield."

This was news to Darcy. "And does Uncle Geoffrey approve?"

"I haven't discussed it with him, but I doubt that he disapproves, otherwise, he wouldn't have agreed to the Netherfield venture. I suspect that Charles might be just the thing for Anne. Someone who comes with his own fortune won't be drawing on the estate, and he's so spineless that Father and Aunt will be able to get him to agree to anything."

"I can't see that it would be attractive to Bingley at all," said Darcy. "He won't be able to have children with Anne and will probably have to name one of your nieces as his heir."

"You're looking at it the wrong way," replied Richard. "He wants an estate so he may legitimately call himself a gentleman—Rosings is a grand estate. With regard to his legacy, I should think he would be happy to get his heir to adopt his name—Bingley-de Bourgh sounds quite well."

"Perhaps, it certainly sounds better than Hughes Ball Hughes which is utterly ridiculous," said Darcy, referring to the boy whose projected name change would acquire him a fortune that dwarfed Darcy's own.

"Yes, they say Hughes will have forty thousand a year when he reaches his majority. That's a tidy sum. They're already calling him Golden Ball at Eton."

"Well, I hope he uses it as responsibly as his grandfather," declared Darcy dismissively. "But I am a little surprised that Bingley has moved on so quickly from Jane Bennet. He is a little fickle, but it is usually distance that causes his interest to wane. He is an amiable fellow, and one I would not disdain as brother-in-law. I had hoped that the dowries I pledged for Elizabeth's sisters would have made Miss Bennet more palatable to the Bingley sisters."

"Well, I'm glad it has not," retorted Richard; "for I fear I am not much competition for him. All I can offer Jane Bennet are connections and the possibility of bearing the next Earl of Matlock."

"What? Will not your father provide you with something on your marriage?"

"He is not able. Everything that is not entailed has been mortgaged to pay for his mistresses. It is not entirely his fault of course; my grandfather was at it before him."

"Really?" asked Darcy. "I had no idea that things were so desperate."

"Of course not. You and your father have worked hard to increase your fortunes, but I'm afraid ours is on the wane."

Darcy bit his lip. "I had no idea that things had come to such a pass. Where will you live?"

"That I have been thinking desperately about. If I invest Jane's dowry, the supplement to my income should enable me to rent a reasonable house just outside of London: Hans Town, for example. That way I will be able to spend most nights with Jane, unless there is another war, of course. I'd better employ a good butler rather than a housekeeper—for security, if nothing else.

I'd have to give up these rides north, and it will be back to parade ground duty; but if I could get Jane Bennet, it would certainly be worth it."

"You could live in my London townhouse," offered Darcy.

"That's very sweet, Darcy, but *you* need to live in your London townhouse."

Darcy stared into the fire for several minutes. There was plenty of room in his townhouse, which was decidedly under-utilised, but he realised his cousin would want some privacy, and things would start to get crowded once Richard's children came along. A moment's reflection inspired a brilliant idea.

"What about the Dower House?" he asked.

"It's funny you should say that," said Richard. "I was just over there the other day. Georgie and Elizabeth were giving it the once over when I dropped in on my way north. It's a very nice house, much better than I would be able to hire down south, but I wouldn't be able to see Jane above once a fortnight, if that; which is not conducive to begetting brats."

"You could resign your commission," suggested Darcy.

"And live on what? Jane's dowry won't stretch that far."

"You could have the Dower House for a peppercorn rent. It's sitting empty, and I have no wish to rent it to anyone else—it would infringe on my privacy."

"Thanks, Darce, but I've no wish to become your pensioner."

"What about transferring to a local militia?"

"Well, that *would* be a comedown in the world, but I suppose I would be willing to trade that for marital felicity. With Napoleon safely installed on Elba, I'll no doubt end up on half-pay soon anyway, which will lessen the difference in income."

"It might also be possible to appoint you to a supplementary position, like Sheriff," said Darcy.

"Well, that would definitely make things sweeter," said Richard smiling; "and I wouldn't need a butler for the Dower House—Jane would be safe enough on the estate."

"I would certainly welcome your company, and no doubt Elizabeth would like to have her sister close. We could play chess more often!" said Darcy tossing off the last of his bumper. "Have you made another move?"

"I can't remember," said Richard vaguely. "Let us go look at the board."

Lizzy had been kicking herself for her ill-judged prank ever since her husband took himself off downstairs. When Georgie and Mrs Annesley quit the sitting room, she retired to her own bedchamber. After Jenny had attired Lizzy in her nightgown and departed, Lizzy had not crawled into bed. Instead, she pulled on a modest wrap and sat down in front of the fire, ostensibly to read.

When, an hour later, she heard the men coming up the stairs, she jumped up and raced to the hall door. Hearing them bid each other goodnight, and the colonel's footsteps receding down the hall, Elizabeth let herself into the hallway. Darcy was standing in front of his bedchamber with his hand resting on the doorknob, seemingly lost in thought.

He looked up when Lizzy's door clicked shut behind her and she skittered down the hallway in her bare feet to meet him.

"Fitzwilliam, I'm sorry if I embarrassed you with the cat's cradle earlier," she whispered so that Georgie, whose room stood opposite, might not hear. "It was meant to be a light-hearted prank to cover the fact that I neglected to get you a Christmas present."

Darcy looked up and down the corridor; then motioned his wife inside his bedchamber before closing the door.

"I apologise for my own reaction," replied Darcy softly. "I was just embarrassed because Georgie was there. You really shouldn't act so freely in front of her or encourage her to behave that way to Henry Anstey. Mrs Annesley is having trouble getting her ready for her come-out, and you're not helping by doing things like that."

Lizzy nodded, but couldn't repress a lump forming in her throat. She and Jane had always been held up as models of propriety compared to their sisters, especially Lydia; and here was Darcy accusing her of leading his sister astray. She didn't think there was the faintest chance of a romance between Georgie and Mr Anstey, but she had to admit that Georgie might try a version of the prank on him that didn't involve the kiss, which would not be very lady-like.

Casting her eyes down, Elizabeth backed from her husband's presence, fumbling for the doorknob. With a 'goodnight', she turned and fled into the corridor.

Darcy stood in the dim light emitted by the hearth, cursing himself for a fool. He had drawn his wife into his bedchamber to ensure their conversation was private, expecting a spirited argument. One part of him acknowledged that he'd fully intended to finish their debate with a kiss or two. Now where was he?—standing alone in the dark. Worse still, he couldn't go after Elizabeth, for he'd spiked his own guns—he couldn't tell his wife to act with more decorum and then back her against a wall.

Sighing, he rang for Finn.

34 Christmas

Darcy awoke to a desire so intense he could hardly think. He struggled to orient himself. He was at Pemberley, the carriage wheel broken, it was Christmas Day, and... *Wednesday.* He groaned, refusing to accept that his thoughtless exchange with his wife last night had blighted any chance of relief for the week. But perhaps all was not lost... He had been tired from his journey... *Surely, Elizabeth would understand?*

He pulled on his banyan without bothering to tie it, let himself into the shared sitting room, and trod stealthily across the frigid space. His fist reached up to the door of his wife's bedchamber, hesitating a moment. Then, gathering his courage, he knocked lightly. Hearing an indistinct reply, he turned the knob and opened the door.

"...The bears were chasing us through the Dower House. We were trying to catch up with Richard because he'd gone ahead to find some candles. Then, when I turned around you were gone! and I realised I had run into a room with only one door..."

Darcy had taken several steps into the bedchamber before he realised with horror that it was Georgie, not Elizabeth, speaking; and that his sister must have crept into his wife's bed. Although he was wearing his banyan, it gaped at the front; his chemise barely covered his embarrassment.

Almost simultaneously, the head closest to him turned; and he perceived, after a heart-stopping moment, that it was Elizabeth. Her eyes widened momentarily as she realised his predicament; then she sat up, interposing her body between Georgie and the sitting room door.

Gratefully, he nodded to her before retreating silently to the sitting room, closing the door noiselessly against Georgie's babble. Having successfully effected his retreat, Darcy sighed heavily, but it sounded more like a groan to his own ears. Upon reaching his own bedchamber, he was startled when Finn materialised silently from the dressing room.

Finn noticed his master jump. "I'm sorry, sir. I've only just come in and thought you were still abed."

"Finn, do you think there is time for a hot bath before church?" asked Darcy in desperation.

"Certainly, sir," replied Finn with a smile.

Although Darcy dressed rapidly afterwards, assisted by his valet, no one would have guessed it from his immaculate appearance. When he descended to the vestibule followed by Finn, the ladies and Mrs Reynolds were donning their cloaks. He was glad to see that Elizabeth was wearing her church cloak and that it became her very well. Knowing his cousin to be a infrequent churchgoer, Darcy did not expect his tardy arrival, and they set off for church without Richard.

The rector was pleased to see Darcy back in the family pew after his trip to Yorkshire. He would have been less sanguine if he had known the master of Pemberley's attendance at the Christmas service was more by accident than design.

The church service was short and pleasant, calling for peace and goodwill towards others. After exchanging Christmas greetings with the rector and the congregation, the Darcys agreed to use their spare time changing into something more comfortable for breakfast.

Darcy donned his riding gear in preparation for a gallop afterwards. Arriving in the breakfast parlour, he found his cousin reading yesterday's paper. "Catching up on the news?" he asked conversationally as he sat down. "I gather you took the opportunity to sleep in after your long ride yesterday."

"Sleep in? It's only eight o'clock, Darcy," replied Richard. "Can't sleep in on Christmas Day! Weren't you up at dawn harassing your parents for your gifts as a boy?"

"No," replied Darcy disdainfully.

Richard rolled his eyes, but he was prevented a riposte by the entrance of Elizabeth and Georgiana, who burst into the room giggling, arm-in-arm, and dressed in white muslins with Tiffany sashes: Elizabeth's of dark green and Georgiana's, red. Ribbons of matching colours bound their hair.

Darcy felt a strange pang of jealousy. *How has my sister managed to get so close to Elizabeth in such a short time?*

Mrs Annesley entered shortly after, still wearing her dark green church dress, but with a MacKillop tartan shawl, which Darcy had never seen before, fastened across one shoulder.

"Is that some sort of new uniform for females?" asked the colonel wryly.

"We are holly, silly!" declared Georgiana.

"Yes, you are a bit prickly!" replied the colonel, returning fire.

"It's the leaves that are prickly," retorted Georgie triumphantly; "and Lizzy is the one wearing green!"

"Touché," said Richard. "Perhaps this will make you sweeter," he added, placing a flat box upon the table.

Georgie opened it to reveal a beautiful coral necklace of the deepest red. "Oh, Richard! It's beautiful!"

Richard clasped it around Georgie's neck, where it hung beautifully against her white skin and black curls, admirably complemented by the Tiffany sash. Georgie admired it in the large parlour mirror.

"And for you, Cousin Elizabeth!" Richard added, slipping a matching box towards her.

The box contained a similar necklace, of pale pink coral. When Elizabeth tried it on, she noticed that the colour looked good against her slightly tanned complexion and that the necklace, which was shorter than Georgie's, sat close to the base of her gracefully thin neck. Clearly Colonel Fitzwilliam was a man of taste.

"Thank you, Cousin Richard, it is beautiful!" she said, giving him a peck on the cheek.

Now Darcy was chagrined—the box of furs he had sent over a week ago had contained his intended Christmas gift for his wife, specifically the church cloak; and the piano had been his gift to Georgie. Nevertheless, he now found himself empty-handed on Christmas morning. Fortunately he was able to at least redeem himself in the eyes of his sister, though it was more due to good luck than good management, and he duly whispered a request to a beckoned footman.

"I gather the muff you sent earlier was my intended present, Fitzwilliam?" Georgie said archly.

"Well, there was that, and the piano… Perhaps I might have something more, but you will have to wait until after breakfast, Georgie," Darcy replied coolly.

His porridge was soon placed in front of him, and they all fell into easy conversation over breakfast, with the colonel injecting items of news and gossip whenever the conversation threatened to wane or became moribund.

Elizabeth added her mite with witty comments but she was unable to add any information and again felt her isolation at Pemberley. Her sister Jane's letters in no way substituted for her conversation; and Elizabeth realised how much she missed her friend Charlotte, who had been her chief source of news from Meryton and, to some extent, the larger world. Disgusted with her friend's practical acceptance of Mr Collin's proposal, Lizzy had not offered to correspond with Charlotte on her departure from Hertfordshire and was now beginning to regret the dropped connection.

After breakfast, Darcy declared that they should all don their cloaks if Georgie wished to receive her Christmas present. He led them out to the drive, where Healy shortly appeared, leading a beautiful horse with a glossy jet-black coat.

Georgie was in raptures and fell upon her brother's chest to give him a solid hug before bounding into the saddle. She then made Elizabeth's heart stop in her chest by setting the horse straight at the large hedge that bordered the drive. Richard gave a hurrah as she sailed over it, while Darcy made an inarticulate sound in the back of his throat, before Georgie flew back over the hedge towards them.

"Now, Georgie," Darcy protested, "you shouldn't have taken her at such a large jump straight off." But secretly he was quite proud of his little sister's horsemanship.

"Where did you get her, Fitz?" asked Georgie as she petted the mare and began to put her through her paces.

"She was one of the Duke of Exersett's hunting string. I got her from one of the mill owners who had purchased her at Tattersall's for his daughter, only to find she was a tad high-spirited for that lady."

Darcy had been quite pleased with the purchase because he had paid a much shorter price than the considerable sum the mare had achieved in the sale yard. The mill owner had cautioned him that the horse might be a bit of a handful for his little sister.

"She is beautiful, Fitz!" declared Georgie. "Let us go for a ride!"

"Only if you put on your riding habit, Georgie," replied Darcy. "I can see your stockings."

After Georgie hurried inside to comply, Darcy, who was already wearing his buckskin breeches, sidled up to Elizabeth. Taking off one dogskin glove, he caught her hand before she could follow the others back into the house. Having come outside in haste, she was not wearing gloves, and her fingers were quite cold. Removing his second glove, he enveloped them in his own large warm hands.

"I regret I have nothing else to give you, Elizabeth. I had not thought to be back so soon and intended to pick up something in the metropolis."

"I did not expect anything else, sir. Both the cloaks were lovely and I have already made much use of the less expensive one."

"Nonetheless, if there is anything your heart desires, let me know, and it shall be yours."

"That is a big promise!" chirped Elizabeth, amused at his confidence in the Darcy coffers. "I might ask for the moon!"

Darcy and Georgie were soon off on their ride. The mare proved more than capable of keeping up with Darcy's stallion, Ajax, who wasted much of his energy in cantankerous capering.

Entering his dressing room on his return from the ride, Darcy changed from his buckskin breeches, setting them aside for Finn to brush, and pulled on a pair of knitted pantaloons. He then opened the top of the cabinet where he kept his valuable accessories. In replacing his watch and fob, which he always wore outside the house, but never inside where he could consult a clock, his eye fell upon the bundle of Diana's letters that resided there.

I really ought to dispose of them, he thought sadly; *now that he I am a married man.*

Picking the letters up, Darcy felt a wretched feeling grip his heart—of some great loss, the same feeling that had gripped him when he had been told of his father's sudden death. Nonetheless, impelled by a sense of the righteousness of his original thoughts—his obligation to Elizabeth—he determinedly grasped the bundle.

Darcy retreated to his bedchamber and briefly considered sitting in front of the hearth there to do the deed, before realising he would not wish to be disturbed by Elizabeth, remote though that possibility was. Instead he returned to his dressing room and, retrieving the key to the family sitting room, unlocked the door in the hall. After passing through, Darcy secured it again behind him.

It had been his intention to set the letters alight using the flint and candle he kept on the mantel, but upon reaching the hearth, he felt the need to read them one last time. Walking into his boyhood room, Darcy sat down on his bed. He'd always found things simpler there, drawing on the comfort of an idyllic childhood when his parents still lived. Flicking off his shoes, he lay back on the counterpane, drew Diana's letters from the pocket of his coat, and untied the bundle.

Although the first letter put him in a mood of pleasant reminiscence, as Darcy read, a sense of loss began to grip him. Still, he found himself smiling occasionally at things Diana had written that evoked pleasant memories; but after reading half the pile he found himself unable to continue. *Seven years of my life—a time when I had thought myself content. Gone... and with nothing to show for it but these scraps of paper.*

Darcy let his arm drop and stared at the ceiling. Then his eyes fell on the books and toys on the shelf. *Another person gone, like Mother and Father.* It was at that moment he realised that he could as much burn these letters as he could burn his childhood playthings.

Getting up, he shook himself, then lifted the lid of his schooling desk and dumped the love notes untidily inside. As he did so, one letter on different paper to the rest caught his eye, and he reached out to it reflexively. Turning it over, he frowned when he saw that it was addressed simply 'To Elizabeth'. Recollection dawned as he read the first lines and realised it was the letter from Badajoz by the Yardley boy. Darcy dropped it like a hot coal. Why had he not left the damned thing in the library at Netherfield?

Casting it down on top of the pile of his own letters, he hastily closed the desk. When he returned to the family room to consult his parents' carriage clock, he discovered himself to be fifteen minutes late for lunch—an unheard-of event. Hurriedly, he took himself off downstairs.

Darcy was ill prepared for his cousin's teasing on his tardiness, but when Richard found Darcy's moodiness to be more determined than usual, he desisted, and partly by way of a distraction, suggested they repair to the library after lunch. Georgie protested, declaring her sitting room the most appropriate place for the afternoon's entertainment—she had prepared a number of carols for them to sing. Richard assured her the men would make their way to her in good time, as soon as they had a drink.

But upon arriving at the library, Richard announced casually that he had made his next cunning chess move, resulting in his cousin rolling his eyes and asking what had suddenly reanimated his interest in the game. Darcy then viewed the board desultorily for a moment, before moving his queen. His hand had barely left the piece before he saw his error.

"No, no!" protested Richard, "You took your hand off!" and he swiftly moved his bishop, declaring check and mate.

Darcy was floored. "You cheated!" he declared.

"Now, now! Are we eleven years old?" returned Richard, thus skilfully avoiding any admission that he had indeed been helped.

Richard had, of course, wanted to divulge Elizabeth's assistance upon conclusion of the match, but she had convinced him this was not a good idea, saying:

"While your cousin could do with a set-down, you must not let him think it has come at the hands of a woman!"

Richard could not help thinking that Elizabeth would make a far better chess opponent for Darcy than himself, and that now was as good a time as any for them to get acquainted in the game. But Elizabeth was thinking better of her clandestine role in the match and could not agree. Her husband's moods had made her more wary.

Although Darcy was at first convinced that the positions of one or more pieces had been surreptitiously altered; his reconstruction of the end of the game soon made him see his error, and he conceded with the best grace he could muster when Richard handed him a snifter of brandy.

When the cousins sat down in front of the fire, Richard managed to lift Darcy's spirits somewhat by getting him to recount in more detail the coup of the mare's purchase in Yorkshire. This, in turn, reminded Darcy of Richard's own purchases, and he praised his cousin for his good taste in necklaces. Richard was not deluded as to the real train of Darcy's thoughts on the subject.

"You are no doubt wondering where I got the money, and why I bothered, but are too polite to say so?" he said. "Well, I pawned my snuff box. It is an old-fashioned and expensive habit, which I have long wished to give up; …had determined that I would do so ever since father told me I must marry; and I have found out that Jane Bennet disapproves of snuff, happily before she ever discovered that I take it, so now the final nail is in the coffin!"

"Hmmph," vouchsafed Darcy, knowing his cousin had tried to give up snuff several times before.

"But I must admit an ulterior motive. Note my cunning plan," Richard continued, leaning closer; "I aim to curry favour with one sister by giving gifts to the other!"

"And carry the correspondence extolling your beneficence as well!" said Darcy. "But your plan has one weakness—you have no idea what the sisters write to each other. They might discuss politics in London!"

"I do not rely on chance!" laughed Richard. "I have asked your wife to recommend me to her sister!

"How unscrupulous you are!" said Darcy.

"All is fair in love and war!" replied the colonel.

By the time they repaired to Georgie's sitting room, this combination of distractions had succeeded in making Darcy more fit for company. The gentlemen arrived upstairs in time to hear Georgie finish a playful piece by Mozart.

"Finally, you are here!" she cried, before insisting they cluster round the piano to sing the carols she had prepared which included *While Shepherds Watched* and *Good King Wencelas*.

During the first carol, Elizabeth tried to sing harmony in alto to Mrs Annesley's soprano, which she did competently enough, despite the fact that alto was not her natural singing range. However, the men's baritone voices so overpowered the ladies' that Elizabeth thought her voice would be better employed assisting Mrs Annesley's soprano in the subsequent carols.

It was either that, she thought wryly, *or stuffing the stocking she had been darning into Colonel Fitzwilliam's mouth.*

Towards the end of the second carol, she saw Darcy stamp on Richard's foot after he issued a particularly loud and slightly flat note and was amused to overhear the following whispered exchange between them during Georgiana's coda:

"What!?" protested the colonel.

"Tone it down!"

"Am I singing too loudly?"

"Perhaps I should ask instead if you are deaf?"

Although a better choral balance was achieved in the third carol after Richard heeded his cousin's advice, Elizabeth believed their ensemble far from being considered accomplished.

"Well, there!" declared Georgie after striking the final note, "Wasn't that lovely? Although Richard I would prefer you stood just a little further away from me next time."

"What a couple of musical snobs you Darcys are," exclaimed Richard. "That was my best church voice!"

"You obviously attend a very large church," remarked Darcy.

"One has to fill the space above the rafters," retorted Richard.

After Georgie requested the gentlemen sit down to hear solo pieces from Mrs Annesley and Elizabeth, her companion gave a creditable rendition of her song, which was generously applauded by the gentlemen. Then it was Elizabeth's turn to sing *Amazing Grace*.

As the first notes sounded, Darcy almost burst out laughing when Richard's jaw dropped open. Having already listened to his wife's soft, sweet soprano in church, he knew her to sing quite well. But as the piece continued and Elizabeth's voice increased in confidence and volume, he became aware that she had been hiding her light under a bushel. Darcy had always considered himself a connoisseur of music, but he had never been physically affected by it before. The combination of his wife's beautiful voice and his carnal knowledge of her now had a powerful effect on him. Images of him kissing her slender neck right above that coral necklace where he could see her throat swelling in song invaded his mind; and before he knew what he was about, his imagination had progressed so much further that he was in near danger of embarrassing himself thanks to his swallowtail coat. Although the cut-away style of the front of the coat showed off his muscular legs toned by riding, it gave a gentleman no quarter if he got excited, particularly in knitted pantaloons.

Darcy was thinking that he might have to abandon his position on the settee, when he happened to notice a book on a side table. Picking this up and pretending to examine the flyleaf, he casually let the volume rest in his lap.

During the course of her singing, Elizabeth was aware that her husband's attention was directed towards her and was gratified by it. She hardly noticed she had the equal attention of Colonel Fitzwilliam. As to the ladies, they were already aware of her singing abilities, which had become readily apparent during their social intercourse over the preceding weeks. In the presence of her husband, Elizabeth really exerted herself. She knew her accomplishments were few, but believed that even Miss Bingley would have had difficulty sneering at her performance. She was pleased that Darcy clearly appreciated this one small talent she possessed as a lady, which to her mind, elevated her above the woman who would merely be the mother of his children. Little did she know that his thoughts were not so refined—because of her talent, her husband was busy ravishing her in his mind.

All afternoon and throughout dinner, Darcy and Elizabeth were supremely conscious of each other's presence. Elizabeth hid her preoccupation well behind wit and élan; and Darcy, not so well, behind something bordering on an uncharacteristic grumpiness. As they read poetry and plays, listened to more of Georgie's music, and had their afternoon tea, they exchanged looks and the occasional touch as their hands brushed on a book or a teacup. Elizabeth, aware she had erred in not locking the hall door of her bedchamber when her husband was in residence, had silently vowed that it would not happen again and sought to silently communicate her wish to make amends.

After dinner, Mrs Reynolds removed the branches of candles from the dinner table, brought in a tray of raisins, doused them with brandy, and set the tray alight in readiness for a game of snapdragon. The colonel proved a true adept at extracting the raisins from the flames, although Darcy ungenerously attributed his cousin's skill to everything from thickened skin to being inured against brandy. Darcy delivered these insults with such a straight face that only his cousin's light-hearted response clued Elizabeth in to the fact that her husband was mostly joking. After Richard single-handedly disposed of half the plate of raisins, Mrs Annesley declared him the undisputed winner, suggesting he would find his true love in the New Year. This prediction made him exchange a smug glance with Elizabeth, whom he had enlightened on his hopes for Jane before lunch.

When the tea was cleared away, Elizabeth saw her chance to make amends to her husband for her matitudinal faux pas. After a series of yawns and winks worthy of her mother, she declared it had been rather a long day and took herself off to bed. Georgiana, who had spent many hours at the piano and was more justified in making such a claim, followed soon after, allowing Darcy to also make a quick exit. The colonel protested but was sanguine to sit down to cards with Mrs Annesley when she declared herself also not quite ready to retire.

Darcy's heart beat fast as he retreated to his bedchamber. Finn appeared promptly to his summons and was surprised to find his master quite chatty as he divested him of his clothes.

"How was your Christmas, Finn?" asked Darcy. "How did you amuse yourself?"

"Very well, sir. I'm teaching Healy how to play piquet."

"Piquet? And how does he get on?"

"Very well, sir," replied Finn, "Very well."

After dismissing his valet, Darcy paced up and down on the rug in front of the hearth in his banyan. *Elizabeth might not be so forward in her preparations as myself,* he thought; *it would not do to go charging in there.* In anticipation of the near fulfilment of his desires, Darcy's sense of humour reasserted itself, and it occurred to him that he was feeling as high-spirited and cantankerous as his horse had been on his morning ride. This thought somehow checked him, and he realised it would not do to let his animal spirits gain the ascendency as he had done during his last encounter with his wife. *But what to do?* He was too eager, and she slower to passion. The serendipity of re-reading Diana's letters that morning then occurred to him. *Yes, if I must employ the arts of dalliance then let it be—better that, than succumbing to my baser nature, using my wife barbarously as I did before fleeing to Yorkshire.*

A glance at the clock on the mantel showed a good half-hour had passed. Darcy padded across the sitting room in his bare feet and knocked at the door.

Elizabeth was waiting for him in bed with her chestnut mane tumbled over her shoulders. She threw the covers aside as he approached and he saw she was wearing a sheer gown that looked like the overdress of a ball gown, but with nothing underneath. Her nipples and the dark triangle of hair between her legs were clearly visible. He felt himself jerk in response. How could he explain to his wife that he needed no provocation without offending her?

Darcy slipped the banyan off, but very sensibly kept his nightshirt on, before hopping into bed beside his wife. After some spirited kissing to which she responded admirably, he began to slide down in the bed, circling her larynx with his tongue, and then sucking the flesh around it into his mouth, as he had longed to do earlier in the music room. He could feel her stroking his back through his nightshirt. He tipped her onto her back to straddle her leg with his knee. As he descended to her nipples, sucking first one through the net of her gown as he played with the other, she brought her fingertips en pointe and began to rake her nails down his back. He descended still further, nestling between her thighs before lifting the hem of her gown above his head to stroke the soft flesh between them while he explored her navel with his tongue. Her fingers reached the nape of his neck and played with the thick curls there. He rang his tongue along the inside of her thigh and then buried his face in her fanny. She jerked.

"Fitzwilliam?"

As his mouth was studiously employed, he did not reply. One of her hands, which had slid to the crown of his head, buried itself in the roots of his hair, and gave a small tug.

"Fitzwilliam? What are you doing? Please talk to me?"

"Mmphh," he vouchsafed, but redoubled his efforts, not getting the response he desired.

"Fitzwilliam, I..." but she could go no further.

He petted her thighs reassuringly, pleased that her body had conquered her mind. She moaned and began squirming beneath his hands. He thrust his head towards her rhythmically, and once her body began moving in time, hoisted himself up to kneel between her thighs. With one slick movement he divested himself of his nightgown, wiping his face with it, before throwing it off the end of the bed. She gasped as he revealed himself, making his heart give an odd little lurch of satisfaction. He towered over her for a moment, feeling his power like a god, before projecting himself over her, suspended on his palms. He introduced himself easily with the work of a few nudges; and then with a few more, buried himself to the hilt, plying her vigorously as she rocked in sympathy with him, calling his name, "Fitz, Fitz", each word a little caress.

Finally, she sighed, and Darcy succumbed with an almighty groan. Exhausted, he descended to his elbows and kissed her brow.

"Elizabeth," he managed, before rolling to the side and going out like a light.

35 Boxing Day

At Netherfield, the Bingley sisters were quite satisfied with their efforts to engage their brother's interest in Miss de Bourgh. They encouraged Charles to carry Anne up and down the stairs and from room to room during their daily routine, deeming the footmen too rough for the purpose. Mr Bingley, whose every sympathy had gone out to the fragile lady from their first acquaintance at Longbourn, now began to refer to her as "his fairy" as he spirited her through the house.

In the evenings, while the Bingley sisters sat down to whist with the earl and Hurst, Charles read poetry to his fairy, getting up occasionally to poke the fire, rearrange the screen, and adjust Miss de Bourgh's blanket. Mrs Jenkinson viewed these ministrations with happy indulgence as it allowed her to continue uninterrupted with her knitting.

During the day, the earl often went off to London, ostensibly on business, but in reality to his mistress's house. He was replaced by Mr Collins, who was also a daily visitor at Netherfield, often accompanied by his betrothed, Charlotte Lucas. Although Mr Collins was tolerated by the Bingley sisters as the necessary emissary of Lady Catherine, Miss Lucas's incursions were at first resented, but as she took the trouble of nursing Miss de Bourgh, the sisters were soon reconciled to her presence when they found themselves at leisure to dispense tea at appropriate times.

Meanwhile, Lady Lucas merrily planned her eldest daughter's wedding. Such a triumph over those Bennets!—her daughter to be the next Mistress of Longbourn! When Charlotte had passed her quarter century without even a hint of an offer, Lady Lucas had sadly admitted to herself that her daughter's future lay in looking after her parents in their old age, following which she must be admitted to the charity of one of her brothers. Lady Lucas could only hope that her younger daughter Mariah did better, encouraging her to dance with all the militia officers. Then luck had finally favoured dear Charlotte!—Along had come Mr Darcy and upset Mrs Bennet's best-laid plans. No doubt if Fanny Bennet had been aware earlier of Mr Darcy's inclination, she would have steered Mr Collins towards Mary and had three daughters married. Instead, she had been caught unawares by Mr Darcy's declaration, and Charlotte had been the beneficiary.

Lady Lucas was quite cognisant that spite had precipitated Mr Collins' declaration to her daughter, but clever Charlotte had exerted herself to engage his affections to such an extent that the clergyman subsequently declared that he had favoured Charlotte all along and only duty had prompted him to request Miss Elizabeth's hand in the first place.

Despite Mr Collins' willingness to defer his wedding until Miss de Bourgh was fully recovered, Lady Catherine had insisted the nuptials go ahead as originally planned and condescended to be present at the ceremony in Meryton. Mr Collins spent more time with his patroness on his wedding day than with his bride. Charlotte handled the neglect with aplomb, looking as well as she could in the slightly over-trimmed dress prepared by her mother.

The wedding breakfast was a success, although the Bingley sisters, who had deigned to grace the nuptials in the company of their *dear* friend Lady Catherine, could not agree. They spent their time pooh-poohing everything from the table decorations to the champagne punch, but then had to listen to Lady Catherine's long-winded opinions on how everything could have been better managed. However, the majority of the guests declared themselves more than satisfied with the feast. The disappointed Mrs Bennet behaved herself as well as could be expected, only giving vent to her general dissatisfaction with the event by whispering disparaging comments to her sister Philips—even at short notice, she observed, her Lizzy's feast had been much better.

The happy couple spent their wedding night at Lucas Lodge—the least said about the evening the better.

Mr Bingley did not attend the wedding. His sisters were eager to enforce his separation from Jane Bennet, and he gracefully acceded to their wishes to keep Miss de Bourgh company when she was deemed not well enough to attend. The earl watched all these manoeuvrings with silent satisfaction. He was quite *au fait* with the machinations of catty women.

When Dr Douglas visited Netherfield on the following day, he finally declared Miss de Bourgh well enough to attempt the journey to Kent. After some discussion, the earl convinced Lady Catherine to spend Christmas with Anne at his townhouse, an invitation which would have surprised his second son and nephew had they been aware of it. But there was method in the earl's madness—he intended to broach the topic of the Bingley boy as a potential mate for Anne.

They all set off for London the day before Christmas Eve—the Bingleys abandoning Netherfield once more for Hurst's townhouse in London. Before departing, the earl had a very satisfactory tête-à-tête with the youngest Bingley sister, who he had quickly ascertained wore the pants in that family, and was hopeful that a deal could be struck if only his sister Catherine could be brought to reason. This he attempted to do after treating her to a very elaborate evening meal of some twenty dishes at his London townhouse.

His sister was at first indignant; while she thought the Bingley sisters well-educated and the brother quite comely, Lady Catherine had no wish to marry her daughter to a family so recently connected to trade. Her grandchild to have mercantile blood? The shades of Rosings would not be thus polluted! The earl forbore to point out that her husband, who was now conveniently dead, had been a banker. Lady Catherine had expected the earl to offer her nephew, Richard, as a groom.

But after assuring his sister than any attempt to get progeny from Anne was hopelessly deluded and tantamount to murder, Lord Geoffrey finally managed to get Lady Catherine to shut up long enough to further delineate his plans—one of his granddaughters to be named Anne's heir, to be moved to Rosings to be brought up as Catherine wished. As this scheme secured Lady Catherine's future in the event of Anne's early demise—cutting out a distant cousin of Sir Lewis's—it put a whole new complexion on the matter. By midnight they had struck a deal, and the earl, feeling slightly queasy—no doubt due to that rich sauce that had accompanied the partridge—was able to head off to his mistress's townhouse.

On the morning of Christmas Eve, Lady Catherine and Anne departed London for Rosings with Dr Douglas in attendance, leaving an invitation for the Bingleys to join them as early as Boxing Day. With a crow to her sister Louisa, Caroline immediately accepted.

Lizzy woke up feeling as warm as a piece of toast and was gratified upon turning over to discover her husband still in bed. She and Jenny had in fact planned quite carefully to achieve this result by stitching a new cover for the bed that was much thicker on her side than on his. She knew that Fitzwilliam disliked it when she snuggled up too close to him. Her efforts, she assured herself, were merely to secure his comfort *and* her own—when she awoke, she liked things to be where she had put them before falling asleep.

Propping her head on her hand, Lizzy surveyed her husband. He looked much younger in slumber, resembling the guileless youth captured in his portrait in the gallery. As she watched him, his eyelids fluttered open, and she noticed what beautiful long lashes he had.

"Good morning," Elizabeth greeted.

Darcy looked confused for a moment before realising he was still in his wife's bed. He sat up and Elizabeth noted with appreciation the body she had mostly only glimpsed by candlelight, except of course for their short interlude before Yorkshire—the incident of the riding crop.

"I beg your pardon," he said. "I guess I must have been tired. What time is it?"

"It is seven. But do not apologize, I'm very glad you did not whisk yourself off like a thief in the night. I always find it disconcerting when you disappear."

"You do?" asked Darcy in some surprise.

"Yes. It would be nice to exchange a few words before you fly away, Cupid."

Lizzy was only teasing of course, but her choice of metaphor pleased

Darcy greatly. Nonetheless, he was at a loss to match her wit so early in the morning and responded simply with:

"Has Mrs Reynolds spoken with you about today's arrangements?"

"We have been preparing baskets for the tenants, although I use that term in the royal sense because Mrs Reynolds has done the bulk of the work. My sole contribution was to borrow some cake trays from my aunt."

"Cake trays?"

"To add a personal touch—I will show you when we go downstairs. I understand the tenants are to come after breakfast, and the countess and several other friends have been invited for lunch."

Lunch. Darcy realised how horribly remiss he had been in trying to abscond to London at Christmas. He *had* previously been absent from the Boxing Day festivities when he had been in residence in London—his housekeeper and steward presided in his stead, distributing largesse to the tenants. But doing so shortly after his marriage would not have been wise.

"Thank you for organising this," he replied. "I should have thought of it myself. Indeed, I wish you had reminded me in a letter."

A spark of annoyance flashed through Elizabeth's mind. She was astonished how *his* oversight had turned into her own, but she answered with equanimity and a smile: "I hardly knew where to direct it. I don't think 'Fitzwilliam Darcy, Yorkshire' would have found you."

Darcy knew his wife was perfectly correct. While he had sent one letter with the furs, he had not apprised her of more than his general direction.

He got up now and pulled on his banyan. As Lizzy watched his attractive butt disappear with some regret, she noticed he had two prominent dimples above the cheeks. She never knew men had dimples there!

After a moment's hesitation Darcy leant over the bed to kiss her cheek, saying, "I'll see you at breakfast."

Lizzy rang for her maid and ordered a bath. While Jenny attended to this, Elizabeth straightened the rather rumpled bed. Discovering Fitzwilliam's discarded nightgown on the floor, she shook her head with a smile, and stuffed it into a bedside drawer. As it smelled rather strongly of herself, she would deliver it later to his room rather than leave it lying around for the maids to discover.

Her bath was rather a quick one, Jenny wanting to array her in one of her church dresses for the Boxing Day festivities. The dress was a new gown from Madame Lafrange, fashioned from a heavy deep red silk from her uncle Gardiner's warehouse. The bodice was figured with gold embroidery. A lighter red silk was draped from the elbows, attached to gold bands. Jenny had chosen a matching amulet to show off the modest décolletage, and Elizabeth's hair was rolled and fastened above her neck with a jewelled clip.

After breakfast, they assembled in the vestibule, all except Colonel Fitzwilliam, who had gone off straight after eating to Matlock to escort his mother over for lunch. Elizabeth showed her husband the tiny madeleines that had been added to each basket, which contained other 'luxury' items, such as manufactured soap, as well as sweets for the children, and various trinkets and toys purchased from the tinker. Darcy would have stolen one of the little cakes to try, but Mrs Reynolds, anticipating his curiosity, produced an extra plate of them before he could raid a basket.

The tenants were shortly shown in, forming a neat line that stretched out the door. Georgie and Elizabeth took turns presenting a basket to each tenant while Darcy conversed with them on various topics ranging from fences to the weather. Elizabeth could not help thinking his conversation rather inane, but the tenants seemed to be pleased with the attentions of the master, and Darcy seemed to know them all by name.

About half the baskets had been dispensed when a family appeared at the doorway with several children. One of them, a handsome boy of about ten, was limping and Lizzy noticed that he winced whenever he put his weight on his left foot. Handing the basket she was holding to Georgie, she walked down the line.

"Good morning," she said pleasantly to the mother. "What fine children you have."

"Good morning, Mrs Darcy," returned the woman, gratified to be singled out.

"I noticed your son is limping?"

"Oh, Ben! Yes, he caught his knee on a nail some weeks ago, and will not let me touch it, but he says it is getting better."

"Will you permit me to look at it, Ben?" asked Elizabeth.

Ben seemed unwilling to comply, but when his mother scowled at him, he acquiesced.

Taking the boy aside, Lizzy seated him on a chair brought by a footman, whereupon the boy lifted the knee of his breeches to reveal a great carbuncle below the kneecap. His mother exclaimed at the state of his leg, scolding him as a silly boy for concealing his hurts.

Lizzy sent her maid for a needle, hot water and some clean rags. Receiving these, she held the needle in a candle to clean it, before kneeling at the boy's feet and lancing the sore. After the initial pain of having his flesh pricked, the boy testified to his immediate relief as the pus spurted from his leg. This was caught with a rag and another warm rag placed over the wound to draw the bad humor out, while Lizzy cleaned and heated the needle once more. Ben was reluctant to submit to more doctoring, but Lizzy coaxed him to allow her to check his wound more thoroughly. Much hissing ensued as she probed the sore and more pus was released from the fissure as she broached some inner cavity. After several more attempts to assess the extent of his hurt, she was obliged to desist when the boy became increasingly sensitive to her explorations, though Lizzy was not confident she had cleaned the wound sufficiently to allow it to heal. Nonetheless, he would stand no more poking; and she was forced to desist, advising him to come back to the house once a day so that she might check on his progress and poultice the wound if necessary.

Although Darcy continued to converse with his tenants throughout this ordeal, he shifted his position to allow himself to watch his wife. Her pose reminded him of his surreptitious observations of her at the Lucases' soirée, when she had tended the little boy who had fallen down the stairs. She looked very graceful kneeling on the footstool that her maid had found for her comfort.

Finally, the baskets were all dispensed, and the tenants went off to the tithe barn, where a space had been cleared for their feast. The men stood to drink their ale while the women sat down to examine the contents of their baskets and trade the items from the tinker as suited their fancy.

As the last of them departed, a carriage appeared in the drive, which was soon revealed to carry Henry Anstey and his parents. They were a little early for lunch; but Henry, who bounded from the carriage and immediately sought out Georgiana, made no secret that his enthusiasm had likely driven their early arrival.

Elizabeth promptly sent the Darcy carriage for her aunt and Miss Dorsey, who had also accepted her invitation to lunch. Before they arrived, the Floreys pre-empted them. As Elizabeth was busy showing the Floreys to the saloon, Darcy's steward handed her aunt and her friend down from their carriage when he happened to arrive at the front door of the great house around the same time.

Finally, a grand carriage appeared, and Darcy and Elizabeth hastened out to greet the Countess of Matlock. Richard, who was accompanying his mother, handed her down. She was dressed in an old-fashioned grand toilette—a grey silk dress with a colourful stomacher, laced over with grey ribbon. Her hair was powdered and adorned with a turban matching the stomacher, decked with feathers. Her appearance, which was worthy of Versailles, was set off to a nicety by her son's dress uniform, but Elizabeth found it all rather overwhelming in the wilds of Derbyshire.

They all sat down to a fine feast with Darcy occupying one end of the table and Elizabeth the other. Richard and Georgie sat down near Elizabeth, who had placed her aunt and Henry Anstey to her immediate left and right. The countess sat on Darcy's right. They were flanked by the Floreys, with Darcy's steward and Mrs Annesley next to them. The other guests occupied the middle of the table, which Mrs Reynolds had extended with one of its extra leaves.

Lady Matlock was a gifted conversationalist, and buoyed by her warm welcome, grand clothes and her surroundings, one would have been hard put to recognize the wan lady who had presented such a pathetic appearance to her son from her bed only a few weeks ago.

Mrs Reynolds and Cook had once again excelled, serving up the remainder of the venison and a pheasant, presented initially with all its feathers. There were trout, baked vegetables, and a tasty mutton tart, which Darcy had not encountered before. He wondered if it was a recipe contributed by Elizabeth.

After lunch, the whole party adjourned to the saloon, where Georgie played, Elizabeth sang, and Miss Florey exhibited on the harp. The bulk of the guests departed after tea, but the countess remained. She had been invited to stay overnight—partly because she was family, but also because she had further to travel, living over ten miles away.

A pleasant afternoon was whiled away in Georgie's sitting room, where the countess devoted much of her time to conversing with Elizabeth. All in all she found Mrs Darcy a pleasant girl, but as Lady Matlock became better acquainted with the circumstances of Elizabeth's family, the countess was at a loss to understand Darcy's choice. She could only assume he had fallen hopelessly in love.

They were all about to sit down to dinner when a rider was heard coming down the drive at speed. Darcy and Richard both went to investigate, the colonel believing he might be being summoned back to the Life Guards. *Surely Napoleon could not have escaped from Elba?*

Richard at first thought his suspicions confirmed when the courier declared he sought Colonel Richard Fitzwilliam, having come from London via Matlock.

Upon unsealing the letter, Richard paled.

"What is it?" asked Darcy anxiously.

"It is from Father's butler, Goring," Richard croaked. "Father has collapsed and may not make it through the night."

36 Richard joins the fray

The countess swooned on hearing the news and was caught simultaneously by Darcy and Richard as she fell, resulting in them knocking their heads together quite soundly.

She recovered quite suddenly, before her maid and vinaigrette could be fetched, when Richard called for his horse—Lady Matlock had several instructions she wished to impart before he left.

After partaking of the soup on his mother's insistence, Richard posted off to London, hoping to arrive before his father departed the world. Darcy undertook to accompany the countess on the morrow. They would travel in his carriage, which was not so luxurious as the countess's, but newer and better sprung.

Georgie was sullen throughout dinner, noticing that no plans were being made for herself or Elizabeth to join them on the journey to London. She confronted her brother at the head of the stairs after the countess went off to her chamber to lie down.

Darcy's reply was decisive. "This is not a jaunt, Georgie. If Uncle Geoffrey dies, I will be entirely preoccupied with the funeral and putting his affairs in order; and you will be in mourning, so you will not be able to go anywhere."

"I don't want to go anywhere," Georgie protested. "I just want to be with *you*."

"Trust me," said Darcy, "you will be more comfortable here at Pemberley with Elizabeth."

And with that he was off, leaving Georgie with nothing to do but slam her bedchamber door.

Darcy arrived in his bedchamber to find Finn packing.

"Oh, they found you!" he said with relief, as Finn hurried forward to pull off his boots. "Mrs Reynolds said she was having trouble locating you."

"I beg your pardon, sir. I was playing piquet with Healy," said Finn, easing his master out of his coat and waistcoat.

"Ah! That's right!" said Darcy, raising his chin as Finn divested him of his cravat. "I should have remembered!"

Finn was very glad the master had not.

"I'm sorry to do this to you," apologized Darcy, grabbing his valise and walking to his bedside table, "but if we could be off first thing in the morning, I would greatly appreciate it."

"No problem, sir," replied Finn from the dressing room, "I have almost finished packing. I have laid a fresh nightgown on the bed, although I thought perhaps you might wish to reuse the one on your pillow, as you did not leave it in the dressing room."

Darcy finally noticed the neatly folded nightgown on his pillow. Picking it up, he discreetly sniffed it, and then realising its provenance, surreptitiously stuffed it under the documents in his valise.

"Thank you, Finn. You did just as you aught," he called.

Donning the new nightgown, Darcy pulled off his breeches, stockings and smalls and deposited them all in the dressing room, just as Finn closed the lid on his trunk.

"All done, sir," said Finn, picking up the discarded clothes. "I will see you in the morning."

"Thank you, Finn," said Darcy. "Goodnight."

Darcy climbed into bed and lay back on the pillows, his mind in turmoil. He knew the bulk of settling the earl's affairs would fall to him—the viscount was determinedly useless, and Richard had not been trained to take his father's place. Although Darcy had a rough notion of the earl's means, his recent discussion with Richard had suggested that the earl's property was heavily encumbered. It was no use trying to think on it further until he knew the exact state of affairs, but his mind could not help running through the possibilities. He could only hope the earl survived long enough to put him in the way of things.

Darcy could feel a knot forming in his stomach—he hated disorder, and he had a horrible feeling that things were not going to be tidy. He was about to put out his candle, though he knew he would probably have trouble getting to sleep, when he heard a small knock at the sitting room door. Elizabeth entered in answer to his summons.

"I thought I might find you staring at the ceiling," she said, as she approached in a quilted dressing gown.

"Is there a problem?" he asked.

"I just came to make sure you are all right. You looked worried at dinner."

"The earl's affairs are likely to be complicated. I dread what I will find."

"I gather Richard's brother is unlikely to be of much help."

"I can only hope that I get there before the earl dies. Perhaps I can salvage something for Richard; but once Robert is in the saddle, there may be nothing that I can do."

There was silence for a moment, before Elizabeth gathered her courage and walked round the foot of the bed. "Do you mind if I hop in?" she asked.

Darcy shook his head in bemusement as his wife climbed into his bed, dressing gown and all.

"I know you don't like me clinging to your back," Elizabeth explained. "I think I should be warm enough in this."

"I'm sorry," apologized Darcy, embarrassed that his reluctance for his wife's nocturnal embraces had been noticed. "I'm just not used to sleeping with someone else."

This statement somewhat puzzled Elizabeth, but she let it pass.

"You want me to go?" asked Elizabeth.

"No! I meant... Richard said you used to sleep with your sister. I suppose you're used to it."

Elizabeth suppressed a smile on hearing the cousins had been discussing her sleeping arrangements with Jane. Then she noticed the uncharacteristic crease between Darcy's brows.

"Are you in pain?"

"No. Well... Yes. It is nothing—a bit of a pain in my gut."

Elizabeth considered him for a moment. "Roll over," she said.

Darcy dutifully presented his back, and she began to rub it.

"Does that feel better?" she asked after a few minutes.

"Yes," he said sleepily. "Shall I snuff the candle?"

"Yes. Goodnight, Fitzwilliam."

"Goodnight, Elizabeth."

Richard arrived, exhausted, in London before sunset the following day and went straight to his father's townhouse in Grosvenor Square. He had barely rapped on the front door before Goring had it open.

"Thank goodness, you are here, sir!" said the butler.

"Does he still live?" asked Richard.

"Yes, sir," said Goring, securing the door. "He is holding on. The doctor says there is some hope."

"How did it happen?" asked Richard, as they began walking briskly across the vestibule and up the stairs.

"He had rather a loud argument with his sister before Christmas, sir, and complained for about a day afterwards that he had indigestion. Then he went off to Curzon Street..."

Richard knew that his father's mistress was established there.

"He arrived back early the following morning in a hackney," continued Goring, "which I thought unusual for him—for he always walks—and then collapsed in my arms in the vestibule."

"So you sent for the doctor right away?"

"Well, Dr Douglas happened to arrive at that moment, sir. I had not been able to secure the door before rushing to the master's aid, and the doctor walked right in. He had come to report to the earl after establishing Miss de Bourgh at Rosings. I wanted to get the earl up to his bed, but the doctor made me lay him straight on the floor, which I thought a trifle unseemly. When he took to pummelling the earl, I wasn't quite sure what to do; but he seemed to know his business, and after ten minutes or so the earl opened his eyes. It took some while, but we eventually got him into bed, and I sent a message for you. Dr Douglas has been here ever since."

Richard blinked at this extraordinary providence through the agency of

Dr Douglas. "And my brother? Has he been sent for?"

"Of course, sir; I sent the best footman on that errand, but he has yet to return. I do not expect that Lord Robert will be easy to find."

They had reached the earl's bedchamber, and belatedly handing his hat to the butler, Richard knocked and entered. His father was asleep in the huge canopied bed. Beside him, Dr Douglas was sprawled in a fauteuil, his eyes closed, looking exhausted. A neatly dressed young woman who had been sitting further away started up when they entered the room, holding a finger to her lips and approaching the doctor. Upon her light touch on his shoulder, Dr Douglas's eyes fluttered open and he stood, motioning that they should retreat to the hall, whereupon he followed them out.

"Miss Smyth will call if I'm needed," Dr Douglas advised Richard. "Your father wants to speak to you, most urgently, but it would be better if he rouses naturally. May I call you as soon as he wakes?"

"Certainly," said Richard. "Is there any hope?"

"It is too early to tell. His heart had stopped when I found him in the vestibule, but he recovered presently. It depends on the extent of the damage. I have seen men live for years after such events, but I do not want to raise your hopes too much. It is unlikely he will recover completely. It is really more a question of how long he has left."

"Thank you, doctor. I understand and am happy just to see him alive. You look fagged yourself."

"I was waiting for your arrival and for my nurse, Miss Smyth, to relieve me. She arrived but an hour ago. If a cot could be set up, I will sleep properly now, but I wish to remain on hand should there by another attack. I will instruct Miss Smyth to wake me and send for you as soon as the earl awakes."

"Certainly," said Richard. "Goring will see to the cot."

As the butler hurried off to extract the colonel's campaign bed from storage, a footman followed Richard to the bedchamber he used on his infrequent overnight stays in the townhouse. He had not been in the bedchamber for years, preferring to stay at Darcy House; but he noticed the room was much the same, with only the positions of some smaller pieces of furniture altered.

By the time Goring returned, Richard had washed and changed into a fresh shirt, the only thing he had packed in his saddlebag besides his shaving kit.

"I'm famished, Goring. Is there anything to eat?"

"The cook says the soup is ready, sir. Will that do until dinner?"

"Certainly, and some brandy if you have it."

"There is only port, sir," replied Goring.

Richard grimaced. "Very well, that will do."

After wolfing the soup, Richard lay down to rest and had only just nodded off when he was summoned to his father's bedchamber.

He entered to find his father's eyes looking strangely dull and sunken.

"Richard," croaked the earl in a weak voice. "I knew I could rely on you."

"Yes, Father. I am here. Darcy and Mother should be here tomorrow."

"Good. I need to get my affairs in order. I fear I am not much longer for this world. And Robert?"

"They are still searching for him, Father. Goring sent the best footman. He said he is intelligent and persistent."

"Fobbing? Yes, he is good. But Richard, how is this thing going with Jane Bennet? I want to see that settled before I die."

Richard paled and would have tried to change the subject, had he not known that his father would persist 'til he got the answer he wanted.

"It is too early, Father," he replied. "She has a tendre for Bingley, and he has only just left Netherfield."

"You are too cautious, Richard, like your mother. Women aren't that hard to get. You just have to ask them."

Richard could hardly think that women would drop into his hands like ripe fruit as they did for his father—their circumstances were vastly different; but he gave his father the only assurance that he could: "I will go to Longbourn as soon as Mother and Darcy arrive. Will that satisfy you?"

"Yes," said the earl, settling back into his pillows. "Now, am I allowed to have anything to eat?"

The countess and Darcy set off from Pemberley at first light, waved off by Elizabeth and a sullen Georgiana, who had to be coaxed from her room by her sister-in-law.

The Darcy coach arrived in London in the late afternoon of the following day. Darcy was surprised his aunt had tolerated the journey so well. She seemed strangely energised as he accompanied her up the steps of the earl's townhouse and rapped on the door. As they waited for the door to be answered, Darcy watched as the countess's maid supervised the unloading of her luggage; then he signalled to the coachman to drive off to his townhouse across the square. Who knew how long he would be detained inside? He would walk back to his townhouse. To his surprise, the door was opened not by the butler, but Richard.

"Goring is upstairs with Father," Richard explained.

"Then he lives?" asked the countess breathily.

"Yes, Mother. He is awake and talking, but you must not exert him too much. He is very weak."

The countess threw off the shepherdess's hat she was wearing and hastened upstairs. Richard and Darcy exchanged glances and hurried after her.

By the time they had reached the earl's bedchamber, the countess had already thrown herself across her husband's chest. Dr Douglas hovered anxiously nearby and was relieved when Richard grabbed his mother by the waist and dragged her backwards to the side of the bed, but she retained a claw-like grasp on her husband's hand.

Lord Matlock merely rolled his eyes at his son and glanced in acknowledgement at Darcy. He then looked at Richard and flicked his eyes towards the door.

"Mother," said Richard dutifully, "you must be very tired after your journey. Come back after you've refreshed yourself—we wouldn't want you to fall ill now..."

"Yes, it is true!" lamented the countess, allowing herself to be escorted from the room by her son. "I will stay by your side, Geoffrey, but it was a long journey, and I *do* feel faint!"

The door had not yet clicked shut when the earl motioned for Darcy to approach the bed.

"Nephew, you must help me put my affairs in order. I have summoned my man of business. He is already downstairs, awaiting your arrival. Speak with him, and devise a plan, then come tell me your thoughts."

"Yes, Uncle," said Darcy, bowing and retreating to the door.

Darcy found the earl's man of business, Mr Havershott, expecting him in the library.

"It is a pleasure to see you again, Mr Darcy," Havershott said, getting up from behind a desk overspread with paper to shake hands. "If you would like to take my chair, I will explain things over your shoulder."

Mr Havershott systematically summarised the state of the entailed properties that would be inherited by the viscount, which although free from encumbrance, required many improvements to increase their profitability. He then went on to detail the other properties that were free from entail, and could possibly have formed the basis of the earl's second son's inheritance, had they not been grossly encumbered. It was clear to Darcy that several of these properties would have to be sold to reduce the earl's debt and provide working capital to halt the downward spiral.

"I'm afraid the earl's friends have also diminished his fortune greatly over the years," continued Mr Havershott, "by asking him to invest in various ventures from racehorses to property. I advised against many of these, of course, but my lord never liked to disappoint his friends..."

"Are you saying the money was poorly invested or swindled?" asked Darcy. "Can any of it be recovered?"

"A combination of things—poor investments, failed ventures, and downright embezzlement. I'm afraid the joint venture you undertook with the earl several years ago was one of the few things that prospered. Some of the money can be recovered, I believe, but most of it is gone forever."

"Then firstly let us talk of how we might do that, and invest the money more wisely. Then we can go over the strategic value of each of the unentailed properties to determine which might be disposed of. Once we have a plan, I will go back to my uncle, but I do not know if he will take my advice."

"I think you might be pleasantly surprised there, sir. You uncle has long expressed an admiration to me on how you took on your father's affairs, but he is a proud man... His illness has at last given him a chance to seek your advice without injury to his dignity. I believe he will acquiesce with your plans and save his friendships by discreetly letting his friends know that his hard-headed nephew has stepped into the breach."

Darcy blushed, suppressing a small smile of gratification. It was to be his only joy over the next few hours as a plan was painstakingly hashed out.

It was an hour before midnight before Darcy finally emerged, having taken dinner with Mr Havershott at the desk in the library. He would have dearly loved to walk back to his townhouse and seek his own bed, but upon discovering that the earl was awake and expecting him, he waited upon his uncle.

Darcy explained his plans carefully, repeating the diplomatic language Mr Havershott had employed, and was gratified to find that the earl's man of business had correctly divined his uncle's reaction. The earl nodded sagely throughout his speech. Then grasping Darcy's bicep through his coat, he thanked him for his trouble and gave permission for him to go ahead.

Bidding his uncle goodnight, Darcy donned his coat and walked wonderingly across the square to his own townhouse. It was a brilliant clear night, and when Darcy looked up at the stars, they almost seemed to confirm to him that the earth had shifted on its axis. Far off, a church bell began to chime midnight. His heart felt warm at the deference his uncle had shown him. It seemed like he had grown ten years older in one day, had finally filled his father's shoes.

Darcy laughed to himself to think that he was rejoicing to be mentally nudging his forties, when it occurred to him that he had never really felt twenty-eight in the first place. It almost seemed like time had frozen when his father died; that he had stayed twenty-one in his head all along while his body aged, his face became thinner and his chin more prominent. Was he finally twenty-eight in his head?

Reaching his bedchamber, he sighed as Finn helped him from his clothes before collapsing on his bed. He had put on a fresh nightgown, but found the one from his valise on his pillow. Hugging it to his chest, he fell asleep.

As promised, Richard Fitzwilliam set off for Hertfordshire in the morning, feeling very much that a declaration to Miss Bennet was premature. So early was his departure—a habit of his military training—that he had no chance of speaking to his cousin Darcy, who was expected back at Matlock House at nine.

Richard spent the entire journey to Longbourn concocting a speech, which he mentally ripped to shreds several times, before finally assembling something that did not sound ridiculous to his own ears. He was so preoccupied with this exercise when passing through St Albans that he would have run down a small dirty boy, somewhat camouflaged against the dust in the road, if his horse had not shied.

It is ironic, Richard thought as the mother jerked the boy off the road; *after all my plotting and scheming over Christmas with Cousin Elizabeth, that I should now be heading for Longbourn without the benefit of her influence.*

He yelled a 'beg your pardon,' over his shoulder and continued, heedless of the invective that was being hurled at him by the woman. *Perhaps she is a fishwife,* he thought wryly, before turning his deliberations back to Jane.

The colonel arrived at Longbourn in time for morning tea, which Miss Bennet dispensed with her usual smiles in the dining room while her mother looked on encouragingly. He could hear the piano playing in the parlour next door where, Mrs Bennet explained, her youngest daughters were learning to waltz with some officers of the militia under the tutelage of their Aunt Gardiner, who was visiting for the festive season.

After eating some very tolerable Christmas pudding that seemed to contain a large amount of brandy and was accompanied by a brandied custard, Richard asked Miss Bennet if she cared for a stroll around the garden.

They donned their cloaks as it was cold outside, although the snow had not yet fallen in Hertfordshire. At least the weather afforded them some privacy, for Mrs Bennet was not about to brave the frigid outdoors. They had barely reached the wilderness when Richard turned and grasped Jane's gloved hands.

"Miss Bennet, I know this seems forward of me, but I was hoping you might consider my suit."

Jane suppressed a gasp.

"Before you give me an answer, I feel obliged to lay my circumstances before you. You will, of course, have realised from my lack of title that I am not the heir—I am in fact the second son. I do not expect to inherit any property, although it is possible that something might come my way from one of my aunts. If and when that occurs is a matter of conjecture. For the moment, I can rely only on my army pay. My current mode of living is only comfortable because of my connections. As an army vagabond, there are any number of noble houses where a bachelor can arrive on the doorstep and expect food or even lodging. All I have had to do is keep myself clothed, mounted and armed. For this reason I have hesitated to take a wife. My family's circumstances have changed that. After ten years, my brother's marriage has produced only daughters. While he may still yet produce a son and heir to the Fitzwilliam line, my father has asked me to marry, and promised to do what he can for me. In short, he hopes my wife will be the mother of the next viscount, who will one day be earl."

Jane's mouth opened in a silent 'o'.

"My mission today has been precipitated by my father's illness. I had planned to return to Longbourn after Christmas to ask you to permit me to court you. But my father had a turn over Christmas and lies gravely ill. He urged me to come here today against my better judgement, in the hope that he might see me settled before he dies. Tell me, Miss Bennet, is there hope?"

Jane, who had been listening attentively throughout this speech, felt her heart warm when the colonel referred to "courtship", only to miss a beat when she realised he had come straight to the point. Overcome with confusion, her smile faltered, before her mind took several very practical strides. She blushed and, assuming her complaisant smile, said:

"Sir, your attention has not gone unnoticed, and I am highly flattered by it. But would it be possible to keep a roof over our heads?"

"Indeed, Jane," he replied, "I would not expect you to accept under any other conditions. It should be possible to rent a small townhouse on the outskirts of London, in Hans Town, if you are agreeable; or it may be possible for me to resign my commission so we may remove to Derbyshire."

"To Derbyshire?" asked Jane in surprise. "Would we perhaps live at your father's country seat?"

"Well, that is a possibility," he said, although he certainly hoped it would not come to that, as he knew his mother could be very difficult where other females were concerned; "but Darcy has offered me the Dower House at Pemberley, which I thought might appeal since you could be near your sister."

"Oh," said Jane, immediately warming to this idea. "But could you support a family if you resigned your commission?"

"The tentative plan is to purchase a commission in a local militia."

"And you would be willing to do this?" she asked.

"If you will agree to be my wife," he said, clasping her hand, "most gladly."

His expression warmed Jane's heart. She had not fallen in love with the colonel in the way she had fallen for Mr Bingley, but her interactions with him had led her to believe he was an estimable man. At that moment, his willingness to upend his life for her struck Jane most forcibly. *What a stark comparison to Mr Bingley's inconstancy!* A tear threatened to escape from her eye at the injustice of her feelings, which she could not control, and she put up her glove to staunch it.

"Well, Colonel Fitzwilliam," said Jane, somewhat tremulously, "I am certainly willing to wed you, whether we live in London or Derbyshire, provided my father gives his permission."

Richard clasped Jane's hand more tightly, but decided he had better seek parental permission before attempting a kiss.

Jane squeezed his hand in return, before venturing a question of her own: "But what of your father? Is his condition so very grave?"

"So grave, Miss Bennet, that if your father agrees, I will ask his permission to take you back to London shortly, to be married at my father's bedside."

Jane gasped and wondered how her mother would take this news. Nonetheless, she walked calmly back to the house with the colonel.

Upon re-entering the dining room, they discovered Jane's Aunt Gardiner pouring herself a cup of tea with an amused look on her face, while Mrs Bennet looked between Jane and the colonel expectantly. The colonel could only assume that their private tête-à-tête had been not so private.

Jane calmly asked her aunt to pour Richard a cup of tea before excusing herself quietly, whereupon she wended her way to her father's library and told him all. He looked solemn upon hearing her rendition of the colonel's circumstances, but agreed to hear the young man's case. Upon perceiving her father's quelling demeanour, Jane did not quite have the courage to mention the urgency of the colonel's suit and could only hope that her lover was a persuasive man.

Returning to the dining room, she gave a discreet nod to Richard.

As if heading for the nearest convenience, the colonel skilfully divested himself of two little Gardiners who had discovered him to be a jolly playmate.

"Are you all right, my dear?" Mrs Gardiner asked Jane, once the colonel departed. "You look a little pale."

"Yes, Aunt," replied Jane. "Although I could do with a cup of tea."

Jane did her best to distract herself by playing with the Gardiner children during what seemed an interminably long interview between Richard and her father.

"Do you think Colonel Fitzwilliam will stay for lunch, Jane dear?" asked her mother, as she directed the housemaid Sarah to set the table.

"I hardly know, Mother..." said Jane in prevarication. But before she could get any farther, a door opened in the hallway, and the sound of men's laughter echoed down the hall. Jane realised with some wonderment that she had never before heard her father laugh in such an unaffected way.

The gentlemen appeared at the dining room door, with her father stepping into the room first.

"Colonel Fitzwilliam can stay for lunch, dear, if it is quick, but he needs to be off to London by half-past one. Can we accommodate him?"

"Certainly," said Mrs Bennet, before scurrying off towards the kitchen yelling, "Hill! Hill!"

The three younger Bennet sisters appeared with two very young militia officers, whom the colonel had not met previously. He judged them to be raw recruits, not much more than fifteen. They looked rather in awe of the colonel's Life Guards uniform as they seated themselves at the foot of the table. Mrs Bennet sat down to the right of her husband, to bring herself into proximity of the colonel on his left. Jane sat next to Richard while Mrs Gardiner seated herself opposite her niece, on Fanny's right.

The soup was on the table in a matter of minutes, and the colonel managed to keep to his timetable by abstaining from dessert. He was not sure he could have eaten any more plum pudding anyway without rolling off his horse.

Throughout lunch, Mrs Bennet interrogated the colonel on his personal life since they had last seen him, prefixing all her impertinent questions with praise of her daughter, Jane. Much to his wife's chagrin, Mr Bennet steered the conversation away from each of these shoals with his sarcastic humour, while Mrs Gardiner did her best to add her wit while smoothing her sister-in-law's ruffled feathers. All of this was punctuated by shrieks and guffaws from the two youngest Bennets and their swains at the far end of the table. In contrast, the four small Gardiners who had been seated at a miniature table to the side were the picture of good table manners.

When he finally got up to go, Richard bid the two older ladies a gracious good-bye before Jane stood to accompany him to the vestibule. Mrs Bennet gave Jane an encouraging wink.

"I can only think your interview with my father went well?" Jane whispered as they escaped into the hall.

"As best as I could have hoped," said Richard. "He wants to sight the settlement before allowing you out the door, but I hope to return for you in two days hence with a Special Licence. Your father says your Aunt Gardiner is due to return to town soon anyway, and he hopes she might accompany you and attend the ceremony. He is sure your mother is going to be disappointed about not having a proper celebration, but in the circumstances... As to what we do afterwards, I will be guided by your wishes. I will have to stay in London until the situation with Father resolves. Perhaps you could return to Longbourn? Or possibly stay with your Aunt Gardiner? Think on what you wish to do."

Richard grasped her hand, and having received the benediction of paternal consent, bent down and finally kissed Jane lightly. As he expected, her lips felt heavenly.

His horse was brought round from the stables and, after donning his roquelaure, Richard mounted. Tipping his hat to his betrothed, he galloped off towards London.

Mrs Bennet had been waiting impatiently to question Jane upon her return to the dining room, so she was quite vexed when Mr Bennet unexpectedly motioned for his wife to follow him to his library. Once they were safely secluded inside, he divulged the news.

But the squire's attempt at discretion was thwarted—the entire house being apprised of Mrs Bennet's response when she shrieked: "Another Special Licence! Why are these young men in such a hurry?"

37 Beggar My Neighbour

On returning to London in the afternoon, Richard anxiously sought out his father. The earl was holding on and was glad for some good news. Whispering in his son's ear, he advised him to seek out Darcy who was in the library working on the settlements.

Arriving at the earl's townhouse early that morning, Darcy had been quite annoyed to find that Richard had gone off empty-handed to Hertfordshire to request Jane's hand.

"Why did you not consult me?" Darcy repined in a whisper when his cousin presented himself in the library.

They moved off to the hearth, so as not to disturb Mr Havershott. "The least I could have done," said Darcy, "was to give you a bottle of brandy for Mr Bennet."

"Well, I wasn't trying to bribe him, Darcy," protested Richard. "It worked out all right. We traded a few jokes, though he did mention that you'd come prepared. Did you *really* give him a book of fairy tales?"

"Mr Bennet was a university don before inheriting Longbourn. That's what he studied at Oxford."

"Heavens above!" cried the colonel. "Fairy tales? Whatever for?"

"Well, they are part of the oral tradition. They are allegories and moralistic tales…"

"Good grief!" smirked the colonel, heading off this lecture. "Are you telling me that Mrs Edgeworth is a plagiarist?"

Darcy viewed his cousin's light-hearted jest with disfavour. "You know," said he, "it's a pity your father didn't send you to university for a couple of years before buying you a lieutenant's commission."

"I'm sure it wouldn't have done me an ounce of good," replied Richard imperturbably.

Darcy decided not to flog that dead horse.

"Well, we've almost finished the settlements," he said, glancing round at two clerks seated at a card table in a corner, making fair copies of the draft.

"Good Lord!" said Richard. "What on earth did you find to settle?"

"I'll explain over dinner. You'd better get off to the Archbishop."

Richard, obeying, met Goring outside the library, and guiltily remembered to enquire of his mother.

"She is taking tea with some friends in the saloon, sir. There has been a constant stream of visitors since this morning."

When Richard poked his head into the saloon, he found his mother holding court amongst all her old crowd. Clearly she was in high croak. Before he could withdraw discreetly, he was summoned into the room to exchange greetings, be inspected, and cooed over—*Such a magnificent uniform!*

He was then sent off on an errand to purchase more macaroons from Gunter's—*All the footmen,* complained his mother, *were attending the earl!*

After escaping the saloon, Richard mounted a fresh horse that had been brought round from the stables and set off for Doctors' Commons via Gunter's, managing to conduct his business at both institutions before they closed.

He arrived back at the townhouse to find his father asleep, and Darcy departed to his own abode, where he'd invited Richard to dinner. After a brief consultation with Dr Douglas, who advised him that his father was as well as could be expected, Richard handed the macaroons to Goring, leaving word that he should be fetched from Darcy's townhouse if necessary.

Skipping back down the stairs, Richard walked briskly across the square. Despite having ridden a good fifty miles that day, he felt strangely energised. He reassured himself it was all in a day's work, before admitting: *It feels strangely like going into battle—a combination of excitement and anxiety.*

As he ran up the steps to Darcy House, Richard could only be thankful that his cousin was there to help him through the ordeal of his father's illness and his own marriage. He wouldn't have known where to start with the paperwork, nor would his brother, Robert—once they managed to find him. *In fact,* Richard acknowledged, *Robert will probably be more a hindrance than a help.*

Having already come to the same conclusion on the previous evening, Darcy had worked hard during the day to finalise the settlements and associated paperwork before Robert could stick his oar in. The earl had agreed to sell several of the encumbered properties to fund a nest egg for any future viscount. The remaining un-entailed properties had been deeded to Richard. They were currently a liability because of the mortgages, but all the retained properties had strategic value—being close to London, or to industrialised areas of the north. Given time, Darcy believed he could turn them to profit.

When Richard finally arrived at Darcy House, he found his cousin organising his own affairs—Darcy still had to rearrange his finances after the Yorkshire deal, and now must stump up the first of the Bennet dowries. Still, Darcy was sanguine—it was worth it to ensure his sister-in-laws married well, and the first five thousand couldn't have gone to a worthier suitor.

Darcy looked up briefly from his desk as Richard let himself into the study. "So it all went well?"

"Heigh-ho," said Richard. "They said the licence should be ready by noon tomorrow. So I guess I now need to find a clergyman."

"Isn't the Duke of Clifton a crony of your father's?" asked Darcy. "His third son was recently ordained."

"And where do you suggest I look for *him*?"

"I believe he's having dinner next door," smiled Darcy.

Richard grinned back. "*Hoowww* convenient," he drawled, before heading to the door.

"Before you go…" said Darcy, lifting a finger.

"Yes?"

"I presume you need to collect your bride. Hadn't you better send a note to Longbourn advising them of your plans?"

Richard smiled sheepishly before taking the offered pen and paper. "Your pardon, I've never had to organise a wedding before, but I guess this is second time round for you."

When Richard went off to ply the knocker next door and thus secure his clergyman, Darcy added his cousin's note to the document bag containing a copy of the settlement, and a footman was duly sent off into the night.

An hour later, the cousins finally sat down to dinner.

"So, here are the settlements," said Darcy, handing over a copy as Richard finished his soup.

Richard's eyebrows went higher with every clause. "But how can this possibly be funded, Darcy?"

"I've worked it all out with Havershott. Some properties will have to be sold and the rest managed more effectively to increase their income. We can build townhouses on the property near Hans Town, and there is a mill right next to one of the properties in Yorkshire that the owner wants to expand."

"Well, that's ironic!" said Richard. "Here I was considering *leasing* in Hans Town and suddenly I'm the landlord! And has Father really agreed to this?"

"Yes, he's already ceded the deeds to you."

Richard was so overcome he could hardly speak. His face underwent several contortions before he composed himself and squeezed Darcy's bicep.

"Darcy, you are the best of fellows!"

Darcy grimaced back in embarrassment and resisted the urge to rub his arm once it was released. But he was spared having to reply to this encomium when the dishes for the second course were laid on the table.

"So what time have you agreed on for the ceremony?" he asked Richard.

"Hopefully around three pm. I'll return to Hertfordshire tomorrow morning to escort Jane back to London. Her Aunt Gardiner will be with her, so I expect they'll go via Cheapside to divest themselves of the children, if nothing else."

This turned out to be pretty much the plan. Richard arrived shortly before Mr Gardiner, who had brought his carriage from London to retrieve his family from their curtailed holiday. What disappointment the children might have felt in learning they were leaving Longbourn early was quickly forgotten when they discovered that Colonel *Fizzwilliam* was to be their new uncle.

When the colonel dismounted, two small Gardiners clamped themselves to each leg; and when he tried to shake them off, they subsided to his boots, so that he was forced to wade to the portico to greet Jane. She laughed at his predicament before Mrs Gardiner appeared and rescued him.

Shortly afterward, Richard arrived at Mr Bennet's library with Darcy's bottle of brandy. During a brief consultation, Mr Bennet praised his modesty in describing his circumstances, before handing him back a signed copy of the marriage settlements. Richard chose to smile sheepishly rather than explain the magic wand Darcy had waved over his affairs. But the colonel was surprised to discover that Jane's father did not intend to accompany them to London to witness the ceremony.

"My brother Gardiner will stand in for me," explained Mr Bennet. "The metropolis and I do not like each other."

With a shake of hands they parted.

Mr Bennet exerted himself sufficiently to come out to the portico to give his eldest daughter a hug before she departed for her new life. Jane clung to him piteously, not knowing when she might see him again, and feeling excessively maudlin about her father's mortality in the light of the earl's circumstances.

"There, there," said Mr Bennet, patting her hand, "we will see each other shortly, and you may write me a letter at any time you choose." But of answering it, he said nothing.

Mrs Bennet was less sanguine. She raced about hugging everyone and exclaiming, alternately sniffling into her handkerchief and bursting into rapturous laughter. As the carriage drew off, she waved her handkerchief and hugged her three remaining daughters.

"Ooh, an earl's son!" she exclaimed. "Who knows, Lydia, you may marry a duke!"

The ceremony went forward as planned at the earl's townhouse at three pm. The Gardiners' carriage arrived in Mayfair at quarter to the hour, and after paying the toll, proceeded to Grosvenor Square.

The Gardiners exchanged glances as they viewed the magnificent townhouse, but Jane only had eyes for the colonel who had appeared at the top step in full dress uniform.

Richard's eyes sparkled as he handed his bride out of the carriage. Jane was once more wearing her gold silk and her mother's pearls, but this ensemble was complemented by a jewelled hair comb and veil loaned to her by Mrs Gardiner, and she carried a huge bouquet of hothouse flowers worthy of her new station in life.

The Gardiner party were escorted into the opulent vestibule, where they met Mr Darcy, who emerged from a room pressing his temples. After exchanging salutations, they proceeded up the grand marble staircase into the earl's bedchamber, which looked as magnificent as any state bedchamber they had ever visited on public days.

Here they encountered the countess, dressed in a grand toilette. She acknowledged them with a look, but held herself aloof, seated near the earl's bedhead. The earl did appear in a bad way, but was propped up in his bed on pillows for the occasion.

Jane and Richard knelt on two footstools that had been arranged nearby to say their responses to the liturgy, delivered by a clergyman so youthful it seemed hardly possible that he shaved.

Afterwards, the earl found the energy to beckon Jane closer, and she planted a chaste kiss on the cheek of her new father-in-law before they all retreated to the hall at the urging of Dr Douglas.

A magnificent cold collation was presided over by the countess, who was glacially polite to Jane and condescending to the Gardiners before retreating to a group of her own friends who were the only other guests at the reception.

Richard was slightly embarrassed by his mother's behaviour, but the deficit was somewhat redressed by Darcy, who greeted Jane with all the solicitude of a brother and far more affability than she had guessed he possessed. When Dr Douglas and the clergyman descended soon after, they fell into such congenial conversation that the countess's cold manners and her equally distant friends were soon forgotten, and the two groups separately celebrated the nuptials and drank champagne.

Once the cake had been cut, Richard managed to draw Jane aside.

"Jane, in all this flurry, we have not spoken of arrangements following the reception. I realise that our wedding has been very precipitate, that I have not wooed you in the way that I had hoped. Please understand if you wish to return to the Gardiners' house tonight, I will be more than happy to ride over there every day to engage your heart, before we live as man and wife."

Jane blushed prettily, but looked her husband steadily in the face as she replied, "Sir, I would not shirk from my marital duties, especially since the rapidity with which we have taken our vows has been driven by your father's concerns for the succession."

Richard was suffused with joy at her words, as they coincided with the dearest wishes of his heart, but he was also amused with the prim way his wife had expressed herself.

Taking Jane's hand, he squeezed it. "Then, Darcy has very generously offered us his townhouse for the honeymoon."

Jane nodded her acceptance of the offer, and the Gardiners, being apprised of the arrangement and not wishing to impose further on the countess, wished their niece all happiness and departed soon after.

The colonel had originally intended to proceed to Darcy House with his bride by walking across the square, as he had done so many times before. But noticing her silk slippers, he had the consideration to send a footman off to summon a chair; and upon the arrival of this vehicle, handed his wife into it before accompanying her on foot on their short journey.

As Jane wended across the square, she anticipated her fate with all the courage and fortitude of the Maid of Orleans. Her calmness and faith in her husband were not misplaced—Colonel Fitzwilliam had thought long and hard, *very hard*, about the best way to induct his wife into her marital duties. He congratulated himself on coming up, so to speak, with an ingenious solution.

Jane had never before used a sedan chair and when it started raining lightly as they proceeded across the square, she was quite astonished when the bearers took it straight up the steps of the Darcy townhouse and through the door, keeping it level all the way. Setting it down on the vestibule floor, they quickly withdrew the poles so she might not soil her dress on alighting, and opened the door of the chair. She thanked them prettily as Richard paid them, whereupon they withdrew their vehicle as efficiently as they had entered.

After Darcy's footmen helped Jane from her coat and the colonel from his boots, a neatly dressed matron and a younger woman stepped forward to introduce themselves as Darcy's housekeeper, Mrs Flowers, and Jane's new maid, Amabel. For despite the countess's coldness, Richard's mother knew what was owing to a lady of the Fitzwilliam clan and had engaged a maid for her daughter-in-law—a competent girl who had served the late mother of one of the countess's friends.

Richard gave them a cheery hello before dismissing them both for the evening—much to Jane's bemusement—but asking Jane's maid to be ready to serve her mistress in the morning.

After the servants had departed, Jane looked around in appreciation at the foyer of the Darcy townhouse, which, although not so ostentatious as its equivalent at Matlock House, was generously proportioned and somehow contrived to seem terribly expensive, despite being sparsely furnished. *Much*, thought Jane, *like the new fashions in men's clothing.*

"Nice, isn't it?" said Richard, as he took her hand and guided her towards the staircase. "Mind that Ming vase. That's a conceit of old Mr Darcy's—worth a king's ransom—nearly knocked that over when I was a kid."

Jane took a step away from it in alarm before they began padding up the thick rug on the steps.

"Was this place furnished by Mr Darcy's parents?" she asked.

"Mostly—Darcy's changed and added or a thing or two, like that landscape," Richard said, pointing to an atmospheric painting on the landing that rather puzzled Jane—she wondered if the artist's eyesight might be failing.

Reaching his bedchamber, Richard carried his wife across the threshold before settling her on a chaise longue. Jane was no lightweight, but he managed this admirably. To her astonishment, he then produced a pack of playing cards.

"Would you care a for a game, Mrs Fitzwilliam?"

Slightly bewildered, Jane gave a nod.

"Do you know *Beggar-My-Neighbour?*" Richard asked, straddling the end of the chaise-longue.

...another nod and a bemused smile.

"Very well," Richard said, dealing; "I propose an additional set of rules: whoever wins a hand by a Jack must take something off, but if you win by a Queen you must take something off the *other* person. Whoever wins by a King may steal a kiss on the lips, but if you win by an ace you may choose to kiss me *anywhere* your heart desires. Do you understand the rules?"

Jane blushed and nodded.

The ensuing card game was without doubt the most memorable of her life. She chose to divest her husband first of the most the trivial things—his gloves, his fob; and kissed him in the most insipid places—his chin, his nose. But Richard played the game in quite a different way. After kissing Jane once soundly on the lips, and a second time above her garter on her right leg, he won the chance to remove something and rather than divest her of a shoe or glove as she had expected, he most provocatively put his hands through the slits of her gown and removed her pockets. This was done with much fumbling and sliding of his hands, which caused Jane to break into a giggle. Once he got her stays off, the game was abandoned, though she was still wearing several items of jewellery and one stocking.

Jane had, of course, been apprised of her marital duties by Mrs Bennet prior to her departure from Hertfordshire, and thankfully her mother had once more been ably assisted by Mrs Gardiner. The substance of this talk was much what it had been for Elizabeth, though Mrs Bennet's attitude was quite different: she clasped her eldest daughter's hand and sympathised with her so piteously that Jane was almost moved to tears before Mrs Gardiner said her piece and assuaged some of Jane's fears.

After her husband snuffed the single candle he had kept burning during their lovemaking, Jane fell asleep in his arms, happy in the knowledge that her aunt's advice had been far more accurate than her mother's.

38 A honeymoon

At breakfast, Jane discovered that not only had Mr Darcy loaned them his townhouse, he had absented himself from it, occupying Richard's room at Matlock House. This, she advised her husband, could not continue. She had never felt entirely comfortable with Mr Darcy—he seemed to inhabit some higher sphere, not only in rank but also in intellect. She had always been more comfortable with gentlemen like Mr Bingley and the colonel— intelligent, but not intimidatingly so. Nonetheless, she refused to drive her brother-in-law from his abode for the duration of their honeymoon and urged her husband to ensure Mr Darcy returned in the evening.

She could only wish that her dear sister Lizzy had accompanied her husband to London to facilitate conversation. She knew the colonel, *her husband!* would shield her from the worst excesses of Mr Darcy's intellect— the snubbing silences when she said some stupid thing, mostly from sheer fright, because she was not generally a stupid woman. But Richard, living so much in the world of men, could not entirely enter into female thoughts. Having inherited her father's intellect, Lizzy was not intimidated by Mr Darcy to the extent she could spar with him in conversation. But she combined these powers with her own sweetness, which did not mock people less intellectually capable than herself. *Well, perhaps occasionally their younger sisters, …and their mother, …and Mr Collins.*

Good grief! thought Jane. *Perhaps Lizzy is more like Mr Darcy than I have heretofore appreciated, and I have only been spared by sisterly grace!*

Richard had pledged himself to help Darcy sort out his father's affairs; and Jane, knowing that his father's illness would preoccupy him, had arranged to spend her days with the Gardiners. After being assisted into the Darcy carriage by her husband for the journey to Gracechurch Street, with her maid on the backward-facing seat and one of Darcy's footmen standing up behind, Jane watched her husband walk back towards Matlock House until the carriage left the square, and he disappeared behind the buildings flanking Grosvenor Street.

As Jane had resolved to write immediately to her sister after settling in at the Gardiners', she began to compose the letter in her head as she drove along.

Dear Lizzy,
  No doubt Mr Darcy has already informed you, and you will think me gone mad, but let me reassure you that I am quite sane, and am now the Honourable Mrs Richard Fitzwilliam.
  I can only guess you will think me as flighty as Lydia or as practical as Charlotte, but while there is some justice in these comparisons, I have every

hope that the future will confirm the soundness of my decision. As you know, I have been aware of the impediments in the way of any future happiness with Mr Bingley from the time of the Netherfield Ball. His indifference to me since Miss de Bourgh departed Longbourn has been distressing. While he continued to treat me with flattering attention every time we met, these meetings were far too few, and once he departed Netherfield for Kent I gave up all hope of him. I do not accuse him of purposely breaking my heart. I believe him too good for that. No, his sin lies in being too easily distracted.

The colonel, on the other hand, has been most constant in his attentions, although they were not overt at first. When Miss de Bourgh was in residence and Mr Bingley and the earl visited frequently, I often looked up to see him watching me. What he was thinking I could not know, but sometimes I fancied I saw disapproval in his face. However, after consulting Charlotte, I began to think his disapproval might not be directed at me; and sure enough, once the other men were gone and he visited alone, he was more forthcoming and particular, to the extent I thought he might be considering courting me.

The thing that most impressed me was his constant good humour. He is not a truly affable man like Mr Bingley—he has directed such looks at some of Kitty and Lydia's intemperate swains that I would not like to be the man who crossed him; but he has been very forbearing with our mother and younger sisters. To me, he has shown only solicitude, and I have every hope of growing to love him most deeply.

He had mentioned several times that his circumstances were not good. At first, I interpreted these pronouncements to indicate he had no serious intentions, but later realised he sincerely wished not to misrepresent his prospects. But how 'not good' for an earl's son compared to our own situation I could hardly know.

My shock when he came to the point so quickly was great. I believe my heart actually stopped for a moment when he asked for my hand. But it was soon clear that the earl's sudden turn had hastened his intentions. When he explained that he would be willing to give up his commission to allow me to live near you in Derbyshire, and bring up our children together, I could not imagine a better picture of domestic felicity. That was what really tipped the balance for me.

My father quickly reassured me, before I left for London, that the colonel's circumstances were really not so bad as he had painted; and that he expected that I would live in more affluence with the colonel than I had at Longbourn as his child. This caused me quite a pang, and I began to cry and reassured him I had lacked for nothing, but he shooed me out of his study, and there was no chance to talk afterwards.

As to our living arrangements, I only look forward to the felicity of being near you once more, dear sister, and having you nearby as our children grow up together. The colonel has told me much of the Dower House and I cannot wait to see it. It seems incredible that everything has worked out so well!

For the moment, I must wait here with Richard, but I hope to be with you soon; or if our stay here is protracted, perhaps Mr Darcy will allow you and Georgiana to join us once the cold weather has abated...

This much Jane had composed before the carriage arrived at Gracechurch Street, where her aunt and her young nephews met her joyfully.

Her aunt was relieved to see Jane greet her with a smile bordering on a grin; a heartening sign from her niece, who was known for her characteristically placid smiles. Upon Jane's announcing her intention of writing directly to her dear sister Lizzy, Mrs Gardiner deposited her in the morning room, closing the door against her intrepid sons, and announcing she would bring in tea at eleven.

After ensuring the children were well occupied and supervised, Mrs Gardiner duly arrived with the tea, and during the subsequent tête-à-tête was confirmed in her opinion that all had gone well on the wedding night.

Upon reaching Matlock House, Richard immediately sought Darcy, ostensibly to thank him for loaning his townhouse, but in reality to bask in the felicity of them now being brothers-in-law, and with such matchless wives! Darcy was pleased to see his cousin feeling so satisfied and felt slightly guilty about bursting his bubble.

"I'm afraid your father has another task for us," broached Darcy.

"What now? Are we to be sent off in search of Robert?"

"No. He wants to finalise the succession at Rosings—Anne needs an heir. I believe he has spoken to you already of his wishes."

"To set up one of my nieces? True, but surely that is a matter of paperwork—Anne revising her will."

"Under the agreement made by your father with Aunt Catherine, your niece must live at Rosings to become familiar with the estate and its management."

"To be brought under Aunt's thumb more like!" scoffed Richard.

"Someone must visit Lady Stanley and deliver the child to Rosings," said Darcy. "Your father had hoped to delegate that duty to Robert, but as he has not appeared..."

"Hell and damnation! Must I be off to Derbyshire again? So much for a honeymoon!"

"I'm sorry, but I agree with your father. Aunt Catherine won't allow the will to be altered until she is sure of the niece. Your father is worried that she may yet force Anne to have a child, regardless of the risk to her health. All Aunt needs is a live birth."

"She'd be a fool to try it," growled Richard. "She'd only end up with a dead daughter and lose Rosings to Lewis de Bourgh's cousin."

"Your father is trying to ensure the future of at least one of his grandchildren as well as save Anne," pointed out Darcy.

Richard sighed. "I know! Damn Robert! As the child's father, it is *his* place to do this! But I will go for Anne."

"Talk to your father now," urged Darcy, "but don't agitate him."

Richard dutifully tripped up the stairs and knocked on the door of the earl's bedchamber. It was answered by Miss Smyth. The earl, who seemed to have slightly more colour in his face, was propped up in bed. He watched his second son approach the bed with a sapient eye.

"Got a spring in your step," he croaked.

"There's a good reason for that, Father. Thank you for your efforts on my behalf. Jane is more than I ever hoped for."

Both men knew the effort to finance the marriage was almost entirely Darcy's, although neither fully appreciated the effort he would go to in the coming weeks and years to ensure Richard's patrimony—in their eyes he seemed to possess a magic wand to wave over their affairs. Still the earl's acquiescence and signature had been crucial, and both father and son knew it.

"You're welcome, Son," said the earl, reaching out to squeeze his second son's forearm before dropping his arm flaccidly on the counterpane.

Richard returned his father's grasp briefly, like a handshake, attempting to cover for his father's weakness—it embarrassed him.

"I understand you want me to go to Derbyshire?" he said.

Haltingly, the earl advised Richard that he had already raised his plan with Lady Stanley in a letter from Netherfield and received her assurances that she approved of the scheme, before coming to terms with his sister at Christmas.

On his father's prompting, Richard sat down at a small secretaire near the earl's bed and wrote a letter to be sent by courier to Miranda, notifying her that he would arrive shortly to collect the child.

The colonel then headed down the stairs to take his leave of Darcy, who was once more ensconced in the library, surrounded by paper. After his cousin wished him God's speed on his journey, Richard mounted his steed to head to Gracechurch Street to tell his bride of the alterations in their plans.

Behind him, Darcy picked up the next prospectus from the stack Mr Havershott had left before reading it through and assigning it to one of the piles in front of him: invest, investigate, or discard. He had wanted to get through the whole pile before meeting Mr Havershott in the City after lunch, but he could see that wish was hopelessly optimistic. Darcy's back ached from the clumps in Richard's horsehair mattress. His own staff rolled his mattress every day, and he knew his housekeepers would never have let a mattress get to such a state. This was one reason Darcy had continued to keep a woman in charge rather than adopting the new fashion for butlers—women paid more attention to details in household matters.

After two hours, Darcy laid his head on his crossed arms for a short nap, imagining Elizabeth rubbing his back—that helped a little. Refreshed, he got up and stretched, then called for tea.

When Mr Gardiner arrived home for lunch during Richard's surprise visit to Gracechurch Street, they all sat down to eat together. During the meal, it was decided that Jane would stay with the Gardiners until her husband returned from his errand, and her maid was sent off in a hackney to retrieve her trunks that had made the opposite journey only the day before.

Mr and Mrs Gardiner stayed at table when Richard got up to depart before dessert, eager to be on his way, and back to his bride's side 'ere long. Jane followed him into the hall, and when he perceived they were alone, he pulled her into the sitting room opposite to take his leave.

"I'm so sorry, my darling," said Richard. "How I wanted to be with you again tonight."

"I know, Richard. I feel the same, but your father may not have much time left on this earth. You are being a good son by honouring his wishes."

"Thank you, Jane, for understanding. You are an angel."

Following a lingering kiss, they reluctantly returned to the hallway, where Jane helped her husband with his cloak and hat. After returning his salute with a wave, she stood on the doorstep as he disappeared into the busy traffic of Gracechurch Street.

Travelling as fast as he dared in the poor weather, Richard arrived in Derbyshire almost two days later, and headed straight for the viscount's estate ten miles south of Wyvern Hall. Chaseley was an Elizabethan manor, less sprawling than Wyvern Hall, but in a similar state of disrepair. It had been added to the earl's estates by marriage, and been the viscount's residence for over two hundred years. The viscountess was waiting for him in the wainscoted drawing room, where a great fire burned in the huge grate.

"Richard," said Lady Stanley, standing as he entered. "How goes the earl?"

"He is still alive," replied the colonel as he kissed his sister-in-law's hand, "and anxious to forward this adoption. Is the child ready?"

"I've summoned her just now. Her trunk is packed. You will have lunch before you go?"

"Gladly, if it can be procured quickly."

The words had scarcely left his mouth when there was a knock, and the door opened to reveal a tall girl of twelve years with a woebegone look on her face. She was accompanied into the room by a maid and a younger girl who both seemed to be almost supporting her.

"Sophia, please spare me the dramatics," said her mother. "We've been through this a hundred times. Rosings is a far grander estate than Chasely—you will be far better off there."

Sophia had not seen Rosings, but she knew her Aunt Catherine and could not agree. "Please, no, Mother!" she pleaded. "Mary wants to go instead!"

The viscountess looked at her younger daughter, who nodded in confirmation. She pursed her lips at her pretty older daughter who was shaping up to be just as unreliable as her father, before looking back at her second eldest. Mary was a plain girl who had inherited the least admirable aspects of both her handsome parents' features; but she was a dutiful child, who seemed to have more of her mother's common sense.

Lady Stanley looked at Richard. "Do you think the earl will object if my second eldest goes instead?"

"I cannot think he has a preference," replied Richard, "any one of 'em will do. Better to send the willing one."

"Very well, Mary, your Uncle Richard is leaving after lunch, so you will have to pack quickly. Go now!"

Mary ran from the room accompanied by the girls' maid, while Sophia fell upon her mother's breast with tearful 'thank yous', much to the viscountess's astonishment. After pushing her handkerchief at the girl, Lady Stanley managed to fob her daughter off by suggesting she help her sister pack.

An hour later, the girl's trunk was loaded onto the viscountess's travelling carriage, and after a curtsey to her mother, ten-year old Mary climbed into the coach, followed by the girls' maid, who carried a basket containing their lunch and some extra provisions.

The viscountess sighed. *One taken care of.*

With a tip of his hat to Lady Stanley, Richard was off, setting the pace for the coach that lumbered behind him. After transferring the girls to a post-chaise in Derby, Colonel Fitzwilliam began the long journey back to London.

39 Here's poison

Lizzy and Georgie spent their first week in Derbyshire well enough after Georgiana had recovered from her sulks about her brother's departure. After breakfasting together, they spent their mornings apart: Georgiana riding and Elizabeth with many tasks: for when Fitzwilliam left for London, Elizabeth had decided her holiday was over. There were so many things she wanted to do—reoccupy the family sitting room, clean up the observatory—and, of course, she needed to visit the tenants. Boxing Day had served as her introduction. Now she had her cloak, there was no excuse not to do her duty.

Her first solo office as mistress of Pemberley was made easy when Ben reappeared to allow her to poultice his knee. Granted he was accompanied by his mother on the first trip, who looked like she had dragged him there by his collar; but he came readily enough afterwards, once he discovered the relief to be had from the searing hot oat poultice Elizabeth applied, drawing out the pus.

Lizzy could only be amused at the use she had made of Fitzwilliam's precious oats. She imagined he would be less fond of porridge if he could glimpse the disgusting, used poultices she threw away. But Ben's knee healed remarkably, and after a week she thought he had been tortured sufficiently to release him into the wild, reminding him to return quickly should his wound take a turn for the worse.

With regard to the abandoned sitting room and observatory, Elizabeth decided the observatory should be her priority—it was in the worse condition, and she had decided the sitting room should be a joint family effort. Indeed, she began to refer to it as the family room to distinguish it from Georgie's sitting room.

Before calling in the chambermaids to remove the dust from the observatory, Elizabeth decided to tackle Lady Anne's desk herself—there were loose papers on it that had been left in situ when Mrs Darcy died. Besides being dusty, these were largely intact. After ridding them of the powdery dust that caked them, Lizzy discovered that Lady Anne had been transcribing an entry from her logbook that contained a drawing, description and positions of a comet she had been observing, into a letter addressed to 'Dear Thomas'. There was also some correspondence from a French astronomer. Lizzy set aside the cleaned documents in the family room, until the observatory was rid of its layer of dust.

Letting the chambermaids loose on the observatory, Elizabeth instructed them to avoid the telescope and its plinth, deciding she should clean the instrument herself to be on the safe side. The maids sieved sand to settle the dust before setting to with their brooms. It was dirty work and Elizabeth could only be glad she spent most of her time on the far side of the arras.

After enquiring with Georgiana, who could not furnish the Christian name of her uncle, Elizabeth consulted The Baronetage. Having discovered that Sir Thomas Fitzwilliam was indeed the Astronomer Royal, she decided to finish transcribing Lady Anne's observations and send them to him. *Who knows? Perhaps they are still of use.*

Her lap desk proved inadequate for this task, being too small to accommodate the logbook as well as a sheet of paper. Looking around the family room, Elizabeth spotted a reasonably large side table. It was too low to use with a chair, but she thought she might contrive by kneeling on a footstool, when she remembered seeing a small Davenport desk in the blue room. Retrieving her writing materials from her lap desk, she found the larger desk suited her purposes admirably and set about her task.

By lunchtime, the maids had cleaned the observatory up to the height of the windows. Inspired by the improvement in the room wrought by their efforts, Elizabeth would have dearly loved to clean the telescope in the afternoon, but she decided this would be antisocial. The maids assured her that they would set to polishing the woodwork with beeswax as soon as they could be spared from the kitchens.

As was their wont, the Darcy ladies spent their afternoon together in Georgie's sitting room. While Georgie played, Lizzy and Mrs Annesley listened and occupied themselves with their own work: Mrs Annesley with handicraft and Lizzy composing an acrostic for Georgiana, as she had done so many times before for her sister Jane. Late in the day, when a note came from Madame Lafrange that more of Elizabeth's dresses were ready for a final fitting, the three ladies decided to visit Lambton the next day.

Georgie's appearance in the village on the following afternoon caused almost as much of a stir as Elizabeth's had upon her marriage. Lizzy noted, to her amusement, that her sister-in-law's visit not only provoked the interest of the women and children of the village, it drew several young men out of the woodwork, no doubt keen to get a glimpse of the heiress. After visiting the dressmaker, the three ladies had a very pleasant afternoon tea with Lizzy's aunt and Miss Dorsey, who had much in common with Mrs Annesley.

When Georgie set out on her ride the next morning with Healy in tow, Elizabeth walked into the observatory with Mrs Reynolds to find the room much improved. The wood gleamed, but the cleanliness of the floor only served as an unfortunate counterpoint to the grimy glass roof. Nevertheless Mrs Reynolds was so impressed with Elizabeth's efforts to rehabilitate the room that she volunteered to help personally. Together, they cleaned the external surface of the telescope and the plinth before the housekeeper was obliged to return to her other duties. But upon leaving, Mrs Reynolds summoned two footmen to clean the windows, first retrieving a large set of wheeled library steps that was stored in a niche of the tower such that they were disguised as part of the wainscoting. Two long poles, used to reach the furthest parts of the windows, were procured from the second level of the tower. The housekeeper then helped Lizzy drape an old sheet over the telescope before hurrying off to supervise the serving of morning tea.

Satisfied with the progress of the footmen, Lizzy sat down once again at the Davenport desk to write a letter to her sister, recounting Darcy's trip to Yorkshire and return for Christmas, skipping the potentially embarrassing revelation that his return had not been from choice but rather forced by circumstances. She spoke of the Christmas presents, Richard's coral necklaces, and Georgie's delight in her new horse.

Beginning the revelation of the gentlemen's departure to London upon the earl's illness, she was forced to mend her pen. As Lizzy had left her lap desk in her bedchamber, she opened the top of the Davenport, hoping to find a penknife inside rather than walk back to her room.

Imagine her surprise when she spotted a letter addressed *"To Elizabeth"*.

At first she thought it must be a missive that her husband had neglected to post to her from Yorkshire, though why it should be in *this* desk rather than in his study she could not guess. Although it bore a seal, it had been opened, suggesting perhaps he had intended to add something. But upon unfolding and reading it, she realised it was not from Fitzwilliam at all, but from Edward Yardley. Indeed, Elizabeth belatedly recognized his handwriting.

The shock of the discovery caused her to drop the letter, as if she had discovered a spider in the desk. It was bizarre. What was a letter from Edward doing in this room? As she stood there staring at the sheet of paper on the floor, a cold feeling crept over her, as a sense of unreality gripped her. It was as if an icy hand had reached from the past and touched her, as if Edward had returned from the grave.

Steadying herself, Elizabeth tried to apply logic to the situation. Her husband had been at Netherfield; had spent a large amount of time in the study. *Perhaps it had got mixed up with Darcy's papers?* Likely the letter had arrived at Netherfield after news of Edward's death, and Sir Laurence had deemed it pointless to deliver it; possibly had thought it might upset her.

Getting up, Elizabeth picked up Edward's letter from the floor and read it through again. She was gripped by melancholy as she did so. *He had been such a good, simple soul!* Tears trickled down her cheeks as she thought of him and their many happy times together in childhood. She had loved Edward like a brother, and thought his youthful declaration of love for her somewhat misguided. But the letter proved his love had stood the test of time, when she thought it had faltered! Could she have loved Edward as a man? Yes, she thought she could have! What heart could withstand such an uncomplicated attachment?

Returning to the desk, Elizabeth saw there were more letters, and picking up a handful of them, she opened the next one eagerly, hoping to read more of Edward's dear words and thus remember him. But the next letter was addressed *'Dearest Wills'* and she was halfway through the first paragraph before she realised she was reading a letter to her husband from his lover.

Elizabeth gasped. Later, she realised that she should have put the letter down at that point, but her eyes were drawn on, as if glued to the paper. There were endearments, poetry, descriptions of their lovemaking and his body, *such metaphors!*—all evidence of a much longer and deeper connection than she shared with her husband. It was signed merely *'D'*.

It was as if Elizabeth had woken in a nightmare, to walk into a room containing all her fears recorded in these letters: Edward had loved her and Fitzwillam did not! Elizabeth dropped the pile of letters as if scalded and staggered backwards, feeling like she had been punched in the stomach. When the back of her legs collided with the small bed in the room, she sat down abruptly and, clutching the edge of the mattress, stared at the scattered paper on the floor.

Curling herself up, she laid her head on the pillow and cried for ten minutes or so. Then, mastering her emotions, Lizzy contemplated the sheets of folded paper on the floor. One part of her wanted to gather those illicit love letters and read their contents, possibly to discover the identity of her husband's lover and the extent of their love affair, but a wiser part of her held her back. Certainly it would be improper to read his letters, but more than that, she thought they would act like poison in her veins.

Getting up, Elizabeth arranged the scattered letters in a neat pile, ready to hide them away once more in the desk. But then, taking the first letter that she had already scanned, Lizzy read it through once more, reasoning that she had already contaminated herself with it. Indeed, Lizzy thought she might be able to deal better with this revelation if she at least knew who she had to contend with—for it occurred to Elizabeth that she had never discovered whether Darcy's lover was male or female. In the weeks since her marriage she had forgotten her father's opinion, convinced that her husband's skills in lovemaking had been acquired through much practise.

Elizabeth parsed the letter in detail: the handwriting was sophisticated, but looked rounded and light on the page; several turns of phrase struck her as feminine, and the descriptions of lovemaking—surely only a female would have described things thus. She reached some poetry, and doubted again—the person was intelligent, learned; *perhaps it was a man after all?*

D. Douglas? Duncan? Diana? Dorothea? Oh, why am I torturing myself?

With a sniff, Elizabeth folded the letter and placed it on top of the pile. Then, seeing a red ribbon in the desk, she tied the letters together with trembling hands, carefully placed the package in a corner of the desk, and closed the lid. She slipped the letter from Edward into her pocket—it was addressed to her, and she would keep it in remembrance of him.

Feeling drained, she gathered her paraphernalia and walked towards the door. Elizabeth knew she should return to the observatory—it would help distract her, but she had neither the inclination nor the energy. Stepping outside, she vowed she would never set foot in Darcy's childhood room again. Closing the door, she locked it.

40 Hatchard's

Elizabeth was thankful there was yet an hour to lunch. She retreated to her bedchamber to lie down, claiming a headache in response to Jenny's solicitude. But she got up an hour later when her maid enquired if she would prefer a tray.

As she descended to the dining room, Elizabeth was determined not to allow her emotional turmoil to show. She steadfastly tried to think happy thoughts, focussing on her dear sister Jane and the many days of felicity they had spent together. At dinner, she succeeded in fooling Mrs Annesley, and Georgie was too engrossed in solving her acrostic to notice anything amiss.

Over the next few days, Elizabeth's emotions fluctuated wildly. She was subdued in the presence of Georgiana and Mrs Annesley, holding herself in check. Their voices somehow seemed softer and muddier, as if they were all immersed in water. She had to remind herself to speak at appropriate times. In private, she alternated between sorrow and anger, and the source of these raw emotions she could hardly understand. Her anger was at first directed towards her husband, but she soon turned it on herself.

Darcy had said from the start that his heart was engaged elsewhere, and she had determined at Longbourn to guard her own heart against him; not to hate or resent him, but to keep her own heart safe. She had tried to cultivate him as a friend—that had seemed the wisest path. But now she had to admit that, despite herself, despite her knowledge of his entanglement, she had fallen in love with him. There could be no other explanation for the torrent of emotions the letters had produced.

Elizabeth had almost screamed with vexation when she had realised it. She had made an odd noise; and Jenny, who had been in the dressing room at the time, had come out to check on her. Elizabeth had grabbed her toe and claimed to have stubbed it.

Lizzy realized that her husband was such a complex character. There was much goodness in him: his attention to his duty, his general lack of vice, his solicitude for his sister and for her... *But oh! He is so self-centred! That,* she thought, *is his chief failing.* She could not really blame him for it: being brought up as the only son, for such a long time the only child on a grand estate, all these factors must have contributed. *It is such a shame!* His good looks, intelligence, and circumstances had made him such an eligible catch for any lady, but had also spoiled him to be the faithful husband of none.

Richard's trip back to London with Mary took two and a half-days—the longest he had ever spent completing the journey. Mary's maid, unused to the bounding motion of the post-chaise, was sick several times during the first few hours; and after stopping twice, they were forced to continue at a slower pace. By the time they had reached London, ten-year old Mary was tending her fifteen-year old abigail, who had continued to dry-retch throughout the journey.

Finally, they arrived in Grosvenor Square, where Richard hoped to find his father still alive. When Goring came out to greet the carriage, he reassured Richard that the earl was holding on. Richard left the butler to deal with the girls, running up the front steps of the townhouse to seek his mother. The countess, who was with her old circle of tabbies in the drawing room, was quite put out that she was expected to greet her grandchild.

"Why on earth did you bring Mary?" she exclaimed. "She is only eight! And where is her governess?"

"She is ten, mother. The eldest one wished to stay with Miranda," said Richard, putting the best complexion on it that he could. "And I expect the three remaining sisters still have use for their governess. Aunt Catherine will no doubt wish to choose her own for the girl. A young maid came with her but she is ill."

"Is it catching?" asked the countess in alarm.

"No, Mother, she is merely ill from the carriage."

"Oh! These peasants! They can never tolerate being in a vehicle! Very well," said the countess, snapping her fan shut. "Send her in!"

Mary was loath to leave her maid, but was convinced to do so when a chambermaid was found to tend the poor abigail.

With her pleasing manners and charming garb—one of Georgiana's cast-offs from some seven years ago—Mary soon had the tabbies in the drawing room cooing over her, offering her tea and cake. Her second best dress was still in good order, very fine; and if it was a little out of date, so were the fashions of the ladies who surrounded her—they could not imagine why anyone would wish to array themselves in the cheap fabrics and formless fashions favoured by the current debutantes.

The little girl was soon summoned to the earl's bedside for her benediction. When Richard led her into the bedchamber, Mary's eyes goggled as she surveyed the earl's enormous bed with its rich trappings. Stopping three feet from the bed, Mary gave a curtsey, upon which the earl beckoned her forward. Her fichu-clad shoulders barely rose above the mattress.

The earl reached out a beringed claw to ruffle the girl's hair, like he had done so many times to his sons in their early youth; but perceiving the neat ringlets there, he gripped her shoulder instead.

"You must not let me down, Mary," croaked the earl, apprised of the substitution of one granddaughter for the other. Exhausted by a single sentence, he fell back upon the pillows, signalling Richard to talk.

Richard, who had flung himself thankfully into a fauteuil, leant forward to address his niece. "Grandpapa has arranged for you to stay three months with Lady Catherine; after which she will either adopt you, or you will return to Derbyshire. Do you understand?"

"Yes, I will do my best to please Aunt Catherine," offered the girl, as if repeating a catechism.

The earl smiled at her and signalled her dismissal, whereupon she followed her uncle Richard into the hall. Once Richard closed the door, the girl looked up at him quizzically. Her attitude made Richard think of a small sparrow.

"Yes?" prompted Richard.

"Will I still be a Fitzwilliam if Aunt Catherine adopts me?"

"Of course, it is your heritage. You will continue to be called Lady Mary, even though Sir Lewis was only a baron. It is your birthright. But like getting married, you will change your surname."

"So Aunt is a lady twice over—once due to her rank as an earl's daughter and secondly as the wife of a baron," observed Mary.

"That's right!" laughed Richard. "Call her Lady *Lady* Catherine and you will get on with her famously!"

Understanding, Mary smiled back.

Against attempting Kent that afternoon, Richard had firmly decided. His butt was sore from riding, and he wanted to see his wife. The languid maid provided a ready excuse. He resolved they would set off early in the morning, requesting the earl's carriage for the journey. It provided a much smoother ride and would hopefully not sicken the maid so much as the post-chaise. Nonetheless, Richard requested that Goring pack a bowl and some water.

After restoring Mary to the countess, Richard sought out Darcy and discovered him in the earl's study.

"You've not been here since I left?" Richard asked incredulously.

"I've been to the City twice and, of course, I have slept; but other than that, yes," replied Darcy, rubbing his forehead with his left hand.

Richard could see that Darcy was exhausted. Dark rings under his eyes made his usually handsome face look haggard. It had always seemed so ironic to Richard that his own father, who had always been profligate in his ways, had outlived Darcy's clean-living father. Watching his cousin with concern, the likely reason for his uncle's untimely demise now occurred to him: Uncle Darcy had always worked hard to increase his fortune; his own father, the earl, had intimated he had done so to make himself worthy of the Lady Anne.

Darcy is under no such obligation, thought Richard, *but is probably motivated instead by duty—a need to fulfil his patrimony.*

Darcy returned his pen to the inkstand.

Well, thought Richard, completing the comparison, *my father's lifestyle has finally caught up with him.* Suddenly feeling his cousin's mortality, Richard remonstrated with him: "Darce, you looked fagged. Come, man, you need to take a break; get outside. It's so dark in here!"

"Will you dine with me, or do you have plans to go to the Gardiners?" asked Darcy in return.

"The Gardiners did invite me to dine and stay overnight on my return to the city, but I could always dine with you and head over there afterwards."

"I would be grateful for the company," admitted Darcy, getting up from the desk. "I have missed someone to talk to."

"Well, that would be a first!" scoffed Richard, surprised that his ungregarious cousin would express such an opinion. "Why don't you come to Rosings? I presume Bingley will still be there."

"I can't; someone needs to stay here with your father, especially if Robert should turn up."

"Have they *still* not found him?" Richard asked incredulously, before adding in an amused voice: "Perhaps he has gone to the moon?"

"Goring has received several notes from Fobbing. We are now apprised of half-a-dozen locations in England where Robert is *not*, but Fobbing must find him eventually."

After sending a footman off to Gracechurch Street, the cousins left Matlock House. Walking slowly back across the square, Richard told the tale of his journey. Darcy was quite surprised to hear the younger daughter had volunteered to come—he thought her a little too small to cope with such responsibility and resolved to speak to her before she departed in the morning.

Following an early dinner, Richard went off to Gracechurch Street, and Darcy was left to his solitude. Unable to bear looking at another business paper, he retreated to his bedchamber, resolving to go to bed early. But despite pulling the used nightshirt from his bedside drawer and hugging it tightly, he was unable to find repose. The stress of having to make so many unfamiliar decisions so quickly was taking its toll.

Pushing the nightshirt under his pillow, Darcy got up and descended to the library, searching for a volume of poetry. Instead, his hand alighted on the novel Georgiana had given him for his birthday. He had only read the first chapter, tossing it aside as a silly thing—a book about nothing. But nothing seemed welcome now; the easily parsed prose more relaxing than the higher flights of poesy.

Padding back up the stairs, Darcy got into bed with his banyan around his shoulders and reacquainted himself with the story of the Dashwoods, whose situation suddenly seemed to have more relevance. After being engrossed in the story for two hours, he could hardly keep his eyes open, and settling down, he fell asleep, hugging his used nightgown.

Richard woke at dawn and had some difficulty extracting himself from his wife's warm bed. With a superhuman effort, he pulled on his clothes, which he had arrayed neatly on a chair—a habit borne from years of looking after himself. Standing, he almost scraped the ceiling of the small chintz-covered bedroom that smelt so deliciously of his wife.

Jane stirred, bereft of the warm arms that had encompassed her during the night. They had not got to sleep 'til well after midnight had chimed. Richard rearranged a blanket that had fallen off the end of the bed over his wife's sleeping form and let himself out of the chamber, tiptoeing down the stairs before being let out the front door by a chambermaid.

Cheapside was already stirring, but not yet crowded—so Richard made good time to Mayfair. He found his niece at breakfast with her maid in the kitchens. The countess, who was still abed, had completely forgotten to arrange her granddaughter's early departure, but fortunately the girl had sought sustenance herself. Mary and her maid sat nibbling tea and toast while Richard ate a bowl of porridge and downed a tankard of ale.

Heading out to the carriage with the girls, Richard was surprised to meet Darcy in the vestibule. He was dressed immaculately in a black coat and hessians with biscuit-coloured breeches and looked more rested, although the dark circles under his eyes were still apparent.

"I want to say a word to Mary before she goes off," explained Darcy.

Richard nodded and stepped out to oversee the carriage prior to their departure. He had decided to accompany the girls in comfort rather than ride.

Darcy crouched down and took his niece's gloved hands. "Mary, if you find yourself unable to live with your Aunt Catherine, I will understand, and do what I can for you. Be nice to your cousin Anne. She has had a hard life."

"I will, Uncle Darcy, and do not worry. I can be good for three months."

Darcy thought the girl seemed to have a twinkle in her eye. He escorted Mary and her maid outside, watching them climb into the carriage. Richard stepped in after them and motioned the maid, who had taken the backward-facing seat, to sit beside her mistress on the backbench so that he could take her place. He could see both girls were agog with the luxuriously appointed carriage. Making sure the maid was acquainted with the location of the bowl, Richard pushed himself back into the backward-facing seat and looked at his cousin.

"If I am not back tonight, it will be tomorrow. Promise me you will take a break while I'm away."

Darcy looked annoyed for a moment before saying, "I had thought of going to Hatchard's for a book on steam engines after my trip to Yorkshire. Will that satisfy you?"

"Admirably," said Richard. He tipped his hat, and they were off.

Darcy walked to the bookshop after lunch. His steps towards Berkeley Square were filled with memories of the many times he had undertaken that journey before. Rather than walk past Gunter's and risk being accosted by the predatory females who loitered there, he kept to the other side of the square and was thus forced to pass by Diana's old doorstep. He noticed the mourning hatchment, commemorating her husband's passing, had finally been removed from above the front door.

So much has changed, and in such a short time! he thought. *She is now safely installed in the Duke of Redford's residence in Belgravia Square.*

Still, he kept on without hesitation, and gaining Piccadilly, turned toward the bookshop. Accustomed to looking neither left nor right in order to avoid awkward social interactions, Darcy failed to notice George Wickham standing near the corner of St James and Piccadilly.

George had been waiting for the past twenty minutes in what warmth the winter sun afforded, loitering not far from the entrance of White's, and hoping to find an acquaintance to sign him into that club or, more likely, Brook's or Boodle's down the street. His senses pricked up when he saw Darcy pass by, and he briefly considered tailing him to see what he could make of the opportunity. His interest lapsed when he saw Darcy pass into Hatchard's—no fun was to be had in a bookshop.

Five minutes later he revised his opinion entirely when a carriage with a ducal crest came up the street, and Her Grace The Duchess of Redford emerged and followed Darcy into Hatchard's.

Darcy was on the first floor, perusing the technical books, when he smelled a familiar scent of jasmine-based perfume. It reminded him so much of the perfume Diana wore, which had been personally concocted for her by Floris of Jermyn Street. He continued reading, convinced his earlier perambulations through Berkeley Square had evoked the memory, but when finally some dainty steps approached, there was no mistaking them. Darcy froze.

"Sir, would you mind passing the blue book on the shelf above you? I am afraid I cannot reach it."

As if in a dream, he looked up from the page he was reading and stared at her.

"On the second shelf from the top, slightly to your left," Diana prompted.

Silently he handed the book down.

She looked through the front matter while he continued to stare; but she kept her head down, and the only view he was afforded was of the fake fruit on her hat. Diana handed the book back. Facing towards him, a sliver of paper peeped from the covers.

"No, I do believe I have it wrong," she said. "It was the brown book beside it that I was looking at yesterday. Could I impose upon you to retrieve that one?"

Darcy carefully laid the blue book on the shelf beside him and retrieved the brown one.

Diana opened the front cover, and after briefly perusing it, looked up again and flashed him a sweet smile. He did not move a muscle.

"Thank you, so much," she said. "It is just as I hoped."

Turning, she retreated down the stairs.

Darcy stood there for a moment, sucking in his breath through his teeth. Then he turned slowly and viewed the blue book, as if he expected it to bite him. Picking it up, he opened it slightly and let the note slide inside, marking the page with his finger before looking around. With the exception of a couple at the far end of the floor, he was alone.

Opening the book properly, he retrieved the note, and unfolding it inside the book, read:

"I sincerely regret the mode of our parting and would like to remain friends. Meet me, when you can, at the usual time."

Dazed, feeling somehow he had encountered an apparition; Darcy stuffed the note into his waistcoat pocket. Replacing the blue book on its shelf, Darcy continued to peruse the books on steam engines, but could not concentrate. Through the fabric of his shirt, he fancied he could feel the slip of paper sitting there, making his skin itch. Losing all patience with his research, he gave up and, picking up the books he was trying to choose between, took all three to the counter.

41 Old friends

Wickham had run across Piccadilly, dodging traffic, and only slowed upon entering Hatchard's. Quickly scanning the ground floor, he ascertained Diana had gone higher. Proceeding smartly up the steps, he had to stop when she came into view, standing still at the top of the flight of stairs, her eyes fixed in front of her. Wickham pulled out his pocket-watch and retreated a couple of steps, pretending to consult it. After a moment, he risked a peek upwards under the brim of his hat and saw she had sat down at one of the desks available to patrons. She scribbled something before standing and proceeding along the first floor.

A couple overtook him on the stairs, and seeing his opportunity, he followed in their footsteps, but he could have cursed aloud when they stopped well short of his quarry to view books. Darcy and Diana were only ten feet away, but there was no way to get closer without risk of being seen. George watched them surreptitiously, using the couple as a screen, before pulling a book from a shelf to justify his continued presence there. When Darcy and Diana both looked up at the bookshelf, Wickham moved quickly into the chair that Diana had occupied. With his back to them, he strained to hear their conversation over that of the nearer couple. Diana seemed to be saying perfectly innocuous things to Darcy, while he wasn't saying anything at all.

Why am I not surprised? thought Wickham. *He is such a looby!*

He risked another peek and narrowly missed looking Diana directly in the eye as she turned to leave, holding a brown book. Fortunately she seemed to be preoccupied. *Oh, who am I kidding anyway? She probably doesn't even remember me.* Only gentlemen with large... *estates* got to tumble Lady Diana...

Wickham reminded himself that Darcy was the one he had to worry about. George didn't want to let him know he was under surveillance *just* yet.

When the couple conveniently drifted in front of him, he peeped round them in time to see Darcy pocketing a note. *Oh, ho! Fitzwilliam! The clandestine affair continues! Naughty boy! And you, a married man!*

The couple moved off, and deciding there was no advantage in continuing to spy on Darcy, Wickham followed them. He saw Diana's coach depart as he came down the stairs before spotting the brown book, discarded on the front counter. Picking it up, he flicked through it. It seemed to be a treatise on drainage ditches. *Good Lord! Trust Darcy to be reading something like this! What a bore he is!*

"Are you interested in that, sir? I was just about to re-shelve it."

Wickham looked up to see the proprietor hovering. "Ah, no," he replied. "I was looking for poetry."

"It generally doesn't come in the quarto format, sir. You'll find most of our holdings on the second floor."

"Thank you," said Wickham. "I've just come from there." And turning on his heel, George left.

Half an hour later Darcy descended with his tomes, which Mr Hatchard added to his account.

"I do hope the volume of fairy tales met with your requirements, Mr Darcy?"

Darcy blinked, having almost forgotten about the book that had passed through his hands so quickly—it seemed to have happened ages ago.

"Thank you, John. It was just what I required."

"And now steam engines," continued Mr Hatchard, as he swiftly wrapped the book in brown paper. "You certainly have diverse tastes."

"Back to business, John," replied Darcy. "I'm afraid I don't have much time for fairy tales."

Darcy walked home in turmoil. He went to his own townhouse first, to drop off the books, and found his hand shaking as he reached up to the knocker. He spent the afternoon engaged in his own business, unable to tackle anything mentally demanding for the earl. Towards the evening, he ventured across the square to his uncle's townhouse—to check on the state of things there before returning to his own establishment for dinner.

Richard did not arrive, and Darcy could only assume he'd been delayed at Rosings. Breaking the promise he had made to himself at Pemberley, Darcy drank rather a lot of brandy after dinner. *Elizabeth is not here*, he reasoned, *and thus I cannot do her any harm*. His potations did allow him to drop off to sleep relatively easily.

Morning, however, saw a return of his agitation. He managed some breakfast, convinced that Richard would show before lunch, and worked in a desultory fashion during the morning. But midday arrived, and still his cousin had not returned. Unable to contemplate anything for lunch, Darcy requested a tray in his study, and then only took tea.

Bereft of Richard's counsel, he tried to decide what he should do himself. Diana had finally offered him the interview he had deeply craved following their unexpected rupture, but given they were both now committed to other people, it seemed rather pointless, didn't it? Or was he being a social idiot once more? She had gently mocked him during their affair for his awkwardness with women. *'We are all the same species, you know!'* she had laughed.

It was true and he knew it. There had not been many women in his life, or at least, not ones he felt he could develop some understanding with, ones who could converse on interesting topics. That was why he had been attracted to Diana in the first place. She had said she wanted to be friends, hadn't she? Was it impossible for him to be friends with a woman? Reassuring himself, Darcy pulled out her note once more and stared at it. It was only then, when he noticed that she had written *'when you can'*, not *'if you can'* or *'if you will'*, that the first glimmer of anger emerged. He felt somewhat like a dog being called to heel.

Much pacing of his study ensued. If she *did* want to be his friend, it would be wrong to reject her—she could quite rightfully scorn him as a misogynist. If he did not want to be her friend now, then his relationship with her could not have been the pure love he had thought it to be, but merely... rutting.

He looked at the clock and saw that it wanted five minutes to three. *Goodness! How did that happen? My mind must have been spinning in circles!* Making his decision, Darcy strode into the foyer and was helped into his coat. After donning the proffered gloves and hat, he took his cane. Descending the front steps three at a time, he hailed the hackney standing in the square and, climbing into it before it came to a halt, issued the direction to Belgravia Square. Darcy could hear his heart pounding in his ears as they drove down Park Lane. He forced himself to take several deep breaths. Arriving at his destination, Darcy handed the jarvey a gold coin, asking him to stand until he got inside, and effected his entrance quite discreetly when Leith came immediately to the front door.

Sitting in the square, Wickham had almost abandoned his vigil. He knew that Darcy's assignations had been for Tuesdays at three, and when quarter past the hour rolled round, he had almost given up—*Darcy is so damned punctilious!* But then the hackney entered the square—the dolt from Derbyshire had showed after all.

Excellent! thought George, *Perhaps I will finally get something from this old game!* George's previous attempts to make good of Darcy's affair had come to nought. Darcy had refused to give him another penny after the £3000 lump sum in lieu of the living of Kympton, as if anyone could survive on that! The earl had told George he would be soundly beaten if he dared to show his face to him again, not that *he* was too much longer for this world, while Diana had merely laughed in his face. Maybe she wouldn't be so nonchalant now she was married to the duke—*he* wasn't witless like the marquis had been. But Wickham rather fancied he'd try Darcy again first—Mrs Darcy brought a new element to the scenario.

It was while he was contemplating this series of happy thoughts that a completely new game occurred to George. *Goddamn!* Why hadn't he thought of it before? Clearly, Darcy was tied by the heels in London until the earl shuffled off his mortal coil, and just as clearly he'd left his new wife at Pemberley, safe on his estate far away from the vices of the metropolis. *But was she safe from an old family friend? the son of a trusted retainer?*

Without waiting for Darcy to emerge, Wickham entered the same hackney Darcy had quit and was off to Hicks Hall, and the road north.

Diana's butler Leith had welcomed Darcy like an old friend and shown him directly into the saloon. The duke's house was magnificent, just as ostentatious as the earl's, but lacking any evidence of decay. Darcy seemed to recall coming there for a ball early in his career, perhaps for one of the duke's younger daughters? Still, candlelight never did justice to a place. Of course, he preferred the more comfortable and less ostentatious refinement imbued by his father on Pemberley and his own townhouse—it seemed somehow more English; but he could appreciate this more Continental grandeur.

Diana got up to welcome him when he entered, and her Papillion gave a sharp yap of recognition also.

"Darcy, how good it is to see you! I heard you got married!" she smiled.

Behind him, he heard Leith close the door.

"Indeed, I heard you also got married," he replied, with only the faintest trace of pique.

She laughed and held out her hand towards him.

Darcy took her ungloved fingers and bowed over Diana's hand, but did not kiss it before releasing her. Standing up, he noticed how low cut her gown was, barely covering the nipples; her modesty only preserved by the diaphanous chemisette she wore underneath. He remembered a similar outfit she had worn early in their acquaintance, which had resulted in their precipitate congress on her settee, leaving a stain. It all seemed so sordid now.

"You said you wished to talk," he said rather stiffly.

"I felt so bad afterwards, about the manner of our parting. You know it was for the best, but I saw you took it hard. I didn't mean to hurt you so."

"You seem terribly solicitous of my heart all of a sudden," replied Darcy.

She gave him a hurt, wan smile, before gesturing to the chessboard. "Come, would you like a game?"

He gave an odd gesture in reply—a simultaneous nod and shrug. They sat down in two opposing fauteuils. The Papillion jumped onto the settee and then a nearby table for a better view, its claws scraping the polish. Diana had sat in front of red and therefore moved her pawn first, while he opened the conversation.

"I didn't know you were interested in agricultural improvements," he remarked.

She laughed. "I went to view the latest volumes of poetry, but I didn't quite make it to the second floor, did I? I must admit I was hoping to run into you sometime. I thought you might have returned to town. How does the earl fare?"

"Not well. A recovery seems unlikely."

That topic closed, a silence briefly reigned.

"So..." continued Diana, "I hear you met your wife in Hertfordshire..."

"News travels fast."

"Miss Bingley was quite vocal in her disapprobation. I gather she did not attend the wedding?"

"By her own choice, so you shouldn't pay any attention to what she says. Her pronouncements are driven by pure spite."

"So it is not, as she says, merely a marriage of convenience?"

A silent rage ripped through Darcy, apparent only in the tightening of the muscles of his jaw. "Bingley would do well to discipline his sister."

"Come, Darcy. We are friends, are we not? We all have to make sacrifices in life. I know you are supremely conscious of your duty."

"My wife's name is Elizabeth. She is the daughter of a country squire. I met her while I was staying with Bingley at Netherfield."

"Respectable," offered Diana, "but not of the first circles."

"No, not of the first circles, but then neither am I," said Darcy defensively.

"You are too modest, my dear. While you lack a title, you may be seen everywhere, *when* you choose to be."

"She is intelligent," continued Darcy, "perhaps not as learned as yourself, but quick-witted and full of élan. I think that is what first caught my notice."

"Of course, and I understand *quite* pretty as well."

"Indeed," said Darcy, not catching the implied slight. "Although, I must admit I failed to truly appreciate her beauty until she gained a competent maid. It is long since I have thought her one of the most beautiful women of my acquaintance." He laid his hand on his bishop, trying to gather his thoughts before committing to a move.

"Really?" said Diana, and with a light stroke on his wrist, her hand rested on top of his. "And does she know how to please you?"

In his confusion, Darcy was only vaguely aware of the growl of the little dog beside him, before a voice rang out:

"Good afternoon, Mr Darcy. It is so good of you to amuse my wife with a game of chess."

Darcy stood rapidly, blushing like a boy who had been caught with his hand in the sweet jar as the Duke of Redford strode into the room through an internal door.

"Your Grace," he said, bowing.

"Has my wife not yet offered you tea?" said the duke, ringing a bell. "How remiss of her!"

"My dear," said Diana to her husband. "Did you forget something?"

"Indeed. I had not been at White's half an hour before I felt home and hearth calling!"

Leith opened the door from the vestibule and, for an instant, looked rather startled on perceiving the duke.

"Some tea, Leith," said the duchess.

"Perhaps I should be going," said Darcy, getting up.

"Not at all," said the duke. "It is long since we have spoken at White's, Darcy. As we are both recently married, I'm sure we have much in common."

So Darcy sat through one of the most uncomfortable afternoon teas of his life, politely answering the duke's questions about his marriage and the earl's illness, before begging off on the earl's sake and hurrying from the room. Retrieving his effects from Leith, Darcy almost ran down the steps and walked rapidly towards Hyde Park. When he encountered an empty hackney on reaching Park Lane, Darcy jumped aboard. Throwing himself back into the seat, he briefly closed his eyes, trying to blot out what had surely been the most embarrassing incident of his life. His hand reached reflexively into his pocket, and he withdrew a lacy handkerchief, fingering a small brown spot in its centre.

42 Regret

For the few minutes it took the hackney to arrive at his townhouse, the majority of Darcy's mind raged against himself for his stupidity, while a small part protested that he had needed to give her the benefit of the doubt.

Alighting in front of his house, Darcy proceeded to run up the steps but was halted by a hail from behind. He turned to see Richard striding across the square.

Darcy stopped and waited for his cousin to reach him. "Is there aught amiss?" he asked.

"Nothing that has not been skew-whiff for the past week or so," replied the colonel. "Where have you been?"

They had reached the front door that had already been opened by the attendant footman upon recognising their voices.

"I took your advice to get out," said Darcy evasively. "Did all go well at Rosings?"

"As well as might be expected," sighed the colonel. "Lady Catherine was at first horrible to her niece. That is why I stayed overnight, hoping to smooth things over."

"Why on earth would she do that?"

"*I don't knooow*," Richard drawled. "She may have been in a bad curl because the Bingleys went off. They apparently had some prior invitation to visit at one of the other great houses."

"So Bingley has decided not to court Cousin Anne."

"I'm not sure Bingley's made a decision in his life," scoffed the colonel. "I've no doubt 'twas his social-climbing sister who dragged him off, but apparently they promised to return in a month. Of course, that would not do for Aunt! Nothing can compare to Rosings!"

"So do you think Mary will cope?"

"Don't worry—Mrs Collins turned up and smoothed Aunt's ruffled feathers. Mary seemed to take it all in her stride and with the help of Mrs Collins, she was well on her way to charming Aunt when I left."

"And how fares Anne?"

"Better than I have ever seen her. I actually got a smile and a bit of conversation."

"So you think Dr Douglas's methods are working?"

"Yes. I wouldn't describe Anne as having roses in her cheeks, but she did not look like death warmed up like she usually does."

The cousins had by this time repaired to the study, where the colonel promptly poured them some brandy while Darcy stirred the fire before leaning against the mantle.

"I've done something stupid," said Darcy quietly.

"Well, that's quite an admission coming from you," said Richard, handing his cousin his glass. "Would you care to explain?"

"I went to see Diana."

"Lord! Whatever possessed you? Frankly, I wouldn't have thought it of you, Darcy."

"It's not what you think. I met her by chance, yesterday in Hatchard's. She said she wanted to talk..."

"About what?" huffed the colonel. "You had seven years of *conversation*!"

Darcy blushed. "She said she regretted the way we had parted; that she wanted to remain friends."

"Oh, you didn't fall for that one!"

"I'm afraid I did."

"What happened?"

"Nothing. The duke walked in."

"My God! What were you doing?"

"Playing chess."

Richard snorted brandy through his nose and burst into laughter. "How risqué!"

"Shut up! It's not funny!"

"Sorry, what happened? Did he cut up at you?"

"He asked me to tea."

Unable to suppress another smirk, Richard covered his mouth with his hand, but his eyes began to water with the effort of keeping a straight face and the after-effects of the brandy.

"I've never been so embarrassed in my whole life!" winced Darcy.

"Blushed, did you?"

"From top to toe."

"Well, you've never been very good at disguise. But if you were only playing chess, what was the problem?

"I shudder to think what would have happened if he hadn't walked in at that moment."

"Trying it on, was she?"

"I should have realised when Leith closed the door..."

In the ensuing silence, only the crackling of the fire could be heard.

"Perhaps this is a good thing," said Richard finally.

"I'm not sure what good can be found in it!" spat Darcy.

"What would you have done if the duke hadn't walked in?" asked Richard.

"We should have had an argument! Our first, ever! I am married! *She* is married!"

"But she was married before..." said the colonel gently.

"It was different!" protested Darcy. "Her husband was incapable..." And then, more lamely, "We fell in love."

"Maybe *you* thought it was different," offered Richard. "You did offer her marriage after all..."

"What are you saying?"

"Darcy, I think you and she had very different perspectives on your affair."

"How so?"

"I didn't want to say anything before—you were upset when it ended; but now you've had a glimpse of Diana's true character..."

Darcy stared at his cousin.

Richard returned his cousin's look earnestly, before continuing quietly: "I know she had a brief affair with Robert..."

"When was this?" asked Darcy, horrified.

"About a year after you started. You were at Pemberley. Robert hit her when he was drunk, and Leith threw him out on his ear."

"Why have you never told me this?" whispered Darcy.

"Darcy, I tried to several times, but you wouldn't hear a bad word about her."

Darcy stared into the fire, shaking his head. "What a fool I have been!"

"We are all fools in love," said Richard, gripping his shoulder.

They sat in silence for a while before Richard re-introduced the subject of his trip to Rosings. After half an hour's inconsequential conversation, he made to get up.

"Darcy, I've promised to have dinner with the Gardiners tonight. I can beg off if you like..."

"No, don't do that."

"Are you sure you're all right?"

"Yes, just disillusioned. I'll walk over to check on your father after dinner."

"Thanks, old man. I'll be back here for breakfast, but send a note if there's an emergency and I'll come straight away."

Darcy took a tray for dinner once more in his study. He ate, but the food tasted like ashes in his mouth. Sitting in front of the fire afterwards, Darcy realised that Diana must have also been seeing the duke prior to their wedding. Of course, some part of him had acknowledged the likelihood of it before, but he had refused to accept it, imagining instead the duke's offer coming out of the blue.

Withdrawing Diana's note from his waistcoat, Darcy threw it in the fire. Watching it curl and burn, he felt a part of himself had drifted away with the smoke; but upon the heels of this thought came another memory. A cold feeling crept over him as Darcy realised that in his haste to return to London following the earl's turn, he had left Diana's letters unburnt in his school desk.

At Pemberley, Elizabeth tried to keep herself busy. She finished transcribing Lady Anne's logbook, even creditably copying her drawings, though Lizzy was no artist. Writing a cover note, she sealed the transcript inside and sent the letter off to Greenwich. She continued to compose acrostics for his sister in the afternoon as Georgie played the piano.

Elizabeth had discovered that underneath her unsophisticated veneer, her sister had an intelligent mind, having studied with a governess until quite recently. Mrs Annesley had replaced that lady when she had gone to keep house for her widowed brother—Fitzwilliam and Richard having decided that a lady who could prepare Georgie for her come-out would be more appropriate than another governess. Elizabeth could not entirely agree. It seemed to her that Georgie needed something more than her music to occupy her mind. Lizzy resolved to teach her chess.

Despite her attempts to keep busy during her time alone, in the observatory and when out walking, Elizabeth's mind constantly mulled over her husband's love letters, like picking at a scab. She knew it had been a mistake to read even that single letter sent to Fitzwilliam by his lover. It was true that curiosity killed the cat.

Two days after the discovery of the letters, Elizabeth woke feeling ill. She almost skipped breakfast, but when Georgie knocked on her door to say good morning, Lizzy accompanied her sister downstairs and felt slightly better after eating.

The next few days saw no improvement, and when her usual breakfast of ham and eggs was placed before her one morning, she was overcome with such a strong wave of nausea that she had to leave the room. Returning after composing herself, she surprised Mrs Reynolds by requesting porridge.

When Elizabeth felt no better after a week, the penny finally dropped. Jenny had attributed her sickness to a lurgy; she—to heart sickness; and finally, when she had thrown up into her chamber pot one morning, the obvious—she had not had a period since she had come to Derbyshire.

Elizabeth could not believe her stupidity. She had been so distracted by her changed circumstances that she had completely failed to notice when her period had not eventuated on schedule a week before Christmas. When she had thought of it briefly after Fitzwilliam departed, she had consoled herself with the belief that the upheaval in her life had likely caused a slight irregularity. It seemed unlikely she would be pregnant after such a short interval.

After consultation with Jenny and Mrs Reynolds, there seemed little doubt—her breasts felt full and sore, another symptom she had vaguely ascribed to her unspecified illness. The truth was Elizabeth had no lurgy or heart sickness—she had been infected by Fitzwilliam Darcy.

On the very day when Elizabeth came to this conclusion, she received a letter from the source of her troubles. Her husband wrote that the earl seemed to be improving, and the doctor held out hope that he might make a recovery, although he warned that the earl would likely be an invalid for what remained of his life. Darcy apologized for his continued absence, but the earl had begged him to set his affairs in order, lest he not recover. Finally he hoped Jane's news would bring her joy, although what he could be referring to Elizabeth could not know. *Perhaps Mr Bingley had returned to Netherfield?* If so, she felt rather sorry for the colonel, not having had time to put in a good word for him.

Still upset by the discovery of her husband's letters, Elizabeth had no wish for his company. Indeed, she felt her composure was not sufficient to face Darcy now—she might not be able to guard her temper. Her pregnancy gave her the perfect excuse. She wrote to him telling him to be easy, that she believed he had done his duty and that she was with child. Stretching the truth slightly, she told him she felt well, and encouraged him to assist his uncle in any way he felt possible.

A letter arrived by return post only four days later in which Darcy expressed his joy and solicitude. Elizabeth's heart gave a strange gurgle as she read his words, but Lizzy reminded herself not to take his words at face value. Her husband urged her to summon the family doctor. This, Elizabeth was not inclined to do at such an early stage, but she was thwarted by Mrs Reynolds—Darcy had also written instructions to his housekeeper, and she would not be swayed from following the master's instructions.

The doctor confirmed their diagnosis. Elizabeth was enceinte.

43 Something wicked

When the colonel arrived for dinner in Gracechurch Street, he found his wife quite distracted.

"Oh! I cannot believe I was so stupid!" cried Jane.

"Whatever is the matter? asked her husband.

"The letter I wrote after our marriage—I'm fairly sure I directed it to Lizzy at "Wyvern Hall" via Lambton!"

"Have I addled your brain?" Richard asked, sneaking a kiss before the Gardiner children could run into the room. "Do not worry. I'm sure the servants will redirect it. *Provided* you wrote 'Elizabeth Darcy' and not 'Elizabeth Bennet'."

"Thankfully, I was not *that* stupid," replied Jane. "I sent another letter off this afternoon summarising the contents of the first should it not arrive; although I certainly hope it does, because it contained all my heartfelt sentiments on our marriage, which I could not hope to reproduce."

"Oh?" said Richard, pulling a mock mournful face and venturing another kiss. "Has marital felicity paled already?"

"You know it has not," said Jane, pushing him playfully away to a respectable distance on hearing her uncle's footsteps in the hall.

"Why, Colonel!" said Mr Gardiner, appearing a moment later. "You *were* able to join us! I gather your mission in Kent went well?"

"As well as could be expected," replied Richard.

"Well, she's a brave lass! Though I remember being sent off to boarding school at much the same age! Still, it is different for a girl to be separated from her family! You would not have liked that, would you, Jane?"

"Uncle, you know that Lizzy and I lived with Lady Yardley for several years when we were much younger!"

"Well, so you did!" laughed her uncle. "In retrospect, it explains rather a lot!"

Retrieving his effects and making all speed to the Saracen's Head Inn, Wickham was lucky enough to secure a place on the mail coach to Manchester, which departed at five in the evening—one of the booked passengers had failed to show and an outside seat was available. George had hoped, of course, to secure a more comfortable inside seat for the journey. Fortunately, he was able to purchase a large frieze coat from a passing ruffian, and a scarf from an old woman with the proceeds of a ring he'd prigged from a recent conquest.

Despite these purchases, he was unable to feel the tip of his nose by the time he finally transferred inside the coach when they stopped briefly at Market Harborough at five in the morning. It was seven in the evening before he descended the coach in Buxton and sought accommodation at the post inn.

Ridding himself of the dirty frieze coat and scarf the next morning, George quite startled the proprietor when he descended for breakfast in all his elegance. True, his nose had still been a trifle red, but a little macquillage had done the trick.

After donning his greatcoat, he hired a whisky to drive to Lambton and thence Pemberley. The eight-year old son of the proprietor of the livery stables accompanied him to bring the equipage back afterwards. Sitting on the backboard, the boy did double duty, holding Wickham's large carpetbag.

George reached Pemberley before noon, and luck favoured him again when he arrived at the front door just as Georgiana Darcy was returning from her morning ride. He saw she had grown very tall but was too mannish in her features to be called pretty, even with her black hair curled into ringlets. The horse she was riding looked like it had cost a pretty penny.

"George!" she said, flying to him and throwing her arms around his neck as she greeted him like a brother. "It is so long since I have seen you!"

As George disentangled himself from Georgie's embrace, he looked up to see Mrs Reynolds viewing him askance.

"Why, Reynolds!" he said, flashing her a winning smile. "It is good to see your familiar face again! My work and studies have kept me away far too long!"

Mrs Reynolds wished it had been longer, but she vouchsafed a "good morning, sir." She was thinking of the problems she'd had with the maids ever since young Wickham had returned from his first term of Eton at the age of fourteen. She had never been able to prove it—the girls would not talk—but the coincidence of his visits and their pregnancies was too great. Nor had the housekeeper been able to broach her suspicions with old Mr Darcy—his fondness for the boy was too blind. Nonetheless, the old master had always provided for the girls unquestioningly by finding husbands for them among his tenant farmers. Soon after Fitzwilliam stepped into his father's shoes, George had gone off to study law and the problem had solved itself... until now.

When Georgie promptly invited George to tea, he silently congratulated himself on getting his foot in the door. Nonchalantly handing his bag to a lackey, he sent the hired whiskey off.

Georgie insisted on having the tea in her sitting room, which Mrs Reynolds could not approve of, and they repaired there to find Mrs Annesley tidying Georgie's sheet music.

George made inconsequential conversation with both ladies until Georgie handed him his tea.

"Is Fitzwilliam out on the estate, Georgie, or burning wax in his study?" George enquired politely.

"Oh no! He is in London, George. Uncle Geoffrey is terribly ill, and brother has gone off to handle his affairs!"

"How terrible!" George exclaimed. "Is it *very* serious?"

"Oh, yes! Richard went dashing off to London almost straight away. Brother left soon after, to escort Aunt!"

"What a shame that I missed him!" bemoaned George. "I had hoped to be here for Christmas, but there was far too much work; and I could not abandon the partners now they are coming to rely on me!"

"Oh! Is your career going well?" asked Georgie excitedly.

George handed over his card with flourish. "I have every hope of being made a junior partner before Easter, Georgie—the first step on the ladder!"

"Oh, how exciting!" said Georgie, viewing the card.

It merely said *'Mr George Wickham, Esquire'*, but for all Georgie's admiration, it might have been gold-plated.

"Is the work very demanding?" she asked.

"Oh, very! It is not for the faint-hearted! Mountains of paper to be read and so many letters to write!"

The sound of a light carriage was heard in the drive.

"Oh! That will be Lizzy back from the tenants!" said Georgie, getting up and running to the hall window.

When George followed Georgiana to the window, he saw a lady wearing a hooded cloak descend from a curricle driven by a groom. A footman had gone out to retrieve a large wooden box from under the seat.

"Come!" said Georgie, grabbing his wrist, "you must meet her!" And laughing, she pulled George down the spiral stairs of the foyer to meet Elizabeth in the vestibule.

Frowning at her charge's forward behaviour, Mrs Annesley struggled to keep up.

Lizzy had paused in the vestibule to pick up three letters from the salver that rested there.

"Elizabeth! Here is George, come to visit us!"

Elizabeth turned to behold the handsomest man she had ever laid eyes on. His wavy blond hair was fashioned into the 'Windswept' style. His sideburns were short and, very unusually, he sported a well-trimmed moustache which emphasised his delicate pink lips. She could not help making the inevitable comparison to her husband, and she had to admit this man was even more handsome than her spouse—so handsome, she thought, that he could even be called beautiful. He was Apollo, and Darcy was Mars.

George flashed her a brilliant smile, which was almost heartfelt. Mrs Darcy had a pretty heart-shaped face, beautiful chestnut hair, and now she was divested of the cloak, he could see that her figure was light and pleasing. He believed he was going to quite *enjoy* seducing her.

"Do the introductions properly please, Georgie," whispered Mrs Annesley.

"I beg your pardon! *Dear* sister," said Georgie archly, "this is Mr George Wickham, Esquire."

George made a very courtly bow.

Elizabeth immediately realised she had been introduced to the young man whose miniature she had seen in the portrait gallery. So Georgie's 'George' was Mr Wickham; and old Mr Darcy's godson was his former steward's son. What had Mrs Reynolds implied? That his heart was not in the right place? What could she mean by that?

"George, this is my new sister, Mrs Elizabeth Darcy, née Bennet, of Longbourn!"

George made an exaggerated start. "But what is this? Fitzwilliam has married! I had no idea!"

"We were married very recently, sir," said Lizzy, "in Hertfordshire."

"Well!" said George, "This *is* a surprise! I had thought… But please accept my sincere congratulations! You have made quite the catch, Mrs Darcy!"

Georgie beamed at this compliment to her brother. Despite her pique with being left alone in Derbyshire, she truly loved and admired Fitzwilliam and merely wished to be with him more often.

"Come upstairs, Lizzy!" begged Georgie. "We were just having tea!"

Lizzy dutifully pocketed her letters, though she was burning to read them—two were from her sister Jane, while the third was from the Astronomer Royal!

Upstairs, Mrs Annesley poured a cup of tea for Lizzy, topping up the strong brew with hot water from a kettle on the hearth.

"George wanted to visit us for Christmas, but was delayed!" said Georgie.

"Do you often visit, Mr Wickham?" enquired Elizabeth.

"Not for several years, I'm afraid, Mrs Darcy. My studies and work have kept me very busy." And then, turning to Georgie, he teased, "You have probably tossed me out of my room like an old rag!"

"Indeed, we have not! All your things are just where you left them! So you may be easy!"

"Do you intend to stay long, Mr Wickham?" asked Elizabeth.

"Please call me, George! I had hoped to stay for up to a month. It is my first break since starting with the firm, but I have been warned that they may not be able to spare me for so long! However! I'm determined to be philosophical about it—to go back stoutly if I'm needed, but enjoy myself here while I may!"

George proceeded to charm all the ladies throughout dinner—quoting poetry and bestowing pretty compliments. His amiability, thought Elizabeth, put Mr Bingley's quite in the shade. Afterwards they listened to Georgie's music, which Mr Wickham praised with enthusiasm, also lauding the wonderful instrument and the delightful sitting room bestowed by her thoughtful brother!

For Lizzy, the evening seemed to last for ever. She wanted nothing more than to read the letters in her pocket and found her eyes occasionally glazing over at Mr Wickham's polite nothings. When Mrs Annesley insisted on Georgie's bedtime, Lizzy breathed a sigh of relief. George bowed politely and took himself off down the hall. His bedchamber apparently was in the far end of the guest wing, a place Lizzy had never ventured.

Retreating to her bedchamber, Elizabeth pulled the letters from her pocket to read them in front of the hearth. She first opened the missives from Jane, and perceiving the one directed to Wyvern Hall to be the older, finally understood the reason for her sister's lack of communication.

"No wonder!" she exclaimed to Jenny as her maid brushed out her hair. "She addressed the first letter very ill!"

"Is it the first letter she has sent to you by post?" enquired her maid.

"No, I believe there was one other, but all the others were carried by Colonel Fitzwilliam, so I suppose she forgot the direction."

Elizabeth then began to read. "Why, Jenny!" she cried. "My sister has married Colonel Fitzwilliam! And they will be coming to live here at Pemberley!"

"Oh, Mrs Darcy! How wonderful! How sly the colonel was! Telling you he merely wished to court her!"

"It is all on account of the earl! He wanted Richard settled! Oh, I am *so* glad! Richard is far more reliable than Mr Bingley was! And now we will all be together!"

In all her excitement, Lizzy completely forgot about the third letter, and while Jenny undressed her, they chattered merrily about cleaning up the Dower House, removing the holland covers from the furniture, and unrolling the rugs. Such fun they would have!

As Lizzy lay down to sleep, her thoughts returned to their unexpected guest. She had to admit that Mr Wickham was everything a lady could want in a gentleman. He was as charming as the colonel and even more handsome than her husband; but Mrs Reynolds' comment nagged at her, and she resolved to seek out the housekeeper on the morrow for further information.

George had hoped for his first chance to get Mrs Darcy alone when Georgie went off on her morning ride. Georgie had entreated him to come along, but he begged off, claiming to have recently hurt his hip. But Mrs Darcy didn't appear at breakfast, and George had almost thought himself thwarted when he spied her out in the formal garden.

On Mrs Reynolds' advice, Lizzy had taken to having breakfast alone in her bedchamber, within easy distance of her chamber pot. She nibbled dry biscuits with a little tea, and this seemed to do the trick of settling her stomach, such that she had even managed to go out in the curricle with

Healy to visit tenants the day before.

She finally remembered her third letter as she nibbled her breakfast and opened it.

Dear Mrs Darcy,

Thank you for sending on my sister's final notes. They are indeed of use to me, although I never had the temerity to ask for them. I believe George Darcy blamed me somewhat for Anne's death, as her pneumonia was likely caught or exacerbated by her late night observations. I know Anne was very loath to light a fire in the observatory because it tarnished the mirrors.

I would indeed find it useful if you could continue Anne's observations. I am unfortunately unable to leave Greenwich myself, but if you are willing, I can send my assistant to show you how to work the telescope, which is of my own design; and how to take the observations. The mirrors will be sadly tarnished and may need to be replaced. Anne used them in rotation, sending them off alternately to Sheffield to be re-polished. My assistant can help with setting this up.

If you wish to proceed, let me know by return mail, and I will send him to you directly,

Yours faithfully,
Sir Thomas Fitzwilliam,
Astronomer Royal.

Imagine her gratification upon reading such a letter from the Astronomer Royal! *Would not her father be chuffed!*

Finishing her breakfast, Lizzy donned her cloak, deciding to take her morning constitutional in the formal garden before re-inspecting the Dower House.

When she reached the mosaic at the centre of the garden, she thought of the kiss she had shared there with Fitzwilliam, unconsciously laying her hand across her belly as she did so.

"Mrs Darcy! What a beautiful day it is!" said George as he came striding towards her.

Elizabeth turned to perceive Mr Wickham. "Indeed, that is why I chose to walk in the garden!" she replied. "The air is frigid, but the sun shines beautifully!"

"You must tell me more about yourself! I am agog to know how you captured the fastidious Fitzwilliam!" George laughed. "We played together as boys, you know, had the same tutor, were brought up as brothers! I know he is not easily pleased!" He gestured to indicate she should continue on her way.

"There is not much to tell!" Elizabeth said, as they began to walk towards the folly. "We met at a ball in Hertfordshire. I got to know him a little better when I stayed at Netherfield for the best part of a week—my sister fell ill while visiting his friend's sisters—and things proceeded from there!"

"It seems impertinent to ask, but how long had you known him when you married?"

Lizzy noticed Mr Wickham had asked anyway, but replied equably, "Well, Mr Bingley took the lease from Michaelmas, so it was about three months."

"Three months!" he laughed. "It seems hardly time to call the banns!"

"We were married by Special Licence."

"Indeed? And did you marry outside your parish?" he enquired.

"No, in the village church at the usual time."

"But, of course!" laughed Mr Wickham. "Special Licences are the fashion in the Ton and nothing less would do for dear Darcy's consequence. But I must congratulate you on your catch! There will be several females gnashing their teeth at you. I may have to gallant you to balls in London to ensure your safety."

"I doubt there will be any need for that Mr Wickham!" Elizabeth laughed in reply.

"Are you fixed in Derbyshire then?"

"For the moment, yes—I do so like the country."

"Well, that is fortunate, indeed!" he smiled. "Since *here* you are!"

They walked on for a few steps before he ventured, "And what does Fitzwilliam consider the chief of your merits?"

Lizzy blushed at this bold question before answering honestly, "I believe that my nursing skills and solicitude for my sister impressed him."

"Ah!" nodded Mr Wickham, knowingly.

They had by now reached the folly and, walking through it, arrived on the other side. The air was cooler there, and Lizzy shivered, suddenly aware of the closeness of the trees, and the fact they were screened from the house.

She turned back, but before she could take a step, Mr Wickham had whipped off his greatcoat and surrounded her with it, imprisoning her as he held it by the lapels.

"And are you not rather lonely, here on your own?" he breathed.

"Thank you, Mr Wickham," said Lizzy shortly, "but I am not cold!"

"But I am sure I saw you shiver!"

"Please put on your coat. It was merely a reaction to this damp place. My cloak is lined with fur, and I would hate for a guest to catch cold," she said meaningfully.

Wickham released her with a bow. He donned his greatcoat and instead offered his arm. This she took in the way of a peace offering, and they wandered back towards the house. As they passed through the centre of the garden, Elizabeth could not resist looking at the statue of Autumn, to assess the resemblance to Mr Wickham. She had to admit that Georgie's imagination had not been overactive in drawing the comparison—the living image was the superior, not only because it was rendered in flesh.

44 Schemes

In the days following his visit to Diana, Darcy went through a torrent of emotions. The discovery that Diana's interest in him might be more physical and less pure than he had believed was a painful one. However, having already grieved for his lost love, he only spent a day or two wallowing in self-pity before progressing rapidly to anger.

How dare she approach him now as if he were some rake! Why, it was monstrous! She had pledged herself to another, and so had he! They had both made their decisions and must move on. As to the extra information that his cousin had imparted—that he was one of many lovers, it was too awful to contemplate. To think he had given his heart to such a woman, while to her he had been only a diversion! He felt foolish, hurt, and betrayed.

Mindful of his duty, Darcy tried to concentrate on his uncle's business, but thoughts of his seven-year affair with Diana obtruded—things they had said and done together, each moment now examined in a new light. He tried to find something, anything, in what she had said that spoke of true affection; but the memories were all clouded with his own perceptions, and he could not obtain a view outside the prism of his own hopeless love.

As he systematically cleared his uncle's desk in consultation with Havershott, it occurred to him that his thoughts of Diana bore a resemblance to this process—it was as if he was tidying his love for Diana away. Each reminiscence was examined, found wanting, and filed for eternity. Each day he walked back to his townhouse stroking the handkerchief in his pocket. Each night he curled up with the nightgown that smelt of Lizzy. It was almost a week before he came to the realisation that he had a wife having his child in Derbyshire, and that he loved her; had loved her for a very long time, but had been too stubborn or inertial to admit it.

Why had he carried the handkerchief around and refused to give it back? Some part of his mind had admitted the attraction, but his more reasonable self refused to participate, conscious that to do so would be a betrayal of his former love—a false love now laid bare by his humiliation at the duke's townhouse. He had been too proud to admit he had made a mistake until Diana had made it clear their attraction was purely physical, not founded on the higher principles he had imagined it.

When had he first felt attracted to Elizabeth? When he saw her climb the ha-ha? When he heard her spirited rendition of *The Taming of the Shrew* at Netherfield? Or had it been when he first encountered her at the Meryton Assembly and steadfastly denied her worthiness to dance with him? Had those sparkling eyes and spirited smile entranced him even then?

As these realisations dawned on him, he wanted nothing more than to fly back to Pemberley to be with his wife, to throw himself at her feet and make up for what he was sure must be his perceived indifference; for now he recognised his restraint for what it was—the determined bridling of his passion for her. He wanted to have her in his bed, hold her in his arms, never let her go—but he could not. He had to stay put to finalise his uncle's affairs.

Surely there could not be more than another week of it? If his uncle lingered after his business was finalised, Darcy determined to excuse himself. Once Havershott was satisfied, he would return to Pemberley—he owed it to his wife and unborn child. Richard could continue the vigil for his father; he must return to his own affairs.

Richard and Jane had returned to Darcy House, so that Richard could be near both Jane and his father. Watching the happy couple bill and coo at each other over meals was almost more than Darcy could bear. That Richard was deeply in love Darcy had no doubt, although the depth of his cousin's emotion surprised him—Darcy had never seen Richard so smitten. What astounded him was Miss Bennet, no, *Mrs Fitzwilliam*. What Darcy had judged to be insipidity in Jane was now revealed to have been restraint—something he could only admire. She seemed rapidly to have developed a very deep and passionate affection for his cousin. This was held in check when Darcy was present, but he'd disturbed them a couple of times and had taken to coughing loudly before entering a room. It occurred to him that if he had courted Elizabeth properly, he might also be the recipient of such attention. He could only watch the progress of their honeymoon with envy.

Darcy's thoughts then began to dwell on his intimate time with Elizabeth, and more painful truths emerged. He had attributed his short fuse during lovemaking to everything but the obvious—the lack of a sheath, her virginity; when the truth was that he was so overpoweringly attracted to his wife that he could barely restrain himself. He could smell her own delightful perfume as he sat there trying to concentrate on writing—the sweet, honey-like smell combined with musk, so much more powerful than Diana's expensive jasmine concoction. Being alone, these thoughts were of course excruciating in their physical effects, but during the day he bore them as well as he could. At night, he gave himself over to his phantom Lizzy and hoped that Finn did not mind too much changing the sheets.

Wickham was not discouraged that his direct approach to seducing Elizabeth Darcy had not worked. It was always worth a try and saved time when it succeeded; but some ladies were demure and required more subtle wooing. George began forwarding his more devious plans for Mrs Darcy's entrapment after lunch.

When the ladies repaired to Georgie's sitting room, he excused himself briefly and slipped into the library. During his enforced time on and in the mail coach, George had been thinking furiously of subtle ways of enlightening Mrs Darcy on the subject of her husband's infidelity. Again, luck had favoured him in Buxton. While his horse was being harnessed at the livery stables, an old biddy had approached him—a street vendor hawking posies and dried flowers. His first impulse to send her off ungraciously was stifled on his lips when she produced a card with a pressed flower stuck to it. Inspiration struck, and he handed over a penny for her wares.

The card, which bore a pressed red rose, he had carefully inscribed on the back with *"Dear Fitz, I burn for you, Diana"*. The copperplate writing, complete with large feminine loops, was so superb he had chuckled with self-satisfaction on completing it. Perusing the newer volumes of poetry in the library, George found a volume of Wordsworth inscribed with *dear* Fitzwilliam's moniker, and carefully slipped the card inside before joining the ladies upstairs.

Upon conclusion of Georgie's after-lunch piano recital, Wickham suggested reading some poetry during their afternoon tea; and the idea finding favour with both Georgie and Mrs Annesley, they all repaired to the library.

George announced himself ready to declaim for their entertainment, but encouraged Mrs Darcy to select a volume for him. Although Elizabeth was willing to help, she declared herself quite unable to make an informed selection—she preferred reading witty plays.

"I must confess that I am rather partial to Wordsworth, Mrs Darcy," declared Wickham, "just like your dear husband. Although, we differ on many points, I find we are quite in agreement on poetry."

Georgie simpered at this worthy sentiment.

Elizabeth selected the single volume of Wordsworth on the shelf, and would have relinquished it immediately to Mr Wickham, had he not insisted that she select a poem for him. Acquiescing with good grace, she opened the book at random, and the card fluttered to the ground on cue. George bent quickly to retrieve it, hoping to hand it directly to her with the flower face-up; but Mrs Darcy was quicker, and standing up, she replaced the card between the books on the shelf so rapidly that George thought she had failed to appreciate its nature. Nonetheless, he knew he would have another opportunity to reintroduce the card.

George's recitation of the verse was superlative. Indeed, he had made a study of many actors on the London stage and might easily have made his living among them had it not been beneath him as a gentleman to do so. Georgie and Mrs Annesley praised him to the skies, although he would have preferred the accolades of Mrs Darcy, who merely smiled politely.

When they parted to rest before dinner, George once more repaired to the library to re-plant his card, but after fruitlessly searching for it on the shelf, he concluded that Mrs Darcy must have taken his bait after all.

At dinner he watched Elizabeth very carefully. Although she was hardly cast down, he fancied she *was* a trifle subdued. Smiling to himself, he prepared for the next phase of his plan.

Elizabeth had returned to the library before dinner to retrieve the card, using the internal stairs that descended from the master sitting room. Its inscription, of course, had not been a pleasant discovery for Elizabeth, but in the light of her earlier knowledge it was not a surprise. Now the phantom had a name—Diana; and a definite sex.

Was she jealous? *Yes*. Elizabeth's first impulse was to tear the card into tiny pieces and stomp on it. This, she observed wryly, was perfectly ridiculous, but might have some cathartic value.

Obviously, Lizzy could not leave the card lying around where the servants or Georgie might find it. Unable to think of anything better to do with it, she let herself into Darcy's childhood room and deposited it under the package of Diana's letters, locking the door again on her retreat. In her haste to be away from the source of her embarrassment, it did not occur to Elizabeth to compare the writing on the card with that of the letters.

George's next opportunity for marital mischief occurred after breakfast the next morning. Georgie had gone off on her morning ride when he observed Mrs Darcy slip into the gallery during his morning perambulations. It was if he had been granted a wish. He walked casually in behind Elizabeth some few minutes later and gave an exaggerated start upon encountering her.

"Why, bless me, Mrs Darcy! You gave me a fright! I thought I was quite alone and was about to begin quoting poetry!"

"Do you often quote poetry, Mr Wickham?"

"Yes, to keep my mind sharp, but I must admit myself momentarily at a loss…"

Looking around at the portraits, he made a grand gesture and ventured: "It is indeed a desirable thing to be descended, but the glory belongs to our ancestors."

Elizabeth frowned. "Plutarch?"

Wickham's eyes widened momentarily. He had hoped to impress Mrs Darcy with his erudition, although he would have incorrectly ascribed the quote to Plato—*one of those Greeks*; but he made a quick recover: "Mrs Darcy!" he smiled; "You are a bluestocking!"

Elizabeth blushed and cast her eyes down. "My father was a fellow at Oxford. I'm afraid some of it rubbed off."

Wickham saw that he had managed to flatter her and was sanguine. He carefully noted this weakness—pride in her own intellectual powers, and determined to capitalise on it. "Can I hope to enlighten you on the identity of any of these august persons? Or are you already acquainted?"

"Mrs Reynolds showed me some portraits of the immediate family, and a miniature of yourself, I might add; but as to the rest, I am quite at sea."

"Well, goodness me, we cannot have that! Am I to assume that you are not yet acquainted with old Mr Darcy, your good husband's father?"

"I'm afraid not, although I assume from the fashions that he is this large portrait next to his son."

"Indeed, so. Done by Sir Joshua Reynolds—no relation to our own dear Reynolds. A remarkable likeness of a venerable man; one of the best men that ever breathed, Mrs Darcy; and the truest friend I ever had. He was my godfather and excessively attached to me. I cannot do justice to his kindness. He was like a father to me after my own father, who was originally in law, died suddenly. As you know, I have chosen to follow in my father's footsteps. He gave up everything to be of use to the late Mr Darcy and devoted all his time to the care of the Pemberley property. He was most highly esteemed by Mr Darcy, a most intimate, confidential friend. Mr Darcy often acknowledged himself to be under the greatest obligations to my father's active superintendence; and when, immediately before my father's death, Mr Darcy gave him a voluntary promise of providing for me, I am convinced that he felt it to be as much a debt of gratitude to my father as an expression of his affection for myself."

"Were you very young when your father passed away?" asked Elizabeth solicitously.

"I was eight, Mrs Darcy. Too young to have lost both my parents, but Mr Darcy did everything in his power to soften the blow, and I believe I was a great comfort to him too, after his own wife died."

"Of course," agreed Elizabeth, "but he would have had the solace of his own children as well."

"As to that I cannot say. Miss Georgie was too young, more of a burden than anything for a widower, poor babe; and as to Fitzwilliam, well... he has always had the dispassionate disposition of his mother, Lady Anne. The Fitzwilliams are a noble line who have ever been celebrated for their coolness. It has stood them in good stead throughout history, particularly in times of war, making them favourites of several kings and elevating them to the earldom."

Wickham could see Elizabeth was considering this statement. He let her stew for a moment before walking a little further along and gesturing at the next portrait. "Here next to Mr Darcy, is Lady Anne's portrait by Gainsborough. You see she has the Fitzwilliam nose, which both her son and daughter have inherited; but they have Mr Darcy's black curly hair. As you can see, Lady Anne had the most beautiful auburn hair. It was very striking. I know only one other lady with hair like it—Lady Diana, the Duchess of Redford, or I should say, Her Grace."

"Lady Diana?" repeated Elizabeth, while reminding herself that Diana was a common name.

"Yes, do you know her?" asked George coolly. "She is a celebrated beauty and a great friend of your husband's."

"No," replied Elizabeth, feeling a coldness steal over her as the words *'celebrated beauty'* echoed in her head. She forced herself to speak, but her voice sounded distant, as if produced by another person. "I am not familiar with many members of the Ton. My father disdains London society and I have never attended any balls there."

"You are not missing much. They are a very snooty lot," declared George.

"So is Lady Diana related to the Fitzwilliams?" asked Elizabeth, hoping against hope that the connection was a family one.

"Well, not closely," replied George, "though the Ton are all somehow related to each other. They are a very inbred lot!" he joked. "No, Lady Diana was a Dawlish. She married a widowed marquis ten years her senior on her come-out, although he met with an accident, poor chap."

"So she was a widow herself before marrying the duke?" asked Elizabeth.

"Yes, for a short time; but her history is an unusual one. Her husband's accident did not kill him, but left him barely alive. He never re-entered society afterwards. I believe both his mind and body were greatly affected to the extent that he was little better than a child. They kept him locked up at his estate, Stanyon, in Somerset. Apparently the marchioness couldn't bear to look at him afterwards. When they married, he was a very handsome man and a non-pareil, rarely beaten at sport or play, quite the catch, you understand."

"How sad," said Elizabeth.

"Quite!" dissimulated George, who actually took pleasure in the misfortunes of the Ton, a set he dearly wished to enter. "He lingered on for years. They must have been very lonely ones for the marchioness, and it is fortunate that she had a friend like your husband to keep her company. They used to meet once a week to play chess."

"Chess?"

"Yes, on Tuesdays, I believe."

Elizabeth had given a slight start at this sally, which Wickham was pleased to observe, although at first he was at a loss to understand it. *Surely Darcy didn't preserve his mistress's rutting schedule with his wife?* thought George. *Oh, that would be too droll!*

"In fact, I believe I passed him, near the duke's residence last Tuesday," mused George, as if to himself. "No doubt he was on his way there."

"Surely, you are mistaken, Mr Wickham. I believe Fitzwilliam is busy dealing with the earl's affairs."

"Perhaps," George conceded, "but remember, all work and no play makes Jack a dull boy."

Elizabeth made no answer, pretending to be studying Lady Anne's portrait. She was fighting back the tears that were pooling in her eyes.

"Yes, Lady Diana is quite the intellectual," continued George. "They say there are very few university-educated men who can rival her in learning. Being independently wealthy, she has had the benefit of the best masters."

"Indeed?"

"Apparently, she can speak Greek and Latin as well as French, and quote any number of poets, both classic and modern. She is also well-versed in philosophy."

"Oh," said Elizabeth quietly, before reminding herself to keep speaking. "And how long has she been married to the duke?"

"Well, it must be over three months now. Though I cannot think why she chose to marry him! It was certainly not the wisest decision of her life."

"How is that?"

"He is a man who very much prefers the company of men. I'm sure he would spend all day at White's if he could."

"It doesn't seem that either of them made a sound decision," observed Elizabeth.

"Well, it was likely one of those cold-blooded marriages of convenience they favour in the Ton," conceded George.

"Oh? Does the duke need a heir?" asked Elizabeth, causing George to smile to himself knowingly—Mrs Darcy having innocently confirmed his supposition on the nature of the Darcys' union.

"No, no. He is well set up that way from his first wife. I would say his first object was likely to have the prettiest female available on his arm for social functions."

"Goodness! And why do you think the duchess remarried if she is independently wealthy?"

"Mrs Darcy! You are universally charming! What is *some* wealth, when one can always have more? The duke's wealth is quite astounding. Besides, Lady Diana was only a marchioness before, whereas now she is a duchess. She could not have done better unless she had married the Prince Regent!"

"I think I would prefer to be happy," said Elizabeth.

"Really? Then I wonder…" said George, carefully examining Mrs Darcy's face, assessing whether he should risk a kiss now.

Perturbed by his proximity, Elizabeth stepped backwards.

"But excuse me," George apologised. "I find myself quite malapropos."

Elizabeth knew the question Mr Wickham had been about to pose and was thankful he had not. "So you grew up here at Pemberley with

Fitzwilliam?" she asked in an attempt to turn the subject.

"You could not have met with a person who knows your husband better than myself," he laughed, breaking the tension. "We were born in the same parish, within the same park; the greatest part of our youth was passed together; inmates of the same house, sharing the same amusements, objects of the same parental care."

"Surely his sister knows him better?" Elizabeth smiled in dispute, a dimple peeping from the peach-like flesh at the corner of her mouth.

Wickham felt a jerk of attraction in the vicinity of his navel as the blood began to pool in his nether regions. "At a distance of twelve years?' he said. "I think not. Ask me anything! Darcy's favourite colour?—*black*. Favourite breakfast?—*porridge*. Favourite shot?—*ten*. I am a font of information, Mrs Darcy," declared George before leaning a little closer and saying conspiratorially, "Use me as you will."

At that moment Mrs Reynolds entered the room and froze upon seeing Mr Wickham's head bent towards the mistress. *A humble servant*, she thought, *would efface themselves at such a moment*. She reflected she was more a *dutiful* servant.

"I beg your pardon, Mrs Darcy. You wanted to see me?"

Elizabeth, turned, her face slightly flushed. "Yes, Reynolds. I was wondering if we should shift this little table to underneath the portrait of Fitzwilliam. I think it will change the focus of the room."

45 Confidences

Although George was a little annoyed at Reynolds' interruption, on reflection he believed it had been fortuitous. As a seducer, he had met with the occasional rebuff; and if he could be faulted on technique, he acknowledged in himself a slight tendency to rush his fences.

He had given Mrs Darcy a courtly bow and gone off to his bedchamber on the pretence of writing some letters. Of course, there were no letters to write, George had abandoned his legal studies years ago to live by his wits. Instead, he drew a pack of cards from his carpetbag and began to absentmindedly shuffle them in front of the hearth as he reviewed his progress with Mrs Darcy.

He believed he was correct in his original surmise—that Darcy had married to beget an heir after Diana discarded him for the duke. No doubt Fitzwilliam thought that a country miss, who could be safely left in Derbyshire, was best for his requirements.

George lost himself for a moment wondering how the awkward Darcy had gone about courting his wife. *What had Elizabeth said?* That they had met at an assembly and got to know each other better when she was nursing her sister? Lord! How he wished he'd been a fly on the wall! *'Dear Miss Elizabeth, you have such a way with a bandage! Would you be my wife?'* George chuckled just imagining it, but acknowledged the truth was likely far more boring—Darcy probably bribed her gouty old father with several fine bottles of port before arranging a generous settlement.

Wickham's mind flicked back to his recent conversation with Mrs Darcy. He fancied he'd scored a very big hit against Darcy with his revelations of Diana. George knew that all pretty females are vain, so he expected to gain traction with Mrs Darcy by dwelling on Diana's beauty. He had not originally intended to say anything on Diana's intellectual aspect. The discovery that Mrs Darcy fancied herself a bit of a bluestocking had been a happy coincidence that allowed him to twist the knife a little harder—there was nothing like jealousy to get a female to reveal her claws.

George also congratulated himself on getting in that reference to Darcy's cold-bloodedness. If the Darcys' marriage was, as he suspected, a marriage of convenience, then he thought it unlikely Darcy and his wife had come to any deep understanding in the few weeks since their marriage—Darcy was a very private person, an extremely difficult person to get to know. From years of baiting and needling him, Wickham knew that Darcy was slow to anger or, for that matter, to show any emotion at all; and he also knew that many people misinterpreted Darcy's sang-froid as lack of feeling; but George appreciated that Darcy's reserve hid a bottomless pit of pent-up emotions that could be drawn on to torture him. The portrait gallery had provided the perfect backdrop to sympathise with Mrs Darcy on her husband's absence and lack of solicitude, under the guise of ancestral enlightenment.

George pretty much fancied that the neglected Mrs Darcy was ready to scratch her husband's eyes out—so ready, that it should be a simple matter to get her to fall into his arms instead.

Finishing his shuffling, George pulled a card at random from the pack, looked at it, and smiled. It was an ace.

In London, Darcy had sat down at the first opportunity after his series of epiphanies to write a very long letter to his wife. It was difficult at first to express his emotions, but after tossing several ruined sheets of paper into the fire, he had decided that to write something, anything, was better than to write nothing at all. He initially spoke of his love for Elizabeth, and his delight that she was having his child.

Breaking off from his missive, Darcy struggled to recall what he had written in his previous letter regarding Elizabeth's pregnancy—so much had happened since then. Although he had expressed his joy and solicitude, in retrospect he could not help wondering if his letter had conveyed the right sentiment. His predominant feelings on first receiving the news had been selfish ones: pride, that he was to be a father, and relief, that he had actually managed to impregnate his wife. After all, when a man had made love as many times as he had, a number well into triple figures, without issue; one couldn't help wondering if one was actually capable of siring a child. It would have indeed been ironic, after all those years of using a sheath with Diana, if he had been unable to impregnate his wife. *But*, he reminded himself, thinking of Richard's information, *there had been other reasons for using the sheath, hadn't there?*

Returning his pen to the paper, Darcy began to backtrack, to trace his growing fascination with Elizabeth at Netherfield. He also tried to discreetly convey the reasons for his odd actions in Derbyshire, such as going off to Yorkshire, without committing anything too risqué to paper.

> *Almost from the earliest moments of our acquaintance, I felt an attraction to you that I steadfastly denied, unwilling to admit myself so fickle. When I told you my heart was already engaged, I thought it true, although the relationship I spoke of had been sundered months previously. Its duration had been so long that I almost considered myself a married man, and like a widower, refused to see the light before me when dwelling on the ashes of my past love.*
>
> *What prompted me to ask you to marry me under such conditions I cannot know—perhaps a small part of me that recognized my attraction to you and grasped hope when I was determined to be morose and stupid. But I thank*

God for that grain of sense.

Since bringing you to Pemberley, that fledgling love has grown into a passionate admiration and regard—something that threatened to overwhelm me. Unprepared for such feelings by anything in my former existence, my response was ridiculous—I ran. Can you forgive me?

My time here in London has given me a new perspective, and I hope to return to you a new man—one who is ready to love and cherish you, as you should be,

Your devoted husband
Fitzwilliam Darcy.

Rereading his letter, he winced at the first clumsily expressed feelings but found that his shaky start was to some extent ameliorated by the genuineness of the sentiment he had managed to convey by the end.

Dipping his pen in the standish, Darcy added a postscript, re-expressing his joy on her pregnancy to Elizabeth and promising to be home within a fortnight.

After rearranging the table in the gallery, Elizabeth had accompanied Mrs Reynolds to the stillroom to select pot-pourri for her bedchamber from the stock the housekeeper kept there. Reynolds had suggested she keep a bowl next to the commode to cover the smell of her morning sickness. Finding herself private with the housekeeper, Elizabeth broached the topic of Mr Wickham.

"Mrs Reynolds, I cannot like Mr Wickham staying here when my husband is absent, though I fear I would be overstepping my authority in sending him on his way."

"I cannot like it either, ma'am, but he *is* old Mr Darcy's godson. He has had a room in the house ever since his own father died, and thus I must treat him like family."

When the housekeeper seemed unwilling to say anything more, Elizabeth pressed her. "Mrs Reynolds, you mentioned something once which suggested you did not think him of good character…"

"No, ma'am."

"Would you care to elaborate?"

"Well, ma'am. I very strongly suspected Mr Wickham of interfering with the maids when he was a youth."

"Do you mean he had his way with them against their will, Mrs Reynolds?"

"I cannot say whether it was against their will or no, Mrs Darcy. However, quite a number of them had to leave service with bairns, and always after Mr Wickham's visits in the summer."

"And do you have any proof of your suppositions, Mrs Reynolds?"

"Only the proof of my eyes, Mrs Darcy. Old Mr Darcy arranged for the girls to marry tenant farmers, and there are several children that have a look of Mr Wickham about them. You may see them for yourself."

Elizabeth could not recall the children the housekeeper mentioned, but she recorded their names in a notebook her aunt had given her to help in her new duties as mistress of Pemberley before slipping it back into her pocket.

"Mrs Reynolds, I know you will keep this confidential, but do you think there is any danger to myself or to Miss Georgiana?"

"It was only ever maids, Mrs Darcy. Some gentlemen think them fair game, though I know that men of the Darcy family have never thought so, not while I have been in service."

"I cannot believe that a man who would do such a thing could call himself a gentleman."

"No, ma'am."

"Well, there is nothing I can do beyond writing Fitzwilliam to notify him that Mr Wickham is present."

"I think that would be best, ma'am."

"I do wish he would take himself off."

"Yes, ma'am."

Elizabeth had begged off spending her afternoon in Georgie's sitting room—she was in no fit state for anyone's company, least of all Mr Wickham's. Fortunately, she had a valid excuse. As Mr Bletchley, the Astronomer Royal's assistant, was arriving on the morrow, she was spending her afternoon in the observatory and had locked the door to the family room to enforce her solitude.

Still the canker of Mr Wickham's words remained. Elizabeth could see that she was no match for the peerless Lady Diana. What was mere prettiness when compared to beauty? A squire's daughter to a marchioness, and now a duchess? A local wit compared to a first-rate mind? It was clear that Lady Diana wanted to have her cake and eat it too—a handsome lover to complement her titled husband. Elizabeth supposed that such women got what they wanted.

It was all so depressing, but the information was not new. Mr Wickham had merely filled in the gaps in her knowledge. The salient point, Elizabeth reminded herself, was that she was not just Fitzwilliam Darcy's wife—she was Mistress of Pemberley and the mother of future Darcys, the continuation of a line. Her portrait would hang in the gallery, perhaps with a baby at her breast as was the current fashion. She had a job to do, and she was determined to do it well.

Wiping the telescope with the cloth in her hand, Elizabeth removed the cover of the eyepiece and peered into it once more. Staring at the dull reflection from the mottled mirror, she reminded herself of her excitement at the visit of the astronomer's assistant and pushed negative thoughts from her head.

A board creaked behind her.

She stood quickly to perceive Mr Wickham ascending stealthily from the lower level of the tower.

"Mr Wickham!"

"Mrs Darcy! What a surprise to find you here!"

"I think your surprise must surely be exceeded by my own," replied Elizabeth dryly.

"I had no idea where you had disappeared to, but I was certainly missing your presence this afternoon," insinuated Mr Wickham. "I'm afraid I had the headache and begged Georgie to allow me walk in the garden to clear my head."

"You head clearly *must* be aching. You are no longer in the garden."

"Indeed!" he smiled, "but perceiving the gardener's door open, I decided to ascend the tower. I must admit a great curiosity to seeing this observatory—Lady Anne was very territorial about it."

"So Fitzwilliam has told me."

"Yes, dear Fitzwilliam," sighed George. "We were great friends as boys, but we grew apart after my father died."

"Really? How was that?" asked Lizzy, turning her back on him and walking towards Lady Anne's desk.

"I'm afraid dear Fitz has a jealous temperament," said Wickham, trailing behind her. "His father was most kind to me after my own father passed away. Mr Darcy treated me like a second son and had every intention of adopting me. Had not his untimely death intervened, I might now be the master of a tidy estate."

"That seems very generous towards a godson," said Lizzy, picking up the book on telescopes.

"Indeed, but Mr Darcy and I shared a special bond. In me, he found a temperament most truly like his own generous self," George said, moving closer. "His own son favoured his noble wife, who was rather a cold person, a true Fitzwilliam."

"I believe you said something about that yesterday. I understood that Lady Anne and Mr George Darcy were very close," said Lizzy, thrusting the book at Mr Wickham. "Would you mind shelving that, over there?" she said, pointing at a high bookshelf.

Wickham looked at the book askance but obeyed. When he turned away from her, Lizzy discreetly pulled the bell-wire summoning Jenny.

"I gather Fitzwilliam told you that," said Wickham, disposing of the book and approaching once more. "I think it would be more accurate to say that for Lady Anne, old Mr Darcy had the deepest respect and admiration, but she did not have a loving disposition. I was a great consolation to Mr Darcy after his wife's death."

"Really?" said Elizabeth, who had done a few calculations since yesterday; "and that would have occurred before Georgie was one and when Fitzwilliam was twelve, while you were…"

"Fourteen. Fitzwilliam, who is two years my junior, was always closer to his mother and couldn't enter into his poor father's feelings at the time. I'm only glad I was able to provide some comfort to old Mr Darcy."

George took a step closer and lowered his voice, "I understand your own position here is quite lonely and am willing to help in any way I can."

Elizabeth pulled a rather large handkerchief from her pocket and blew her nose noisily, causing George to retreat.

"That is a rather large handkerchief, Mrs Darcy," he observed.

"It is one of my husband's," she smiled. "They are so much more practical than the tiny lacy ones that females are required to carry round."

They heard the swish of the arras and turned to perceive Jenny. She looked rather puzzled to find Mr Wickham with the mistress, and unable to parse the situation, she merely curtsied.

"Ah, Jenny!" said Elizabeth with genuine relief. "Can you help me with the second mirror? I wanted to polish it before Mr Bletchley arrives. If you could take the other side, I've prepared a table in my chambers."

"Mr Wickham," Lizzy continued, handing him her chatelaine, "would you mind opening the sitting room door for me?"

George could only comply.

After setting the mirror on a hall table, Elizabeth retrieved her chatelaine, and locked the sitting room door behind them.

"How is your head, Mr Wickham?" she asked solicitously. "Would you like some laudanum?"

"No, I believe I have recovered, Mrs Darcy. Thank you for your solicitude. I am ready to re-join this afternoon's piano recital."

"Wonderful. I'll just get the maids started with this mirror and will join you."

After locking the door to her bedchamber, Lizzy pulled the bell-wire to summon Mrs Reynolds before turning to Jenny.

"I've no idea how to polish this mirror, ma'am," said her bemused handmaid. "Should we use the silver polish?"

"Nor do I," laughed Elizabeth, "and I certainly wouldn't ask you to adopt a chambermaid's duties. Mr Wickham found me alone, which was quite inappropriate. Hence I summoned you to play chaperone. How did you get through the locked door? Did Reynolds open it for you?"

"No, I ran around and came up through the servants' stairs into the nursery."

"Thank you for your quick thinking," praised Elizabeth.

When Mrs Reynolds arrived, Elizabeth took her to the master sitting room where they had a detailed discussion about improving security. It was unnerving that one could not feel safe behind a locked door.

As promised, Elizabeth returned to Georgie's sitting room afterwards, judging there to be safety in numbers. While she did not believe Mr Wickham would impose upon her, he was certainly doing enough to set tongues wagging if she was not careful. She had not felt so pursued since Mr Collins' unwelcome attentions.

Before dinner, Elizabeth sat down to write a letter to her husband apprising him of Mr Wickham's arrival. Had duty not dictated it, she would have delayed this letter until she was in a better mood—the revelations about his mistress were too recent. No words of love found their way to the page, but Elizabeth's missive did contain a remarkably concise summary of the latest tenant dispute and her proposed solution. She laid the letter on the salver in the vestibule, ready to be taken to the receiving office in the morning, before going in to dinner.

A little after midnight, Wickham stole down the servants' stairs and scooped Elizabeth's letter up. Reaching his room, he read it quickly, smiled at its unromantic contents and tossed it in the hearth.

A day later he was entertained to intercept a letter coming in the other direction. This proved too hilarious to burn. George tucked it into his waistcoat so he could re-peruse Fitzwilliam's heartfelt throbbings at leisure. But the letter did contain one important piece of information: Darcy would be home in a fortnight; George would have to work quickly.

46 Mr Bletchley

George's original intention in visiting Pemberley had been to cause a little havoc in the Darcy household. He knew that most women were susceptible to his charms, having spent the years since his Cambridge days living out of the pockets of a succession of rich widows, and spicing his life with the occasional extramarital affair with an agreeable beauty. He had entertained hopes of making Mrs Darcy his next liaison. That would surely have caused Fitzwilliam some grief. Imagine if George's own child had ended up heir to Pemberley! It would have been too sweet after the shabby way Darcy had treated him after his father's death. Four thousand pounds to support him through his legal studies! Who could live on that?

After two more days trying to steal time alone with Mrs Darcy, George had to admit defeat. That damned fellow from the observatory had arrived on the first day—a short ill-looking fellow with a long face. Mrs Darcy didn't seem to mind spending time alone with him, though George supposed that, given his hideous aspect, no-one would suspect him of being her cicisbeo.

It was clear from Fitzwilliam's letter that Mrs Darcy was already expecting. A shame. Furthermore, George's revelations on Darcy's infidelity did not seem to be having the desired effect on his wife. After a promising start when he thought he was making some progress, she had shown herself to be rather refractory to his disclosures.

Perhaps Mrs Darcy already suspects her husband's extra-marital involvement? Or stay... Could it be that Darcy has already disclosed his relationship with Diana to her? It is just the sort of damned foolish thing that he would do. What is he fond of saying? 'Disguise is my abhorrence.'

Certainly it appeared that Mrs Darcy was one of those phlegmatic females who considered it their duty to guard home and hearth while their husbands gallivanted around London! Such a woman might prove rather intractable to seduction. She remained polite, but George could tell he was making no headway. It was as if her soft, pliant exterior hid a core of iron.

Now, watching Georgie play the piano, a new project occurred to George, and he mentally kicked himself for being so slow in conceiving it. Georgiana Darcy had a considerable dowry, and he could not imagine her upright brother casting his only sister off because of a mésalliance. *In short, the man who married her would be set for life. And how far is the Scottish border?—a mere one hundred and sixty miles.*

True, George had always thought of Georgie as a baby, which is exactly what she had been when he'd been sent off from Pemberley to Eton at fourteen. She was still only half his age of thirty. But she *was* fifteen; and she was tall and could pass for a woman, though she remained as flat as a tack despite her maid's attempts to create something passing for a décolletage.

Getting up, George walked towards her. "Georgie, can I turn the pages for you?"

Georgie blushed.

Mrs Annesley was quite discomposed to find Mr Wickham sitting beside her charge when she re-entered the sitting room. *Could a woman not use the chamber pot in peace?*

Declaring himself fit the next day, Mr Wickham proposed joining Georgie on her morning ride. Although Healy always accompanied Miss Darcy, the addition of Mr Wickham prompted Mrs Annesley to request a horse saddled for herself also. She set off with the party mounted on Georgie's old slug.

During the days of Mr Bletchley's visit, Elizabeth's time was spent almost wholly with him. The astronomer's assistant had announced he could devote only a week to making the telescope operational and instructing Mrs Darcy in its use.

Both primary mirrors were found to be severely tarnished. The one fitted to the telescope, which was in the worse condition, was removed and sent post-haste to Sheffield for polishing, with instructions that it should be returned in no later than five days. The second mirror, which had been stored in a cupboard, was in better nick, and Mr Bletchley decided it would have to suffice for their instructional observations until the re-polished mirror was returned.

In the evenings, Mr Bletchley tutored Elizabeth in the workings of the telescope while Jenny sat by, stitching and occasionally casting a bemused eye on the proceedings. Mr Bletchley was surprised to discover that Elizabeth had some knowledge of astronomy. She already knew of the Messier objects, and thus could avoid these annoying phenomena when searching for comets, planets and supernovae. She was quick to learn how to set the telescope using coordinates, and to drive its movement with the clockwork device the Astronomer Royal had invented. Furthermore, she was a pleasure to instruct, so unlike the snooty and arrogant young men who visited Greenwich from the universities, who were sure that they already knew everything. Her delight when he demonstrated that the telescope could be elevated from below by a winding mechanism to make observations near the horizon had been most gratifying.

All-in-all Mrs Darcy was a most apt pupil, and by the time Mr Bletchley was due to leave at the end of the week, he was satisfied she would be able to make meaningful observations to contribute to the Astronomer Royal's work. By Friday, he had shown her how to fit the re-polished mirror, sent the other mirror off to Sheffield, and got in two nights of practical observation with the new mirror.

For her part, Elizabeth could not have been more pleased with Mr Bletchley's visit. The distraction had lifted her depression about her lukewarm relationship with her husband. She thought she would, in time, get over her jealously of his mistress, which she realised was based on the tendre she had recently developed for him. With Jane nearby, she felt she could live quite tolerably as a neglected wife. The life she had mapped out for herself as mistress of Pemberley, sometime companion to Fitzwilliam Darcy, and mother of his children would be a full one; but it had hitherto lacked anything to engage her higher faculties. She could now see this void being filled by her work for the Astronomer Royal as superintendent of what was still one of the best telescopes in England.

Upon Mr Bletchley's return to London, Elizabeth was a little worried that Mr Wickham might renew his unwanted attentions. She had not been sure if he was just flirting or if he meant something more, but Mrs Reynolds' information had been sufficient to worry her that he might be looking for casual diversion. Perhaps he considered married women, along with chambermaids, to be in the category of 'women who could be trifled with'. She had heard of such men through Charlotte.

As she had received no reply to her letter to Fitzwilliam advising him of Mr Wickham's presence, Elizabeth still had no authority to make some excuse to send him off—such as they wished to renovate the guest wing; but it did occur to her that she and Georgie might temporarily flee to Matlock on some pretext if he continued to bother her. Fortunately, upon Mr Bletchley's departure, Elizabeth discovered that Mr Wickham seemed to have given up his assiduous attentions, and she had every hope that he would soon decamp.

For Lizzy, the advent of Mr Wickham had produced bittersweet reflections on her relationship with her husband. While she had been fleetingly taken by the combination of Mr Wickham's disastrously good looks and charming manner, his criticism of her husband had raised her hackles. At first she had attributed her ire to the unexpected passion she had developed for her husband, but on continued reflection, she believed there was a perfectly rational explanation for it—for better or for worse, her fortunes were tied to Fitzwilliam. Why this interloper thought she would risk her future by dallying with him, she could not at first comprehend, but she later reasoned that Mr Wickham probably hadn't even bothered to think about it, as the risk to himself was small. She concluded therefore that Mr Wickham was a selfish trifler who only considered his own pleasure.

Inevitably she found herself comparing Mr Wickham to her husband. She had initially believed that the 'love' she had developed for Fitzwilliam was nothing more than a physical attraction to him, arising naturally from his good looks and their intimate relations. But she had to admit that she wasn't the least attracted to Mr Wickham, who was far better looking. If she thought about it, she believed Fitzwilliam's good looks were more on par with her own. Some gallant fellows had called her a beauty, but she hardly thought she would ever inspire anyone to pick up a brush like Lady Hamilton had. Similarly, Fitzwilliam was good looking, but Mr Wickham… Yes, she could imagine an artist being inspired by him. But, while she could appreciate Mr Wickham's beauty, it held no allure for her—there was something about Fitzwilliam she found inherently attractive: that hooked nose and the combination of his curved lips and pronounced chin quite put Mr Wickham's classic good looks in the shade.

Another aspect of her husband intrigued her: Elizabeth also thought she had begun to understand him to some extent. What she had originally thought arrogance, she now believed a kind of social awkwardness. He didn't like attending social functions and was only comfortable in the company of those he knew well. He probably would be happiest sitting beside the hearth with his family. She, on the other hand, could appreciate such domestic bliss but did enjoy a party. She thought Darcy would be able to enjoy social life if he just had a companion to help him navigate it; by her ease and liveliness, his manners might be improved. Would she ever get a chance to test her theory in London? It seemed unlikely.

Elizabeth could not help but find it ironic that Fitzwilliam had chosen a mistress who was considered an intellectual. Lizzy had always sought to win her father's approval by improving herself through reading and had been slightly resentful that as a female, barred from university, she could never hope to attain the respect from her father that she craved. But if Mr Wickham could be believed, the duchess had used her wealth to buy an education that rivalled that available at any university. Could not Lizzy use her pin money to do just the same? Elizabeth thought that by pursuing such a course, she might not only raise her own self-esteem, she might be able to garner the respect of her father *and* her husband.

In short, Lizzy began to comprehend that Fitzwilliam Darcy was exactly the man who, in disposition and talents, would most suit her; but, she reflected sadly, she had come into his life too late to convince him of that.

In London, Darcy was having breakfast with Richard and Jane when a harried footman arrived, breathlessly requesting their immediate presence at Matlock House.

Dropping their cutlery, the men promptly answered the summons by abandoning the table and Jane, and sprinting across the square. They arrived in the vestibule to pandemonium. From upstairs, the wails of the countess emanated from the open door of the earl's bedchamber. Several ladies who were friends of the countess stood whispering in the vestibule, but stopped abruptly upon perceiving Richard and Darcy.

Taking the stairs in several leaps, Richard arrived in his father's bedchamber to find Doctor Douglas closing his father's eyes. Swiftly following his cousin in a more decorous fashion by running up the steps one at a time, Darcy walked in behind him. Miss Smyth was fruitlessly trying to comfort the countess.

"I'm sorry, there is nothing I can do," apologized the doctor to Richard. "He really is gone this time."

Richard nodded his acceptance. "Come, Mother. I think you should lie down. Perhaps Dr Douglas can give you some laudanum…"

"Where is Robert?" wailed the countess. "I need Robert!"

This irked Richard. Robert was now the earl, and despite all his misdemeanours, his ascendency had begun. Who had been around to visit his mother all these years? *Richard*. And who did she call for? *Robert*. Primogeniture won again.

As the senior executor of the earl's will, it fell to Darcy to organise the funeral while Richard and Jane dealt with the distress of the earl's household. A notice was immediately placed in the gazette, the hatchment placed, and the earl's body embalmed and laid out in his study, after which a succession of visitors, both friends and old enemies, attended the townhouse in a steady stream.

When Robert had still not been located three days later, they decided to proceed with the funeral regardless. Breaking with tradition, the earl had requested to be laid to rest in London. His reasons were two-fold: the family tomb at Wyvern Hall was full and falling down besides; and the earl had expressed a wish to be interred in London where he had spent most of his life. Although he had purchased a plot in the graveyard of St George's Hanover Square, he had not yet commissioned the tomb, not anticipating his untimely demise. Darcy had thus arranged for the earl to be interred in a lead-lined coffin in a nearby spot while the tomb was constructed.

The day of the funeral was chill and miserable. The family party consisted only of Richard, Darcy and Mr Gardiner who was attending on behalf of Mr Bennet; the earl's brother hadn't spoken to him in years and Lady Stanley's father was unable to attend due to his gout. However, a number of the earl's friends turned up to see their friend off. All proceeded uneventfully until the bearers began to lower the coffin into the grave.

The top had barely sunk beneath the surface of the earth when the earl's mistress appeared from behind a nearby tomb dressed in a black domino. Before anyone had time to protest that a woman should not be at the graveside, *and such a woman!* she threw herself on top of the casket. At this point Richard could not help noticing that underneath the domino, she was wearing an amazingly gaudy purple silk gown and rather fetching black stockings with scarlet clocks. Landing with a dainty thud, she so startled one of the younger bearers that he lost his grip on the length of black silk that he was using to help lower the coffin into the grave. The casket swayed, and but for the seven other stalwarts, might have crashed into the pit.

Mr Gardiner, hastening to their assistance, grasped the lady's upper arms to haul her back, but was met with spirited resistance and a theatrical performance of hysterics worthy of Drury Lane. The colonel hesitated to join the fray for a moment, hoping momentarily that the coffin might crash six feet under and break her silly neck, thus saving them some trouble. But he took pity on Mr Gardiner. Grabbing one of the damsel's wrists, he gave her a rough jerk, propelling her upwards. Despite Mr Gardiner's larger purchase on the lady, she somehow contrived to collapse into Richard's arms, but had little chance to rest there before she was pushed roughly away to arm's length, where she stood swaying uncertainly.

Throughout these proceedings Darcy remained still as a statue. A close observer might have noticed a slight roll of his eyes under lowered lids. However, he did finally bat an eyelid when Lord Robert Fitzwilliam, 11th Earl of Matlock, suddenly appeared, dressed in rather gaudy town clothes with a multi-caped greatcoat thrown round his shoulders.

The 10th earl's mistress promptly collapsed into *his* arms, causing him to ejaculate, "Well, you silly wench, what are *you* doing here?"

He then announced to his brother, as if he had just happened upon him at White's, "I'd better deal with this then," and picking the damsel up, carted her off.

Richard, who stared at his brother's behaviour with an open mouth, had the presence of mind to indicate to Fobbing, who had also appeared a respectful distance from the graveside, that he should continue to dog his brother's footsteps.

The rest of the interment proceeded without interruption, which, after such a debacle, Darcy could only be thankful for.

The funeral party then proceeded back to Matlock House for a cold collation. As Robert had been 'found' it was anticipated that the reading of the will could proceed, but the rest of the party had to await Lord Robert's pleasure. A street urchin had arrived at Matlock House shortly after their return from St George's, bearing a pencilled note from Fobbing, indicating he was awaiting developments in the kitchens at Curzon Street.

Two hours later, Robert arrived, partook of a little ale and cold ham and received the condolences of the guests, before retiring to the study with the rest of the immediate family to hear the reading of the will. The fact that he had failed to see his father for a last time before the coffin was sealed seemed to bother him not a wit.

As soon as the study doors closed, the dowager countess clung to her son, the new earl, most piteously.

"Oh, Robert!" she sobbed. "Thank goodness you have returned to set things to right!"

This statement, which caused Richard and Darcy to exchange a glance, was met with, "Quite" by Robert.

However, once the will was read by Mr Havershott, Robert's urbanity was slightly rocked by its contents, which could be summarised thus:

To my first son, Robert, all his entitlements as earl;
To my second son, Richard, my gratitude, my watch, and the following properties...;
To my nephew, Fitzwilliam Darcy, my admiration and esteem.

After Havershott finished reading the various codicils, Robert approached Richard.

"Well, you seem to have done pretty well by hanging 'round father's deathbed," he sneered.

To which Richard coolly replied. "Pity you didn't turn up earlier then."

"Now, boys," intervened the countess. "There is no need for rancour. Your father did give a little to Richard, but the properties were small ones, which do not even boast a decent house. Do not begrudge your brother, Robert. You and I will do very well here in Matlock House, while your family is well-housed at Chasely."

"I'm not sure what gave you that idea, Mother. I presumed you would be going back to Wyvern Hall," replied the heir.

"Not at all, Robert. I only resided there to avoid having your father's mistresses continually underfoot in Curzon Street."

"Well, now you will have *my* mistresses continually underfoot in Curzon Street," her son retorted.

Although the countess was slightly affronted by her son's discourteous speech, she replied evenly, "Well, as you are my son and *not* my husband, I expect I shall bear it as well as I can—blood is thicker than water."

"No, no, mother. I'm afraid you will rather cramp my style," averred Robert. "I will not demand that you decamp to the Dower House at Wyvern, for I know 'tis falling down. I have no wish to rusticate at my countryseat, so I will very generously let you reside there. Count your blessings. I intend to make Matlock House my principal residence. Your speedy removal to the country is appreciated."

Darcy, who could see that the dowager was not going down without a fight, judged it a good time to remove to his own domicile. Casting an apologetic glance at Richard, he bowed to his relatives and departed.

When Richard joined him an hour later at Darcy House, he found his cousin in his study.

"Well, did you get that spat sorted?" asked Darcy.

"No, Mother refuses to budge," replied Richard; "and Robert went off to White's to avoid the screaming. He says she has a week to depart, after which he will put her bodily into the carriage."

"Charming. And what excuse did he give for not appearing earlier?"

"Merely that he was trying to avoid his creditors. He knew Fobbing was following him but gave him the slip several times, believing him to be an agent of the usurers."

"Oh, *pish*. Surely he recognized one of his father's own servants!"

"Well, possibly not. Fobbing's only been with us for ten years."

"I don't believe it. I suppose he eventually got wind of your father's death and decided his credit problems were solved."

"Pretty much; which they are, at least temporarily."

Darcy grimaced and checked his watch. "Are you for lunch?"

"Not really hungry," replied Richard, "but I'll sit down with you and Jane."

They found Jane awaiting them in the dining room, reading a letter.

"Is that from Longbourn?" asked Richard.

Jane looked at him quizzically, before realising that her husband did not know that her mother was illiterate. "No, it's from Lizzy," she replied.

This statement stopped Darcy in his tracks, for he suddenly realised that he had not received a response from Lizzy to his heartfelt letter. After patiently waiting for a week for a reply, reassuring himself that five days was the minimum turnaround he could expect, the earl's death had been very distracting. Now, the fact that a reply hadn't come after ten days made him worry anew. Could it be that Elizabeth had rejected his apology?

"What news from your sister?" asked Richard of his wife.

"Well, the astronomer's assistant has come and gone, and an annoying person called Mr Wickham has turned up…"

"*What?!*" thundered Darcy.

Jane almost dropped the letter in fright. She looked at her husband in trepidation.

Richard grabbed Darcy's arm to calm him. "What does she say of Wickham?" asked Richard softly. "Is he staying in Lambton?"

"Well, no," replied Jane. "He is staying in his old room at Pemberley."

"My God!" said Darcy, staggering. "It never occurred to me that he would have the effrontery to turn up there after our rupture! I should have advised Mrs Reynolds! They know nothing of what went on in London!"

"That cuckoo!" spat Colonel Fitzwilliam.

"I must go to Pemberley!" said Darcy. "Immediately!"

47 Revelations

Darcy had run off into the hall like a madman, hallooing for Finn.

"Who is Mr Wickham?" asked Jane in consternation.

"He hates Darcy," replied Richard, "and would do anything to injure him."

"But why?" asked Jane, unable to comprehend such wickedness.

"They grew up together. Mr Wickham is the steward's son, and old Mr Darcy stood as godfather to him. Uncle Darcy was rather taken with George, who was named for him, to the extent that George got it into his head that Mr Darcy favoured him more than his own son. Certainly he was more demonstrative towards George than Fitzwilliam, but I believe it was partly in compensation for the loss of George's parents."

Jane's mouth had opened in a silent, 'oh!'

"George did something bad when he was fourteen and Mr Darcy sent him off to Eton. I never found out what it was. He continued to come home in the holidays up until Darcy's father died, but broke with the family when he discovered Uncle Darcy hadn't left him a legacy in his will as he'd expected. He has continued to harry Fitzwilliam over the years. It's astonishing that he has just appeared at the family's estate, expecting to be taken back in! But one should never put anything past George."

Jane was at a loss to know what to say.

"Jane," Richard said, falling to his knee. "This bodes no good. I must go to Pemberley with Darcy. I fear for your sister and also Georgiana. Wickham is a bad man."

Fear brought tears to Jane's eyes. "Of course, Richard! You must do what is necessary!"

Richard asked Jane to read the parts of the letter concerning Mr Wickham to him, lest they contain important information. Rather than do this, she pressed the missive into his hands, assuring him there was nothing in it that could not be shared with him directly. He scanned the relevant passages quickly before tucking the letter into his breast pocket and giving his wife a reassuring hug.

Richard's first impulse was to immediately send his wife back to Gracechurch Street in the Darcy carriage, but Jane refused to delay their own departure thus. She offered instead to take a hackney with a footman and her maid if need be, but thought she would be quite safe staying at Darcy House with the servants. When Darcy reappeared, it was settled—Jane would stay in Grosvenor Square. Darcy then sought Mrs Flowers while the Fitzwilliams retreated upstairs to gather Richard's belongings.

Downstairs, Darcy found his housekeeper busy preparing food for their departure. In reply to his queries as to whether Mrs Reynolds had mentioned Mr Wickham in any of the correspondence sent from Pemberley, Mrs Flowers was chagrined to report that she had not received any correspondence from Mrs Reynolds for over a fortnight and would have mentioned this strange occurrence to the master had not the earl's death intervened.

By the time Darcy had checked his desk and written a short note to Havershott, footsteps on the stairs and Finn's voice in the vestibule alerted him to his valet's readiness for their departure. He was donning his greatcoat when Richard joined him in the vestibule carrying his effects.

With a quick farewell to Jane, the cousins were off. Finn, who was sharing the carriage on the forward seat, quickly closed his eyes, as if settling down to sleep.

Once the carriage was swaying across Hampstead Heath and Finn lightly snoring, Darcy sought further information on Wickham from Richard. "What do you think he means by going to Pemberley like this at such a time?"

"He knows you are preoccupied here in London and seeks to take advantage of it," replied Richard.

"But how? He could only importune the women for their pin money or steal the silver..."

Richard inwardly sighed at Darcy's naivety. "You know his habits, Darcy—he is a seducer. Surely you see his object is likely to be to cuckold you; or worse, and this is what I really fear, that his object is Georgie."

Darcy paled. As familiar as he was with Wickham, he could never second-guess him. His own mind was wholly unacquainted with evil and could not sympathise at all with George's perfidious schemes. "What did Elizabeth say in her letter?" he asked.

"Merely that he is there and annoying her," replied Richard, handing over the missive.

When Darcy found no further information about Wickham on perusing it, he let his hand drop to his knee as he stared into space.

"Wait!" said Richard, "there is something written on the outside, near the seal." He leant over to read *'All my love, Aunt Amelia.'* "What does that mean?" he asked Darcy.

"Elizabeth's great aunt lives in Lambton," replied Darcy. "I suppose she was visiting, or Lizzy visited her."

The cousins sat in silence as the carriage swayed, both impatient to be in Derbyshire.

"Darcy?"

"Yes?"

"What exactly did Wickham do? Why did your father send him away?"

"Well, it was Lady Adversane, Richard. You know that."

"The incident with our clothes when we were swimming? It seems a bit harsh."

"It was more than that, Richard. That was just the start. Wickham visited Lady Adversane almost every night, all throughout that winter. He'd arrive back at Pemberley at any hour of the morning, always stopping by my room to tell me of his exploits—what a big man he was."

Richard rolled his eyes and urged his cousin to continue.

"Lord Adversane was furious when he came back in the summer and found out. He arrived at Pemberley as mad as a bull. I was in the library and could hear him yelling at my father through the heavy oak doors to the study."

"Lord! What a to-do!"

"Father was mortified. He was incredulous at first, but Lord Adversane had actually caught them at it, so there was no denying it. The worst thing was that father blamed me for not alerting him earlier."

"You didn't tell actually him that you knew?" asked Richard incredulously.

"He asked me and I told the truth. But, how could I have gone to him? I couldn't speak on such a subject to my father! I was twelve years old! If Lord Adversane had trouble convincing him, what would he have said if I'd come to him with such a tale?"

"So that's why he sent Wickham away..." mused Richard.

"Yes, the youngest Adversane boy is his."

"You're joking!" said Richard, mentally subtracting ages, before concluding, "Well, I suppose he doesn't look like his brothers."

"No, but fortunately he looks like Lady Adversane."

"So your father thought Eton would straighten Wickham out, did he?"

"Yes, and he went to the grave with that misguided idea. George certainly did a good job afterwards convincing him that butter wouldn't melt in his mouth. Father got to thinking it had all been Lady Adversane's fault."

"Well, with the age difference, that's not surprising."

"Let's just say George didn't improve afterwards. The things he got up to at college would make your hair stand on end."

"You could try me."

"I don't want to talk about it," said Darcy snappishly.

"So what happened when your father died?"

"George was still ploughing through his ecclesiastical studies..." Darcy stopped before continuing as an aside, "Well, that was a poor choice of words."

Richard snorted.

"He'd failed his finals and was about to re-sit them for the third time when Father died. He was livid when he discovered he'd been left nothing but the preferment of the best living. Clearly, he had no intention of being a clergyman at all. He came to me the day after the funeral saying that Father had pushed him down that path and that he wanted a career in law like his own father."

"So you gave him the money in lieu."

"Yes, but that wasn't all. Two days after he left, Mrs Reynolds told me that Father's Ming vase was missing."

"What? But you got it back? It's sitting in the hall at Darcy House."

"No, Richard. There was a pair of them. The other was kept in my father's study at Pemberley. Besides the family jewels, which were kept under lock and key, those vases were the most valuable objects my father possessed."

"Correction, *you* possessed. So given I've never seen such a vase in the study, I gather you *didn't* get it back?"

"There didn't seem much point in going after it. By the time we discovered its disappearance, George would have arrived in London and would surely have disposed of it before I could even find him."

"So, he's a thief as well as a seducer," concluded Richard.

"Yes. Once Reynolds told me of the vase, it occurred to me that a number of my things had gone missing over the years; little things like cravat pins—the sort of thing that a servant could easily drop. I particularly missed the one that my father gave me for my sixteenth birthday. It had a small ruby—was the first pin I possessed with a precious stone. The footman was so apologetic. He searched and searched for it. It never occurred to me that George might be taking them 'til the vase went missing; and it was so unnecessary—Father gave him a perfectly respectable allowance when we were growing up, the same as mine. I couldn't think what to do with the half of it."

"I suspect he gambled even then," confided Richard; "but as to the vase, you had just given him the draft for three thousand pounds, so he couldn't have been in want of money. He must have taken it out of spite."

"Perhaps," conceded Darcy.

"I told you not to give him that lump sum."

"I know, Richard. I'm sorry," sighed Darcy. "You were right, but you can't know how much I wanted him out of my life."

Richard gave his cousin's arm a squeeze.

"I didn't know how much 'til he went to Eton," Darcy continued. "We had grown up together. He was like a brother to me. It wasn't 'til he was gone, that I realised how much *better* everything was when he wasn't around. I could have cried when Father said I would have to share rooms with him at Cambridge. He thought I could help George study; finally pass his exams. You can't know what it's like to have a shadow like that constantly ruining your life."

"You forget I have a brother named Robert," remarked Richard dryly.

That brought Darcy up short. "I'm sorry, that was selfish of me. Your situation is far more pitiable."

"Not at all. You have a thorn in your side whereas I am of no consequence—the spare. But we digress. Wickham continued to dog you."

"At first, he left me alone. He took lodgings in Half Moon Street. I thought at the time this was strange—above his means, and too far from the City. But in retrospect, it is clear he always planned a life for himself as a man about town—something in the style of Brummel. I would run into him occasionally, hanging around the clubs in St James or in Bond Street."

"So the bet at White's about your virginity was the first time he'd bothered you after your father's death?"

"Yes. He seemed still to be in funds then and only did it for sport. But about a year afterwards, he came to me demanding money, saying he would spill the beans to Uncle about Diana."

"I can't think why he thought my father would mind at all," said Richard. "He would probably have given you a medal!"

"Well, *I* would have minded, but I didn't want to give in to George's bullying. The number of times he got me in trouble with Father over stupid little things that I'd done, like back-answering our tutor... I refused to give in."

"You know, I think he *must* have approached Father, threatening to make your affair public... Remember the day that Father delivered his ultimatum regarding us marrying? He said something *then* about dipping your wick in Berkeley Square..."

"Perhaps," said Darcy, "although I suppose word gets round anyway. It's a small world."

"And there is something else..." recalled Richard. "I was once was with Father when we encountered Wickham upon emerging from White's. He slunk off when Father glared at him, like the low-life he is, but I remember my father saying he would like to 'whip that fellow to within an inch of his life'. I thought it strange at the time—I was surprised that my father was even aware of Wickham's existence."

"It wouldn't have surprised me if George tried blackmailing the earl after he failed with me," sighed Darcy. "Then there was that doxy who kept running into me. She turned out to be an associate of George's..."

"Which doxy?"

"I believe her name was Mrs Younge. She introduced herself to me one day in Hatchard's, claiming to know my Aunt Catherine. For a while it seemed I couldn't move without encountering her. At first, I thought she was no different to the other young widows who occasionally intruded themselves to my notice, although she was remarkably persistent. But then I saw her with George in Green Park one day, and the penny dropped."

"Yes, he's certainly done his best to leech on you over the years."

"Unsuccessfully. He's done far better with rich widows. I thought he'd found his pot of gold when he took up with that Yarrow woman."

"Lord, she's as ugly as sin! But certainly *very* rich."

"Indeed, but I believe it must have ended. He wouldn't be trying this else."

The revelations on Wickham's character petered out and the cousins took to staring out their respective windows.

For Darcy, once the disclosures finished, the self-recriminations began as true anxiety set in. Why had he not informed Mrs Reynolds to specifically bar George from Pemberley? He had never dreamed George would ever return. He should have ordered George's effects to be packed up and given to the parish...

Darcy fidgeted with the signet on his hand. Why had Elizabeth not replied to his letter? Surely she would not succumb to Wickham's blandishments? Her letter to Jane claimed she found George annoying, but neither had she replied to Darcy's apology. She must surely be angry with him—racing off first to Yorkshire and then to London soon afterwards. Was he too late to set their marriage to rights? Darcy's stomach cramped with anxiety.

Sitting on the forward seat, Finn was not asleep as he appeared to be, but taking in all this new information. He had his own story of Mr Wickham, which he could not, of course, contribute. He was only glad that *he* had not succumbed to Mr Wickham's blandishments.

He remembered the incident all too well, occurring at that painful time in his life when Fred Mitcham, his love to end all loves, had spurned him and departed to work for the earl. Finn had lapsed into smoking again, as he occasionally did when he felt fragile, and always hated himself for it. He'd been puffing on a cigarillo at the base of the area steps late one evening, wearing a dustcoat to keep the smell off his clothes, when the most beautiful man he had ever met had peered over the railings from the street.

"Ah! There is nothing like the aroma of a good cigarillo!" the young man had declared, before asking if he could join him.

Finn had thought he might be dreaming, and wasn't sure if he had even replied. The fellow had let himself through the gate and settled on the step above him, before reaching out and gently taking the cigarillo from his hand. They had shared it 'til the stub burnt Finn's fingers, chatting about the different varieties of cigarillo to be had. All the while, Finn had stared at his companion's face, wondering that such beauty existed outside of a painting.

It was only when the young man got up to go that Finn noticed that the fashionable clothes he was wearing were slightly shabby and concluded he was some ganymede, discreetly departing one of the houses of the square under darkness.

The fellow held out his hand, and Finn clasped it. "I'm George," he said cheerily, before taking himself off. "Hope to see you again soon."

Mrs Flowers had pounced on him once he'd let himself back inside the house. "Mr Finn, do you have a moment?"

He'd hardly had time to divest himself of the dustcoat.

She had invited him into her office and then surprised him by shutting the door afterwards. That had made him sweat a little—the only woman Finn felt comfortable with in such close quarters was his mother.

"Mr Finn, situated as my office is, I couldn't help overhearing your conversation just now. Do you know that young man?"

"No, Mrs Flowers. I've never met him before. He said his name was George."

"That's right. George Wickham, and he is trouble."

She'd then gone on to summarise Mr Wickham's connection with the family, including Mrs Reynolds' suspicions of his preying on the chambermaids, plus some additional information she'd never told a soul and trusted he never would either—she'd overhead Mr Wickham trying to blackmail the master. She couldn't tell him more and would go to the grave with the secret, but Mr Wickham was *not* a man to be trusted.

Finn had thanked her politely, said he would be on his guard, and wandered off, sadly reflecting that he'd known George was too good to be true. But when he'd divested the master of his clothes before bed that night, he'd silently vowed that George Wickham would never get to the master through him. He'd die first.

Finn had avoided the area steps for the next month to discourage Mr Wickham's pretensions. He had next seen George three months later upon emerging from Manton's after his weekly shooting session there. As a gentleman's gentleman, Finn still kept to some of the pastimes of his youth—it reminded him of better days, before his father had left his mother penniless. After the old man had gone off, Finn had left school to go into service, and had regularly sent his entire wage back to his mother in Ireland. But once he'd started with Mr Darcy, there had been a little left over to amuse himself, and shooting his pistols had become one of his chief pleasures.

When they met again after the space of three months, Finn found his memory had not exaggerated George's good looks—he was as beautiful as ever and looking spruce in fine clothes, laughing with his companions. George hadn't even recognised Finn when they passed in the street. Clearly he had other fish to fry.

As Finn sat on the carriage seat, feigning sleep, his determination to protect his master reasserted itself. George had stepped across the line.

With Darcy's own team starting the journey from London, Harry drove for all he was worth. The coachman was unaware of their mission, but he knew something was wrong, and that the master was returning to Derbyshire with all haste. The Darcy carriage drove on into the night as far as Stoney Stratford where they reluctantly stopped at The Green Man. With only one coachman and no moonlight, they would likely come to grass before reaching Derbyshire if they tried to press on.

They were up before first light in the morning; and as the sky began to lighten, set off on the next stage. Richard and Finn fell back asleep, waking again when the morning sun poured into the carriage; but Darcy stared out the window, his face rigid with anxiety while his fingers twirled the pencil he had drawn from his pocket at a furious pace, as if he was turning the wheels of the carriage himself. His knee bounced up and down impatiently.

They travelled like the Mail, only stopping to change horses, relieve themselves and grab what food and drink they could from the boys who ran out into the yard. Despite their hectic pace, the day seemed to drag on forever. Richard's attempts to break the tension by starting conversations were met with stony silence by Darcy, and he gave up after his first few sallies.

Near sunset, they were approaching Matlock, and Darcy thought they might make Pemberley that night when a huge storm broke, and they were forced to take refuge at Wyvern Hall. They came within an inch of disaster coming up the drive when a gigantic tree branch came crashing down behind them, startling the horses and narrowly missing the carriage.

All night the storm raged and threatened to go on into the morning, but the thunder and lightening ceased just after dawn, giving way to a steady rain. Richard had gone out with some of the tenant farmers soon afterwards to clear the drive. Half an hour later they were off.

At Pemberley, Elizabeth had woken early due to her morning sickness and uncharacteristically shot her bolt before she could take her tea and biscuits. Jenny blamed the storm, which had given way to a light drizzle.

Feeling better on her empty stomach, Elizabeth had dressed and sat in front of the pier glass between the great windows while Jenny brushed her hair. Watching the sky outside lighten as the storm clouds parted, Elizabeth caught a glimpse of something white in her peripheral vision; but when she turned her attention to the formal garden below, nothing moved. She had ascribed the phenomenon to a passing bird, when, with only a peremptory knock, Mrs Reynolds burst into the room.

"Mrs Darcy," she huffed; "your pardon, but Miss Georgie is gone."

48 The bandbox

Lizzy had immediately concluded that she had glimpsed Georgiana's white dress disappearing through the folly and had run for her boots.

"Where is Mr Wickham?" she asked the housekeeper as she kicked her slippers off.

"Gone from his room, ma'am, and his carpet bag too!"

"Your hair, Mrs Darcy," protested Jenny, as she trailed after her mistress with the brush.

"A bonnet, Jenny!" returned Elizabeth, "immediately!"

"What do you intend, ma'am?" asked Mrs Reynolds, wringing her hands. "Should I send for the steward?"

"I think I just saw Georgie run through the folly, Reynolds," replied Elizabeth, pushing her feet into her boots. "Where does that lane behind the folly go?"

"The lane goes to Tideswell, ma'am. It joins the road to Manchester at Whaley Bridge."

Elizabeth's heart gave a lurch in her chest. *Manchester! Good Lord, if Georgie has gone with George, then his object is likely Gretna Green!*

She stood up, and taking the bonnet, jammed it onto her head over her unbound hair. Jenny gaped at her.

"My cloak, Jenny! Quickly!" said Elizabeth as she made for the door, tying the ribbons of her bonnet.

"Mrs Darcy!" said Mrs Reynolds, finally perceiving Elizabeth intended running after Georgie herself. "I'm sure the steward could be here in half an hour."

Her words fell on Elizabeth's heels. Grabbing her cloak, Elizabeth had fled down the servants' stairs that led directly to the garden.

Elizabeth flung the cloak around herself as she emerged from the house, not stopping to do up the fastenings but holding it together as she ran. As she fled across the formal garden, Elizabeth cursed herself for a simpleton—George had likely stopped bothering her because he had moved on to Georgie! She had not guessed it. Every time she had been present, George seemed to be merely teasing Georgie in a light-hearted condescending way, but he *had* started riding with her sister-in-law in the mornings. She thought they had been adequately chaperoned.

After Lizzy ran through the folly and around the pond, she came out onto the verge that bordered the lane. A post-chaise was waiting on the gravel, and a short distance from it, George and Georgie appeared to be arguing over a bandbox—its contents spilled on the ground.

"Fuck the bandbox, Georgie! I'll buy you a new bloody bonnet once we're married."

"But George! It's all I've got except the clothes I'm wearing!"

"Just get in the carriage, girl," he said, pushing her roughly towards it. "We need to go!"

Heaving a sigh of relief that she'd managed to intercept the pair, Lizzy ran towards them.

"Oh, Georgie!" she called across the intervening distance, "I'm so glad I caught up with you! You mustn't run off like this, you know. It's not at all the thing!"

George's head jerked up like a jack-in-the-box, and he glared at Georgie in an *I-told-you-so* kind of way.

"Oh, Lizzy," called Georgie over her shoulder, as George proceeded to frog-march her to the carriage, "I know! But Fitzwilliam is *so* unfair to George, we thought this would be best."

George wasn't about to be distracted by a female gabfest. Opening the door, he pushed Georgiana roughly inside; his movements punctuated by protesting squawks from the girl.

Elizabeth was a little disturbed by Georgie's speech; it was obvious that her sister was completely under Mr Wickham's thumb. Clearly, she was going to have to reason with George. She hurried onwards and had almost reached the carriage when George turned back towards her, pulling a pistol from his coat, but keeping it close to his body, so that it was hidden from Georgie in the coach.

"You shouldn't walk alone so early in the morning, you know, Mrs Darcy," he muttered through his teeth. "You might encounter desperate poachers."

Lizzy stopped short and looked at the gun in disbelief. It had not escaped her notice that she was no longer 'Elizabeth' but had reverted to 'Mrs Darcy'.

"Back off, or I'll shoot you on the spot," George said in a low voice, his face twisted into an expression of hatred; "and leave that wretch you call a husband, a widower. He has led such a blessed life, it would do him good to encounter some hardship."

This statement, combined with his expression, truly shocked Elizabeth. It revealed a whole new aspect of George that was much blacker than Mrs Reynolds had painted him, and a very deep antipathy towards Darcy. Quaking inside, Lizzy knew she had to make an effort to stop him. Persuasion was her only device.

"Don't be silly, George," replied Lizzy, more confidently than she felt. "Mrs Reynolds knows I've run after you. I don't believe you will pull that trigger—you'd swing from Tyburn if you ever did such a thing."

"Brave words, Mrs Darcy," said George, seeing she was not to be cowed; "But perhaps it would be better if you came along with us anyway. I can cause Fitz far more embarrassment this way. Fancy his wife abandoning him for a lover!"

When George turned back to the carriage, Georgiana, who had been watching this interchange from the carriage without catching all of George's words, finally saw the pistol and found her voice.

"George, what are you doing!?" she cried. "That pistol isn't loaded is it?"

"I thought I saw a rabbit," replied George conversationally, before continuing, "Your delightful sister-in-law has decided to lend us countenance;" whereupon he stepped round Elizabeth and motioned her into the carriage.

Elizabeth bit her lip in vexation. Why had she been so impetuous?

When the Darcy carriage arrived at Pemberley in a cloud of dust, Mrs Reynolds raced down the front steps wringing her hands.

"What has happened?" asked Darcy, turning pale. Behind Mrs Reynolds in the vestibule, he could see Mrs Annesley looking ten years older—her face a horrible shade of grey. Beside her, Jenny was crying.

"Oh, Master," said Mrs Reynolds, lowering her voice so the other servants could not hear, "Miss Georgiana has gone missing, and so has George Wickham, who was staying here."

Darcy drew his breath in through his teeth, his worst fears confirmed. "Where is my wife?" he demanded, disturbed she had not been the first to greet him.

"She ran after them!" hissed Mrs Reynolds. "I tried to stop her, sir, but she thought she could catch them."

"When did this happen?"

"Not an hour ago, sir!"

"And she has not returned? Why has no one searched for her?"

"Stevens went after her, sir. She ran through the folly, but he could not find her. I sent word to your steward, but he has not yet arrived."

"The folly?" repeated Darcy, before turning to Richard; "then they must have taken the back road."

Darcy rounded on Stevens, who had edged up upon catching his name. "You're supposed to accompany Mrs Darcy everywhere," he growled.

"Your pardon, sir," replied Stevens wretchedly, knowing he was going to lose his place after all these years; "but Mrs Darcy was off 'ere I knew what she was at, and she runs fast for a lady. I got there in time to see a carriage making off down the road, but she was gone. I found a band-box, sir, but left it to mark the spot."

"And you could not find Mrs Darcy?"

"She is gone, sir; in the carriage, I am sure, willy-nilly. Her footsteps go no further."

The colonel now whispered in Darcy's ear. "If George is aiming for Gretna, then they've likely taken the back road through Chapel and will join the main road at Whaley Bridge. He won't get a decent change of horses before Whaley Bridge."

Darcy nodded his understanding but felt sick to his stomach. *Had both his wife and his sister now abandoned him?*

"We need horses!" he cried at the grooms, who had run out to tend to the Darcy carriage. "Bring Ajax!"

Healy raced back to the stables to comply, while Richard retrieved his gauntlets, spurs and sword from his baggage.

Ajax and Miss Georgie's mare were soon brought around.

"Get up behind me, Stevens," cried Darcy, mounting his horse; "and show me the spot."

Darcy galloped off, with Stevens up behind, thundering round the house and through the formal garden, heedless of the box hedges. The colonel was hard on his heels.

Finn, meanwhile, who had been sitting on the forward seat of the carriage, climbed down and looked at Healy.

"Get the master's racing curricle, Healy!" he said.

"What for?" retorted Healy. "The master's gone off on his horse."

"We are going to use it," stated Finn calmly.

"I can't do that! The master will skin me."

"Do as I say, this instant!" said Finn, pulling rank.

After a moment's hesitation, Healy raced back to the stables.

Finn turned to the second footman who, in the absence of the guiding hand of Stevens, hovered in the vestibule, unsure whether he was meant to be invisible or not. "Come here, you looby, and help me with this trunk!" Finn said.

The footman raced to Finn's assistance, but the trunk Finn unloaded from the carriage belonged to himself, not the master. After setting it on the ground, Finn unlocked it and threw back the lid. Rummaging in the bottom of the trunk, he produced a large flat box of shagreen. This he handed reverently to the footman before trying to reverse somewhat the devastation he had wrought on his carefully folded clothes. He then locked his trunk, received the box back from the footman, and waited impatiently for Healy to return with the vehicle.

"Take the trunks inside," he gestured imperiously at the footman, who was watching all these strange goings on in a kind of stupor.

The under-footmen were summoned, and the carriage was duly being unloaded when Healy reappeared driving the curricle with four horses harnessed.

Finn climbed in with some misgivings. "I thought these things were meant to be drawn by two horses," he said, as they set off down the drive.

"They go faster with four," Healy replied, concentrating on the first switchback.

"Are you sure you know how to drive this thing with four?" asked Finn as they went round with inches to spare.

Healy, who was highly affronted by Finn's lack of confidence in him, ignored this remark.

Realising his faux pas, Finn continued: "Have you any idea where this Wickham would go?"

"Why, yes," said Healy, who was sharp-eared enough to have caught what the colonel had whispered to Darcy. "The only decent road to Gretna from here goes through Manchester. It's about 170 miles."

"Why are we going this way?"

"If they're headed for Whaley Bridge, we'll go faster on the good road. It becomes the post road after Buxton."

"Do you think we can catch them with an hour's start?"

"Of course!" cried Healy.

As they reached the crest of the hill, Healy flicked the ribbons and the horses set off at a spanking pace. He cracked the whip to wind them up down the straight.

"What's that, then?" Healy asked, flicking his eyes to the shagreen box on Finn's lap.

"My duelling pistols," replied Finn.

When Richard and Darcy arrived at the lane, Stevens got down to point out the carriage tracks and trampled grass.

The colonel, meanwhile, had dismounted to examine the bandbox.

"We don't need to know how many bonnets she's missing, Richard," said Darcy sarcastically, as Ajax cavorted, impatient to keep going.

"Well, hopefully not many," said Richard coolly, as he remounted his horse, "cause she left her money behind."

Darcy's eyes widened as he watched Richard toss a red purse in one hand.

"I wonder how much money Wickham has in his pocket," Darcy speculated.

"Hopefully not much," replied Richard. "Wouldn't it be wonderful if he got stranded at Whaley Bridge?"

They looked at each other meaningfully and then spurred their horses into action.

Stopping occasionally to ask farmhands if they'd seen a post-chaise, Richard soon learnt that George had hired only two post horses. It was obvious to his pursuers that Wickham had expected to get clean away. Indeed, George believed he had intercepted all mail between Derbyshire and London, and was completely unaware that Elizabeth's aunt had kindly offered to carry a letter for Jane to the receiving office after her visit four days ago.

As they continued their pursuit, the cousins thought they glimpsed the yellow body of the coach in the distance once or twice as they came down past Tisda, but mostly they had to rely on report to judge the closing distance to their quarry.

Upon reaching Whaley Bridge, they discovered that George had indeed been delayed there—the carriage had departed not five minutes before, with four horses harnessed. Given the length of the delay, the cousins thought it likely that George had been obliged to sell something to pay for the change.

As she watched Pemberley disappear into the distance, Elizabeth could not help thinking bitterly of how grossly she had erred in her handling of Mr Wickham. Chief among her regrets was not chaperoning Georgie more assiduously; and in particular, she begrudged the time she had spent with Mr Bletchley and the telescope, when she should have been safeguarding his sister-in-law from the perfidious Mr Wickham. She tried to put these useless recriminations aside in favour of thinking of a way to thwart George's plans.

Turning towards the couple on the forward-facing seat, she watched as George clasped Georgie's hand and smiled at her, magically transforming from the devil who had bundled Elizabeth into the carriage into an adoring gentleman. Georgie smiled back at him guilelessly. Wickham's pistol had disappeared, presumably into the offside pocket of his greatcoat.

"Mr Wickham, perhaps it would be better if you sat on the forward seat. We may encounter friends of the family during our journey," suggested Elizabeth.

George rolled his eyes but grudgingly swapped places. Georgie smiled in apology at George but accepted the rearrangement with equanimity.

Elizabeth first thought of how she might escape the carriage at a posting stop, but she quickly realized she could not abandon Georgie; and unless George left them alone, she would likely have trouble convincing her sister to give up the elopement. Other schemes, like bribing the post-boys with her non-existent money, or objecting at the ceremony over the anvil flitted through her head—all of them desperate and unlikely to succeed.

In the end, Elizabeth decided the best plan was to remain vigilant and hope that some situation might arise, through opportunity or a mistake on Mr Wickham's part, which would allow her to foil his scheme. For the moment it would be better to pretend compliance.

Elizabeth's first ray of hope came when she discovered that Mr Wickham was not in funds. There'd been hell to pay just before Whaley Bridge when George discovered Georgie had no money, having left her purse in the abandoned bandbox.

"Why the hell don't you have a pocket?" he spat.

"But George, Mrs Annesley says they spoil the line of a dress!"

Elizabeth might have found the combination of George's vulgar tongue and Georgie's polite fastidiousness deeply amusing, if she wasn't thinking furiously of how she might contrive to turn the situation to her advantage. She, of course, had no inkling that her husband and cousin were racing to her succour, thinking them still in London.

But George was not to be thwarted by a lack of cash. Used to the exigencies of paying gambling debts, he knew the location of every pawnbroker between Derbyshire and London. George directed the post-boy to an establishment in the direction of Taxal where he hocked the buckles on Georgie's shoes. He was obliged to force Mrs Darcy to accompany him into the dealer's premises, lest she be up to some mischief in the carriage; but funds were duly obtained at the cost of a twenty-minute delay.

Elizabeth felt frustrated when she arrived back at the carriage, having been unable to think of anything to thwart Mr Wickham during their unscheduled stop. But unbeknownst to her, the delay had been sufficient to close the narrowing gap between the post-chaise and the two independent pursuits.

George was more worried that the abduction of Elizabeth might have precipitated a pursuit by Darcy's steward. So when they finally arrived at the posting house, he ordered four horses to be harnessed for the next stage. Of course, Mrs Darcy *might* have been lying about telling the servants of her whereabouts, but George thought it would be better to make all haste, at least as far as Manchester, where he could go to ground if necessary. It might be safer to compromise Georgie before he got to the border.

Arriving at the posting house soon after the post-chaise departed, the colonel was forced to change his horse—Georgie's mare not being up to his weight over such a long distance; but Ajax was holding up and they were soon off again. Fifteen minutes out of Whaley Bridge, the gentlemen, now galloping, caught up with the carriage.

Healy and Finn, whose route on the post road had merged with their quarry's at Whaley Bridge, were not much farther behind. They watched as the colonel put on a burst of speed and drawing his sword, yelled, "Halt in the name of the King!" at the post-boys.

The post-boys, perceiving the colonel's white gauntlets and seeing a flash of his resplendent uniform beneath his roquelaure, immediately drew rein.

"Drive on dammit!" yelled George in defiance at the boys as the post-chaise slowed. Pulling a pistol from his pocket, he let down one of the nearside windows and took aim at the colonel as Richard grabbed for the nearside leader's bit.

Elizabeth, unwilling to have her relative fired upon with impunity, threw herself against George, a little late, but sufficient to disturb his aim as the pistol discharged.

The shot threw up dust near the hooves of the colonel's mount, causing the horse to start and rear. But the colonel, who was a veteran of the Penisular campaign, was not to be dislodged from his saddle by such a trifle.

Having come up behind the contretemps, Finn had indicated to Healy to pull up behind a tree on the verge, a good fifty yards behind the postchaise. Retrieving his pistols, he jumped down and ran along the ditch on the roadside towards the chaise.

Upon seeing his wife struggling with George, Darcy dismounted as the carriage drew to a halt and ran towards the nearside door to defend Elizabeth, while Finn ran towards the offside door.

George pushed back savagely at Elizabeth for her interference, and already off balance, she twisted and fell. Catching her head on the brass door handle, she slumped to the floor of the carriage. Wickham grabbed his second pistol, and would have aimed again at the colonel, had not Darcy called to him:

"George! What are you doing? You do not honestly think you will get away with this do you?"

Wickham swung round, intent now on the man his mentor, Mr Darcy, had encouraged him to think of as a brother. He raised his gun.

As the barrel of the pistol came level with his chest, Darcy looked into George's eyes and saw something barely human there. He knew in an instant he had miscalculated in calling George's attention to himself and would pay with his life. In a fraction of a second that seemed to spin out to infinity, a profound stab of regret gripped him. He was not ready to meet his maker—there was a sense of unfinished business. His wife might be pregnant with his heir, but his overwhelming feeling was that he had made a mess of things. He, who had always believed himself so competent, would go to the grave amid scandal, a blot on the Darcy lineage who could, at best, be forgotten by the family—the brother who had failed to protect his sister; the husband who had neglected his wife; the heir who had died shortly after coming into his patrimony; the father who never lived to see his child. The one wish that flitted through Darcy's mind was that he could tell his wife and sister how sorry he was.

In the same instant, Finn reached the offside door of the carriage and taking one step to the left to keep his master out of his line of fire, he raised his pistol, reached past Georgiana, and fired through the open window of the carriage.

George jerked upwards and fell on top of Elizabeth.

A deathly silence followed the deafening report of the pistol inside the closed space of the cabin. The carriage jobbed forwards as the postilions fought to control the spooked horses. Finn wrenched at the door handle of the offside door with his left hand, but it was stuck fast.

Finally reaching the nearside door, Darcy opened it to stare in horror at the bodies on the floor, before directing his gaze at Georgiana who had squeezed herself tightly into the far corner of the carriage with her legs drawn up on the seat, too terrified to scream.

The colonel arrived a fraction of a second later. Bumping his cousin out of the way with his shoulder, he wrenched the door fully open. Seeing George had been hit in the shoulder, Richard grabbed him by the heels of his boots and pulled him out of the carriage, eliciting a shriek of pain from Wickham when his injured shoulder caught on the door. The shriek quickly turned to the squeal of a stuck pig when Richard twisted George's body unceremoniously to free him of the carriage; and ended in a grunt when Wickham hit the dirt, knocking the wind out of him.

Darcy threw himself into the space vacated by Wickham to see Elizabeth sprawled on the floor of the carriage, spattered in blood. Crawling over her, his heart skipped a beat as he searched for her pulse.

Having determined she was yet alive, he discovered with relief that the large amount of blood on her gown did not appear to be her own, but Wickham's. Releasing his breath, he turned his attention to her face, but her bloodless blue lips sent a chill down his spine.

"Elizabeth, Elizabeth!" he called.

His wife lay silent and unresponsive. It was then he noticed the tiny amount of blood at her temple. Pushing his hand into her hair, he was horrified when he withdrew his fingers bloodied.

"What is the matter?" asked the colonel, who had relinquished the unconscious Wickham to Finn and was peering over Darcy's shoulder. "Is she injured?"

"Her head," whispered Darcy, fighting to hold back tears.

The colonel stepped over Darcy into the carriage and lay along the carriage seat to reach Elizabeth.

He noted the blood on Darcy's hand, the dark mark forming near Elizabeth's temple, and gently prised open her eyelids, one at a time.

"We must get a doctor," he said. "At the very least she has a concussion."

Richard looked at Georgie. "What happened? Did Wickham hit her?"

"He pushed her," said Georgie. "She fell. I think her head hit the door-handle."

The colonel fingered the edges on the door-handle and grimaced.

With some difficulty, they extracted Elizabeth from the carriage and laid her on the floor of the curricle, which Healy walked carefully to a nearby inn.

49 The inn

The proprietors of the Blue Boar listened in some incredulity to the tale Richard spun about Wickham accidentally shooting himself when he tried to plug a bird from the carriage. The lady had apparently hit her head upon the door handle of the carriage when the horses jobbed at the report. But they opened up the two poor rooms the inn boasted for the injured lady and gentleman when Darcy silently handed them two golden guineas.

His 'young cousin', the colonel went on to relate of Wickham, had just received news of the sudden loss of his mother, and they were journeying to Manchester to arrange her funeral. As they had been riding outside the carriage, they had no idea their cousin had been drinking until he had pulled one of the carriage pistols from its holster upon seeing a large bird. He really was in a bad way, having taken his mother's loss very hard.

"I heard two shots not one," muttered the wife to her husband, as she set more water on to boil in the kitchen.

"You just busy yourself with some clean rags like the colonel asked you, Hannah," adjured her husband as he stoked the fire. "The tall gentleman in black is Mr Darcy of Pemberley, and if he says half a dozen shots were one, then they were."

One of the post-boys had volunteered to ride back to Whaley Bridge to fetch the gentry-doctor upon being apprised of the injuries to the lady and gentleman. He had his horse out of its traces in a matter of a minute and set off with another of Darcy's guineas in his pocket.

When the post-boy returned with the doctor in tow an hour later, Darcy insisted he see the unconscious Elizabeth first, although Richard knew there was little the physician could do for her.

"Her pulse is weak, which is worrying. Her eyes do not respond properly to light," said the doctor. "She has an injury to her brain; but how serious it is, there is no way of knowing. She must be kept still in bed until she wakes."

"How long will that be?" asked Darcy anxiously, holding the hand of his unconscious wife.

"It could be hours, or weeks," said the doctor, uncomfortably aware that it could also be never.

Wickham, who had regained consciousness shortly after being deposited on the bed, had gladly accepted brandy from the colonel's hip flask to dull the pain, prior to the colonel packing the wound in his shoulder. George could only wonder at Richard's solicitude after the rough treatment he had received at his hands. He supposed it was the closest he was likely to get to an apology. More alcohol was appropriated from the taproom once the flask was exhausted, though of a significantly lower quality.

In fact, it had been Richard's aim to get Wickham suitably drunk by the time the doctor arrived to lend credence to his drunken cousin-bird story. For the moment, the colonel was thinking of proprieties and would deal with Wickham later.

On attending George, the doctor complimented the colonel on his skilful packing of the wound as he prepared to extract the ball. Despite his inebriated state, Wickham was a poor patient, who had to be held down during this operation—Richard at his head, and Finn at his feet.

"He is a very lucky man," said the doctor, when George finally passed out, dosed heavily with laudanum. "The ball barely missed the axillary artery..."

Finn, who had withstood the gore of the operation stoically, paled at this. Shooting wafers at Manton's was one thing, but shooting people was quite something else. Based on a theoretical knowledge of duelling, he'd aimed for a non-lethal shot to the shoulder. He wasn't sure he would have the courage to do it again after seeing the results.

"...but he should pull through," concluded the doctor.

"Pity," muttered the colonel under his breath.

The doctor had then gone off to attend a yeoman with a broken leg, who had been awaiting his pleasure all the while; assuring his noble clients he would return in the morning to check on the lady and gentleman.

After the colonel departed briefly to check on Darcy, Finn picked up the ruined clothes cut from George's upper body—a once beautiful coat and waistcoat. The doctor had slit them down one side when George had been unable to tolerate them being removed in a more conventional manner. Finn's valet-sensibilities rued the destruction of such beautiful garments—clothes that were much finer than anything he had ever possessed. The waistcoat was embroidered in autumn colours, and Mr Wickham had teamed it with a green tailcoat that matched one of the threads. To Finn's mind, the ensemble perfectly blended the sumptuousness of the fashions of yesteryear with the clean lines of the clothes popularised by Mr Brummel. Mr Finn could certainly not fault Mr Wickham's taste in clothes. Tracing the beautiful embroidery of the French waistcoat with his fingers, he felt something in the lining. Turning the garment inside out, he discovered a letter in an inner pocket. It was in the master's handwriting, directed to Mrs Darcy, leaving Finn to wonder how it came to be in Mr Wickham's possession. Flipping it over, he was further perturbed to see that it had been unsealed.

When the colonel returned shortly after, Finn handed the letter over. "I found this in Mr Wickham's pocket, sir. It is unsealed, but I assure you I have not read it."

Taking the proffered letter, the colonel raised his eyebrows slightly upon recognising the significance of it. "Ah!" he said, "was there any other correspondence?"

"Not that I noticed, sir," replied Finn. "I happened upon that in a inner pocket of his waistcoat when I was folding it."

"Very well. Thank you, Finn. If you could watch Mr Wickham 'til dinner, I'll take over afterwards. Please search the remainder of Mr Wickham's effects. He has a tendency to be light-fingered."

"Yes, sir."

Upon leaving the room, Richard's first impulse was to return the letter directly to Darcy, but having just poked his head into Elizabeth's room where Darcy waited anxiously, he thought better of it. Taking the letter to a window on the stair, he unfolded it and began to read. He was touched by his cousin's sentiments and so relieved that he appeared to have finally moved on from Diana. Anger towards Wickham, however, was his chief sentiment on refolding the letter. *How dare George try to come between Fitzwilliam and his wife!* Richard stood by the window, thinking for some time.

Meanwhile, Darcy and Georgiana were maintaining a bedside vigil for the unconscious Elizabeth. Georgie sat miserably in the room's sole chair while her brother knelt at his wife's beside, his head collapsed on his left arm, while his right hand clasped that of his inanimate wife. When the innkeeper's wife intruded to suggest Georgie lie down on a cot she had prepared in her own bedchamber, Georgie made no demur. With a silent glance at her despondent brother, she took herself off.

Georgie was, of course, feeling terrible. She descried her lack of judgement in not immediately discerning George to be the evil man that he had clearly shown himself to be as soon as he had suggested they elope— she knew it had been wrong, but his arguments had seemed so convincing. Worse still, despite his behaviour to both herself and Elizabeth during the entire farrago, she realised she had been making excuses for him right up until the moment he had shot at Cousin Richard. In short, she had behaved like a ninny and almost got her brother, his wife and her cousin killed. Would Fitzwilliam ever forgive her?

Finding himself alone with his wife, Darcy closed the door and crawled onto the narrow bed beside Elizabeth. Suddenly, she who had seemed the picture of health—walking three miles to tend her sister at Netherfield, climbing the ha-ha—seemed now so fragile, and it was all his fault. He clasped her to him, comforted by her warmth and thinking she could not slip from life if he held her close. Occasionally he felt her pulse but it remained weak.

Several hours passed in a blur. Darcy lost all sense of time despite putting his pocket watch, propped open, on the bedside table. He occasionally referred to it, telling himself she must wake soon. Sometimes when it seemed like an hour had passed, it was only five minutes since he'd last looked at it. Another time, he thought fifteen minutes had gone by, but the watch declared it to be an hour. He got up on the hour to rinse out the rag on Elizabeth's head, soaking it again in the bowl of vinegar left by the landlady, before laying it across her brow.

When the room dimmed, Darcy lit the tallow candle on the bedside table before taking off his boots and crawling back beside Elizabeth. Finally there was a knock at the door, and Richard stepped in to tell him dinner was ready.

"I'm not eating 'til she wakes," returned Darcy.

Richard grimaced, but nodded silently. He would argue with Darcy tomorrow if he continued his fast. Closing the door softly, he escorted a wan Georgie down to the coffee room.

While Richard ate, Georgie only picked at her food silently.

"Why are you sad?" asked Richard suddenly.

Georgie gaped at him in amazement.

"Well?" prompted Richard.

"Elizabeth is hurt badly, and it is all my fault! What if she doesn't recover? I will have killed my brother's wife and ruined any chance of Fitz's happiness. I could never forgive myself!"

"And what of Wickham?"

"What of him?" Georgiana spat. "I never want to see him again! How could he attempt to kill you and Fitzwilliam! You three were childhood friends! I thought we could all be happy together, but he is quite mad!"

"Yes," said Richard, "fit to be tied. We may yet have to commit him to Bedlam to ensure he doesn't bother you and Fitz again." Privately Richard thought Wickham was fit to be hanged.

"I certainly wouldn't go anywhere with him again, Richard," assured Georgie.

"Unfortunately, Georgie, this is only one of a series of schemes by which Wickham has tried to leech money out of your brother…"

"Oh," said Georgie, who had already begun to wonder if George's motives had been mercenary. Her fragile womanly confidence promptly crumbled to dust, leaving her feeling very much a green girl.

Richard proceeded to relate a sanitised version of Wickham's lifestyle during the years he had been missing. Georgie was quite shocked to discover George had abandoned his studies in law quite long ago and had never worked in that profession, particularly given the confident way he had spoken of it. Clearly, George had made that all up.

Afterwards, Richard had given his cousin a hug and escorted her upstairs to her cot. Georgie didn't much fancy sleeping in the same room as the proprietress of the inn, but in the circumstances, she didn't think it politic to complain.

After seeing his cousin to the door of her bedchamber, Richard returned to Finn and encouraged him to go downstairs for dinner.

"Then get some sleep, Finn, while I watch over Wickham. Come back at two in the morning, so I can catch some sleep myself."

An hour after Finn left, Wickham stirred.

"Oh, so you are babysitting, are you?" he sneered at Richard upon perceiving him in the dim light afforded by the single tallow candle. "I thought Darcy's valet got to do all the dirty work."

"I must admit that Darcy has a priceless valet, but if he hadn't taken you down, someone else would have," replied the colonel equably.

"Oh, yes?" Wickham scoffed. "You and your regiment, perhaps? A fat lot of good your swords will do you! What a bunch of sissies you are!"

"I hadn't realised you'd taken to pistols George, although you did like to brandish your toy one when we played pirates."

"Yes, well some of us grew up and had to make our way in the world."

"You've been making your way in the world under a series of petticoats," retorted Richard.

"You should talk! Prancing round the edge of the battlefield! Life Guards don't go anywhere near the real action!"

"I believe I recently spent some time in the Peninsula. Perhaps I was dreaming," replied the colonel.

There was a silence as they regarded each other balefully.

"So what prompted you to turn up?" asked George, curious to know of the flaw in his plan.

"Don't you ever read newspapers, George? My father died. Thought you'd take advantage of his illness, did you? Thought Darcy tied by the heels in London?"

"I never let a chance go by," replied George in an offhand manner. "So the old earl is dead, is he? Well, he was a better man than you or Robert will ever be."

"I cannot deny it," returned Richard calmly.

"He had real spunk!" declared George, warming to his theme. "He was worthy of the Fitzwilliam name! Whereas you two are as colourless as your mother! The Hansfords were always dull as dishwater and only ever got ahead by playing lickspittle to the King! Everybody says so!"

The colonel refused to rise to the bait. "So what are your plans, George? Your incursions upon Darcy cannot continue. I will not allow it."

"Big words! Darcy owes me and you know it!"

"Hmm," returned the colonel, considering this statement for a while before finally looking up. "Well, the doctor has asked me to change your bandages once more," he said, ringing for the chambermaid; "so I suppose we should get it over and done with now."

"At least, you're a decent nurse," sneered George, casting what he should have been grateful for as a slight. "Though this bandage is damn tight!"

"Yes, I fancy I saved a few lives over the years. More men die after the battle than during it," the colonel observed philosophically.

The chambermaid arrived with the hot water and rags, blushing at the handsome man's dishabille. She had turned to leave when the colonel called her back.

"Stay and assist me, will you?" he asked.

She nodded and smiled at George. He leered back.

"Ouch! What the hell are you doing?" he demanded as a sharp pain lanced from his wound.

"Now, who's the sissy?" replied the colonel, slipping his hand into his pocket. "I barely touched you."

The wound was cleaned and bound up again.

"It feels looser than before," George complained.

"Weren't you just complaining it was too tight?" remarked the colonel. "Do you want some more laudanum?"

"Yes, if it will help me sleep. I'm damned uncomfortable," whinged George.

The colonel thanked the maid for her services and poured out the draft.

George soon nodded off and sometime after midnight the colonel also fell asleep in his chair. He was roused at two when Finn arrived to take his watch. Getting up to meet him at the door, Richard was surprised to see that the valet was accompanied by Darcy's groom, Healy.

Richard stepped outside the bedchamber and closed the door.

"Is there a problem?" he asked, viewing the pair.

"I've come to take Finn's watch for him," explained Healy. "I'm plenty rested."

"That's not necessary, Healy," interjected Finn. "The colonel asked me to take the watch."

"No, no," said Richard, considering. "Healy will do. I merely forgot there were four of us. Finn can take over after breakfast. We won't be going anywhere 'til the doctor has cleared Mrs Darcy to travel. Better to share the burden of watching Wickham. I don't want him to escape. I believe Darcy will bring charges against him."

Richard, in fact, thought nothing of the sort, since he knew Georgie's reputation could only be tarnished by such an action, but he retired for the night to a cot set up in the coffee room, sanguine.

He was woken at seven when Healy burst into the room.

"Colonel, you'd better come quick! Mr Wickham's dead."

50 Karma

The colonel raced up the stairs behind Healy to find Finn had already drawn the sheet over Wickham's head.

Richard pulled back the cloth to gaze on his childhood friend once more. George looked like some pale angel—his face deadly white and his lips bloodless. The bandage round George's shoulder was soaked with blood.

"It looks like he bled to death during the night," said the colonel calmly.

"I suppose I will have to stand my trial," said Finn, looking almost as pale as George.

"No, Finn. We will stick to our story. The post-boys did not see you fire. They merely saw Wickham fire at me, and I have explained that was an accident. As far as the doctor knows, Wickham shot himself accidentally while trying to shoot birds. If anyone is at fault here, it is myself for not fastening the bandage sufficiently tightly. He was complaining that it was too tight. It will be death by misadventure. Do not touch him until the doctor arrives."

"Yes, sir."

Richard knocked on the door of the Darcys' bedchamber, intending to apprise his cousin of the situation before the physician called. He was a little perturbed when no answer was forthcoming. Cautiously, he opened the door to see his cousin lying alongside his wife—Elizabeth underneath the covers and Darcy, squeezed beside her on the narrow bed, lying atop them. They were both still wearing their clothes. The physician had suggested that Elizabeth be moved as little as possible, and merely bade the proprietress loosen her stays. Darcy had likely kept his clothes on in sympathy, though he had finally taken his boots off. As Richard watched, Elizabeth's eyelids fluttered open. She stared at him uncomprehendingly for a moment.

"Colonel Fitzwilliam..." she said, confused and unable to recognize her surroundings. "Where am I?"

"What is the last thing you remember, Cousin Elizabeth?" said Richard, approaching the bed and crouching.

Elizabeth paused, remembering brushing her hair after the storm, pulling on her boots, anxiety... "Running after Georgiana. Wickham had a pistol, and he forced me into the carriage... What happened?"

This conversation was enough to rouse Darcy, who propped himself up beside Elizabeth and leant over to kiss her forehead. "Thank God," he murmured.

Suppressing a puckish smile, Richard turned his attention back to Elizabeth: "We left London soon after the earl's funeral when Jane apprised us that George Wickham was at Pemberley. We missed you by about an hour and set off immediately in pursuit, catching up with the post-chaise just past Whaley Bridge. You fell and hit your head when we stopped the carriage."

"How stupid of me! Have I been insensible long?" she asked.

"For the best part of a day. We took you to the nearest inn and called the doctor. He should be here again soon to check on your progress. He will be very glad that you are awake. You had us all worried."

Elizabeth attempted to sit up, but upon shifting her head, groaned.

"Oh dear! I fear I'm getting a splitting headache!"

"Best to stay lying down," advised the colonel, "at least until the doctor has seen you."

Darcy slid from the small space between the wall and Elizabeth, jumping up to wet the cloth again with vinegar, then laying it across Elizabeth's brow.

After a small knock, the door opened to admit Georgie.

"Oh, you are awake!" she cried, "I'm so glad you're all right!"

"Softly, softly, Georgie," cautioned Richard. "Cousin Elizabeth has a headache. Can you sit with her for a while?"

Darcy would have protested, but Richard indicated discreetly he wished to talk to him outside.

After closing the door on the ladies, they walked a few steps away before Richard whispered, "Wickham died in the night."

Darcy was speechless for a moment before uttering, "God help me. I cannot be sorry."

The doctor was pleased to find Elizabeth awake, but unsurprised by her headache, for which he'd had the forethought to bring powders. He cautioned she should not be moved until her headache had resolved without the benefit of any medicine, if at all possible, to which advice Darcy acceded his willingness to abide.

On being led to his second patient, the physician was quite shocked to discover George had passed away during the night. Examining his body, the doctor declared the artery must have been compromised after all. Secretly, he was rather worried he might have nicked the vessel inadvertently when digging out the pellet.

"Had he bled much when you changed the dressings?" he asked the colonel.

"No, it was around nine when I changed them, was it not?" Richard asked the chambermaid, whom he had asked to attend lest the doctor needed to ask her any questions.

"Yes, sir. He was fine then, though a bit grumpy."

"He was complaining that the bandage was too tight, and against my better judgement, I loosened it. You would think that I, with my years in the Peninsula, would know better; but as you said, he seemed fine. I sat with him until two, when Healy took over."

"And he was alive then?" asked the doctor.

"Yes, snoring," replied the colonel, "as I'd given him the largest dose of laudanum you recommended, complaining of the pain as he was."

"It's all my fault!" said Healy, who had stepped quietly into the room with Finn. "I noticed when he stopped snoring, but was only glad he'd ceased making such a racket. The tallow candle had burnt down, and the landlady hadn't left another, so I didn't notice he was gone 'til dawn."

"Do not be too hard on yourself, Healy," replied the colonel. "This whole debacle was completely unnecessary, and it is George who has been the chief architect of his own demise. I'm only glad his mother was not alive to see it."

The doctor was only too glad that nobody was blaming him, which was too often the case, even when he had moved heaven and earth to save the patient. After writing out the death certificate, he instructed the chambermaid on how to lay out the body before expressing his condolences and bidding the colonel good day. He promised to return in the afternoon to check on Mrs Darcy.

After giving Healy an encouraging slap on the back and telling him not to take the misfortune to heart, Richard once more summoned Darcy from his room to discuss the funeral arrangements.

"I suppose we ought to bury him at Pemberley next to his father," replied Darcy.

"We ought to bury him at the crossroads," retorted Richard; "but I suppose I'd be satisfied to get him underground anywhere. Have you told Georgie?"

"No."

"Then let me do it. Has she had breakfast?"

"No."

"I'll take her down to the coffee room. Shall I get them to send up a tray?"

"Elizabeth's fallen back asleep," replied Darcy.

"I'll send one up anyway," declared the colonel.

Returning to his wife, Darcy had sent Georgie off and sat next to Elizabeth in the dim room—the landlady having hung an oilcloth across the window in deference to Elizabeth's headache.

"What has happened?" came her voice out of the gloom.

Believing his wife to have been asleep, Darcy gave an involuntary start. "Nothing!" he blurted before thinking.

"There is something you are not telling me," declared Elizabeth quietly.

"I beg your pardon. I was merely worried for your sensibilities and your head," apologized Darcy. "Unfortunately, Richard gave you the abbreviated version of what occurred yesterday. I'm afraid that Wickham is dead."

Elizabeth suppressed a gasp. "But how?"

"The story we have retailed is that he shot himself while drunk, trying to shoot a bird. He died last night of his wound."

"How terrible! Did you... Was there a duel?"

"No. It was all over in a flash—literally," replied Darcy. "Wickham tried to shoot Richard when he pulled over the carriage. You tussled with him and were knocked senseless as a result."

"Well, thank goodness for that," joked Elizabeth. 'I thought you were going to say that *I* shot him."

Darcy's eyes widened in surprise.

"Was that joke in poor taste?" asked Elizabeth. "You must excuse me, I've been knocked on the head! Obviously, I am not to know *who* shot Mr Wickham!"

"I'll tell you when we get home," assured Darcy. "For the moment, the doctor has recorded misadventure, which should avoid an inquest. Given Georgiana's involvement, I'm keen that it stay that way."

"I see. So if the sheriff does turn up, I can honestly say I was knocked stupid," replied Elizabeth.

"Yes," replied Darcy.

"Perhaps I was stupid before I was knocked," replied Elizabeth sadly. "I'm so sorry, Fitzwilliam. George was bothering me, but I had no idea he'd moved on to Georgie. He started riding with her in the mornings, but they were chaperoned by both Mrs Annesley and Healy."

"Do not blame yourself, my dear," returned Fitzwilliam. "The error is chiefly my own—I knew what a blackguard George was, but I never thought to ban him from Pemberley. It never occurred to me that he would have the effrontery to ever turn up there. I have been totally remiss in exposing you and Georgie to his machinations."

"It seems that Mr Wickham was way too clever for all of us," said Elizabeth sadly. "Have you spoken to Georgie?"

"No. Richard said he would advise her of George's death over breakfast."

"I meant with regard to what did or did not occur before the elopement," explained Elizabeth.

Darcy paled. Having stopped the carriage before nightfall, it had not occurred to him that he might yet be too late. His silence spoke volumes.

"Perhaps you'd better send her to me after breakfast," advised Elizabeth.

"My dear, I would not like to impose upon you in your current state. The doctor is returning this afternoon; perhaps he...?"

"Goodness, no!" replied Elizabeth. "If George hasn't managed to get under her skirts, you certainly don't want the doctor there. Think of her sensibilities."

A knock at the door saved Darcy from having to reply to this sally, and when the proprietress entered with a tray, he managed a lame, "thank you" to his wife.

The landlady had brought up fresh baked scones with jam and cream, and a pot of tea, which she deposited gingerly on the side table. She then removed the oilcloth from the window so they could 'see what they were about' before going off.

Elizabeth thought the scones looked delicious and was glad her morning sickness wasn't plaguing her. She managed to eat two, while Darcy polished off half-a-dozen and still felt ravenous, thinking wistfully of ham and eggs.

After Darcy had replaced the oilcloth on the window, Elizabeth gratefully lay down again, while Darcy settled into the chair.

"Oh, and by the way," he said as an afterthought, "The story is that George was our cousin. We were all travelling to Manchester to attend George's mother's funeral. You and Georgie had gone ahead with George. I was delayed with Richard at Pemberley on unexpected business with my steward."

"Very well," said Elizabeth, gratefully closing her eyes once more.

Richard had waited 'til Georgie finished her tea and scones before divulging news of George's death. Her reaction spoke volumes regarding the depth of Georgie's tendre for George and left Richard wondering whether anyone would have ever been so upset at news of his own demise on some foreign battlefield. Richard spent the next hour calming a hiccupping Georgie as she poured out the story of her girlish adoration for George, which had developed during his end of term visits to Pemberley prior to her father's death. Her youthful admiration for George's handsome person had developed into full-blown infatuation when George had noticed her sufficiently to talk to her in the garden once or twice.

With some gentle questions, Richard discovered that George's courtship of Georgie had consisted of nothing more than quoting some bad poetry and picking a few flowers for her during their rides together. As one of her guardians, this news provided him with significant relief, and he spent a good half-hour petting and coddling Georgie before suggesting she help care for her sister-in-law.

After a quick discussion with Darcy, Richard set off with Healy for Whaley Bridge to engage the services of the local parson and an undertaker for George. Although the post-boys had taken the nag he had hired back to Whaley Bridge, he still needed to retrieve Georgie's mare.

Meanwhile, Finn had gone through Wickham's carpetbag and discovered the colonel's suspicions were entirely founded. Hidden between George's accoutrements, which included a cosmetic case that would have been the envy of any actor, Finn discovered the master's silver standish, letter knife, and several items of cutlery that Mrs Reynolds was no doubt missing.

Finn had been shooed out of Wickham's bedchamber by the

proprietress of the inn, who insisted that the washing and laying out of George's body was women's work, but they allowed him to return to attire the body for burial. This they accomplished together, and with the combination of George's elegant clothes and his cosmetics, Finn achieved something approaching perfection.

When Finn retired from the room upon perceiving Healy drive up to the inn with the parson in the curricle, the two women paused briefly to contemplate George.

"Lor', what a shame!" declared the chambermaid.

Hannah could only concur. "Foolish young man!" she said sorrowfully.

Then she draped an oilcloth over the window, lit a candle, and withdrew to let the parson do his work.

The undertaker had taken Wickham's body off to Whaley Bridge after lunch, allowing Finn to prepare the bedchamber for occupation by the master and the colonel in the evening. The landlady had slit the mattress in the yard, pulling out around half of the kapok to stuff into the new ticking she'd sewn. The rest of the mattress would have to be burnt. The floor was scrubbed, the room aired, and fresh herbs gathered so that the smell of death was almost undetectable to Finn's sensitive nostrils. Although quarters were cramped, nobody got to sleep on a chair that night.

The sheriff had also arrived after lunch, and after talking to the colonel and Darcy, gave his condolences and left, satisfied with their version of events. Indeed, Mr Darcy's general demeanour and attention to the burial of his cousin had long ago assuaged the proprietress's concerns that there was anything havey-cavey about George's demise, and she could only be sorry that a respectable gentleman had been saddled with such a ramshackle young man for a cousin.

Healy had gone off in the curricle in the afternoon to retrieve fresh clothes for the family and the Darcy carriage. He arrived back with Jenny, whose joy on being reunited with her mistress was evident.

The doctor deemed Mrs Darcy fit for travel the following day, but upon readying the mistress for the journey home, Jenny was appalled to find that her injuries were not confined to her head. Changing her chemise, they discovered that Elizabeth had sustained severe bruising to her torso and legs, which she had hitherto been unaware of. She begged Jenny not to mention it to Darcy, lest he call back the doctor and strand them in the inn any longer—she longed to be back home.

The undertaker had hired a courier in Whaley Bridge to transport George's coffin, and the sad cortège returned to Pemberley that afternoon.

51 Aftermath

Darcy's relief on retrieving his wife and sister largely unhurt was overwhelmed by his guilt upon Wickham's death until George was finally laid to rest. Regardless of George's bad behaviour, they had grown up together, and Darcy could not help thinking he had mismanaged the situation from go to whoa for things to have come to such a pass.

George's funeral proceeded without ceremony, and he was interred beside his father in the churchyard at Pemberley, a place generally reserved for trusted retainers. The colonel had argued that George should be buried in unconsecrated ground, but Darcy, who did not want even a hint of scandal, prevailed.

It was only afterwards that Darcy began to appreciate the true cost of Wickham's malfeasance. He had not seen Mrs Annesley since his precipitate departure in pursuit of George. As both Georgie and Elizabeth kept to their beds 'til after the funeral, he had not missed her. But when Georgie returned to her sitting room the following day to play mournful tunes, her companion's absence became noticeable. It was then that Darcy remembered Mrs Annesley's grey face during those panicked moments when he had returned to Pemberley.

"She is not well, sir," replied Mrs Reynolds to his enquiry at breakfast.

Elizabeth, who had only just emerged from the sickroom herself after the tiring journey back from Whaley Bridge, promised to look in on her. She found Mrs Annesley so far from well that she summoned the family physician from Buxton to examine her. He determined that she'd had an attack of angina.

Against Elizabeth's wishes, Darcy then suggested Dr Gordon also check the mistress following her recent head injury. As the physician had arrived very early in the morning, Darcy delayed his morning ride so that he might speak to him personally after the consultation. He received the good doctor in his study.

"For the moment she needs bed rest," Dr Gordon recommended. "But it is not just the head injury; she has substantial bruising across her abdomen. Given her state, I am little worried. It's possible she may lose the baby. Only time will tell."

"What will happen?" asked Darcy, paling.

"If she does miscarry, she will start bleeding, probably within the next two weeks. The bleeding will be heavier than her normal courses, something between that and a full birth. She'll deliver the unviable child. Notify me as soon as it starts. I'll ensure a good midwife attends her and will come at critical time points."

Darcy closed his eyes briefly. "Thank you, Dr Gordon."

The next week was one of unenviable tension for both Elizabeth and Darcy. Lizzy refused to stay in her bed, saying she felt perfectly fine; but her morning sickness continued to be noticeably absent, and this, she thought, could only have two diametrically opposed causes: either the pregnancy had proceeded past the nauseous stage, or she had lost the child as the doctor feared. Darcy became more than usually silent and began chewing his nails. Neither of them spoke of the situation to the other.

One evening, six days after their return to Pemberley, Lizzy excused herself from dinner. It had begun.

Darcy got up immediately from the table when Mrs Reynolds informed him, advising him that the doctor had already been summoned. Pale-faced, he left the room without speaking a word.

After Darcy departed, Georgie wondered aloud what could be ailing her sister-in-law, commenting also on her brother's seeming overreaction. Richard quietly explained the situation. Distraught, Georgie would have followed her brother upstairs, but was held back by her cousin. She promptly burst into tears and was inconsolable for the next hour. Richard stroked her hair, and told her that there was no way of knowing if her sister's misfortune arose from their ill-starred journey, but Georgie already felt herself culpable in precipitating Mrs Annesley's seizure.

Richard could only be glad he had delayed his return to London on the basis of Georgie's flagging spirits—Darcy now had enough to contend with on his own. He'd written to Jane several days ago, advising her of his continued sojourn in Derbyshire and promising to return as soon as he was able. He'd also written to his commanding officer, advising him of his intention to resign his commission and asking him to let him know of anyone interested in purchasing it.

Upstairs, Darcy paced the adjacent shared sitting room while the doctor examined Elizabeth. Upon leaving Elizabeth's chamber to join him, the doctor shook his head sadly.

"I'm very sorry, sir. There is no hope for the child, but she is young, and hopefully will pull through. However, as the family physician, there is one other thing I need to mention…"

"Yes?"

"She may not be able to conceive again. With a natural miscarriage the chances are good, provided there is no pre-existing condition; but these ones that are caused by accidents can be especially traumatic. God willing, it will not be the case, but I feel I should forewarn you."

Darcy's heart sank. "Thank you, doctor."

Elizabeth, who had tiptoed to the adjoining door behind the doctor to hear the verdict through the keyhole, crouched there, frozen for a moment, tears beading in her eyes. The sound of Jenny coming through the service door sent her hurrying back to bed. Her maid had come with fresh rags and hot water.

After staring into space for some minutes after the doctor's departure, Darcy pulled himself together and knocked on the door of his wife's chamber. Jenny would have sent him on his way, but Mrs Reynolds forestalled her when Darcy indicated to them that he wished a moment alone with his wife. Both the servants withdrew to the dressing room.

Reaching Elizabeth's bedside, Darcy drew up the bed steps, and clasping Elizabeth's hand, sat down upon them beside her.

Her face was stony, her lips drawn in a thin line. "I heard the doctor," she said quietly. "You can divorce me."

Darcy's heart froze. "Why would I want to do that?" he said with false cheerfulness, giving her hand a squeeze.

"You married me to produce an heir, and I have failed," she replied.

He swallowed, feeling as if something was stuck in his throat. "Let us not talk of this. You are upset."

"Henry the eighth divorced his wife for that reason. The Duke of Devonshire also divorced the duchess, although I believe the case there was different."

"Hush, Lizzy. You are overwrought. I do not wish to divorce you."

"I think I could be quite content to live in a tidy cottage somewhere."

"Please, Lizzy, stop. Perhaps I should call the doctor back. You need some laudanum."

"Fitzwilliam, *I know*."

"Yes, Lizzy; I realise you heard the doctor, but he mentioned it merely as a possibility. It is not set in stone."

"No, Fitzwilliam I *know*... about Diana," she added in a whisper.

The silence was deafening. You could have heard a pin drop. Minutes seemed to tick by.

Finally, Darcy found his voice—he'd already discovered his letters tied in a neat bundle when he was sure he had left them in a state of disorder on his precipitate departure for London. "I suppose you found the letters," he said in a halting manner. "Forgive me for leaving them lying about. I meant to dispose of them at Christmas... Then I had to go off suddenly... I'm sorry, *truly* sorry."

"I am sorry too, and am justly served for reading them, although you must understand that I only read one of them in its entirety before realising what it was. I was working on the telescope and found the letter from Edward first, you see... "

She was unable to say anything more. She knew she would burst out sobbing if she tried to continue.

Darcy sat there, unable to think of anything appropriate to say to ameliorate the situation. A numbness seemed to be spreading from his heart to his limbs.

Time's Up, Mr Darcy

Jenny peeked timidly from the dressing room. "Please, sir, we really need to tend to the mistress."

His face a mask, Darcy got up and reluctantly left the room on wooden legs. Closing the door behind him, he paused for a moment before setting off down the hall towards the door of his parents' sitting room, gaining momentum as he went. Finding the door fast, he banged impotently with his fist on the wooden panels before striding back to his dressing room, where he flung several things aside before finding the key in the top of his cabinet.

Letting himself into the room, Darcy ran to his childhood bedchamber, flung open the top of the Davenport desk, untied the red ribbon, and began ripping Diana's letters to shreds. The pieces fell like a maelstrom about his feet until he'd destroyed every sheet of paper down to the last inch. He then grabbed the red ribbon that had tied them, tried to tear that too, and not succeeding, hit his head repeatedly on the doorframe in frustration until he was grabbed suddenly from behind by Richard, who had come upstairs to see Georgie to her bedchamber.

"Darcy! Darcy! What are you doing?" Richard yelled. He had never seen his cousin in such state.

"What am I doing?" yelled Darcy back, trying to wrestle himself free from his cousin's grip. "What does it matter what I'm doing?! I've lost her!"

"Calm down!" yelled Richard, pinning Darcy against a wall. "Mrs Reynolds says she'll probably be all right. It's just the child, Darcy! She's just lost the child!"

"You don't understand, Richard," Darcy said, tears welling from his eyes. "I've lost Elizabeth! She knows about Diana!"

They stared at each other for a moment before Richard sighed: "I suppose Wickham was poisoning her mind, trying to cut a wheedle with her..."

"No, Richard. It was me," said Darcy in a small voice. "I left Diana's letters lying around..."

Richard suddenly realised they were surrounded by shredded paper.

"Oh, God, Darcy!" he said, releasing his cousin.

Darcy slid down the wall, his head collapsing onto his knees. Bursting out sobbing, he drew his arms over his head to hide his face.

Richard sat down unsteadily on the side of the bed, picking up a card that had somehow survived the devastation.

After a time, Darcy grew calmer. He wiped his eyes, only to discover his hand red with his own blood. In a daze, he pulled his handkerchief from his pocket and began to mop his injured forehead.

"Well!" said Richard, looking at the card. "Did Diana really write stuff like this to you?"

He handed it to Darcy, who closed his eyes as if in pain.

"Oh Lord!" said Darcy. "What a wretch George was! That isn't Diana's writing! No doubt this is one of his many schemes to undermine my relationship with my wife! No wonder Elizabeth never wrote back when I wrote to telling her how much I loved her. Between my carelessness and George's scheming, she probably thinks I'm the biggest cad in England."

"No, Darcy. She didn't write because she never had your letter! See here?" Richard said, withdrawing Darcy's letter from his jacket with his free hand. "Wickham took it! Finn found it in his waistcoat!"

"Oh, heavens!" said Darcy. "Mrs Flowers hadn't received anything from Mrs Reynolds either. George was probably intercepting all the mail! What a rotter he was!"

"Bloody hell!" growled Richard, incensed at the depth of Wickham's perfidy. "It's like a bad play! I ought to go and disinter the beast!"

They sat in silence for a while until Richard, seeing Darcy was smearing blood all over his forehead, pressed his own handkerchief to his cousin's head to stem the flow.

"What a mess I've made of my life!" said Darcy wretchedly. "What should I do? Elizabeth wants a divorce…"

"No, no, no!" said Richard, shaking his head. "She's upset because of the baby! You've got to fix things up! Tell her that you love her; that you made a mistake, just like in the letter!"

"You don't understand, Richard! Dr Gordon says she may not be able to have any children."

"Oi! That is harsh!" sighed Richard, losing himself in thought. "I suppose Elizabeth is offering to stand aside, so you can marry again? It might be possible if you sought an annulment rather than a divorce… But is that what you want?"

"No," croaked Darcy. "I love her."

Silence stretched between them.

"But it is not the end of the world!" said Richard eventually. "Georgie may produce an heir, or you could adopt someone, just like Anne is doing!"

Darcy nodded, but did not say a word.

"You need to decide what you want most, Darcy: a child of your own or Elizabeth. It is noble of her to step aside. I know you will be generous to her if you choose to follow that path."

"There is no question," Darcy replied hoarsely. "I cannot, *will not* live without her! And your father is not here to bully me into any other position!"

"True!" said Richard. "Good man! So you must go tell her! But first we need to fix you up!"

They had gone off to procure a needle and thread for Darcy's split head, which oozed blood every time he stopped pressing on it with the handkerchief. Finn had gone quite pale upon seeing the master; but after watching Richard try to stitch up the wound, he had to intervene and finished the operation himself.

Richard had cleansed the wound with brandy from his hip flask, and after Finn tied off the thread, he surreptitiously took a couple of swigs from the colonel's flask to settle his stomach. Finn washed the blood out of Darcy's hair and arranged it to cover the wound before tying a fresh cravat and sending him on his way.

Darcy had knocked timidly on Elizabeth's bedchamber door while Richard leaned against the wainscoting along the hall in silent support. Mrs Reynolds answered the door and would have turned him away, but he was firm in demanding admittance. Jenny hastily rearranged the counterpane and looked affronted. Darcy ignored them both.

Elizabeth was lying on her side, facing away from him, towards the window. Quietly he approached the bed and, without stopping to remove his boots, Darcy lay down behind his wife and clasped her shoulder, much as he had done at the inn near Whaley Bridge. She turned her head slightly in question when she detected his presence.

"Elizabeth," he whispered into her ear. "I have come to tell you that I love you."

Mrs Reynolds grabbed Jenny's arm and pulled her once more into the dressing room.

"The letter from Edward..." he explained; "I found it at Netherfield in the library. I should have given it to you, but... It was with some other correspondence from the Yardley boys to their mother. I believe it was likely delivered at the same time as the official notice of their deaths. I doubt Lady Yardley ever saw the correspondence."

Darcy's hand slid down her arm to grasp his wife's hand. "I didn't want to upset you by showing it to you belatedly, to open old wounds. But once I'd read it—realised there'd been an understanding between the two of you, I thought that you might know what it was like to lose a lover."

"I don't understand, Fitzwilliam," said Elizabeth haltingly. "Are you saying that Diana is dead?"

"No, Elizabeth. She jilted me."

"Then the lady you are in love with... the lady you visit in London... is that someone else?"

Darcy closed his eyes. "There is no one else, Elizabeth. There was only ever Diana, and you."

"But you said when you proposed that your heart belonged to someone else..."

Darcy mentally kicked himself for his morose stupidity before continuing: "It was already over then, Elizabeth. I was just having difficulty getting over it. I am finished with Diana. It is done, in the past."

He rubbed Elizabeth's palm with his thumb. "I love *you*, Elizabeth. I know you think I married you for convenience, I thought so once too; but I believe I was taken with you from the time I saw you climb the ha-ha. I was just too stupid to admit it."

"That's very sweet, Fitzwilliam," said Elizabeth with a sniff, "but you don't have to rewrite history."

In desperation, Darcy reached into his pocket and pulled out a folded handkerchief, which he dropped in front of his wife, like some offering. Elizabeth wiped a tear from her eye with her finger before looking at it and recognising it as the one she had lost at Netherfield. Picking it up, she opened it to reveal the small spot of blood in the centre.

"Did Mr Bingley find my handkerchief?" she asked, bewildered.

"It was never lost, Elizabeth. I had it all along."

"I don't understand."

"Please believe me. I love you, Elizabeth. I have loved you for a long time. Diana left me before I ever went to Netherfield. I had asked her to marry me, but she married a duke instead. It took me some time to get over it."

"So you didn't visit a woman in London?"

Darcy sighed. "Did Wickham tell you this?"

"Yes."

"I did visit Diana once, Elizabeth. I needed to see her once more, to sort a few things out."

A look of pain crossed Elizabeth's face, and Darcy immediately regretted his words until he realised that his wife was clutching her belly.

"Does it hurt?" he asked.

"Mmm," she assented, momentarily unable to speak.

"Would it help if I rubbed your back?" asked Darcy, remembering the time she had rubbed his back.

Releasing her hand, he massaged her back tentatively.

"No. Please stop. It's tender," said Elizabeth, and Darcy ceased rubbing and withdrew his hands.

"But the warmth is nice," she continued, and he placed them gently back on.

"Like this?" he asked, spreading his palms on her lower back.

Elizabeth sighed as the warmth spread through her. It really did seem to lessen the pain.

Five minutes later, Mrs Reynolds came back into the room carrying a small table. Seeing their confidences were at an end, she hauled the sheet and counterpane up at the far end of the bed, erecting a low wall between herself and Mr Darcy. Then straddling Mrs Darcy's hips with the table legs, she pulled the covers back over, making a small tent above the mistress's body.

"Fitzwilliam, you really need to leave," said Mrs Reynolds, and Darcy knew it was true because she had pulled rank on him, addressing him as she had done in his childhood.

Kissing Elizabeth's upper arm sadly, he withdrew. As he exited to the hall, Darcy saw the midwife there, waiting with her bag.

The doctor arrived an hour later, and a cot was set up for him in the master sitting room.

Darcy spent a wretched night. He had lost his child and possibly the affections of his wife too. Had he said enough to redeem himself? He did not know. He got up occasionally to check on the progress of his wife, but he was barred entry to Elizabeth's chamber and sent back to his own room with the same message—that things were proceeding normally and were as well as could be expected.

There was light rain the next morning—the sort of drizzle that would not normally deter Darcy from his morning ride, but he had no enthusiasm for it. Richard sought him out when he did not come down for breakfast, but when Darcy evinced no enthusiasm for eating, his cousin, for once, did not argue.

Richard realised then that sending Darcy back to fix things with his wife on the previous night had not been sufficient to remediate the situation. He supposed the timing was poor, but he also realised his cousin had probably not had the words or eloquence required. Richard knew Darcy had a tendency to retreat into himself when he was hurt. Where Richard would have employed all his arts to retrieve the situation, Darcy was likely struck dumb. But Darcy *had* managed to express his feelings in the letter that Wickham had stolen, which was even now sitting in Richard's pocket—probably the poor chap had slaved over the thing. He wished it were possible to slip it to Elizabeth's maid, but no doubt she was beleaguered with the current situation.

Darcy and Richard stood together in the hallway near the top of the stairs, occasionally glancing towards Elizabeth's chamber whenever a bump or voice fooled them into believing the door might open. Georgiana also had not emerged from her chamber. A sapping ennui seemed to pervade the whole house.

Within this silence, the sound of a four-horse carriage some way off along the drive rang like a clarion call, despite the muting influence of the rain. Richard thought there was something familiar about the sound, and when the carriage came into view he saw that it belonged to his mother. Wondering what could have brought her to Pemberley, Richard raced downstairs only to find his wife stepping from the carriage followed by her maid.

"Jane, what are you doing here?" he asked in some alarm.

"Do not fear," said Jane. "There is nothing wrong! I merely

accompanied your mother to Derbyshire. The poor countess! Robert wasn't being very nice, but I managed to convince him to loan us the earl's carriage to allow his mother to return to Wyvern Hall. The countess very kindly offered me her own carriage to finish the journey to Pemberley!"

Richard stared at his wife in amazement. When had his mother ever done anything nice for anyone? Not only had he married the most beautiful woman in England, she was also a miracle worker!

"I hope you are not upset," she said, unnerved by her husband's uncharacteristic silence. "It seemed I could be of more use in Derbyshire than in London. I thought I could perhaps help cheer Georgiana up after her disappointment!"

Richard gave his wife a hug. "You couldn't have come up at a better time! I'm afraid things have not been going well for your sister. She has lost her baby."

"Oh, no!" Jane exclaimed.

They moved inside and sought out privacy in the saloon, where Richard proceeded to tell Jane the whole story of the Wickham debacle. Jane had, of course, known her sister was pregnant, having been informed around the same time that Elizabeth had advised Darcy. She was devastated that tragedy had struck when everything had seemed on the verge of being perfect, but quickly rallied when her husband suggested her intervention was needed.

Richard explained that Elizabeth had suggested a divorce on the grounds that she might no longer be able to bear children, but that Darcy was determined to keep her regardless. Choosing not to mention anything of Diana, Richard assured Jane that Darcy had become very close to his wife during their short marriage, but was very poor at expressing his feelings. He then revealed Darcy's letter, which had been purloined by Wickham.

"Can you give it to her, Jane?" asked Richard. "Darcy can't go into the room, but you can."

"Of course, Richard," said Jane, tucking the letter into her muff and kissing the tip of his nose. "Please take me to her."

52 Rapproachment

If Darcy had spent a wretched night, it was nothing to Elizabeth's. Whenever she felt too sorry for herself, she tried to focus on the fact that no better care was likely to be found in all England than she was receiving from Mrs Reynolds, Jenny and Doctor Gordon. She was sad, but she was not frightened, feeling sure she could pull through this disaster.

Did she regret her impetuous decision to run after Georgie? No. The cost had been high, but she was sure she had saved her little sister from a lifetime of misery. Without Elizabeth's company, Georgie might have been compromised and had to marry that wretched man, although Lizzy was convinced that Darcy and Richard would have moved heaven and earth to avoid such a union if possible.

Still, if Georgie had not lost her purse when she dropped the bandbox; if Jane had not received Lizzy's letter; if Aunt Amelia had not visited that day and kindly offered to post it so that it arrived just in time... it did not bear thinking about. Fate and everyone else's goodness had conspired against George, overwhelming his singularly determined evil.

And what of herself? Had she overreacted when she offered Darcy a divorce? Elizabeth realised her judgment was likely impaired due to the trauma of her situation; but she believed that, in the circumstances, it had been the right thing to do. Darcy needed an heir, and she merely wanted to lead a comfortable and fulfilling life; and there were so many ways she could do that—as Jane's companion-governess, for example, like they had originally planned.

Provided Darcy honoured the arrangement to pay her sisters' dowries; honoured Elizabeth's sacrifice to Georgie's well-being; then her marriage, however short, would have been a positive thing in the grand scheme of things; and if there was one thing she had learned about Fitzwilliam Darcy during the time they had shared, it was that he was an honourable man who *tried* to do the right thing.

Still, Elizabeth felt miserable and unwanted despite Fitzwilliam's sudden protestations of love. She had shoved her old handkerchief under her pillow when Fitzwilliam had left the room, unwilling to believe in his change of heart; but occasionally, during moments of relative privacy, she got the handkerchief out and looked at it.

What Fitzwilliam had said seemed incredible, and she could not help ascribing his declaration to maudlin sympathy. Could it really be possible that he had already been in love with her when he asked her to marry him? When she thought about all the things he had done and said, particularly in Hertfordshire, it seemed scarcely possible. Yet there remained the handkerchief and his explanation for his possession of it. Try as she might—and Elizabeth did think of some fantastical stories—the most parsimonious explanation for that scrap of linen sitting in front of her was that he was telling the truth. Mr Haughty-Taughty Fitzwilliam Darcy had fallen in love with Miss Nobody Bennet from Hertfordshire—she of the dowdy chemisette and slightly embarrassing relations. By Occam's razor, he loved her.

Elizabeth could only wonder at someone being so confused. As a student of character, she found it difficult to understand that one's own feelings could be such a mystery, but she supposed that some people, even intelligent ones, might be incapable of self-reflection. *Certainly Mr Wickham seemed to lack that ability,* Lizzy thought dismally; *or no, perhaps he had just lacked any sense of ethics.*

To be fair, Elizabeth had to admit there was a time when she had been blind to her own love for Fitzwilliam Darcy. Love could be insidious, creeping up on you. Lizzy had not realised she had fallen in love with him until she admitted her jealousy of Diana. She had spent the weeks since that realisation quashing her love, putting it back in the box from which it had escaped. She had been determined to damp it down to a fondness, which could be managed without embarrassing fits of ill temper.

As for her husband, she still had trouble seeing evidence of his love—flying as he had, so soon after their marriage, to Yorkshire and then to London. She suspected he was confusing love with lust, compounded with the guilt of not being on hand at a critical juncture, when his sister needed him. Possibly he also regretted, and felt needlessly culpable, for her own injury.

Elizabeth appreciated his sympathy, but *she* had chosen to run after George and Georgie; and she freely admitted she would do it again. She was not the sort of person who could stand idly by when action was needed to prevent a loved one from coming to harm. She had taken a chance and paid dearly for it, but idleness in such a situation was what she would have regretted most of all—the thought that she might have done something, but had not tried.

More importantly, Fitzwilliam's sympathy was not enough to sustain a doomed relationship. Elizabeth was sure he would later regret not taking the opportunity to move on and find a mother for his heir, just as Henry had eventually regretted Catherine of Aragon.

Very early in the morning, events had reached their logical conclusion—Elizabeth had delivered the lost babe, and Jenny had spirited away the tiny thing in a bundle of rags. Dr Gordon seemed to become most anxious then; but an hour or so later, if the clock could be believed, for it seemed to take forever, Lizzy heard the physician whisper to Mrs Reynolds that he believed the mistress was out of the woods. Elizabeth had managed to fall asleep for a while then.

When she woke, Elizabeth thought she must be dreaming, for she could hear her sister Jane talking to Mrs Reynolds. But upon opening her eyes she saw it was no dream—Jane was hurrying towards her, wearing a pelisse, and carrying a muff.

"Oh, Jane, how I have needed you!" Elizabeth said, hugging her sister and finally letting herself cry.

"Yes, I am here now! Everything will be all right!" said Jane.

And it was quite amazing, for no sooner were the words out of her sister's mouth, than the sun broke through the clouds and lit up the room. Lizzy gasped in amazement and Jane just hugged her sister. Based on Richard's information, Jane had been seriously worried about the extent of Elizabeth's injuries and was overjoyed to see her all in one piece. She caressed the yellow bruise near Lizzy's left temple. Mrs Reynolds offered to bring tea, and Lizzy suddenly realised she was quite ravenous.

Then Jane sat down, and after the doctor and servants had disappeared, she demanded Lizzy's version of events, everything since they had parted after the wedding, all the things too private to be written down. They stopped briefly when breakfast arrived and began again once they were alone in the room. Jane then spoke of her own happiness, and the felicity she envisaged, living together with her sister at Pemberley. Finally they spoke of the elephant in the room.

"Lizzy," said Jane, "Richard believes that Darcy truly loves you. They are like brothers and know each other as well as you and I. Darcy is not just feeling sorry for you. He wrote you a letter from London, but Mr Wickham took it. Richard found it in his waistcoat after his death. He apologises for reading it, but knowing that things between the two of you are at sixes and sevens, Richard thinks it's important for you to read it now."

Jane had then handed over the missive and gone off to the chamber pot, letting her sister read Darcy's letter alone. Elizabeth read it and read it again, scarcely able to believe her eyes. With a strong prejudice against everything he might say, she pored over his account of what had happened at Netherfield: how he had watched her and listened to her, captivated from the start but unwilling to admit it. She turned over the paper she was holding, wondering if this was something Darcy and Richard had cooked up for the moment, but the stains and the creases on it convinced her that the letter was what it purported to be; and the clumsiness of its opening lines surely bespoke of her own awkward husband, that dear man, *who was hopelessly in love with her*. Tears started to her eyes. Lizzy was so engrossed in her own thoughts that she failed to notice that Jane had crept back into the room.

"So you see, you cannot possibly think of breaking with him," said Jane softly, caressing her sister's hair, "because you will break his heart. Plus you will break mine, because I am determined to be happy here."

Lizzy gave a great sigh and hugged her sister. Then Jane rang for Jenny so that Elizabeth could have a bath before they admitted Darcy. Jenny only put a little water into the bottom of the tub, as Dr Gordon had instructed, and Lizzy knelt, supported on either side by Jane and Jenny.

Afterwards, trying to pamper Elizabeth, they wrapped her in the new dressing gown that her Aunt Amelia had brought as a belated Christmas present on the day she had carried the letter back to Lambton. It had been made to order by Madame Lafrange from the finest silk that had come from the Gardiners' warehouse. Jenny had tied apricot ribbons in Elizabeth's chestnut hair to match the gown and put a little macquillage on the bruise on the side of her face.

Darcy, who had been dragged out riding by his cousin after all—'to give the ladies some space'—was called in from the hall and admitted, smelling of horse and carrying his infamous riding crop. He came forward timidly, unsure of his welcome, and upon Elizabeth holding out her arms, rushed into them, hugging her tightly, riding crop and all. Jane crept out of the room behind him.

Overcome with emotion, he was unable to speak.

"Ah!" Elizabeth joked, covering the awkward moment, "the handkerchief thief returns! You know you can be hanged or transported for such."

Darcy was taken aback for a moment at his wife's ability to jest at such a time. With his arms still round her shoulders, he drew back to look at her. Then realising she did not wish him to speak of their misfortune, he found his voice and attempted to reply in kind: "Not if you are a gentleman. Besides, I gave you one of equal value, so it was more of a swap."

Darcy kissed her gently then and, taking her hand, promised to never leave her again. That was when Elizabeth noticed the stitches in his forehead.

"What have you done to yourself?" she asked.

"I ran into a doorpost," he said sheepishly.

Elizabeth pulled some of his curls down to hide the stitches, before caressing the stubble on his jaw. Darcy brought his hand up to the soft skin of her jaw to mirror her action and looked at her so earnestly that Elizabeth almost burst out crying. Regaining her composure, she complained that he smelt of horse and sent him off before things got too maudlin.

Darcy departed to change, but returned half an hour later carrying the chessboard. Jane quietly put down the book she had been reading aloud and went off down the hall to Georgie's sitting room, where she could hear her sister-in-law playing mournful tunes on the piano.

"I hear from Richard that you have already defeated me once," said Darcy.

"Oh, what a scamp he is!" replied Elizabeth. "He promised to never tell! But that victory doesn't count because it was won under false pretences."

"Oh?" said Darcy.

"Yes, you thought you were playing your cousin, instead of a far more formidable opponent, and thus underestimated the opposition."

"Really?" said Darcy. "Those are very big words!"

Two hours later she defeated him again, in more honourable circumstances.

While Jane had been helping to bathe Lizzy, Darcy and Richard had gathered up the fragments of the torn love letters in Darcy's childhood room and burnt them in the hearth of the family sitting room. Richard had been about to throw George's counterfeit card into the flames when he thought better of it and tucked it quietly into his jacket. After sneaking down to Darcy's study later that night to obliterate the writing, Richard went out early the next morning and pushed the card with its single red rose into the newly turned sod of George's grave.

"There you are, mate," he said quietly, "I expect that's the only flower you'll be getting, and it's more than you deserve."

Indeed, no other bloom was ever placed on Mr Wickham's grave, even though several of his natural children regularly ran through the graveyard, oblivious that their father lay there.

53 To get back up again

A tragedy is not forgotten in a week or even a month, but time heals all wounds. Lizzy was not completely assured that her husband's newly professed love was strong enough to abide a barren wife, but Jane had at least convinced her to give marital felicity a chance.

Much to Lizzy's annoyance, Doctor Gordon recommended she spend a week in bed, which she felt completely unnecessary; but she bowed to the pressure. Elizabeth was saved from falling into a lethargy by Jane's reading and a series of chess games with her husband.

While George Wickham might have knocked her head and bruised her body, Elizabeth's wounds were chiefly in her mind. She tried not to think of the loss of her child, following her dictum of remembering only things from the past that gave her pleasure. She chose instead to hide behind slightly hollow jests for the first difficult few weeks.

Despite the effort made by Darcy to demonstrate his love to his wife by solicitude, the situation between them was at first slightly cool. Darcy realised he could not magically reverse the damage he had done to their relationship in the first weeks of their marriage before his epiphany. Winning back his wife's love would take time. His contrition was genuine, but he was not good at expressing his feelings; nor did he wish to open old wounds by speaking of how much he regretted his affair with Diana. Richard agreed it was enough that Elizabeth should know that the entanglement was over. Moreover, his cousin reminded Darcy that actions speak louder than words and encouraged him to be more demonstrative, but Lizzy was in no mood for lovemaking.

Jane and Richard, who lived for the first month in the main house, were instrumental in smoothing the waters between Darcy and Elizabeth once Lizzy emerged from the sick room. Each understood the complex characters of their respective relatives, softened every edge, and worked to establish an atmosphere of amity. Richard covered for Darcy's silence and Jane, for Lizzy's slightly awkward jokes—which were more characteristic of her father than herself—knowing her sister needed time to recover her equanimity.

Rather than give in to her unquiet mind, Lizzy chose to immerse herself in activity. Although the Dower House had been cleaned in preparation for its occupation, and the rugs unrolled, most of the furniture that had previously resided there had been taken off to the main house years ago, and Lizzy had waited until her sister arrived before redistributing it. Knowing that Richard's finances were limited, Elizabeth thought she could help Jane furnish the old house cheaply using the existing furniture by claiming she wished to redecorate her own house.

Thus a month passed by preparing the Dower House for Jane and Richard—choosing furniture from the main house; having footmen cart it to the Dower House and having them cart back some of the pieces that did not work. Richard and Darcy watched all this activity with bemusement but wisely chose not to interfere.

A week after Jane's arrival, Richard had formally resigned his commission. Three weeks later, he had received notice the commission had been purchased for a very good price after some spirited bidding between a lieutenant-colonel and a very ambitious major, both eager to advance themselves despite the reduced opportunities of peacetime. Richard found it harder to part with his uniform, which he tucked lovingly into a trunk at the end of their bed. The proceeds from the sale of his Life Guards commission allowed him to purchase the rank of brigadier in the Derbyshire militia, enabling the very aged incumbent to retire in some comfort, and Jane to reupholster the furniture in the colours of her choice.

Finally, the ladies deemed the Dower House fit for occupation and the Fitzwilliams took up residence, leaving the Darcys to navigate their relationship themselves.

After church the following Sunday, Darcy took Elizabeth for a walk through the formal garden, as he had done during the first week of their marriage.

"I'm afraid we clipped a few of the box hedges, riding through here in haste when we went charging in pursuit of you and Georgie," he said ruefully.

"No matter," Lizzy replied. "It will grow back in time."

"We can change it if you wish. We could rip the box hedges out and do something completely different. Perhaps a gravity-fed fountain?"

"Well, that is an interesting idea, and you must tell me exactly how it works sometime, but your mother designed this garden, and I'm sure it has some sentimental value to you. I must say, my interests lie more in the practical—I have a fancy to expand the kitchen garden at the end of the guest wing."

He smiled, remembering when he had proposed to Elizabeth upon encountering her gathering simples by the River Lea on that misty morning.

"So you can pick herbs to take back to your hut on chicken legs," he added.

"Exactly," she said.

In spring, Lizzy made good on her plans; a decorative kitchen garden in the shape of a large leaf was constructed with paths delineating the veins. It was very pleasant to walk between the redolent beds. A spectacular overview of its clever design could be appreciated from the master guest room, which had formerly housed Mr George Wickham.

The resumption of marital relations between the Darcys required navigation of some shoals. Darcy, plagued by guilt, initially kept away from his wife's bed, unsure how long it would take Elizabeth to physically recover and certainly unwilling to ask his family physician such a question. When her husband had not returned to her bed by Tuesday week, Lizzy sought him out. She spent the night in his bed, cuddled within his arms, both of them wearing their cambric nightgowns. It was not particularly comfortable, but a rapprochement had been made.

In the morning, Elizabeth chucked her husband on his chin, and after a lingering kiss, Darcy agreed to resume his practice of visiting her on Tuesdays.

A month later, he found her cambric gown had been replaced by one of Jenny's more adventurous negligées, and his own cambric gown was also promptly abandoned, but thankfully not for a negligée. Darcy now felt sufficiently comfortable with his wife to adopt his habit of sleeping au naturel in her presence, as was his custom when he slept alone. Elizabeth could only shake her head at his willingness to be naked on cold nights, but given he was far more tolerant of her habit of clinging to his back when the weather was frosty, she was not going to suggest he rug up.

Fortunately, Doctor Gordon's worries proved needlessly dire. When Lizzy found herself pregnant a few months later, the trauma of her first loss began to fade. After the quickening, Lizzy began to relax and return to her old self. The love for Fitzwilliam she had once been determined to quash blossomed again. The bump that was swelling in her body was her connection to him.

One morning at the breakfast table, as he ate his porridge, Darcy caught her staring at his face and brought his napkin up to his chin, lest he had left some milk there.

While appreciating his fine features, Lizzy had also been wondering how a man who was so smart—for she daily learned of Darcy's cleverness in his fields of business—could also be so clueless about some things. As a student of character, she had begun to understand that intelligence has not a single aspect, but many. As outstanding as Fitzwilliam was in his cleverness for business, there were many other ways his more practical cousin Richard outshone him. Understanding her husband's faults and weaknesses only made Elizabeth feel more tenderly towards him. She suddenly felt a stab of determination to protect him from life's slings and arrows. After the footman had left with an empty salver, Elizabeth reached out to caress the edge of his ear.

Darcy looked at her quizzically, but she merely smiled and dropped her hand to the table, stroking the last knuckle of his index finger.

He smiled shyly back.

For some reason that seemed to have no practical basis in nature that she could think of, Elizabeth's pregnancy made her want her husband even more. He, at first, was reluctant to participate given her delicate condition, until she had screamed at him that she was not made of china and forced his compliance. The result had been such a heated session that after opening his eyes the following morning and finding his wife staring at him dreamily, Darcy had laughed.

"What's so funny?" Elizabeth asked her husband archly.

"You certainly don't take no for an answer," he grinned in reply.

"My goodness," she said, stroking his bristly cheek. "You have dimples on your face too!"

"Too?" replied Darcy. "Who is this other person I am being compared to?"

"Jealousy does not become you," she chided. "I meant you have dimples on your face, just like your bottom," and saying this she reached around and gave him a smart slap behind, before placing her fingers in the indentations on his lower back.

"I was not aware that I had dimples on my bottom," he said, stretching his hand back to his derrière and trying to reclaim Lizzy's hand.

This she would not allow, and instead she guided his hand to the indentations to prove her point. "You see? One, two."

"I believe you are correct, Mrs Darcy. You are a never-ending source of improved self-awareness. You may turn me into a philosopher."

"I sincerely doubt that," said Lizzy dryly. "Better stick to your numbers."

The restrictions of Tuesdays were soon forgotten.

In her gravid state, Lizzy suddenly rediscovered her desire to redecorate the family sitting room and the nursery beside it, and dragged her husband from his study to discuss how they should go about it.

"The paintings of these boys in this room, do I assume correctly that they are all you?"

"Indeed."

"And they were painted by your mother?"

"No, my father. I believe Mother thought he spent too much time in his study. After seeing a sketch he'd made of one of the carriages he was considering purchasing, she recommended he learn to paint formally from a tutor, as a means of relaxation. He didn't like drawing animate objects at first, finding them boring."

"Ah! I see! But he chose to make an exception when the subject was his son."

Darcy blushed slightly and confirmed it was true.

"But not his daughter?" enquired Elizabeth, noting the absence of any portraits of Georgiana.

"He gave up painting when my mother died. That one on the right was painted when I was twelve, just before her death. I suppose Georgie was still too young to pose."

"One should never give up," Elizabeth replied, giving Darcy's forearm a squeeze, before moving swiftly to a discussion of how they should rearrange and update the furniture.

Later she spied the book of poetry near the well-used wing chair by the hearth and, considering his father's hobby of painting, said to Darcy: "But tell me, what do you do for relaxation?"

"Well, I read!" replied her husband.

"But not even novels!" retorted his wife. "Dear me! That will not do! Your mother's philosophy is quite right; you need to do something more creative!"

After much thought, Darcy decided to collect insects. He enjoyed mounting and classifying them using the Linnaean system, which he had learnt of at a Royal Society lecture. This turned out to be a happy choice, which employed many a quiet evening while his wife was busy with the telescope. Later, when their children grew older, Darcy spent many joyous hours dashing round the gardens and countryside with them, chasing six-legged creatures, particularly those that could fly, with a butterfly net.

Based on both her husband's and Richard's behaviour, Lizzy decided that men were in fact still children at heart and she was glad that having their own children gave the cousins a chance to indulge their childish aspects under the guise of looking after their offspring.

As for Jane and Richard, the domestic arrangements that were settled upon for the Dower House were quite novel. In addition to Jane's maid, it was decided that the Fitzwilliams would initially only keep two servants: a chambermaid and a footman. All their meals would be taken in the main house with the Darcys, reducing the Fitzwilliams' expenses and adding to the felicity of all.

Jane and Richard *were* occasionally absent from breakfast at the main house, choosing to stay in bed—clearly Richard was tired from his exertions on the previous day in the militia. Whenever this happened, Mrs Reynolds quietly sent a tray to the Dower House at an appropriately late hour.

After a year adjusting to his new job as brigadier of the Derbyshire militia, Richard finally felt able to part with his Life Guard's uniform. When a captain who was close to his own size agreed to purchase it, Jane helped her husband pack it up to be couriered back to London.

"I'm keeping my sword," said Richard, "I hope you don't mind. It's worth a pretty penny, but my father had it engraved with the Fitzwilliam motto when I joined."

"Of course, not," said Jane, giving him a hug as she looked at the lethal weapon her husband held in his hands.

"I believe that is Latin," she said, reading the engraving on the blade near the hilt. "*'Quicquid necesse est'*. Did I say it right? I learnt a little French, so I believe I know what it means, but perhaps you'd like to translate."

"'Whatever it takes'," said Richard, and putting down his sword, he kissed his wife.

54 Visitors

Many letters were sent back and forth between Pemberley and Gracechurch Street arranging a visit by the Gardiners in the summer. The Gardiners' four young children were to be left in the care of their cousins at Longbourn while their parents made a tour of Derbyshire, using Pemberley as their base. Initially the Gardiners intended to spend a week at Pemberley before exploring all the celebrated beauties of Matlock, Chatsworth, Dovedale, and the Peak; venturing for a day trip to the Peak with the Darcys, before accompanying Aunt Amelia and Miss Dorsey to Dovedale, and staying overnight with Jane and Richard at Wyvern Hall when they all visited the dowager countess, who had greatly improved in civility towards her favourite daughter-in-law.

The day of the Gardiners' arrival was anticipated with some delight by both Bennet sisters, but nothing could have equalled their surprise when, after their aunt and uncle stepped from the carriage, who should descend but their father. Jane and Elizabeth threw themselves upon Mr Bennet with exclamations of heartfelt joy, hugs and a few tears, which quite astonished him and from which he did his best to speedily extract himself.

"Now, now girls," he tut-tutted. "It has been but six months or so since we last saw one another, not years! You are sadly crushing my waistcoat!"

"But, Papa," exclaimed Jane, "you must forgive us. We had no idea you were accompanying Aunt and Uncle and are quite overcome!"

"Yes," said Lizzy, smiling at her aunt, who had been their sole correspondent, "you have been most sly, and since when have you been worried about the state of your waistcoat, Papa?"

It was soon explained that the Gardiners had been on the verge of abandoning their trip to Derbyshire. They had arrived at Longbourn only to discover that Mrs Bennet and her two youngest daughters, who had been in Brighton since February, had failed to return to Hertfordshire to fulfil their promised babysitting duties. After following the militia that had been stationed in Meryton to the Regent's favourite seaside resort at the invitation of Colonel Forster's new young wife, the three Bennet ladies were unwilling to relinquish the mad social whirl of an encampment of soldiers.

Rather than engage in tiresome explanations during the following afternoon tea, Mr Bennet surrendered a letter from Mrs Bennet, transcribed by Kitty. Taking this from her father, Lizzy proceeded to read it aloud, mostly for Jane's information. She managed to imbue Mrs Bennet's missive with so much of her mother's character that she soon had Jane and the Gardiners stifling giggles. Mrs Bennet *'was sure that her girls were an inch away from very eligible matches: Kitty with a Major Harpenden, who had been very particular; and Lydia with a Colonel Kimpton!'*

Mrs Gardiner had then explained how they had managed to travel to Derbyshire after all. In response to Mrs Bennet's potentially holiday-wrecking bombshell, Mary had staunchly declared herself ready to mind all four Gardiner children, but this Mrs Gardiner could not allow. Having already given their two nannies leave to visit their respective parents, she knew the four children would be too much for Mary to handle. The Gardiners had almost admitted defeat and headed back to London, when who should arrive in a gig, but Charlotte.

Mrs Collins was in Hertfordshire for a month, having journeyed there to attend the wedding of one of her brothers. Her husband had been unable to accompany her, unwilling to leave Lady Catherine's side, of which more anon. Taking tea with Mary and the Gardiners, Charlotte had instantly declared herself willing to help Mary at Longbourn; and when Mr Bennet had been apprised of Mrs Collins' offer by Mr Gardiner, he had just as quickly accepted it with a twisted smile, saying it would allow the future mistress of Longbourn a chance to become acquainted with her property and serve its current mistress right for neglecting her duty. Mr Bennet had then had the happy notion of accompanying the Gardiners to Derbyshire, having a fancy to see the library at Pemberley that he had heard so much of, but just as assuredly avoiding a house full of young children.

Mrs Gardiner was particularly gratified to stay with her nieces at Pemberley, a place she had visited once or twice on public days, having formerly passed some years of her life in Lambton. Being very young when she had visited, she only had jumbled memories of a single trip, but with the help of her Aunt Amelia who visited the next day, these were swiftly decomposed into two separate events, her most striking memory being her awe upon encountering the huge vestibule with its spiral staircase.

The next morning, Elizabeth was keen to show the Gardiners the grounds. They set off together with her husband for a walk, with Stevens trailing behind. Entering the woods and bidding adieu to the river for a while, they ascended some of the higher grounds, from which, in spots where the opening of the trees gave the eye power to wander, were many charming views of the valley, the opposite hills, with the long range of woods overspreading many, and occasionally, part of the stream. Mr Gardiner expressed a wish of going round the whole park, but feared it might be beyond a walk, prompting Mr Darcy to reveal that it was ten miles round and could only be easily circumnavigated in a day on horseback or in a carriage. It settled the matter; and they pursued the accustomed circuit; which brought them again, after some time, in a descent among hanging woods, to the edge of the water, and one of its narrowest parts. They crossed it by a simple bridge, in character with the general air of the scene. It was a spot less adorned than any they had yet visited, and the valley, here contracted into a glen, allowed room only for the stream and a narrow walk amidst the rough coppice-wood that bordered it.

They took their way towards the house on the opposite side of the river, in the nearest direction, but their progress was slow. Mr Gardiner, though seldom able to indulge the taste, was very fond of fishing, and was so much engaged in watching the occasional appearance of some trout in the water, and talking to Mr Darcy about them, that they advanced but little.

The conversation soon turned to fishing, and Elizabeth heard her husband invite her uncle, with the greatest civility, to fish there as often as he chose during his stay, offering at the same time to supply him with fishing tackle, and pointing out those parts of the stream where there was usually most sport.

Having not been present on the sole occasion when Darcy had previously conversed with the Gardiners over the lunch he had shared with them at Gracechurch Street during their short engagement, Elizabeth could not but be pleased at the ready understanding that seemed to develop so quickly between her husband, usually so reticent with guests, and Mr Gardiner. It was consoling that Darcy should know she had some relations for whom there was no need to blush. Elizabeth listened most attentively to all that passed between them and gloried in every expression, every sentence of her uncle, which marked his intelligence, his taste, or his good manners.

Mr Bennet, on the other hand, spent almost the entire duration of his visit in the library at Pemberley, exploring the large number of volumes collected there, the work of many generations. When he did join them for meals, Elizabeth found her father much better behaved in the absence of her mother. In the evenings, he was often kept company in the library by his son-in-law, while the rest of the party enjoyed more social entertainment upstairs. Lizzy occasionally poked her head into the library to find them sitting in the wing chairs on either side of the hearth, reading companionably, the silence broken only by the crackling of the fire. She would smile and quietly sneak away.

One day, when the Fitzwilliams and Gardiners had gone off with Georgiana to Wyvern Hall, and her husband had gone out with his steward, Lizzy crept down to the library via the internal stair from the master sitting room with *The Satyricon*.

"I have brought your book back, Papa," she said, returning the volume.

"Why, thank you, my dear," Mr Bennet said, placing it on a pile of books he intended to borrow from his son-in-law. "And did you find it useful?"

"Well, let us say it was educational," said his favourite daughter, blushing a little, "though perhaps not as relevant as you might have supposed."

"Ah!" said Mr Bennet in understanding; "So much the better for you then, eh?"

To which sally, Elizabeth really *did* blush.

On leaving Pemberley, Mr Bennet declared that he had now seen the famous library and, finding it quite satisfactory, could die happy.

Soon after the Gardiners' departure, Darcy ventured to London to attend to some business and, as usual, Finn accompanied his master. Although he never showed it openly, Finn was feeling more than a little downcast at that time because his romance with Healy had not outlasted the arrival of a new kitchen maid who was quite taken with the young groom.

Finn had consoled himself by discovering the talents of Madame Lafrange in Lambton. In recognition of his valued services to the Darcys, Finn had received a considerable raise; and he had kept what remained of Wickham's clothes in the hope that some of them might be sized to fit him in London. The breeches, which were too tight, he had given to Healy. However, the master's continued rustication somewhat limited Finn's opportunities to have these garments altered, until he discovered the dressmaker in Lambton was quite up to the task. She worked a small miracle on Wickham's ruined waistcoat by replacing the ripped side with narrow matching plain panels. The tailcoat she was unable to remediate because of the difficulty in matching the distinctive green fabric, but she made an excellent replacement with some similar material she sourced in Sheffield.

On that fateful trip to London, it just so happened that, in an attempt to cheer himself up, Finn had worn the ensemble to Manton's shooting gallery one morning after his master had gone off on business to the City. He was lining up his next shot when he was startled by a long, low whistle.

"*Whew*, that is some waistcoat!"

Finn, immediately recognising that voice, lowered his pistol and spun round.

"Well, look what the cat dragged in," he drawled upon perceiving his ex-lover, Fred Mitcham, looking as handsome as ever. "What are you doing here?"

"I heard you liked putting holes in things," retorted Mitcham. "In fact, that you were quite the hero in Derbyshire."

"Things are strangely exaggerated at such a distance," pooh-poohed Finn, before observing Mitcham's empty hands. "You seem to have forgotten your gun."

"Oh, don't worry!" grinned Mitcham. "I've still got it."

Finn almost blushed.

"No," continued Mitcham, "I thought I'd wander round and let you know that I've started work again for Mr Darcy. Can't say I liked working for the new earl that much."

"As First Footman?" enquired Finn, "Holloway won't be happy about that!"

"No, as both a footman and a groom, so I'll be travelling between here and Pemberley as the master sees fit. I did both jobs for the earl. Got more versatile under him so to speak."

Finn smiled broadly.

55 Love blossoms

By autumn, Jane and Richard had a son; and by Christmas, the Darcys had a daughter.

Fitzwilliam could not have been more pleased with his *petit paquet*, and once his daughter learned to sit on his lap, many a pair of his breeches were soiled before she was properly potty-trained. But Darcy liked nothing more than to hold his daughter in his arms and sniff her chestnut hair. Lizzy teased him jokingly that he was attempting to determine paternity.

The summer after the Gardiners' visit, Elizabeth employed the first of many tutors to extend her spotty education. At first she studied the classics—Latin, Greek and philosophy; until she realised she was emulating the list of Diana's interests as enumerated by Mr Wickham. Thereafter Elizabeth discovered her true inclination was for mathematics, particularly geometry, which was of tremendous utility in her astronomical calculations and also, strangely enough, dressmaking.

Lizzy and Darcy continued to grow in intimacy. By the time their daughter had reached the age of one, their understanding of each other's minds had advanced considerably. Although Elizabeth no longer received tuition in philosophy, she maintained an interest in it by reading Lady Anne's books in the library; and this, along with her work with Darcy's uncle in astronomy, made Fitzwilliam realise that his wife was equal in understanding to his mother, whom he had greatly admired.

Sneaking past the arras one crisp autumn night, Darcy asked Elizabeth where she had gained her knowledge of astronomy.

"My father had quite a nice refractor. We used to look at stars together."

"I remember..." he said, drawing forward and running his hand along the barrel of the telescope, "sitting on my mother's lap when I was very small, being shown the stars. I liked the clusters... like jewels... I believe there was one called the Beehive..."

"Oh, M44! Yes, that is one of my favourites."

"Em forty-four?" he repeated.

"Yes, that is the designation given by Messier in his catalogue. It would have appeared in the first catalogue because there were forty-five included. Your mother had a copy. It has been superseded by the Herschels' General Catalogue."

Elizabeth walked towards a bookshelf. "Yes! Here it is."

Thereafter, they spent many nights stargazing once the children were in bed. After Lizzy finished her practical observations on comets and planets, they looked at useless but pretty objects, some of them catalogued by Messier. Lizzy even communicated some new ones she discovered to the Astronomer Royal and was delighted when one of her suggested names appeared in the astronomical bulletin.

On cloudy nights, once the children had settled down, they sat in the master sitting room reading, with Lizzy's feet tucked under her husband's warm thighs.

For her part, Elizabeth realised that her husband had an analytical mind of the first order. This she gleaned from talking to him of his business dealings, but also from their chess games. With the benefit of her father's training, Lizzy beat her husband almost unvaryingly for the first few months of their competition. But her husband soon brought himself up to her level, and after a year his victories were more frequent than her own.

Fitzwilliam never did remember not to call his wife "my dear" but Elizabeth forgave him his short memory on the topic. She realised her request was an unreasonable one based on her father's behaviour, for which Fitzwilliam was blameless. What she really objected to was her father's disrespectful behaviour towards her mother. The fact that Fitzwilliam treated her as his intellectual equal—played chess with her, let her pursue her observations with the telescope—showed that he respected her.

On the day she'd first realised this, they had been sitting together reading in the master sitting room after the Sunday service. It was a miserable day outside—the sort of day when one is glad just to be snug, out of the weather. Elizabeth had spontaneously leant over and given her husband a hug.

"I love you," she said.

The tips of Darcy's ears had gone quite pink and an infinitesimal smile had formed on his lips. "I love you, too," he replied softly.

They remembered that day fondly for many years to come as the beginning of their marital bliss.

As to their physical intimacy, some time after the birth of their first child Darcy finally mastered his volcanism. Around the same time, Lizzy was largely divested of her shyness. She claimed no mother could give birth without losing it to some extent.

Once Darcy had himself under better control, the benefit of his years with Diana became more apparent. Lizzy came to realise that her husband's knowledge of lovemaking was far more extensive than she had previously realised. As much as she enjoyed some of these interludes, Elizabeth thought their most memorable trysts were the spontaneous ones. Of course, she occasionally liked to play tricks on her husband, like wriggling at crucial moments, just to let him know who was *really* in control.

56 Of Georgie and Rosings

Jane's arrival at Pemberley might have resulted in Georgie returning to the lonely existence she endured before her brother's wedding. But both Jane and Elizabeth had too much sensibility and kindness to allow that. They were careful to include their younger sister-in-law in all their schemes. Nonetheless, Georgie initially had trouble recovering her normally cheerful demeanour, and both Bennet sisters exerted themselves to buoy Georgie's easily crushed spirits of youth. Jane began riding with her regularly, mounted on Georgie's 'old slug.'

"He is such a beautiful horse!" exclaimed Jane, when Healy first led the gelding from the stable. "How could you bear to part with him?"

Georgie averred she much preferred her Firefly, petting her high-bred mare as she coquetted, well aware she was being praised. Jane did not at all mind that Starlight—for that was the gelding's name—did not fancy lifting his hocks too far; she didn't really care to take a tilt at regular stitchers and suggested that Georgie refrain from doing so in her company.

"Go jump hedges with your brother, Georgie. He can bring you back on a hurdle. Not me!"

Indeed, Georgie did ride more adventurously when accompanied by her brother or cousin rather than Jane, but never came to grief.

For her part, Jane was particularly struck by Georgie's beautiful piano playing, and unlike Lizzy, who had abandoned the keyboard when faced by such excellence, Jane was inspired to try harder, even though she realised she would never equal Georgie. To Jane, the ability to produce such beautiful music was enough. Georgie proved an apt tutor and within a year, Jane had eclipsed Mary as the most proficient Bennet on the pianoforte.

Lizzy attempted to honour her resolution of teaching Georgie to play chess. This required a great deal of patience on her part, a quality that she did not consider amongst her strongest points, but which, she reminded herself, she would do well to cultivate. Fortunately, Richard stepped in, and proved a better partner for Georgie in the first fifty or so games it took before she began to regularly defeat him. Thereafter Lizzy and Darcy were more worthy opponents, though only in casual games. They reserved their full prowess for games against each other.

Mrs Annesley's angina continued to bother her. She retired to live with her brother when his wife died, six months after the Darcy's marriage. Although Dr Gordon explained to Georgie that her companion's seizure had been inevitable, she always blamed herself for precipitating the event, sending Mrs Annesley poorly executed craft projects she had slaved over every Christmas as evidence of her contrition.

Although Georgie had trouble recovering her spirits after the Whaley

Bridge debacle, the birth of the first of the Darcy children at Christmas set her on the path to recovery, and the three sisters eventually became boon companions until Georgie married years later.

Georgie never lost her child-like interest in the clever fairy tales that her sister-in-law could invent, weaving traditional tales with incidents in their own lives. When Fitzwilliam did occasionally go off to London alone on business, Georgie would often crawl into Lizzy's bed early in the morning to hear another story, and thus precipitated an embarrassing incident when her brother came home early on horseback one moonlit night. Finding Lizzy's door unexpectedly barred against her on the following morning, Georgie knocked.

"Go away, Georgie!" yelled Fitzwilliam.

Outside the door, Georgie instantly fired up in response to her brother's harsh words, but her flush of anger quickly turned to a blush on realising the reason for her brother's location in Elizabeth's bedchamber, however vague her understanding of what went on there. Stifling a nervous giggle as she retreated to her sitting room, Georgie was soon engrossed in her piano playing, giving Elizabeth and Fitzwilliam a pleasant score to their lovemaking.

The Darcys and the Fitzwilliams embarked on their first London season for Georgiana's come-out at the age of twenty. Uncharacteristically, all their children went too. Georgie was not a success, despite the support of Jane and Elizabeth. Although a number of men expressed interest in courting her, some of them quite eligible matches, she offended around half of them by saying gauche things at inappropriate moments, reminding Lizzy of Fitzwilliam's behaviour in Hertfordshire.

After acquiring a reputation as an arrogant bluestocking, Georgie eventually made a match in Derbyshire where she married Captain Henry Anstey, who had joined the army upon Napoleon's return. She found him remarkably improved by this experience, despite the loss of one eye and two fingers of his right hand at Waterloo, quite different from the annoying boy who would not loan her his Diablo. They eventually had three sons, who all liked Aunt Lizzy's fairy stories.

With regards to events at Rosings, the Bingleys eventually returned to Kent after Caroline's attempt to snare a viscount came to naught. However they left again shortly after, when Miss Bingley discovered the nature of Mary Fitzwilliam's position in the household. Lady Catherine had been so pleased with her great niece that she had allowed Anne to formally adopt Mary only two months after her arrival.

Following an ear-splitting argument during which Caroline accused Lady Catherine of luring them to Rosings under false pretences, the Bingleys decamped. After discoursing on the ingratitude of the parvenu for hours after their departure, Lady Catherine collapsed the next day and died six months later, following her brother to the hereafter within the year.

Mr Bingley eventually returned to Netherfield without his relatives in the summer. He rode immediately over to Longbourn to take his potluck with them but was disappointed to find Jane absent.

"I hope Miss Bennet is well? " he asked Mrs Bennet. "Is she visiting in Meryton with Miss Lydia?"

"But have you not heard, Mr Bingley? Jane was married just after Christmas to Mr Darcy's cousin, the colonel. But of course you know him—he stayed at Netherfield."

Mr Bingley went quite pale.

"Lydia, also, married quite recently, to Mr Denny of the militia. He is a lieutenant in the Hussars now and looks *very well* in his new uniform. Mary is Miss Bennet now," added Mrs Bennet hopefully.

Mr Bingley left shortly after coffee and did not renew his lease on Netherfield at Michaelmas.

Anne de Bourgh married Dr Douglas in a quiet ceremony attended only by Richard, Lady Mary Fitzwilliam-de Bourgh and the Collins, exactly six months after Lady Catherine's death. Under her husband's care, Anne lived to the age of forty-three.

The following Easter, Elizabeth visited Rosings with Darcy when he made his annual trip there to deal with the business of the estate, as had been his habit before the rupture caused by his marriage.

Anne, who knew nothing of estate business, was profuse in her thanks to her cousin, and Darcy was amazed to see her looking so well. She confided to him that her husband had prescribed a special diet for her, but to Darcy's mind this turned out to be nothing more than ordinary food. Apparently his aunt had quacked his cousin with a series of fashionable 'health' diets that had been anything but.

Elizabeth was able to renew her friendship with Charlotte, spending many happy days at the parsonage while Mr Collins attended his new patroness at Rosings. Inevitably there were shared dinners at Rosings, during which Darcy could not help notice Mr Collins continually comparing the Parsonage to Pemberley. In a quiet moment when they were alone, Darcy asked his wife what she thought he meant by it. Darcy was completely astonished to discover that Elizabeth's cousin had been a rival for her affections, but admitted that considering the entail, her cousin's pretensions were not entirely preposterous. Nonetheless, the next time the parson made a similar comparison, Darcy asked him, in his most condescending manner, to refrain from making comparisons to an estate he knew only by hearsay, and would likely never see.

Charlotte had difficulty suppressing a smile. Mr Collins was so startled by Mr Darcy's striking adoption of his Aunt Catherine's demeanour that he apologised profusely and never dared to mention the subject again.

57 The season

The Darcys and Fitzwilliams spent the bulk of the next four years in Derbyshire, with one of the men occasionally venturing to London for special business, but always alone, leaving the other to guard home and hearth. Once Georgie came out, the families began to spend the season together in London, where they all managed to squeeze into Darcy House.

Two months before embarking on their first London season, Darcy had arrived in the City to manage his joint real estate investments with Richard. In seeking out various title deeds, Darcy realised that the expensive parure he had purchased for Diana was still sitting in the safe in his study. He had completely forgotten about it.

Darcy had briefly contemplated selling it, knowing his wife would prefer something practical, such as new mirrors for her telescope. That idea was swiftly abandoned after a trip to Rundall and Bridge, where he discovered the resale value of the gems, particularly the more expensive emeralds, was a fraction of what he had paid for them. While Darcy had plenty of money, he never wasted it. The jewellers convinced him that resetting the stones in a new arrangement was a far more sensible option, and Darcy went off considering several designs, none of which caught his fancy.

In the end it was Finn who suggested a design to grace Elizabeth's long slender neck—more in the way of an elaborate choker than a pendant. A worthy implementation of this amazing piece ended up requiring around twice the number of stones in the original parure, but when Darcy saw the finished necklace on his wife, he begrudged not a penny of it.

Of course, once Finn had designed the necklace, he could not let Mrs Darcy wear it with *any* old dress, and a grand conspiracy was hatched with Madame Lafrange to design a gown to complement it. For this confection an amazing silk that shone blue from the weft and green from the warp was sourced from London, which Madame proposed to drape à la polonaise to show off its iridescent hues. A custom-made wide cincture that clasped under the bust, decorated with peacock feathers, would complete the ensemble.

Given Darcy's blessing, the dress was constructed in great secrecy in Lambton using Mrs Darcy's measurements. When the time came for it to be fitted, Elizabeth was escorted to the village by Jenny and Finn and requested to don a blindfold before entering the modiste's premises.

After Jenny transported the finished gown to London with all the care required had it been made of glass, the occasion chosen by the Bennet sisters for the debut of this fashion tour de force was Lady Sefton's Ball.

Still in ignorance of the garb she was to wear and knowing only that Jenny and Finn were beside themselves with excitement, Lizzy submitted meekly when she was blindfolded again once the time came to don the dress. If Elizabeth thought she would finally get to see her apparel as Jenny applied some paint to her face, she was sadly mistaken. Mrs Flowers retrieved a powdering gown from the depths of some cupboard and this was carefully draped over the dress before the blindfold was removed.

Finally, with her face appropriately powdered and painted, and her hair arranged in a coiffure worthy of a Chinese empress, Lizzy was at last able to view the transformation wrought by Finn and Jenny. Her sister Jane had arrived for the grand unveiling accompanied by Georgiana.

Elizabeth's first thought upon seeing herself in the pier glass illuminated by two branches of candles was that she would look magnificent sitting upon an Arabian charger in Astley's amphitheatre. But before she could express her reservations, Jane had gasped and rushed up to her.

"Oh, Elizabeth! You look beautiful!" she exclaimed.

"Just like a princess!" gushed Georgie.

This brought a smile to Elizabeth's lips as she recalled the exclamation of the tenant's child on her first Sunday in Pemberley's chapel. Although Elizabeth suspected that Jenny and Finn had primed her sisters, she was divested of this notion when Darcy came into the room. As Fitzwilliam was incapable of subterfuge, her husband's reaction spoke volumes. He stopped suddenly just inside the threshold of her bedchamber, as if he had run into a wall of glass, and froze in an attitude that was a very creditable imitation of one of the handsome Greek statues in the British museum, although with more clothes on.

"Does she not look beautiful?" Jane prompted.

"Yes," Darcy croaked, and then suddenly remembering the jewels, he mutely held out the box, still rooted to the spot.

Lizzy stepped forward to receive the parure and evinced a startled "oh!" when she opened the lid. "Fitzwilliam, they're beautiful!" she managed. "Would you help me put them on?"

Darcy attempted to clasp the choker round his wife's neck with trembling hands, but this was only eventually achieved when Jane assisted him. Finally, Jenny retrieved the matching earrings and Mrs Darcy was deemed ready for the evening.

The Darcys arrived downstairs to find Richard piggy-backing his son and nephew simultaneously; or more particularly, one year old George was on his uncle's shoulders while a giggling two-year old Geoffrey clung precariously to his father's back. Their sisters provided an enthusiastic chorus for the merriment, jumping up and down on the furniture.

"Oh, Richard! Do be careful!" Jane said, bustling up to him in her pale blue silk. "The children may puke on your uniform!"

Richard, who had expected to be admonished for his careless handling of his progeny, stifled a laugh at his wife's altered priorities. He was fairly disdainful of his Derbyshire militia uniform after the past glories of his Life Guards' days. Nonetheless, he dutifully handed the children over to Nurse so he could survey his beautiful wife.

Jane was looking exquisite in a pale blue watered silk with a sapphire pendant round her neck, generously loaned from the Fitzwilliam jewel casket by the dowager countess. No matter that the jewels were only paste. Richard wasn't about to enlighten any of the females of his family about his father's disclosures regarding the contents of that box. Rightfully the "jewels" belonged to the new Lady Matlock anyway, but Miranda had not insisted her mother hand over the family heirlooms, preferring to live in retirement in the country, far away from Robert. Perhaps his sister-in-law had guessed that the stones were mere trumpery. After all, Robert would surely have prigged them by now if they were real. Nonetheless, Richard was grateful to the eleventh countess for her generosity. Jane looked magnificent; so much so, that when their nurse began herding the children upstairs for bed, Richard Fitzwilliam yawned, said he was feeling rather fatigued, and perhaps Mrs Fitzwilliam would like to retire early with him?

Jane surreptitiously pinched him before kissing their children goodnight. Then, brushing some lint off Richard's shoulder that had likely been introduced by the horseplay, she pulled her ermine shawl around her neck, threaded her arm through his, and squeezed his gloved hand. While Richard's militia uniform did not achieve the magnificence of his Life Guards' uniform, he still managed to look impressive in it.

"Georgie, how pretty you look in that ball gown!" said Richard, finally noticing his cousin; "and that red sash complements that beautiful coral necklace admirably! Where did you get such an exquisite piece?"

Georgie performed a mock curtsey. "You know very well that you gave it to me for Christmas, Cousin Richard! But thank you for noticing the sash. I spent a whole day searching for a ribbon that matched the necklace exactly!"

Stepping into the hall with his wife, Richard's eyes popped when he saw Elizabeth, who had retreated into the hallway to shunt the children upstairs.

"Why Cousin Elizabeth, dare I say it? You look as pretty as a peacock!"

"As long as I don't sound like one!" riposted Elizabeth. "They are the most dreadful sounding birds!"

"Yes," agreed the brigadier pensively, "those ones that Aunt Catherine had at Rosings used to give me nightmares!"

Of course, when Darcy had first laid eyes on his wife's magnificence, it had occurred to him that she was an incarnation of the goddess Juno, the peacock being her familiar. A suaver man might have made this allusion, but for once Darcy was glad for his tied tongue. Given his history with another member of the pantheon, it would not have been a happy comparison. Instead, he contented himself with stooping to give Elizabeth a chaste kiss on her rouged cheek while his hand rested lightly but possessively on her back.

The Darcys and Fitzwilliams then ventured out into the night and, by the light of flambéaux, stepped into the Darcy carriage for the short drive to Belgravia Square.

As they proceeded down Park Lane, Darcy recalled another journey along that thoroughfare to see Diana and his subsequent discomfiture when the duke had returned home. Feeling her husband's hands tense, Lizzy stroked his gloves, earning her a grateful glance. She knew Fitzwilliam hated socialising but didn't realise his trepidation arose from the worry that he might encounter Diana at the ball, close as it was to the Duke of Redford's domicile. Despite Wickham's disclosures, Elizabeth had never bothered to enquire the direction of the duchess.

Lady Sefton's Ball was, as usual, a crush. All eyes in their immediate vicinity turned towards them when the Darcys and Fitzwilliams were announced.

"By Jove, she's got a king's ransom round her neck," exclaimed Mr Fothergill, standing with a companion in an alcove.

"Egads, I've never known Darcy to be so extravagant," added Mr Fancot. "Why, all he'll ever play at White's is silver loo!"

While the dandies were surveying the hardware, a gaggle of ladies observed the Bennet sisters' progress from a balcony.

"They are sisters from a modest estate in Hertfordshire," commented Lady Sefton.

"My goodness," said Lady Campbellreigh from behind her fan, "it is the Gunning sisters all over again! But at least they are English!"

"Well, they have hardly snared an earl and two dukes!" retorted Lady Jersey. "Although I suppose the way the current Earl of Matlock is going, his brother may end up stepping into his shoes. That would make one earl."

"To my mind," observed Lady Hitchin, "Darcy's cousin has snagged the prettier bride."

"Possibly," replied Lady Sefton; "but everyone knows that men administer to their vanity by favouring women who resemble themselves. Darcy's wife looks like she could be his sister."

"An interesting observation," replied Lady Hitchin. "There is something of Lady Anne Darcy about his wife, despite her diminutive stature. I suppose one might call Georgiana Darcy handsome, but she is an unfortunate combination of her handsome parents' features. It seems her brother inherited all their good looks. He must surely be infatuated to have bought his wife such a necklace."

"I heard he had it specially commissioned; designed it himself," said Lady Campbellreigh.

"Hmmph. Well, it is worthy of the Crown Jewels. I suppose it will be dubbed the Darcy Necklace," observed Lady Jersey drily.

After the introductions were made, a gaggle of young men and several older ones lined up to dance with the Bennet sisters and a few were polite enough to engage Georgie. Any rakes who dared to approach the ladies were given a hard stare by Darcy and Richard. For the most part, these gentlemen went off in search of other game. The exception was the notorious Duke of Andover, who flashed an evil grin back at the cousins before claiming a dance with both Bennet sisters anyway. But as the duke kept the line and was getting old anyway, they did not call him out.

Darcy reserved the waltz with Elizabeth for himself. No one but he was going to be putting their hands on his wife's waist. They made a beautiful couple as they performed the steps.

"Well I had no idea Darcy could dance so well!" commented Lady Sefton.

"I had no idea he could dance at all!" joked Lady Jersey.

It was three in the morning when the Darcy carriage arrived back in Grosvenor Square. Darcy would have preferred to have fled the Sefton's Ball on the stroke of midnight but was restrained by Richard.

"Let the ladies stay longer. They are enjoying themselves."

After bidding Jane, Richard and a sleepy Georgie goodnight on the first floor landing, Darcy and Elizabeth ascended the stairs to their chambers on the second floor. Darcy would have escorted his wife to her bedchamber door but she forestalled him.

"Is there any room in your bed tonight, Fitzwilliam?" Elizabeth asked with a seraphic smile.

Darcy instantly broke into a wide grin and pulled her towards his chamber. Quickly closing the door behind him, he grasped his wife in a determined clinch. Once they came up for air, Darcy tugged at his cravat and Elizabeth kicked off her shoes, but before she could divest herself of any further garments, she noticed the door of Darcy's dressing room open a crack. Finn poked his head out and fixed her with an anguished look.

"Excuse me, Fitzwilliam. I just need to use your dressing room for a moment..." explained Elizabeth, disappearing within and closing the door behind her.

"What is it, Finn?" she whispered urgently. "Do you want the necklace?"

"No, ma'am, the ceinture - the peacock feathers are very delicate!"

Elizabeth allowed Finn to divest her of the belt and asked him to tell Jenny to go to bed. Pulling off her heavy earrings, she returned to Fitzwilliam's bedchamber.

Darcy was down to his breeches and stockings and grabbed her urgently for another kiss. This proved a little more than either of them could bear and, moving quickly, he twisted his wife round in his arms and urged her, chest down, onto the mattress. Rucking up the polonaise at the back, he pushed into her from behind, giving an exclamation of delight to find her ready for him.

After minutes of mutual pure bliss, Darcy collapsed on top of Lizzy and rolled to the side.

"Oh Lord!" he said as he slipped the tiny silk cap sleeve off Elizabeth's shoulder to caress her skin. "I've been wanting to do that all night!"

Elizabeth caressed the scar on her husband's forehead with her thumb. Darcy, who was a little embarrassed about the blemish, had grown his hair longer at the front to cover it. But for Elizabeth, it was special—Richard had told her the truth behind Darcy's encounter with the doorpost.

"Well I'm glad you let me have my little moment of glory," responded Elizabeth, running her fingers through the black locks of his fringe. "But I must admit it was a pleasant denouement for the evening."

Darcy stretched with satisfaction and closed his eyes.

"Don't you dare fall asleep before you've helped me out of these clothes!" Elizabeth admonished. "I've sent Jenny to bed."

Darcy willingly complied and stripped his wife to her birthday suit. After removing her last stocking, he delicately bit the nail of her big toe, flashing her a wolfish grin. Finally he removed his own stockings.

"Haven't you forgotten something?" Elizabeth asked as he stretched himself out on the bed beside her.

"Well, no," Darcy replied, eyeing the necklace that still graced Elizabeth's neck. "I've a fancy to make love to you again while you're wearing that."

And he did.

Collapsing back on the pillows afterwards, Darcy snuggled up to his wife. "I wish I could get someone to paint you just as you are now," he said, planting a kiss above the clasp of her choker; "but I suppose I would have to kill the artist afterwards because he had seen you au naturel."

Lizzy laughed. "I'm sure you wouldn't be able to find an artist to paint such a scandalous picture! Even the Italian artists used male models for their nudes."

Darcy did not like to say he had seen several such contemporary paintings, some of them proudly displayed at White's.

"I suppose I had better take it off," he remarked.

His recent exercise having markedly steadied his hand, Darcy had the choker off in a trice. Discarding it carelessly on a side table, he spooned behind his wife, having finally discovered the joys of snuggling two years into his marriage.

They had just closed their eyes when a shriek from Jane below stairs suggested the Fitzwilliams were not quite ready for slumber.

"Oh, how I will tease Jane about that tomorrow!" said Lizzy, and they drifted off to sleep.

58 Of things past

One can never erase the past, and occasionally Diana intruded into Darcy's life, often when he least expected it.

Spotting Diana at balls had Darcy walking quickstep in the other direction. His behaviour had Diana ruing her own actions. She thought she had been quite noble in letting her young lover get on with his own life and really would have liked to remain friends with him.

The sad truth was that her marriage to the duke was not a success. After paying a lot of attention to Diana when he was wooing her, the duke neglected his wife somewhat after their nuptials, preferring to talk and bet in the company of his peers at White's. Every attempt by Diana to discreetly recruit a new cicisbeo was thwarted by the duke until, five years after their marriage, Diana scandalised the Ton by fleeing to the country to live at her estate in Somerset with her butler, Leith.

The duke then went through lengthy divorce proceedings that dragged through the courts for over ten years, twice the length of his actual marriage. He had a debilitating stroke shortly after wedding his third wife, a young debutante, who then proceeded to cuckold him far less discreetly than Diana had ever attempted.

One particular interaction with Diana is worthy of note. Six years into the Darcy's marriage, a crate marked "fragile" arrived at Darcy House during the season. When Fitzwilliam opened it in his study, he discovered it contained a Ming vase matching the one in the vestibule of Darcy House. Upon unsealing the note that accompanied it, Darcy discovered only a single word—*'Sorry'*, on the outer sheet. The inner sheet contained the following explanation:

> *"I came across this beautiful Ming vase at an auction house. My interest was piqued when the auctioneer told me he had seen only one other like it—at Darcy House. I remember you told me there was a pair, and that one had disappeared from Pemberley after your father's death. If the hallmarks are indeed the same, I would like you to keep this as an apology, as I believe it may rightfully be your property.*
>
> *D"*

Darcy's first inclination was to return the vase, but Lizzy demurred. After checking the hallmarks, she wrote the thank you note to Diana herself. The vase was returned to Pemberley but resided thereafter in the gallery, where it matched the ox-blood paint on the wall so well that Lizzy concluded that the room had been originally decorated to house it.

The original bliss that the eldest Bennet sisters had envisaged at Longbourn, living together in the same household, came to fruition. Granted, they weren't exactly living under the same roof, nor was Lizzy governess to Jane's children, but neither sister was about to quibble with details.

For the males of Pemberley, domestic bliss was captured by the following exchange one summer's evening as the men sat on the back steps, watching their children chase each around the formal garden.

"You liar!" said Darcy, seemingly apropos of nothing, but prompted by the previous night's dinner, for which Jane had arrived in a beautiful new gown, prompting panegyrics throughout the meal from her husband.

"I beg your pardon!" said Richard.

"I distinctly remember you saying at Netherfield that you would never marry a beautiful woman and now you boast of it!"

"Ah! But you miss the salient point!"

"Which is?"

"That was before I discovered Jane was not only the most beautiful woman in England but also the most trustworthy!"

"A nice riposte, but you are wrong because I have married the most beautiful woman in England," retorted Darcy.

"While I admit your wife is good-looking," returned his cousin without hesitation, "you are sadly deluded, and must be *truly* besotted."

Ten years after their marriage, the Darcys and Fitzwilliams took the children to visit their grandparents in Hertfordshire.

Netherfield had been vacated by the Mudgleys after their seven year stint there, and Darcy had hired it for the winter quarter, so the children could celebrate Christmas at Longbourn. On the fifteenth day of Advent, Jane and Richard had gone off to a party at Aunt Philips', for which Darcy had expressed no enthusiasm. Lizzy and Darcy had stayed at Netherfield 'to mind the children' who were in fact quite competently supervised by two nannies and a governess.

Thus, after dinner, Darcy and Lizzy found themselves alone in the saloon. Lizzy took out her notebook and began to compose riddles for her eldest daughter, who was remarkably adept at solving them. Darcy had picked up a book, but his wife could not help noticing that his attention was not fixed on it.

"Is there a problem?" she asked.

"I remember you sitting in that exact chair ten years ago when you came to tend Jane during her illness."

"Yes, it is a coincidence, is it not? For I was composing an acrostic on that occasion too, only for Jane."

"I'm not sure I could have added one and one together on that night,

Time's Up, Mr Darcy

for I was admiring you."

"Oh? You had a strange way of showing it. I thought you were deploring my grubby fingers."

"Really?" Darcy echoed. "I only noticed how slender and shapely your hands were... *Were* they grubby?"

"Yes," she said. "From my pencil."

"What a pity," he said, getting up from his chair. "If I'd noticed, I would have offered to clean them."

And saying this, he took her hand; and before she he had any notion of his purpose, he had pulled her index finger into his mouth up to the second knuckle.

Lizzy had quite forgotten herself and, once she was sensible, was only glad they had not been interrupted; but Darcy had planned ahead—the key to the saloon door was in his waistcoat pocket, residing over the back of a chair.

Lizzy was always glad they took the opportunity to lease Netherfield for that short period, because her mother passed away the following year after a short illness. As little as she and her mother had in common, Elizabeth knew it was the end of an era.

Given that all his daughters were married, Mr Bennet decided to relinquish Longbourn to the Collins prior to his death and return to Oxford rather than live on his own.

A few years later, Lizzy and Jane ventured to Trinity College to surprise their father for his birthday. The porter was kind enough to take Mr Bennet's daughters to the common room where the fellows of the college very graciously admitted the ladies for their father's birthday celebration.

They were introduced to a colleague of Mr Bennet's, a Mr Baxter, who spent the evening engaged in light-hearted banter with their father. Jane was so glad that their father had found such a good friend to ease the burden of his old age, but Lizzy had been more perceptive. It had not escaped her notice that when they entered the room, where ladies were generally not permitted, Mr Baxter and her father had been holding hands.

One last piece of the puzzle fell into place for Lizzy, and her father's advice on her engagement finally made sense.

FINIS

By the River Lea
Invoke Euripides
Will you wed me?
Met in the mist
Tantalising lady
My children to bear
Here all alone but
Mine ever after
Destined to be

Made in the USA
Lexington, KY
13 May 2017